NOT A PENNY MO

AND

HONOUR AMONG THIEVES

Jeffrey Archer's writing career has spanned almost thirty years. His bestselling novels, which range from *Not a Penny More, Not a Penny Less* to *Kane and Abel* and *The Eleventh Commandment*, have sold over 120 million copies throughout the world.

In August 2001, he was sentenced to four years in prison for perjury. During that time he wrote three highly praised and bestselling works of non-fiction entitled *Prison Diaries*. He was released in July 2003.

He is married with two children and lives in London and Granchester.

ALSO BY JEFFREY ARCHER

NOVELS

Shall We Tell The President?
Kane & Abel
The Prodigal Daughter
First Among Equals
A Matter of Honour
As the Crow Flies
The Fourth Estate
The Eleventh Commandment
Sons of Fortune
False Impression

The Gospel According to Judas by Benjamin Iscariot
(with Frank Moloney)

SHORT STORIES

A Quiver Full of Arrows
Twelve Red Herrings
The Collected Short Stories
To Cut a Long Story Short
Cat O'Nine Tales

PLAYS

Beyond Reasonable Doubt
Exclusive
The Accused

PRISON DIARIES

Volume One – Belmarsh: Hell
Volume Two – Wayland: Purgatory
Volume Three – North Sea Camp: Heaven

SCREENPLAYS

Mallory: Walking off the Map
False Impression

JEFFREY ARCHER

NOT A PENNY MORE, NOT A PENNY LESS

AND

HONOUR AMONG THIEVES

PAN BOOKS

Not a Penny More, Not a Penny Less first published 1976 by Jonathan Cape Ltd.
First published in paperback 1977 by Coronet.
First published by Pan Books 2003.
Honour Among Thieves first published 1993 by HarperCollins Publishers.
First published in paperback 1994 by HarperCollins.
First published by Pan Books 2003.

This omnibus first published 2008 by Pan Books
an imprint of Pan Macmillan, a division of Macmillan Publishers Limited
Pan Macmillan, 20 New Wharf Road, London N1 9RR
Basingstoke and Oxford
Associated companies throughout the world
www.panmacmillan.com

ISBN 978-0-330-45777-4

3 5 7 9 8 6 4 2

A CIP catalogue record for this book is available from the British Library.

Printed and bound in Great Britain by
CPI Mackays, Chatham ME5 8TD

NOT A PENNY MORE, NOT A PENNY LESS

AND

HONOUR AMONG THIEVES

NOT A PENNY MORE, NOT A PENNY LESS

To Mary

AND THE FAT MEN

Author's Note

I acknowledge all the help I received from so many people in writing this book and wish to thank them: David Niven, Jr, who made me do it, Sir Noel and Lady Hall who made it possible, Adrian Metcalfe, Anthony Rentoul, Colin Emson, Ted Francis, Godfrey Barker, Willy West, Madame Tellegen, David Stein, Christian Neffe, Dr John Vance, Dr David Weeden, the Rev. Leslie Styler, Robert Gasser, Professor Jim Bolton, and Jamie Clark; Gail and Jo for putting it together; and my wife, Mary, for the hours spent correcting and editing.

PROLOGUE

'Jörg expect $7 million from Crédit Parisien in the No. 2 account by 6 pm tonight, Central European time, and place it with first-class banks and triple "A" commercial names. Otherwise, invest it in the over-night Euro-dollar market. Understood?'

'Yes, Harvey.'

'Place $1 million in the Banco do Minas Gerais, Rio de Janeiro, in the names of Silverman and Elliott and cancel the call loan at Barclays Bank, Lombard Street. Understood?'

'Yes, Harvey.'

'Buy gold on my commodity account until it reaches $10 million and then hold until you receive further instructions. Try and buy in the troughs and don't rush – be patient. Understood?'

'Yes, Harvey.'

Harvey Metcalfe realised that the last instruction was unnecessary. Jörg Birrer was one of the most conservative bankers in Zürich and, more important to Harvey, had over the past twenty-five years proved to be one of the shrewdest.

'Can you join me at Wimbledon on Tuesday, June

25th at 2 pm, Centre Court, my usual debenture seat?'

'Yes, Harvey.'

The telephone clicked into place. Harvey never said goodbye. He had never understood the niceties of life and it was too late to start learning now. He picked up the phone, dialled the seven digits which would give him the Lincoln Trust in Boston, and asked for his secretary.

'Miss Fish?'

'Yes, sir.'

'Remove the file on Prospecta Oil and destroy it. Destroy any correspondence connected with it and leave absolutely no trace. Understood?'

'Yes, sir.'

The telephone clicked again. Harvey Metcalfe had given similar orders three times in the last twenty-five years and by now Miss Fish had learnt not to question him.

Harvey breathed deeply, almost a sigh, a quiet exhalation of triumph. He was now worth at least $25 million, and nothing could stop him. He opened a bottle of Krug champagne 1964, imported from Hedges & Butler of London. He sipped it slowly and lit a Romeo y Julieta Churchill, which an Italian immigrant smuggled in for him in boxes of two hundred and fifty once a month from Cuba. He settled back for a mild celebration. In Boston, Massachusetts, it was 12.20 pm – nearly time for lunch.

*

In Harley Street, Bond Street, the King's Road and Magdalen College, Oxford, it was 6.20 pm. Four men, unknown to each other, checked the market price of Prospecta Oil in the final edition of the London *Evening Standard*. It was £3.70. All four of them were rich men, looking forward to consolidating their already successful careers.

Tomorrow they would be penniless.

1

MAKING A MILLION legally has always been difficult. Making a million illegally has always been a little easier. Keeping a million when you have made it is perhaps the most difficult of all. Henryk Metelski was one of those rare men who had managed all three. Even if the million he had made legally came after the million he had made illegally, Metelski was still a yard ahead of the others: he had managed to keep it all.

Henryk Metelski was born on the Lower East Side of New York on May 17th, 1909, in a small room that already slept four children. He grew up through the Depression, believing in God and one meal a day. His parents were from Warsaw and had emigrated from Poland at the turn of the century. Henryk's father was a baker by trade and had soon found a job in New York, where immigrant Poles specialised in baking black rye bread and running small restaurants for their countrymen. Both parents would have liked Henryk to be an academic success, but he was never destined to become an outstanding pupil at his high school. His natural gifts lay elsewhere. A cunning, smart little boy, he was far more interested in the control of the underground school market in cigarettes and liquor than in stirring tales of the American Revolution and the Liberty Bell. Little Henryk never believed for one moment that the best things in life were free, and the pursuit of money and power came as naturally to him as the pursuit of a mouse to a cat.

When Henryk was a pimply and flourishing fourteen-year-old, his father died of what we now know to be cancer. His mother outlived her husband by no more than a few months, leaving the five children to fend for themselves. Henryk, like the other four, should have gone into the district orphanage for destitute children, but in the mid-1920s it was not hard for a boy to disappear in New York – though it was harder to survive. Henryk became a master of survival, a schooling which was to prove very useful to him in later life.

He knocked around the Lower East Side with his belt tightened and his eyes open, shining shoes here, washing dishes there, always looking for an entrance to the maze at the heart of which lay wealth and prestige. His first chance came when his room-mate Jan Pelnik, a messenger boy on the New York Stock Exchange, put himself temporarily out of action with a sausage garnished with salmonella. Henryk, deputed to report his friend's mishap to the Chief Messenger, upgraded food-poisoning to tuberculosis, and talked himself into the ensuing vacancy. He then changed his room, donned a new uniform, lost a friend, and gained a job.

Most of the messages Henryk delivered during the early twenties read 'Buy'. Many of them were quickly acted upon, for this was a boom era. He watched men of little ability make fortunes while he remained nothing more than an observer. His instincts directed him towards those individuals who made more money in a week on the Stock Exchange than he could hope to make in a lifetime on his salary.

He set about learning how to master the way the Stock Exchange operated, he listened to private conversations, opened sealed messages and found out which closed company reports to study. By the age of eighteen he had four years' experience of Wall Street: four years which most messenger boys would have spent simply walking across crowded floors, delivering little pink pieces of paper; four years which to Henryk Metelski were the equivalent of a Master's Degree from the Harvard Business School. He was not to know that one day he would lecture to that august body.

One morning in July 1927 he was delivering a message from Halgarten & Co, a well-established brokerage house, making his usual detour via the washroom. He had perfected a system whereby he could lock himself into a cubicle, study the message he was carrying, decide whether the information was of any value to him and, if it was, immediately telephone Witold Gronowich, an old Pole who managed a small insurance firm for his fellow countrymen. Henryk reckoned to pick up an extra $20 to $25 a week for the inside knowledge he supplied. Gronowich, in no position to place large sums on the market; never let any of the leaks lead back to his young informant.

Sitting on the lavatory seat, Henryk began to realise that this time he was reading a message of considerable importance. The Governor of Texas was about to grant the Standard Oil Company permission to complete a pipeline from Chicago to Mexico, all other public bodies involved having already agreed to the proposal. The market was aware that the company had been trying to obtain this final permission for nearly a year, but the general view was that the Governor would turn it down. The message was to be passed direct to John D. Rockefeller's broker, Tucker Anthony, immediately. The granting of this permission to build a pipeline would open up the entire North to a ready supply of oil, and that could only mean increased profits. It was obvious to Henryk that Standard Oil stock must rise steadily on the market once the news had broken, especially as Standard Oil already controlled 90 per cent of the oil refineries in America.

In normal circumstances Henryk would have sent on this information direct to Mr Gronowich, and was about to do so when he noticed a rather overweight man, who was also leaving the washroom, drop a piece of paper. As there was no one else about at the time, Henryk picked it up and retreated back into his private cubicle, thinking that at best it would reveal another piece of information. In fact, it was a cheque for $50,000 made out to cash from a Mrs Rose Rennick.

Henryk thought quickly, and not on his feet. He left the washroom at speed and was soon standing outside on Wall Street itself. He made his way to a small coffee-shop on Rector Street and sat there pretending to drink a Coca-Cola while he carefully worked out his plan. He then proceeded to act on it.

First, he cashed the cheque at a branch of the Morgan Bank on the south-west side of Wall Street, knowing that in his smart uniform as a messenger at the Exchange he would easily pass as a carrier for some distinguished firm. He then returned to the Exchange and acquired from a floor broker 2,500 Standard Oil shares at \$$19\frac{7}{8}$, leaving himself $126.61 change after brokerage charges. He placed the $126.61 in a Checking Account with the Morgan Bank. Then, waiting in tense anticipation for an announcement from the Governor's office, he put himself through the motions of a normal day's work, too preoccupied with Standard Oil even to make a detour via the washroom with the messages he carried.

No announcement came. Henryk could not know that the news was being held up until the Exchange had officially closed at 3 pm in order to allow the

Governor himself to buy shares anywhere and everywhere he could lay his grubby hands on them. Henryk went home that night petrified that he had made a disastrous mistake. He had visions of losing his job and everything he had built up over the past four years. Perhaps he would even end up in jail.

He was unable to sleep that night and became steadily more restless in his small open-windowed but airless room. At 1 am he could stand the uncertainty no longer, so he jumped out of bed, shaved, dressed and took a subway to Grand Central Station. From there he walked to Times Square where with trembling hands he bought the first edition of the *Wall Street Journal*. For a moment he couldn't take in the news, although it was shrieking at him in banner headlines:

GOVERNOR GRANTS OIL PIPELINE RIGHTS
TO ROCKEFELLER

and a secondary headline:

HEAVY TRADING EXPECTED IN STANDARD OIL SHARES

Dazed, Henryk walked to the nearest all-night café, on West 42nd Street, and ordered a large hamburger and French fries, which he covered in ketchup and nibbled at like a man eating his last breakfast before facing the electric chair, rather than his first on the way to fortune. He read the full details of Rockefeller's coup on page one, which spread over to page fourteen, and by 4 am he had bought the first three editions of the *New York Times* and the first two editions of the *Herald Tribune.* The lead story was the same in each. Henryk hurried home, giddy and elated, and changed into his uniform. He arrived at the Stock Exchange at 8 am and went through the motions of a day's work, thinking only of how to carry out the second part of his plan.

When the Stock Exchange opened officially, Henryk went over to the Morgan Bank and requested a loan of $50,000 against the security of his 2,500 Standard Oil shares, which had opened that morning at $21¼. He placed the loan in his Checking Account and instructed the bank to issue him a draft for the $50,000 to be made out to Mrs Rose Rennick. He left the bank and looked up the address and telephone number of his unwitting benefactor.

Mrs Rennick, a widow who lived off the investments left by her late husband, lived in a small apartment on 62nd Street, which Henryk knew to be one of the most fashionable parts of New York. The call from a Henryk Metelski, asking to see her on an urgent private matter, came as something of a surprise to her, but a final mention of Halgarten & Co. gave her a little more confidence and she agreed to see him at the Waldorf-Astoria at 4 pm that afteroon.

Henryk had never been inside the Waldorf-Astoria, but after four years on the Stock Exchange there were few prominent hotels or restaurants he had not heard mentioned in other people's conversations. He realised that Mrs Rennick was more likely to have tea with him there than to see a man with a name like Henryk Metelski in her own apartment, especially as his Polish accent was more pronounced over the telephone than it was face to face.

As Henryk stood in the thickly carpeted lobby of the Waldorf, he blushed at his sartorial naïveté. Imagining that everybody was staring at him, he buried his short, amply-covered frame in an elegant chair in the Jefferson Room. Some of the other patrons of the Waldorf were amply covered too, but Henryk felt that *Pommes de Terre Maître d'Hôtel* were more likely to have caused their obesity than French fries. Vainly wishing he had put a little less grease on his black wavy hair and a little more on his down-at-heel shoes, he scratched nervously at an irritating pustule on the side of his mouth and waited. His suit, in which he felt so assured and prosperous among his friends, was shiny, skimpy, cheap and loud. He did not blend in with the décor, still less with the patrons of the hotel, and, feeling inadequate for the first time in his life, he picked up a copy of the *New Yorker*, hid behind it, and prayed for his guest to arrive quickly. Waiters fluttered deferentially with instinctive superciliousness. One, he noticed, did nothing more than circle the tearoom delicately proffering lump sugar from silver tongs in a white-gloved hand: Henryk was enormously impressed.

Rose Rennick arrived a few minutes after four, accompanied by two small dogs and wearing an outrageously large hat. Henryk thought she looked over sixty, overweight, overmade-up and overdressed, but she had a warm smile and appeared to know everyone, as she moved from table to table, chatting to the regular Waldorf-Astoria set. Eventually reaching what she had rightly assumed to be Henryk's table, she was rather taken aback, not only to find him so strangely dressed, but also looking even younger than his eighteen years.

Mrs Rennick ordered tea while Henryk recited his well-rehearsed story: there had been an unfortunate mistake with her cheque, which had been wrongly credited to his firm at the Stock Exchange on the previous day; his boss had instructed him to return the cheque immediately and to say how much they regretted the unfortunate error. Henryk then passed over the draft for $50,000, and added that he would lose his job if she insisted on taking the matter any further, as he had been entirely responsible for the mistake. Mrs Rennick had, in fact, only been informed of the missing cheque that morning and did not realise that it had been cashed, as it would have taken a few days to clear her account. Henryk's perfectly genuine anxiety as he stumbled through his tale would have convinced a far more critical observer of human nature than Mrs Rennick. Readily she agreed to let the matter drop, only too pleased to have her money returned; as it was in the form of a draft from the Morgan Bank, she had lost nothing. Henryk breathed a sigh of relief and for the first time that day began to relax and enjoy himself. He even called for the waiter with the sugar and silver tongs.

After a respectable period of time had passed, Henryk explained that he must return to work, thanked Mrs Rennick for her co-operation, paid the bill and left. Outside on the street he whistled with relief. His new shirt was soaked in sweat (Mrs Rennick would have called it perspiration), but he was out in the open and could breathe freely again. His first major operation had been a success.

He stood on Park Avenue, amused that the venue for his confrontation with Mrs Rennick had been the Waldorf, the very hotel where John D. Rockefeller, the President of Standard Oil, had a suite. Henryk had arrived on foot and used the main entrance, while Mr Rockefeller had earlier arrived by subway and taken his private lift to the Waldorf Towers. Although few New Yorkers were aware of it, Rockefeller had had his own private station built fifty feet below the Waldorf-Astoria to save him travelling the eight blocks to Grand Central Station, there being no stop between there and 125th Street. (The station remains to this day, but as no Rockefellers live at the Waldorf-Astoria, the train never stops there.) While Henryk had been discussing his $50,000 with Mrs Rennick, Rockefeller had been considering an investment of $5,000,000 with Andrew W. Mellon, President Coolidge's Secretary of the Treasury, fifty-seven floors above him.

The next morning Henryk returned to work as usual. He knew he had only five days' grace to sell the shares and clear his debt with the Morgan Bank and the stockbroker, as an account on the New York Stock Exchange runs for five business days or seven calendar days. On the last day of the account the shares were standing at $23¼. He sold at $23⅛, and cleared his overdraft of $49,625 and, after expenses, realised a profit of $7,490 which he left deposited with the Morgan Bank.

Over the next three years, Henryk stopped ringing Mr Gronowich, and started dealing for himself, in small amounts to begin with, but growing larger as he gained in experience and confidence. Times were still good, and while he didn't always make a profit, he had learnt to master the occasional bear market as well as the more common bull. His system in the bear market was to sell short – not a practice considered to be entirely ethical in business. He soon mastered the art of selling shares he didn't own in expectation of a subsequent fall in their price. His instinct for market trends refined as rapidly as did his taste for clothes, and the guile learnt in the backstreets of the Lower East Side always stood him in good stead. Henryk soon discovered that the whole world was a jungle – sometimes the lions and tigers wore suits.

When the stock market collapsed in 1929 Henryk had turned his $7,490 into $51,000 of liquid assets, having sold on every share he possessed the day after the Chairman of Halgarten & Co jumped out of one of the Stock Exchange windows. Henryk had got the message. With his newly acquired income he had moved into a smart apartment in Brooklyn and started driving a rather ostentatious red Stutz. Henryk realised at an early age that he had come into the world with three main disadvantages – his name, background and impecunity. The money problem was solving itself, and now the time had come to expunge the other two. To that end, he had made an application to change his name by court order to Harvey David Metcalfe. When the application was granted, he ceased all further contact with his friends from the Polish community, and in May 1930 he came of age with a new name, new background, and very new money.

It was later that year at a football game that he first met Roger Sharpley and discovered that the rich have their problems too. Sharpley, a young man from Boston, had inherited his father's company, which specialised in the import of whisky and the export of furs. Educated at Choate and later in Dartmouth College, Sharpley had all the assurance and charm of the Boston set, so often envied by his fellow countrymen. He was tall and fair, looked as if he came from Viking stock, and with his air of the gifted amateur, found most things came easily to him – especially women. He was in every way a total contrast to Harvey. Although they were poles apart, the contrast acted like a magnet and attracted the one to the other.

Roger's only ambition in life was to become an

officer in the Navy, but after graduating from Dartmouth he had had to return to the family business because of his father's ill-health. He had only been with the firm a few months when his father died. Roger would have liked to have sold Sharpley & Son to the first bidder, but his father had made a codicil to his will to the effect that if the firm were sold before Roger's fortieth birthday (that being the last day one can enlist for the US Navy), the money gained from the sale would be divided equally among his other relatives.

Harvey gave Roger's problem considerable thought, and after two lengthy sessions with a skilful New York lawyer, suggested a course of action to Roger: Harvey would purchase 49 per cent of Sharpley & Son for $100,000 and the first $20,000 profit each year. At the age of forty, Roger could relinquish the remaining 51 per cent for a further $100,000. The Board would consist of three voting members – Harvey, Roger and one nominated by Harvey, giving him overall control. As far as Harvey was concerned, Roger could join the Navy and need only attend the annual shareholders' meeting.

Roger could not believe his luck. He did not even consult anyone at Sharpley & Son, knowing only too well that they would try to talk him out of it. Harvey had counted on this and had assessed his quarry accurately. Roger gave the proposition only a few days' consideration before allowing the legal papers to be drawn up in New York, far enough away from

Boston to be sure the firm did not learn what was going on. Meanwhile, Harvey returned to the Morgan Bank, where he was now looked upon as a man with a future. Since banks deal in futures, the manager agreed to help him in his new enterprise with a loan of $50,000 to add to his own $50,000, enabling Harvey to acquire 49 per cent of Sharpley & Son, and become its fifth President. The legal documents were signed in New York on October 28th, 1930.

Roger left speedily for Newport, Rhode Island, to commence his Officers Training programme in the US Navy. Harvey left for Grand Central Station to catch the train for Boston. His days as a messenger boy on the New York Stock Exchange were over. He was twenty-one years of age and the President of his own company.

What looked like disaster to most, Harvey could always turn into triumph. The American people were still suffering under Prohibition, and although Harvey could export furs, he could no longer import whisky. This had been the main reason for the fall in the company profits over the past decade. But Harvey soon found that with a little bribery, involving the Mayor of Boston, the Chief of Police and the Customs officials on the Canadian border, plus a payment to the Mafia to ensure that his products reached the restaurants and speak-easies, somehow the whisky imports went up rather than down. Sharpley & Son lost its more respectable and long-serving staff, and replaced them with animals better-suited to Harvey Metcalfe's particular jungle.

From 1930 to 1933 Harvey went from strength to strength, but when Prohibition was finally lifted by President Roosevelt after overwhelming public demand, the excitement went with it, Harvey allowed the company to continue to deal in whisky and furs while he branched out into new fields. In 1933 Sharpley & Son celebrated a hundred years in business. In three years Harvey had lost 97 years of goodwill and doubled the profits. It took him five years to reach his first million and only another four to double the sum again, which was when he decided the time had come for Harvey Metcalfe and Sharpley & Son to part company. In twelve years from 1930 to 1942, he had built up the profits from $30,000 to $910,000. He sold the company in January 1944 for $7,000,000, paying $100,000 to the widow of Captain Roger Sharpley of the US Navy and keeping $6,900,000 for himself.

Harvey celebrated his thirty-fifth birthday by buying at a cost of $4 million a small, ailing bank in Boston called the Lincoln Trust. At the time it boasted a profit of approximately $500,000 a year, a prestigious building in the centre of Boston and an unblemished and somewhat boring reputation. Harvey intended to change both its reputation and its balance sheet. He enjoyed being the President of a bank – but it did nothing to improve his honesty. Every dubious deal in the Boston area seemed to emanate from the

Lincoln Trust, and although Harvey increased the bank's profits to $2 million per annum during the next five years, his personal reputation was never in credit.

Harvey met Arlene Hunter in the winter of 1949. She was the only daughter of the President of the First City Bank of Boston. Until then Harvey had never taken any real interest in women. His driving force had always been making money, and although he considered the opposite sex a useful relaxation in his free time, on balance he found them an inconvenience. But having now reached what the glossy magazines referred to as middle age and having no heir to leave his fortune to, he calculated that it was time to find a wife who would present him with a son. As with everything else that he had wanted in his life, he considered the problem very carefully.

Harvey had first run into Arlene when she was thirty-one: quite literally, when she had backed her car into his new Lincoln. She could not have been a greater contrast to the short, uneducated, overweight Pole. She was nearly six feet tall, slim and although not unattractive, she lacked confidence and was beginning to think that marriage had passed her by. Most of her school friends were already on their second divorces and felt rather sorry for her. Harvey's extravagant ways came as a welcome change after her parents' prudish discipline, which she often felt was to blame for her awkwardness with men of her own age. She had only had one affair – a disastrous failure, thanks to her total innocence – and until Harvey arrived, no one had seemed to be willing to give her a second chance. Arlene's father did not approve of Harvey, and showed it, which only made him more attractive to her. Her father had not approved of any of the men she had associated with, but on this occasion he was right. Harvey on the other hand realised that to marry the First City Bank of Boston with the Lincoln Trust could only be of long-term benefit to him, and with that in mind he set out, as he always did, to conquer. Arlene didn't put up much of a battle.

Arlene and Harvey were married in 1951 at a wedding more memorable for those who were absent than those who attended. They settled into Harvey's Lincoln home outside of Boston and very shortly afterwards Arlene announced she was pregnant. She gave Harvey a daughter almost a year to the day after their marriage.

They christened her Rosalie, and she became the centre of Harvey's attention; his only disappointment came when a prolapse closely followed by a hysterectomy prevented Arlene from bearing him any more children. He sent Rosalie to Bennetts, the most expensive girls' school in Washington, and from there she was accepted at Vassar to major in English. This even pleased old man Hunter, who had grown to tolerate Harvey and adore hs granddaughter. On gaining her degree, Rosalie continued her education at the

Sorbonne, after a fierce disagreement with her father concerning the type of friends she was keeping, particularly the ones with long hair who didn't want to go to Vietnam – not that Harvey had done much during the Second World War, except to cash in on every shortage. The final crunch came when Rosalie dared to suggest that morals were not to be decided only by length of hair or political views. Harvey missed her, but refused to admit the fact to Arlene.

Harvey had three loves in his life: the first was still Rosalie, the second was his paintings, and the third his orchids. The first had started the moment his daughter was born. The second was a love that had developed over many years and had been kindled in the strangest way. A client of Sharpley & Son was about to go bankrupt while still owing a fairly large sum of money to the company. Harvey got wind of it and went round to confront him, but the rot had already set in and there was no longer any hope of securing cash. Determined not to leave empty-handed, Harvey took with him the man's only tangible asset – a Renoir valued at $10,000.

Harvey's intention was to sell the picture quickly before it could be proved that he was a preferred creditor, but he became so entranced with the fine brushwork and the delicate pastel shades that his only desire was to own more. When he realised that pictures were not only a good investment, but that he actually liked them as well, his collection and his love grew hand in hand. By the early 1970s, Harvey had a Manet, two Monets, a Renoir, two Picassos, a Pissarro, a Utrillo, a Cézanne, as well as most of the recognised lesser names, and he had become quite a connoisseur of the Impressionist period. His one remaining desire was to possess a Van Gogh, and only recently he had failed to acquire *L'Hôpital de St Paul à St Remy* at the Sotheby-Parke Bernet Gallery in New York, when Dr Armand Hammer of Occidental Petroleum had outbid him – $1,200,000 had been just a little too much for Harvey.

Earlier, in 1966, he had failed to acquire Lot 49, *Mademoiselle Ravoux*, from Christie, Manson & Woods, the London art dealers; although the Rev. Theodore Pitcairn, representing the Lord's New Church in Bryn Athyn, Pennsylvania, had pushed him over the top, he had only whetted his appetite further. The Lord giveth, and on that occasion the Lord had taken away. Although it was not fully appreciated in Boston, it was already recognised in the art world that Harvey had one of the finest Impressionist collections in the world, almost as widely admired as that of Walter Annenberg, President Nixon's Ambassador to London who, like Harvey, had been one of the few people to build up a major collection since the Second World War.

Harvey's third love was his prize collection of orchids, and he had three times been a winner at the New England Spring Flower Show in Boston, twice beating old man Hunter into second place.

*

Harvey now travelled to Europe once a year. He had established a successful stud in Kentucky and liked to see his horses run at Longchamp and Ascot. He also enjoyed watching Wimbledon, which he considered was still the greatest tennis tournament in the world. It amused him to do a little business in Europe at the same time, giving him the opportunity to make some more money for his Swiss bank account in Zürich. He did not need a Swiss account, but somehow he got a kick out of doing Uncle Sam. Although Harvey had mellowed over the years and cut down on his more dubious deals, he could never resist the chance to take a risk if he thought the reward was likely to be big enough. One such golden opportunity presented itself in 1964 when Her Majesty's Government invited applications for exploration and production licences in the North Sea. At that time neither the British Government nor the civil servants involved had any idea of the future significance of North Sea oil, or the role it would eventually play in British politics. If the Government had known that in 1978 the Arabs would be holding a pistol to the heads of the rest of the world, and the British House of Commons would have eleven Scottish Nationalist Members of Parliament, it would surely have reacted in a totally different way.

On May 13th, 1964, the Secretary of State for Power laid before Parliament 'Statutory Instrument – No. 708 – Continental Shelf – Petroteum'. Harvey read this particular document with great interest, thinking that it might well be a means of making an exceptional killing. He was particularly fascinated by Paragraph 4 of the document, which read:

> Persons who are citizens of the United Kingdom and Colonies and are resident in the United Kingdom or who are bodies corporate incorporated in the United Kingdom may apply in accordance with these Regulations for:
>
> (a) production licence; or,
> (b) an exploration licence.

When he had studied the Regulations in their entirety, he had to sit back and think hard. Only a small amount of money was required to secure a production and exploration licence. As Paragraph 6 went on to point out:

> (1) With every application for a production licence there shall be paid a fee of two hundred pounds with an additional fee of five pounds for every block after the first ten in respect whereof that application is made.
>
> (2) With every application for an exploration licence there shall be paid a fee of twenty pounds.

Harvey couldn't believe it. How easy it would be to use such a licence to create an impression of a vast enterprise! For a few hundred dollars he could be alongside such names as Shell, BP, Total, Gulf and Occidental.

Harvey went over the Regulations again and again, hardly believing that the British Government could release such potential for so small an investment. Only the application form, an elaborate and exacting document, now stood in his way. Harvey was not a British subject, none of his companies was British and he realised he would have problems of presentation. He decided that his application must therefore be backed by a British bank and that he would set up a company whose directors would win the confidence of the British Government.

With this in mind, early in 1964, he registered at Companies House in England a firm called Prospecta Oil, using Malcolm, Bottnick and Davis as his solicitors and Barclays Bank, who were already the Lincoln Trust's representative in Europe, as his bankers. Lord Hunnisett became Chairman of the company and several distinguished public figures joined the Board, including two ex-Members of Parliament who had lost their seats when the Labour Party won the 1964 Election. Prospecta Oil issued 2,000,000 10-pence shares at one pound, which were all taken up for Harvey by nominees. He also deposited $500,000 in the Lombard Street branch of Barclays Bank.

Having thus created the front, Harvey then used Lord Hunnisett to apply for the licence from the British Government. The new Labour Government elected in October 1964 was no more aware of the significance of North Sea oil than the earlier Conservative administration. The Government's requirements for a licence were a rent of £12,000 a year for the first six years, 12½ per cent revenue tax, and a further Capital Gains tax on profits; but as Harvey's plan was to reap profits for himself rather than the company that presented no problems.

On May 22nd, 1965, the Minister of Power published in the *London Gazette* the name of Prospecta Oil among the fifty-two companies granted production licences. On August 3rd, 1965, Statutory Instrument No. 1531 allocated the actual areas. Prospecta Oil's was 51° 50′ 00″ N: 2° 30′ 20″ E, a site adjacent to one of BP's holdings.

Then Harvey sat back, waiting for one of the companies which had acquired North Sea sites to strike oil. It was a longish wait but Harvey was in no hurry, and not until June 1970 did BP make a big commercial strike in their Forties Field. BP had already spent over $1 billion in the North Sea and Harvey was determined to be one of the main beneficiaries. He was now on to another winner, and immediately set the second part of his plan in motion.

Early in 1972 he hired an oil rig which, with much flourish and advance publicity, he had towed out to the Prospecta Oil site. Having hired the rig on the basis of being able to renew the contract if he made a successful strike, he engaged the minimum number of workers allowed by the Government Regulations, and then proceeded to drill to 6,000 feet. After this drilling had been completed he released from the company's employment all those involved, but told Reading &

Bates, from whom he had rented the rig, that he would be requiring it again in the near future and therefore would continue to pay the rental.

Harvey then released Prospecta Oil shares on to the market at the rate of a few thousand a day for the next two months, all from his own stock, and whenever the financial journalists of the British Press rang to ask why these shares were steadily rising, the young public relations officer at Prospecta Oil's city office would say, as briefed, that he had no comment to make at present but there would be a press statement in the near future; some newspapers put two and two together and made about fifteen. The shares climbed steadily from 10 pence to nearly £2 under the guidance of Harvey's chief executive in Britain, Bernie Silverman, who, with his long experience of this kind of operation, was only too aware of what his boss was up to. Silverman's main task was to ensure that nobody could show a direct connection between Metcalfe and Prospecta Oil.

In January 1974 the shares stood at £3. It was then that Harvey was ready to move on to the third part of his plan, using Prospecta Oil's enthusiastic new recruit, a young Harvard graduate called David Kesler, as the fall-guy.

2

DAVID PUSHED his glasses back on to the bridge of his nose and read the advertisement in the Business Section of the *Boston Globe* again, to make sure he was not dreaming. It could have been tailor-made for him:

> Oil Company based in Great Britain, carrying out extensive work in the North Sea off Scotland, requires a young executive with experience in the stock market and/or financial marketing. Salary $25,000 a year. Accommodation supplied. Based in London. Apply Box No. 217A.

Knowing it could lead to other openings in an expanding industry, David thought it sounded like a challenge and wondered if they would consider him experienced enough. He recalled what his tutor in European affairs used to say: 'If you must work in Great Britain, better make it the North Sea. With their union problems, there's nothing else great about the country.'

David Kesler was a lean, clean-shaven young American, with a crew cut which would have been better suited to a lieutenant in the Marines, a fresh complexion and an unquenchable earnestness. David wanted to succeed in business with all the fervour of the new Harvard Business School graduate. He had spent six years in all at Harvard, the first four studying mathematics for his Bachelor degree, and the last two across the Charles River at the Business School. Recently graduated and armed with a BA and an MBA, he was looking for a job that would reward him for the exceptional capacity for hard work he knew he possessed. Never a brilliant scholar, he envied those natural academics among his classmates who mastered post-Keynesian economic theories like children learning their multiplication tables. David had worked ferociously for six years, only lifting his nose far enough from the grindstone to fit in a daily workout at the gymnasium and the occasional weekend watching Harvard Jocks defending the honour of the university on the football field or on the basketball court. He would have enjoyed playing himself, but that would have meant less time for study.

He read the advertisement again, and then typed a carefully prepared letter to the box number. A few days passed before a reply came, summoning him for an interview at a local hotel on the following Wednesday at 3.00.

David arrived at 2.45 pm at the Copley Hotel on Huntingdon Avenue, the adrenalin pumping through his body. He repeated the Harvard Business School motto to himself as he was ushered into a small private room: look British, think Yiddish.

Three men, who introduced themselves as Silverman, Cooper and Elliott, interviewed him. Bernie Silverman, a short, grey-haired, check-tied New Yorker with a solid aura of success, was in charge. Cooper and Elliott sat and watched David silently.

Silverman spent a considerable time giving David an enticing description of the company's background and its future aims. Harvey had trained Silverman carefully and he had at his well-manicured fingertips all the glib expertise needed by the right-hand man in a Metcalfe coup.

'So there you have it, Mr Kesler. We're involved in one of the biggest commercial opportunities in the world, drilling for oil in the North Sea off Scotland. Our company, Prospecta Oil, has the backing of a group of banks in America. We have been granted licences from the British Government and we have the financing. But companies are made not by money, Mr Kesler, but by people – it's as simple as that. We're looking for a man who will work night and day to help put Prospecta Oil on the map, and we'll pay the right man a top salary to do just that. If we offer you the position, you'll be working in our London office under the immediate direction of our Managing Director, Mr Elliott.'

'Where are the company headquarters?'

'New York, but we have offices in Montreal, San Francisco, London, Aberdeen, Paris and Brussels.'

'Is the company looking for oil anywhere else?'

'Not at the moment,' answered Silverman. 'We're

sinking millions into the North Sea after BP's successful strike, and the fields around us have so far had a one-in-five success ratio, which is very high in our business.'

'When would you want the successful applicant to start?'

'Some time in January, when he's completed a government training course on management in oil,' said Richard Elliott. The slim, sallow No. 2 sounded as if he was from Georgia. The government course was a typical Harvey Metcalfe touch – maximum credibility for minimum expense.

'And the company apartment,' said David, 'where's that?'

Cooper spoke:

'You'll have one of the company flats in the Barbican, a few hundred yards away from our London City office.'

David had no more questions – Silverman had covered everything and seemed to know exactly what he wanted.

Ten days later David received a telegram inviting him to join Silverman for lunch at the 21 Club in New York. When David arrived at the restaurant, he recognised a host of well-known faces at nearby tables and felt new confidence: his host obviously knew what he was about. Their table was in one of the small alcoves selected by businessmen who prefer their conversations to remain confidential.

Silverman was genial and relaxed. He stretched

the conversation out a little, discussing irrelevancies, but finally, over a brandy, offered David the position in London. David was delighted: $25,000 a year, and the chance to be involved with a company which obviously had such an exciting future. He did not hesitate in agreeing to start his new appointment in London on January 1st.

David Kesler had never been to England before: how green the grass was, how narrow the roads, how closed in by hedges and fences were the houses! It felt like Toy Town after the vast highways and large automobiles of New York. The small flat in the Barbican was clean and impersonal and, as Mr Cooper had said, convenient for the office a few hundred yards away in Threadneedle Street.

Prospecta's offices consisted of seven rooms on one floor of a large Victorian building; Silverman's was the only office with a prestigious air about it. There was a tiny reception area, a telex room, two rooms for secretaries, a larger room for Mr Elliott and another small one for himself. It seemed very poky to David, but as Silverman was quick to point out, office rent in the City of London was $30 a square foot compared with $10 in New York.

Bernie Silverman's secetary, Judith Lampson, ushered David through to the well appointed office of the Chief Executive. Silverman sat in a large black swivel chair behind a massive desk, which made him look like a midget. By his side were positioned four telephones, three white and one red. David was later to learn that the important-looking red telephone was directly connected to a number in the States, but he never actually discovered to whom.

'Good morning, Mr Silverman. Where would you like me to start?'

'Bernie, please call me Bernie. Take a seat. Notice the change in the price of the company's shares in the last few days?'

'Oh, yes,' enthused David. 'Up a half to nearly $6. I suppose it's because of our new bank backing and the other companies' successful strikes?'

'No,' said Silverman in a low tone designed to give the impression that no one else must hear this part of the conversation, 'the truth is that we've made a big strike ourselves, but we haven't yet decided when to announce it. It's all in this geologist's report.' He threw a smart, colourful document over his desk.

David whistled under his breath. 'What are the company's plans at the moment?'

'We'll announce the strike,' said Silverman quietly, picking at his India rubber as he talked, 'in about three weeks' time, when we're certain of the full extent and capacity of the hole. We want to make some plans for coping with the publicity and the sudden inflow of money. The shares will go through the roof, of course.'

'The shares have already climbed steadily. Perhaps some people already know?'

'I guess that's right,' said Silverman. 'The trouble with that black stuff is once it comes out of the ground you can't hide it.' Silverman laughed.

'Is there any harm in getting in on the act?' asked David.

'No, as long as it doesn't harm the company in any way. Just let me know if anyone wants to invest. We don't have the problems of inside information in England – none of the restrictive laws we have in America.'

'How high do you think the shares will go?'

Silverman looked him straight in the eye and then said casually, '$20.'

Back in his own office, David carefully read the geologist's report that Silverman had given him: it certainly looked as if Prospecta Oil had made a successful strike, but the extent of the find was not, as yet, entirely certain. When he had completed the report, he glanced at his watch and cursed. The geologist's file had totally absorbed him. He threw the report into his briefcase and took a taxi to Paddington Station, only just making the 6.15 train. He was due in Oxford for dinner with an old classmate from Harvard.

On the train down to the university city he thought about Stephen Bradley, who had been a friend in his Harvard days and had generously helped David and other students in mathematics classes that year. Stephen, now a visiting Fellow at Magdalen College, was undoubtedly one of the most brilliant scholars of

David's generation. He had won the Kennedy Memorial Scholarship to Harvard and later in 1970 the Wister Prize for Mathematics, the most sought-after award in the mathematical faculty. Although in monetary terms this award was a derisory $80 and a medal, it was the reputation and job offers it brought with it that made the competition so keen. Stephen had won it with consummate ease and nobody was surprised when he was successful in his application for a Fellowship at Oxford. He was now in his third year of research at Magdalen. His papers on Boolean algebra appeared at short intervals in the *Proceedings of the London Mathematical Society*, and it had just been announced that he had been elected to a Chair in Mathematics back at his alma mater, Harvard, to commence in the fall.

The 6.15 train from Paddington arrived in Oxford an hour later and the short taxi ride from the station down New College Lane brought him to Magdalen at 7.30. One of the College porters escorted David to Stephen's rooms, which were spacious, ancient, and comfortably cluttered with books, cushions and prints. How unlike the antiseptic walls of Harvard, thought David. Stephen was there to greet him. He didn't seem to have changed one iota. His suit seemed to hang off his tall, thin, ungainly body; no tailor would ever have employed him as a dummy. His heavy eyebrows protruded over his out-of-date round-rimmed spectacles, which he almost seemed to hide behind in his shyness. He ambled over to David and welcomed him, one minute an old man, the next younger than his thirty years. Stephen poured David a Jack Daniels and they settled down to chat. Although Stephen never looked upon David as a close friend at Harvard, he had enjoyed coaching him and always found him eager to learn; besides, he always welcomed an excuse to entertain Americans at Oxford.

'It's been a memorable three years, David,' said Stephen, pouring him a second drink. 'The only sad event was the death of my father last winter. He took such an interest in my life at Oxford and gave my academic work so much support. He's left me rather well off, actually . . . Bath plugs were obviously more in demand than I realised. You might be kind enough to advise me on how to invest some of the money, because at the moment it's just sitting on deposit in the bank. I never seem to have the time to do anything about it, and when it comes to investments I haven't a clue.'

That started David off about his demanding new job with Prospecta Oil.

'Why don't you invest your money in my company, Stephen. We've had a fantastic strike in the North Sea, and when they announce it the shares are going to go through the roof. The whole operation would only take a month or so and you could make the killing of a lifetime. I only wish I had some of my own money to put into it.'

'Have you had the full details of the strike?'

'No, but I've seen the geologist's report, and that makes pretty good reading. The shares are already going up fast and I'm convinced they'll reach $20. The problem is that time is already running out.'

Stephen glanced at the geologist's report, thinking he would study it carefully later.

'How does one go about an investment of this sort?' he asked.

'Well, you find a respectable stockbroker, buy as many shares as you can afford and then wait for the strike to be announced. I'll keep you informed on how things are going and advise you when I feel is the best time to sell.'

'That would be extremely thoughtful of you, David.'

'It's the least I can do after all the help you gave me with maths at Harvard.'

'Oh, that was nothing. Let's go and have some dinner.'

Stephen led David to the college dining hall, an oblong, oak-panelled room covered in pictures of past Presidents of Magdalen, bishops and academics. The long wooden tables at which the undergraduates were eating filled the body of the hall, but Stephen shuffled up to the High Table and offered David a more comfortable seat. The students were a noisy, enthusiastic bunch – Stephen didn't notice them, but David was enjoying the whole experience.

The seven-course meal was formidable and David wondered how Stephen kept so thin with such daily temptations. When they reached the port, Stephen suggested they return to his rooms rather than join the crusty old dons in the Senior Common Room.

Late into the night, over the rubicund Magdalen port, they talked about North Sea oil and Boolean algebra, each admiring the other for his mastery of his subject. Stephen, like most academics, was fairly credulous outside the bounds of his own discipline. He began to think that an investment in Prospecta Oil would be a very astute move on his part.

In the morning, they strolled down Addison's Walk near Magdalen Bridge, where the grass grows green and lush by the Cherwell. Reluctantly, David caught a taxi at 9.45 leaving Magdalen behind him and passing New College, Trinity, Balliol and finally Worcester, where he saw scrawled across the college wall, '*c'est magnifique mais ce n'est pas la gare*'. He caught the 10.00 am train back to London. He had enjoyed his stay at Oxford and hoped he had been able to help his old Harvard friend, who had done so much for him in the past.

'Good morning, David.'

'Good morning, Bernie. I thought I ought to let you know I spent the evening with a friend at Oxford, and he may invest some money in the company. It might be as much as $250,000.'

'That's fine, David, keep up the good work. You're doing a great job.'

Silverman showed no surprise at David's news, but once back in his own office he picked up the red telephone.

'Harvey?'

'Yes.'

'Kesler seems to have been the right choice. He may have talked a friend of his into investing $250,000 in the company.'

'Good. Now listen carefully. Brief my broker to put 40,000 shares on the market at just over $6 a share. If Kesler's friend does decide to invest in the company, mine will be the only large block of shares immediately available.'

After a further day's consideration, Stephen noticed that the shares of Prospecta Oil moved from £2.75 to £3.05 and decided the time had come to invest in what he was now convinced must be a winner. He trusted David, and had been impressed by the glossy geologist's report. He rang Kitcat & Aitken, a firm of stockbrokers in the City, and instructed them to buy $250,000-worth of shares in Prospecta Oil. Harvey Metcalfe's broker released 40,000 shares when Stephen's request came on to the floor of the stock exchange and the transaction was quickly completed. Stephen's purchase price was £3.10.

After investing his father's inheritance, Stephen spent the next few days happily watching the shares climb to £3.50, even before the expected announcement. Though Stephen didn't realise it, it was his own investment that had caused the shares to rise. He began to wonder what he would spend the profit on even before he had realised it. He decided not to cash in immediately, but hold on; David thought the shares would reach $20, and in any case he had promised to tell him when to sell.

Meanwhile, Harvey Metcalfe began to release a few more shares on to the market, because of the interest created by Stephen's investment. He was beginning to agree with Silverman that David Kesler, young, honest, and with all the enthusiasm of a man in his first appointment, had been an excellent choice. It was not the first time Harvey had used this ploy, keeping himself well away from the action while placing the responsibility on inexperienced, innocent shoulders.

At the same time, Richard Elliott, acting as the company spokesman, leaked stories to the press about large buyers coming into the market, which in itself occasioned a flood of small investors and kept the price steady.

One lesson a man learns in the Harvard Business School is that an executive is only as good as his health. David never felt happy without a regular medical check-up; he rather enjoyed being told he was in good shape, but perhaps should take things a little easier. His secretary, Miss Rentoul, had therefore made an appointment for him with a Harley Street doctor.

Dr Robin Oakley was by anyone's standards a successful man. At thirty-seven he was tall and handsome, with a head of dark hair that looked as if it would never recede. He had a classic strong face and the self-assurance that came from proven success. He still played squash twice a week, which helped him look enviably younger than his contemporaries. Robin had remained fit since his Cambridge days, which he left with a Rugby Blue and an upper-second-class degree. He had gone on to complete his medical training at St Thomas's, where once again his Rugby football rather than his medical skill brought him into prominence with those who decide the future careers of young men. When he qualified, he went to work as an assistant to a highly successful Harley Street practitioner, Dr Eugene Moffat. Dr Moffat was successful not so much in curing the sick as in charming the rich, especially middle-aged women, who came to see him again and again however little seemed to be wrong with them. At fifty guineas a visit that had to be regarded as success.

Moffat had chosen Robin Oakley as his assistant for exactly those qualities which he himself displayed, and which had made him so sought-after. Robin Oakley was unquestionably good-looking, personable, well-educated – and just clever enough. Robin settled very well into Harley Street and the Moffat system, and when the older man died suddenly in his early sixties, he took over his mantle with the ease with which a crown prince would take over a throne. Robin continued to build up the practice, losing none of Moffat's ladies other than by natural causes, and did remarkably well for himself. He had a wife and two sons, a comfortable country house a few miles outside Newbury in Berkshire, and a considerable saving in blue chip securities. He never complained at his good fortune and enjoyed life, at the same time being, he had to confess, a little bored with it all. He was beginning to find that the bland role of sympathetic doctor was almost intolerably cloying. Would the world come to an end if he admitted that he neither knew nor cared just what was causing the minute patches of dermatitis on Lady Fiona Fisher's diamond-studded hands? Would the Heavens descend if he told the dreaded Mrs Page-Stanley that she was a malodorous old woman in need of nothing more medically taxing than a new set of dentures? And would he be struck off if he personally administered to the nubile Miss Lydia de Villiers a good dose of what she so clearly indicated she desired?

David Kesler arrived on time for his appointment. He had been warned by Miss Rentoul that in England doctors and dentists cancel if you are late and still charge you.

He stripped and lay on Robin Oakley's couch. The doctor took his blood pressure, listened to his heart, and made him put out his tongue, an organ that seldom stands up well to public scrutiny. As he tapped and poked his way over David's body, they chatted.

'What brings you to work in London, Mr Kesler?'

'I'm with an oil company in the City. I expect you've heard of us – Prospecta Oil?'

'No,' said Robin. 'Can't say I have. Bend your legs up, please.' He hit David's knee-caps smartly, one after the other, with a patella hammer. The legs jumped wildly.

'Nothing wrong with those reflexes.'

'You will, Dr Oakley, you will. Things are going very well for us. Watch out for our progress in the papers.'

'Why?' said Robin, smiling, 'Struck oil, have you?'

'Yes,' said David quietly, pleased with the impression he was creating, 'as a matter of fact we've done just that.'

Robin prodded David's abdomen for a few seconds. 'Good muscular wall, not fat, no sign of an enlarged liver. Young man, you're in good physical shape.'

Robin left him in the examination room to get dressed and thoughtfully wrote out a brief report on Kesler for his records, while his mind dwelt on deeper things. An oil strike.

Harley Street doctors, although they routinely keep private patients waiting for three-quarters of an hour in a gas-fired waiting-room equipped with one out-of-date copy of *Punch*, never let them feel rushed once they are in the consulting room. Robin had no intention of rushing Mr Kesler.

'There's very little wrong with you, Mr Kesler. Some signs of anaemia, which I suspect are caused by nothing more than overwork and your recent rushing about. I'm going to give you some iron tablets which should quickly take care of that. Take two a day, morning and night.' He scribbled an illegible prescription for the tablets and handed it to David.

'Many thanks. It's kind of you to give me so much of your time.'

'Not at all. How are you finding London?' asked Robin. 'Very different from America, I expect.'

'Sure – the pace is much slower. Once I've mastered how long it takes to get something done here I'll be halfway to victory.'

'Do you have many friends in London?'

'No,' replied David, 'I have one or two buddies at Oxford from my Harvard days, but I haven't yet made contact with many people in London.'

Good, thought Robin, here is a chance for me to find out a little more about the oil game, and spend some time with a man who makes most of his patients look as if they had both feet in the grave. It might even shake me out of my lethargy. He continued, 'Would you care to join me for lunch later in the week? You might like to see one of our antique London clubs.'

'How very kind of you.'

'Excellent. Will Friday suit you?'

'It certainly will.'

'Then let's say one o'clock at the Athenaeum Club in Pall Mall.'

David returned to his City desk, picking up his tablets on the way. He took one immediately. He was beginning to enjoy his stay in London. Silverman seemed pleased with him, Prospecta Oil was doing well and he was already meeting some interesting people. Yes, he felt this was going to be a very happy period in his life.

On Friday at 12.45 pm, David arrived at the Athenaeum, a massive white building on the corner of Pall Mall, overlooked by a statue of the Duke of York. David was amazed by the size of the rooms and his commercial mind could not help wondering what price they would fetch as office space. The place appeared to be full of moving waxworks who, Robin later assured him, were in fact distinguished generals and diplomats.

They lunched in the Coffee Room, dominated by a Rubens of Charles II, and talked about Boston, London, squash, and their shared passion for Katharine Hepburn. Over coffee, David readily told Robin the details of the geologist's findings on the Prospecta Oil site. The shares had now climbed to £3.60 on the London Stock Exchange, and were still going up.

'Sounds like a good investment,' said Robin, 'and as it's your own company, it might be worth the risk.'

'I don't think there's much of a risk,' said David, 'as long as the oil is actually there.'

'Well, I'll certainly consider it most seriously over the weekend.'

They parted on the steps of the Athenaeum, David to a conference on the Energy Crisis organised by the *Financial Times*, Robin to his home in Berkshire. His two young sons were back from prep school for the weekend and he was looking forward to seeing them again. How quickly they had passed from babies to toddlers, to boys; soon they would be young men, he thought. And how reassuring to know their future was secure. Perhaps he should make that future a little more secure by investing in David Kesler's company. He could always put the money back into blue chip shares once the strike had been announced.

Bernie Silverman was also pleased to hear the possibility of a further investment.

'Congratulations, my boy. We're going to need a lot of capital to finance the pipe-laying operations, you know. Pipe-laying can cost $2 million per mile. Still, you're playing your part. I've just had word from head office that we are to give you a $5,000 bonus for your efforts. Keep up the good work.'

David smiled. This was business in the proper Harvard tradition. If you bring home the results, you get the rewards.

'When will the strike be officially announced?' he asked.

'Some time in the next few days.'

David left Silverman's office with a glow of pride.

Silverman immediately contacted Harvey Metcalfe on the red phone, and he set the routine in motion once again. Metcalfe's brokers released on to the market 35,000 shares at £3.73 and approximately 5,000 each day on to the open market, always being able to feel when the market had taken enough and thus keeping the price steady. Once again, the shares climbed when Dr Oakley invested heavily in the market, this time to £3.90, keeping David, Robin and Stephen all happy. They were not to know that Harvey was releasing more shares each day because of the interest they had caused, and that this was now creating a market of its own.

David decided to spend some of his bonus on a painting for his little flat in the Barbican, which he felt was rather grey. About $2,000, he thought, something that was going to appreciate in value. David quite enjoyed art for art's sake, but he liked it even more for business's sake. He spent Friday afternoon tramping around Bond Street, Cork Steet and Bruton Street, the home of the London art galleries. The Wildenstein was too expensive for his pocket and the Marlborough too modern for his taste. The painting he finally picked out was at the Lamanns Gallery in Bond Street.

The gallery, just three doors away from Sotheby's,

consisted of one vast room with a worn grey carpet and red faded wallpaper. As David was later to learn, the more worn the carpet, the more faded the walls, the greater the success and reputation of the gallery. There was a staircase at the far end of the room, against which some unregarded paintings were stacked, backs to the world. David sorted through them on a whim and found, to his delight, something that appealed to him.

It was an oil by Leon Underwood called *Venus in the Park.* The large, rather sombre canvas contained about six men and women sitting on metal chairs at circular tea-tables. Among them, in the foreground, was a comely naked woman with generous breasts and long hair. Nobody was paying her the slightest attention and she sat gazing out of the picture, face inscrutable, a symbol of warmth and love in indifferent surroundings. David found her utterly compelling.

The gallery proprietor, Jean-Pierre Lamanns, advanced on him, adorned in an elegantly tailored suit, as befitted a man who rarely received cheques for less than a thousand pounds. At thirty-five, he could afford the little extravagances of life, and his Gucci shoes, Yves St Laurent tie, Turnbull & Asser shirt and Piaget watch left no one, especially women, in any doubt that he knew what he was about. He was an Englishman's vision of a Frenchman, slim and neat with longish, dark wavy hair and deep brown eyes that hinted at being a little sharp. He was capable of being pernickety and demanding, with a wit that was often as cruel as it was amusing, which may have been one of the reasons why he had not married. There certainly had been no shortage of applicants. Customers, however, saw only his charming side. As David wrote out his cheque, Jean-Pierre rubbed his forefinger backwards and forwards over his fashionable moustache, only too happy to discuss the picture.

'Underwood is one of the greatest sculptors and artists in England today. He even tutored Henry Moore, you know. I believe he is underestimated because of his dislike of journalists and the press, whom he describes as nothing more than drunken scribblers.'

'Hardly the way to endear oneself to the media,' murmured David, as he handed over the cheque for £850, feeling agreeably prosperous. Although it was the most expensive purchase he had ever made, he felt the picture was a good investment and, more important, he liked it.

Jean-Pierre took David downstairs to show him the Impressionist and Modern collection he had built up over many years, continuing to enthuse about Underwood. They celebrated David's first acquisition over a whisky in Jean-Pierre's office.

'What line of business are you in, Mr Kesler?'

'I work with a small oil company called Prospecta Oil, who are exploring prospects in the North Sea.'

'Had any success?' enquired Jean-Pierre, a little too innocently.

'Well, between the two of us, we're rather excited

about the future. It's no secret that the company shares have gone from £2 to nearly £4 in the last few weeks, but no one knows the real reason.'

'Would it be a good investment for a poor little art dealer like myself?' asked Jean-Pierre.

'I'll tell you how good an investment I think it is,' said David. 'I am putting $3,000 in the company on Monday, which is all I have left in the world – now that I've captured Venus, that is. We'll shortly be making a rather important announcement.'

A twinkle came into Jean-Pierre's eye. To one of his Gallic subtlety, a nod was as good as a wink. He did not pursue the line of conversation any further.

'When's the strike going to be announced, Bernie?'

'I'm expecting it early next week. We've had a few problems. Nothing we can't lick, though.'

That gave David some relief, as he had taken up 500 shares himself that morning, investing the remaining $3,000 from his bonus. Like the others, he was hoping for a quick profit.

'Rowe Rudd.'

'Frank Watts, please. Jean-Pierre Lamanns.'

'Good morning, Jean-Pierre. What can we do for you?'

'I want to buy 25,000 Prospecta Oil.'

'Never heard of them. Hold on a minute . . . New

company, very low capital. A bit risky, J.-P. I wouldn't recommend it.'

'It's all right, Frank, I only want them for two or three weeks, then you can sell. I've no intention of holding on to them. When did the account start?'

'Yesterday.'

'Right. Buy this morning and sell them before the end of the account, or earlier. I'm expecting an announcement next week, so once they go over £5 you can get rid of them. No need to be greedy, but buy them in my company name, I don't want the deal traced back to me – it might embarrass the informant.'

'Right, sir. Buy 25,000 Prospecta Oil at market price and sell before the last day of the account, or sooner if instructed.'

'Correct, I'll be in Paris all next week looking at pictures, so don't hesitate to sell once they go over £5.'

'Right, J.-P. Have a good trip.'

The red telephone rang.

'Rowe Rudd are looking for a substantial block of shares. Do you know anything about it?'

'No idea, Harvey. It must be David Kesler again. Do you want me to speak to him?'

'No, say nothing. I've released another 25,000 shares at £3.90. Kesler's only got to do one more big one and I'll be out. Prepare our plan for seven days before the end of this Stock Exchange account.'

'Right, boss. You know quite a few people are also buying in small amounts.'

'Yes, just as before, they all have to tell their friends they're on to a good thing. Say nothing to Kesler.'

'You know, David,' said Richard Elliott, 'you work too hard. Relax. We're going to have enough work on our hands when the announcement's made.'

'I guess so,' said David. 'Work's just a habit with me now.'

'Well, why don't you take tonight off and join me for a spot of something at Annabel's?'

David was flattered by the invitation to London's most exclusive nightclub and accepted enthusiastically.

David's hired Ford Cortina looked somewhat out of place that evening in Berkeley Square among the double-parked Rolls Royces and Mercedes. He made his way down the little iron staircase into the basement, which at one time must have been no more than the servants' quarters for the elegant town house above. Now it was a splendid club, with a restaurant, discothèque and a small elegant bar, the walls covered in old prints and pictures. The main dining-room was dimly lit and crowded with small tables, most of them already occupied. The décor was Regency and extravagant. Mark Birley, the owner, had in the short period of ten years made Annabel's the most sought-after club in London, with a waiting list for membership of well over a thousand. The discothèque was playing in the far corner of a crowded dance floor, on which you couldn't have parked two Cadillacs. Most of the couples were dancing very close to each other – they had little choice. David was somewhat surprised to observe that nearly all of the men on the floor were about twenty years older than the girls they held in their arms. The head waiter, Louis, showed David to Richard Elliott's table, realising it was David's first visit to the club by the way he stared at all the personalities of the day. Oh well, thought David, perhaps one day they'll be staring at me.

After an exceptionally good dinner Richard Elliott and his wife joined the crowd on the dance floor, while David returned to the little bar surrounded by comfortable red settees and struck up a conversation with someone who introduced himself as James Brigsley. Even if he did not treat the whole world as such, Mr Brigsley certainly treated Annabel's as a stage. Tall, blond and aristocratic, his eyes alight with good humour, he seemed at ease with everyone around him. David admired his assured manner, something he had never acquired and feared he never would. His accent, even to David's untutored ears, was resonantly upper-class.

David's new acquaintance talked of his visits to the States, flattering him by remarking how much he had always liked the Americans. After some time, David was able quietly to ask the head waiter who the Englishman was.

'He's Lord Brigsley, the eldest son of the Earl of Louth, sir.'

What do you know, thought David, lords look like anyone else, especially when they've had a few drinks. Lord Brigsley was tapping David's glass.

'Would you care for another?'

'Thank you very much, my lord,' said David.

'Don't bother with all that nonsense. The name's James. What are you doing in London?'

'I work for an oil company. You probably know my Chairman, Lord Hunnisett. I've never met him myself, to tell you the truth.'

'Sweet old buffer,' said James. 'His son and I were at Harrow together. If you're in oil, perhaps you can tell me what to do with my Shell and BP shares.'

'Hold on to them,' said David. 'It's sensible to remain in any commodities, especially oil, as long as the British Government doesn't get greedy and try to take control of the assets themselves.'

Another double whisky arrived. David was beginning to feel just slightly tipsy.

'What about your own company?' enquired James.

'We're rather small,' said David, 'but our shares have gone up more than any other oil company in the last three months. Even so, I suspect they've nowhere near reached their zenith.'

'Why?' demanded James.

David glanced round and lowered his voice to a confidential whisper.

'Well, I expect you realise that if you make an oil strike in a big company it can only put the percentage of your profits up by a tiny amount. But if you make a strike in a small company, naturally that profit will be reflected as a considerably larger percentage of the whole.'

'Are you telling me you've made a strike?'

'Perhaps I shouldn't have said that,' said David. 'I'd be obliged if you'd treat that remark in confidence.'

David could not remember how he arrived home or who put him to bed, and he appeared rather late in the office the next morning.

'I am sorry, Bernie, I overslept after a very good evening with Richard at Annabel's.'

'Doesn't matter a bit. Glad you enjoyed yourself.'

'I hope I wasn't indiscreet, but I told some lord, whose name I can't even remember, that he ought to invest in the company. I may have been a little too enthusiastic.'

'Don't worry, David, we're not going to let anyone down and you need the rest. You've been working your ass off.'

James Brigsley left his London flat in Chelsea and took a taxi to his bank, Williams & Glyn's. James was an extrovert by nature and at Harrow his only real love had been acting; but when he had left school, his father had refused to allow him to go on the stage and insisted that he complete his education at Christ Church, Oxford, where again he took a greater interest in the Dramatic Society than in gaining a degree in his chosen subjects of Politics, Philosophy and Economics. James had never mentioned to anyone since leaving Oxford the class of degree he managed to secure, but for better or worse the fourth-class Honours degree was later abolished. After Oxford he joined the Grenadier Guards, which gave him considerable scope for his histrionic talent. This was indeed to be James's introduction to society life in London, and he succeeded as well as a personable, rich young viscount might be expected to do in the circumstances.

When he had completed his two years in the Guards, the earl gave him a 250-acre farm in Hampshire to occupy his time, but James did not care for the coarser country life. He left the running of the farm to a manager and once again concentrated on his social life in London. He would dearly have liked to go on the stage, but he knew the old man still considered Mrs Worthington's daughter's ambition an improper one for a future peer of the realm. The fifth earl didn't think a great deal of his eldest son one way and another, and James did not find it easy to persuade his father that he was shrewder than he was given credit for. Perhaps the inside information David Kesler had let slip after a few drinks would give him the opportunity to prove his old dad wrong.

In Williams & Glyn's fine old building in Birchin Lane, James was ushered into the manager's office.

'I should like to borrow some money against my farm in Hampshire,' said Lord Brigsley.

Philip Izard, the manager, knew Lord Brigsley well and was also acquainted with his father. Although he had respect for the earl's judgment, he did not have a great deal of time for the young lord. Nevertheless, it was not for him to query a customer's request, especially when the customer's family was one of the longest-standing in the bank's history.

'Yes, my lord, what sum do you have in mind?'

'Well, it seems that farmland in Hampshire is worth about £1,000 an acre and is still climbing. Why don't we say £150,000? I should then like to invest the money in shares.'

'Will you agree to leave the deeds with the bank as security?' enquired Izard.

'Yes, of course. What difference does it make to me where they are?'

'Then I am sure we will find it acceptable to advance you a loan of £150,000 at 2 per cent above base rate.'

James was not at all sure what base rate was, but he knew that Williams & Glyn's were as competitive as everyone else in such matters and that their reputation was beyond dispute.

'Thank you,' said James. 'Please acquire for me 35,000 shares in a company called Prospecta Oil.'

'Have you checked carefully into this company, my lord?' enquired Izard.

'Yes, of course I have,' said Lord Brigsley, very sharply. He was not in awe of the bank-managerial class.

In Boston, Harvey Metcalfe was briefed over the telephone by Silverman of the meeting in Annabel's between David Kesler and a nameless peer who seemed to have more money than sense. Harvey released 40,000 shares on to the market at £4.80. Williams & Glyn's acquired 35,000 of them and, once again, the remainder was taken up by small investors. The shares rose a little. Harvey Metcalfe was now left with only 30,000 shares of his own, and over the next four days he was able to dispose of them all. It had taken him fourteen weeks to off-load his entire stock in Prospecta Oil at a profit of just over $6 million.

On the Friday morning, the shares stood at £4.90 and Kesler had, in all innocence, occasioned four large investments: Harvey Metcalfe studied them in detail before putting through a call to Jörg Birrer.

Stephen Bradley had bought 40,000 shares at $6.10

Dr Robin Oakley had bought 35,000 shares at $7.23

Jean-Pierre Lamanns had bought 25,000 shares at $7.80
James Brigsley had bought 35,000 shares at $8.80
David Kesler himself had bought 500 shares at $7.25.

Among them they had purchased 135,500 shares at a cost of just over $1 million. They had also kept the price rising, giving Harvey the chance to off-load all his own stock on to a natural market.

Harvey Metalfe had done it again. His name was not on the letterhead and now he possessed no shares. Nobody would be able to place any blame on him. He had done nothing illegal; even the geologist's report contained enough ifs and buts to pass in a court of law. As for David Kesler, Harvey could not be blamed for his youthful over-enthusiasm. He had never even met the man. Harvey Metcalfe opened the bottle of Krug Privée Cuvée 1964, imported from Hedges & Butler of London. He sipped it slowly, then lit a Romeo y Julieta Churchill, and settled back for a mild celebration.

David, Stephen, Robin, Jean-Pierre and James celebrated at the weekend as well. Why not? Their shares were at £4.90 and David had assured them all that they would reach £10. On Saturday morning David ordered his first bespoke suit from Aquascutum, Stephen tut-tutted his way through the end-of-vacation examination papers he had set his freshmen students, Robin attended his sons' prep school Sports Day, Jean-Pierre re-framed a Renoir, and James Brigsley went shooting, convinced that at last he had one in the eye for his father.

3

David arrived at the office at 9 am on Monday to find that the front door was locked. He could not understand it. The secretaries were supposed to be in by 8.45.

After waiting around for over an hour, he walked to the nearest telephone box and dialled Bernie Silverman's home number. There was no reply. He then rang Richard Elliott at home: the ringing tone continued. He rang the Aberdeen office with the same result. He decided to return to the office. There must be a simple explanation, he thought. Was he daydreaming? Or was it Sunday? No – the streets were jammed with people and cars.

When he arrived back at the office a young man was nailing up a board. '2,500 sq ft to let. Apply Conrad Ritblat.'

'What do you think you are doing?' David demanded.

'The old tenants have given notice and left. We're looking for new ones. Are you interested in looking over the property?'

'No,' said David, backing away in panic. 'No, thank you.'

He raced down the street, sweat beginning to show on his forehead, praying that the telephone box would still be empty.

He flicked quickly through the L–R directory and looked up Bernie Silverman's secretary, Judith Lampson. This time there was a reply.

'Judith, in God's name, what's going on?' His voice would have left her in no doubt how anxious he was.

'No idea,' replied Judith. 'I was given my notice on Friday night with a month's pay in advance and no explanation.'

David dropped the telephone. The truth was slowly beginning to dawn on him although he still wanted to believe there was some simple explanation. Whom could he turn to? What should he do?

He returned in a daze to his flat in the Barbican. The morning post had arrived in his absence. It included a letter from the landlords of his flat:

Corporation of London,
Barbican Estate Office,
London EC2
01–628–4341

Dear Sir,

We are sorry to learn you will be leaving at the end of the month, and would like to take this opportunity of thanking you for the payment of rent in advance.

We should be pleased if you would kindly deposit the keys at this office at your earliest covenience.

Yours faithfully,

C. J. Caselton,
Estate Manager

David stood frozen in the middle of the room, gazing at his new Underwood with sudden loathing.

Finally, fearfully, he dialled his stockbrokers.

'What price are Prospecta Oil this morning?'

'They've dipped to £3.80,' replied the broker.

'Why have they fallen?'

'I've no idea, but I'll make some enquiries and ring you back.'

'Please put my 500 shares on the market immediately.'

'500 Prospecta Oil at market price. Yes, sir.'

David put the phone down. It rang a few minutes later. It was his broker.

'They've only made £3.50 – exactly what you paid for them.'

'Would you credit the sum to my account at Lloyd's Bank, Moorgate Branch?'

'Of course, sir.'

David did not leave the flat for the rest of the day or night. He lay on his bed chain-smoking, wondering what he ought to do next, sometimes looking out of his little window over a rain-drenched City of banks, insurance companies, stockbrokers and public companies – his own world, but for how much longer? In the morning, as soon as the market opened, he rang his broker again, in the hope that they would have some new information.

'Can you give me any more news on Prospecta Oil?' His voice was tense and weary now.

'The news is bad, sir. There's been a spate of heavy selling and the shares have dropped to £2.80 on the opening of business this morning.'

'Why? What the hell's going on?' His voice rose with every word.

'I've no idea, sir,' replied a calm voice that always made one per cent, win or lose.

David replaced the receiver. All those years at Harvard were about to be blown away in a puff of smoke. An hour passed, but he did not notice it.

He ate lunch in an inconspicuous restaurant and read a disturbing report in the *London Evening Standard* by its City Editor, David Malbert, headlined 'The Mystery of Prospecta Oil'. By the close of the Stock Exchange at 4 pm the shares had fallen to £1.60.

David spent another restless night. He thought with pain and humiliation of how easily two months of good salary, a quick bonus and a good deal of smooth talk had bought his unquestioning belief in an enterprise that should have excited all business suspicion. He felt sick as he recalled his man-to-man tips on Prospecta Oil, whispered confidentially into willing ears.

On Wednesday morning, dreading what he knew he was bound to hear, David once again rang the broker. The shares had collapsed to £1 and there was no longer a market for them. He left the flat and walked over to Lloyd's Bank where he closed his account and drew out the remaining £1,345. The cashier smiled at him as she passed over the notes, thinking what a successful young man he must be.

David picked up the final edition of the *Evening Standard* (the one marked '7RR' in the right-hand corner). Prospecta Oil had dropped again, this time to 25 pence. Numbed, he returned to his flat. The housekeeper was on the stairs.

'The police have been round enquiring after you, young man,' she said haughtily.

David climbed the stairs, trying to look unperturbed.

'Thank you, Mrs Pearson. I guess it's another parking fine I forgot to pay.'

Panic had now taken over completely: David never felt so small, so lonely and so sick in his life. He packed everything he owned into a suitcase, except the painting, which he left hanging on the wall, and booked a one-way ticket to New York.

4

Stephen Bradley was delivering a lecture on group theory at the Mathematics Institute in Oxford to a class of third-year undergraduates the morning David left. Over breakfast he had read with horror in the *Daily Telegraph* of the collapse of Prospecta Oil. He had immediately rung his broker, who was still trying to find out the full facts for him. He then phoned David Kesler, who seemed to have vanished without trace.

The lecture Stephen was delivering was not going well. He was preoccupied, to say the least. He could only hope that the undergraduates would misconstrue his absentmindedness as brilliance, rather than recognise it for what it was – total despair. He was at least thankful that it was his final lecture of the Hilary term.

Stephen looked at the clock at the back of the lecture theatre every few minutes, until at last it pointed to the hour and he was able to return to his rooms in Magdalen College. He sat in his old leather chair wondering where to start. Why the hell had he put everything into one basket? How could he, normally so logical, so calculating, have been so recklessly stupid and greedy? He had trusted David, and still found it hard to believe that his friend was in any way involved with the collapse. Perhaps he shouldn't have taken for granted that someone he had befriended at Harvard must automatically be right. There had to be a simple explanation. Surely he must be able to get all his money back. The telephone rang. Perhaps it was his broker with more concrete news.

As he picked up the phone, he realised for the first time that the palms of his hands were slippery with sweat.

'Stephen Bradley.'

'Good morning, sir. I am sorry to bother you. My name is Detective Inspector Clifford Smith of the Fraud Squad, Scotland Yard. I was wondering if you would be kind enough to see me this afternoon?'

Stephen hesitated, thinking wildly for a minute that he might have done something criminal by investing in Prospecta Oil.

'Certainly, Inspector,' he replied uncertainly, 'would you like me to travel to London?'

'No, sir,' replied the Inspector, 'we'll come to you. We can be in Oxford by 4 pm, if that's convenient.'

'I'll expect you then. Goodbye, Inspector.'

Stephen replaced the receiver. What could they want? He knew little of English law and hoped he was not going to be involved with the police as well. All this just six months before he was due to return to

Harvard as a professor. Stephen was even beginning to wonder if that would materialise.

The Detective Inspector was about 5 ft 11 in in height, and somewhere between forty-five and fifty. His hair was turning grey at the sides, but brilliantine toned it in with the original black. His shabby suit, Stephen suspected, was more indicative of a policeman's pay than of the Inspector's personal taste. His heavy frame would have fooled most people into thinking he was rather slow. In fact, Stephen was in the presence of one of the few men in England who fully understood the criminal mind. Time and time again he had been the man behind the arrest of international defrauders. He had a tired look that came from years of putting men behind bars for major crimes, only to see them freed again shortly after and living comfortably off the spoils of their shady transactions. In his opinion, crime did pay. The department was so understaffed that some of the smaller fry even got away scot-free; often the office of the Director of Public Prosecutions would decide it would be too expensive to follow the case through to a proper conclusion. On other occasions. the Fraud Squad simply did not have the back-up staff to finish the job properly.

The Detective Inspector was accompanied by Detective Sergeant Ryder, a considerably younger man – 6 ft 1 in, thin in body and face. His large brown eyes had a more innocent look against his sallow skin. He was at least a little better dressed than the Inspector, but then, thought Stephen, he probably wasn't married.

'I'm sorry about this intrusion, sir,' began the Inspector, after he had settled himself comfortably in the large armchair usually occupied by Stephen, 'but I'm making enquiries into a company called Prospecta Oil. Now before you say anything, sir, we realise that you had no personal involvement in the running of this company or indeed its subsequent collapse. But we do need your help, and I would prefer to ask you a series of questions which will bring out the points I need answered, rather than have you just give me a general assessment. I must tell you, sir, you don't have to answer any of my questions if you don't want to.'

Stephen nodded.

'First, sir, what made you invest such a large amount in Prospecta Oil?'

The Inspector had in front of him a sheet of paper with a list of all the investments made in the company over the past four months.

'The advice of a friend,' replied Stephen.

'Mr David Kesler, no doubt?'

'Yes.'

'How do you know Mr Kesler?'

'We were students at Harvard together and when he took up his appointment in England to work for an oil company, I invited him down to Oxford for old times' sake.'

Stephen went on to detail the full background of his association with David, and the reason he had been willing to invest such a large amount. He ended his explanation by asking if the Inspector thought that David was criminally involved in the rise and fall of Prospecta Oil.

'No, sir. My own view is that Kesler, who incidentally has made a run for it and left the country, is no more than the dupe of bigger men. But we would still like to question him, so if he contacts you, please let me know immediately. Now, sir,' the Inspector continued, 'I'm going to read you a list of names and I would be obliged if you could tell me whether you have ever met, spoken to or heard of any of them . . . Harvey Metcalfe?'

'No,' said Stephen.

'Bernie Silverman?'

'I've never met or spoken to him, but David did mention his name in conversation when he dined with me here in college.'

The Detective Sergeant was writing down everything Stephen said, slowly and methodically.

'Richard Elliott?'

'The same applies to him as Silverman.'

'Alvin Cooper?'

'No,' said Stephen.

'Have you had any contact with anyone else who was involved in the company?'

'No.'

For well over an hour the Inspector quizzed

Stephen on minor points, but he was unable to give him very much help, although he had kept a copy of the geologist's report.

'Yes, we are in possession of one of those documents, sir,' said the Inspector, 'but it's cleverly worded. I doubt if we'll be able to rely much on that for evidence.'

Stephen sighed and offered the two men some whisky and poured himself a donnish dry sherry.

'Evidence against whom or for what, Inspector?' he said as he returned to his chair. 'It's clear to me that I've been taken for a sucker. I probably don't need to tell you what a fool I've made of myself. I put my shirt on Prospecta Oil because it sounded like a sure-fire winner, and ended up losing everything I had without having a clue what to do about it. What in heaven's name has been going on in Prospecta Oil?'

'Well, sir,' said the Inspector, 'you'll appreciate there are aspects of the case I'm not at liberty to discuss with you. Indeed, there are some things that aren't very clear to us yet. But the game isn't a new one, and this time it's been played by an old pro, a very cunning old pro. It works something like this: a company is set up or taken over by a bunch of villains who acquire the majority of the shares. They invent a plausible story about a new discovery or super product that will send the shares up, whisper it in a few willing ears, release their own shares on to the market and let them be snapped up by the likes of you, sir, at a higher price. Then they clear off with the profit they have made, after which the shares collapse because the company has no real substance. As often as not, it ends with dealings in the shares being suspended on the stock market, and finally in the compulsory liquidation of the company. That hasn't happened yet in this case, and it may not. The London Stock Exchange is only just recovering from the Caplan fiasco and they don't want another scandal on their hands. I'm sorry to say that we can hardly ever recover the money, even if we produce enough evidence to nail the villains. They have it all stashed away all over the world before you can say Dow-Jones Index.'

Stephen groaned. 'My God, you make it all sound so appallingly simple, Inspector. The geologist's report was a fake, then?'

'Not exactly, sir. Very impressively worded and well presented, but with plenty of ifs and buts; and one thing is for certain; the DPP's office is hardly likely to spend millions finding out if there *is* any oil in that part of the North Sea.'

Stephen buried his head in his hands and mentally cursed the day he met David Kesler.

'Tell me, Inspector, who put Kesler up to this? Who was the real brains behind it all?'

The Inspector realised only too well the terrible agony Stephen was going through. During his career he had faced many men in the same position, and he was grateful for Stephen's co-operation.

'I'll answer any questions I feel cannot harm my

own enquiry,' said the Inspector. 'But it's no secret that the man we'd like to nail is Harvey Metcalfe.'

'Who's Harvey Metcalfe, for God's sake?'

'He's a first-generation American who's had his fingers in more dubious deals in Boston than you've had hot dinners. Made himself a multi-millionaire and a lot of other people bankrupt on the way. His style is so professional and predictable now we can smell the man a mile off. It will not amuse you to learn that he is a great benefactor of Harvard – does it to ease his conscience, no doubt. We've never been able to pin anything on him in the past, and I doubt if we'll be able to this time either. He was never a director of Prospecta Oil, and he only bought and sold shares on the open market. He never, as far as we know, even met David Kesler. He hired Silverman, Cooper and Elliott to do the dirty work, and they found a bright enthusiastic young man all freshly washed behind the ears to sell their story for them. I'm afraid it was a bit unlucky for you, sir, that the young man in question was your friend, David Kesler.'

'Never mind him, poor sod,' said Stephen. 'What about Harvey Metcalfe? Is he going to get away with it again?'

'I fear so,' said the Inspector. 'We have warrants out for the arrest of Silverman, Elliott and Cooper. They all beat it off to South America. After the Ronald Biggs fiasco I doubt if we'll ever get an extradition order to bring them back, even though the American and Canadian police also have warrants out for them. They were fairly cunning too. They closed the London office of Prospecta Oil, surrendered the lease and returned it to Conrad Ritblat, the estate agents, and gave notice to both secretaries with one month's pay in advance. They cleared the bill on the oil rig with Reading & Bates. They paid off their hired hands, Mark Stewart in Aberdeen, and took the Sunday morning flight to Rio de Janeiro, where there was $1 million in a private account waiting for them. Another two or three years, after they've spent all the money, and they'll undoubtedly turn up again with different names and a different company. Harvey Metcalfe rewarded them well and left David Kesler holding the baby.'

'Clever boys,' said Stephen.

'Oh, yes,' said the Inspector, 'it was a neat little operation. Worthy of the talents of Harvey Metcalfe.'

'Are you trying to arrest David Kesler?'

'No, but as I said we would like to question him. He bought and sold 500 shares, but we think that was only because he believed in the oil strike story himself. In fact, if he was wise, he would return to England and help the police with their enquiries, but I fear the poor man has panicked under pressure and made a bolt for it. The American police are keeping an eye out for him.'

'One last question,' said Stephen. 'Are there any other people who made such fools of themselves as I did!'

The Inspector gave this question long consideration. He had not had as much success with the other big investors as he had had with Stephen. They had all been evasive about their involvement with Kesler and Prospecta Oil. Perhaps if he released their names it might bring them out in some way.

'Yes, sir, but . . . you must understand that you never heard about them from me.'

Stephen nodded.

'For your own interest you could find out what you need to know by making some discreet enquiries through the Stock Exchange. There were four main punters, of whom you were one. Between the four of you you lost approximately $1 million. The others were a Harley Street doctor, Robin Oakley, a London art dealer called Jean-Pierre Lamanns, and a farmer, the unluckiest of all, really. As far as I can gather, he mortgaged his farm to put up the money. Titled young gentleman: Viscount Brigsley. Metcalfe's snatched the silver spoon out of his mouth, all right.'

'No other big investors?'

'Two or three banks burnt their fingers badly, but there were no other private investors above £10,000. What you, the banks and the other big investors did was to keep the market buoyant long enough for Metcalfe to off-load his entire holding.'

'I know, and worse, I foolishly advised some of my friends to invest in the company as well.'

'Er . . . there are two or three small investors from Oxford, yes sir,' said the Inspector, looking down at the sheet of paper in front of him, 'but don't worry –

we won't be approaching them. Well, that seems to be all. It only leaves me to thank you for your co-operation and say we may be in touch again some time in the future. In any case, we'll keep you informed of developments, and I hope you'll do the same for us.'

'Of course, Inspector. I do hope you have a safe journey back to town.' The two policemen downed their drinks and left.

Stephen could never recall if it was while sitting in his armchair looking out at the Cloisters, or later in bed that night, that he decided to employ his academic mind to carry out a little research on Harvey Metcalfe and his fellow dupers. His grandfather's advice to him, when as a small child he failed to win their nightly game of chess, floated across his mind: Stevie, don't get cross, get even. He was pleased he had given his final lecture and finished work for the term, and as he fell asleep at 3 am only one name was on his lips: Harvey Metcalfe.

5

Stephen awoke at about 5.30 am. He seemed to have been heavily, dreamlessly asleep, but as soon as he came to, the nightmare started again. He forced himself to use his mind constructively, to put the past firmly behind him and see what could be done about the future. He washed, shaved, dressed and missed college breakfast, occasionally murmuring to himself 'Harvey Metcalfe'. He then pedalled to Oxford station on an ancient bicycle, his preferred mode of transport in a city blocked solid with juggernaut lorries and full of unintelligible one-way systems. He left Ethelred the Unsteady padlocked to the station railings. There were as many bicycles standing in the ranks as there are cars in other railway stations.

He caught the 8.17 train so favoured by those who commute from Oxford to London every day. All the people at breakfast seemed to know each other and Stephen felt like an uninvited guest at someone else's party. The ticket collector bustled through the buffet car and clipped Stephen's first-class ticket. The man opposite Stephen produced a second-class ticket from behind his copy of the *Financial Times*. The collector clipped it grudgingly.

'You'll have to return to a second-class compartment when you've finished your breakfast, sir. The restaurant car is first-class, you know.'

Stephen considered the implication of these remarks as he watched the flat Berkshire countryside jolt past, and his coffee cup lurched unsampled in its saucer before he turned his mind to the morning papers. *The Times* carried no news of Prospecta Oil that morning. It was, he supposed, an insignificant story, even a dull one. Not kidnap, not arson, not even rape; just another shady business enterprise collapsing – nothing there to hold the attention of the front page for more than one day. Not a story he would have given a second thought to himself but for his own involvement, which gave it all the makings of a personal tragedy.

At Paddington he pushed through the ants rushing round the forecourt, glad that he had chosen the closeted life of a university or, more accurately, that it had chosen him. Stephen had never come to terms with London – he found the city large and impersonal, and he always took a taxi everywhere for fear of getting lost on the buses or the underground. Why didn't the English number their streets so Americans would know where they were?

'*The Times* office, Printing House Square.'

The cabby nodded and moved his black Austin deftly down the Bayswater Road, alongside a rain-sodden Hyde Park. The crocuses at Marble Arch looked sullen and battered, splayed wetly on the close grass. Stephen was impressed by London cabs: they never had a scrape or mark on them. He had once been told that cab-drivers are not allowed to pick up fares unless their vehicles are in perfect condition. How different from New York's battered yellow monsters, he thought. The cabby proceeded to swing down Park Lane to Hyde Park Corner, past the House of Commons and along the Embankment. The flags were out in Parliament Square. Stephen frowned. What was the lead story he had read over so inattentively in the train? Ah yes, a meeting of Commonwealth leaders. He supposed he must allow the world to go about its daily business as usual.

Stephen was unsure how to tackle the problem of checking Harvey Metcalfe out. Back at Harvard he would have had no trouble, first making a bee-line for his father's old friend Hank Swaltz, the business correspondent of the *Herald American*. Hank would be sure to have supplied him with the inside dope. The diary correspondent of *The Times*, Richard Compton-Miller, was by no means as appropriate a contact, but he was the only British press man Stephen had ever met. Compton-Miller had been visiting Magdalen the previous spring to write a feature on the time-honoured observance of May Day in Oxford. The choristers on the top of the College tower had sung the Miltonian salute as the sun peeped over the horizon on May 1st:

Hail, bounteous May, that doth inspire
Mirth and youth and warm desire.

On the banks of the river beneath Magdalen bridge where Compton-Miller and Stephen had stood, several couples had clearly been inspired.

Later, Stephen had been more embarrassed than flattered by his appearance in the resulting piece written by Compton-Miller for *The Times* diary: academics are sparing with the word brilliant, but journalists are not. The more self-important of Stephen's Senior Common Room colleagues had not been amused to see him described as the brightest star in a firmament of moderate luminescence.

The taxi pulled into the forecourt and came to a stop by the side of a massive hunk of sculpture by Henry Moore. *The Times* and the *Observer* shared a building with separate entrances, *The Times*'s by far the more prestigious. Stephen asked the sergeant behind the desk for Richard Compton-Miller, and was directed to the fifth floor and then to his little private cubicle at the end of the corridor.

It was only a little after 10 am when Stephen arrived, and the building was practically deserted. Compton-Miller later explained that a national newspaper does not begin to wake up until 11 am and generally indulges itself in a long lunch hour until about 3. Between then and putting the paper to bed, about 8.30 pm for all but the front page, the real work is done. There is usually a complete change of staff, staggered from 5 pm onwards, whose job it is to watch for major news stories breaking during the night. They always have to keep a wary eye on what is happening in America, because if the President makes an important statement in the afternoon in Washington they are already going to press in London. Sometimes the front page can change as often as five times during the night; in the case of the assassination of President Kennedy, news of which first reached England about 7 pm on the evening of November 22nd, 1963, the entire front page had to be scrapped to make way for the tragedy.

'Richard, it was kind of you to come in early for me. I didn't realise that you started work so late. I rather take my daily paper for granted.'

Richard laughed. 'That's OK. We must seem a lazy bunch to you, but this place will be buzzing at midnight when you're tucked up in bed and sound asleep. Now, how can I help you?'

'I'm trying to do a little research on a fellow countryman of mine called Harvey Metcalfe. He's a substantial benefactor of Harvard, and I want to flatter the old boy by knowing all about him when I return.' Stephen didn't care very much for the lie, but these were strange circumstances he now found himself in.

'Hang on here and I'll go and see if we have anything in the cutting room on him.'

Stephen amused himself by reading the headlines pinned up on Compton-Miller's board – obviously stories he had taken some pride in: 'Prime Minister to Conduct Orchestra at Royal Festival Hall', 'Miss World loves Tom Jones', 'Muhammad Ali says "I will be Champion Again"'.

Richard returned fifteen minutes later, carrying a thickish file.

'Have a go at that, Descartes. I'll be back in an hour and we can have some coffee.'

Stephen nodded and smiled gratefully. Descartes never had to solve the problems he was facing.

Everything Harvey Metcalfe wanted the world to know was in that file, and a little bit he didn't want the world to know. Stephen learned of his yearly trips to Europe to visit Wimbledon, of the success of his horses at Ascot and of his pursuit of Impressionist pictures for his private art collection. William Hickey of the *Daily Express* had on one occasion titillated his readers with a plump Harvey clad in Bermuda shorts and a report that he spent two or three weeks a year on his private yacht at Monte Carlo, gambling at the Casino. The Metcalfe fortune was in his opinion too new to be respectable. Stephen wrote down meticulously all the facts he thought relevant and was studying the photographs when Richard returned.

He took Stephen off to have some coffee in the canteen on the same floor. Cigarette smoke swirled mistily round the girl at the cashier's desk at the end of the self-service counter.

'Richard, I don't quite have all the information I might need. Harvard want to touch this man for quite a large sum: I believe they are thinking in terms of about $1 million. Where could I find out some more about him?'

'*New York Times*, I should imagine,' said Compton-Miller. 'Come on, we'll give Terry Robards a visit.'

The *New York Times* office in London was also on the fifth floor of *The Times* building in Printing House Square. Stephen thought of the vast *New York Times* building on 43rd Street and wondered if the London *Times* had a reciprocal arrangement, and was secreted away in their basement. Terry Robards turned out to be a wiry American wearing a perpetual smile. Terry immediately made Stephen feel at ease, a knack he had developed almost subconsciously over the years and which was a great asset when digging a little deeper for stories.

Stephen repeated his piece about Metcalfe. Terry laughed.

'Harvard aren't too fussy where they get their money from, are they? That guy has discovered more legal ways of stealing money than the Internal Revenue Service.'

'You don't say,' said Stephen innocently.

The *New York Times* file on Harvey was voluminous. 'Metcalfe's rise from Messenger Boy to Millionaire', as one headline put it, was documented admirably. Stephen took further careful notes. The details of Sharpley & Son fascinated him, as did the facts on some war-time arms dealing and the background of his wife Arlene and their daughter Rosalie. There was a picture of both of them, but the daughter was only fifteen at the time. There were also long reports of two court cases some twenty-five years past, in which Harvey had been charged with fraud but never convicted, and a more recent case in 1956 concerning a share transfer scheme in Boston. Again Harvey had escaped the law, but the District Attorney had left the jury in little doubt of his views on Mr Metcalfe. The most recent press stories were all in the gossip columns: Metcalfe's paintings, his horses, his orchids, his daughter's success at Vassar and his trips to Europe. Of Prospecta Oil there was not a word. Stephen had to admire Harvey's ability to conceal his more dubious activities from the press.

Terry invited his fellow expatriate to lunch. Newsmen always like new contacts and Stephen looked like a promising one. He asked the cabby to go to Whitfield Street. As they inched their way out of the City into the West End, Stephen hoped that the meal would be worth the journey. He was not disappointed.

Lacy's restaurant was airy and bedecked with clean linen and young daffodils. Terry said it was greatly favoured by press men. Margaret Costa, the cookery writer and her chef husband, Bill Lacy, certainly knew their onions. Over delicious watercress soup followed by *Médaillons de veau à crême au calvados* and a bottle of *Château de Péronne 1972*, Terry became quite expansive on the subject of Harvey Metcalfe. He had interviewed him once at Harvard on the occasion of the opening of Metcalfe Hall, which included a gymnasium and four indoor tennis courts.

'Hoping to get himself an honorary degree one day,' said Terry cynically, 'but not much hope, even if he gives a billion.'

Stephen noted the words thoughtfully.

'I guess you could get some more facts on the guy at the American Embassy,' said Terry. He glanced at his watch. 'No, hell, the library closes at 4 pm. Too late today. Time I got back to the office now America's awake.'

Stephen wondered if press men ate and drank like that every day. They made University dons look positively celibate – and however did they manage to get a paper out?

Stephen fought his way on to the 5.15 train to return with the Oxford-bound commuters, and only when he was alone in his room did he begin to study the results of his day's work. Though exhausted, he forced himself to sit at his desk until he had prepared the first neat draft of a dossier on Harvey Metcalfe.

Next day Stephen again caught the 8.17 to London, this time buying a second-class ticket. The ticket collector repeated his piece about leaving the restaurant car after he had finished his meal.

'Sure,' said Stephen, as he toyed with the remains of his coffee for the rest of the hour-long journey, never shifting from first-class. He was pleased with himself: he had saved £2, and that was exactly how Harvey Metcalfe would have behaved.

At Paddington he followed Terry Robard's advice and took a taxi to the American Embassy, a vast monolithic building which sprawls over 250,000 square feet and is nine storeys high, stretching the entire length of one side of Grosvenor Square. It was not, however, as elegant as the American Ambassador's magnificent official residence, Winfield House in Regents Park, where Stephen had been summoned to drinks last year, which was once the private home of Barbara Hutton before it was sold to the American government in 1946. Certainly, either of them was large enough for seven husbands, thought Stephen.

The entrance to the Embassy Reference Library on the ground floor was firmly shut. Stephen was reduced to a close study of the plaques on the wall in the corridor outside, honouring recent Ambassadors to the Court of St James. Reading backwards from Walter Annenberg, he had reached Joseph Kennedy when the doors of the library swung open, not unlike a bank. The prim girl behind a sign marked 'enquiries' was not immediately forthcoming on the subject of Harvey Metcalfe.

'Why do you require this information?' she asked sharply.

This threw Stephen for a moment, but he quickly recovered. 'I'm returning to Harvard in the fall as a professor and I feel I should know more about his involvement with the university. I'm at present a Visiting Fellow at Magdalen College, Oxford.'

Stephen's answer motivated the girl to immediate action and she produced a file within a few minutes. Though by no means as racy as the *New York Times*'s, it did put figures on the amounts Harvey Metcalfe had donated to charity and gave precise details of his gifts to the Democratic Party. Most people do not divulge the exact amount they give to political parties, but Harvey only knew about lights – no one seemed to have told him about bushels.

Having finished his research at the Embassy, Stephen took a taxi to the Cunard offices in St James's Square and spoke to a booking clerk and from there on to Claridge's in Brook Street, where he spent a few minutes with the duty manager. A telephone call to Monte Carlo completed his research. He travelled back to Oxford on the 5.15.

Stephen returned to his college rooms. He felt he now knew as much about Harvey Metcalfe as anyone, except perhaps for Arlene and Detective Inspector Clifford Smith of the Fraud Squad. Once again he stayed up into the early hours completing his dossier, which now ran to over forty typewritten pages.

When the dossier was finally completed he went to bed and fell into a deep sleep. He rose again early in the morning, strolled across the Cloisters to a Common Room breakfast and helped himself to eggs, bacon, coffee and toast. He then took his dossier to the Bursar's office where he made four copies of every document, ending up with five dossiers in all. He strolled back across Magdalen Bridge, admiring as always the trim flower beds of the University Botanic Gardens beneath him on his right, and called in at Maxwell's Bookshop on the other side of the bridge.

Stephen returned to his rooms with five smart files all of different colours. He then placed the five dossiers in the separate files and put them in a drawer of his desk which he kept locked. Stephen had a tidy and methodical mind, as a mathematician must: a mind the like of which Harvey Metcalfe had never yet come up against.

Stephen then referred to the notes he had written after his interview with Detective Inspector Smith and rang Directory Enquiries, asking for the London addresses and telephone numbers of Dr Robin Oakley, Jean-Pierre Lamanns and Lord Brigsley. Directory Enquiries refused to give him more than two numbers at any one time. Stephen wondered how the GPO expected to make a profit. In the States the Bell Telephone Company would happily have given him a dozen telephone numbers and still ended with the inevitable 'You're welcome'.

The two he managed to wheedle out of his reluctant informant were Dr Robin Oakley at 122 Harley Street, London W1, and Jean-Pierre Lamanns at the Lamanns Gallery, 40 New Bond Street, W1. Stephen then dialled Directory Enquiries a second time and requested the number and address of Lord Brigsley.

'No one under Brigsley in Central London,' said

the operator. 'Maybe he's ex-Directory. That is, if he really is a lord,' she sniffed.

Stephen left his study for the Senior Common Room, where he thumbed through the latest copy of *Who's Who* and found the noble lord:

> BRIGSLEY, Viscount; James Clarence Spencer; b. 11 Oct. 1942; Farmer; *s* and *heir* of 5th Earl of Louth, *cr* 1764, *qv*. *Educ*: Harrow; Christ Church, Oxford (BA). Pres. Oxford University Dramatic Society. Lt Grenadier Guards 1966–68. *Recreations*: polo (not water), shooting. *Address*: Tathwell Hall, Louth, Lincs. *Clubs*: Garrick, Guards.

Stephen then strolled over to Christ Church and asked the secretary in the Treasurer's office if she had in her records a London address for James Brigsley, matriculated 1963. It was duly supplied as 119 King's Road, London SW3.

Stephen was beginning to warm to the challenge of Harvey Metcalfe. He left Christ Church by Peckwater and the Canterbury Gate, out into the High and back to Magdalen, hands in pockets, composing a brief letter in his mind. Oxford's nocturnal slogan-writers had been at work on a college wall again: 'Deanz meanz feinz' said one neatly painted graffito. Stephen, the reluctant Junior Dean of Magdalen, responsible for undergraduate discipline, smiled. If they were funny enough he would allow them to remain for one term, if not, he would have the porter scrub them out immediately. Back at his desk, he wrote down what had been in his mind.

Magdalen College,
Oxford.
April 15th

Dear Dr Oakley,
I am holding a small dinner party in my rooms next Thursday evening for a few carefully selected people.
I would be delighted if you could spare the time to join me, and I think you would find it worth your while to be present.

Yours sincerely,
Stephen Bradley

PS: I am sorry David Kesler is unable to join us.
Black Tie: 7.30 for 8 pm.

Stephen changed the sheet of letter paper in his old Remington typewriter and addressed similar letters to Jean-Pierre Lamanns and Lord Brigsley. Then he sat thinking for a little while before picking up the internal telephone.

'Harry?' he said to the head porter. 'If anyone rings the lodge to ask if the college has a fellow called Stephen Bradley, I want you to say, "Yes, sir, a new Mathematics Fellow from Harvard, already famous for his dinner parties." Is that clear, Harry?'

'Yes, sir,' said Harry Woodley, the head porter.

He had never understood Americans – Dr Bradley was no exception.

All three men did ring and enquire, as Stephen had anticipated they might. He himself would have done the same in the circumstances. Harry remembered his message and repeated it carefully, although the callers still seemed a little baffled.

'No more than me, or is it I?' muttered the head porter.

Stephen received acceptances from all three during the next week, James Brigsley's arriving last, on the Friday. The crest on his letter paper announced a promising motto: *ex nihilo omnia.*

The butler to the Senior Common Room and the college chef were consulted, and a meal to loosen the tongues of the most taciturn was planned:

Coquilles St Jacques	Pouilly Fuissé 1969
Carrée d'agneau en croûte	Feux St Jean 1970
Casserôle d'artichauts et champignons	
Pommes de terre boulangère	
Griestorte with raspberries	Barsac Ch. d'Yquem 1927
Camembert frappé	Port Taylor 1947
Café	

Everything was ready; all Stephen could do now was wait for the appointed hour.

On the stroke of 7.30 pm on the appointed Thursday Jean-Pierre arrived. Stephen admired the elegant dinner-jacket and large floppy bow-tie that his guest wore, while he fingered his own little clip-on, surprised that Jean-Pierre Lamanns, who had such obvious savoir-faire, could also have fallen victim to Prospecta Oil. Stephen plunged into a monologue on the significance of the isosceles triangle in modern art while Jean-Pierre stroked his moustache. It was not a subject Stephen would normally have chosen to speak on without a break for five minutes, and he was only saved from the inevitability of more direct questions from Jean-Pierre by the arrival of Dr Robin Oakley. Robin had lost a few pounds in the past month, but Stephen could see why his practice in Harley Street was a success. He was, in the words of H. H. Munro, a man whose looks made it possible for women to forgive any other trifling inadequacies. Robin studied his shambling host, wondering whether he dared to ask immediately if they had ever met before. No, he decided; he would leave it a little and hope perhaps some clue as to why he had been invited would materialise during dinner. The David Kesler P.S. worried him.

Stephen introduced him to Jean-Pierre and they chatted while their host checked the dinner-table. Once again the door opened, and with a little more respect than previously displayed, the porter announced, 'Lord Brigsley'. Stephen walked forward to greet him, suddenly unsure whether he should bow or shake hands. Although James did not know anyone present at the strange gathering, he showed no signs of discomfort and entered easily into the conversation. Even Stephen was impressed by James's relaxed line of small talk, although he couldn't help recalling his academic results when at Christ Church and wondered whether the noble lord would in fact be an asset to his plans.

The culinary efforts of the chef worked their intended magic. No guest could possibly have asked his host why the dinner party was taking place while such delicately garlic-flavoured lamb, such tender almond pastry, such excellent wine, were still to hand.

Finally, when the servants had cleared the table and the port was on its way round for the second time, Robin could stand it no longer:

'If it's not a rude question, Dr Bradley.'

'Do call me Stephen.'

'Stephen, may I ask what is the purpose of this select little gathering?'

Six eyes bored into him demanding an answer to the same question.

Stephen rose and surveyed his guests. He walked around the table twice before speaking and then started his discourse by recalling the entire history of the past few weeks. He told them of his meeting in that very room with David Kesler, his investment in Prospecta Oil, followed soon afterwards by the visit of the Fraud Squad, and their disclosure about Harvey Metcalfe. He ended his carefully prepared speech with the words, 'Gentlemen, the truth is that the four of us are in the same bloody mess.' He felt that sounded suitably British.

Jean-Pierre reacted even before Stephen could finish what he was saying.

'Count me out. I couldn't be involved in anything quite so ridiculous as that. I am a humble art dealer, not a speculator.'

Robin Oakley also jumped in before Stephen was given the chance to reply:

'I've never heard anything so preposterous. You must have contacted the wrong man. I'm a Harley Street doctor – I don't know the first thing about oil.'

Stephen could see why the Fraud Squad had had trouble with these two and why they had been so thankful for his co-operation. They all looked at Lord Brigsley, who raised his eyes and said very quietly:

'Absolutely right on every detail, Dr Bradley, and I'm in more of a pickle than you. I borrowed £150,000 to buy the shares against the security of my small farm in Hampshire and I don't think it will be long before the bank insists that I dispose of it. When they do and my dear old pa, the fifth earl, finds out, it's curtains for me unless I become the sixth earl overnight.'

'Thank you,' said Stephen. As he sat down, he turned to Robin and raised his eyebrows interrogatively.

'What the hell,' said Robin. 'You're quite right – I was involved. David Kesler was a patient of mine and in a rash moment I invested £100,000 in Prospecta Oil as a temporary advance against my securities. God only knows what made me do it. As the shares are only worth 50 pence I'm stuck with them. I have a shortfall at my bank which they're beginning to fuss about. I also have a large mortgage on my country home in Berkshire and a heavy rent on my Harley Street consulting-room, a wife with expensive tastes and two boys at the best private prep school in England. I've hardly slept a wink since Detective Inspector Smith visited me two weeks ago.' He looked up. His face had drained of colour and the suave self-confidence of Harley Street had gone. Slowly, they all turned and stared at Jean-Pierre.

'All right, all right,' he admitted, 'me too. I was in Paris when the damned thing folded under me, so now, I'm stuck with the useless shares. £80,000 borrowed against my stock at the gallery. And what's worse, I advised some of my friends to invest in the bloody company too.'

Silence enveloped the room. It was Jean-Pierre who broke it again:

'So what do you suggest, Professor,' he said sarcastically. 'Do we hold an annual dinner to remind us what fools we've been?'

'No, that was not what I had in mind.' Stephen hesitated, realising that what he was about to suggest was bound to cause even more commotion. Once again he rose to his feet, and said quietly and deliberately:

'We have had our money stolen by a very clever man who has proved to be an expert in share fraud. None of us is knowledgeable about stocks and shares, but we are all experts in our own fields. Gentlemen, I therefore suggest we steal it back.

' – NOT A PENNY MORE AND NOT A PENNY LESS.'

A few seconds' silence was followed by uproar.

'Just walk up and take it I suppose?' said Robin.

'Kidnap him,' mused James.

'Why don't we just kill him and claim the life insurance?' said Jean-Pierre.

Several moments passed. Stephen waited until he had complete silence again, and then he handed round the four dossiers marked 'Harvey Metcalfe' with each of their names below. A green dossier for Robin, a blue one for James and a yellow for Jean-Pierre. The red master copy Stephen kept for himself. They were all impressed. While they had been wringing their hands in unproductive dismay, it was obvious that Stephen Bradley had been hard at work.

Stephen continued:

'Please read your dossier carefully. It will brief you on everything that is known about Harvey Metcalfe. Each of you must take the document away and study the information, and then return with a plan of how we are, between us, to extract $1,000,000 from him without his ever being aware of it. All four of us must come up with a separate plan. Each may involve the other three in his own operation. We will return here in fourteen days' time and present our conclusions. Each member of the team will put $10,000 into the kitty as a float and I, as the mathematician, will keep a running account. All expenses incurred in retrieving our money will be added to Mr Metcalfe's bill, starting with your journey down here this evening and the cost of the dinner tonight.'

Jean-Pierre and Robin began to protest again, but it was James who stopped the proceedings, by simply saying:

'I agree. What have we got to lose? On our own we've no chance at all: together we might just tweak the bastard.'

Robin and Jean-Pierre looked at each other, shrugged and nodded.

The four of them settled down to discuss in detail the material Stephen had acquired over the past few days. They left the college a little after midnight, each agreeing to have a plan ready for the Team's consideration in fourteen days' time. None of them was quite sure where it all might end, but each was relieved to know he was no longer on his own.

Stephen decided that the first part of the Team versus Harvey Metcalfe had gone as well as he could have wished. He only hoped his co-conspirators would now get down to work. He sat in his armchair, stared at the ceiling and continued thinking.

6

Robin retrieved his car from the High Street, not for the first time in his life being thankful for the 'Doctor on Call' sticker which always gave him an extra degree of freedom when parking. He headed back towards his home in Berkshire. There was no doubt about it, Stephen Bradley was a very impressive man; Robin was determined to come up with something that would ensure that he played his full part.

Robin let his mind linger a little on the delightful prospect of recovering the money he had so ill-advisedly entrusted to Prospecta Oil and Harvey Metcalfe. It must be worth a try: after all, he might as well be struck off the register of the General Medical Council for attempted robbery as for bankruptcy. He wound the window of the car down a little way to dispel the last delicious effects of the claret and considered Stephen's challenge more carefully.

The journey between Oxford and his country house passed very quickly. His mind was so preoccupied with Harvey Metcalfe that when he arrived home to his wife there were large sections of the journey that he could not even remember. Robin had only one talent to offer, apart from his natural charm, and he hoped that he was right in thinking that particular talent was the strength in his armour and a weakness in Harvey Metcalfe's. He began to repeat aloud something that was written on page 16 of Stephen's dossier, 'One of Harvey Metcalfe's recurrent worries is . . .'

'What was it all about, darling?'

His wife's voice brought Robin quickly to his senses and he locked the briefcase containing the green Metcalfe dossier.

'You still awake, Mary?'

'Well, I'm not talking in my sleep, love.'

Robin had to think quickly. He had not yet steeled himself to tell Mary the details of his foolish investment, but he had let her know about the dinner in Oxford, not at that time realising it was in any way connected with Prospecta Oil.

'It was a tease, sweetheart. An old friend of mine from Cambridge has been appointed a lecturer at Oxford, so he dragged a few of his contemporaries down for dinner and we had a damn good evening. Jim and Fred from my old college were there, but I don't expect you remember them.'

A bit weak, thought Robin, but the best he could do at 1.15 in the morning.

'Sure it wasn't some beautiful girl?' said Mary.

'I'm afraid Jim and Fred could hardly be described as beautiful, even by their loving wives.'

'Do lower your voice, Robin, or you'll wake the children.'

'I'm going down again in two weeks time to . . .'

'Oh, come to bed and tell me about it at breakfast.'

Robin was relieved to be let off the hook until the morning. He clambered in beside his fragrant silk-clad wife and ran his finger hopefully down her vertebral column to her coccyx.

'You'll be lucky, at this time of night,' she mumbled.

They both slept.

Jean-Pierre had booked himself in at the Eastgate Hotel in the High. There was to be an undergraduate exhibition the next day at the Christ Church Art Gallery. Jean-Pierre was always on the look-out for new young talent which he could contract to the Lamanns Gallery. It was the Marlborough Gallery, a few doors away from him in Bond Street, that had taught the London art world the astuteness of buying up young artists and being closely identified with their careers. But for the moment, the artistic future of his gallery was not uppermost in Jean-Pierre's mind: its very survival was threatened, and the quiet American don from Magdalen had offered him the chance of redress. He settled down in his comfortable hotel bedroom, oblivious of the late hour, reading his dossier and working out where he could fit into the jigsaw. He was not going to allow two Englishmen and a Yank to beat him. His father had been relieved at Rochefort by the British in 1918 and released from a prisoner-of-war camp near Frankfurt by the Americans in 1945. Nothing was going to stop him being a full participant in this operation. He read his yellow dossier late into the night: the germ of an idea was beginning to form in his mind.

James made the last train from Oxford and looked for an empty carriage where he could settle down to study the blue dossier. He was a worried man: he was sure the other three would each come up with a brilliant plan and, as had always seemed to be the case in the past, he would be found lacking. He had never been under any real pressure before – everything had come to him so easily; now it had all gone just as easily. A foolproof scheme for relieving Harvey Metcalfe of some of his excess profits was not James's idea of an amusing pastime. Still, the awful vision of his father discovering that the Hampshire farm was mortgaged up to the hilt was always there to keep his mind on the job. But fourteen days was such a short time: where on earth should he begin? He was not a professional man like the other three and had no particular skills to offer. He could only hope that his stage experience might come in useful at some point.

He bumped into the ticket collector, who was not surprised to find James was the holder of a first-class ticket. The quest for an empty compartment was in vain. James concluded that Richard Marsh must be trying to run the railways at a profit. Whatever next?

Still more aggravating, they would probably give him a knighthood for his pains.

The next best thing to an empty compartment, James always thought, was one containing a beautiful girl – and this time his luck was in. One of the compartments was occupied by a truly stunning creature who looked as if she was alone. The only other person in the carriage was a middle-aged lady reading *Vogue*, who showed no signs of knowing her travelling companion. James settled down in the corner with his back to the engine, realising he could not study the Metcalfe dossier on the train. They had all been sworn to total secrecy, and Stephen had cautioned them against reading the dossiers in anyone else's company. James feared that of the four of them he was going to find it the most difficult to remain silent: a companionable man, he found secrets rather burdensome. He touched his overcoat pocket, the one holding the dossier in the envelope supplied by Stephen Bradley. What an efficient man he was, thought James. Alarmingly brainy, too. He was bound to have a dozen clever plans ready for consideration by the next meeting. James frowned and stared out of the window hoping some serendipitous idea would strike him. Instead he found himself studying the reflection of the profile of the girl sitting opposite him . . .

She had a shiny bob of dark brown hair, a slim straight nose and her large hazel eyes seemed fixed on the book she held in her lap. James wondered if she was as entirely oblivious of his presence as she appeared to be, and reluctantly decided that she was. His eyes slipped down to the gentle curve of her breast, softly encased in angora. He craned his neck slightly to see what sort of legs the reflection had. Damn it, she was wearing boots. He looked back at the face again. It was now looking back at him, faintly amused. Embarrassed, he switched his attention to the third occupant of the carriage, the unofficial chaperone in front of whom James lacked the courage even to strike up a conversation with the beautiful profile.

In desperation he stared at the cover of the middle-aged lady's *Vogue*. Another beautiful girl. And then he looked more carefully. It wasn't another girl, it was the same girl. To begin with, he could hardly believe his eyes, but a quick check against the genuine article left him in no doubt. As soon as *Vogue* was relinquished in favour of *Queen*, James leant across and asked the chaperone if he might be allowed to read it.

'Station bookstalls are closing earlier and earlier,' he said idiotically. 'I couldn't get anything to read.'

The chaperone agreed reluctantly.

He turned to the second page. 'Cover: Picture yourself like this . . . black silk georgette dress with chiffon handkerchief points. Ostrich-feather boa. Turban with flower, matching dress. Made to measure by Zandra Rhodes. Anne's hair by Jason at Vidal Sassoon. Photograph by Lichfield. Camera: Hasselblad.'

James was quite unable to picture himself like that. But at least he now knew the girl's name, Anne. The next time the real-life version looked up, he showed her by sign language that he had spotted the photograph. She smiled briefly at James and then returned to her book.

At Reading station the middle-aged lady left, taking *Vogue* with her. Couldn't be better, mused James. Anne looked up, faintly embarrassed, and smiled hopefully at the few passers-by walking up and down the corridor looking for a seat. James glared at them as they passed. No one entered the carriage. James had won the first round. As the train gathered speed he tried his opening gambit, which was quite good by his normal standards:

'What a super picture on the front of *Vogue* taken by my old friend Patrick Lichfield.'

Anne Summerton looked up. She was even more beautiful than the picture James had referred to. Her dark hair, cut softly in the latest Vidal Sassoon style, her big hazel eyes and faultless skin gave her a gentle look that James found irresistible. She had that slim, graceful body that all leading models need to earn their living, but Anne also had a presence that most of them would never have. James was quite stunned and wished she would say something.

Anne was used to men trying to pick her up but she was rather taken aback by the remarks about Lord Lichfield. If he was a friend, it would be offhand not to be at least polite. On a second glance she found James's diffidence rather charming. He had used the self-deprecating approach many times with great success, but this time it was perfectly genuine. He tried again.

'It must be a hell of a job being a model.'

What a bloody silly line, he thought. Why couldn't he just say to her, I think you're absolutely fantastic? Can we talk a little and if I still think you're fantastic perhaps we can take it from there? But it never worked that way. He knew he would have to go through the usual routine.

'It's bearable if the contracts are good,' she replied, 'but today's been particularly tiring.' Her voice was gentle, and the faint transatlantic accent appealed to James. 'I've been smiling my head off all day, modelling an advertisement for Close-Up toothpaste: the photographer never seemed to be satisfied. The only good thing about it was that it ended a day earlier than expected. How do you know Patrick?'

'We were fags together at Harrow in our first year. He was rather better than me at getting out of work.'

Anne laughed – a gentle, warm laugh. It was obvious he knew Lord Lichfield.

'Do you see much of him now?'

'Occasionally at dinner parties, but not regularly. Does he photograph you a lot?'

'No,' said Anne, 'the cover picture for *Vogue* was the only time.'

As they chatted on, the thirty-five-minute journey between Reading and London seemed to pass in a flash. Walking down the platform of Paddington Station with Anne, James ventured:

'Can I give you a lift home? My car is parked round the corner in Craven Street.'

Anne accepted, relieved not to have to search for a taxi at that late hour.

James drove her home in his Alfa Romeo. He had already decided that he could not hold on to that particular luxury for much longer with petrol going up and cash flow going down. He chattered merrily all the way to her destination, which turned out to be a block of flats in Cheyne Row overlooking the Thames; much to Anne's surprise he just dropped her off at the front door and said goodnight. He did not even ask for her telephone number and he only knew her Christian name. In fact, she did not have any idea what his name was. Pity, she thought as she closed the front door; he had been a rather pleasant change from the men who worked on the fringe of the advertising media, who imagined they had an automatic right to a girl's compliance just because she posed in a bra.

James knew exactly what he was doing. He had always found a girl was more flattered if he called her when she least expected it. His tactics were to leave the impression that she had seen the last of him, especially when the first meeting had gone well. He returned to his home in the King's Road and considered the situation. Unlike Stephen, Robin and

Jean-Pierre, with thirteen days to go, he still had no ideas for defeating Harvey Metcalfe. But he was hatching plans for Anne.

On waking in the morning, Stephen began to do a little more research. He started with a close study of the way the university was administered. He visited the Vice-Chancellor's office in the Clarendon Building, where he spent some time asking strange questions of his personal secretary, Miss Smallwood. She was most intrigued. He then left for the office of the University Registrar, where he was equally inquisitive. He ended the day by visiting the Bodleian Library, and copying out some of the University Statutes. Among other outings during the next fourteen days was a trip to the Oxford tailors, Shepherd and Woodward, and a full day at the Sheldonian Theatre to watch the brief ceremony as a batch of students took their Bachelor of Arts degrees. Stephen also studied the layout of the Randolph, the largest hotel in Oxford. This he took some considerable time over, so much so that the manager became inquisitive and Stephen had to leave before he became suspicious. His final trip was a return journey to the Clarendon to meet the Secretary of the University Chest, and to be taken on a guided tour of the building by the porter. Stephen warned him that he anticipated showing an American around the building on the day of Encaenia, but remained vague.

'Well, that won't be easy . . .' began the porter. Stephen carefully and deliberately folded a pound note and passed it to the porter '. . . though I'm sure we'll be able to work something out, sir.'

In between his trips all over the university city, Stephen did a lot of thinking in the big leather chair and a lot more writing at his desk. By the fourteenth day his plan was perfected and ready for presentation to the other three. He had put the show on the road, as Harvey Metcalfe might have said, and he intended to see it had a long run.

Robin rose early on the morning after the Oxford dinner, and avoided awkward questions from his wife at breakfast about his experience the night before. He travelled up to London as soon as he could get away, and on arrival in Harley Street was greeted by his efficient secretary-cum-receptionist, Miss Meikle.

Elspeth Meikle was a dedicated, dour Scot who looked upon her work as nothing less than a vocation. Her devotion to Robin, not that she ever called him that even in her own mind, was obvious for all to see.

'I want as few appointments as possible over the next fourteen days, Miss Meikle.'

'I understand, Dr Oakley,' she said.

'I have some research to carry out and I don't want to be interrupted when I'm alone in my study.'

Miss Meikle was somewhat surprised. She had always thought of Dr Oakley as a good physician, but had never known him in the past to over-indulge in research work. She padded off noiselessly in her white-shod feet to admit the first of a bunch of admirably healthy ladies to Dr Oakley's clinic.

Robin disposed of his patients with less than dignified speed. He went without lunch and began the afternoon by making several telephone calls to the Boston Infirmary and several to a leading gastro-enterologist for whom he had been a houseman at Cambridge. Then he pressed the buzzer to summon Miss Meikle.

'Could you pop round to H. K. Lewis for me, Miss Meikle, and put two books on my account. I want the latest edition of Polson and Tattersall's *Clinical Toxicology* and Harding Rain's book on the bladder and abdomen.'

'Yes, sir,' she said, quite unperturbed at the thought of interrupting her lunchtime sandwich to fetch them.

They were on his desk before he had completed his calls, and he immediately started reading long sections of them carefully. The following day he cancelled his morning clinic and went to St Thomas's Hospital to watch two of his old colleagues at work. His confidence in the plan he had formulated was growing. He returned to Harley Street and wrote some notes on the techniques he had observed that morning, much as he had done in his student days. He paused to remember the words Stephen had used:

'Think as Harvey Metcalfe would. Think for the

first time in your life, not as a cautious professional man, but as a risk-taker, as an entrepreneur.'

Robin was tuning in to Harvey Metcalfe's wavelength, and when the time came he would be ready for the American, the Frenchman and the lord. But would they be willing to fall in with his plan? He looked forward to their meeting.

Jean-Pierre returned from Oxford the next day. None of the youthful artists had greatly impressed him, though he had felt that Brian Davis's still life showed considerable promise and had made a mental note to keep an eye on his future work. When he arrived back in London he started, like Robin and Stephen, on his research. A tentative idea that had come to him in the Eastgate Hotel was beginning to germinate. Through his numerous contacts in the art world he checked all the buying and selling of major Impressionist paintings over the previous twenty years and made a list of the pictures which were currently thought to be on the market. He then contacted the person who held it in his power to set his plan in motion. Fortunately the man whose help he most needed, David Stein, was in England and free to visit him: but would he fall in with the plan?

Stein arrived late the following afternoon and spent two hours with Jean-Pierre privately in his little room in the basement of the Lamanns Gallery. When he left Jean-Pierre was smiling to himself. A final afternoon spent at the German Embassy in Belgrave Square, followed by a call to Dr Wormit of the Preussischer Kulturbesitz in Berlin and a further one to Mme Tellegen at the Rijksbureau in The Hague, gave him all the information he required. Even Metcalfe would have praised him for the final touch. There would be no relieving the French this time. The American and the Englishman had better be up to scratch when he presented his plan.

On waking in the morning the last thing James had on his mind was an idea for outwitting Harvey Metcalfe. His thoughts were fully occupied with more important things. He telephoned Patrick Lichfield at home.

'Patrick?'

'Yes,' mumbled a voice.

'James Brigsley.'

'Oh, hello James. Haven't seen you for some time. What are you doing waking a fellow up at this filthy hour?'

'It's 10 am Patrick.'

'Is it? It was the Berkeley Square Ball last night and I didn't get to bed until four. What can I do for you?'

'You took a picture for *Vogue* of a girl whose first name was Anne.'

'Summerton,' said Patrick without hesitation. 'Got her from the Stacpoole Agency.'

'What's she like?'

'No idea,' said Patrick. 'I thought she was awfully nice. She just thought I wasn't her type.'

'Obviously a woman of taste, Patrick. Now go back to sleep.' James put the phone down.

Anne Summerton was not listed in the telephone directory – so that ploy had failed. James remained in bed, scratching the stubble on his chin, when a triumphant look came into his eye. A quick flip through the S–Z directory revealed the number he required. He dialled it.

'The Stacpoole Agency.'

'Can I speak to the manager?'

'Who's calling?'

'Lord Brigsley.'

'I'll put you through, my lord.'

James heard the phone click and the voice of the manager.

'Good morning, my lord. Michael Stacpoole speaking. Can I help you?'

'I hope so, Mr Stacpoole. I have been let down at the last moment and I'm looking for a model for the opening of an antique shop and I'll need a classy sort of bird. You know the kind of girl.'

James then described Anne as if he had never met her.

'We have two models on our books who I think would suit you, my lord,' offered Stacpoole. 'Pauline Stone and Anne Summerton. Unfortunately, Pauline is in Birmingham today for the launching of the new

Allegro car and Anne is completing a toothpaste session in Oxford.'

'I need a girl today,' James said. How he would have liked to have informed Stacpoole that Anne was back in town. 'If you find either of them are free for any reason, perhaps you would ring me at 735–7227.'

James rang off, a little disappointed. At least, he thought, if nothing comes of it today he could start planning his part in the Team versus Harvey Metcalfe. He was just resigning himself to that when the phone rang. A shrill, high-pitched voice announced:

'This is the Stacpoole Agency. Mr Stacpoole would like to speak to Lord Brigsley.'

'Speaking,' said James.

'I'll put you through, my lord.'

'Lord Brigsley?'

'Yes.'

'Stacpoole here, my lord. It seems Anne Summerton is free today. When would you like her to come to your shop?'

'Oh,' said James, taken aback for a second. 'The shop is in Berkeley Street, next to the Empress Restaurant. It's called Albemarle Antiques. Perhaps we could meet outside at 12.45?'

'I'm sure that will be acceptable, my lord. If I don't ring you back in the next ten minutes, you can assume the meeting is on. Perhaps you'd be kind enough to let us know if she's suitable. We normally prefer you to come to the office, but I'm sure we can make an exception in your case.'

'Thank you,' said James and put the phone down, pleased with himself.

James stood on the west side of Berkeley Street in the doorway of the Mayfair Hotel so that he could catch Anne arriving. When it came to work, Anne was always on time, and at 12.40 pm she appeared from the Piccadilly end of the street. Her skirt was of the latest elegant length, but this time James could see that her legs were as slim and shapely as the rest of her. She stopped outside the Empress Restaurant and looked in bewilderment at the Brazilian Trade Centre on her right and the Rolls Royce showrooms of H. R. Owen on her left.

James strode across the road, a large grin on his face.

'Good morning,' he said casually.

'Oh hello,' said Anne, 'what a coincidence.'

'What are you doing here all alone and looking lost?' said James.

'I'm trying to find a shop called Albemarle Antiques. You don't know it by any chance? I must have the wrong street. As you go in for knowing lords, you might know the owner, Lord Brigsley?'

James smiled:

'I am Lord Brigsley.'

Anne looked surprised and then burst out laughing. She realised what James had done and was flattered by the compliment.

They lunched together at the Empress, James's favourite eating place in town. He explained to Anne why it had been Lord Clarendon's favourite restaurant as well – 'Ah,' he had once declared, 'the millionaires are just a little fatter, and the mistresses are just a little thinner, than in any other restaurant in town.'

The meal was a triumph and James had to admit that Anne was the best thing that had happened to him for a long time. After lunch she asked where the agency should send their account.

'With what I have in mind for the future,' replied James, 'they'd better be prepared for a large bad debt.'

7

Stephen wrung James warmly by the hand the way the Americans will and presented him with a large whisky on the rocks. Impressive memory, thought James, as he took a gulp to give himself a little Dutch courage, and then joined Robin and Jean-Pierre. By unspoken mutual consent, the name of Harvey Metcalfe was not mentioned. They chattered inconsequentially of nothing in particular, each clutching his own dossier, until Stephen summoned them to the table. Stephen had not, on this occasion, exercised the talents of the college chef and the butler to the Senior Common Room. Instead, sandwiches, beer and coffee were stacked neatly on the table, and the college servants were not in evidence.

'This is a working supper,' said Stephen firmly, 'and as Harvey Metcalfe will eventually be footing the bill, I've cut down considerably on the hospitality. We don't want to make our task unnecessarily harder by eating our way through hundreds of dollars per meeting.'

The other three sat down quietly as Stephen took out some closely-typed sheets of paper.

'I'll begin,' he said, 'with a general comment. I've been doing some further research into Harvey Metcalfe's movements over the next few months. He seems to spend every summer doing the same round of social and sporting events. Most of the details are already well documented in your files. My latest findings are summarised on this separate sheet which should be added as page 38A of your dossiers. It reads:

> Harvey Metcalfe will arrive in England on the morning of June 21st on board the QE2, docking at Southampton. He has already reserved the Trafalgar Suite for his crossing and booked a Rolls Royce from Guy Salmon to take him to Claridge's. He will stay there for two weeks in the Royal Suite and he has his own debenture tickets for every day of the Wimbledon Championships. When they are over he flies to Monte Carlo to stay on his yacht *Messenger Boy* for another two weeks. He then returns to London and Claridge's to see his filly, Rosalie, run in the King George VI and Queen Elizabeth Stakes. He has a private box at Ascot for all five days of Ascot Week. He returns to America on a Pan American jumbo jet from London Heathrow on July 29th, flight No. 009 at 11.15 to Logan International Airport, Boston.'

The others attached page 38A to their dossiers, aware once again how much detailed research Stephen had undertaken. James was beginning to feel ill, and it certainly was not the excellent salmon sandwiches that were causing his discomfort.

'The next decision to be taken,' said Stephen, 'is to allocate the times during Metcalfe's trip to Europe when each plan will be put into operation. Robin, which section would you prefer?'

'Monte Carlo,' said Robin without hesitation. 'I need to catch the bastard off his home ground.'

'Anyone else want Monte Carlo?'

Nobody spoke.

'Which would you prefer, Jean-Pierre?'

'I'd like Wimbledon fortnight.'

'Any other takers?'

Again, nobody spoke. Stephen continued:

'I'm keen to have the Ascot slot myself and the short time before he returns to America. What about you, James?'

'It won't make any difference what period I have,' said James rather sheepishly.

'Right,' said Stephen.

Everybody, except James, seemed to be warming to the exercise.

'Now expenses. Have all of you brought your cheques for $10,000? I think it's wise to think in dollars as that was the currency Harvey Metcalfe worked in.'

Each member of the Team passed over a cheque to Stephen. At least, thought James, this is something I can do as well as the others.

'Expenses to date?'

Each passed a chit to Stephen again and he began to work out figures on his stylish little HP 65 calculator, the digits glowing red in the dimly-lit room.

'The shares cost us $1 million. Expenses to date $142, so Mr Metcalfe is in debt to us to the tune of $1,000,142. Not a penny more and not a penny less,' he repeated. 'Now to our individual plans. We will take them in the order of execution.' Stephen was pleased with that word. 'Jean-Pierre, Robin, myself and finally James. The floor is yours, Jean-Pierre.'

Jean-Pierre opened a large envelope and took out four sets of documents. He was determined to show that he had the measure of Stephen as well as of Harvey Metcalfe. He handed round photographs and road maps of the West End and Mayfair. Each street was marked with a number, indicating how many minutes it took to walk. Jean-Pierre explained his plan in great detail, starting with the crucial meeting he had had with David Stein, and ending with the roles the others would have to carry out.

'All of you will be needed on the day. Robin will be the journalist, James the representative from Sotheby's, and Stephen, you will act as the purchaser. You must practise speaking English with a German accent. I shall also require two tickets for the whole of Wimbledon fortnight on the Centre Court opposite Harvey Metcalfe's debenture box.'

Jean-Pierre consulted his notes.

'That is to say, opposite box No. 17. Can you arrange that, James?'

'No problem. I'll have a word with Mike Gibson, the Club referee, in the morning.'

'Good. Finally, then, you must all learn to operate

these little boxes of tricks. They are called Pye Pocketfones and don't forget that the use and ownership of them are illegal.'

Jean-Pierre produced four miniature sets and handed three to Stephen.

'Any questions?'

There was a general murmur of approval. There were going to be no loose ends in Jean-Pierre's plan.

'My congratulations,' said Stephen. 'That should get us off to a good start. Now, how about you, Robin?'

Robin relayed the story of his fourteen days. He reported on his meeting with the specialist, and explained the toxic effects of anticholinesterase drugs.

'This one will be hard to pull off; we'll have to be patient and wait for the right opportunity. But, we must stay prepared every moment Metcalfe is in Monte Carlo.'

'Where will we be staying in Monte Carlo?' asked James. 'I usually go to the Metropole. Better not make it there.'

'No, it's all right, James, I have provisional reservations at the Hôtel de Paris from June 29th to July 4th. However, before that you are all to attend several working sessions at St Thomas's Hospital.'

Diaries were consulted, and a series of meetings agreed upon.

'Here is a copy of Houston's *Short Textbook of Medicine* for each of you. You must all read the chapter on severe cuts and bruises. I don't want any of you to stick out like sore thumbs when we're all dressed in white. You, Stephen, will come to Harley Street the week after next for an intensive medical course, as you must be totally convincing as a doctor.'

Robin had chosen Stephen because he felt that with his academic mind he would pick up the most in the short time available.

'Jean-Pierre, you must attend a gaming club every evening for the next month and learn exactly how baccarat and blackjack are played, and how to continue playing for several hours at a time without losing money. It'll help if you get hold of Peter Arnold's *The Encyclopedia of Gambling* from Hatchards. James, you will learn to drive a small van through the rush hour traffic, and you are also to report to Harley Street next week so that we can try a dry run together.'

All eyes were wide open. If they pulled that one off they could do anything. Robin could see the anxiety in their faces.

'Don't worry,' he said, 'my profession has been carried on by witch-doctors for a thousand years. People never argue when they're confronted with a trained man, and you, Stephen, are going to be a trained man.'

Stephen nodded. Academics could be equally naïve. Hadn't that been exactly what had happened to all of them with Prospecta Oil?

'Remember,' said Robin, 'Stephen's comment at the bottom of page 33 of the dossier . . . "At all times we must think like Harvey Metcalfe".'

Robin gave a few more details of how certain rocedures were to be carried out. He then answered demanding questions for twenty-eight minutes. Finally, Jean-Pierre softened:

'I thought none of you would beat me, but Robin's plan is brilliant. If we get the timing right we'll only need an ounce of luck.'

James was beginning to feel distinctly uneasy as his time drew nearer. He rather wished he had never accepted the invitation to dinner in the first place and regretted being the one to urge the others to take up Stephen's challenge. At least the duties he had been given in the first two operations were well within his scope.

'Well, gentlemen,' said Stephen, 'you've both risen admirably to the occasion, but my proposals will make more demands on you.'

Stephen began to reveal the fruits of his research during the past two weeks and the substance of his plan. They all felt rather like students in the presence of a professor. Stephen's lecturing tone was not intentional; it was a manner he had developed, and like so many academics, he was unable to switch it off in private company. He produced a calendar for Trinity Term and outlined how the university weeks worked, the role of its Chancellor, Vice-Chancellor, the Registrar and the Secretary of the University Chest. Like Jean-Pierre, he supplied maps to each member of the Team, this time of Oxford. He had carefully marked a route from the Sheldonian Theatre to Lincoln

College, and from Lincoln to the Randolph Hotel, and had drawn up a contingency plan if Harvey Metcalfe insisted on using his car, despite the one-way system.

'Robin, you must study what the Vice-Chancellor does at Encaenia. It won't be like Cambridge; the two universities do everything similarly but not identically. You must know the route he's likely to take on that day and his habits backwards. I've arranged for a room at Lincoln to be at your disposal on the final day. Jean-Pierre, you will study and master the duties of the Registrar at Oxford and know the alternative route marked on your map so that you never come face to face with Robin. James, you must know how the Secretary of the University Chest goes about his work – the location of his office, which banks he deals with and how the cheques are cashed. You must also know the routes he's likely to take on the day of Encaenia as if they were part of your father's estate. I have the easiest role on the day, because I will be myself in everything but name. You must all learn how to address each other correctly and we'll have a dress rehearsal in the ninth week of term, on a Tuesday when the university is fairly quiet. Any questions?'

Silence reigned, but it was a silence of respect. All could see that Stephen's operation would demand split-second timing and that they would have to run through it several times to cover all contingencies. But if they were convincing they could hardly fail.

'Now, the Ascot part of my plan is simple. I will

only want Jean-Pierre and James inside the Members' Enclosure. I shall need two Enclosure tickets which I'm hoping you can acquire, James.'

'You mean badges, Stephen,' corrected James.

'Oh, do I?' said Stephen. 'I also require someone in London to send the necessary telegram. That'll have to be you, Robin.'

'Agreed,' said Robin.

For nearly an hour the others asked several questions of detail in order to be as familiar with the plan as Stephen was.

James asked no questions and his mind began to drift, hoping the earth would swallow him up. He even began to wish that he had never met Anne, although she was hardly to blame. In fact, he could not wait to see her again. What was he going to say when they . . .

'James, wake up,' said Stephen sharply. 'We're all waiting.'

Six eyes were now fixed on him. They had produced the ace of hearts, diamonds and spades. But had he the ace of trumps? James was flustered and poured himself another drink.

'You bloody upper-class twit,' said Jean-Pierre, 'you haven't got an idea, have you?'

'Well, actually, I've given the problem a lot of thought, but nothing seemed to come.'

'Useless – worse than useless,' said Robin.

James was stammering helplessly. Stephen cut him short.

'Now listen, James, and listen carefully. We meet here again in twenty-one days' time. By then we must know each other's plans backwards. One error could blow the whole thing. Do you understand?'

James nodded – he was determined not to let them down in that.

'And what's more,' said Stephen firmly, 'you must have your own plan ready for scrutiny. Is that also clear?'

'Yes,' mumbled James unhappily.

'Any other questions?' said Stephen.

There were none.

'Right. We go through the three individual operations again in full.'

Stephen ignored the muttered protests.

'Remember, we're up against a man who isn't used to being beaten. We won't get a second chance.'

For an hour and a half they went through the details of each operation in the order of action. First, Jean-Pierre during Wimbledon fortnight: second, Robin in Monte Carlo: third, Stephen during and after Ascot.

It was late and they were all weary when they finally rose from the table. They departed sleepily, each with several tasks to carry out before their next meeting. Each went his separate way, but all were due to meet again the following Friday in the Jericho Theatre of St Thomas's Hospital.

8

THE NEXT TWENTY DAYS turned out to be an exacting time for all four of them. Each had to master the other plans as well as organising his own. Friday brought them all together for the first of many sessions at St Thomas's Hospital, which would have been entirely successful if James had managed to stay on his feet. It was not the sight of blood that daunted him – the sight of the knife was enough. The only virtue from James's standpoint was that he once again avoided having to explain why he had not come up with any ideas of his own.

The next week was almost full time, with Stephen in Harley Street taking a potted course in one particular field of medicine at a fairly high level.

James spent several hours driving an old van through the heavy traffic from St Thomas's to Harley Street, preparing for his final test in Monte Carlo, which he felt could only be considerably easier. He also returned to Oxford for a week, learning how the Secretary of the University Chest's office operated, and also studying the movements of the Secretary himself, Mr Caston.

Jean-Pierre, at a cost to Mr Metcalfe of $25 and a 48-hour wait, became an overseas member of The Claremont, London's most distinguished gaming club, and passed his evenings watching the wealthy and lazy play baccarat and blackjack, their stakes often reaching $1,000. After three weeks of watching he ventured to join the Golden Nugget casino in Soho, where the stakes rarely exceeded £5. By the end of the month he had played for 56 hours, but so conservatively that he was only showing a small loss.

James's overriding worry was still his personal contribution. The more he grappled with the problem, the less he came to grips with it. He turned it over and over in his mind, even when he was travelling through London at high speed. One night after returning the van to Carnie's in Lots Road, Chelsea, he drove his Alfa Romeo over to Anne's flat by the river, wondering if he dared confide in her.

Anne was preparing a special meal for James. She was aware that he not only appreciated good food, but had taken it for granted all his life. The home-made gazpacho was smelling good and the *Coq au vin* was all but ready. Lately she had found herself avoiding modelling assignments out of London as she did not care to be away from James for any length of time. She was also conscious that he was the first man for some time that she would have been willing to go to bed with – and to date he had made no efforts to leave the dining-room.

James arrived carrying a bottle of Beaune Montée

Rouge 1971 – even his wine cellar was fast diminishing. He only hoped it would last long enough for the plans to come to fruition. Not that he felt an automatic right to a part of the bounty while he failed to contribute his own plan.

Anne looked stunning. She was wearing a long black dress of some soft material that tantalised James with the reticence with which it outlined her shape. She wore no makeup or jewellery, and her heavy hair gleamed in the candlelight. The meal was a triumph for Anne, and James started wanting her badly. She seemed nervous, spilling a little ground coffee as she filtered two strong tiny cups. What was in her mind? He did not want to blunder with unwanted attentions. James had had much more practice at being loved than at being in love. He was used to adulation, to ending up in bed with girls who made him shudder in the cold clear light of morning. Anne affected him in an entirely different way. He wanted to be close to her, to hold her and to love her. Above all, he wanted her to be there in the morning.

Anne cleared away the supper, avoiding James's eye, and they settled down to brandy and Lena Horne singing 'I Get Along Without You Very Well'. She sat, hands clasped round her knees on the floor at James's feet, staring into the fire. Tentatively, he put out a hand and stroked her hair. She sat unresponsive for a moment and then bent her head back and stretched out her arm to bring his face down to hers. He responded, leaning forward and stroking her cheek and nose with his mouth, holding her head in his hands, his fingers gently exploring her ears and neck. Her skin smelled faintly of jasmine and her open mouth glinted in the firelight as she smiled up at him. He kissed her and slid his hands down on to her body. She felt soft and slight under his hands. He caressed her breasts gently, and moved down beside her, his body pressing against hers. Wordlessly, he reached behind her and unzipped her dress and watched it fall to the ground. He stood up, his eyes never leaving hers, and undressed quickly. She glanced at his body and smiled shyly.

'Darling James,' she said softly.

After they had made love, like two people in love and not as lovers, Anne settled her head on James's shoulder and stroked the hair on his chest with a fingertip.

'What's the matter, James? I know I'm rather shy. But it will . . .'

'You were beautiful. God knows, you were perfect. That's not the problem . . . Anne, I have to tell you something, so just lie back and listen.'

'You're married.'

'No, it's far worse than that.' James lay silent for a moment, lit a cigarette and inhaled deeply. There are occasions in life when revelation is made easier by circumstance; it all came out in an unco-ordinated jumble. 'Anne darling, I've made a bloody fool of myself by investing a vast sum of money with a bunch of crooks who've stolen it. I haven't even told my family – they'd be terribly distressed if they ever found out. To make matters better or worse, I've got myself involved with three other chaps who found themselves in the same predicament, and now we're all trying to get our money back. They're nice fellows, full of bright ideas, but I haven't a clue how to begin to keep my part of the bargain. What with the worry of being £150,000 down the drain and having to keep racking my brain for a good idea, I'm half frantic. You're the only thing that's kept me sane the last month.'

'James, start again, but slower this time,' said Anne.

Thus James revealed the entire history of Prospecta Oil from his meeting with David Kesler at Annabel's to his invitation to dine with Stephen Bradley at Magdalen, finally explaining why he had been driving a hired van like a maniac through the rush hour. The only detail James left out was the name of their intended victim, as he felt that by withholding that he was not completely violating his bond of secrecy with the rest of the Team.

Anne inhaled very deeply.

'I hardly know what to say. It's incredible. It's so unbelievable that I believe every word.'

'I feel better just for telling someone, but it would be terrible if the others ever found out.'

'James, you know I won't say a word to anyone. I'm just so very sorry you're in such a mess. You must let me see if I can come up with an idea. Why don't we work together without letting the others know?'

James felt better already.

She began stroking the inside of his leg. Twenty minutes later, they sank into a blissful sleep, dreaming up plans to defeat Harvey Metcalfe.

9

In Lincoln, Massachusetts, Harvey Metcalfe began to prepare for his annual trip to England. He intended to enjoy himself thoroughly and expensively. He had plans for transferring some more money from his numbered accounts in Zürich to Barclays Bank, Lombard Street, ready to buy yet another stallion from one of the Irish stables to join his stud in Kentucky. Arlene had decided not to accompany him on this trip: she did not care too much for Ascot and even less for Monte Carlo. In any case, it gave her the chance to spend some time with her ailing mother in Vermont, who still had little respect for her prosperous son-in-law.

Harvey checked with his secretary that all the arrangements for the holiday had been completed. There was never any need to check up on Miss Fish, it was simply a habit on Harvey's part. Miss Fish had been with him for twenty-five years, from the days when he had first taken over the Lincoln Trust. Most of the respectable staff had walked out on Harvey's arrival, or shortly afterwards, but Miss Fish had remained, nursing in her unalluring bosom ever fainter hopes of eventual marriage to Harvey. By the time Arlene appeared on the scene, Miss Fish was an able and completely discreet accomplice without whom Harvey could hardly have operated. He paid her accordingly, so she swallowed her chagrin at the thought of another Mrs Metcalfe, and stayed put.

Miss Fish had already booked the short flight to New York and the Trafalgar Suite on the *QE2*. The trip across the Atlantic was almost the only total break Harvey ever had from the telephone or telex. The bank staff were instructed to contact the great liner only in dire emergency. On arrival at Southampton it would be the usual Rolls Royce to London and the private suite at Claridge's, which Harvey judged to be one of the last English hotels, along with the Connaught and Browns, where his money allowed him to mix with what he called 'class'.

Harvey flew to New York in high good humour, relaxing and drinking a couple of Manhattans on the way. The arrangements on board ship were as impeccable as ever. The Captain, Peter Jackson, always invited the occupant of the Trafalgar Suite or the Queen Anne Suite to join him on the first night out at the Captain's table. At $1,250 a day for the suites it could hardly be described as an extravagant gesture on Cunard's part. On such occasions, Harvey was always on his best behaviour, although even that struck most onlookers as somewhat brash.

One of the Italian stewards was detailed to arrange a little diversion for Harvey, preferably in the shape of a tall blonde with a large bosom. The going rate for the night was $200, but the Italian could charge Harvey $250 and still get away with it. At 5 ft 7 in and 227 lb, Harvey's chances of picking up a young thing in the discothèque were slender, and by the time he had lashed out on drinks and dinner, he could have spent almost as much money and achieved absolutely nothing. Men in Harvey's position do not have time for that sort of failure and expect everything in life to have its price. As the voyage was only five nights, the steward was able to keep Harvey fully occupied, although he felt it was just as well that Harvey had not booked a three-week Mediterranean cruise.

Harvey spent his days catching up with the latest novels he had been told he must read and also taking a little exercise, a swim in the morning and a painful session in the gymnasium during the afternoon. He reckoned to lose 10 lb during the crossing, which was pleasing, but somehow Claridge's always managed to put it back on again before he returned to the States. Fortunately, his suits were tailored by Bernard Weatherill of Dover Street, Mayfair, who by dint of near-genius and impeccable skill made him look well-built rather than distinctly fat. At £300 per suit it was the least he could expect.

When the five days were drawing to a close, Harvey was more than ready for land again. The women, the exercise and the fresh air had quite revived him and he had lost all of 11 lb on the crossing.

He felt a good deal of this must have come off the night before, which he had spent with a young Indian girl who had made the *Kama Sutra* look like a Boy Scout's handbook.

One of the advantages of real wealth is that menial tasks can always be left to someone else. Harvey could no longer remember when he last packed or unpacked a suitcase, and when the ship docked at the Ocean Terminal it came as no surprise to him to discover everything packed and ready for Customs – a $100 bill for the head steward seemed to bring men in little white coats from every direction.

Harvey always enjoyed disembarking at Southampton. The English were a race he liked, though he feared he would never understand them. He found them always so willing to be trodden on by the rest of the world. Since the Second World War, they had relinquished their colonial power in a way no American business man would have ever considered for an exit from his own boardroom. Harvey had finally given up trying to understand the British way of business during the 1967 devaluation of the pound. Every jumped-up speculator on the face of the globe had taken advantage of the inside knowledge. Harvey knew on the Tuesday morning that Harold Wilson was going to devalue any time after Friday, 5 pm Greenwich Mean Time, when the Bank of England closed for the weekend. On the Thursday even the junior clerk at the Lincoln Trust knew. It was no wonder that the Old Lady of Threadneedle

Street was raped and despoiled of an estimated £1½ billion over the next few days. Harvey had often thought that if only the British could liven up their boardrooms and get their tax structure right, they might end up being the richest nation in the world, instead of a nation which, as *The Economist* had stated, could now be taken over by the Arabs with ninety days of oil revenue. While the British flirted with socialism and still retained a *folie de grandeur*, they seemed doomed to sink into insignificance. But still Harvey adored them.

He strode down the gangplank like a man with a purpose. Harvey had never learnt to relax completely, even when he was on vacation. He could spend just about four days away from the world, but if he had been left on the *QE2* any longer he would have been negotiating to buy the Cunard Steamship Company. Harvey had once met the Chairman of Cunard, Vic Matthews, at Ascot and had been baffled to hear him harking on the prestige and reputation of the company. Harvey had expected him to brag about the balance sheet. Prestige interested Harvey, of course, but he always let people know how much he was worth first.

Customs clearance was given with the usual speed. Harvey never had anything of consequence to declare on his European trips, and after they had checked two of his Gucci suitcases, the other seven were allowed through without inspection. The chauffeur opened the door of the white Rolls Royce Corniche. The vehicle sped through Hampshire and into London in a little over two hours, which gave Harvey time for a rest before dinner.

Albert, the head doorman at Claridge's, stood smartly to attention and saluted as the car drew up. He knew Harvey of old and was aware that he had come, as usual, for Wimbledon and Ascot. Albert would undoubtedly receive a 50 pence tip every time he opened the white Rolls door. Harvey didn't know the difference between a 50 pence and 10 pence piece – a difference which Albert had welcomed since the introduction of decimalisation in Britain. Moreover, Harvey always gave Albert £5 at the end of Wimbledon fortnight if an American won the singles title. An American invariably reached the finals, so Albert always placed a bet with Ladbrokes on the other finalist and won either way. Gambling appealed to both Harvey and Albert; only the sums involved were different.

Albert arranged for the luggage to be sent up to the Royal Suite, which during the year had already been occupied by King Constantine of Greece, Princess Grace of Monaco and Emperor Hailé Selassie of Ethiopia, all with considerably more conviction than Harvey. But Harvey still considered that his annual holiday at Claridge's was more assured than theirs.

The Royal Suite is on the first floor at Claridge's and can be reached by an elegant sweeping staircase from the ground floor, or by a commodious lift with its own seat. Harvey always took the lift up and walked down. At least that way he convinced himself he was taking some exercise. The suite itself consists of four rooms: a small dressing-room, a bedroom, a bathroom, and an elegant drawing-room overlooking Brook Street. The furniture and pictures make it possible for you to believe that you are still in Victorian England. Only the telephone and television dispel the illusion. The room is large enough to be used for cocktail parties or by visiting heads of state to entertain large parties. Henry Kissinger had received Harold Wilson there only the week before. Harvey enjoyed the thought of that. It was about as close as he was going to get to either man.

After a shower and change of clothes, Harvey glanced through his waiting mail and telexes from the bank, which were all routine. He took a short nap before going down to dine in the main restaurant.

There in the large foyer was the usual string quartet, looking like out-of-work refugees from Hungary. Harvey even recognised the four musicians. He had reached that time in life when he did not like change; the management of Claridge's, aware that the average age of their customers was over fifty, catered accordingly. François, the head waiter, showed Harvey to his usual table.

Harvey managed a little shrimp cocktail and a medium fillet steak with a bottle of Mouton Cadet. As he leaned forward to study the sweets trolley, he did not notice the four young men eating in the alcove on the far side of the room.

Stephen, Robin, Jean-Pierre and James all had an excellent view of Harvey Metcalfe. He would have had to bend double and move slightly backwards to have any sight of them.

'Not exactly what I expected,' commented Stephen.

'Put on a bit of weight since those photographs you supplied,' said Jean-Pierre.

'Hard to believe he's real after all this preparation,' remarked Robin.

'The bastard's real enough,' said Jean-Pierre, 'and a million dollars richer because of our stupidity.'

James said nothing. He was still in disgrace after his futile efforts and excuses at the last full briefing, although the other three had to admit that they did receive good service wherever they went with him. Claridge's was proving to be no exception.

'Wimbledon tomorrow,' said Jean-Pierre. 'I wonder who'll win the first round?'

'You will of course,' chipped in James, hoping to soften Jean-Pierre's acid comments about his own feeble efforts.

'We can only win your round, James, if we ever fill in an entry form.'

James sank back into silence.

'I must say, looking at the size of Metcalfe we ought to get away with your plan, Robin,' said Stephen.

'If he doesn't die of cirrhosis of the liver before we're given the chance,' replied Robin. 'How do you feel about Oxford now you've seen him, Stephen?'

'I don't know yet. I'll feel better when I've belled the cat at Ascot. I want to hear him speak, watch him in his normal environment, get the feel of the man. You can't do all that from the other side of the dining-room.'

'You may not have to wait too long. This time tomorrow we may know everything we need to know – or all be in West End Central Police Station,' said Robin. 'Maybe we won't even pass Go, let alone collect £200.'

'We have to – I can't afford bail,' said Jean-Pierre.

When Harvey had downed a large snifter of Rémy Martin VSOP he left his table, slipping the head waiter a crisp new pound note.

'The bastard,' said Jean-Pierre with great feeling. 'It's bad enough knowing he's stolen our money, but it's humiliating having to watch him spend it.'

The four of them prepared to leave, the object of their outing achieved. Stephen paid the bill and carefully added the sum to the list of expenses against Harvey Metcalfe. Then they left the hotel separately and as inconspicuously as possible. Only James found this difficult as all the waiters and porters insisted on saying 'Good night, my lord.'

Harvey took a stroll round Berkeley Square and did not even notice the tall young man slip into the doorway of Moyses Stevens, the florists, for fear of being spotted by him. Harvey could never resist asking a policeman the way to Buckingham Palace, just to compare his reaction with that of a New York cop, leaning on a lamp post, chewing gum, holster on hip. As Lenny Bruce had said on being deported from England, 'Your pigs is so much better than our pigs'. Yes, Harvey liked England.

He arrived back at Claridge's at about 11.15 pm, showered and went to bed – a large double bed with that glorious feel of clean sheets. There would be no women for him at Claridge's or, if there were, it would be the last time he would find the Royal Suite available to him during Wimbledon or Ascot. The room moved just a little, but then after five days on an ocean liner it was unlikely to be still for a couple of nights. He slept well in spite of it, without a worry on his mind.

10

HARVEY ROSE AT at 7.30 am, a habit he could not break, but he did allow himself the holiday luxury of breakfast in bed. Ten minutes after he had called room service, the waiter arrived with a trolley laden with half a grapefruit, bacon and eggs, toast, steaming black coffee, a copy of the previous day's *Wall Street Journal*, and the morning edition of *The Times*, *Financial Times* and *International Herald Tribune*.

Harvey was not sure how he would have survived on a European trip without the *International Herald Tribune*, known in the trade as the 'Trib'. This unique paper, published in Paris, is jointly owned by the *New York Times* and the *Washington Post*. Although only one edition of 120,000 copies is printed, it does not go to press until the New York Stock Exchange is closed. Therefore, no American need wake up in Europe out of touch. When the *New York Herald Tribune* folded in 1966, Harvey had been among those who advised John H. Whitney to keep the *International Herald Tribune* going in Europe. Once again, Harvey's judgment had been proved sound. The *International Herald Tribune* went on to absorb its faltering rival, the *New York*

Times, which had never been a success in Europe. From then on the paper went from strength to strength.

Harvey ran an experienced eye down the Stock Exchange lists in the *Wall Street Journal* and the *Financial Times*. His bank now held very few shares as he, like Jim Slater in England, had suspected that the Dow-Jones Index would collapse and had therefore gone almost entirely liquid, holding only some South African gold shares and a few well-chosen stocks about which he had inside information. The only monetary transaction he cared to undertake with the market so shaky was to sell the dollar short and buy gold, so that he caught the dollar on the way down and gold on the way up. There were already rumours in Washington that the President of the United States had been advised by his Secretary of the Treasury, George Schultz, to allow the American people to buy gold on the open market later that year or early the following year. Harvey had been buying gold for the past fifteen years: all the President was going to do was to stop him from breaking the law. Harvey was of the opinion that the moment the Americans were able to buy gold, the bubble would burst and the price of gold would recede – the real money would be made while the speculators anticipated the rise, and Harvey intended to be out of gold well before it came on to the American market. Once the President made it legal, Harvey couldn't see a profit in it.

Harvey checked the commodity market in Chicago. He had made a killing in copper a year before. Inside information from an African ambassador had made this possible – information the ambassador had imparted to too many people. Harvey had not been surprised to read that he had later been recalled to his homeland and shot.

He could never resist checking the price of Prospecta Oil, now at an all-time low of $\$^1/_8$: there could be no trading in the stock, simply because there would only be sellers and no buyers. The shares were virtually worthless. He smiled sardonically and turned to the sports page of *The Times*.

Rex Bellamy's article on the forthcoming Wimbledon Championships tipped John Newcombe as favourite and Jimmy Connors, the new American star who had just won the Italian Open, as the best outside bet. The British press wanted the 39-year-old Ken Rosewall to win. Harvey could well remember the epic final between Rosewall and Drobny in 1954, which had run to 58 games. Like most of the crowd, he had supported the 33-year-old Drobny, who had finally won after three hours of play, 13–11, 4–6, 6–2, 9–7. This time, Harvey wanted history to repeat itself and Rosewall to win, though he felt the popular Australian's chance had slipped by during the ten years when the professionals were barred from Wimbledon. Still, he saw no reason why the fortnight should not be a pleasant break, and perhaps there might be an American victor even if Rosewall couldn't manage it.

Harvey had time for a quick glance at the art reviews before finishing his breakfast, leaving the papers strewn over the floor. The quiet Regency furniture, the elegant service and the Royal Suite did nothing for Harvey's habits. He padded into the bathroom for a shave and a shower. Arlene told him that most people did it the other way round – showered and then ate breakfast. But, as Harvey pointed out to her, most people did things the other way round from him, and look where it got them.

Harvey habitually spent the first morning of Wimbledon fortnight visiting the Summer Exhibition at the Royal Academy in Piccadilly. He would then follow this with visits to most of the West End's major galleries – Agnew's, Tooths, the Marlborough, Wildenstein – all within easy walking distance of Claridge's. This morning would be no exception. If Harvey was anything, he was a creature of habit, which was something the Team were quickly learning.

After he had dressed and bawled out room service for not leaving enough whisky in his cabinet, he headed down the staircase, emerged through the swing door on to Davies Street and strode off towards Berkeley Square. Harvey did not observe a studious young man with a two-way radio on the other side of the road.

'He's left the hotel by the Davies Street entrance,' said Stephen quietly to his little Pye Pocketfone, 'and he's heading towards you, James.'

'I'll pick him up as he comes into Berkeley Square, Stephen. Robin, can you hear me?'

'Yes.'

'I'll let you know as soon as I spot him. You stay put at the Royal Academy.'

'Right you are,' said Robin.

Harvey strolled round Berkeley Square, down into Piccadilly and through the Palladian arches of Burlington House. With a bad grace, he stood and queued with the assorted humanity in the forecourt, shuffling past the Astronomical Society and the Society of Antiquaries. He did not see another young man opposite standing in the entrance of the Chemical Society, deep in a copy of *Chemistry in Britain.* Finally, Harvey made it up the red-carpeted ramp into the Royal Academy itself. He handed the cashier £5.00 for a season ticket, realising that he would probably want to return at least three or four times. He spent the rest of the morning studying the 1,182 pictures, none of which had been exhibited anywhere else in the world before the opening day, in accordance with the stringent rules of the Academy. Despite that ruling, the Hanging Committee had still had over 5,000 pictures to choose from.

On the opening day of the exhibition the month before, Harvey had acquired, through his agent, a watercolour by Alfred Daniels of the House of

Commons for £350 and two oils by Bernard Dunstan of English provincial scenes for £125 each. The Summer Exhibition was still, in Harvey's estimation, the best value in the world. Even if he did not want to keep all the pictures himself, they made wonderful presents when he returned to the States. The Daniels reminded him of a Lowry he had bought some twenty years before at the Academy for £80: that had turned out to be another shrewd investment.

Harvey made a special point of looking at the Bernard Dunstans in the Exhibition. Of course, they were all sold. Dunstan was one of the artists whose pictures always sold in the first minutes of the opening day. Although Harvey had not been in London on that day, he had had no difficulty in buying what he wanted. He had planted a man at the front of the queue, who had obtained a catalogue and marked those artists he knew Harvey could resell easily if he made a mistake and keep if his judgment were right. When the exhibition opened on the dot of 10 am, the agent had gone straight to the purchasing desk and acquired the five or six pictures he had marked in the catalogue before he or anyone other than the Academicians had seen them. Harvey studied his vicarious purchases with care. On this occasion he was happy to keep them all. If there had been one that did not quite fit in with his collection, he would have returned the picture for resale, undertaking to purchase it if nobody else showed any interest. In twenty years he had acquired over a hundred pictures by this method and returned a mere dozen, never once failing to secure a resale. Harvey had a system for everything.

At 1 pm, after a thoroughly satisfactory morning, he left the Royal Academy. The white Rolls Royce was waiting for him in the forecourt.

'Wimbledon.'

'Shit.'

'What did you say?' queried Stephen.

'S.H.I.T. He's gone to Wimbledon, so today's down the drain,' said Robin.

That meant Harvey would not return to Claridge's until at least seven or eight that evening. A rota had been fixed for watching him, and Robin accordingly picked up his Rover 3500 V8 from a parking meter in St James's Square and headed off to Wimbledon. James had obtained two tickets for every day of the Championships opposite Harvey Metcalfe's debenture box.

Robin arrived at Wimbledon a few minutes after Harvey and took his seat in the Centre Court, far enough back in the sea of faces to remain inconspicuous. The atmosphere was already building up for the opening match. Wimbledon seemed to be getting more popular every year and the Centre Court was packed to capacity. Princess Alexandra and the Prime Minister were in the Royal Box awaiting the entrance of the gladiators. The little green scoreboards at the southern end of the court were flashing up the names of Kodeš and Stewart as the umpire took his seat on the high chair in the middle of the court directly overlooking the net. The crowd began to applaud as the two athletes, both dressed in white, entered the court carrying four rackets each. Wimbledon does not allow its competitors to dress in any colour other than white, although they had relaxed a little by permitting the trimming of the ladies' dresses to be coloured.

Robin enjoyed the opening match between Kodeš and an unseeded player from the United States, who gave the champion a hard time before losing to the Czech 6–3, 6–4, 9–7. Robin was sorry when Harvey decided to leave in the middle of an exciting doubles match. Back to duty, he told himself, and followed the white Rolls at a safe distance to Claridge's. On arriving, he telephoned James's flat, which was being used as the Team's headquarters in London, and briefed Stephen.

'May as well call it a day,' said Stephen. 'We'll try again tomorrow. Poor old Jean-Pierre's heart-beat reached 150 this morning. He may not last many days of false alarms.'

When Harvey left Claridge's the following morning he went through Berkeley Square into Bruton Street and then on into Bond Street, stopping only 50 yards from Jean-Pierre's gallery. But he turned east instead of west and slipped into Agnew's, where he had an appointment with Sir Geoffrey Agnew, the head of the family firm, for news of Impressionist pictures on the market. Sir Geoffrey was anxious to get away to another meeting and could only spend a few minutes with Harvey. He had nothing worthwhile to offer him.

Harvey left Agnew's soon afterwards clutching a small consolation prize of a maquette by Rodin, a mere bagatelle at £800.

'He's coming out,' said Robin, 'and heading in the right direction.' Jean-Pierre held his breath, but Harvey stopped once again, this time at the Marlborough Gallery to study their latest exhibition of Barbara Hepworth. He spent over an hour appreciating her beautiful work, but decided the prices were now outrageous. He had bought two Hepworths only ten years before for £800. The Marlborough was now asking between £7,000 and £10,000 for her work. So he left and continued up Bond Street.

'Jean-Pierre?'

'Yes,' replied a nervous voice.

'He's reached the corner of Conduit Street and he's about 50 yards away from your front door.'

Jean-Pierre prepared his window, removing the Graham Sutherland watercolour of the Thames and the Boatman.

'He's turned left, the bastard,' said James, who was stationed opposite the gallery. 'He's walking down Bruton Street on the right-hand side.'

Jean-Pierre put the Sutherland back on the easel in the window and retired to the lavatory, muttering to himself:

'I can't cope with two shits at once.'

Harvey meanwhile stepped into an inconspicuous entrance on Bruton Street and climbed the stairs to Tooths, more hopeful of finding something in a gallery which had become famous for its Impressionists. A Klee, a Picasso and two Salvador Dalis – not what Harvey was looking for. Though very well executed, the Klee was not as good as the one in his dining-room in Lincoln, Massachusetts. Besides, it might not fit in with any of Arlene's decorative schemes. Nicholas Tooth, the managing director, promised to keep his eyes open and ring Harvey at Claridge's should anything of interest turn up.

'He's on the move again, but I think he's heading back to Claridge's.'

James willed him to turn round and return in the direction of Jean-Pierre's gallery, but Harvey strode purposefully towards Berkeley Square, only making a detour to the O'Hana Gallery. Albert, the head door-man, had told him there was a Renoir in the window, and indeed there was. But it was only a half-finished canvas which Renoir had obviously used for a practice run or had disliked enough to leave unfinished. Harvey was curious as to the price and entered the gallery.

'£30,000,' said the assistant, as if it was $10 and a snip at that.

Harvey whistled through the gap between his front teeth. It never ceased to amaze him that an inferior picture by a first-rank name could fetch £30,000 and an outstanding picture by an artist with no established reputation could only bring a few hundred dollars. He thanked the assistant and left.

'A pleasure, Mr Metcalfe.'

Harvey was always flattered by people who remembered his name. But hell, they ought to remember – he had purchased a Monet from them last year for £62,000.

'He's definitely on his way back to the hotel,' said James.

Harvey spent only a few minutes in Claridge's, picking up one of their famous specially prepared luncheon hampers of caviar, beef, ham and cheese sandwiches and chocolate cake for later consumption at Wimbledon.

James was next on the rota for the Championships and decided to take Anne with him. Why not – she knew the truth. It was Ladies' Day and the turn of Billie Jean King, the vivacious American champion, to take the court. She was up against the unseeded American, Kathy May, who looked as if she was in for a rough time. The applause Billie Jean received was unworthy of her abilities, but for some reason she had never become a Wimbledon favourite. Harvey was accompanied by a guest who James thought had a faintly mid-European look.

'Which one is your victim?' asked Anne.

'He's almost exactly opposite us talking to the man in a light grey suit who looks like a government official from the EEC.'

'The short fat one?' asked Anne.

'Yes,' said James.

Whatever comments Anne made were interrupted by the umpire's call of 'Play' and everyone's attention focused on Billie Jean. It was exactly 2 pm.

'Kind of you to invite me to Wimbledon, Harvey,' said Jörg Birrer. 'I never seem to get the chance for much relaxation nowadays. You can't leave the market for more than a few hours without some panic breaking out somewhere in the world.'

'If you feel that way it's time for you to retire,' said Harvey.

'No one to take my place,' said Birrer. 'I've been chairman of the bank for ten years now and finding a successor is turning out to be my hardest task.'

'First game to Mrs King. Mrs King leads by one game to love in the first set.'

'Now, Harvey, I know you too well to expect this invitation to have been just for pleasure.'

'What an evil mind you have, Jörg.'

'In my profession I need it.'

'I just wanted to check how my three accounts stand and brief you on my plans for the next few months.'

'Game to Mrs King. Mrs King leads by two games to love in the first set.'

'Your No. 1 official account is a few thousand dollars in credit. Your numbered commodity account'

– at this point Birrer unfolded a small piece of unidentifiable paper with a set of neat figures printed on it – 'is short by $3,726,000, but you are holding 37,000 ounces of gold at today's selling price of $135 an ounce.'

'What's your advice on that?'

'Hold on, Harvey. I still think your President is either going to announce a new gold standard or allow your fellow-countrymen to buy gold on the open market some time next year.'

'That's my view too, but I'm still convinced we want to sell a few weeks before the masses come in. I have a theory about that.'

'I expect you're right, as usual, Harvey.'

'Game to Mrs King. Mrs King leads by three games to love in the first set.'

'What are your charges on my overdraft?'

'One-and-a-half per cent above inter-bank rate, which at present is 13.25, and therefore we're charging you 14.75 per cent per annum, while gold is rising in price at nearly 70 per cent per annum. It can't go on that way; but there are still a few months left in it.'

'OK,' said Harvey, 'hold on until November 1st and we'll review the position again then. Coded telex as usual. I don't know what the world would do without the Swiss.'

'Just take care, Harvey. Do you know there are more specialists in our police force on fraud than there are for homicide?'

'You worry about your end, Jörg, and I'll worry

about mine. The day I get uptight about a few underpaid bureaucrats from Zürich who haven't got any balls, I'll let you know. Now, enjoy your lunch and watch the game. We'll have a talk about the other account later.'

'Game to Mrs King. Mrs King leads by four games to love in the first set.'

'They're very deep in conversation,' said Anne. 'I can't believe they're enjoying the match.'

'He's probably trying to buy Wimbledon at cost price,' laughed James. 'The trouble with seeing the man every day is that one begins to have a certain respect for him. He's the most organised man I've ever come across. If he's like this on holiday, what the hell is he like at work?'

'I can't imagine,' said Anne.

'Game to Miss May. Mrs King leads by four games to one in the first set.'

'No wonder he's so overweight. Just look at him stuffing that cake down.' James lifted his Zeiss binoculars. 'Which reminds me to ask, darling, what have you brought for lunch?'

Anne dug into her hamper and unpacked a crisp salad in French bread for James. She contented herself with nibbling a stick of celery.

'Getting far too fat,' she explained. 'I'll never get into those winter clothes I'm supposed to be modelling next week.' She touched James's knee and smiled. 'It must be because I'm so happy.'

'Well, don't get too happy. I prefer you thin.'

'Game to Mrs King. Mrs King leads by five games to one in the first set.'

'This is going to be a walkover,' said James. 'It so often is in the opening match. People only come to see if the champion's in good form, and I think she'll be very hard to beat this year now she's after Helen Moody's record of eight Wimbledon championships.'

'Game and first set to Mrs King by six games to one. Mrs King leads one set to love. New balls, please. Miss May to serve.'

'Do we have to watch him all day?' asked Anne.

'Yes, we must make sure he returns to the hotel and doesn't change his plans suddenly or anything silly like that. If we miss our chance when he walks past Jean-Pierre's gallery, we may not get another one.'

'What do you do if he does decide to change his plans?'

'God knows, or to be more accurate, Stephen knows – he's the mastermind.'

'Game to Mrs King. Mrs King leads by one game to love in the second set.'

'Poor Miss May, she's about as successful as you are, James. How is the Jean-Pierre operation looking?'

'Awful. Metcalfe hasn't been anywhere near the gallery. He was within 30 yards of the window today and marched off in the opposite direction. Poor Jean-Pierre nearly had heart failure. But we're more hopeful of tomorrow. So far he seems to have covered Piccadilly and the top end of Bond Street, and the one thing we can be sure of with Harvey Metcalfe is that he's thorough. So he's almost bound to cover our bit of territory at one time or another.'

'You should all have taken out life insurance for $1 million, naming the other three as beneficiaries,' said Anne, 'and then if one of you had a heart attack, the others would all get their money back.'

'It's no laughing matter, Anne. It's bloody nerve-racking while you're hanging around, especially when you have to wait for him to make all the moves.'

'Game to Mrs King. Mrs King leads by two games to love in the second set and by one set to love.'

'How about your own plan?'

'Nothing. Useless. And now we've started on the others I seem to have less time to concentrate on my own.'

'Why don't I seduce him?'

'Not a bad idea, but you'd have to be pretty special to get £100,000 out of him, when he can hang around outside the Hilton or in Shepherd Market and get it for £30. If there's one thing we've learnt about that gentleman it's that he expects value for money. At £30 a night it would take you just under fifteen years to repay my share, and I'm not sure the other three would be willing to wait that long. In fact, I'm not sure they'll wait another fifteen days.'

'We'll think of something, don't worry,' said Anne.

'Game to Miss May. Mrs King leads by two games to one and by one set to love.'

'Well, well. Miss May has managed another game. Excellent lunch, Harvey.'

'A Claridge's special,' said Harvey, 'so much better than getting caught up with the crowds in the restaurant where you can't even watch the tennis.'

'Billie Jean is making mincemeat of the poor girl.'

'No more than I expected,' said Harvey. 'Now, Jörg, to my second numbered account.'

Once again the unidentifiable piece of paper that bore a few numbers appeared. It is this discretion of the Swiss that leads half the world, from heads of state to Arab sheiks, to trust them with their money. In return the Swiss maintain one of the healthiest economies in the world. The system works, so why go elsewhere? Birrer spent a few seconds studying the figures.

'On April 1st – only you could have chosen that day, Harvey – you transferred $7,486,000 to your No. 2 account which was already in credit $2,791,428. On April 2nd, on your instructions, we placed $1 million in the Banco do Minas Gerais in the names of Mr Silverman and Mr Elliott. We covered the bill with Reading & Bates for the hire of the rig for $420,000 and several other bills amounting to $104,112, leaving your present No. 2 account standing at $8,753,316.'

'Game to Mrs King. Mrs King leads three games to one in the second set and by one set to love.'

'Very good,' said Harvey.

'The tennis or the money?' said Birrer.

'Both. Now, Jörg, I anticipated needing about $2

million over the next six weeks. I want to purchase one or two pictures in London. I have seen a Klee that I quite like and there are still a few galleries I want to visit. If I'd known the Prospecta Oil venture was going to be such a success, I'd have outbid Armand Hammer at the Sotheby-Parke Bernet for that Van Gogh last year. I shall also need some ready cash for some new horses at the Ascot Blood Stock Auctions. My stud's running down and it's still one of my greatest ambitions to win the King George and Elizabeth Stakes.' (James would have winced if he could have heard Harvey describe the race so inaccurately.) 'My best result so far, as you know, was third place, and that's not good enough. This year I've entered Rosalie, my best filly for years. If I lose I'll have to build up the stud again, but I'm damn well going to win this year.'

'Game to Mrs King. Mrs King leads four games to one and by one set to love.'

'So is Mrs King, it seems,' said Birrer. 'I'll brief my senior cashier that you're likely to be drawing large amounts over the next few weeks.'

'Now I don't wish the remainder to lie idle, so I want you to purchase more gold carefully over the next few months, with a view to off-loading it in the New Year. If the market does take a downward turn, I'll phone you in Zürich. At the close of business each day you are to loan the outstanding balance on an overnight basis to first-class banks and triple "A" commercial names.'

'What are you going to do with it all, Harvey, if those cigars don't get you first?'

'Oh, lay off, Jörg. You sound like my doctor. I've told you a hundred times, next year I retire, I quit, finito.'

'I can't see you dropping out of the rat race voluntarily, Harvey. It pains me to think how much you're worth now.'

Harvey laughed.

'I can't tell you that, Jörg. It's like Aristotle Onassis said – if you can count it, you haven't got any.'

'Game to Mrs King. Mrs King leads by five games to one and by one set to love.'

'How's Rosalie? We still have your instructions to pass the accounts on to her in Boston if anything should happen to you.'

'She's well. Phoned me this morning to tell me she won't be able to join me at Wimbledon because she's tied up with her work. I expect she'll end up marrying some rich American and won't need it. Enough of them have asked her. Can't be easy for her to decide if they like her or my money. I'm afraid we had a row about that a couple of years back and she still hasn't forgiven me.'

'Game, set and match to Mrs King: 6–1, 6–1.'

Harvey, Jörg, James and Anne joined in the applause while the two women left the court, curtseying in front of the Royal Box to the President of the All England Club, His Royal Highness, The Duke of Kent. Harvey and Jörg Birrer stayed for the next match, a doubles, and then returned to Claridge's together for dinner.

James and Anne had enjoyed their afternoon at Wimbledon and when they had seen Harvey safely back to Claridge's, accompanied by his mid-European friend, they returned to James's flat.

'Stephen, I'm back. Metcalfe is settled in for the night. On parade at 8.30 tomorrow morning.'

'Well done, James. Maybe he'll bite then.'

'Let's hope so.'

The sound of running water led James to the kitchen in search of Anne. She was elbow-deep in suds, attacking a soufflé dish with a scourer. She turned and brandished it at him.

'Darling, I don't want to be offensive about your daily, but this is the only kitchen I've ever been in where you have to do the washing up before you make the dinner!'

'I know. She only ever cleans the clean bits of the flat. Her work load's getting lighter by the week.'

He sat on the kitchen table, admiring her slim body.

'Will you scrub my back like that if I go and have a bath before dinner?'

'Yes, with a scourer.'

*

The water was deep and comfortably hot. James lay back in it luxuriously, letting Anne wash him. Then he stepped dripping out of the bath.

'You're a bit overdressed for a bathroom attendant, darling,' he said. 'Why don't we do something about it?'

Anne slipped out of her clothes while James dried himself. When he went into the bedroom, Anne was already huddled under the sheets.

'I'm cold,' she said.

'Fear not,' said James. 'You're about to be presented with your very own six-foot hot water bottle.'

She took him in her arms.

'Liar, you're freezing.'

'And you're lovely,' said James, trying to hold on to every part of her at once.

'How's your plan going, James?'

'I don't know yet, I'll tell you in about twenty minutes.'

She didn't speak again for nearly half an hour, when she said:

'Out you get. The baked cheese will be ready by now and in any case I want to remake the bed.'

'No need to bother about that, you silly woman.'

'Yes, there is. Last night I didn't sleep at all. You pulled all the blankets over to your side and I just watched you huddled up like a self-satisfied cat while I froze to death. Making love to you isn't at all what Harold Robbins promised it would be.'

'When you've finished chattering, woman, set the alarm for 7 am.'

'Seven am? You don't have to be at Claridge's until 8.30.'

'I know, but I want to go to work on an egg.'

'James, you really must give up your undergraduate sense of humour.'

'Oh, I thought it was rather funny.'

'Yes, darling. Why don't you get dressed before the dinner is burnt to a cinder?'

James arrived at Claridge's at 8.29 am. Whatever his own inadequacies, he was determined not to fail the others in their plans. He tuned in to check that Stephen was in Berkeley Square and Robin in Bond Street.

'Morning,' said Stephen. 'Had a good night?'

'Bloody good,' said James.

'Sleep well, did you?' asked Stephen.

'Hardly a wink.'

'Stop making us jealous,' said Robin, 'and concentrate on Harvey Metcalfe.'

James stood in the doorway of Slater's, the furriers, watching the early morning cleaners leave for home and the first of the office staff arriving.

Harvey Metcalfe was going through his normal routine of breakfast and the papers. Just before he had gone to bed he had a telephone call from his wife in Boston and another from his daughter during breakfast the next morning, which started his day well. He decided to continue his pursuit of an Impressionist picture in some of the other galleries in Cork Street and Bond Street. Perhaps Sotheby's would be able to help him.

He left the hotel at 9.47 am at his usual brisk pace.

'Action stations.'

Stephen and Robin snapped out of their daydreaming.

'He's just entered Bruton Street. Now he's heading for Bond Street.'

Harvey walked briskly down Bond Street, past the territory he had already covered.

'Only 50 yards off now, Jean-Pierre,' said James. 'Forty yards, 30 yards, 20 yards . . . Oh no, damn it, he's gone into Sotheby's. There's only a sale of medieval painted panels on there today. Hell, I didn't know he was interested in them.'

He glanced up the road at Stephen, padded out and aged to the condition of a wealthy, middle-class business man for the third day in a row. The cut of the collar and the rimless glasses proclaimed him as West German. Stephen's voice came over the speaker:

'I am going into Jean-Pierre's gallery. James, you stay north of Sotheby's on the far side of the street and report in every fifteen minutes. Robin, you go inside and dangle the bait under Harvey's nose.'

'But that's not in the plan, Stephen,' stammered Robin.

'Use your initiative and get on with it, otherwise

all you'll be doing is taking care of Jean-Pierre's heart condition and receiving no fees. Right?'

'Right,' said Robin nervously.

Robin walked into Sotheby's and made a surreptitious bee-line for the nearest mirror. Yes, he was still unrecognisable. Upstairs, he spotted Harvey near the back of the sale room, and planted himself on a nearby seat in the row behind him.

The sale of medieval painted panels was well under way. Harvey knew he ought to like them, but could not bring himself to condone the Gothic partiality for jewellery and bright, gilded colours. Behind him, Robin hesitated but then struck up a quiet-voiced conversation with his neighbour.

'Looks all very fine to me, but I've no knowledge of the period. I'm so much happier with the modern era. Still, I must think of something appropriate to say for my readers.'

Robin's neighbour smiled politely.

'Do you have to cover all the auctions?'

'Almost all – especially when there may be surprises. In any case, at Sotheby's you can always find out what's going on everywhere else. Only this morning one of the assistants gave me a tip that the Lamanns Gallery may have something special in the Impressionist field.'

Robin beamed the whispered information carefully at Harvey's right ear and then sat back and waited to see if it had created any effect. Shortly afterwards, he was rewarded by the sight of Harvey squeezing out of his row to leave. Robin waited for three more lots to be auctioned, then followed him, fingers crossed.

Outside, James had been keeping a patient vigil.

'10.30 – no sign of him.'

'Roger.'

'10.45 – still no sign of him.'

'Roger.'

'11.00 – he's still inside.'

'Roger.'

'11.12 action stations, action stations.'

James slipped quickly into the Lamanns Gallery as Jean-Pierre once again removed from his window the Sutherland watercolour of the Thames and the Boatman, and replaced it with an oil by Van Gogh, as magnificent an example of the master's work as a London gallery had ever seen. Now came the acid test: the litmus paper was walking purposefully down Bond Street towards it.

The picture had been painted by David Stein, who had achieved notoriety in the art world for faking 300 paintings and drawings by well-known Impressionists, for which he had received a total of $864,000 and, later, four years. He was only exposed when he put on a Chagall exhibition at the Niveaie Gallery in Madison Avenue in 1969. Unknown to Stein, Chagall himself was in New York at the time for an exhibition at the museum in Lincoln Center where two of his most famous works were on display. On being informed of the Niveaie exhibition, Chagall furiously reported the pictures to the District Attorney's office as fakes. Stein had already sold one of the imitation Chagalls to Louis D. Cohen at a price of nearly $100,000, and to this day there is a Stein Chagall and a Stein Picasso at the Galleria d'Arte Moderna in Milan. Jean-Pierre was confident that what Stein had achieved in the past in New York and Milan he could now repeat in London.

Stein had continued to paint Impressionist pictures, but now signed them with his own name; thanks to his indubitable talent he was still making a handsome living. He had known and admired Jean-Pierre for several years and when he heard the story of Metcalfe and Prospecta Oil, he agreed to produce a Van Gogh for $10,000 and to sign the painting with the master's famous 'Vincent'.

Jean-Pierre had gone to considerable lengths to identify a Van Gogh that had vanished in mysterious circumstances, so that Stein could resurrect it to tempt Harvey. He had started with de la Faille's comprehensive *oeuvres* catalogue, *The Works of Vincent Van Gogh*, and selected from it three pictures that had hung in the National Gallery in Berlin prior to the Second World War. In de la Faille, they were entered under Nos. 485, *Les Amoureux* (*The Lovers*), 628, *La Moisson* (*The Harvest*), and 766, *Le Jardin de Daubigny* (*The Garden of Daubigny*). The last two were known to have been bought in 1929 by the Berlin Gallery, and *Les Amoureux* probably bought around the same time. At the start of the war, all three had disappeared.

Jean-Pierre then contacted Professor Wormit of

the Preussischer Kulturbesitz. The Professor, a world authority on missing works of art, was able to rule out one of the possibilities, *Le Jardin de Daubigny*; soon after the war it apparently had reappeared in the collection of Siegfried Kramarsky in New York, though how it got there remains a mystery. Kramarsky had subsequently sold the painting to the Nichido Gallery in Tokyo, where it now hangs. The Professor confirmed that the fate of the other two Van Goghs remained unknown.

Next Jean-Pierre turned to Madame Tellegen-Hoogendoorm of the Dutch Rijksbureau voor Kunsthistorische Documentatie. Madame Tellegen was the acknowledged authority on Van Gogh and gradually, with her expert help, Jean-Pierre pieced together the story of the missing paintings. They had been removed, along with many others, from the Berlin National Gallery in 1937 by the Nazis, despite vigorous protests from the Director, Dr Hanfstaengl, and the Keeper of Paintings, Dr Hentzen. The paintings, stigmatised by the philistinism of the National Socialists as degenerate art, were stored in a depot in the Kopenickerstrasse in Berlin. Hitler himself visited the depot in January 1938, and legalised the proceedings as an official confiscation.

What happened to the two Van Goghs after that, nobody knows. Many of the Nazi-confiscated works were quietly sold abroad by Joseph Angerer, an agent of Hermann Goering, to obtain much-needed foreign currency for the Führer. Some were disposed of in a sale organised by the Fischer Art Gallery in Lucerne on June 30th, 1939. But many of the works in the depot in the Kopenickerstrasse were simply burned, stolen, or are still missing.

Jean-Pierre managed to obtain black-and-white reproductions of *Les Amoureux* and *La Moisson*: no colour positives survive, if they were ever made. It seemed to Jean-Pierre unlikely that any colour reproductions of two paintings last seen in 1938 would exist anywhere. He therefore settled down to choose between the two.

Les Amoureux was the larger of the two, at 76 × 91 cm. However, Van Gogh did not seem to have been satisfied with it. In October 1889 (letter No. 556) he referred to 'a very poor sketch of my last canvas'. Moreover, it was impossible to guess the colour of the background. *La Moisson*, in contrast, had pleased Van Gogh. He had painted the oil in September 1889 and written of it, 'I feel very much inclined to do the reaper once more for my mother' (letter No. 604). He had in fact already painted three other very similar pictures of a reaper at harvest time. Jean-Pierre was able to obtain colour transparencies of two of them, one from the Louvre and the other from the Rijksmuseum, where they now hang. He studied the sequence. The position of the sun, and the play of light on the scene, were practically the only points of difference. Jean-Pierre was therefore able to see in his mind's eye what *La Moisson* must have looked like in colour.

Stein agreed with Jean-Pierre's final choice and he studied the black-and-white reproduction of *La Moisson* and the colour transparencies of its sister paintings long and minutely before he set to work. He then found an insignificant late-nineteenth-century French work, and skilfully removed the paint from it, leaving a clean canvas except for a vital stamp on the back which even Stein could not have reproduced. He marked on the canvas the exact size of the picture, 48.5 × 53 cm and selected a palette knife and brush of the type that Van Gogh had favoured. Six weeks later *La Moisson* was finished. Stein varnished it, and baked it for four days in an oven at a gentle 85°F to age it. Jean-Pierre provided a heavy gilt Impressionist frame and it was well ready for Harvey Metcalfe's scrutiny.

Harvey, acting on his overheard tip, could see no harm in dropping into the Lamanns Gallery. He was about five paces away when he first caught sight of the picture being taken out of the window. He could not believe his eyes. A Van Gogh, without a doubt, and a superlative one at that. *La Moisson* had actually been on display for only two minutes.

Harvey almost ran into the gallery, only to discover Jean-Pierre deep in conversation with Stephen and James. None of them took any notice of him. Stephen was addressing Jean-Pierre in a guttural accent.

'170,000 guineas seems high, but it is a fine example. Can you be sure it is the picture that disappeared from Berlin in 1937?'

'You can never be sure of anything, but you can see on the back of the canvas the stamp of the Berlin National Gallery, and the Bernheim Jeune have confirmed they sold it to the Germans in 1927. The rest of its history is well chronicled back to 1890. It seems certain that it was looted from the museum in the upheaval of the war.'

'How did you come into possession of the painting?'

'From the private collection of a member of the British aristocracy who wishes to remain anonymous.'

'Excellent,' said Stephen. 'I would like to reserve it until 4 pm when I will bring round a cheque for 170,000 guineas from the Dresdner Bank AG. Will that be acceptable?'

'Of course, sir,' replied Jean-Pierre. 'I will place a red dot on it.'

James, in the sharpest of suits and a dashing trilby, hovered knowledgeably behind Stephen.

'It certainly is a marvellous example of the master's work,' he remarked ingratiatingly.

'Yes. I took it round to Julian Barron at Sotheby's and he seemed to like it.'

James retreated mincingly to the end of the gallery, relishing his role as a connoisseur. At that moment Robin walked in, a copy of the *Guardian* sticking out of his pocket.

'Good morning, Mr Lamanns. I heard a rumour at Sotheby's about a Van Gogh which I'd always thought must be in Russia. I'd like to write a few paragraphs about the history of the painting and how you came into possession of it for tomorrow's paper. Is that OK by you?'

'I should be delighted,' said Jean-Pierre, 'although actually I have just reserved the picture for Herr Drosser, the distinguished German dealer, at 170,000 guineas.'

'Very reasonable,' said James knowingly from the end of the gallery. 'I think it's the best Van Gogh I have seen in London since *Mademoiselle Ravoux* and I'm only sorry my house won't be auctioning it. You're a lucky man, Mr Drosser. If you ever decide to sell it, don't hesitate to contact me.' James handed Stephen a card and smiled at Jean-Pierre.

Jean-Pierre watched James. It was a fine performance. Robin began to take notes in what he hoped looked like shorthand and again addressed Jean-Pierre.

'Do you have a photograph of the picture?'

'Of course.'

Jean-Pierre opened a drawer and took out a colour photograph of the picture with a typewritten description attached. He handed it to Robin.

'Do watch the spelling of Lamanns, won't you? I get so bored with being confused with a French motor car race.'

He turned to Stephen.

'So sorry to keep you waiting, Herr Drosser. How would you like us to despatch the picture?'

'You can send it to me at the Dorchester tomorrow morning, room 120.'

'Certainly, sir.'

Stephen started to leave.

'Excuse me, sir,' said Robin, 'can I take the spelling of your name?'

'D.R.O.S.S.E.R.'

'And may I have permission to quote you in my article?'

'You may. I am with my purchase very pleased. Good day, gentlemen.'

Stephen bowed his head smartly, and departed. He stepped out into Bond Street and to the horror of Jean-Pierre, Robin and James, Harvey, without a moment's hesitation, also walked out.

Jean-Pierre collapsed heavily on his Georgian mahogany desk and looked despairingly at Robin and James.

'God Almighty, the whole thing's a fiasco. Six weeks of preparation, three days of agony, and then he walked out on us.' Jean-Pierre looked at *La Moisson* angrily.

'I thought Stephen assured us that Harvey would stay and bargain with Jean-Pierre. It's in his character,' mimicked James plaintively. 'He'd never let the picture out of his sight.'

'Who the hell thought up this bloody silly enterprise?' muttered Robin.

'Stephen,' they all cried together, and rushed to the window.

'What an interesting maquette by Henry Moore,' said an impeccably corseted middle-aged lady, her hand firmly placed on the bronze loin of a naked acrobat. She had slipped unnoticed into the gallery while the three had been grumbling. 'How much are you asking for it?'

'I will be with you in a minute, madam,' said Jean-Pierre. 'Oh hell, I think Metcalfe's following Stephen. Get him on the pocket radio, Robin.'

'Stephen, can you hear me? Whatever you do, don't look back. We think Harvey's only a few yards behind you.'

'What the hell do you mean he's only a few yards behind me? He's meant to be in the gallery with you buying the Van Gogh. What are you playing at?'

'Harvey didn't give us a chance. He walked straight out after you before any of us could continue as planned.'

'Very clever. Now what am I meant to do?'

Jean-Pierre took over:

'You'd better go to the Dorchester just in case he is actually following you.'

'I don't even know where the Dorchester is,' yelped Stephen.

Robin came to his rescue:

'Take the first right, Stephen, and that'll bring you into Bruton Street, keep walking as straight as you can until you reach Berkeley Square. Stay on the line, but don't look back or you may turn into a pillar of salt.'

'James,' said Jean-Pierre, thinking on his feet for the first time in his life. 'You take a taxi immediately to the Dorchester and book room 120 in the name of Drosser. Have the key ready for Stephen the moment he walks through the door, then make yourself scarce. Stephen, are you, still there?'

'Yes.'

'Did you hear all that?'

'Yes. Tell James to book 119 or 121 if 120 is not available.'

'Roger,' replied Jean-Pierre. 'Get going, James.'

James bolted out of the gallery and barged in front of a woman who had just hailed a taxi, a thing he had never done before.

'The Dorchester,' he hollered, 'as fast as you can go.'

The taxi shot off.

'Stephen, James has gone and I'm sending Robin to follow Harvey so he can keep you briefed and guide you to the Dorchester. I'm staying put. Everything else OK?'

'No,' said Stephen, 'start praying. I've reached Berkeley Square. Where now?'

'Across the garden then continue down Hill Street.'

Robin left the gallery and ran all the way to Bruton Street until he was only 50 yards behind Harvey.

'Now about the Henry Moore,' said the well-corseted lady.

'Screw Henry Moore,' said Jean-Pierre, not even looking around.

The steel-reinforced bosom heaved.

'Young man, I have never been spoken to in . . .'

But Jean-Pierre had already reached the lavatory, and closed the door.

'You're crossing South Audley Street now, then continue into Deanery Street. Keep going, don't turn right or left and don't whatever you do look back. Harvey is still about 50 yards behind you. I'm a little more than 50 yards behind him,' said Robin. Passers-by stared at the man talking into his little instrument.

'Is Room 120 free?'

'Yes, sir, they checked out this morning, but I'm not sure if it's ready for occupancy yet. I think the maid may still be clearing the room. I'll have to check, sir,' said the tall receptionist in the morning suit, which indicated that he was a senior member of the floor staff.

'Oh, don't worry about that,' said James, his German accent far better than Stephen's. 'I always have that room. Can you book me in for one night? Name's Drosser, Herr – um – Helmut Drosser.'

He slipped a pound over the counter.

'Certainly, sir.'

'That's Park Lane, Stephen. Look right – the big hotel on the corner straight in front of you is the Dorchester. The semi-circle facing you is the main entrance. Go up the steps, past the big man in the green overcoat, and through the revolving door and you'll find reception on your right. James ought to be there waiting for you.'

Robin was grateful that the annual dinner of the Royal Society for Medicine had been held at the Dorchester last year.

'Where's Harvey?' bleated Stephen.

'Only 40 yards behind you.'

Stephen quickened his pace, ran up the steps of the Dorchester and pushed through the revolving door so hard that the other residents coming out found themselves on the street faster than they had planned. Thank God, James was standing there holding a key.

'The lift's over there,' said James, pointing. 'You've only chosen one of the most expensive suites in the hotel.'

Stephen glanced in the direction James had indicated and turned back to thank him. But James was already heading off to the American Bar to be sure he was well out of sight when Harvey arrived.

Stephen left the lift at the first floor and found that the Dorchester, which he had never entered before, was as traditional as Claridge's, its thick royal blue and golden carpets leading to a magnificently appointed corner suite which overlooked Hyde Park. He collapsed into an easy chair, not quite sure what to expect next. Nothing had gone as planned.

Jean-Pierre waited at the gallery, James sat in the American Bar and Robin loitered by the side of Barclays Bank, Park Lane, a mock-tudor building 50 yards from the entrance of the Dorchester.

'Have you a Mr Drosser staying at this hotel? I think it's room 120,' barked Harvey.

The receptionist looked through the card index.

'Yes, sir. Is he expecting you?'

'No, but I'll have a word with him on the house phone.'

'Of course, sir. If you'd be kind enough to go through the small archway on your left you will find five telephones. One of them is a house phone.'

Harvey marched through the archway as directed.

'Room 120,' he instructed the operator, who sat in his own little section, wearing the green Dorchester uniform with golden castles on the lapels.

'Cubicle No. 1, please, sir.'

'Mr Drosser?'

'Speaking,' said Stephen, summoning up his German accent for a sustained effort.

'My name is Harvey Metcalfe. I wonder if I could come up and have a word with you? It's about the Van Gogh you bought this morning.'

'Well, it's a little inconvenient at the moment. I am about to take a shower and I do have a lunch appointment.'

'I won't keep you more than a few minutes.'

Before Stephen could reply, the telephone clicked. A few moments later there was a knock on the door. Stephen's legs wobbled. He answered it nervously. He had changed into a white Dorchester dressing-gown and his brown hair was somewhat dishevelled and darker than normal. It was the only disguise he could think of at such short notice as the original plan had not allowed for a face-to-face meeting with Harvey.

'Sorry to intrude, Mr Drosser, but I had to see you immediately. I know you have just purchased a Van Gogh from the Lamanns Gallery and I was hoping that, as you are a dealer, you might be willing to sell it on for a quick profit.'

'No, thank you,' said Stephen, relaxing for the first time. 'I've wanted a Van Gogh for my gallery in Munich for many years. I'm sorry, Mr Metcalfe, it's not for sale.'

'Listen, you paid 170,000 guineas for it. What's that in dollars?'

Stephen paused.

'Oh, about $435,000.'

'I'll give you $15,000 if you release the picture to me. All you have to do is ring the gallery and tell them that the picture is now mine and that I will cover the bill.'

Stephen sat silent, not sure how to handle the situation without blowing it. Think like Harvey Metcalfe, he told himself.

'$20,000 in cash and you've got a deal.'

Harvey hesitated. Stephen's legs wobbled again.

'Done,' said Harvey. 'Ring the gallery immediately.'

Stephen picked up the telephone.

'Can you get me the Lamanns Gallery in Bond Street as quickly as possible, please – I have a lunch appointment.'

A few seconds later the call came through.

'Lamanns Gallery.'

'I would like to speak to Mr Lamanns.'

'At last, Stephen. What the hell is happening your end?'

'Ah, Mr Lamanns, this is Herr Drosser. You remember, I was in your gallery earlier this morning.'

'Of course I remember, you fool. What are you going on about, Stephen? It's me – Jean-Pierre.'

'I have a Mr Metcalfe with me.'

'Christ, I'm sorry, Stephen. I didn't . . .'

'And you can expect him in the next few minutes.'

Stephen looked towards Harvey who nodded his assent.

'You are to release the Van Gogh I purchased this morning to Mr Metcalfe and he will give you a cheque for the full amount, 170,000 guineas.'

'Out of disaster, triumph,' said Jean-Pierre quietly.

'I'm very sorry I shall not be the owner of the picture myself, but I have, as the Americans would say, had an offer I can't refuse. Thank you for the part you played,' said Stephen and put the telephone down.

Harvey was writing out a cheque to cash for $20,000.

'Thank you, Mr Drosser. You have made me a happy man.'

'I am not complaining myself,' said Stephen honestly. He escorted Harvey to the door and they shook hands.

'Goodbye, sir.'

'Good day, Mr Metcalfe.'

Stephen closed the door and tottered to the chair, almost too weak to move.

Robin and James saw Harvey leave the Dorchester. Robin followed him in the direction of the gallery, his hopes rising with each stride. James took the lift to the first floor and nearly ran to Room 120. He banged on the door. Stephen jumped at the noise. He didn't feel he could face Harvey again. He opened the door.

'James, it's you. Cancel the room, pay for one night and then join me in the cocktail bar.'

'Why? What for?'

'A bottle of Krug 1964 Privée Cuvée.'

One down and three to go.

11

JEAN-PIERRE was the last to arrive at Lord Brigsley's King's Road flat. He felt he had earned the right to make an entrance. Harvey's cheque had been cleared and the Lamanns Gallery account was for the moment $447,560 in credit. The painting was in Harvey's possession and the heavens had not yet fallen in. Jean-Pierre had cleared more money in two months of crime than he had in ten years of legitimate trading.

The other three greeted him with the acclaim normally reserved for a sporting hero, and a glass of James's last bottle of Veuve Clicquot 1959.

'We were lucky to pull it off,' said Robin.

'We weren't lucky,' said Stephen. 'We kept our nerve under pressure, and the one thing we've learned from the exercise is that Harvey can change the rules in the middle of the game.'

'He almost changed the game, Stephen.'

'Agreed. So we must always remember that we shall fail unless we can be as successful, not once, but four times. We must not underestimate our opponent just because we've won the first round.'

'Relax, Professor,' said James. 'We can get down

to business again after dinner. Anne came in this afternoon especially to make the salmon mousse, and it won't go down well with Harvey Metcalfe.'

'When am I going to meet this fabulous creature?' asked Jean-Pierre.

'When this is all over and behind us.'

'Don't marry her, James. She's only after our money.'

They all laughed. James hoped the day would come when he could tell them she had known all along. He produced the *boeuf en croûte* and two bottles of Echezeaux 1970. Jean-Pierre sniffed the sauce appreciatively.

'On second thoughts she ought to be seriously considered if her touch in bed is half as deft as it is in the kitchen.'

'You're not going to get the chance to be the judge of that, Jean-Pierre. Content yourself with admiring her French dressing.'

'You were quite outstanding this morning, James,' said Stephen, steering the conversation away from Jean-Pierre's pet subject. 'You should go on the stage. As a member of the British aristocracy, your talent's simply wasted.'

'I've always wanted to, but my old pa is against it. Those who live in expectation of a large inheritance must expect to have to toe the filial line.'

'Why don't we let him play all four parts in Monte Carlo?' suggested Robin.

The mention of Monte Carlo sobered them up.

'Back to work,' said Stephen. 'We have so far received $447,560. Expenses with the picture and an unexpected night at the Dorchester were $11,142 so Metcalfe still owes us $563,582. Think of what we've still lost, not of what we've gained. Now for the Monte Carlo operation, which depends upon split-second timing and our ability to sustain our roles for several hours. Robin will bring us up to date.'

Robin retrieved the green dossier from the brief-case by his side and studied his notes for a few moments.

'Jean-Pierre, you must grow a beard, starting today, so that in three weeks' time you'll be unrecog-nisable. You must also cut your hair very short.' Robin grinned unsympathetically at Jean-Pierre's grimace. 'Yes, you'll look absolutely revolting.'

'That,' said Jean-Pierre; 'will not be possible.'

'How are the baccarat and blackjack coming on?' continued Robin.

'I have lost $37 in five weeks, which includes my member's fee at the Claremont and the Golden Nugget.'

'It all goes on expenses,' said Stephen. 'That puts the bill up to $563,619.'

The others laughed. Only Stephen's lips did not move. He was in sober earnest.

'James, how is your handling of the van going?'

'I can reach Harley Street from St Thomas's in 14 minutes. I should be able to do the actual run in Monte Carlo in about 11 minutes, though naturally

I shall want to do some practice runs the day before. To start with I'll have to master driving on the wrong side of the road.'

'Strange how everybody except the British drives on the wrong side of the road,' observed Jean-Pierre.

James ignored him.

'I'm not sure of all the continental road signs either.'

'They are detailed in the Michelin guide that I gave you as part of my dossier.'

'I know, but I'll still feel easier when I've experienced the actual run and not just studied maps. There are quite a few one-way streets in Monaco and I don't want to be stopped going down the wrong one with Harvey Metcalfe unconscious in the back.'

'Don't worry. You'll have ample time when we're there. So, that only leaves Stephen, who's about the most competent medical student I've ever had. You're confident of your newly acquired knowledge, I hope?'

'About as confident as I am with your American accent, Robin. Anyway, I trust that Harvey Metcalfe will be in no state of mind to worry about such trivialities by the time we meet up.'

'Don't worry, Stephen. Believe me, he wouldn't even register who you were if you introduced yourself as Herr Drosser with a Van Gogh under both arms.'

Robin handed round the final schedule of rehearsals for Harley Street and St Thomas's, and once again consulted the green file.

'I've booked four single rooms on different floors

at the Hôtel de Paris and confirmed all the arrangements with the Centre Hospitalier Princesse Grace. The hotel is reputed to be one of the best in the world – it's certainly expensive enough – but it's convenient for the Casino. We fly to Nice on Monday, the day Harvey is due to arrive on his yacht.'

'What do we do for the rest of the week?' enquired James innocently.

Stephen resumed control:

'We master the green dossier backwards, frontwards and sideways for a full dress rehearsal on Friday. The most important thing for you, James, is to get a grip of yourself and let us know what you intend to do.'

James sank back into gloom.

Stephen closed his file briskly.

'That seems to be all we can cover tonight.'

'Hang on, Stephen,' said Robin. 'Let's strip you off once more. I'd like to see if we can do it in 90 seconds.'

Stephen lay down slightly reluctantly in the middle of the room, and James and Jean-Pierre swiftly and carefully removed all his clothes.

'Eighty-seven seconds. Excellent,' said Robin, looking down at Stephen, naked except for his watch. 'Hell, look at the time. I must get back to Newbury. My wife will think I have a mistress and I don't fancy any of you.'

Stephen dressed himself quickly while the others prepared to leave. A few minutes later, James stood by the front door, watching them depart one by one. As soon as Stephen was out of sight, he bounded downstairs into the kitchen.

'Did you listen?'

'Yes, darling. They're all rather nice and I don't blame them for being cross with you. They're being very professional about the whole venture, while you sounded like the only amateur. We'll have to think up something good for you to match them. We've over a week before Mr Metcalfe goes to Monte Carlo and we must use the time constructively.'

James sighed: 'Well, let's enjoy tonight. At least this morning was a triumph.'

'Yes, but not yours. Tomorrow we work.'

12

'Passengers for flight 017 to Nice are now requested to board the aircraft at gate No. 7,' boomed the loudspeaker at Heathrow's No. 1 terminal.

'That's us,' said Stephen.

The four of them took the escalator to the first floor, and walked down the long corridor. After being searched for guns, bombs, and whatever else terrorists are searched for, they proceeded down the ramp.

They sat separately, never speaking or even looking at each other. Stephen had warned them that the flight could well be sprinkled with Harvey's friends, and each imagined himself to be sitting next to the closest of them.

James gazed moodily at the cloudless sky and brooded. He and Anne had read every book they could lay their hands on that even hinted at stolen money or successful duplicity, but they had found nothing they could plagiarise. Even Stephen, in between being undressed and practised upon at St Thomas's, was becoming daunted by the task of finding a winning plan for James.

The Trident touched down at Nice at 13.40, and

the train journey from Nice to Monte Carlo took them a further twenty minutes. Each member of the team made his own way to the elegant Hôtel de Paris in the Place du Casino. At 7 pm they were all present in room 217.

'All settled into your rooms?'

The other three nodded. 'So far, so good,' said Robin. 'Right, let's go over the timing. Jean-Pierre, you will go to the Casino tonight and play a few hands of baccarat and blackjack. Try to acclimatise to the place and learn your way around. In particular, master any variations in the rules there might be from the Claremont, and be sure you never speak in English. Do you foresee any problems?'

'No, can't say I do, Robin. In fact I may as well go now and start rehearsing.'

'Don't lose too much of our money,' said Stephen.

Jean-Pierre, resplendent in beard and dinner-jacket, grinned and slipped out of room 217 and down the staircase, avoiding the lift. He walked the short distance from the hotel to the famous Casino.

Robin continued:

'James, you take a taxi from the Casino to the hospital. On arrival you will leave the meter running for a few minutes and then return to the Casino. You can normally rely on a taxi to take the shortest route, but to be sure, tell the driver it's an emergency. That'll give you the opportunity of seeing which traffic lanes he uses under pressure. When he's returned you to the Casino, walk the route from there to the hospital and back. Then you can assimilate it in your own time. After you've mastered that, repeat the same procedure for the route between the hospital and Harvey's yacht. Never enter the Casino or even get close enough to the boat to be seen. Being seen now means being recognised later.'

'What about my knowledge of the Casino on the night of the operation?'

'Jean-Pierre will take care of that. He'll meet you at the door because Stephen won't be able to leave Harvey. I don't think they will charge you the 12 franc entrance fee if you're wearing a white coat and carrying a stretcher, but have it ready to be sure. When you've completed the walk, go to your room and stay there until our meeting at 11 am tomorrow. Stephen and I will also be going to the hospital to check that all the arrangements have been carried out as cabled from London. If at any time you see us, ignore us.'

As James left room 217, Jean-Pierre arrived at the Casino.

The Casino stands in the heart of Monte Carlo overlooking the sea, surrounded by the most beautiful gardens. The present building has several wings, the oldest of which was designed by Charles Garnier, the architect of the Paris Opera House. The gambling rooms, which were added in 1910, are linked by an atrium to the Salle Garnier in which operas and ballets are performed.

Jean-Pierre marched up the marble staircase to the

entrance and paid his 12 francs. The gambling rooms are vast, full of the decadence and grandeur of Europe at the turn of the century. Massive red carpets, statues, paintings and tapestries give the building an almost regal appearance and the portraits lend an air of a country home still lived in. Jean-Pierre found the clientèle were of all nationalities: Arabs and Jews played next to each other at the roulette wheel and chatted away with an ease that would have been unthinkable at the United Nations. Jean-Pierre felt totally relaxed in the unreal world of the wealthy. Robin had assessed his character accurately and given him a role he could master with aplomb.

Jean-Pierre spent over three hours studying the layout of the Casino – its gambling rooms, bars and restaurants, the telephones, the entrances and exits. Then he turned his attention to the gambling itself. He discovered that two shoes of baccarat were played in the Salons Privés at 3 pm and 11 pm, and learned from Pierre Cattalano, the head of the public relations department of the Casino, which of the private rooms Harvey Metcalfe preferred to play in.

Blackjack is played in the Salon des Amériques from 11 am daily. There are three tables, and Jean-Pierre's informant told him that Harvey always played on table No. 2, seat No. 3. Jean-Pierre played a little blackjack and baccarat, to discover any slight variations in rules there might be from the Claremont. In fact there were none, as the Claremont still adheres to French rules.

Harvey Metcalfe arrived noisily at the Casino just after 11 pm, leaving a trail of cigar ash leading to his baccarat table. Jean-Pierre, inconspicuous at the bar, watched as the head croupier first showed Harvey politely to a reserved seat, and then walked through to the Salon des Amériques to the No. 2 blackjack table and placed a discreet white card marked '*Réservé*' on one of the chairs. Harvey was clearly a favoured client. The management knew as well as Jean-Pierre which games Harvey Metcalfe played. At 11.27 pm Jean-Pierre left quietly and returned to the solitude of his hotel room where he remained until 11 am the next day. He phoned no one and did not use room service.

James's evening also went well. The taxi-driver was superb. The word 'emergency' brought out the Walter Mitty in him: he travelled through Monte Carlo as if it were nothing less than the Rally itself. When James arrived at the hospital in 8 minutes 44 seconds, he genuinely felt a little sick and had to rest for a few minutes in the Entrée des Patients before returning to the taxi.

'Back to the Casino, but much slower, please.'

The journey back along the Rue Grimaldi took just over eleven minutes and James decided he would settle for trying to cover it in about ten. He paid off the taxi-driver and carried out the second part of his instructions.

Walking to the hospital and back took just over an hour. The night air was gentle on his face, and the streets crowded with lively chattering people. Tourism is the chief source of income for the Principality, and the Monégasques take the welfare of their visitors very seriously. James passed innumerable little pavement restaurants and souvenir shops stocked with expensive trinkets of no significance that once bought would be forgotten or lost within a week. Noisy groups of holiday-makers strolled along the pavements, their multilingual babel forming a meaningless chorus to James's thoughts of Anne. On arrival back at the Casino. James then took a taxi to the harbour to locate *Messenger Boy*, Harvey's yacht, and from there once more to the hospital. He then walked the same route and, like Jean-Pierre, he was safely in his room before midnight, having completed his first task.

Robin and Stephen found the walk to the hospital from their hotel took a little over 40 minutes. On arrival Robin asked the receptionist if he could see the superintendent.

'The night superintendent is now on duty,' said a freshly starched French nurse. 'Who shall I say is asking him for?'

Her English pronunciation was excellent and they both avoided a smile at her slight mistake.

'Doctor Wiley Barker of the University of California.'

Robin began to pray that the French superintendent would not happen to know that Wiley Barker, President Nixon's physician and one of the most respected surgeons in the world, was actually touring

Australia at the time lecturing to the major universities.

'*Bonsoir, Docteur Barker. Monsieur Bartise à votre service. Votre visite fait grand honneur à notre hôpital humble.*'

Robin's newly acquired American accent stopped any further conversation in French.

'I would like to check the layout of the theatre,' said Robin, 'and confirm that we have it provisionally booked for tomorrow from 11 pm to 4 am for the next five days.'

'That is quite correct, *Docteur Barker*,' said the superintendent, looking down at a clip-board. 'The theatre is off the next corridor. Will you follow me, please?'

The theatre was not dissimilar to the one the four of them had been practising in at St Thomas's – two rooms with a rubber swing door dividing them. The main theatre was well equipped and a nod from Robin showed Stephen that it had all the instruments he required. Robin was impressed. Although the hospital had only some 200 beds, the theatre itself was of the highest standard. Rich men had obviously been ill there before.

'Will you be requiring an anaesthetist or any nurses to assist you, *Docteur Barker*?'

'No,' said Robin. 'I have my own anaesthetist and staff but I will require a tray of laparotomy instruments to be laid out every night. However, I will be able to give you at least an hour's warning before you need make any final preparations.'

'That's plenty of time. Will there be anything else, sir?'

'Yes, the special vehicle I ordered. Can it be ready for my driver at 12 pm tomorrow?'

'Yes, *Docteur Barker*. It will be in the small car park behind the hospital and your driver can pick up the keys from the reception.'

'Can you recommend an agency from which I can hire an experienced nurse for post-operative care?'

'*Bien sûr*, the Auxiliaire Médical of Nice will be only too happy to oblige – at a certain price, of course.'

'Of course,' said Robin. 'And that reminds me to ask, have all your expenses been dealt with?'

'Yes, *Docteur*. We received a cheque from California last Thursday for $7,000.'

Robin had been very pleased with that touch. It had been so simple. Stephen had contacted his bank at Harvard and asked them to send a draft from the First National City Bank in San Francisco to the hospital secretary at Monte Carlo.

'Thank you all for your help, Monsieur Bartise. You have been most obliging. Now you do understand that I am not quite sure which night I shall be bringing my patient in. He's a sick man, although he doesn't know it, and I have to prepare him for the operation.'

'Of course, *mon cher Docteur*.'

'Finally, I would appreciate it if you would tell as few people as possible that I am in Monte Carlo. I am trying to snatch a holiday at the same time as working.'

'I understand, Docteur Barker. You can be assured of my discretion.'

Robin and Stephen bade farewell to Monsieur Bartise and took a taxi back to the hotel.

'I'm always slightly humiliated by how well the French speak our language compared with our grasp of theirs,' said Stephen.

'It's all the fault of you bloody Americans,' said Robin.

'No, it isn't. If France had conquered America, your French would be excellent. Blame it on the Pilgrim Fathers.'

Robin laughed. Neither of them spoke again until they reached room 217 for fear of being overheard. Stephen had no doubts about the responsibility and risk they were taking with Robin's plan.

Harvey Metcalfe was on the deck of his yacht, sunbathing and reading the morning papers. *Nice-Matin*, irritatingly enough, was in French. He read it laboriously, with the aid of a dictionary, to see if there were any social events to which he ought to get himself invited. He had gambled late into the night, and was enjoying the sun's rays on his fleshy back. If money could have obtained it, he would have been 6 ft and 170 lb with a handsome head of hair, but no amount of suntan oil would stop his balding dome from burning, so he covered it with a cap inscribed with the words 'I'm sexy'. If Miss Fish could see him now . . .

At 11 am, as Harvey turned over and allowed the sun to see his massive stomach, James strolled into room 217 where the rest of the Team were waiting for him.

Jean-Pierre reported on the layout of the Casino and Harvey Metcalfe's habits. James brought them up to date on the result of his race through the city the night before and confirmed that he thought he could cover the distance in just under eleven minutes.

'Perfect,' said Robin. 'Stephen and I took 15 minutes by taxi from the hospital to the hotel so if Jean-Pierre warns me immediately the balloon goes up in the Casino, I should have enough time to see that everything is ready before you all arrive.'

'I do hope the balloon will be going down, not up, in the Casino,' remarked Jean-Pierre.

'I have booked an agency nurse to be on call from tomorrow night. The hospital has all the facilities I require. It'll take about two minutes to walk a stretcher from the front door to the theatre, so from the moment James leaves the car park I should have at least 16 minutes to prepare myself. James, you'll be able to pick up the vehicle from the hospital car park at 12 pm. The keys have been left in reception in the name of Dr Barker. Do a couple of practice runs and no more. I don't want you causing interest by looking conspicuous. And could you leave this parcel in the back, please.'

'What is it?'

'Three long white laboratory coats and a stethoscope for Stephen. While you're at it, better check that you can unfold the stretcher easily. When you've finished the two runs, put the vehicle back in the car park and return to your room until 11 pm. From then through to 4 am you'll have to wait in the car park until you get the "action stations" or "all clear" signal from Jean-Pierre. Everybody buy new batteries for your transmitters. I don't want the whole plan to collapse for the sake of a ten-penny battery. I'm afraid there's nothing much for you to do, Jean-Pierre until this evening, except relax. I hope you have some good books in your room.'

'Can't I go to the Princess Cinema and see François Truffaut's *La Nuit Américaine*? I just adore Jacqueline Bisset. *Vive la France*.'

'My dear Jean-Pierre, Miss Bisset's from Reading,' said James.

'I don't care. I still want to see her.'

'A frog he would a-wooing go,' said James mockingly.

'But why not?' said Robin. 'The last thing Harvey will do is take in an intellectual French film with no sub-titles. Hope you enjoy it – and good luck tonight, Jean-Pierre.'

Jean-Pierre left for his room as quietly as he had come, leaving the rest of them together in room 217.

'Right, James. You can do your practice runs any time that suits you. Just make sure you're wide awake tonight.'

'Fine. I'll go and pick up the keys from the hospital reception. Let's just hope nobody stops me for a real emergency.'

'Now, Stephen, let's go over the details again. There's more than money to lose if we get this wrong. We'll start from the top. What do you do if the nitrous oxide falls below five litres . . .'

'Station check – station check – operation Metcalfe. This is Jean-Pierre. I am on the steps of the Casino. Can you hear me, James?'

'Yes. I am in the car park of the hospital. Out.'

'Robin here. I am on the balcony of room 217. Is Stephen with you, Jean-Pierre?'

'Yes. He's drinking on his own at the bar.'

'Good luck and out.'

Jean-Pierre carried out a station check every hour on the hour from 7 pm until 11 pm, merely to inform Robin and James that Harvey had not arrived.

Eventually, at 11.16, he did show up, and took his reserved place at the baccarat table. Stephen stopped sipping his tomato juice and Jean-Pierre moved over and waited patiently by the table for one of the men seated on the left or right of Harvey to leave. An hour passed by. Harvey was losing a little, but continued to play. So did the tall thin American on his right and the Frenchman on his left. Another hour and still no movement. Then suddenly the Frenchman on the left of Metcalfe had a particularly bad run, gathered his few remaining chips and left the table. Jean-Pierre moved forward.

'I am afraid, Monsieur, that that seat is reserved for another gentleman,' said the banker. 'We do have an unreserved place on the other side of the table.'

'It's not important,' said Jean-Pierre, who backed away, not wanting to be remembered, cursing the deference with which the Monégasques treat the wealthy. Stephen could see from the bar what had happened and made furtive signs to leave. They were all back in room 217 just after 2 am.

'What a bloody silly mistake. *Merde, merde, merde.* I should have thought of reservations the moment I knew Harvey had one.'

'No, it was my fault. I don't know anything about how casinos work and I should have queried it during rehearsals,' said Robin, stroking his newly acquired moustache.

'No one is to blame,' chipped in Stephen. 'We still have three more nights, so no need to panic. We'll just have to work out how to overcome the seating problem, but for now we'll all get some sleep and meet again in this room at 10 am.'

They left, a little depressed. Robin had sat waiting in the hotel on edge for four hours. James was cold and bored in the hospital car park, Stephen was sick of tomato juice and Jean-Pierre had been on his feet by the baccarat table waiting for a seat that wasn't even available.

Once again Harvey lounged in the sun. He was now a light pink and was hoping to be a better colour towards the end of the week. According to his copy of the *New York Times*, gold was still climbing and the Deutschmark and the Swiss franc remained firm, while the dollar was on the retreat against every currency except sterling. Sterling stood at $2.42. Harvey thought a more realistic price was $1.80 and the sooner it reached that the better.

Nothing new, he thought, when the sharp ring of a French telephone roused him. He never could get used to the sound of foreign telephones. The attentive steward bustled out on deck with the instrument on an extension lead.

'Hi, Lloyd. Didn't know you were in Monte . . . why don't we get together? . . . 8 pm? . . . Me too . . . I'm even getting brown . . . Must be getting old . . . What? . . . Great, I'll see you then.'

Harvey replaced the receiver and asked the steward for a large whisky on the rocks. He once again settled down happily to the morning's financial bad news.

'That seems to be the obvious solution,' said Stephen.

They all nodded their approval.

'Jean-Pierre will give up the baccarat table and book a place next to Harvey Metcalfe on his blackjack table in the Salon des Amériques and wait for him to change games. We know both the seat numbers Harvey plays at and we'll alter our own plans accordingly.'

Jean-Pierre dialled the number of the Casino and asked to speak to Pierre Cattalano:

'*Réservez-moi la deuxième place à la table 2 pour le vingt-et-un ce soir et demain soir, s'il vous plaît.*'

'*Je pense que cette place est déjà réservée, Monsieur. Un instant, s'il vous plaît, je vais vérifier.*'

'*Peut-être que 100 francs la rendra libre,*' replied Jean-Pierre.

'*Mais certainement, Monsieur. Présentez-vous à moi dès votre arrivée, et le nécessaire sera fait.*'

'*Merci,*' said Jean-Pierre and replaced the receiver. 'That's under control.'

Jean-Pierre was visibly sweating, though had his call had no other outcome than to secure him a reserved seat, not a drop of perspiration would have appeared. They all returned to their rooms.

When the clock in the town square struck twelve, Robin was waiting quietly in room 217, James stood in the car park humming 'I Get Along Without You Very Well', Stephen was at the bar of the Salon des Amériques toying with yet another tomato juice and Jean-Pierre was at seat No. 2 on table No. 2, playing blackjack. Both Stephen and Jean-Pierre saw Harvey come through the door, chatting to a man in a loud-checked jacket which only a Texan could have worn outside his own back yard. Harvey and his friend sat down together at the baccarat table. Jean-Pierre beat a hasty retreat to the bar.

'Oh, no. I give up.'

'No, you don't,' whispered Stephen. 'Back to the hotel.'

Spirits were very low when they were all assembled in room 217, but it was agreed that Stephen had made the right decision. They could not risk the entire exercise being carefully observed by a friend of Harvey's.

'The first operation is beginning to look a bit too good to be true,' said Robin.

'Don't be silly,' said Stephen. 'We had two false alarms then, and the entire plan had to be changed at the last minute. We can't expect him just to walk in and hand over his money. Now snap out of it, all of you, and go and get some sleep.'

They returned to their separate rooms, but not to much sleep. The strain was beginning to tell.

'That's enough I think, Lloyd. A goodish evening.'

'For you, you mean, Harvey, not for me. You are one of nature's winners.'

Harvey patted the checked shoulder expansively. If anything pleased him more than his own success, it was other people's failure.

'Do you want to spend the night on my yacht, Lloyd?'

'No thanks. I must get back to Nice. I have a meeting in Paris, France, tomorrow lunch. See you soon, Harvey – take care of yourself.' He dug Harvey in the ribs jocularly. 'That's a fair-sized job.'

'Goodnight, Lloyd,' said Harvey, a little stiffly.

The next evening Jean-Pierre did not arrive at the Casino until 11 pm. Harvey Metcalfe was already at the baccarat table minus Lloyd. Stephen was at the bar looking angry, and Jean-Pierre glanced at him apologetically as he took his seat at the blackjack table. He played a few hands to get the feel, trying to keep his losses fairly limited without drawing attention to the modesty of his stakes. Suddenly Harvey left the baccarat table and stalked into the Salon des Amériques, glancing at the roulette tables as he passed more out of curiosity than interest. He detested games of pure chance, and considered baccarat and blackjack games of skill. He headed to table No. 2 seat No. 3, on Jean-Pierre's left. Jean-Pierre felt his adrenalin start pumping round and his heart-beat rise up to 120 again. Stephen left the Casino for a few minutes to warn James and Robin that Harvey had moved to the blackjack table and was now sitting next to Jean-Pierre. He then returned to the bar and waited.

There were seven punters at the blackjack table. On box No. 1, a middle-aged lady smothered in diamonds, who looked as if she might be passing time while her husband played roulette or perhaps baccarat. On box No. 2, Jean-Pierre. On Box No. 3, Harvey. On Box No. 4, a dissipated young man with the world-weariness that usually goes with a large unearned income. On box No. 5, an Arab in full robes. On box No. 6, a not-unattractive actress who was clearly resting, Jean-Pierre suspected, with the occupant of box No. 5; and on box No. 7, an elderly straight-backed aristocratic Frenchman in evening dress.

'A large black coffee,' Harvey drawled to the slim waiter in his smart brown jacket.

Monte Carlo does not allow hard liquor to be sold at the tables or girls to serve the customers. In direct contrast to Las Vegas, the Casino's business is gambling, not booze or women. Harvey had enjoyed Vegas when he was younger, but the older he became the more he appreciated the sophistication of the French. He had grown to prefer the formal atmosphere and decorum of this particular Casino. Although at the No. 3 table only he, the aristocratic Frenchman and Jean-Pierre wore dinner-jackets, it was frowned upon by the management to be dressed in any way that might be described as casual.

A moment later, piping hot coffee in a large golden cup arrived at Harvey's side. Jean-Pierre eyed it nervously while Harvey placed 100 francs on the table next to Jean-Pierre's 3-franc chip, the minimum and maximum stake allowed. The dealer, a tall young man of not more than thirty, who was proud of the fact that he could deal a hundred hands in an hour, slipped the cards deftly out of the shoe. A king for Jean-Pierre, a four for Harvey, a five for the young man on Harvey's left and a six for the dealer. Jean-Pierre's second card was a seven. He stuck. Harvey drew a ten and also stuck. The young man on Harvey's left also drew ten and asked the dealer to twist again. It was an eight – bust.

Harvey despised amateurs in any field and even fools know you don't twist if you have twelve or more when the dealer's card face up is a three, four, five or six. He grimaced slightly. The dealer dealt himself a ten and a six. Harvey and Jean-Pierre were winners. Jean-Pierre ignored the fate of the other players.

The next round was unwinnable. Jean-Pierre stuck at eighteen, two nines which he chose not to split as the dealer had an ace. Harvey stuck on eighteen, an eight and a jack, and the young man on the left bust again. The bank drew a queen – 'Black Jack' – and took the table.

The next hand gave Jean-Pierre a three, Harvey a seven and the young man a ten. The dealer drew himself a seven. Jean-Pierre drew an eight and doubled his stake to 6 francs and then drew a ten – vingt-et-un. Jean-Pierre did not blink. He realised he was playing well and that he must not draw attention to himself, but let Harvey take it for granted. In fact Harvey hadn't even noticed him: his attention was riveted on the young man on his left, who seemed anxious to make a gift to the management on every hand. The dealer continued, giving Harvey a ten and the young man an eight, leaving them both no choice but to stick. The dealer drew a ten, giving himself seventeen. He paid Jean-Pierre, left Harvey's stake and paid the young man. The management was happy to pay the young man occasionally, if only to keep him sitting there all night.

There were no more cards left in the shoe. The dealer made a great show of re-shuffling the four packs and invited Harvey to cut the cards before replacing them in the shoe. They slipped out again: a ten for Jean-Pierre, a five for Harvey, a six for the young man and a four for the dealer. Jean-Pierre drew an eight. The cards were running well. Harvey drew a ten and stuck at fifteen. The young man drew a ten and asked for another card. Harvey could not believe his eyes and whistled through the gap in his front teeth. Sure enough, the next card was a king. The young man was bust. The dealer dealt himself a jack and then an eight, making twenty-two, but the young man had learned nothing from it. Harvey stared at him. When would he discover that, of the fifty-two cards in the pack, no less than sixteen have a face value of ten?

Harvey's distraction gave Jean-Pierre the opportunity he had been waiting for. He slipped his hand into his pocket and took the prostigmin tablet Robin had given him into the palm of his left hand. He sneezed, pulling his handkerchief from his breast pocket in a well-rehearsed gesture with his right hand. At the same time, he quickly and unobtrusively dropped the tablet into Harvey's coffee. It would, Robin had assured him, be an hour before it took effect. To begin with Harvey would only feel a little sick; then he would get rapidly worse until the pain was too much to bear, before finally collapsing in absolute agony.

Jean-Pierre turned to the bar, gripped his right-hand fist three times and then placed it in his pocket. Stephen left immediately and warned Robin and James from the steps of the Casino that the prostigmin tablet was in Metcalfe's drink. It was now Robin's turn to be tested under pressure. First he rang the hospital and asked the sister on duty to have the theatre in full preparation. Then he rang the nursing agency and asked for the nurse he had booked to be waiting in the hospital reception in exactly ninety minutes' time. He sat alone, nervously waiting for another call from the Casino.

Stephen returned to the bar. Harvey had started to feel a little sick, but was loath to leave. Despite the growing pain, his greed was forcing him to play on. He drank the rest of this coffee and ordered another one, hoping it would clear his head. The coffee did not help and Harvey began to feel steadily worse. An ace and a king followed by a seven, a four and a ten, and then two queens helped him to stay at the table. Jean-Pierre forced himself not to look at his watch. The dealer gave Jean-Pierre a seven, Harvey another ace and the young man a two. Quite suddenly, almost exactly on the hour, Harvey could bear the pain no longer. He tried to stand up to leave the table.

'*Le jeu a commencé, Monsieur*,' the dealer said formally.

'Go stuff yourself,' said Harvey and collapsed to the ground, gripping his stomach in agony. Jean-Pierre sat motionless while the croupiers and gamblers milled around helplessly. Stephen fought his way through the circle which had gathered round Harvey.

'Stand back, please. I am a doctor.'

The crowd moved back quickly, relieved to have a professional man on the scene.

'What is it, Doctor?' gasped Harvey, who felt the end of the world was about to come.

'I don't know yet,' replied Stephen. Robin had warned him that from collapse to passing out might be as short a time as ten minutes, so he set to work fast. He loosened Harvey's tie and took his pulse. He then undid his shirt and started feeling his abdomen.

'Have you a pain in the stomach?'

'Yes,' groaned Harvey.

'Did it come on suddenly?'

'Yes.'

'Can you try and describe the quality of the pain? Is it stabbing, burning or gripping?'

'Gripping.'

'Where is it most painful?'

Harvey touched the right side of his stomach. Stephen pressed down the tip of the ninth rib, making Harvey bellow with pain.

'Ah,' said Stephen, 'a positive Murphy's sign. You probably have an acutely inflamed gall-bladder. I'm afraid that may mean gallstones.' He continued to palpate the massive abdomen, gently. 'It looks as if a stone has come out of your gall-bladder and is passing down the tube to your intestine – it's the squeezing of that tube that's giving you such a dreadful pain. I'm afraid your gall-bladder and the stone must be removed at once. I can only hope there is someone at the hospital who can perform an emergency operation.'

Jean-Pierre came in bang on cue:

'Doctor Wiley Barker is staying at my hotel.'

'Wiley Barker, the American surgeon?'

'Yes, yes,' said Jean-Pierre. 'The chap who's been taking care of Nixon.'

'My God, what a piece of luck. We couldn't have

anyone better, but he might turn out to be very expensive.'

'I don't give a damn about expense,' wailed Harvey.

'Well, it might be as high as $50,000.'

'I don't care if it's $100,000,' screamed Harvey. At that moment he would have been willing to part with his entire fortune.

'Right,' said Stephen. 'You, sir,' looking at Jean-Pierre, 'ring for an ambulance and then contact Doctor Barker and ask if he can get to the hospital immediately. Tell him it's an emergency. This gentleman requires a surgeon of the highest qualifications.'

'You're damn right I do,' said Harvey, and passed out.

Jean-Pierre left the Casino and called over his transmitter:

'Action stations. Action stations.'

Robin left the Hôtel de Paris and took a taxi. He would have given $100,000 to change places with the driver, but the car was already moving relentlessly towards the hospital. It was too late to turn back now.

James smashed the ambulance into first gear and rushed to the Casino, siren blaring. He was luckier than Robin. With so much to concentrate on he didn't have time to consider the consequences of what he was doing.

Eleven minutes and forty-one seconds later he arrived, leapt out of the driver's seat, opened the back door, gathered the stretcher and rushed up the Casino steps in his long white coat. Jean-Pierre was standing expectantly on the top step waiting for him. No words passed between them as he guided James quickly through the Salon des Amériques where Stephen was bending over Harvey. The stretcher was placed on the floor. It took all three of them to lift Harvey Metcalfe's 227 lb on to the canvas. Stephen and James picked up the stretcher and took him quickly through to the waiting ambulance, followed by Jean-Pierre.

'Where are you going with my boss?' demanded a voice.

Startled, the three of them turned round. It was Harvey Metcalfe's chauffeur, standing by the white Rolls Royce. After a moment's hesitation, Jean-Pierre took over.

'Mr Metcalfe has collapsed and has to go to hospital for an emergency operation. You must return to the yacht immediately, tell the staff to have his cabin ready and await further instructions.'

The chauffeur touched his cap and ran to the Rolls Royce. James leapt behind the wheel, while Stephen and Jean-Pierre joined Harvey in the back of the vehicle.

'Hell, that was close. Well done, Jean-Pierre. I was speechless,' admitted Stephen.

'It was nothing,' said Jean-Pierre, sweat pouring down his face.

The ambulance shot off like a scalded cat. Stephen and Jean-Pierre both replaced their jackets with the long white laboratory coats left on the seat and Stephen put the stethoscope round his neck.

'It looks to me as if he's dead,' said Jean-Pierre.

'Robin says he isn't,' said Stephen.

'How can he tell from four miles away?'

'I don't know. We'll just have to take his word for it.'

James screeched to a halt outside the entrance to the hospital. Stephen and Jean-Pierre hurried their patient through to the operating theatre. James returned the ambulance to the car park and quickly joined the others in the theatre.

Robin, scrubbed up and gowned, was there to meet them at the door and while they were strapping Harvey Metcalfe to the operating table in the small room next to the theatre, he spoke for the first time:

'All of you, change your clothes. And Jean-Pierre, you scrub up as instructed.'

All three of them changed and Jean-Pierre started to wash immediately – a long, laborious process which Robin had firmly taught him must never be cut short. Post-operative septicaemia formed no part of his plan. Jean-Pierre appeared from the scrubbing-up room ready for action.

'Now, relax. We've done this nine times already. Just carry on exactly as if we were still in St Thomas's.'

Stephen moved behind the mobile Boyles machine. For four weeks he had been training as an anaesthetist: he had rendered James and a faintly protesting Jean-Pierre unconscious twice each in practice runs at St Thomas's. Now was his chance to exercise his new powers over Harvey Metcalfe.

Robin removed a syringe from a plastic packet and injected 250 mg of thiopentone into Harvey's arm. The patient sank back into a deep sleep. Quickly and efficiently Jean-Pierre and James undressed Harvey and then covered him in a sheet. Stephen placed the mask from the Boyles machine over Metcalfe's nose. The two flow-meters on the back of the machine showed 5 litres of nitrous oxide and 3 litres of oxygen.

'Take his pulse,' said Robin.

Stephen placed a finger in front of the ear just above the lobe to check the pre-auricular pulse. It was 70.

'Wheel him through into the theatre,' instructed Robin.

James pushed the trolley into the next room until it was just under the operating lights. Stephen trundled the Boyles machine along behind them.

The operating theatre was windowless and coldly sterile. Gleaming white tiles covered every wall from floor to ceiling, and it contained only the equipment needed for one operation. Jean-Pierre had covered Harvey with a sterile green sheet, leaving only his head and left arm exposed. One trolley of sterile instruments, drapes and towels had been carefully laid out by the theatre nurse, and stood covered with a sterile sheet. Robin hung the bottle of intravenous fluid from a standard near the head of the table and taped the end of the tubing to Harvey's left arm to complete the preparation. Stephen sat at the head of the table with the Boyles machine and adjusted the face-mask over Harvey's mouth and nose. Only one of the three massive operating lights hanging directly over Harvey had been turned on, causing a spotlight effect on the protruding bulge of his abdomen.

Eight eyes stared down on their victim. Robin continued:

'I shall give exactly the same instructions as I did in all our rehearsals, so just concentrate. First, I shall clean the abdomen with a skin preparation of iodine.'

Robin had all the instruments ready on the side of the table next to Harvey's feet. James lifted the sheet and folded it back over Harvey's legs, then he carefully removed the sterile sheet covering the trolley of instruments and poured iodine into one of the small basins. Robin picked up a swab in a pair of forceps and dipped it in the iodine solution. With a swift action up, down, and over the abdomen, he cleaned about 1 square foot of Harvey's massive body, throwing the swab into a bin and repeating the action with a fresh one. Next he placed a sterile towel below Harvey's chin, covering his chest, and another over his hips and thighs. A third one he placed lengthways along the left-hand side of his body and a final one along the right-hand side, leaving a 9 inch square of flabby belly exposed. He put a towel clip on each corner to secure them safely and then placed the laparotomy drapes over the prepared site. Robin was now ready.

'Scalpel.'

Jean-Pierre placed what he would have called a knife firmly in Robin's outstretched palm, as a runner might when passing a baton. James's apprehensive eyes met Jean-Pierre's across the operating table, while Stephen concentrated on Harvey's breathing. Robin hesitated only for a second and then made a 10 cm paramedian incision, reaching about 3 cm into the fat. Robin had rarely seen a larger stomach: he could probably have gone as far as 8 cm deep without reaching the muscle. Blood started flowing everywhere, which Robin stopped with diathermy. No sooner had he finished the incision and stanched the flow of blood than he began to stitch up the patient's wound with a 3/0 interrupted plain catgut for ten stitches.

'That will dissolve within a week,' he explained.

He then closed the skin with a 2/0 interrupted plain silk, using an atraumatic needle. Then he cleaned the wound, removing the patches of blood that still remained. Finally, he placed a medium self-adhesive wound dressing over his handiwork.

James took off the drapes and sterile towels and placed them in the bin while Robin and Jean-Pierre put Metcalfe into a hospital gown and carefully packed his clothes in a grey plastic bag.

'He's coming round,' said Stephen.

Robin took another syringe and injected 10 mg of diazepam.

'That will keep him asleep for at least 30 minutes,' he said, 'and in any case, he'll be ga-ga for about three hours and won't remember much of what has happened. James, fetch the ambulance immediately and bring it round to the front of the hospital.'

James left the theatre and changed back into his clothes, a procedure which he could now perform in 90 seconds. He disappeared to the car park.

'Now, you two, get changed and then place Harvey very carefully in the ambulance and Jean-Pierre, wait in the back with him. Stephen, you carry out your next assignment.'

Stephen and Jean-Pierre changed quickly, back into their long white coats and wheeled the slumbering Harvey Metcalfe gently towards the ambulance. Once safely in, Stephen ran to the public telephone by the hospital entrance, checked a piece of paper in his wallet and dialled.

'Hello, *Nice-Matin*? My name's Terry Robards of the *New York Times*. I'm here on holiday, and I have a great little story for you . . .'

Robin returned to the operating theatre and wheeled the trolley of instruments he had used to the sterilising room, and left them there to be dealt with by the hospital theatre staff in the morning. He picked up the plastic bag containing Harvey's clothes and, going through to the changing room, quickly removed his operating gown, cap and mask and put on his own clothes. He went in search of the theatre sister, and smiled charmingly at her.

'All finished, *ma soeur.* I have left the instruments by the steriliser. Please thank Monsieur Bartise for me once again.'

'*Oui, Monsieur. Notre plaisir. Je suis heureuse d'être à même de vous aider. Votre infirmière de l'Auxiliaire Médicale est arrivée.*'

A few moments later, Robin walked to the ambulance, accompanied by the agency nurse. He helped her into the back.

'Drive very slowly and carefully to the harbour.'

James nodded and set off at funeral pace.

'Nurse Faubert.'

'Yes, Docteur Barker.' Her hands were tucked primly under her blue cape, and her French accent was enchanting. Robin thought Harvey would not find her ministrations unwelcome.

'My patient has just had an operation for the removal of a gall stone and will need plenty of rest.'

With that Robin took out of his pocket a gall stone the size of an orange with a hospital tag on it which read 'Harvey Metcalfe'. Robin had in fact acquired the huge stone from St Thomas's Hospital, the original owner being a 6 ft 6 in West Indian bus conductor on the No. 14 route. Stephen and Jean-Pierre stared at it in disbelief. The nurse checked her new charge's pulse and respiration.

'If I were your patient, Nurse Faubert,' said Jean-Pierre, 'I should take good care never to recover.'

By the time they arrived at the yacht, Robin had briefed the nurse on diet and rest, and told her that he would be round to see his patient at 11 am the next day. They left Harvey sleeping soundly in his large cabin, stewards and staff clucking attentively.

James drove the other three back to the hospital, deposited the ambulance in the car park and left the keys with reception. The four of them then headed back to the hotel by separate routes. Robin was the last to arrive at room 217, just after 3.30 am. He collapsed into an armchair.

'Will you allow me a whisky, Stephen?'

'Yes, of course.'

'Good God, he meant it,' said Robin, and downed a large Johnny Walker before handing the bottle over to Jean-Pierre.

'He will be all right, won't he?' said James.

'You sound quite concerned for him. Yes, he can have his ten stitches out in a week's time and all he'll have is a nasty scar to brag about to his friends. I must get some sleep. I have to see our victim at 11 tomorrow morning and the confrontation may well be harder than the operation. You were all great tonight. My God, am I glad we had all those sessions at St Thomas's. If you're ever out of work and I need a croupier, a driver and an anaesthetist, I'll know who to ring.'

The others left and Robin collapsed on to his bed, exhausted. He fell into a deep sleep and woke just after 8 the next morning, to discover he was still fully dressed. That had not happened to him since his days as a young houseman, when he had been on night duty after a fourteen-hour day without a break. Robin had a long soothing bath in very hot water. He dressed and put on a clean shirt and suit, ready for his face-to-face meeting with Harvey Metcalfe. His newly acquired moustache and rimless glasses and the success of the operation made him feel a little like the famous surgeon he was impersonating. The other three all appeared during the next hour to wish him luck and elected to wait in room 217 for his return. Stephen had checked them all out of the hotel and booked a flight to London for late that afternoon. Robin left, again taking the staircase rather than the lift. Once outside the hotel, he walked a little way before hailing a taxi to drive him to the harbour.

It was not hard to find the *Messenger Boy*. She was a gleaming, newly painted 100-footer lying at the east end of the harbour. She sported a massive Panamanian flag on her stern mast, which Robin assumed must be for tax purposes. He ascended the gangplank and was met by Nurse Faubert.

'*Bonjour, Docteur Barker.*'

'Good morning, Nurse. How is Mr Metcalfe?'

'He has had a very peaceful night and is having a light breakfast and making a few telephone calls. Would you like to see him now?'

'Yes, please.'

Robin entered the magnificent cabin and faced the

man he had spent eight weeks plotting and planning against. He was talking into the telephone:

'Yes, I'm fine, dear. But it was an A-1 emergency at the time. Don't worry, I'll live,' and he put the telephone down. 'Doctor Barker, I have just spoken to my wife in Massachusetts and told her that I owe you my life. Even at 5 am she seemed pleased. I understand that I had private surgery, a private ambulance and that you saved my life. Or that's what it says in *Nice-Matin*.'

There was the old picture of Harvey in Bermuda shorts on the deck of the *Messenger Boy*, familiar to Robin from his dossier. The headline read '*Millionaire s'évanouit au Casino*' over '*La Vie d'un Millionnaire Américain a été sauvée par une Opération Urgente Dramatique*!' Stephen would be pleased.

'Tell me, Doctor,' said Harvey with relish, 'was I really in danger?'

'Well, you were on the critical list, and the consequences might have been fairly serious if we hadn't removed this from your stomach.' Robin took out the inscribed gall stone from his pocket with a flourish.

Harvey's eye grew large as saucers.

'Gee, have I really been walking round with that inside me all this time? Isn't that something? I can't thank you enough. If ever I can do anything for you, Doctor, don't hesitate to call on me.' He offered Robin a grape. 'Look, you're going to see me through this thing, aren't you? I don't think the nurse fully appreciates the gravity of my case.'

Robin thought fast.

'I'm afraid I'm not free to do that, Mr Metcalfe. My holiday finishes today and I have to return to California. Nothing urgent: just a few elective surgeries and a rather heavy lecture schedule.' He shrugged deprecatingly. 'Not exactly earth-shattering but it helps me keep up a way of life I have grown accustomed to.'

Harvey sat bolt upright, tenderly holding his stomach.

'Now you listen to me, Doctor Barker. I don't give a damn about a few students. I'm a sick man and I need you here until I've fully recovered. I'll make it worth your while to stay, don't you worry. I never grudge the money where my health is concerned, and what's more if it will persuade you, I'll make the cheque out to cash. The last thing I want Uncle Sam to know is how much I'm worth.'

Robin coughed delicately, wondering how American doctors approached the ticklish subject of fees with their patients.

'The cost could be rather high if I'm not to be out of pocket by staying. It might be as much as $80,000.' Robin drew a deep breath.

Harvey didn't blink.

'Sure. You're the best. That's not a lot of money to stay alive.'

'Very well. I'll get back to my hotel and see if it's possible to rearrange my schedule for you.'

Robin retreated from the sick-room and the white

Rolls Royce took him back to the hotel. In room 217 they all sat staring at Robin in disbelief as he completed his story.

'Stephen, for Christ's sake, the man's a raving hypochondriac. He wants me to stay on here while he convalesces. None of us planned for that.'

Stephen looked up coolly:

'You'll stay here and play ball. Why not give him value for money – at his own expense, of course. Go on, get on the blower and tell him you'll be round to hold his hand every day at 11 am. We'll just have to go back without you. And keep the hotel bill down, won't you?'

Robin picked up the telephone . . .

Three young men left the Hôtel de Paris after a long lunch in room 217, allowing themselves another bottle of Krug '64, and then returned to Nice Airport in a taxi, catching BA flight 012 at 16.10 to London Heathrow. They were once again in separate seats. One sentence remained on Stephen's mind from Robin's reported conversation with Harvey Metcalfe.

'If ever I can do anything for you, don't hesitate to call me at any time.'

Robin visited his patient once a day, borne in the white Corniche with white-walled tyres and a chauffeur in a white uniform. Only Harvey could be quite so brash, he thought. On the third, Nurse Faubert asked for a private word with him.

'My patient,' she said plaintively, 'is making improper advances when I change his dressing.'

Robin allowed Dr Wiley Barker the liberty of an unprofessional remark.

'Can't say I altogether blame him. Still, be firm, Nurse. I'm sure you must have encountered that sort of thing before.'

'*Naturellement*, but never from a patient only three days after major surgery. His constitution, it must be *formidable*.'

'I tell you what, let's catheterise him for a couple of days. That'll cramp his style.' She smiled. 'It must be pretty boring for you cooped up here all day,' Robin continued. 'Why don't you come and have a spot of supper with me after Mr Metcalfe has gone to sleep tonight?'

'I should love to, *Docteur*. Where shall I meet you?'

'Room 217, Hôtel de Paris,' said Robin unblushingly. 'Say 9 pm.'

'I'll look forward to it, *Docteur*.'

'A little more Chablis, Angeline?'

'No more, thank you, Wiley. That was a meal to remember. I think, maybe, you have not yet had everything you want?'

She got up, lit two cigarettes and put one in his

mouth. Then she moved away, her long skirt swinging slightly from the hips. She wore no bra under her pink shirt. She exhaled smokily and watched him.

Robin thought of the blameless Doctor Barker in Australia, of his wife and children in Newbury, and the rest of the Team in London. Then he put them all out of his mind.

'Will you complain to Mr Metcalfe if I make improper advances to you?'

'From you, Wiley,' she smiled, 'they will not be improper.'

Harvey made a talkative recovery, and Robin removed the stitches gravely on the sixth day.

'That seems to have healed very cleanly, Mr Metcalfe. Take it easy, and you should be back to normal by the middle of next week.'

'Great. I have to get over to England right away for Ascot week. You know, my horse Rosalie is favourite this year. I suppose you can't join me as my guest? What if I have a relapse.'

Robin suppressed a smile.

'Don't worry. You're getting along fine. Sorry I can't stay to see how Rosalie performs at Ascot.'

'So am I, Doc. Thanks again, anyway. I've never met a surgeon like you before.'

And you're not likely to again, thought Robin, his American accent beginning to fray at the edges. He bid his adieus to Harvey with relief and to Angeline with regret, and sent the chauffeur back from the hotel with a copper-plate bill:

Dr Wiley Franklin Barker
presents his Compliments to
Mr Harvey Metcalfe
and begs to inform him that the Bill for
Professional Services rendered is
$80,000
in respect of surgery and post-operative treatment.

The chauffeur was back within the hour with a cash cheque for $80,000. Robin bore it back to London in triumph.

Two down and two to go.

13

THE FOLLOWING DAY, Friday, Stephen sat on Robin's examination couch in Harley Street and addressed the troops.

'The Monte Carlo operation was a total success in every way, thanks to Robin keeping his cool. The expenses were fairly high, though. The hospital and hotel bills totalled $11,351, while we received $80,000. Therefore, we've had $527,560 returned to us, and expenses so far have come to $22,530, which leaves Mr Metcalfe still in debt to the tune of $494,970. Does everyone agree with that?'

There was a general murmur of approval. Their confidence in Stephen's arithmetic was unbounded, although in fact, like all algebraists, he found working with figures somewhat tedious.

'Incidentally, Robin, however did you manage to spend $73.50 on dinner last Wednesday night? What did you have, caviar and champagne?'

'Something a little out of the ordinary,' admitted Robin. 'It seemed to be called for at the time.'

'I'd bet more than I laid out in Monte Carlo that I know who joined you for dinner, and I bet she shared more than a table with you too,' said Jean-Pierre, taking his wallet out of his pocket. 'Here you are Stephen, 219 francs – my winnings from the Casino on Wednesday night. If you'd left me alone in peace, we needn't have bothered with Robin's butchery. I could have won the whole amount back on my own. I think the least I deserve is Nurse Faubert's telephone number.'

Jean-Pierre's remarks went straight over Stephen's head.

'Well done, Jean-Pierre, it'll all come off expenses. At today's exchange rate, your 219 francs,' he paused for a moment and tapped out on his calculator, 'is worth $46.76. That brings the expenses down to $22,483.24.

'Now, my plans for Ascot are simple. James has acquired two badges for the Members' Enclosure at a cost of $10. We know that Harvey Metcalfe also has a badge, as all owners do, so as long as we get our timing right and make it look natural, he should once again fall into our trap. James will keep us briefed on the walkie-talkie and will follow the movements of Metcalfe from his arrival to his leaving. Jean-Pierre will wait by the entrance of the Members' Enclosure and follow him in. Robin will send the telegram from Heathrow Airport at 1 pm, so Harvey ought to receive it during lunch in his private box. That part of the plan is easy. It's if we manage to lure him to Oxford that we all have to be on our toes. I must confess, it'd make a pleasant change if Ascot were to work first time.'

Stephen grinned widely.

'That would give us much needed extra time to go over the Oxford plan again. Any questions?'

'You don't need us for part (*a*) of the Oxford plan, only (*b*)?' asked Robin, checking Stephen's notes.

'That's right. I can manage part (*a*) on my own. In fact, it will be better if you all remain in London on that night, well out of the way. Our next priority must be to think up some ideas for James or he might, heaven preserve us, even think up something for himself. I'm becoming very concerned about this,' continued Stephen, 'because once Harvey returns to America we'll have to deal with him on his own ground. To date he's always been at the venue of our choosing. James would stick out like a sore thumb in Boston, even though he's the best actor of the four of us. In Harvey's words, "It would be a whole different ball game".'

James sighed lugubriously and studied the Axminster carpet.

'Poor old James – don't worry, you drove that ambulance like a trooper,' said Robin.

'Perhaps you could learn to fly a plane and then we could hijack him,' suggested Jean-Pierre.

Miss Meikle did not approve of the laughter coming from Doctor Oakley's room and she was glad to see the oddly assorted trio leave. When she had closed the door finally on James she returned to Robin's room.

'Will you see your patients now, Doctor Oakley?'

'Yes, if I must, Miss Meikle.'

Miss Meikle pursed her lips. Whatever had come over him? It must be those dreadful types he had started mixing with lately. He had become so unreliable.

'Mrs Wentworth-Brewster – Doctor Oakley will see you now, and I'll have the pills for your trip to Italy ready for you when you come out.'

Stephen returned for a few days' recuperation to Magdalen College. He had started the entire exercise eight weeks before and two of the Team had succeeded far beyond his expectations. He was conscious that he must crown their efforts with something that would live on in the legends of Oxford long after his departure.

Jean-Pierre returned to work in his gallery in Bond Street. Since he only had to deliver one sentence at Ascot he was not going to be overtaxed, although part (*b*) of Stephen's Oxford plan kept him nightly in front of a mirror rehearsing his role.

James took Anne down to Stratford-upon-Avon for the weekend. The Royal Shakespeare Company obliged with a sparkling performance of *Much Ado about Nothing* and afterwards, walking along the banks of the Avon, James proposed. Only the royal swans could have heard her reply. The diamond ring James had noticed in the window of Cartier while he had been waiting for Harvey Metcalfe to join Jean-Pierre in the gallery, looked even more beautiful on her slender finger. James's happiness seemed complete. If only he could come up with a plan and shock them all, he would want for nothing. He discussed it with Anne again that night, considering new ideas and old ones, still getting nowhere.

But an idea was beginning to formulate in her mind.

14

On Monday morning James drove Anne back to London and changed into the most debonair of his suits. Anne had to return to work, despite James's suggestion that she should accompany him to Ascot. She felt the others would not approve of her presence and would suspect that James had confided in her.

Although James had not told her the details of the Monte Carlo exercise, Anne knew every step of the planned proceedings at Ascot and she could tell that James was nervous. Still, she would be seeing him that night and would know the worst by then. James looked lost. Anne was only thankful that Stephen, Robin and Jean-Pierre held the baton most of the time in this relay team – but the idea that was taking shape in her mind just might surprise them all.

Stephen rose early and admired his grey hair in the mirror. The result had been expensively achieved the previous day in the hairdressing salon of Debenhams. He dressed carefully, putting on his one respectable grey suit and blue checked tie. These were brought out for all special occasions, ranging from a talk to students at Sussex University to a dinner with the American Ambassador. No one had told him the colours clashed and the suit sagged unfashionably at the elbow and knees, because by Stephen's standards it was elegance itself. He travelled from Oxford to Ascot by train, while Jean-Pierre came from London by car. They met up with James at the Belvedere Arms at 11 am, almost a mile from the course.

Stephen immediately telephoned Robin to confirm that all three of them had arrived and asked for the telegram to be read over to him.

'That's perfect, Robin. Now travel to Heathrow and send it at exactly 1 pm.'

'Good luck, Stephen. Grind the bastard into the dust.'

Stephen returned to the others and confirmed that Robin had the London end under control.

'Off you go, James, and let us know the minute Harvey arrives.'

James downed a bottle of Carlsberg and departed. The problem was that he kept bumping into friends and he could hardly explain why he was prevented from joining them.

Harvey arrived at the members' car park just after midday, his white Rolls Royce shining like a Persil advertisement. The car was being stared at by all the racegoers with an English disdain which Harvey mistook for admiration. He led his party to the private box. His newly tailored suit had taxed the ingenuity of Bernard Weatherill to the utmost. A red carnation in his buttonhole and a hat to cover his bald head left him nearly unrecognisable, and James might have missed him had it not been for the white Rolls Royce. James followed the little group at a careful distance until he saw Harvey enter a door marked 'Mr Harvey Metcalfe and Guests'.

'He's in his private box,' said James.

'Where are you?' asked Jean-Pierre.

'Directly below him on the ground level by a course bookmaker called Sam O'Flaherty.'

'No need to be rude about the Irish, James,' said Jean-Pierre. 'We'll be with you in a few minutes.'

James stared up at the vast white stand, which accommodated 10,000 spectators in comfort and gave an excellent view of the racecourse. He was finding it hard to concentrate on the job in hand as once again he had to avoid relations and friends. First was the Earl of Halifax, and then that frightful girl he had so unwisely agreed to take to Queen Charlotte's Ball last spring. What was the creature's name? Ah yes. The Hon. Selina Wallop. How appropriate. She was wearing a mini-skirt that was a good four years out of fashion and a hat which looked as if it could never come into fashion. James jammed his trilby over his ears, looked the other way and passed the time by chatting to Sam O'Flaherty about the 3.20, the King George VI and Queen Elizabeth Stakes. O'Flaherty quoted the latest odds on the favourite at the top of his voice:

'Rosalie at 6:4, owned by that American, Harvey Metcalfe, and ridden by Pat Eddery.'

Eddery was on the way to becoming the youngest-ever champion jockey – and Harvey always backed winners.

Stephen and Jean-Pierre joined James at the side of Sam O'Flaherty's bag. His tick-tack man was standing on an upturned orange box beside him and swinging his arms like a semaphore sailor aboard a sinking ship.

'What's your fancy, gentlemen?' Sam asked the three of them.

James ignored Stephen's slight frown of disapproval.

'£5 each way on Rosalie,' he said, and handed over a crisp £10 note, receiving in return a little green card with the series number and 'Sam O'Flaherty' stamped right across the middle.

'I must presume, James, this is an integral part of your as yet undisclosed plan,' said Jean-Pierre. 'What I should like to know is, if it works, how much do we stand to make?'

'£9.10 after tax if Rosalie wins,' chipped in Sam O'Flaherty, his stub cigar bobbing up and down in his mouth as he spoke.

'Hardly a great contribution towards $1 million, James. Well, we're off to the Members' Enclosure. Let us know the moment Harvey leaves his box. My guess is that around 1.45 he'll come and look at the runners and riders for the two o'clock, so that gives us a clear hour.'

The waiter opened another bottle of Krug 1964 and began pouring it for Harvey's guests; three bankers, two economists, a couple of ship-owners and a distinguished City journalist.

Preferring his guests to be famous and influential, Harvey always invited people who would find it almost impossible to refuse because of the business he might put their way. He was delighted with the company he had assembled for his big day. Senior among them was Sir Howard Dodd, the ageing chairman of the merchant bank that bore his name, but which actually referred to his great-grandfather. Sir Howard was 6 ft 2 in, as straight as a ramrod, and looked more like a Grenadier Guard than a respectable banker. The only thing he had in common with Harvey was the hair, or lack of hair, on his balding head. His young assistant, Jamie Clark, accompanied him. Just over thirty and extremely bright, he was there to be sure his chairman did not commit the bank to anything he might later regret. Although he had a sneaking admiration for Harvey, Clark did not think him the sort of customer the bank should do business with. Nevertheless, he was far from averse to a day at the races.

The two economists, Mr Colin Emson and Dr Michael Hogan from the Hudson Institute, were there to brief Harvey on the parlous state of the British economy. They could not have been more different. Emson was a totally self-made man who had left school at fifteen and educated himself. Using his social contacts, he had built up a company specialising in taxation, which had been remarkably successful thanks to the British Government's habit of putting through a new Finance Act every few weeks. Emson was 6 ft tall, solid and genial, game to help the party along whether Harvey lost or won. Hogan, in contrast, had been to all the right places – Winchester, Trinity College, Oxford, and the Wharton Business School in Pennsylvania. A spell with McKinsey, the management consultants, in London had made him one of the best-informed economists in Europe. Those who observed his slim, sinewy body would not have been surprised to learn that he had been an international squash player. Dark-haired, with brown eyes that rarely left Harvey, he found it hard not to show his contempt; this was his fifth invitation to Ascot – Harvey, it seemed, was never going to take no for an answer.

The Kundas brothers, second-generation Greeks who loved racing almost as much as ships, could hardly be told apart, with their black hair, swarthy skins and heavy dark eyebrows. It was difficult to guess how old they were, and nobody knew how much they were worth. They probably did not know themselves. Harvey's final guest, Nick Lloyd of the *News of the World*, had come along to pick up any dirt he could about his host. He had come near to exposing Metcalfe in the mid-sixties, but another scandal had kept less juicy stories off the front page for several weeks, and by then Harvey had escaped. Lloyd, hunched over the inevitable triple gin with a faint suggestion of tonic, watched the motley bunch with interest.

'Telegram for you, sir.'

Harvey ripped it open. He was never neat about anything.

'It's from my daughter Rosalie. It's cute of her to remember, but damn it all, I named the horse after her. Come on everybody, let's eat.'

They all took their seats for lunch – cold vichyssoise, pheasant and strawberries. Harvey was even more loquacious than usual, but his guests took no notice, aware he was nervous before the race and knowing that he would rather be a winner of this trophy than any he could be offered in America. Harvey himself could never understand why he felt that way. Perhaps it was the special atmosphere of Ascot which appealed to him so strongly – the combination of lush green grass and gracious surroundings, of elegant crowds and an efficiency of organisation which made Ascot the envy of the racing world.

'You must have a better chance this year than ever before, Harvey,' said the senior banker.

'Well, you know, Sir Howard, Lester Piggott is riding the Duke of Devonshire's horse, Crown Princess, and the Queen's Horse, Highclere, is the joint favourite, so I can't afford to over-estimate my chances. When you've been third twice before, and then favourite and not placed, you begin to wonder if one of your horses is going to make it.'

'Another telegram, sir.'

Once again Harvey's fat little finger ripped it open.

'"All the best wishes and good luck for the King George VI and Queen Elizabeth Stakes". It's from the staff of your bank, Sir Howard. Jolly good show.'

Harvey's Polish-American accent made the English expression slightly ridiculous.

'More champagne, everybody.'

Another telegram arrived.

'At this rate, Harvey, you'll need a special room at the Post Office.' There was laughter all round at Sir Howard's feeble joke. Once again Harvey read it out aloud:

'"Regret unable to join you Ascot. Heading soonest California. Grateful look out for old friend Professor Rodney Porter, Oxford Nobel Prize Winner. Don't let English bookies stitch you up. Wiley B., Heathrow Airport". It's from Wiley Barker. He's the guy who did stitch me up in Monte Carlo. He saved my life. He took out a gall stone the size of that bread roll you're eating, Dr Hogan. Now how the hell am I supposed to find this Professor Porter?' Harvey turned to the head waiter. 'Find my chauffeur.'

A few seconds later the smartly-clad Guy Salmon flunkey appeared.

'There's a Professor Rodney Porter of Oxford here today. Go find him.'

'What does he look like, sir?'

'How the hell do I know,' said Harvey. 'Like a professor.'

The chauffeur regretfully abandoned his plans for an afternoon at the railings and departed, leaving Harvey and his guests to enjoy the strawberries, the champagne and the string of telegrams that were still arriving.

'You know if you win, the cup will be presented by the Queen,' said Nick Lloyd.

'You bet. It'll be the crowning moment of my life to win the King George and Elizabeth Stakes and meet Her Majesty The Queen. If Rosalie wins, I'll suggest my daughter marries Prince Charles – they're about the same age.'

'I don't think even you will be able to fix that, Harvey.'

'What'll you do with the odd £81,000 prize money, Mr Metcalfe?' asked Jamie Clark.

'Give it to some charity,' said Harvey, pleased with the impression the remark made on his guests.

'Very generous, Harvey. Typical of your reputation.' Nick Lloyd gave Michael Hogan a knowing look. Even if the others didn't, they both knew what was typical of his reputation.

The chauffeur returned to report that there was no trace of a solitary professor anywhere in the champagne bar, balcony luncheon room or the paddock buffet, and that he'd been unable to gain access to the Members' Enclosure.

'Naturally not,' said Harvey rather pompously. 'I shall have to find him myself. Drink up and enjoy yourselves.'

Harvey rose and walked to the door with the chauffeur. Once he was out of earshot of his guests, he said, 'Get your ass out of here and don't give me any crap about not being able to find him or you can find something for yourself – another job.'

The chauffeur bolted. Harvey turned to his guests and smiled.

'I'm going to look at the runners and riders for the 2 o'clock.'

'He's leaving the box now,' said James.

'What's that you're saying?' asked an authoritative voice he recognised. 'Talking to yourself, James?'

James stared at the noble Lord Somerset, 6 ft 1 in and still able to stand his full height, an MC and a DSO in the First World War. He still exuded enthusiastic energy although the lines on his face suggested that he had passed the age at which the Maker had fulfilled his contract.

'Oh hell. No, sir, I was just . . . em . . . coughing.'

'What do you fancy in the King George VI and Queen Elizabeth Stakes?' asked the peer of the realm.

'Well, I have put £5 each way on Rosalie, sir.'

*

'He seems to have cut himself off,' said Stephen.

'Well, buzz him again,' said Jean-Pierre.

'What's that noise, James? Have you taken to a hearing-aid or something?'

'No, sir. It's . . . it's . . . it's a transistor radio.'

'Those things ought to be banned. Bloody invasion of privacy.'

'Absolutely right, sir.'

'What's he playing at, Stephen?'

'I don't know – I think something must have happened.'

'Oh my God, it's Harvey heading straight for us. You go into the Members' Enclosure, Stephen, and I'll follow you. Take a deep breath and relax. He hasn't seen us.'

Harvey marched up to the official blocking the entrance to the Members' Enclosure.

'I'm Harvey Metcalfe, the owner of Rosalie, and this is my badge.'

The official let Harvey through. Thirty years ago, he thought, they would not have let him into the Members' Enclosure if he'd owned every horse in the race. Then racing at Ascot was only held on four days a year, jolly social occasions. Now it was twenty-four days a year and big business. Times had changed.

Jean-Pierre followed closely, showing his pass without speaking to the official.

A photographer broke away from stalking the outrageous hats for which Ascot has such a reputation, and took a picture of Harvey just in case Rosalie won the King George VI Stakes. As soon as his bulb flashed he rushed over to the other entrance, where Linda Lovelace, the star of *Deep Throat*, the film running to packed houses in New York but banned in England, was trying to enter the Members' Enclosure. In spite of being introduced to a well-known London banker, Richard Szpiro, just as he was entering the Enclosure, she was not succeeding. She was wearing a top hat and morning suit with nothing under the top coat, and no one was going to bother with Harvey while she was around. When Miss Lovelace was quite certain that every photographer had taken a picture of her attempting to enter the Enclosure she left, swearing at the top of her voice, her publicity stunt completed.

Harvey returned to studying the horses as Stephen moved up to within a few feet of him.

'Here we go again,' said Jean-Pierre in French and went smartly over to Stephen and, standing directly between the two of them, shook Stephen's hand warmly, declaring in a voice that was intended to carry:

'How are you, Professor Porter? I didn't know you were interested in racing.'

'I'm not really, but I was on my way back from a seminar in London and thought it a good opportunity to see how . . .'

'Professor Porter,' cried Harvey. 'I'm honoured to make your acquaintance, sir, my name is Harvey Metcalfe from Boston, Massachusetts. My good friend, Dr Wiley Barker, who saved my life, told me you'd be here today on your own, and I'm going to make sure you have a wonderful afternoon.'

Jean-Pierre slipped away unnoticed. He could not believe how easy it had been. The telegram had worked like a charm.

'Her Majesty The Queen; His Royal Highness The Duke of Edinburgh; Her Majesty Queen Elizabeth The Queen Mother; and her Royal Highness The Princess Anne are now entering the Royal Box.'

The massed bands of the Brigade of Guards struck up the National Anthem:

'God Save the Queen.'

The crowd of 25,000 rose and sang loyally out of tune.

'We should have someone like that in America,' said Harvey to Stephen, 'to take the place of Richard Nixon. We wouldn't have any Watergate problems then.'

Stephen thought his fellow American was being just a little unfair. Richard Nixon was almost a saint by Harvey Metcalfe's standards.

'Come and join me in my box, Professor, and meet my other guests. The damned box cost me £750, we may as well fill it. Have you had some lunch?'

'Yes, I've had an excellent lunch, thank you,' Stephen lied – something else Harvey had taught him. He had stood by the Members' Enclosure for an hour, nervous and pensive, unable even to manage a sandwich, and now he was starving.

'Well, come and enjoy the champagne,' roared Harvey.

On an empty stomach, thought Stephen.

'Thank you, Mr Metcalfe. I am a little lost. This is my first Royal Ascot.'

'This isn't Royal Ascot, Professor. It's the last day of Ascot Week, but the Royal Family always comes to see the King George and Elizabeth Stakes, so everybody dresses up.'

'I see,' said Stephen timidly, pleased with his deliberate error.

Harvey collared his find and took him back to the box.

'Everybody, I want you to meet my distinguished friend, Rodney Porter. He's a Nobel Prize Winner, you know. By the way, what's your subject, Rod?'

'Biochemistry.'

Stephen was getting the measure of Harvey. As long as he played it straight, the bankers and shippers, and even the journalists, would never doubt that he was the cleverest thing since Einstein. He relaxed a little and even found time to fill himself with smoked salmon sandwiches when the others were not looking.

Lester Piggott won the 2 o'clock on Olympic Casino and the 2.30 on Roussalka, achieving his 3,000th win. Harvey was getting steadily more nervous. He talked incessantly without making much sense. He had sat through the 2.30 without showing any interest in the result and consumed more and more champagne. At 2.50 he called for them all to join him in the Members' Enclosure to look at his famous filly. Stephen, like the others, trailed behind him in a little pseudo-royal entourage.

Jean-Pierre and James watched the procession from a distance.

'He's too deep in to climb out now,' said Jean-Pierre.

'He looks relaxed enough to me,' replied James. 'Let's make ourselves scarce. We can only get under his feet.'

They headed into the champagne bar, which was filled with red-faced men who looked as if they spent more time drinking than they did watching the racing.

'Isn't she beautiful, Professor? Almost as beautiful as my daughter. If she doesn't win today I don't think I'm ever going to make it.'

Harvey left his little clique to have a word with the jockey, Pat Eddery, to wish him luck. Peter Walwyn, the trainer, was giving final instructions before the jockey mounted and left the Enclosure. The ten horses were then paraded in front of the stand before the race, a custom only carried out at Ascot for the King George VI and Queen Elizabeth Stakes. The gold, purple and scarlet colours of Her Majesty The Queen's horse Highclere led the procession, followed by Crown Princess, who was giving Lester Piggott a little trouble. Directly behind her came Rosalie, looking very relaxed, fresh and ready to go. Buoy and Dankaro trotted behind Rosalie, with the outsiders Mesopotamia, Ropey and Minnow bringing up the rear. The crowd rose to cheer the horses and Harvey beamed with pride, as if he owned every horse in the race.

'. . . and I have with me today the distinguished American owner, Harvey Metcalfe,' said Julian Wilson into the BBC TV outside-broadcast camera. 'I'm going to ask him if he'd be kind enough to give me his views on the King George VI and Queen Elizabeth Stakes, for which he has the joint favourite, Rosalie. Welcome to England, Mr Metcalfe. How do you feel about the big race?'

'It's a thrill to be here, just to participate in the race once again. Rosalie's got a great chance. Still, it's not winning that matters. It's taking part.'

Stephen flinched. Baron de Coubertin, who had first made that remark when opening the 1896 Olympics, must have turned in his grave.

'The latest betting shows Rosalie to be the joint favourite with Her Majesty The Queen's horse Highclere. How do you feel about that?'

'I'm just as worried about the Duke of Devonshire's Crown Princess. Lester Piggott is always hard to beat on a great occasion. He won the first two races and he'll be all set for this one – Crown Princess is a fine little filly.'

'Is a mile and a half a good distance for Rosalie?'

'Results this season show it's definitely her best distance.'

'What will you do with the £81,240 prize money?'

'The money is not important, it hasn't even entered my mind.'

It had certainly entered Stephen's mind.

'Thank you, Mr Metcalfe, and the best of luck. And now over for the latest news of the betting.'

Harvey moved back to his group of admirers and suggested that they return to watch the race from the balcony just outside his box.

Stephen was fascinated to observe Harvey at such close quarters. He had become nervous and even more mendacious than usual under pressure – not at all the icy, cool operator they had all feared him to be. This man was human, susceptible and could be beaten.

They all leant over the rails watching the horses being put into the stalls. Crown Princess was still giving a little trouble while all the others waited. The tension was becoming unbearable.

'They're off,' boomed the loudspeaker.

As twenty-five thousand people raised glasses to their eyes, Harvey said, 'She's got a good start – she's well placed,' continuing to give everybody a running commentary until the last mile, when he became silent. The others also waited in silence, intent on the loudspeaker.

'They're into the straight mile – Minnow leads the field around the bend – with Buoy and Dankaro, looking relaxed, just tucked in behind him – followed by Crown Princess, Rosalie and Highclere . . .

'As they approach the six-furlong marker – Rosalie and Crown Princess come up on the stand side with Highclere making a bid . . .

'Five furlongs to go – Minnow still sets the pace; but is beginning to tire as Crown Princess and Buoy make up ground . . .

'Half a mile to go – Minnow still just ahead of Buoy, who has moved up into second place, perhaps making her move too early . . .

'Three furlongs from home – they're quickening up just a little – Minnow sets the pace on the rails – Buoy and Dankaro are now about a length behind – followed by Rosalie, Lester Piggott on Crown Princess and the Queen's filly Highclere all making ground . . .

'Inside the two-furlong marker – Highclere and Rosalie move up to challenge Buoy – Crown Princess is right out of it now . . .

'A furlong to go . . .'

The commentator's voice rose in pitch and volume.

'It's Joe Mercer riding Highclere who hits the front, just ahead of Pat Eddery on Rosalie – two hundred yards to go – they're neck and neck – one hundred yards to go – it's anybody's race and on the line it's a photo finish between the gold, purple and scarlet colours of Her Majesty the Queen and the black-and-green check colours of the American owner, Harvey Metcalfe – M. Moussac's Dankaro was third.'

Harvey stood paralysed, waiting for the result. Even Stephen felt a little sympathy for him. None of Harvey's guests dared to speak for fear they might be wrong.

'The result of The King George VI and The Queen Elizabeth Stakes.' Once again the loudspeaker boomed out and silence fell over the whole course:

'The winner is No. 5, Rosalie.'

The rest of the result was lost in the roar of the crowd and the bellow of triumph from Harvey. Pursued by his guests, he raced to the nearest lift, pressed a pound note into the lift-girl's hand and shouted 'Get this thing moving.' Only half of his guests managed to jump in with him. Stephen was among them. Once they reached the ground floor, the lift gates opened and Harvey came out like a thoroughbred, past the champagne bar, through the rear of the Members' Enclosure into the Winners' Enclosure, and flung his arms round the horse's neck, almost unseating the jockey. A few minutes later he triumphantly led Rosalie to the little white post marked 'FIRST'. The crowd thronged around him, offering their congratulations.

The Clerk of the Course, Captain Beaumont, stood by Harvey's side, briefing him on the procedure that would be followed when he was presented. Lord Abergavenny, the Queen's Representative at Ascot, accompanied Her Majesty to the Winners' Enclosure.

'The winner of The King George VI and The Queen Elizabeth Stakes – Mr Harvey Metcalfe's Rosalie.'

Harvey was in a dream world. Flash-bulbs popped and film cameras followed him as he walked towards the Queen. He bowed and received his trophy. The Queen, resplendent in a turquoise silk suit and matching turban that could only have been designed by Norman Hartnell, said a few words, but for the first time in his life Harvey was speechless. Taking a pace backwards, he bowed again and returned to his place accompanied by loud applause.

Back in his box the champagne flowed and everybody was Harvey's friend. Stephen realised this was not the moment to try anything clever. He must bide his time and watch his quarry's reaction to these changed circumstances. He stayed quietly in a corner, letting the excitement subside, and observed Harvey carefully.

It took another race before Harvey was half back to normal and Stephen decided the time had now come to act. He made as if to leave.

'Are you going already, Professor?'

'Yes, Mr Metcalfe. I must return to Oxford and mark some scripts before tomorrow morning.'

'I always admire the work you boys put in. I hope

you enjoyed yourself?' Stephen avoided Shaw's famous riposte, 'I had to, there was nothing else to enjoy'.

'Yes, thank you, Mr Metcalfe. An amazing achievement. You must be a very proud man.'

'Well, I guess so. It's been a long time coming, but it all seems worthwhile now . . . Rod, it's too bad you have to leave us. Can't you stay on a little longer and join my party at Claridge's tonight?'

'I should have liked that, Mr Metcalfe, but you must visit me at my college at Oxford and allow me to show you the university.'

'That's swell. I have a couple of days after Ascot and I've always wanted to see Oxford, but I never seem to have found the time.'

'It's the university Garden Party next Wednesday. Why don't you join me for dinner at my college on Tuesday evening and then we can spend the following day looking at the university and go on to the Garden Party?' Stephen scribbled a few directions on a card.

'Fantastic. This is turning out to be the best vacation I've ever had in Europe. How are you getting back to Oxford, Professor?'

'By train.'

'No, no,' said Harvey. 'My Rolls Royce will take you. It'll be back well in time for the last race.'

And before Stephen could protest, the chauffeur was called for.

'Take Professor Porter back to Oxford and then return here. Have a good trip, Professor. I'll look forward to seeing you next Tuesday at 8 pm. Great meeting you.'

'Thank you for a wonderful day, Mr Metcalfe, and congratulations on your splendid victory.'

Seated in the back of the white Rolls Royce on his way to Oxford, the car which Robin had boasted he and he alone would travel in, Stephen relaxed and smiled to himself. Taking a small notebook from his pocket he made an entry:

'Deduct 98 pence from expenses, the price of a single second-class ticket from Ascot to Oxford.'

15

'Bradley,' said the Senior Tutor, 'you're going a bit grey at the edges, dear boy. Is the office of Junior Dean proving too much for you?'

Stephen had wondered whether any of the Senior Common Room would think the change in the colour of his hair worthy of comment. Dons are seldom surprised by anything their colleagues do.

'My father went grey at an early age, Senior Tutor, and there seems to be no way of defying heredity . . .'

'Ah well, dear boy, you'll look all the more distinguished at next week's Garden Party.'

'Oh yes,' replied Stephen, who had been thinking of nothing else. 'I'd quite forgotten about that.'

He returned to his rooms where the rest of the Team were assembled and waiting for their next briefing.

'Wednesday is the day of the Encaenia and the Garden Party,' began Stephen without as much as a 'Good morning, gentlemen'. His students made no protest. 'Now the one thing we've learnt about our millionaire friend is that when we take him away from his own environment he still continues to assume he knows everything. We've now shown that his bluff can be called, as long as we know what's going to happen next week and he doesn't. It's only the same skill he used when promoting Prospecta Oil – always keeping one step ahead of us. Now, we're going to keep two steps ahead of him by having a rehearsal today and a full dress-rehearsal tomorrow.'

'Time spent on reconnaissance is seldom wasted,' muttered James. It was about the only sentiment he could recall from his Army Cadet days at Harrow.

'Haven't had to spend much time on reconnaissance for your plan, have we?' chipped in Jean-Pierre.

Stephen ignored the interruptions.

'Now, the whole process on the day will take about seven hours for me and four hours for you, which includes the time required for make-up; we'll need an extra session on that from James the day before.'

'How often will you need my two sons?' asked Robin.

'Only once, on the Wednesday. Too many runs at it will make them look stiff and awkard.'

'When do you imagine Harvey will want to return to London?' enquired Jean-Pierre.

'I rang Guy Salmon to check their timetable and they've been instructed to have him back at Claridge's by 7 pm, so I've assumed we have only until 5.30.'

'Clever,' said Robin.

'It's awful,' said Stephen. 'I even think like the man now. Right, let's go over the whole plan once again. We'll take it from the red dossier, halfway down page 16. When I leave All Souls . . .'

On Sunday and Monday they carried out full rehearsals. By the Tuesday they knew every route Harvey could take and where he would be at any given moment of the day from 9 am to 5.30 pm. Stephen hoped he had covered every eventuality. He had little choice. They were only going to be allowed one crack at this one. Any mistakes like Monte Carlo and there would be no second chance. The dress-rehearsal went to a second.

'I haven't worn clothes like this since I was six years old and attending a fancy-dress party,' said Jean-Pierre. 'We're going to be anything but inconspicuous.'

'There'll be red and blue and black all round you on the day,' said Stephen. 'It's like a circus for peacocks. No one will give us a second look, not even you, Jean-Pierre.'

They were all nervous again, waiting for the curtain to go up. Stephen was glad they were on edge: he had no doubt that the moment they relaxed with Harvey Metcalfe, they would be found out.

The Team spent a quiet weekend. Stephen watched the College Dramatic Society's annual effort in Magdalen gardens, Robin took his wife to Glyndebourne and was uncommonly attentive, Jean-Pierre read *Goodbye Picasso* by David Douglas Duncan, and

James took Anne to Tathwell Hall in Lincolnshire, to meet his father, the fifth earl.

Even Anne was nervous that weekend.

'Harry?'

'Doctor Bradley.'

'I have an American guest dining with me in my rooms tonight. His name is Harvey Metcalfe. When he arrives will you see he is brought over to my rooms, please.'

'Certainly, sir.'

'And one small thing. He seems to have mistaken me for Professor Porter of Trinity College. Don't correct the mistake, will you? Just humour him.'

'Certainly, sir.'

Harry retreated into the Porter's Lodge shaking his head sadly. Of course, all academics went dotty in the end, but Dr Bradley had been afflicted at an unusually tender age.

Harvey arrived at eight. He was always on time in England. The head porter guided him through the cloisters and up the old stone staircase to Stephen's rooms.

'Mr Metcalfe, sir.'

'How are you, Professor?'

'I'm well, Mr Metcalfe. Good of you to be so punctual.'

'Punctuality is the politeness of princes.'

'I think you'll find it is the politeness of kings, and, in this particular instance, of Louis XVIII.' For a moment Stephen forgot that Harvey wasn't a pupil.

'I'm sure you're right, Professor.'

Stephen mixed him a large whisky. His guest's eyes took in the room and settled on the desk.

'Gee – what a wonderful set of photographs. You with the late President Kennedy, another with the Queen and even the Pope.'

That touch was due to Jean-Pierre, who had put Stephen in contact with a photographer who had been in jail with his artist friend David Stein. Stephen was already looking forward to burning the photographs and pretending they had never existed.

'Let me give you another to add to your collection.'

Harvey pulled out of his inside coat pocket a large photograph of himself receiving the trophy for the King George VI and Queen Elizabeth Stakes from the Queen.

'I'll sign it for you, if you like.'

Without waiting for a reply, he scribbled an exuberant signature diagonally across the Queen.

'Thank you,' said Stephen. 'I can assure you I will treasure it with the same affection as I do my other photographs. I certainly appreciate you sparing the time to visit me here, Mr Metcalfe.'

'It's an honour for me to come to Oxford, and this is such a lovely old college.'

Stephen really believed he meant it, and he suppressed the inclination to tell Harvey the story of the late Lord Nuffield's dinner at Magdalen. For all Nuffield's munificence to the university, the two were never on entirely easy terms. When a manservant assisted the guest's departure after a college feast, Nuffield took the proffered hat ungraciously. 'Is this mine?' he said, disdainfully. 'I wouldn't know, my lord,' was the rejoinder, 'but it's the one you came with.'

Harvey was gazing a little blankly at the books on Stephen's shelves. The disparity between their subject matter, pure mathematics, and the putative Professor Porter's discipline, biochemistry, happily failed to arrest him.

'Do brief me on tomorrow.'

'Surely,' said Stephen. Why not? He had briefed everyone else. 'Let me first call for dinner and I'll go through what I've planned for you and see if it meets with your approval.'

'I'm game for anything. I feel ten years younger since this trip to Europe – it must've been the operation – and I'm thrilled about being here at Oxford University.'

Stephen wondered if he really could stand seven hours of Harvey Metcalfe, but for another $250,000 and his reputation with the rest of the Team . . .

The college servants brought him shrimp cocktail.

'My favourite,' said Harvey. 'How did you know?'

Stephen would have liked to say, 'There's very little I don't know about you,' but he satisfied himself with, 'A fortunate guess. Now, if we meet up at 10 tomorrow morning we can take part in what is thought to be the most interesting day in the university calendar. It's called Encaenia.'

'What's that?'

'Well, once a year at the end of Trinity Term, which is the equivalent of the summer term in an American university, we celebrate the ending of the university year. There are several ceremonies followed by a magnificent Garden Party, which will be attended by the Chancellor and Vice-Chancellor of the University. The Chancellor is the former British Prime Minister, Harold Macmillan, and the Vice-Chancellor is Mr Habakkuk. I'm hoping it will be possible for you to meet them both, and we should manage to cover everything in time for you to be back in London by 7 pm.'

'How did you know I had to be back by 7?'

'You warned me at Ascot.' Stephen could lie very quickly now. He was afraid that if they did not get their million soon he would end up a hardened criminal.

Harvey enjoyed his meal, which Stephen had planned almost too cleverly, each course featuring one of Harvey's favourite dishes. After Harvey had drunk a good deal of after-dinner brandy (price £7.25 per bottle, thought Stephen) they strolled through the quiet Magdalen Cloisters past the Song School. The sound of the choristers rehearsing a Gabrieli mass hung gently in the air.

'Gee, I'm surprised you allow record players on that loud,' said Harvey.

Stephen escorted his guest to the Randolph Hotel, pointing out the iron cross set in Broad Street outside Balliol College, said to mark the spot on which Archbishop Cranmer was burnt at the stake for heresy in 1556. Harvey forbore to say that he had never even heard of the reverend gentleman.

Stephen and Harvey parted on the steps of the Randolph.

'See you in the morning, Professor. Thanks for a great evening.'

'My pleasure. I'll pick you up at 10 am. Sleep well – you have a full day ahead of you tomorrow.'

Stephen returned to Magdalen and immediately called Robin.

'All's well, but I nearly went too far. The meal was altogether too carefully chosen – I even had his favourite brandy. Still, it'll keep me on my toes tomorrow. We must remember to avoid overkill. See you then, Robin.'

Stephen reported the same message to Jean-Pierre and James before falling gratefully into bed. The same time tomorrow he would be a wiser man, but would he be a richer one?

16

At 5 am the sun rose over the Cherwell, and those few Oxonians who were about that early would have been left in no doubt as to why the connoisseurs consider Magdalen to be the most beautiful college at either Oxford or Cambridge. Nestling on the banks of the river, its perpendicular architecture is easy on the eye. King Edward VII, Prince Henry, Cardinal Wolsey, Edward Gibbon and Oscar Wilde had all passed through its portals. But the only thing that was passing through Stephen's mind as he lay awake that morning was the education of Harvey Metcalfe.

He could hear his own heart-beat, and for the first time he knew what Robin and Jean-Pierre had been through. It seemed a lifetime since their first meeting only three months before. He smiled to himself at the thought of how close they had all become in their common aim of defeating Harvey Metcalfe. Although Stephen, like James, was beginning to have a sneaking admiration for the man, he was now even more convinced that Metcalfe could be outmanoeuvred when he was not on home ground. For over two hours Stephen lay motionless in bed, deep in thought, going over his plan again and again. When the sun had climbed over the tallest tree, he rose, showered, shaved and dressed slowly and deliberately, his mind still on the day ahead.

He made his face up carefully to age himself by fifteen years. It took him a considerable time, and he wondered whether women had to struggle as long in front of the mirror to achieve the opposite effect. He donned his gown, a magnificent scarlet, proclaiming him a Doctor of Philosophy of the University of Oxford. It amused him that Oxford had to be different. Every other university abbreviated this universal award for research work, to PhD. In Oxford, it was DPhil. He studied himself in the mirror.

'If that doesn't impress Harvey Metcalfe, nothing ever will.'

And what's more, he had the right to wear it. He sat down to study his red dossier for the last time. He had read the closely typewritten pages so often that he practically knew them by heart.

He avoided breakfast. Looking nearly fifty, he would undoubtedly have caused a stir amongst his colleagues, though probably the older dons would have failed to observe anything unusual in his appearance.

Stephen headed out of the college into the High, unnoticed among the thousand or so other graduates all dressed like fourteenth-century archbishops. Anonymity on that particular day was going to be easy. That, and the fact that Harvey would be bemused by the strange traditions of the ancient university, were the two reasons why Stephen had chosen Encaenia for his day of battle.

He arrived at the Randolph at 9.55 am and informed one of the younger bell-boys that his name was Professor Porter and that he had come to pick up Mr Metcalfe. Stephen took a seat in the lounge. The young man scurried away and returned moments later with Harvey.

'Mr Metcalfe – Professor Porter.'

'Thank you,' said Stephen. He made a mental note to return and tip the bell-boy. That touch had been useful, even if it was only part of his job.

'Good morning, Professor,' said Harvey, taking a seat. 'So tell me, what have I let myself in for?'

'Well,' said Stephen, 'Encaenia begins officially when all the notables of the university take a breakfast of champagne, strawberries and cream at Jesus College, which is known as Lord Nathaniel Crewe's Benefaction.'

'Who's this Lord Crewe guy? Will he be at the breakfast?'

'Only in spirit; the great man died some three hundred years ago. Lord Nathaniel Crewe was a doctor of the university and the Bishop of Durham, and he left £200 a year to the university as a Benefaction to provide the breakfast and an oration which we shall hear later. Of course, the money he willed no longer covers expenses nowadays, with rising prices and inflation, so the university has to dip into its own pocket to continue the tradition. When breakfast is over there is a procession and parade to the Sheldonian Theatre.'

'What happens then?'

'The parade is followed by the most exciting event of the day. The presentation of the Honorands for degrees.'

'The what?' said Harvey.

'The Honorands,' said Stephen. 'They are the distinguished men and women who have been chosen by the senior members of the university to be awarded Oxford honorary degrees.' Stephen looked at his watch. 'In fact, we must leave now to be sure of having a good position on the route from which to watch the procession.'

Stephen rose and guided his guest out of the Randolph Hotel. They strolled down the Broad and found an excellent spot just in front of the Sheldonian Theatre, where the police cleared a little space for Stephen because of his scarlet gown. A few minutes later the procession wound into sight round the corner from the Turl. The police held up all the traffic and kept the public on the pavement.

'Who are the guys in front carrying those clubs?' enquired Harvey.

'They are the University Marshal and the Bedels. They are carrying maces to safeguard the Chancellor's procession.'

'Jesus; of course it's safe. This isn't Central Park, New York.'

'I agree,' said Stephen, 'but it hasn't always been so over the past three hundred years, and tradition dies hard in England.'

'And who's that behind the Bedel fellows?'

'The one wearing the black gown with gold trimmings is the Chancellor of the University, accompanied by his page. The Chancellor is the Right Honourable Harold Macmillan, who was Prime Minister of Great Britain in the late '50s and early '60s.'

'Oh yes, I remember the guy. Tried to get the British into Europe but De Gaulle wouldn't have it.'

'Well, I suppose that's one way of remembering him. Now, he's followed by the Vice-Chancellor, Mr Habakkuk, who is also the Principal of Jesus College.'

'You're losing me, Professor.'

'Well, the Chancellor is always a distinguished Englishman who was educated at Oxford; but the Vice-Chancellor is a leading member of the university itself and is usually chosen from the heads of one of the colleges.'

'Got it, I think.'

'Now, after him, we have the University Registrar, Mr Caston, who is a fellow of Merton College. He is the senior administrator of the university, or you might look on him as the university's top civil servant. He's directly responsible to the Vice-Chancellor and Hebdomadal Council, who are the sort of cabinet for the university. Behind them we have the Senior Proctor, Mr Campbell of Worcester College, and the

Junior Proctor, the Reverend Doctor Bennett of New College.'

'What's a Proctor?'

'For over 700 years the Proctors have been responsible for decency and discipline in the university.'

'What? Those two old men take care of 9,000 rowdy youths?'

'Well, they are helped by the bulldogs,' said Stephen.

'Ah, that's better, I suppose. A couple of bites from an old English bulldog would keep anyone in order.'

'No, no,' protested Stephen, trying desperately not to laugh. 'The name bulldog is given to the men who help the Proctors keep order. Now, finally in the procession you can observe that tiny crocodile of colour: it consists of heads of colleges who are doctors of the university, doctors of the university who are not heads of colleges and the heads of colleges who are not doctors of the university, in that order.'

'Listen, Rod, all doctors mean to me is pain and money.'

'They are not that sort of doctor,' replied Stephen.

'Forget it. I love everything but don't expect me to understand what it's all about.'

Stephen watched Harvey's face carefully. He was drinking the scene in and had already become quieter.

'The long line will now proceed into the Sheldonian Theatre and all the people in the procession will take their places in the hemicycle.'

'Excuse me, sir, what type of cycle is that?'

'The hemicycle is a round bank of seats inside the theatre, distinguished only by being the most uncomfortable in Europe. But don't you worry. Thanks to your well-known interest in education at Harvard I've managed to arrange special seats for us and there will just be time for us to secure them ahead of the procession.'

'Well, lead the way, Rod. Do they really know what goes on at Harvard here?'

'Why yes, Mr Metcalfe. You have a reputation in university circles as a generous man interested in financing the pursuit of academic excellence.'

'Well, what do you know.'

Very little, thought Stephen.

He guided Harvey to his reserved seat in the balcony, not wanting his guest to be able to see the individual men and women too clearly. The truth of the matter was that the senior members of the university in the hemicycle were so covered from head to toe in gowns and caps and bow-ties and bands, that even their mothers would not have recognised them. The organist played his final chord and the guests settled.

'The organist,' said Stephen, 'is from my own college. He's the Choragus, the leader of the chorus, and Deputy Professor of Music.'

Harvey could not take his eyes off the hemicycle and the scarlet-clad figures. He had never seen a sight like it in his life. The music stopped and the Chancellor rose to address the assembled company in vernacular Latin.

'*Causa hujus convocationis est ut . . .*'

'What the hell's he saying?'

'He's telling us why we're here,' explained Stephen. 'I'll try and guide you through it.'

'*Ite Bedelli,*' declared the Chancellor, and the great doors opened for the Bedels to go and fetch the Honorands from the Divinity School. There was a hush as they were led in by the Public Orator, Mr J. G. Griffith, who presented them one by one to the Chancellor, enshrining the careers and achievements of each in polished and witty Latin prose.

Stephen's translation, however, followed a rather more liberal line and was embellished with suggestions that their doctorates were as much the result of financial generosity as of academic prowess.

'That's Lord Amory. They're praising him for all the work he has done in the field of education.'

'How much did he give''

'Well, he *was* Chancellor of the Exchequer. And there's Lord Hailsham. He has held eight Cabinet positions, including Secretary of State for Education and finally Lord Chancellor. Both he and Lord Amory are receiving the degree of Doctor of Civil Law.'

Harvey recognised Dame Flora Robson, the actress, who was being honoured for a distinguished lifetime in the theatre; Stephen explained that she was receiving the degree of Doctor of Letters, as was the Poet Laureate, Sir John Betjeman. Each was presented with his scroll by the Chancellor, shaken by the hand and then shown to a seat in the front row of the hemicycle.

The final Honorand was Sir George Porter, Director of the Royal Institution and Nobel Laureate. He received his honorary degree of Doctor of Science.

'My namesake, but no relation. Oh well, nearly through,' said Stephen. 'Just a little prose from John Wain, the Professor of Poetry, about the benefactors of the university.'

Mr Wain delivered the Crewian Oration, which took him some twelve minutes, and Stephen was grateful for something so lively in a language they could both understand. He was only vaguely aware of the recitations of undergraduate prize winners which concluded the proceedings.

The Chancellor of the university rose and led the procession out of the hall.

'Where are they all off to now?' asked Harvey.

'They are going to have lunch at All Souls, where they will be joined by other distinguished guests.'

'God, what I would give to be able to attend that.'

'I have arranged it,' replied Stephen.

Harvey was quite overwhelmed.

'How did you fix that, Professor?'

'The Registrar was most impressed by the interest you have shown in Harvard and I think they hope you might find it possible to assist Oxford in some small way, especially after your wonderful win at Ascot.'

'What a great idea. Why didn't I think of that?'

Stephen tried to show little interest, hoping that by the end of the day he would have thought of it. He had learnt his lesson on overkill. The truth was that the Registrar had never heard of Harvey Metcalfe, but because it was Stephen's last term at Oxford he had been put on the list of invitations by a friend who was a Fellow of All Souls.

They walked over to All Souls, just across the road from the Sheldonian Theatre. Stephen attempted, without much success, to explain the nature of All Souls to Harvey. Indeed, many Oxonians themselves find the college something of an enigma.

'Its corporate name,' Stephen began, 'is the College of All Souls of the Faithful Departed of Oxford, and it resonantly commemorates the victors of Agincourt. It was intended that masses should forever be said there for the repose of their souls. Its modern role is unique in academic life. All Souls is a society of graduates distinguished either by promise or achievement, mostly academic, from home and abroad, with a sprinkling of men who have made their mark in other fields. The college has no undergraduates, and generally appears to the outside world to do much as it pleases with its massive financial and intellectual resources.'

Stephen and Harvey took their places among the hundred or more guests at the long table in the noble Codrington Library. Stephen spent the entire time ensuring that Harvey was kept fully occupied and was not too obvious. He was thankfully aware that on such occasions people never remember whom they meet or what they say, and happily introduced Harvey to everyone around as a distinguished American philanthropist. He was fortunately placed some way from the Vice-Chancellor, the Registrar and the Secretary of the University Chest.

Harvey was quite overcome by the new experience and was content just to listen to the distinguished men around him – which surprised Stephen, who had feared he would never stop talking. When the meal was over and the guests had risen, Stephen drew a deep breath and played one of his riskier cards. He deliberately marched Harvey up to the Chancellor.

'Chancellor,' he said to Harold Macmillan.

'Yes, young man.'

'May I introduce Mr Harvey Metcalfe from Boston. Mr Metcalfe, as you will know, Chancellor, is a great benefactor of Harvard.'

'Yes, of course. Capital, capital. What brings you to England, Mr Metcalfe?'

Harvey was nearly speechless.

'Well, sir, I mean Chancellor, I came to see my horse Rosalie run in the King George and Elizabeth Stakes.'

Stephen was now standing behind Harvey and made signs to the Chancellor that Harvey's horse had won the race. Harold Macmillan, as game as ever and never one to miss a trick, replied:

'Well, you must have been very pleased with the result, Mr Metcalfe.'

'Well, sir, I guess I was lucky.

'You don't look to me the type of man who depends on luck.'

Stephen took his career firmly in both hands.

'I am trying to interest Mr Metcalfe in supporting some research we are doing at Oxford, Chancellor.'

'What a good idea.' No one knew better than Harold Macmillan, after seven years of leading a political party, how to use flattery on such occasions. 'Keep in touch, young man. Boston was it, Mr Metcalfe? Do give my regards to the Kennedys.'

Macmillan swept off, resplendent in his academic dress. Harvey stood dumbfounded.

'What a great man. What an occasion. I feel I'm part of history. I just wish I deserved to be here.'

Having completed his task, Stephen was determined to escape before any mistakes could be made. He knew Harold Macmillan would shake hands with and talk to over a thousand people that day and the chances of his remembering Harvey were minimal. In any case, it would not much matter if he did. Harvey was, after all, a genuine benefactor of Harvard.

'We ought to leave before the senior members, Mr Metcalfe.'

'Of course, Rod. You're the boss.'

'I think that would be courtesy.'

Once they were out on the street Harvey glanced at his large Jaeger le Coultre watch. It was 2.30 pm.

'Excellent,' said Stephen, who was running three minutes late for the next rendezvous. 'We have just over an hour before the Garden Party. Why don't we take a look at one or two of the colleges.'

They walked slowly up past Brasenose College and Stephen explained that the name really meant 'brass nose' and that the famous original brass nose, a sanctuary knocker of the thirteenth century, was still mounted in the hall. A hundred yards further on, Stephen directed Harvey to the right.

'He's turned right, Robin, and he's heading towards Lincoln College,' said James, well hidden in the entrance of Jesus College.

'Fine,' said Robin and checked his two sons. Aged seven and nine, they stood awkwardly, in unfamiliar Eton suits, ready to play their part as pages, unable to understand what Daddy was up to.

'Are you both ready?'

'Yes, Daddy,' they replied in unison.

Stephen continued walking slowly towards Lincoln, and they were no more than a few paces away when Robin appeared from the main entrance of the college in the official dress of the Vice-Chancellor, bands, collars, white tie and all. He looked fifteen years older and as much like Mr Habakkuk as possible. Perhaps not quite so bald, thought Stephen.

'Would you like to be presented to the Vice-Chancellor?' asked Stephen.

'That would be something,' said Harvey.

'Good afternoon, Vice-Chancellor, may I introduce Mr Harvey Metcalfe.'

Robin doffed his academic cap and bowed. Stephen returned the compliment in like manner. Robin spoke before Stephen could continue:

'Not the benefactor of Harvard University?'

Harvey blushed and smiled at the two little boys who were holding the Vice-Chancellor's train. Robin continued:

'This is a pleasure, Mr Metcalfe. I do hope you are enjoying your visit to Oxford. Mind you, it's not everybody who's fortunate enough to be shown around by a Nobel Laureate.'

'I've enjoyed it immensely, Vice-Chancellor, and I'd like to feel I could help this university in some way.'

'Well, that is excellent news.'

'Look, gentlemen, I'm staying here at the Randolph Hotel. It would be my great pleasure if you could all have tea with me later this afternoon.'

Robin and Stephen were thrown for a moment. He'd done it again – the unexpected. Surely the man realised that on the day of Encaenia the Vice-Chancellor did not have a moment free to attend private tea parties.

Robin recovered first.

'I'm afraid that would be difficult. One has so many responsibilities on a day like this, you understand. Perhaps you could join me in my rooms at the

Clarendon Building? That would give us a chance to have a more private discussion?'

Stephen immediately picked up the lead:

'How kind of you, Vice-Chancellor. Will 4.30 be convenient?'

'Yes, yes, that will be fine, Professor.'

Robin tried not to look as if he wanted to run a mile. Although they had only been standing there for about five minutes, to him it seemed a lifetime. He had not objected to being a journalist, or an American surgeon, but he genuinely hated being a Vice-Chancellor. Surely someone would appear at any moment and recognise him for the fraud he was. Thank God most of the undergraduates had gone home the week before. He began to feel even worse when a tourist started taking photos of him.

Now Harvey had turned all their plans upside down. Stephen could only think of Jean-Pierre and of James, the finest string to their dramatic bow, loitering uselessly in fancy dress behind the tea tent at the Garden Party in the grounds of Trinity College, waiting for them.

'Perhaps it might be wise, Vice-Chancellor, if we were to invite the Registrar and the Secretary of the University Chest to join us?'

'First-class idea, Professor. I'll ask them to be there. It isn't every day we're visited by such a distinguished philanthropist. I must take my leave of you now, sir, and proceed to my Garden Party. An honour to have made your acquaintance, Mr Metcalfe, and I look forward to seeing you again at 4.30.'

They shook hands warmly, and Stephen guided Harvey towards Exeter College while Robin darted back into the little room in Lincoln that had been arranged for him. He sank heavily into a seat.

'Are you all right, Daddy?' asked his elder son, William.

'Yes, I'm fine.'

'Do we get the ice cream and Coca-Cola you promised us if we didn't say a word?'

'You certainly do,' said Robin.

Robin slipped off all the paraphernalia – the gown hood, bow-tie and bands – and placed them back in the suitcase. He returned to the street just in time to watch the real Vice-Chancellor, Mr Habakkuk, leave Jesus College on the opposite side of the road, obviously making his way towards the Garden Party. Robin glanced at his watch. If they had run five minutes late the whole plan would have struck disaster.

Meanwhile, Stephen had done a full circle and was now heading towards Shepherd & Woodward, the tailor's shop which supplies academic dress for the university. He was, however, preoccupied with the thought of getting a message through to James. Stephen and Harvey came to a halt in front of the shop window.

'What magnificent robes.'

'That's the gown of a Doctor of Letters. Would you like to try it on and see how you look?'

'That would be great. But would they allow it?' said Harvey.

'I'm sure they won't object.'

They entered the shop, Stephen still in his full academic dress as a Doctor of Philosophy.

'My distinguished guest would like to see the gown of a Doctor of Letters.'

'Certainly, sir,' said the young assistant, who was not going to argue with a Fellow of the University.

He vanished to the back of the shop and returned with a magnificent red gown with grey facing and a black, floppy velvet cap. Stephen forged on, brazen-faced.

'Why don't you try them on, Mr Metcalfe? Let's see what you would look like as an academic.'

The assistant was somewhat surprised. He wished Mr Venables would return from his lunch break.

'Would you care to come through to the fitting-room, sir?'

Harvey disappeared. Stephen slipped out on to the road.

'James, can you hear me? Oh hell, for God's sake answer, James.'

'Cool down, old fellow. I'm having a deuce of a time putting on this ridiculous gown, and in any case, our rendezvous isn't for another seventeen minutes.'

'Cancel it.'

'Cancel it?'

'Yes, and tell Jean-Pierre as well. Both of you report to Robin and meet up as quickly as possible. He will fill you in on the new plans.'

'New plans. Is everything all right, Stephen?'

'Yes, better than I could have hoped for.'

Stephen clicked off his speaker and rushed back into the tailor's shop.

Harvey reappeared as a Doctor of Letters; a more unlikely sight Stephen had not seen for many years.

'You look magnificent.'

'What do they cost?'

'About £100, I think.'

'No, no. How much would I have to give . . . ?'

'I have no idea. You would have to discuss that with the Vice-Chancellor after the Garden Party.'

Harvey took a long look at himself in the mirror, and then returned to the dressing-room while Stephen thanked the assistant, asked him to wrap up the gown and cap and send them to the Clarendon building to be left with the porter in the name of Sir John Betjeman. He paid cash. The assistant looked even more bewildered.

'Yes, sir.'

He was not sure what to do, except continue praying for Mr Venables' arrival. His prayers were answered some ten minutes later, but by then Stephen and Harvey were well on their way to Trinity College and the Garden Party.

'Mr Venables, I've just been asked to send the full DLitt. dress to Sir John Betjeman at the Clarendon Building.'

'Strange. We kitted him out for this morning's ceremony weeks ago. I wonder why he wants a second outfit.'

'He paid cash.'

'Well, send it round to the Clarendon, but be sure it's in his name.'

When Stephen and Harvey arrived at Trinity College shortly after 3.30, the elegant green lawns, the croquet hoops having been removed, were already crowded with over a thousand people. The members of the university wore an odd hybrid dress: best lounge suits or silk dresses topped with gowns, hoods and caps. Cups of tea and crates of strawberries and cucumber sandwiches were disappearing rapidly.

'What a swell party this is,' said Harvey unintentionally mimicking Frank Sinatra. 'You certainly do things in style here, Professor.'

'Yes, the Garden Party is always rather fun. It's the main social event of the university year, which as I explained, is just ending. Half the senior members here will be snatching an afternoon off from reading examination scripts. Exams for the final-year undergraduates have only just ended.'

Stephen observed the Vice-Chancellor, the Registrar and the Secretary of the University Chest carefully, and steered Harvey well away from them, introducing him to as many of the older members of the university as possible, hoping they would not find the encounter too memorable. They spent just over three-quarters of an hour moving from person to person, Stephen feeling rather like an aide-de-camp to an incompetent dignitary whose mouth must be kept shut for fear of a diplomatic incident. Despite Stephen's anxious approach, Harvey was clearly having the time of his life.

'Robin, Robin, can you hear me?'

'Yes, James.'

'Where are you?'

'I'm in the Eastgate Restaurant: come and join me here and bring Jean-Pierre.'

'Fine. We'll be there in five minutes. No, make it ten. With my disguise, I'd better go slowly.'

Robin paid his bill. The children had finished their reward, so he took them out of the Eastgate to a waiting car and instructed the driver, who had been hired especially for the day, to return them to Newbury. They had played their part and now could only get in the way.

'Aren't you coming home with us, Dad?' demanded Jamie.

No, I'll be back later tonight. Tell your mother to expect me about seven.'

Robin returned to the Eastgate to find Jean-Pierre and James hobbling towards him.

'Why the change of plan?' asked Jean-Pierre. 'It's taken me over an hour to get dressed and ready.'

'Never mind. You're still in the right gear. We had a stroke of luck. I chatted up Harvey in the street and the cocky bastard invited me to tea with him at the Randolph Hotel. I said that would be impossible, but asked him to join me at the Clarendon. Stephen suggested that you two should be invited along as well.'

'Clever,' said James. 'No need for the deception at the Garden Party.'

'Let's hope it's not too clever,' said Jean-Pierre.

'Well, at least we can do the whole damn charade behind closed doors,' said Robin, 'which ought to make it easier. I never did like the idea of walking through the streets with him.'

'With Harvey Metcalfe nothing is ever going to be easy,' said Jean-Pierre.

'I'll get myself into the Clarendon Building by 4.15,' continued Robin. 'You will appear a few minutes after 4.20, Jean-Pierre, and then you, James, about 4.25 pm. But keep exactly to the same routine, act as if the meeting had taken place, as originally planned, at the Garden Party and we had all walked over to the Clarendon together.'

Stephen suggested to Harvey that they should return to the Clarendon Building, as it would be discourteous to be late for the Vice-Chancellor.

'Sure.' Harvey glanced at his watch. 'Jesus, it's 4.30 already.'

They left the Garden Party and walked quickly down towards the Clarendon Building at the bottom of the Broad, Stephen explaining en route that the Clarendon was a sort of Oxford White House where all the officers and officials of the university had their rooms.

The Clarendon is a large, imposing eighteenth-century building which could be mistaken by a visitor for another college. A few steps lead up to an impressive hallway, and on entering you realise you are in a magnificent old building which has been converted for use as offices, with as few changes as possible.

When they arrived the porter greeted them.

'The Vice-Chancellor is expecting us,' said Stephen.

The porter had been somewhat surprised when Robin had arrived fifteen minutes earlier and told him that Mr Habakkuk had asked him to wait in his room; even though Robin was in full academic dress, the porter kept a beady eye on him, not expecting the Vice-Chancellor or any of his staff to return from the Garden Party for at least another hour. The arrival of Stephen gave him a little more confidence. He well remembered the pound he had received for his guided tour of the building.

The porter ushered Stephen and Harvey through to the Vice-Chancellor's rooms and left them alone, tucking another pound note into his pocket.

The Vice-Chancellor's room was in no way pretentious and its beige carpet and pale walls would have given it the look of any middle-ranking civil servant's office, had it not been for the magnificent picture of a village square in France by Wilson Steer which hung over the marble fireplace.

Robin was staring out of the vast windows overlooking the Bodleian Library.

'Good afternoon, Vice-Chancellor.'

Robin spun round. 'Oh, welcome, Professor.'

'You remember Mr Metcalfe?'

'Yes, indeed. How nice to see you again.' Robin shuddered. All he wanted to do was to go home. They chatted for a few minutes. Another knock and Jean-Pierre entered.

'Good afternoon, Registrar.'

'Good afternoon, Vice-Chancellor, Professor Porter.'

'May I introduce Mr Harvey Metcalfe.'

'Good afternoon, sir.'

'Registrar, would you like some . . .'

'Where's this man Metcalfe?'

The three of them stood, stunned, as a man looking ninety entered the room on sticks. He hobbled over to Robin, winked, bowed and said:

'Good afternoon, Vice-Chancellor,' in a loud, crotchety voice.

'Good afternoon, Horsley.'

James went over to Harvey and prodded him with his sticks as if to make sure he was real.

'I have read about you, young man.'

Harvey had not been called young man for thirty years. The others stared at James in admiration. None of them knew that in his last year at university James had played *L'Avare* to great acclaim. His Secretary of the Chest was simply a repeat performance, and even Molière would have been pleased with it. James continued:

'You have been most generous to Harvard.'

'That's very kind of you to mention it, sir,' said Harvey respectfully.

'Don't call me sir, young man. I like the look of you – call me Horsley.'

'Yes, Horsley, sir,' blurted Harvey.

The others were only just able to keep a straight face.

'Well, Vice-Chancellor,' continued James. 'You can't have dragged me halfway across the city for my health. What's going on? Where's my sherry?'

Stephen wondered if James was overdoing it, but looking at Harvey saw that he was evidently captivated by the scene. How could a man so mature in one field be so immature in another, he thought. He was beginning to see how Westminster Bridge had been sold to at least four Americans in the past twenty years.

'Well, we were hoping to interest Mr Metcalfe in the work of the university and I felt that the Secretary of the University Chest should be present.'

'What's this chest?' asked Harvey.

'Sort of treasury for the university,' replied James,

his voice loud, old and very convincing. 'Why don't you read this?' and he thrust into Harvey's hand an Oxford University Calendar, which Harvey could have obtained at Blackwell's bookshop for £2 as indeed James had.

Stephen was not sure what move to make next when, happily for him, Harvey took over.

'Gentlemen, I would like to say how proud I am to be here today. This has been a wonderful year for me. I was present when an American won Wimbledon, I finally obtained a Van Gogh. My life was saved by a wonderful, wonderful surgeon in Monte Carlo and now here I am in Oxford surrounded by all this history. Gentlemen, it would give me a great deal of pleasure to be associated with this famous university.'

James took the lead again:

'What have you in mind?' he shouted at Harvey, adjusting his hearing-aid.

'Well, sir, I achieved my life's ambition when I received the King George and Elizabeth trophy from your Queen, but the prize money, well, I would like to use that to make a benefaction to your university.'

'But that's over £80,000,' gasped Stephen.

'£81,240 to be exact, sir. But why don't I call it $250,000.'

Stephen, Robin and Jean-Pierre were speechless. James alone was left to command the day. This was the opportunity he had needed to show why his great-grandfather had been one of Wellington's most respected generals.

'We accept. But it would have to be anonymous,' said James. 'I think I can safely say in the circumstances that the Vice-Chancellor would inform Mr Harold Macmillan and Hebdomadal Council, but we would not want a fuss made of it. Of course, Vice-Chancellor, I would ask you to consider an honorary degree.'

Robin was so conscious of James's obvious control of the entire situation that he could only add:

'How would you recommend we go about it, Horsley?'

'Cash cheque, so nobody can trace the money back to Mr Metcalfe. We can't have those bloody men from Cambridge chasing him for the rest of his life. Same way as we did for Sir David – no fuss.'

'I agree,' said Jean-Pierre, not having the vaguest idea what James was talking about. Neither, for that matter, had Harvey.

James nodded to Stephen, who left the Vice-Chancellor's office and made his way to the porter's room to enquire if a parcel had been left for Sir John Betjeman.

'Yes, sir. I don't know why they left it here. I'm not expecting Sir John.'

'Don't worry,' said Stephen. 'He's asked me to pick it up for him.'

Stephen returned to find James holding forth to Harvey on the importance of keeping his donation as a bond between himself and the university.

Stephen undid the box and took out the magnificent gown of a Doctor of Letters. Harvey turned red with embarrassment and pride as Robin placed it on his shoulders, chanting '*De mortuis nil nisi bonum. Dulce et decorum est pro patria mori. Per ardua ad astra. Nil desperandum.*'

'Many congratulations,' bellowed James. 'A pity we could not have organised this to be part of today's ceremony, but for such a munificent gesture as yours we could hardly wait another year.'

Brilliant, thought Stephen, Laurence Olivier could not have done better.

'That's fine by me,' said Harvey, as he sat down and made out a cheque to cash. 'You have my word that this matter will never be mentioned to anyone.'

None of them believed that.

They stood in silence as Harvey rose and passed the cheque to James.

'No, sir.' James transfixed him with a glare.

The others looked dumbfounded.

'The Vice-Chancellor.'

'Of course,' said Harvey. 'Excuse me, sir.'

'Thank you,' said Robin, his hand trembling as he received the cheque. 'A most gracious gift, and you may be sure we shall put it to good use.'

There was a loud knock on the door. They all looked round terrified except for James, who was now ready for anything. It was Harvey's chauffeur. James had always hated the pretentious white uniform with the white hat.

'Ah, the efficient Mr Mellor,' said Harvey. 'Gentlemen, I guarantee he's been watching every move we've made today.'

The four froze, but the chauffeur had clearly made no sinister deductions from his observations.

'Your car is ready, sir. You wanted to be back at Claridge's by 7 pm to be in good time for your dinner appointment.'

'Young man,' bellowed James.

'Yes, sir,' whimpered the chauffeur.

'Do you realise you are in the presence of the Vice-Chancellor of this university?'

'No, sir. I'm very sorry, sir.'

'Take your hat off immediately.'

'Yes, sir.'

The chauffeur removed his hat and retreated to the car, swearing under his breath.

'Vice-Chancellor, I sure hate to break up our party, but as you've heard I do have an appointment . . .'

'Of course, of course, we understand you're a busy man. May I once again officially thank you for your most generous donation, which will be used to benefit many deserving people.'

'We all hope you have a safe journey back to the States and will remember us as warmly as we shall remember you,' added Jean-Pierre.

Harvey moved towards the door.

'I will take my leave of you now, sir,' shouted

James. 'It will take me twenty minutes to get down those damned steps. You are a fine man and you have been most generous.'

'It was nothing,' said Harvey expansively.

True enough, thought James, nothing to you, but everything to us.

Stephen, Robin and Jean-Pierre accompanied Harvey from the Clarendon to the waiting Rolls.

'Professor,' said Harvey, 'I didn't quite understand everything the old guy was saying.' As he spoke he shifted the weight of his heavy robes on his shoulders self-consciously.

'Well, he's very deaf and very old, but his heart's in the right place. He wanted you to know that this has to be an anonymous donation as far as the university is concerned, though, of course, the Oxford hierarchy will be informed of the truth. If it were to be made public all sorts of undesirables who have never done anything for education in the past would come trooping along on the day of Encaenia wanting to buy an honorary degree.'

'Of course, of course. I understand. That's fine by me,' said Harvey. 'I want to thank you for a swell day, Rod, and I wish you all the luck for the future. What a shame our friend Wiley Barker wasn't here to share it all.'

Robin blushed.

Harvey climbed into the Rolls Royce and waved enthusiastically to the three of them as they watched the car start effortlessly on its journey back to London.

Three down and one to go.

'James was brilliant,' said Jean-Pierre. 'When he first came in I didn't know who the hell it was.'

'I agree,' said Robin. 'Let's go and rescue him – he's truly the hero of the day.'

They all three ran up the steps, forgetting that they looked somewhere between the ages of fifty and sixty, and rushed back into the Vice-Chancellor's room to congratulate James, who lay silent in the middle of the floor. He had passed out.

In Magdalen an hour later, with the help of Robin and two large whiskies, James was back to his normal health.

'You were fantastic,' said Stephen, 'just at the point when I was beginning to lose my nerve.'

'You would have received an Academy Award if we could have put it on screen,' said Robin. 'Your father will have to let you go on the stage after that performance.'

James basked in his first moment of glory for three months. He could not wait to tell Anne.

'Anne.' He quickly looked at his watch. 'Six-thirty.

Oh hell, I must leave at once. I'm meant to be meeting Anne at eight. See you all next Monday in Stephen's rooms for dinner. By then I'll try to have my plan ready.'

James rushed out of the room.

'James.'

His face reappeared round the door. They all said in chorus: 'Fantastic.'

He grinned, ran down the stairs and leapt into his Alfa Romeo, which he now felt they might allow him to keep, and headed towards London at top speed.

It took him 59 minutes from Oxford to the King's Road. The new motorway had made a considerable difference since his undergraduate days. Then the journey had taken anything from an hour and a half to two hours through High Wycombe or Henley.

The reason for his haste was that the meeting with Anne was most important and under no circumstances must he be late; tonight he was due to meet her father. All James knew about him was that he was a senior member of the Diplomatic Corps in Washington. Diplomats always expect you to be on time. He was determined to make a good impression on her father, particularly after Anne's successful weekend at Tathwell Hall. The old man had taken to her at once and never left her side. They had even managed to agree on a wedding date, subject, of course, to the approval of Anne's parents.

James had a quick cold shower and removed all his make-up, losing some sixty years in the process.

He had arranged to meet Anne for a drink at Les Ambassadeurs in Mayfair before dinner, and as he put on his dinner-jacket he wondered if he could make it from the King's Road to Hyde Park Corner in 12 minutes: it would require another Monte Carlo. He leapt into his car, revving it quickly through the gears, shot along to Sloane Square, through Eaton Square, up past St George's Hospital, round Hyde Park Corner into Park Lane, and arrived at 7.58 pm.

'Good evening, my lord,' said Mr Mills, the club owner.

'Good evening. I'm dining with Miss Summerton and I've had to leave my car double-parked. Can you take care of it?' said James, dropping the keys and a pound note into the doorman's white-gloved hand.

'Delighted, my lord. Show Lord Brigsley to the private rooms.'

James followed the head porter up the red staircase and into a small Regency room where dinner had been laid for three. He could hear Anne's voice in the next room. She came through, looking even more beautiful than usual in a floating mint-green dress.

'Hello, darling. Come on, I want you to meet Daddy.'

James followed Anne into the next room.

'Daddy, this is James. James, this is my father.'

James went red and then white, and then he felt green.

'How are you, my boy. I've heard so much about you from Rosalie that I can't wait to get acquainted.'

17

'CALL ME HARVEY.'

James stood aghast and speechless. Anne jumped into the silence.

'Would you like a whisky, James?'

James found his voice with difficulty.

'Thank you.'

'I want to know all about you, young man,' continued Harvey, 'what you get up to and why I've seen so little of my daughter in the past few weeks, though I think I can guess the answer to that.'

James drank the whisky in one gulp and Anne quickly refilled his glass.

'You see so little of your daughter because I'm always modelling, which means that I'm very rarely in London.'

'I know, Rosalie . . .'

'James knows me as Anne, Daddy.'

'We christened you Rosalie. It was a good enough name for your mother and me and it ought to be good enough for you.'

'Daddy, whoever heard of a top European model

calling herself Rosalie Metcalfe? All my friends know me as Anne Summerton.'

'What do you think, James?'

'I was beginning to think I didn't know her at all,' replied James, recovering slowly. It was obvious that Harvey did not suspect a thing. He had not seen James face to face at the gallery, he had never seen him at Monte Carlo or Ascot, and James had looked ninety years of age at Oxford earlier in the day. He was beginning to believe he had got away with it. But how the hell could he tell the others at their Monday meeting that the final plan, his plan, would be to outwit not Harvey Metcalfe, but his future father-in-law?

'Shall we go through to dinner?'

Harvey did not wait for a reply. He marched on into the adjoining room.

'Rosalie Metcalfe,' whispered James fiercely, 'you've got some explaining to do.'

Anne kissed him gently on the cheek.

'You're the first person who's given me the chance to beat my father at anything. Can't you forgive me? . . . I do love you . . .'

'Come on, you two. Anyone would think you'd never met before.'

Anne and James joined Harvey for dinner. James was amused by the sight of the shrimp cocktail and remembered how Stephen had regretted that touch at Harvey's Magdalen dinner.

'Well, James, I understand you and Anne have fixed a date for the wedding.'

'Yes, sir, if it meets with your approval.'

'Of course I approve. I was hoping Anne would marry Prince Charles after I'd won the King George and Elizabeth Stakes, but an earl will have to do for my only daughter.'

They both laughed, neither of them thinking it was remotely funny.

'I wish you'd come to Wimbledon this year, Rosalie. Imagine, me there on Ladies' Day and the only company I had was a boring old Swiss banker.'

Anne looked at James and grinned.

The waiters cleared the table and wheeled in a trolley bearing a crown of lamb in immaculate cutlet frills, which Harvey studied with great interest.

'Still,' said Harvey, chattering on, 'it was thoughtful of you to ring me at Monte Carlo, my dear. I really thought I was going to die, you know. James, you wouldn't have believed it. They removed a gall stone the size of a baseball from my stomach. Thank God, the operation was performed by one of the greatest surgeons in the world, Wiley Barker, the President's surgeon. He saved my life.'

Harvey promptly undid his shirt and revealed a 4-inch scar across his vast stomach.

'What do you think of that, James?'

'Remarkable.'

'Daddy, really. We're having dinner.'

'Stop fussing, honey. It won't be the first time James has seen a man's stomach.'

It's not the first time I've seen that one, thought James.

Harvey pushed his shirt back into his trousers and continued:

'Anyway, it was really kind of you to phone me.' He leant over and patted her hand. 'I was a good boy too. I took your advice and kept that nice Doctor Barker on for another week in case any complications arose. Mind you, the price these doctors . . .'

James dropped his wine glass. The claret covered the tablecloth with a red stain.

'I'm so sorry.'

'You all right, James?'

'Yes, sir.'

James looked at Anne in silent outrage. Harvey was quite unperturbed.

'Bring a fresh tablecloth and some more wine for Lord Brigsley.'

The waiter opened a fresh bottle of claret and James decided it was his turn to have a little fun. Anne had been laughing at him for three months. Why shouldn't he tease her a little, if Harvey gave him the chance? Harvey was still talking.

'You a racing man, James?'

'Yes, sir, and I was delighted by your victory in the King George VI and Queen Elizabeth Stakes – for more reasons than you realise.'

In the diversion caused by the waiters clearing the table, Anne whispered *sotto voce*:

'Don't try to be too clever, darling – he's not as stupid as he sounds.'

'Well, what do you think of her?'

'I beg your pardon, sir?'

'Rosalie.'

'Magnificent. I put £5 each way on her.'

'Yes, it was a great occasion for me and I was sorry you missed it, Rosalie, because you would have met the Queen and a nice guy from Oxford University called Professor Porter.'

'Professor Porter?' enquired James, burying his face in his wine glass.

'Yes, Professor Porter, James. Do you know him?'

'No, sir, I can't say I do, but didn't he win a Nobel Prize?'

'He sure did and he gave me a wonderful time at Oxford. I enjoyed myself so much I ended up presenting the university with a cheque for $250,000 to be used for research of some kind, so he should be happy.'

'Daddy, you know you're not meant to tell anybody about that.'

'Sure, but James is family now.'

'Why can't you tell anyone else, sir?'

'Well, it's a long story, James, but it was quite an honour for me. You do understand this is highly confidential, but I was Professor Porter's guest at Encaenia. I lunched at All Souls with Mr Harry Macmillan, your dear old Prime Minister, and then I attended the Garden Party, and afterwards I had a meeting with the Vice-Chancellor in his private rooms along with the Registrar and the Secretary of the University Chest. Were you at Oxford, James?'

'Yes, sir. The House.'

'The House?' queried Harvey.

'Christ Church, sir.'

'I'll never understand Oxford.'

'No, sir.'

'You must call me Harvey. Well, as I was saying, we all met at the Clarendon and they stammered and stuttered and they were totally lost for words, except for one funny old guy, who was ninety if he was a day. The truth is that those people just don't know how to approach millionaires for money, so I put them out of their embarrassment and took over. They'd have gone on all day about their beloved Oxford, so eventually I had to shut them up and simply wrote out a cheque for $250,000.'

'That was very generous, Harvey.'

'I'd have given them $500,000 if the old boy had asked. James, you've gone quite white. Do you feel all right?'

'I'm sorry. Yes, I'm fine. I was quite carried away with your description of Oxford.'

Anne joined in:

'Daddy, you made an agreement with the Vice-Chancellor that you would keep your gift as a bond between the university and yourself, and you must promise never to repeat that story again.'

'I think I shall wear the robes for the first time

when I open the new Metcalfe library at Harvard in the fall.'

'Oh, no sir,' stammered James a little too quickly, 'that wouldn't be quite the thing. You should only wear full robes in Oxford on ceremonial occasions.'

'Gee, what a shame. Still, I know what sticklers you English are for etiquette. Which reminds me, we ought to discuss your wedding. I suppose you two will want to live in England?'

'Yes, Daddy, but we'll visit you every year and when you make your annual trip to Europe you can come and stay with us.'

The waiters cleared the table again and reappeared with Harvey's favourite strawberries. Anne tried to steer the conversation to domestic issues and stop her father returning to what he'd been up to during the past two months, while James did everything to get him back on the subject.

'Coffee or liqueur, sir?'

'No, thank you,' said Harvey. 'Just the check. I thought we'd have a drink in my suite at Claridge's, Rosalie. I have something to show you both. It's a bit of a surprise.'

'I can't wait, Daddy. I love surprises. Don't you, James?'

'Normally yes, but I think I've had enough for one day.'

*

James left them and drove the Alfa Romeo to Claridge's garage so that Anne could have a few moments alone with her father. They strolled along Curzon Street, arm in arm.

'Isn't he wonderful, Daddy?'

'Yeah, great guy. Didn't seem too bright to begin with but he cheered up as the meal went on. And fancy my little girl turning out to be a genuine English lady. Your Momma's tickled pink and I'm pleased that we've patched up our silly quarrel.'

'Oh, you helped a lot, Daddy.'

'I did?' queried Harvey.

'Yes, I managed to get things back into perspective during the last few weeks. Now tell me, what is your little surprise?'

'Wait and see, honey. It's your wedding present.'

James rejoined them at the entrance to Claridge's. He could tell from Anne's look that Harvey had given him the seal of parental approval.

'Good evening, sir. Good evening, my lord.'

'Hi there, Albert. Could you fix some coffee and a bottle of Rémy Martin to be sent up to my suite?'

'Right away, sir.'

James had never seen the Royal Suite before. Off the small entrance room, there is a master bedroom on the right and a sitting-room on the left. Harvey took them straight to the sitting-room.

'Children, you are about to see your wedding present.'

He threw the door open in dramatic style and there on the far wall, facing them, was the Van Gogh. They both stared, quite unable to speak.

'That's exactly how it left me,' said Harvey. 'Speechless.'

'Daddy.' Anne swallowed. 'A Van Gogh. But you've always wanted a Van Gogh. You've dreamed of possessing one for years. I couldn't possibly deprive you of it now, and anyway I couldn't think of having anything as valuable as that in my house. Think of the security risk – we don't have the protection you have.' Anne stammered on. 'We couldn't let you sacrifice the pride of your collection, could we, James?'

'Absolutely not,' said James with great feeling. 'I wouldn't have a moment's peace with that on the premises.'

'Keep the painting in Boston, Daddy, in a setting worthy of it.'

'But I thought you'd love the idea, Rosalie.'

'I do, I do, Daddy, I just don't want the responsibility, and in any case Mother must have the chance to enjoy it too. You can always leave it to James and me if you like.'

'What a great idea, Rosalie. That way we can both enjoy the painting. Now I shall have to think of another wedding present. She nearly got the better of me then, James, and she hasn't done that in twenty-four years.'

'Well, I've managed it two or three times lately, Daddy, and I'm still hoping I shall do it once more.'

Harvey ignored Anne's remark and went on talking.

'That's the King George and Elizabeth trophy,' he said, pointing to a magnificent bronze sculpture of a horse and jockey with his hoop and quartered cap studded with diamonds. 'The race is so important they present a new trophy every year – so it's mine for life.'

James was thankful that the trophy at least was genuine.

The coffee and brandy arrived and they settled down to discuss the wedding in detail.

'Now, Rosalie, you must fly over to Lincoln next week and help your mother with the arrangements, otherwise she'll panic and nothing will get done. And, James, you let me know how many people you'll have coming over and I'll put them up at the Ritz. The wedding will be in Trinity Church, Copley Square, and we'll have a real English-style reception afterwards back in my home in Lincoln. Does all that make sense, James?'

'Sounds wonderful. You're a very well organised man, Harvey.'

'Always have been, James. Find it pays in the long run. Now, you and Rosalie must get the details sewn up before she comes over next week; you may not have realised it, but I'm returning to America tomorrow.'

Page 38A of the blue dossier, thought James.

James and Anne spent another hour chatting

about the wedding arrangements and left Harvey just before midnight.

'I'll see you first thing in the morning, Daddy.'

'Goodnight, sir.'

James shook hands and left.

'I told you he was super.'

'He's a fine young man and your mother will be very pleased.'

James said nothing to Anne in the lift on the way down because two other men stood beside them in silence, also intent on reaching the ground floor. But once they were in the Alfa Romeo he took Anne by the scruff of her neck, threw her across his legs, and spanked her so hard that she didn't know whether to laugh or cry.

'What's that for?'

'Just in case you ever forget after we're married who's the head of this household.'

'You male chauvinist pig, I was only trying to help.'

James drove at furious speed to Anne's flat.

'What about all your so-called background – "My parents live in Washington and Daddy's in the Diplomatic Corps",' James mimicked. 'Some diplomat.'

'I know, darling, but I had to think of something once I'd realised who it was you were up against.'

'What in hell's name am I going to tell the others?'

'Nothing. You invite them to the wedding, explain that my mother is American and that's why we're getting married in Boston. I'd give the earth to see their faces when they discover who your father-in-law is. In any case, you still have a plan to think of and you can't possibly let them down.'

'But the circumstances have changed.'

'No, they haven't. The truth of the matter is that they've all succeeded and you've failed, so you be sure you think of a plan by the time you reach America.'

'It's obvious now that we wouldn't have succeeded without your help.'

'Nonsense, darling. I had nothing to do with Jean-Pierre's scheme. I just added some background colour here and there – Promise you'll never spank me again?'

'Certainly I will, every time I think of that picture, but now, darling . . .'

'James, you're a sex maniac.'

'I know, darling. How do you think we Brigsleys have reared tribes of little lords for generations?'

Anne left James early the next morning to spend some time with her father, and they both saw him off at the airport on the midday flight to Boston. Anne could not resist asking in the car on the way back what James had decided to tell the others. She could get no response other than:

'Wait and see. I'm not having it changed behind my back. I'm only too glad you're off to America on Monday.'

18

Monday was a double hell for James. First, he had to see Anne off on the morning TWA flight for Boston, and then he had to spend the rest of the day preparing for the Team meeting in the evening. The other three had now completed their operations and would be waiting to hear what he had come up with. It was twice as hard now he knew that the victim was to be his father-in-law, but he realised that Anne was right and he could not put that forward as an excuse. Nevertheless, he still had to relieve Harvey of $250,000. To think he could have done it with one sentence at Oxford. That was another thing he could not tell the rest of the Team.

As Oxford had been Stephen's victory, the Team dinner was at Magdalen College and James travelled out of London just after the rush hour, past the White City Stadium and on down the M40 to Oxford.

'You're always last, James,' said Stephen.

'Sorry, I've been up to my eyes . . .'

'Preparing a good plan, I hope,' said Jean-Pierre.

James didn't answer. How well they all knew each other now, he thought. In twelve weeks James felt he had come to know more about these three men than any of the so-called friends he'd known for twenty years. For the first time he understood why his father continually referred back to friendships formed during the war with men he normally would never have met. He began to realise how much he was going to miss Stephen when he returned to America. Success was, in fact, going to split them up.

James would have been the last to go through the agony of another Prospecta Oil, but it had certainly had its compensations.

Stephen could never treat any occasion as a celebration, and as soon as the servants had brought in the first course and left, he banged the table with a spoon and declared that the meeting was in progress.

'Make me a promise,' said Jean-Pierre.

'What's that?' asked Stephen.

'When we have every last penny back, I can sit at the top of the table and you won't speak until you're spoken to.'

'Agreed,' said Stephen, 'but not until we do have every last penny. The position at the moment is that we've received $777,560. Expenses on this operation have totalled $5,178, making a grand total of $27,661.24. Therefore, Metcalfe still owes us $250,101.24.'

Stephen handed round a copy of the current balance sheet.

'These sheets are to be added to your own folders as pages 63C. Any questions?'

'Yes, why were the expenses so high for this operation?' asked Robin.

'Well, over and above the obvious things,' said Stephen, 'the truth is that we've been hit by the floating exchange rate of sterling against the dollar. At the beginning of this operation you could get $2.44 to the pound. This morning I could only get $2.32. I'm spending in pounds but charging Metcalfe in dollars at the going rate.'

'Not going to let him off with one penny, are you?' said James.

'Not one penny. Now, before we go on I should like to place on record . . .'

'This gets more like a meeting of the House of Commons every time,' said Jean-Pierre.

'Stop croaking, frog,' said Robin.

'Listen, you Harley Street pimp.'

Uproar broke out. The college scouts, who had seen some rowdy gatherings in their time, wondered if they would have to be called in to help before the evening was completed.

'Quiet,' the sharp, senatorial voice of Stephen brought them all back to order. 'I know you're in high spirits, but we still have to get $250,101.24.'

'We must on no account forget the 24 cents, Stephen.'

'You weren't as noisy the first time you had dinner here, Jean-Pierre:

The man that once did sell the lion's skin
While the beast liv'd, was killed with hunting him.'

The table was silent.

'Harvey still owes the Team money and it'll be just as hard to acquire the last quarter as it was with the first three-quarters. Before I hand over to James, I'd like to place on record that his performance at the Clarendon was nothing less than brilliant.'

Robin and Jean-Pierre banged the table in appreciation and agreement.

'Now, James, we're all ears.'

Once again the room fell into silence.

'My plan is nearly complete,' began James.

The others looked disbelieving.

'But I have something to tell you, which I hope will allow me a short respite before we carry it out.'

'You're going to get married.'

'Quite right, Jean-Pierre, as usual.'

'I could tell the moment you walked in. When do we meet her, James?'

'Not until it's too late for her to change her mind, Jean-Pierre.'

Stephen consulted his diary.

'How much reprieve are you asking for?'

'Well, Anne and I are getting married on August 3rd, in Boston. Anne's mother is American,' explained James, 'and although Anne lives in England, it would please her mother if she was married at home. Then there'll be the honeymoon and after that we anticipate returning to England on August 25th. My plan for Mr Metcalfe ought to be carried out on September 15th, the closing day of the Stock Exchange account.'

'I'm sure that's acceptable, James. All agreed?'

Robin and Jean-Pierre nodded.

James launched into his plan.

'I shall require a telex and seven telephones. They'll need to be installed in my flat. Jean-Pierre will have to be in Paris at the Bourse, Stephen in Chicago on the commodity market and Robin in London at Lloyds. I will present a full blue dossier as soon as I return from my honeymoon.'

They were all struck dumb with admiration and James paused for dramatic effect.

'Very good, James,' said Stephen. 'We'll await the details with interest. What further instructions do you have?'

'First, Stephen, you must know the opening and closing price of gold in Johannesburg, Zürich, New York and London each day for the next month. Jean-Pierre, you must know the price of the Deutschmark, the French franc and the pound against the dollar every day during the same period, and Robin must master a telex machine and PBX 8-line switchboard by September 2nd. You must be as competent as an international operator.'

'Always get the easy jobs, Robin, don't you?' said Jean-Pierre.

'You can . . .'

'Shut up, both of you,' said James.

Their faces registered surprise and respect.

'I've made notes for all of you to work on.'

James handed two typewritten sheets to each member of the Team.

'You add these to your dossiers as pages 74 and 75 and they should keep you occupied for at least a month. Finally, you're all invited to the wedding of Miss Anne Summerton to James Brigsley. I shan't bother issuing you with formal invitations at such short notice, but I've reserved seats for us on a 747 on the afternoon of August 2nd and we're all booked in at the Ritz in Boston for the night. I hope you'll honour me by being ushers.'

Even James was impressed by his own efficiency. The others received the plane tickets and instructions with astonishment.

'We'll meet at the airport at 3 pm and during the flight I shall test you on your dossier notes.'

'Yes, sir,' said Jean-Pierre.

'Your test, Jean-Pierre, will be in both French and English, as you'll be required to converse in two languages over a trans-Atlantic telephone, and appear expert on foreign currency exchange.'

There were no more jokes about James that evening, and as he travelled back up the motorway he felt a new man. Not only had he been the star of the Oxford plan; now he had the other three on the run. He would come out on top and do his old pa yet.

19

For a change James was the first to arrive at a meeting and the others joined him at Heathrow. He had gained the upper hand and was determined not to lose it. Robin arrived last, clutching an armful of newspapers.

'We're only going to be away for two days,' said Stephen.

'I know, but I always miss the English papers, so I've brought enough for tomorrow as well.'

Jean-Pierre threw his arms up in Gallic despair.

They checked their luggage through the No. 3 Terminal and boarded the British Airways 747 flight to Logan International Airport.

'It's more like a football ground,' said Robin, stepping for the first time inside a jumbo jet.

'It holds 350 people. About the size of the crowds most of your English clubs deserve,' said Jean-Pierre.

'Cut it out,' said James sternly, not realising that they were both nervous passengers and were only trying to relieve the tension. Later, during take-off, they both pretended to read, but as soon as the plane reached 30,000 feet and the little white light that says 'fasten seat-belts' switched off, they were back in top form.

The Team chewed its way stolidly through a plastic dinner of cold chicken and Algerian red wine.

'I do hope, James,' said Jean-Pierre, 'that your father-in-law will feed us a little better.'

After the meal James allowed them to watch the film, but insisted that as soon as it was over they must prepare to be tested one by one. Robin and Jean-Pierre moved back fifteen rows to watch *The Sting*. Stephen stayed in his seat to be grilled by James.

James handed Stephen a typewritten sheet of forty questions on the price of gold all over the world and the market movements during the past four weeks. Stephen completed it in twenty-two minutes, and it came as no surprise to James to find that every answer was correct: Stephen had always been the backbone of the Team, and it was his logical brain that had really defeated Harvey Metcalfe.

Stephen and James dozed intermittently until Robin and Jean-Pierre returned, when they were given their forty questions. Robin took thirty minutes over his and scored 38 out of 40. Jean-Pierre took twenty-seven minutes and scored 37.

'Stephen got 40 out of 40,' said James.

'He would,' said Jean-Pierre.

Robin looked a little sheepish.

'And so will you by September 2nd. Understood?'

They both nodded.

'Have you seen *The Sting*?' asked Robin,

'No,' replied Stephen. 'I rarely go to the cinema.'

'They're not in our league. One big operation, and they don't even keep the money.'

'Go to sleep, Robin.'

The meal, the film and James's quizzes had taken up most of the six-hour flight and they all nodded off in the last hour, to be woken suddenly by:

'This is your captain speaking. We are approaching Logan International Airport and our flight is running twenty minutes late. We expect to land at 7.15 in approximately ten minutes. We hope you have enjoyed your flight and will travel again with British Airways.'

Customs took a little longer than usual as they all three had brought presents for the wedding and did not want James to know what they were. They had considerable trouble in explaining to the customs officer why one of the two Piaget watches had inscribed on the back: 'Part of the illicit profits from Prospecta Oil – the three who had plans.'

When they finally escaped the customs official, they found Anne standing at the entrance by a large Cadillac waiting to chauffeur them to the hotel.

'Now we know why it took you so long to come up with something: you were genuinely distracted. Congratulations, James, you're entirely forgiven,' said Jean-Pierre, and threw his arms round Anne as only a Frenchman could. Robin introduced himself and kissed her gently on the cheek. Stephen shook hands with her rather formally. They bustled into the car, Jean-Pierre sitting next to Anne.

'Miss Summerton,' stuttered Stephen.

'Do call me Anne.'

'Will the reception be at the hotel?'

'No,' replied Anne, 'at my parents' house, but there'll be a car to pick you up and take you there after the wedding. Your only responsibility is to see that James gets to the church by 3.30. Other than that you have nothing to worry about. While I think of it, James, your father and mother arrived yesterday and they're staying with my parents. We thought it might not be a good idea for you to spend this evening at home because Mother's flapping about everything.'

'Anything you say, darling.'

'If you should change your mind between now and tomorrow,' said Jean-Pierre, 'I find myself available. I may not be blessed with noble blood, but there are one or two compensations we French can always offer.'

Anne smiled to herself. 'You're a little late, Jean-Pierre. In any case, I don't like beards.'

'But I only . . .' began Jean-Pierre.

The others glared at him.

At the hotel they left Anne and James alone while they went to unpack.

'Do they know, darling?'

'They haven't the slightest idea,' replied James. 'They're going to get the surprise of their life tomorrow.'

'Is your plan ready?'

'Wait and see.'

'Well, I have one,' said Anne. 'When's yours scheduled for?'

'September 13th.'

'I win then – mine's for tomorrow.'

'What, you weren't meant to . . .'

'Don't worry. You just concentrate on getting married . . . to me.'

'Can't we go somewhere?'

'No, you terrible man. You can wait until tomorrow.'

'I do love you.'

'Go to bed, you silly thing. I love you too, but I must go home, otherwise nothing'll be ready.'

James took the lift to the seventh floor and joined the others for coffee.

'Anyone for blackjack?'

'Not with you, you pirate,' said Robin. 'You've been tutored by the biggest crook alive.'

The Team were in top form and looking forward to the wedding. In spite of the transatlantic time dislocation they didn't depart for their separate rooms until well after midnight. Even then, James lay awake for some time, turning over the same question in his mind:

'I wonder what's she's up to this time?'

20

Boston in August is as beautiful a city as any in America, and the Team enjoyed a large breakfast in James's room.

'I don't think he looks up to it,' said Jean-Pierre. 'You're the captain of the Team, Stephen. I volunteer to take his place.'

'It'll cost you $250,000.'

'Agreed,' said Jean-Pierre.

'You don't have $250,000,' said Stephen. 'You have $187,474.69, being one quarter of what's been raised so far, so my decision is that James must be the bridegroom.'

'It's an Anglo-Saxon plot,' said Jean-Pierre, 'and when James has successfully completed his plan and we have the full amount, I shall re-open negotiations.'

They sat talking and laughing for a long time over the toast and coffee. Stephen regarded them fondly, regretting how rarely they would meet once, *if*, he corrected himself sternly, James's operation were accomplished successfully. If Harvey Metcalfe had ever had a team like this on his side instead of against him, he would have been the richest man in the world.

'You're dreaming, Stephen.'

'Yes, I'm sorry. I mustn't forget that Anne has put me in charge.'

'Here we go again,' said Jean-Pierre. 'What time shall we report, Professor?'

'One hour from now, fully dressed to inspect James and take him to the church. Jean-Pierre, you will go and buy four carnations – three red ones and one white. Robin, you will arrange for the taxi and I shall take care of James.'

Robin and Jean-Pierre left, singing the *Marseillaise* lustily in two different keys. James and Stephen watched them depart.

'How are you feeling, James?'

'Great. I'm only sorry that I didn't complete my plan before today.'

'Doesn't matter at all. September 13th will be quite early enough. In any case, the break will do us no harm.'

'We'd never have managed it without you. You know that, don't you, Stephen? We'd all be facing ruin and I wouldn't even have met Anne. We all owe you so much.'

Stephen stared fixedly out of the window, unable to reply.

*

'Three red and one white,' said Jean-Pierre, 'as instructed, and I presume the white one is for me.'

'Pin it on James. Not behind his ear, Jean-Pierre.'

'You look fantastic, but I still fail to see what the lady sees in you,' said Jean-Pierre. Although the four of them were ready to leave, they still had half an hour to kill before the taxi was due. Jean-Pierre opened a bottle of champagne and they toasted James's health, the Team's health, Her Majesty The Queen, the President of the United States, and finally, with simulated reluctance, the President of France. Having finished the bottle, Stephen thought it wise for them to leave immediately and dragged the other three down to the waiting taxi.

'Keep smiling, James. We're with you.'

And they bundled him into the back.

The taxi took only a few minutes to reach Trinity Church, Copley Square, and the driver was not unhappy to be rid of the four of them.

'Three-fifteen pm. Anne will be very pleased with me,' said Stephen.

He escorted the bridegroom to the front pew on the right-hand side of the church, while Jean-Pierre made eyes at the prettiest of the girls. Robin helped hand out the wedding sheets while one thousand overdressed guests waited for the bride.

Stephen had just come to Robin's aid on the steps of the church and Jean-Pierre had joined them, suggesting they took their seats, when the Rolls Royce arrived. They were riveted to the steps by the beauty of Anne in her Balenciaga wedding gown. Her father stepped out behind her. She took his arm and proceeded to climb the steps.

The three stood motionless, like sheep in the stare of a python.

'The bastard.'

'Who's been conning who?'

'She must have known all along.'

Harvey beamed vaguely at them as he walked past with Anne on his arm. They proceeded down the aisle.

'Good God,' thought Stephen. 'He didn't recognise any of us.'

They took their places at the back of the church, out of earshot of the vast congregation. The organist stopped playing when Anne reached the altar.

'Harvey can't know,' said Stephen.

'How do you work that out?' asked Jean-Pierre.

'Because James would never have put us through this unless he'd passed the test himself at some earlier date.'

'Good thinking,' whispered Robin.

'I require and charge you both, as ye will answer at the dreadful day of judgment when the secrets of all hearts shall be disclosed . . .'

'I'd like to know one or two secrets right now,' said Jean-Pierre. 'To start with, how long has she known?'

'James Clarence Spencer, wilt thou have this

woman to thy wedded wife, to live together after God's ordinance in the Holy estate of Matrimony? Wilt thou love her, comfort her, honour and keep her, in sickness and in health and, forsaking all other, keep thee only unto her, so long as ye both shall live?'

'I will.'

'Rosalie Arlene, wilt thou have this man to thy wedded husband, to live . . .'

'I think,' said Stephen, 'we can be sure that she's a fully fledged member of the Team; otherwise we could never have succeeded at Monte Carlo or Oxford.'

'. . . so long as ye both shall live?'

'I will.'

'Who giveth this woman to be married to this man?'

Harvey bustled forward and took Anne's hand and gave it to the priest.

'I, James Clarence Spencer, take thee, Rosalie Arlene, to my wedded wife . . .'

'And what's more, why should he recognise us when he's only seen each of us once, and not as we really are,' continued Stephen.

'And thereto I plight thee my troth.'

'I, Rosalie Arlene, take thee, James Clarence Spencer, to my wedded husband . . .'

'But he must have a chance of working it out if we hang around,' said Robin.

'Not necessarily,' said Stephen. 'No need to panic. Our secret has always been to catch him off home ground.'

'But now he's on home ground,' said Jean-Pierre.

'No, he isn't. It's his daughter's wedding day and it's totally strange to the man. Naturally, we avoid him at the reception, but we don't make it too obvious.'

'You'll have to hold my hand,' said Robin.

'I will,' volunteered Jean-Pierre.

'Just remember to act naturally.'

'. . . and thereto I give thee my troth.'

Anne was quiet and shy, her voice only just reaching the astonished three at the back. James's was clear and firm:

'With this ring I thee wed, with my body I thee worship, and with all my worldly goods I thee endow . . .'

'And with some of ours too,' said Jean-Pierre.

'In the name of the Father, and of the Son and of the Holy Spirit. Amen.'

'Let us pray,' intoned the priest.

'I know what I'm going to pray,' said Robin. 'To be delivered out of the power of our enemy and from the hands of all that hate us.'

'O Eternal God, Creator and Preserver of all mankind . . .'

'We're near the end now,' said Stephen.

'An unfortunate turn of phrase,' offered Robin.

'Silence,' said Jean-Pierre. 'I agree with Stephen. We've got the measure of Metcalfe, just relax.'

'Those whom God hath joined together let no man put asunder.'

Jean-Pierre continued mumbling to himself, but it didn't sound like a prayer.

The blast of Handel's Wedding March from the organ brought them all back to the occasion. The ceremony was over and Lord and Lady Brigsley walked down the aisle watched by two thousand smiling eyes. Stephen looked amused, Jean-Pierre envious, and Robin nervous. James smiled beatifically as he passed them.

After a ten-minute session for the photographers on the steps of the church, the Rolls Royce carried the newly married couple back to the Metcalfes' house in Lincoln. Harvey and the Countess of Louth took the second car, and the Earl and Arlene, Anne's mother, took the third. Stephen, Robin and Jean-Pierre followed some twenty minutes later, still arguing the pros and cons of bearding the lion in his own den.

Harvey Metcalfe's Georgian house was magnificent, with an oriental garden leading down to a lake, great beds of roses and in the conservatory his pride and joy, his collection of rare orchids.

'I never thought I'd see this,' said Jean-Pierre.

'Nor me,' said Robin, 'and now that I have, I'm not too happy.'

'Let's run the gauntlet,' said Stephen. 'I suggest that we join the receiving line at well-separated intervals. I'll go first. Robin, you come second, at least twenty places behind, and Jean-Pierre, you come third, at least twenty places behind Robin, and *act naturally*. We're just friends of James's from England. Now, when you take your places in the queue, listen to the conversation. Try and find someone who's a close friend of Harvey's and jump immediately in front of them. When it comes to your turn to shake hands, Harvey's eyes will already be on the next person because he won't know you and will want to talk to them. That way we should escape.'

'Brilliant, Professor,' said Jean-Pierre.

The queue seemed interminably long. A thousand people shuffled past the outstretched hands of Mr and Mrs Metcalfe, the Earl and Countess of Louth, and Anne and James. Stephen eventually made it and passed with flying colours.

'So glad you could come,' said Anne.

Stephen did not reply.

'Good to see you, Stephen.'

'We all admire your plan, James.'

Stephen slipped into the main ballroom and hid behind a pillar on the other side of the room, as far as he could be from the multi-storey wedding cake in the centre.

Robin was next and avoided looking Harvey in the eyes.

'How kind of you to come all this way,' said Anne.

Robin mumbled something under his breath.

'Hope you've enjoyed yourself today, Robin?'

James was obviously having the time of his life. After being put through it in the same way by Anne, he was relishing the Team's discomfiture.

'You're a bastard, James.'

'Not too loud, old fellow. My mother and father might hear you.'

Robin slipped through to the ballroom and, after a search behind all the pillars, found Stephen.

'Did you get through all right?'

'I think so, but I don't want to see him ever again. What time is the plane back?'

'Eight pm. Now don't panic. Keep your eye out for Jean-Pierre.'

'Bloody good thing he kept his beard,' said Robin.

Jean-Pierre shook hands with Harvey, who was already intent on the next guest as Jean-Pierre had, by shameless queue-barging, managed to secure a place in front of a Boston banker who was obviously a close friend of Harvey's.

'Good to see you, Marvin.'

Jean-Pierre had escaped. He kissed Anne on both cheeks, whispered in her ear, 'Game, set and match to James,' and went off in search of Stephen and Robin. He forgot his original instructions when he found himself face to face with the chief bridesmaid.

'Did you enjoy the wedding?' she asked.

'Of course. I always judge weddings by the bridesmaids, not the bride.'

She blushed with pleasure.

'This must have cost a fortune,' she continued.

'Yes, my dear, and I know whose,' said Jean-Pierre, slipping his arm around her waist.

Four hands grabbed a protesting Jean-Pierre and unceremoniously dragged him behind the pillar.

'For God's sake, Jean-Pierre. She's not a day over seventeen. We don't want to go to jail for rape of a juvenile as well as theft. Drink this and behave yourself.' Robin thrust a glass of champagne into his hand.

The champagne flowed and even Stephen had a little too much. They were all clinging to their pillar for support by the time the toast-master called for silence.

'My lords, ladies and gentlemen. Pray silence for the Viscount Brigsley, the bridegroom.'

James made an impressive speech. The actor in him took over and the Americans adored it. Even his father had a look of admiration on his face. The toast-master then introduced Harvey, who spoke long and loud. He cracked his favourite joke about marrying off his daughter to Prince Charles, at which the assembled guests roared heartily as they always do at weddings, even for the weakest joke. He ended by calling the toast for the bride and groom.

When the applause had died down, and the hubbub of chatter had struck up again, Harvey took an envelope from his pocket and kissed his daughter on the cheek.

'Rosalie, here's a little wedding present for you, to

make up for letting me keep the Van Gogh. I know you'll put it to good use.'

Harvey passed her the white envelope. Inside there was a cheque for $250,000. Anne kissed her father with genuine affection.

'Thank you, Daddy, I promise you James and I will use it wisely.'

She hurried off in pursuit of James, whom she found besieged by a group of American matrons:

'Is it true you're related to the Queen . . .?'

'I never met a real live lord . . .'

'I do hope you'll invite us over to see your castle . . . ?'

'There are no castles in the King's Road,' said James relieved to be rescued by Anne.

'Darling, can you spare me a minute?'

James excused himself and followed Anne, but they found it almost impossible to escape the crowd.

'Look,' she said. 'Quickly.'

James took the cheque.

'Good God – $250,000.'

'You know what I'm going to do with it, don't you?'

'Yes, darling.'

Anne hunted for Stephen, Robin and Jean-Pierre, which was not an easy task as they were still hidden behind a pillar in the far corner. She was eventually guided to the spot by the subdued but spirited rendering of 'Who Wants to be a Millionaire?' issuing from behind it.

'Can you lend me a pen, Stephen?'

Three pens shot out for her use.

She took the cheque from the middle of her bouquet and wrote on its back, 'Rosalie Brigsley – pay Stephen Bradley'. She handed it to him.

'Yours, I believe.'

The three of them stared at the cheque. She was gone before they could even comment.

'What a girl our James has gone and married,' said Jean-Pierre.

'You're drunk, you frog,' said Robin.

'How dare you, sir, suggest that a Frenchman could get drunk on champagne. I demand satisfaction. Choose your weapons.'

'Champagne corks.'

'Quiet,' said Stephen. 'You'll give yourselves away.'

'Well now, tell me, Professor, what's the latest financial position?'

'I'm just working it out now,' said Stephen.

'What?' said Robin and Jean-Pierre together, but they were too happy to argue.

'He still owes us $101 and 24 cents.'

'DISGRACEFUL,' said Jean-Pierre. 'Burn the place down.'

Anne and James left to change, while Stephen, Robin and Jean-Pierre forced down some more champagne. The toast-master announced that the bride and groom would be leaving in approximately fifteen minutes and requested the guests to gather in the main hall and courtyard.

'Come on, we must watch them go,' said Stephen. The drink had given them new confidence and they took their places near the car.

It was Stephen who heard Harvey say, 'God damn it. Do I have to think of everything?' and watched him look round his guests until his eyes fell on the trio. Stephen's legs turned to jelly as Harvey's finger beckoned him.

'Hey, you, weren't you an usher?'

'Yes, sir.'

'Rosalie is going to leave at any moment and there are no flowers for her. God knows what's happened to them, but there are no flowers. Grab a car. There's a florist half a mile down the road, but hurry.'

'Yes, sir.'

'Say, don't I know you from somewhere?'

'Yes, sir, I mean, no sir. I'll go and get the flowers.'

Stephen turned and fled. Robin and Jean-Pierre, who had been watching horrified, thinking that Harvey had at last rumbled them, ran after him. When he reached the back of the house, Stephen came to a halt and stared at the most beautiful bed of roses. Robin and Jean-Pierre shot straight past him, stopped, turned round and staggered back.

'What the hell are you up to – picking flowers for your own funeral?'

'It's only Metcalfe's wishes. Somebody forgot the flowers for Anne and I have five minutes to get them, so start picking.

'*Mes enfants*, do you see what I see?'

The others looked up. Jean-Pierre was staring rapturously at the conservatory.

Stephen rushed back to the front of the house, the prize orchids in his arms, followed by Robin and Jean-Pierre. He was just in time to pass them over to Harvey before James and Anne came out of the house.

'Magnificent. They're my favourite flowers. How much were they?'

'$100,' replied Stephen, without thinking.

Harvey handed over two $50 bills. Stephen retreated sweating, to join Robin and Jean-Pierre.

James and Anne fought their way through the crowd. No man in the gathering could take his eyes off her.

'Oh Daddy, orchids, how beautiful.' Anne kissed Harvey. 'You've made this the most wonderful day in my life . . .'

The Rolls Royce moved slowly down the drive away from the large crowd on its way to the airport, where James and Anne were to catch the flight to San Francisco, their first stop on the way to Hawaii. As the car glided round the house, Anne stared at the empty conservatory and then at the flowers in her arms. James did not notice. He was thinking of other things.

'Do you think they'll ever forgive me?' he said.

'I'm sure they'll find a way, darling. But do let me into a secret. Did you really have a plan?'

'I knew you wouldn't be able to resist asking me that, and the truth is . . .'

The car purred effortlessly along the highway and only the chauffeur heard his reply.

Stephen, Robin and Jean-Pierre watched the guests dispersing, most of them saying their goodbyes to the Metcalfes.

'Don't let's risk it,' said Robin.

'Agreed,' said Stephen.

'Let's invite him out to dinner,' said Jean-Pierre.

The other two grabbed him and threw him into a taxi.

'What's that you have under your morning coat, Jean-Pierre?'

'Two bottles of Krug *dix-neuf cent soixante-quatre.* It seemed such a shame to leave them there on their own. I thought they might get lonely.'

Stephen instructed the driver to take them back to the hotel.

'What a wedding. Do you think James ever had a plan?' asked Robin.

'I don't know, but if he has it will only have to bring in $1.24.'

'We should have retrieved the money he made from his win on Rosalie at Ascot,' mused Jean-Pierre.

After packing and signing out of the hotel, they took another taxi to Logan International Airport and, with considerable help from the British Airways staff, managed to board the plane.

'Damn,' said Stephen. 'I wish we hadn't left without the $1.24.'

21

ONCE ON BOARD, they drank the champagne Jean-Pierre had captured at the wedding. Even Stephen seemed content, although he did occasionally revert to the theme of the missing $1.24.

'How much do you imagine this champagne cost?' teased Jean-Pierre.

'That's not the point. Not a penny more, not a penny less.'

Jean-Pierre decided he would never understand academics.

'Don't worry, Stephen. I've every confidence that James's plan will bring in $1.24.'

Stephen would have laughed, but it gave him a headache.

'To think that girl knew everything.'

On arrival at Heathrow, they had little trouble in clearing customs. The purpose of the trip had never been to bring back gifts. Robin made a detour to W. H. Smiths and picked up *The Times* and the *Evening*

Standard. Jean-Pierre bargained with a taxi-driver about the fare to central London.

'We're not some bloody Americans who don't know the rate or the route and can be easily fleeced,' he was saying, still not yet sober.

The taxi-driver grumbled to himself as he nosed his black Austin towards the motorway. It was not going to be his day.

Robin read the papers happily, one of those rare people who could read in a moving car. Stephen and Jean-Pierre satisfied themselves with watching the passing traffic.

'Jesus Christ.'

Stephen and Jean-Pierre were startled. They had rarely heard Robin swear. It seemed out of character.

'God Almighty.'

This was too much for them, but before they could enquire, he began to read out loud:

'"BP announced a strike in the North Sea which is likely to produce 200,000 barrels of oil a day. The strike is described by their Chairman, Sir Eric Drake, as a major find. The British Petroleum Forties Field is one mile from the so far unexplored Prospecta Oil field and rumours of a bid by BP have sent Prospecta Oil shares to a record high of $12.25 at the close of business."'

'Nom de Dieu,' said Jean-Pierre. 'What do we do now?'

'Oh well,' said Stephen. 'I suppose we'll have to work out a plan for how to give it all back.'

HONOUR AMONG THIEVES

To Geoffrey and Babs

PART ONE

'When *in the Course of human events. . .'*

1

NEW YORK,
February 15th 1993

ANTONIO CAVALLI stared intently at the Arab, who he considered looked far too young to be a Deputy Ambassador.

'One hundred million dollars,' Cavalli said, pronouncing each word slowly and deliberately, giving them almost reverential respect.

Hamid Al Obaydi flicked a worry bead across the top of his well-manicured thumb, making a click that was beginning to irritate Cavalli.

'One hundred million is quite acceptable,' the Deputy Ambassador replied in a clipped English accent.

Cavalli nodded. The only thing that worried him about the deal was that Al Obaydi had made no attempt to bargain, especially as the figure the American had proposed was double that which he had expected to get. Cavalli had learned from painful experience not to trust anyone who didn't bargain. It inevitably meant that they had no intention of paying in the first place.

'If the figure is agreed,' he said, 'all that is left to discuss is how and when the payments will be made.'

The Deputy Ambassador flicked another worry bead before he nodded.

'Ten million dollars to be paid in cash immediately,' said Cavalli, 'the remaining ninety million to be deposited in a Swiss bank account as soon as the contract has been carried out.'

'But what do I get for my first ten million?' asked the Deputy Ambassador, looking fixedly at the man whose origins were as hard to hide as his own.

'Nothing,' replied Cavalli, although he acknowledged that the Arab had every right to ask. After all, if Cavalli didn't honour his side of the bargain, the Deputy Ambassador had far more to lose than just his government's money.

Al Obaydi moved another worry bead, aware that he had little choice – it had taken him two years just to get an interview with Antonio Cavalli. Meanwhile, President Clinton had settled into the White House, while his own leader was growing more and more impatient for revenge. If he didn't accept Cavalli's terms, Al Obaydi knew that the chances of finding anyone else capable of carrying out the task before July the fourth were about as promising as zero coming up on a roulette wheel with only one spin left.

Cavalli looked up at the vast portrait that dominated the wall behind the Deputy Ambassador's desk. His first contact with Al Obaydi had been only days after the war had been concluded. At the time the American had refused to deal with the Arab, as few people were convinced that the Deputy Ambassador's leader would still be alive by the time a preliminary meeting could be arranged.

As the months passed, however, it began to look to Cavalli as if his potential client might survive longer than President Bush. So an exploratory meeting was agreed.

The venue selected was the Deputy Ambassador's office in New York, on East 79th Street. Despite being a little too public for Cavalli's taste, it had the virtue of proving the credentials of the party claiming to be willing to invest one hundred million dollars in such a daring enterprise.

'How would you expect the first ten million to be paid?' enquired Al Obaydi, as if he were asking a real estate agent about a down-payment on a small house on the wrong side of the Brooklyn Bridge.

'The entire amount must be handed over in used, unmarked hundred-dollar bills and deposited with our bankers in Newark, New Jersey,' said the American, his eyes narrowing. 'And Mr Obaydi,' Cavalli added, 'I don't have to remind you that we have machines that can verify . . .'

'You need have no anxiety about us keeping to our side of the bargain,' interrupted Al Obaydi. 'The money is, as your Western cliché suggests, a mere drop in the ocean. The only concern I have is whether you are capable of delivering your part of the agreement.'

'You wouldn't have pressed so hard for this meeting if you doubted we were the right people for the job,' retorted Cavalli. 'But can I be as confident about you putting together such a large amount of cash at such short notice?'

'It may interest you to know, Mr Cavalli,' replied the Deputy Ambassador, 'that the money is already lodged in a safe in the basement of the United Nations building. After all, no one would expect to find such a vast sum deposited in the vaults of a bankrupt body.'

The smile that remained on Al Obaydi's face indicated that the Arab was pleased with his little witticism, despite the fact that Cavalli's lips hadn't moved.

'The ten million will be delivered to your bank by midday tomorrow,' continued Al Obaydi as he rose from the table to indicate that, as far he was concerned, the meeting was concluded. The Deputy Ambassador stretched out his hand and his visitor reluctantly shook it.

Cavalli glanced up once again at the portrait of Saddam Hussein, turned, and quickly left.

When Scott Bradley entered the room there was a hush of expectancy.

He placed his notes on the table in front of him, allowing his eyes to sweep around the lecture hall. The room was packed with eager young students holding pens and pencils poised above yellow legal pads.

'My name is Scott Bradley,' said the youngest Professor in the Law School, 'and this is to be the first of fourteen lectures on Constitutional Law.' Seventy-four faces stared down at the tall, somewhat dishevelled man who obviously hadn't noticed that the top button of his shirt was missing and who couldn't have made up his mind which side to part his hair that morning.

'I'd like to begin this first lecture with a personal statement,' he announced. Some of the pens and pencils were laid to rest. 'There are many reasons to practise law in this country,' he began, 'but only one which is worthy of you, and certainly only one that interests me. It applies to every facet of the law that you might be interested in pursuing, and it has never been better expressed than in the engrossed parchment of The Unanimous Declaration of the Thirteen United States of America.

' "We hold these truths to be self-evident, that all men are created equal, that they are endowed by their Creator with certain inalienable Rights, that among these are Life, Liberty and the pursuit of Happiness." That one sentence is what distinguishes America from every other country on earth.

'In some aspects, our nation has progressed mightily

since 1776,' continued the Professor, still not having referred to his notes as he walked up and down tugging the lapels of his well-worn Harris tweed jacket, 'while in others we have moved rapidly backwards. Each of you in this hall can be part of the next generation of law makers or law breakers –' he paused, surveying the silent gathering, '– and you have been granted the greatest gift of all with which to help make that choice, a first-class mind. When my colleagues and I have finished with you, you can if you wish go out into the real world and ignore the Declaration of Independence as if it were worth no more than the parchment it was written on, outdated and irrelevant in this modern age. Or,' he continued, 'you may choose to benefit society by upholding the law. That is the course great lawyers take. Bad lawyers, and I do not mean stupid ones, are those who begin to bend the law, which, I submit, is only a step away from breaking it. To those of you in this class who wish to pursue such a course I must advise that I have nothing to teach you, because you are beyond learning. You are still free to attend my lectures, but "attending" is all you will be doing.'

The room was so silent that Scott looked up to check they hadn't all crept out. 'Not my words,' he continued as he stared at the intent faces, 'but those of Dean Thomas W. Swan, who lectured in this theatre for the first twenty-seven years of this century. I see no reason not to repeat his philosophy whenever I address an incoming class of the Yale Law School.'

The Professor opened the file in front of him for the first time. 'Logic,' he began, 'is the science and art of reasoning correctly. No more than common sense, I hear you say. And nothing so uncommon, Voltaire reminds us. But those who cry "common sense" are often the same people who are too lazy to train their minds.

'Oliver Wendell Holmes once wrote: "The life of the law has not been logic, it has been experience." ' The pens and pencils began to scratch furiously across the yellow pages, and continued to do so for the next fifty minutes.

When Scott Bradley had come to the end of his lecture, he closed his file, picked up his notes and marched quickly out of the room. He did not care to indulge himself by remaining for the sustained applause that had followed his opening lecture for the past ten years.

Hannah Kopec had been considered an outsider as well as a loner from the start, although the latter was often thought by those in authority to be an advantage.

Hannah had been told that her chances of qualifying were slim, but she had now come through the toughest part, the twelve-month physical, and although, despite her background, she had never killed anyone – six of the last eight applicants had – those in authority were now convinced she was capable of doing so. Hannah knew she could.

As the plane lifted off from Tel Aviv's Ben Gurion airport for Heathrow, Hannah pondered once again what had caused a twenty-five-year-old woman at the height of her career as a model to want to apply to join the Institute for Intelligence and Special Tasks – better known as Mossad – when she could have had her pick of a score of rich husbands in a dozen capitals.

Thirty-nine Scuds had landed on Tel Aviv and Haifa during the Gulf War. Thirteen people had been killed. Despite much wailing and beating of breasts, no revenge had been sought by the Israeli Government because of some tough political bargaining by James

Baker, who had assured them that the Coalition forces would finish the job. The American Secretary of State had failed to fulfil his promise. But then, as Hannah often reflected, Baker had not lost his entire family in one night.

The day she was discharged from hospital, Hannah had immediately applied to join Mossad. They had been dismissive of her request, assuming she would, in time, find that the wound healed. Hannah visited the Mossad headquarters every day for the next two weeks, by which time even they acknowledged that the wound remained open and, more importantly, was still festering.

In the third week they reluctantly allowed her to join a course for trainees, confident that she couldn't hope to survive for more than a few days, and would then return to her career as a model. They were wrong a second time. Revenge for Hannah Kopec was a far more potent drug than ambition. For the next twelve months she worked hours that began before the sun rose and ended long after it had set. She ate food that would have been rejected by a tramp and forgot what it was like to sleep on a mattress. They tried everything to break her, and they failed. To begin with the instructors had treated her gently, fooled by her graceful body and captivating looks, until one of them ended up with a broken leg. He simply didn't believe Hannah could move that fast. In the classroom the sharpness of her mind was less of a surprise to her instructors, though once again she gave them little time to rest.

But now they'd come onto her own ground.

Hannah had always, from a young age, taken it for granted that she could speak several languages. She had been born in Leningrad in 1968, and when fourteen years later her father died, her mother immediately applied for an emigration permit to Israel. The new liberal wind that was blowing across the Baltics made it possible for her request to be granted.

Hannah's family did not remain in a kibbutz for long: her mother, still an attractive, sparkling woman, received several proposals of marriage, one of which came from a wealthy widower. She accepted.

When Hannah, her sister Ruth and brother David took up their new residence in the fashionable district of Haifa, their whole world changed. Their new stepfather doted on Hannah's mother and lavished gifts on the family he had never had.

After Hannah had completed her schooling she applied to universities in America and England to study languages. Mama didn't approve, and had often suggested that with such a figure, glorious long black hair and looks that turned the heads of men from seventeen to seventy, she should consider a career in modelling. Hannah laughed and explained that she had better things to do with her life.

A few weeks later, after Hannah had returned from an interview at Vasser, she joined her family in Paris for their summer holiday. She also planned to visit Rome and London, but she received so many invitations from attentive Parisians that when the three weeks were over she found she hadn't once left the French capital. It was on the last Thursday of their holiday that the Mode Rivoli Agency offered her a contract that no amount of university degrees could have obtained for her. She handed her return ticket to Tel Aviv back to her mother and remained in Paris for her first job. While she settled down in Paris her sister Ruth was sent to finishing school in Zurich, and her brother David took up a place at the London School of Economics.

In January 1991, the children all returned to Israel to celebrate their mother's fiftieth birthday. Ruth was now a student at the Slade School of Art; David was completing his studies for a PhD; and Hannah was appearing once again on the cover of *Elle*.

At the same time the Americans were massing on the Kuwaiti border, and many Israelis were becoming anxious about a war, but Hannah's stepfather assured them that Israel would not get involved. In any case, their home was on the north side of the city and therefore immune to any attack.

A week later, on the night of their mother's fiftieth birthday, they all ate and drank a little too much, and then slept a little too soundly. When Hannah eventually woke, she found herself strapped down in a hospital bed. It was to be days before they told her that her mother, brother and sister had been killed instantly by a stray Scud, and only her stepfather had survived.

For weeks Hannah lay in that hospital bed planning her revenge. When she was eventually discharged her stepfather told her that he hoped she would return to modelling, but that he would support her in whatever she wanted to do.

Hannah informed him that she was going to join Mossad.

It was ironic that she now found herself on a plane to London that, under different circumstances, her brother might have been taking to complete his studies at the LSE. She was one of eight trainee agents being despatched to the British capital for an advanced course in Arabic. Hannah had already completed a year of night classes in Tel Aviv. Another six months and the Iraqis would believe she'd been born in Baghdad. She could now think in Arabic, even if she didn't always think like an Arab.

Once the 757 had broken through the clouds, Hannah stared down at the winding River Thames through the little porthole window. When she had lived in Paris she had often flown over to spend her mornings working in Bond Street or Chelsea, her afternoons at Ascot or Wimbledon, her evenings at Covent Garden or the Barbican. But on this occasion she felt no joy at returning to a city she had come to know so well.

Now, she was only interested in an obscure sub-faculty of London University and a terraced house in a place called Chalk Farm.

2

ON THE JOURNEY BACK to his office on Wall Street, Antonio Cavalli began to think more seriously about Al Obaydi and how they had come to meet. The file on his new client supplied by their London office, and updated by his secretary Debbie, revealed that although the Deputy Ambassador had been born in Baghdad, he had been educated in England.

When Cavalli leaned back, closed his eyes and recalled the clipped accent and staccato delivery, he felt he might have been in the presence of a British Army officer. The explanation could be found in Al Obaydi's file under Education: The King's School, Wimbledon, followed by three years at London University reading law. Al Obaydi had also eaten his dinners at Lincoln's Inn, whatever that meant.

On returning to Baghdad, Al Obaydi had been recruited by the Ministry of Foreign Affairs. He had risen rapidly, despite the self-appointment of Saddam Hussein as President and the regular placement of Ba'ath Party apparatchiks in posts they were patently unqualified to fill.

As Cavalli turned another page of the file, it became obvious that Al Obaydi was a man well capable of adapting himself to unusual circumstances. To be fair, that was something Cavalli also prided himself on. Like Al Obaydi he had studied law, but in his case at Columbia University in New York. When that time of the year came round for graduates to fill out their applications to join leading law firms, Cavalli was always shortlisted when the partners saw his grades, but once they realised who his father was, he was never interviewed.

After working fourteen hours a day for five years in one of Manhattan's less prestigious legal establishments, the young Cavalli began to realise that it would be at least another ten years before he could hope to see his name embossed on the firm's masthead, despite having married one of the senior partners' daughters. Tony Cavalli didn't have ten years to waste, so he decided to set up his own law practice and divorce his wife.

In January 1982 Cavalli and Co. was incorporated, and ten years later, on April 15th 1992, the company declared a profit of $157,000, paying its tax demand in full. What the company books did not reveal was that a subsidiary had also been formed in 1982, but not incorporated. A firm that showed no tax returns, and despite its profits mounting year on year, could not be checked up on by phoning Dun & Bradstreet and requesting a complete VIP business report. This subsidiary was known to a small group of insiders as 'Skills' – a company that specialised in solving problems that could not be taken care of by thumbing through the Yellow Pages.

With his father's contacts, and Cavalli's driving ambition, the unlisted company soon made a reputation for handling problems that their unnamed clients had previously considered insoluble. Among Cavalli's latest assignments had been the recovery of taped conversations between Sinatra and Nancy Reagan that were due to be published in *Rolling Stone* and the theft of a Vermeer from Ireland for an eccentric South American collector. These coups were discreetly referred to in the company of potential clients.

The clients themselves were vetted as carefully as if they were applying to be members of the New York Yacht Club because, as Tony's father had often pointed out, it would only take one mistake to ensure that he would spend the rest of his life in less pleasing surroundings than 23 East 75th Street, or their villa in Lyford Cay.

Over the past decade, Tony had built up a small network of representatives across the globe who supplied him with clients requiring a little help with a more 'imaginative' proposition. It was his Lebanese contact who had been responsible for introducing the man from Baghdad, whose proposal unquestionably fell into this category.

When Tony's father was first briefed on the outline of Operation 'Desert Calm' he recommended that his son demand a fee of one hundred million dollars to compensate for the fact that the whole of Washington would be at liberty to observe him going about his business.

'One mistake,' the old man warned him, licking his lips, 'and you'll make more front pages than the second coming of Elvis.'

Once he had left the lecture theatre, Scott Bradley hurried across Grove Street Cemetery, hoping that he might reach his apartment in St Ronan Street before being accosted by a pursuing student. He loved them all – well, almost all – and he was sure that in time he would allow the more serious among them to stroll back to his rooms in the evenings for a drink and to talk long into the night. But not until they were well into their second year.

Scott managed to reach the staircase before a single would-be lawyer had caught up with him. But then, few of them knew that he had once covered four hundred metres in 48.1 seconds when he'd anchored the Georgetown varsity relay team. Confident he had escaped, Scott leapt up the staircase, not stopping until he reached his apartment on the third floor.

He pushed open the unlocked door. It was always unlocked. There was nothing in his apartment worth stealing – even the television didn't work. The one file that would have revealed that the law was not the only field in which he was an expert had been carefully secreted on his bookshelf between Tax and Torts. He failed to notice the books that were piled up everywhere or the fact that he could have written his name in the dust on the sideboard.

Scott closed the door behind him and glanced, as he always did, at the picture of his mother on the sideboard. He dumped the pile of notes he was carrying by her side and retrieved the mail poking out from under the door. Scott walked across the room and sank into an old leather chair, wondering how many of those bright, attentive faces would still be attending his lectures in two years' time. Forty per cent would be good – thirty per cent more likely. Those would be the ones for whom fourteen hours' work a day became the norm, and not just for the last month before exams. And of them, how many would live up to the standards of the late Dean Thomas W. Swan? Five per cent, if he was lucky.

The Professor of Constitutional Law turned his attention to the bundle of mail he held in his lap. One from American Express – a bill with the inevitable hundred free offers which would cost him even more money if he took any of them up; an invitation from Brown to give the Charles Evans Hughes Lecture on the Constitution; a letter from Carol reminding him she hadn't seen him for some time; a circular from a firm of stockbrokers who didn't promise to double his money but . . .; and finally a plain buff envelope postmarked Virginia, with a typeface he recognised immediately.

He tore open the buff envelope and extracted the single sheet of paper which gave him his latest instructions.

Al Obaydi strolled onto the floor of the General Assembly and slipped into a chair directly behind his Head of Mission. The Ambassador had his earphones on and was pretending to be deeply interested in a speech being delivered by the Head of the Brazilian Mission. Al Obaydi's boss always preferred to have confidential talks on the floor of the General Assembly: he suspected it was the only room in the United Nations building that wasn't bugged by the CIA.

Al Obaydi waited patiently until the older man flicked one of the earpieces aside and leaned slightly back.

'They've agreed to our terms,' murmured Al Obaydi, as if it was he who had suggested the figure. The Ambassador's upper lip protruded over his lower lip, the recognised sign among his colleagues that he required more details.

'One hundred million,' Al Obaydi whispered. 'Ten million to be paid immediately. The final ninety on delivery.'

'"Immediately"?' said the Ambassador. 'What does "immediately" mean?'

'By midday tomorrow,' whispered Al Obaydi.

'At least Sayedi anticipated that eventuality,' said the Ambassador thoughtfully.

Al Obaydi admired the way his superior could always make the term 'my master' sound both deferential and insolent at the same time.

'I must send a message to Baghdad to acquaint the Foreign Minister with the details of your triumph,' added the Ambassador with a smile.

Al Obaydi would also have smiled, but he realised the

Ambassador would not admit to any personal involvement with the project while it was still in its formative stage. As long as he distanced himself from his younger colleague for the time being, the Ambassador could continue his undisturbed existence in New York until his retirement fell due in three years' time. By following such a course he had survived almost fourteen years of Saddam Hussein's reign while many of his colleagues had conspicuously failed to become eligible for their state pension. To his knowledge one had been shot in front of his family, two hanged and several others posted as 'missing', whatever that meant.

The Iraqi Ambassador smiled as his British counterpart walked past him, but he received no response for his trouble.

'Stuck-up snob,' the Arab muttered under his breath.

The Ambassador pulled the earpiece back over his ear to indicate that he had heard quite enough from his number two. He continued to listen to the problems of trying to preserve the rainforests of Brazil, coupled with a request for a further grant from the UN of a hundred million dollars.

Not something he felt Sayedi would be interested in.

Hannah would have knocked on the front door of the little terraced house, but it was opened even before she had closed the broken gate at the end of the pathway. A dark-haired, slightly overweight lady, heavily made-up and with a beaming smile came bustling out to greet her. Hannah supposed she would have been about the same age as her mother, had Mama still been alive.

'Welcome to England, my dear. I'm Ethel Rubin,' she announced in gushing tones. 'I'm sorry my husband's not here to meet you, but I don't expect him back from his chambers for another hour.' Hannah was about to speak when Ethel added, 'But first let me show you your room, and then you can tell me all your plans.' She picked up one of Hannah's bags and led her inside. 'It must be such fun seeing London for the first time,' she said as they climbed the stairs, 'and there will be so many exciting things for you to do during the next six months.'

As each sentence poured out Hannah became aware that Ethel Rubin had no idea why she was in London.

After she had unpacked and taken a shower Hannah joined her hostess in the sitting room. Mrs Rubin chatted on, barely listening to Hannah's intermittent replies.

'Do you know where the nearest gym is?' Hannah had asked.

'My husband should be back at any moment,' Mrs Rubin replied. But before she could get the next sentence out, the front door swung open and a man of about five foot three with dark, wiry hair and even darker eyes almost ran into the room. Once Peter Rubin had introduced himself and asked how her flight had been he didn't waste any words suggesting that Hannah might have come to London to enjoy the social life of the metropolis. Hannah quickly learned that Peter Rubin didn't ask any questions he realised she couldn't answer truthfully. Although Hannah felt sure Mr Rubin knew no details of her mission, he was obviously aware that she hadn't come to London on a package holiday.

Mrs Rubin, however, didn't allow Hannah to get to bed until well after midnight, by which time she was exhausted. Once her head had touched the pillow she slept soundly, unaware of Peter Rubin explaining to his wife in the kitchen that in future their guest must be left in peace.

3

THE DEPUTY AMBASSADOR'S chauffeur slipped out of the UN's private garage and headed west through the Lincoln Tunnel under the Hudson in the direction of New Jersey. Neither Al Obaydi nor he spoke for several minutes while the driver continually checked his rear-view mirror. Once they were on the New Jersey Turnpike he confirmed that no one was following them.

'Good,' was all Al Obaydi offered. He began to relax for the first time that day, and started to fantasise about what he might do if the ten million dollars were suddenly his. When they had passed a branch of the Midlantic National Bank earlier, he had asked himself for the thousandth time why he didn't just stop the car and deposit the money in a false name. He could be halfway across the globe by the following morning. That would certainly make his Ambassador sweat. And, with an ounce of luck, Saddam would be dead long before they caught up with him. And then who would care?

After all, Al Obaydi didn't believe, not even for one moment, that the great leader's outrageous plan was feasible. He had been hoping to report back to Baghdad after a reasonable period of time that no one reliable or efficient enough could be found to carry out such a bold coup. And then the Lebanese gentleman had flown into New York.

There were two reasons why Al Obaydi knew he could not touch one dollar of the money stuffed into the golf bag that rested on the seat beside him. First, there were his mother and younger sister, who resided in Baghdad in relative comfort and who, if the money suddenly disappeared, would be arrested, raped, tortured and hanged – the only explanation being that they had collaborated with a traitor. Not that Saddam ever needed an excuse to kill anyone, especially someone he suspected might have betrayed him.

Secondly, Al Obaydi – who fell on his knees five times daily, faced east and prayed that Saddam would eventually die a traitor's death – could not help observing that Gorbachev, Thatcher and Bush had found it considerably more difficult than the great Sayedi to cling on to power.

Al Obaydi had accepted from the moment he had been handed this assignment by the Ambassador that Saddam would undoubtedly die peacefully in his bed while his own chances of survival – the Ambassador's favourite word – were slim. And once the money had been paid over, if Antonio Cavalli failed to carry out his side of the bargain, it would be Al Obaydi who was called back to Baghdad on some diplomatic pretext, arrested, summarily tried and found guilty. Then all those fine words his law professor at London University had uttered would turn out to be so much sand in the desert.

The driver swung off the turnpike and headed for the centre of Newark as Al Obaydi's thoughts returned to what the money was being used for. The idea had all the hallmarks of his President. It was original, required daring, raw courage, nerve and a fair degree of luck. Al Obaydi still gave the plan no more than a one per cent chance of even reaching the starting blocks, let alone the finishing tape. But then, some people in the State Department had only given Saddam a one per cent chance of surviving Operation Desert Storm. And if the great Sayedi could pull this off, the United States would become a laughing stock and Saddam would have guaranteed himself a place in Arab history alongside Saladin.

Although Al Obaydi had already checked the exact location of the building, he instructed the driver to stop two blocks west of his final destination. An Iraqi getting out of a large black limousine right in front of the bank would be enough of an excuse for Cavalli to pocket the money and cancel the deal. Once the car had stopped, Al Obaydi climbed over the golf bag and out onto the pavement on the kerb side. Although he only had to cover a couple of hundred yards to the bank, this was the one part of the journey that he considered was a calculated risk. He checked up and down the street. Satisfied, he dragged the golf bag out onto the pavement and humped it up onto his shoulder.

The Deputy Ambassador felt he must have looked an incongruous sight as he marched down Martin Luther King Drive in a Saks Fifth Avenue suit with a golf bag slung over his shoulder.

Although it took less than two minutes to cover the short distance to the bank, Al Obaydi was sweating profusely by the time he reached the front entrance. He climbed up the well-worn steps and walked through the revolving door. He was met by two armed men who looked more like sumo wrestlers than bank clerks. The Deputy Ambassador was quickly guided to a waiting lift that closed the moment he stepped inside. The door slid open only when he reached the basement. As Al Obaydi stepped out he came face to face with another man, bigger, if anything, than the two who had originally greeted him. The giant nodded and led him towards a door at the end of a carpeted corridor. As he approached, the door swung open and Al Obaydi entered a room to find twelve men waiting expectantly round a large table. Although conservatively dressed and silent, none of them looked like bank tellers. The door closed behind him and he heard a lock turning. The man at the head of the table stood up and greeted him.

'Good morning, Mr Al Obaydi. I believe you have something to deposit for one of our customers.'

The Deputy Ambassador nodded and handed over the golf bag without a word. The man showed no surprise. He had seen valuables transported in everything from a crocodile to a condom.

He was, however, surprised by the weight of the bag as he humped it up onto the table, spilled out the contents and divided the spoils among the other eleven men. The tellers began counting furiously, making up neat piles of ten thousands. No one offered Al Obaydi a seat, so he remained standing for the next forty minutes, with nothing to do but watch them go about their task.

When the counting had been completed, the chief teller double-checked the number of piles. One thousand exactly. He smiled, a smile that was not directed at Al Obaydi but at the money, then looked up in the direction of the Arab and gave him a curt nod, acknowledging that the man from Baghdad had made the down-payment.

The golf bag was then handed back to the Deputy Ambassador, as it had not been part of the deal. Al Obaydi felt slightly stupid as he slung it over his shoulder. The chief teller touched a buzzer under the table and the door behind him was unlocked.

One of the men who had first met Al Obaydi when he had entered the bank was standing waiting to escort him back to the ground floor. By the time the Deputy Ambassador stepped out onto the street, his guide had already disappeared.

With an enormous sigh of relief, Al Obaydi began to

stroll the two blocks back to his waiting car. He allowed himself a small smile of satisfaction at the professional way he had carried out the whole exercise. He felt sure the Ambassador would be pleased to learn that there had been no mishaps. He would undoubtedly take most of the praise when the message was relayed back to Baghdad that 'Operation Desert Calm' had begun.

Al Obaydi collapsed on the sidewalk before he realised what had hit him: the golf bag had been wrenched from his shoulder before he could react. He looked up to see two youths moving swiftly down the street, one of them clutching their prize.

The Deputy Ambassador had been wondering how he was going to dispose of it.

Tony Cavalli joined his father for breakfast a few minutes after seven the following morning. He had moved back into their brownstone on 75th and Park soon after his divorce. Since his retirement, Tony's father spent most of his time pursuing his lifelong hobby of collecting rare books, manuscripts and historical documents. He had also spent many hours passing on to his son everything he'd learned as a lawyer, concentrating on how to avoid wasting too many years in one of the state's penitentiaries.

Coffee and toast were served by the butler as the two men went about their business.

'Nine million dollars has been placed in forty-seven banks across the country,' Tony told his father. 'Another million has been deposited in a numbered account with Franchard et cie in Geneva, in the name of Hamid Al Obaydi,' he added, buttering a piece of toast.

The father smiled at the thought of his son using an old ploy he had taught him so many years before.

'But what will you tell Al Obaydi when he asks how

his ten million is being spent?' the unofficial chairman of Skills enquired.

For the next hour, Tony took his father through Operation Desert Calm in great detail, interrupted only by the occasional question or suggestion from the older man.

'Can the actor be trusted?' he asked before taking another sip of coffee.

'Lloyd Adams still owes us a little over thirty thousand dollars,' Tony replied. 'He hasn't been offered many scripts lately – a few commercials . . .'

'Good,' said Cavalli's father. 'But what about Rex Butterworth?'

'Sitting in the White House waiting for his instructions.'

His father nodded. 'But why Columbus, Ohio?' he asked.

'The surgical facilities there are exactly what we require, and the Dean of the Medical School has the ideal qualifications. We've had his office and home bugged from top to bottom.'

'And his daughter?'

'We've got her under twenty-four-hour surveillance.'

The chairman licked his lips. 'So when do you press the button?'

'Next Tuesday, when the Dean is due to make a keynote speech at his daughter's school.'

The butler entered the room and began to clear the table.

'And how about Dollar Bill?' asked Cavalli's father.

'Angelo is on his way to San Francisco to try and convince him. If we're going to pull this off we'll need Dollar Bill. He's the best. In fact no one else comes close,' added Cavalli.

'As long as he's sober,' was all the chairman said.

4

THE TALL, ATHLETIC MAN stepped off the plane into the US Air terminal at Washington National Airport. He carried only hand luggage, so he didn't have to wait at the baggage carousel where someone might recognise him. He needed just one person to recognise him – the driver who was picking him up. At six foot one, his fair hair tousled and with almost chiselled fine features, and dressed in light blue jeans, cream shirt and a dark blue blazer, he made many women rather hope that he would recognise them.

The back door of an anonymous black Ford was opened as soon as he came through the automatic doors into the bright morning sunlight.

He climbed into the back of the car without a word and made no conversation during the twenty-five-minute journey that took him in the opposite direction to the capital. The forty-minute flight always gave him a chance to compose his thoughts and prepare his new persona. Twelve times a year he made the same journey.

It had all begun when Scott was a child back in his home town of Denver, and he had discovered his father was not a respectable lawyer but a criminal in a Brooks Brothers suit, a man who, if the price was right, could always find a way round the law. His mother had spent years protecting her only child from the truth, but when her husband was arrested, indicted and finally sentenced to seven years, the old excuse 'there must have been some misunderstanding' no longer carried any conviction.

His father survived three years in prison before dying of what was described in the coroner's report as a heart attack, without any explanation being given for the marks around his throat. A few weeks later, his mother did die of a heart attack, while he was coming to the end of his third year at Georgetown studying law. Once the body had been lowered into the grave and the sods of earth hurled on top of the coffin, he left the cemetery and never spoke of his family again.

When the final rankings were announced, Scott Bradley was placed first in the graduating class, and several universities and leading law firms contacted him to ask about his plans for the future. To the surprise of his contemporaries, Scott applied for an obscure professorship at Beirut University. He didn't explain to anyone why he needed a clean break with the past.

Appalled by the low standard of the students at the university and bored by the social life, Scott began to fill his hours by attending courses on everything from the Islamic religions to the history of the Middle East. When three years later the university offered him the Chair of American Law, he knew it was time to return to the United States.

A letter from the Dean of the Law Faculty at Georgetown suggested he should apply for a vacant professorship at Yale. He wrote the following day and packed his bags when he received their reply.

Once he had taken up his new post, whenever he was asked the casual question, 'What do your parents do?' he would simply reply, 'They're both dead and I'm an only child.' There was a certain type of girl who delighted in this knowledge – they assumed he would need mothering. Several of them entered his bed, but none of them became part of his life.

But he hid nothing from the people he was summoned to see twelve times a year. They couldn't tolerate deception of any kind, and were highly suspicious of his real motives when they learned of his father's criminal record. He told them simply that he wished to make amends for his father's disgrace, and refused to discuss the subject any further.

At first they didn't believe him. After a time they took him on his own terms, but it was still to be years before they trusted him with any classified information. It was when he started coming up with solutions for problems in the Middle East that the computer couldn't handle that they began to stop doubting his motives. When the Clinton Administration was sworn in, the new team welcomed Scott's particular expertise.

Twice recently he had penetrated the State Department itself to advise Warren Christopher. He had been amused to see Mr Christopher suggest on the early-evening news a solution to the problem of sanctions-busting by Saddam that he had put to him earlier that afternoon.

The car turned off Route 123 and drew to a halt outside a pair of massive steel gates. A guard came out to check on the passenger. Although the two men had seen each other regularly over the past nine years, the guard still asked to see his credentials.

'Welcome back, Professor,' the uniformed man finally offered before saluting.

The driver proceeded down the road and stopped outside an anonymous office block. The passenger climbed out of the car and entered the building through a turnstile. His papers were checked once again, followed by another salute. He walked down a long corridor with cream walls until he reached an unmarked oak door. He gave a gentle knock and entered before waiting for a reply.

A secretary was sitting behind a desk on the far side of the room. She looked up and smiled. 'Go right in, Professor Bradley, the Deputy Director is expecting you.'

Columbus School for Girls, Columbus, Ohio, is one of those establishments that prides itself on discipline and scholarship, in that order. The headmistress would often explain to parents that it was impossible to have the second without the first.

Breaking school rules could, in the headmistress's opinion, only be considered in rare circumstances. The request that she had just received fell into such a category.

That night, the graduating class of '93 was to be addressed by one of Columbus's favourite sons, T. Hamilton McKenzie, Dean of the Medical School at Ohio State University. His Nobel Prize for Medicine had been awarded for the advances he had made in the field of plastic and reconstructive surgery. T. Hamilton McKenzie's work on war veterans from Vietnam and the Gulf had been chronicled from coast to coast, and there were men in every city who, thanks to his genius, had been able to return to normal lives. Some lesser mortals who had trained under the Nobel Laureate used their skills to help women of a certain age appear more beautiful than their maker had originally intended. The headmistress of Columbus felt confident that the girls would only be interested in the work T. Hamilton McKenzie had done for 'our gallant war heroes', as she referred to them.

The school rule that the headmistress had allowed to be waived on this occasion was one of dress. She had agreed that Sally McKenzie, head of student government and captain of lacrosse, could go home one hour early from afternoon class and change into clothes of a casual but suitable nature to accompany her father when he addressed the class later that evening. After all, the headmistress had learned the previous week that Sally had won an endowed national scholarship to Oberlin College to study medicine.

A car service had been called with instructions to pick Sally up at four o'clock. She would miss one hour of school, but the driver had confirmed that he would deliver father and daughter back by six.

As four chimed on the chapel clock, Sally looked up from her desk. A teacher nodded and the student gathered up her books. She placed them in her bag, and left the building to walk down the long drive in search of the car. When Sally reached the old iron gates at the entrance to the drive, she was surprised to find the only car in sight was a Lincoln Continental stretch limousine. A chauffeur wearing a grey uniform and a peaked cap stood by the driver's door. Such extravagance, she knew only too well, was not the style of her father, and certainly not that of the headmistress.

The man touched the peak of his hat with his right hand and enquired, 'Miss McKenzie?'

'Yes,' Sally replied, disappointed that the long winding drive prevented her classmates from observing the whole scene.

The back door was opened for her. Sally climbed in and sank into the luxurious leather upholstery.

The driver jumped into the front, pressed a button and the window that divided the passenger from the driver slid silently up. Sally heard the safety lock click into place.

She allowed her mind to drift as she glanced out of the misty windows, imagining for a moment that this was the sort of lifestyle she might expect once she left Columbus.

It was some time before the seventeen-year-old girl realised the car wasn't actually heading in the direction of her home.

Had the problem been posed in textbook form, T. Hamilton McKenzie would have known the exact course of action to be taken. After all, he lived 'by the book', as he so often told his students. But when it happened in real life, he behaved completely out of character.

Had he consulted one of the senior psychiatrists at the university, they would have explained that many of the anxieties he'd kept suppressed over a long period of time had, in his new circumstances, been forced to the surface.

The fact that he adored his only child, Sally, was clear for all to see. So was the fact that for many years he had become bored with, almost completely uninterested in, his wife Joni. But the discovery that he was not good under pressure once he was outside the operating theatre – his own little empire – was something he could never have accepted.

T. Hamilton McKenzie became at first irritated, then exasperated, and finally downright angry when his daughter failed to return home that Tuesday evening. Sally was never late, or at least not for him. The journey by car from Columbus should have taken no more than thirty minutes, even in the rush-hour traffic. Joni would have picked Sally up if she hadn't fixed her hair appointment so late. 'It's the only time Julian could fit me in,' she explained. She always left everything to the last minute. At 4.50 T. Hamilton McKenzie phoned Columbus School for Girls to check there had been no late change of plan.

Columbus doesn't change its plans, the headmistress would have liked to tell the Nobel Laureate, but satisfied herself with assuring him that Sally had left school at four o'clock, and that the limousine company had phoned an hour before to confirm that they would be waiting for her at the end of the drive by the main school gates.

Joni kept repeating in that Southern accent he had once found so attractive, 'She'll be here at any minute, jus' you wait. You can always rely on our Sally.'

Another man, who was sitting in a hotel room on the other side of town and listening to every word they exchanged, poured himself a beer.

By five o'clock, T. Hamilton McKenzie had taken to looking out of the bedroom window every few moments, but the path to their front door lay obstinately unbeaten.

He had hoped to leave at 5.20 p.m., allowing himself enough time to arrive at the school with ten or fifteen minutes to spare. If his daughter did not appear soon, he would have to go without her. He warned his wife that nothing would stop him leaving at 5.20 p.m.

At 5.20 p.m. T. Hamilton McKenzie placed the notes for his speech on the hall table and began pacing up and down the front path as he waited for his wife and daughter to come from opposite directions. By 5.25 p.m., neither of them was at his side and his famous 'cool' was beginning to show distinct signs of steaming.

Joni had taken some considerable time to select an appropriate outfit for the occasion, and was disappointed when she appeared in the hall that her husband didn't even seem to notice.

'We'll have to go without her,' was all he said. 'If Sally hopes to be a doctor one day, she'll have to learn that people have a tendency to die when you keep them waiting.'

'Shouldn't we give her just a li'l longer, honey?' asked Joni.

'No,' he barked, and without even looking back set off for the garage. Joni spotted her husband's notes on the hall table and stuffed them into her handbag before she pulled the front door closed and double-locked it. By the time she reached the road, her husband was already waiting behind the wheel of his car, drumming his fingers on the gear lever.

They drove in silence towards Columbus School for Girls. T. Hamilton McKenzie checked every car heading towards Upper Arlington to see if his daughter was in the back seat.

A small reception party, led by the headmistress, was waiting for them at the foot of the stone steps at the school's main entrance. The headmistress walked forward to shake hands with the distinguished surgeon as he stepped out of the car, followed by Joni McKenzie. Her eyes searched beyond them for Sally. She raised an eyebrow.

'Sally never came home,' Dr McKenzie explained.

'She'll probably join us in a few minutes, if she's not already here,' suggested his wife. The headmistress knew Sally was not on the school premises, but did not consider it courteous to correct the guest of honour's wife, especially as she had just received a call from the car service that required an explanation.

At fourteen minutes to six they walked into the headmistress's study, where a young lady of Sally's age offered the guests a choice of dry sherry or orange juice. McKenzie suddenly remembered that in the anxiety of waiting for his daughter he had left his notes on the hall table. He checked his watch and realised that there wasn't enough time to send his wife back for them. In any case, he was unwilling to admit such an oversight in front of this particular gathering. Damn it, he thought. Teenagers are never an easy audience, and girls are always the worst. He tried to marshal his thoughts into some sort of order.

At three minutes to six, despite there still being no sign of Sally, the headmistress suggested they should all make their way to the Great Hall.

'Can't keep the girls waiting,' she explained. 'It would set a bad example.'

Just as they were leaving the room, Joni took her husband's notes out of her handbag and passed them over to him. He looked relieved for the first time since 4.50.

At one minute to six, the headmistress led the guest of honour onto the stage. He watched the four hundred girls rise and applaud him in what the headmistress would have described as a 'ladylike' manner.

When the applause had faded away, the headmistress raised and lowered her hands to indicate that the girls should be seated again, which they did with the minimum of noise. She then walked over to the lectern and gave an unscripted eulogy on T. Hamilton McKenzie that would have surely impressed the Nobel Committee. She talked of Edward Zeir, the founder of modern plastic surgery, of J.R. Wolte and Wilhelm Krause, and reminded her pupils that T. Hamilton McKenzie had followed in their great tradition by advancing the still-burgeoning science. She said nothing about Sally and her many achievements while at the school, although it had been in her original script. It was still possible to be punished for breaking school rules even if you had just won an endowed national scholarship.

When the headmistress returned to her place in the centre of the stage, T. Hamilton McKenzie made his way to the lectern. He looked down at his notes, coughed, and then began his dissertation.

'Most of you in the audience, I should imagine, think plastic surgery is about straightening noses, removing double chins and getting rid of bags from under your eyes. That, I can assure you, is not plastic but cosmetic surgery. Plastic surgery,' he continued – to the disappointment, his wife suspected, of most of those seated in front of him – 'is something else.' He then lectured for forty minutes on z-plasty, homograting, congenital malformation and third-degree burns without once raising his head.

When he finally sat down, the applause was not quite as loud as it had been when he had entered the room. T. Hamilton McKenzie assumed that was because showing their true feelings would have been considered 'unladylike'.

On returning to the headmistress's study, Joni asked the secretary if there had been any news of Sally.

'Not that I am aware of,' replied the secretary, 'but she might have been seated in the hall.'

During the lecture, versions of which Joni had heard a hundred times before, she had scanned every face in the room, and knew that her daughter was not among them.

More sherry was poured, and after a decent interval T. Hamilton McKenzie announced that they ought to be getting back. The headmistress nodded her agreement and accompanied her guests to their car. She thanked the surgeon for a lecture of great insight, and waited at the bottom of the steps until the car had disappeared from view.

'I have never known such behaviour in all my days,' she declared to her secretary. 'Tell Miss McKenzie to report to me before chapel tomorrow. The first thing I want to know is why she cancelled the car I arranged for her.'

* * *

Scott Bradley also gave a lecture that evening, but in his case only sixteen students attended, and none of them was under the age of thirty-five. Each was a senior CIA field officer, and as fit as any quarterback in America. When they talked of logic, it had a more practical application than the one suggested when Scott lectured his younger students at Yale.

These men were all operating in the front line, stationed right across the globe. Often Professor Bradley pressed them to go over, detail by detail, decisions they had made under pressure, and whether those decisions had achieved the result they'd originally hoped for.

They were quick to admit their mistakes. There was no room for personal pride – only pride in the service was considered acceptable. When Scott had first heard this sentiment he thought they were being corny, but after nine years of working with them in the classroom and in the gym, he'd learned otherwise.

For over an hour Bradley threw test cases at them, at the same time suggesting ways of how to think logically, always weighing known facts with subjective judgement before reaching any firm conclusion.

Over the past nine years, Scott had learned as much from them as they had from him, but he still enjoyed helping them put his knowledge to practical use. Scott had often felt he too would like to be tested in the field, and not simply in the lecture theatre.

When the session was over, Scott joined them in the gym for another workout. He climbed ropes, pumped iron and practised karate exercises, and they never once treated him as anything other than a full member of the team. Anyone who patronised the visiting professor from Yale often ended up with more than their egos bruised.

Over dinner that night – no alcohol, just Quibel –

Scott asked the Deputy Director if he was ever going to be allowed to gain some field experience.

'It's not a vacation job, you know,' came back Dexter Hutchins' reply as he lit up a cigar. 'Give up Yale and join us full time and then perhaps we'll consider the merits of allowing you out of the classroom.'

'I'm due for a sabbatical next year,' Bradley reminded his superior.

'Then take that trip to Italy you've always been promising yourself. After dining with you for the last seven years, I think I know as much about Bellini as ballistics.'

'I'm not going to give up trying for a field job – you realise that, Dexter, don't you?'

'You'll have to when you're fifty, because that's when we'll retire you.'

'But I'm only thirty-six . . .'

'You rise too easily to make a good field officer,' said the Deputy Director, puffing away at his cigar.

When T. Hamilton McKenzie opened the front door of his house, he ignored the ringing phone as he shouted, 'Sally? Sally?' at the top of his voice, but he received no response.

He finally snatched the phone, assuming it would be his daughter. 'Sally?' he repeated.

'Dr McKenzie?' asked a calmer voice.

'Yes, it is,' he said.

'If you're wondering where your daughter is, I can assure you that she's safe and well.'

'Who is this?' demanded McKenzie.

'I'll call later this evening, Dr McKenzie, when you've had time to calm down,' said the quiet voice. 'Meanwhile, do not, under any circumstances, contact the police or any private agency. If you do, we'll know immediately, and will be left with no choice but to return your lovely daughter –' he paused '– in a coffin.' The phone went dead.

T. Hamilton McKenzie turned white, and in seconds was covered in sweat.

'What's the matter, honey?' asked Joni, as she watched her husband collapse onto the sofa.

'Sally's been kidnapped,' he said, aghast. 'They said not to contact the police. They're going to call again later this evening.' He stared at the phone.

'Sally's been kidnapped?' repeated Joni in disbelief.

'Yes,' snapped her husband.

'Then we ought to tell the police right away,' Joni said, jumping up. 'After all, honey, that's what they're paid for.'

'No, we mustn't. They said they'd know immediately if we did, and would send her back in a coffin.'

'A coffin? Are you sure that's what they said?' Joni asked quietly.

'Damn it, of course I'm sure, but they told me she'll be just fine as long as we don't talk to the police. I don't understand it. I'm not a rich man.'

'I still think we ought to call the police. After all, Chief Dixon's a personal friend.'

'No, no!' shouted McKenzie. 'Don't you understand? If we do that they'll kill her.'

'All I understand,' replied his wife, 'is that you're out of your depth and our daughter is in great danger.' She paused. 'You should call Chief Dixon right now.'

'No!' repeated her husband at the top of his voice. 'You just don't begin to understand.'

'I understand only too well,' said Joni, her voice remarkably calm. 'You intend to play Chief of Police for Columbus as well as Dean of the Medical School, despite the fact that you're quite unqualified to do so. How would you react if a State Trooper marched into your operating theatre, leaned over one of your patients and demanded a scalpel?'

T. Hamilton McKenzie stared coldly at his wife, and assumed it was the strain that had caused her to react so irrationally.

The two men listening to the conversation on the other side of town glanced at each other. The man with earphones said, 'I'm glad it's him and not her we're going to have to deal with.'

When the phone rang again an hour later both T. Hamilton McKenzie and his wife jumped as if they had been touched by an electric wire.

McKenzie waited for several rings as he tried to compose himself. Then he picked up the phone. 'McKenzie,' he said.

'Listen to me carefully,' said the quiet voice, 'and don't interrupt. Answer only when instructed to do so. Understood?'

'Yes,' said McKenzie.

'You did well not to contact the police as your wife suggested,' continued the quiet voice. 'Your judgement is better than hers.'

'I want to talk to my daughter,' interjected McKenzie.

'You've been watching too many late-night movies, Dr McKenzie. There are no heroines in real life – or heroes, for that matter. So get that into your head. Do I make myself clear?'

'Yes,' said McKenzie.

'You've wasted too much of my time already,' said the quiet voice. The line went dead.

It was over an hour before the phone rang again, during which time Joni tried once more to convince her husband that they should contact the police. This time T. Hamilton McKenzie picked up the receiver without waiting. 'Hello? Hello?'

'Calm down, Dr McKenzie,' said the quiet voice. 'And this time, listen. Tomorrow morning at 8.30 you'll leave home and drive to the hospital as usual. On the way you'll stop at the Olentangy Inn and take any table in the corner of the coffee shop that is not already occupied. Make sure it can only seat two. Once we're confident that no one has followed you, you'll be joined by one of my colleagues and given your instructions. Understood?'

'Yes.'

'One false move, Doctor, and you will never see your daughter again. Try to remember, it's you who are in the business of extending life. We're in the business of ending it.'

The phone went dead.

5

HANNAH WAS SURE that she could carry it off. After all, if she couldn't deceive them in London, what hope was there that she could do so in Baghdad?

She chose a Tuesday morning for the experiment, having spent several hours reconnoitring the area the previous day. She decided not to discuss her plan with anyone, fearing that one of the Mossad team might become suspicious if she were to ask one question too many.

She checked herself in the hall mirror. A clean white T-shirt and baggy sweater, well-worn jeans, sneakers, tennis socks and her hair looking just a little untidy.

She packed her small, battered suitcase – the one family possession they'd allowed her to keep – and left the little terraced house a few minutes after ten o'clock. Mrs Rubin had gone earlier to do what she called her 'big shop', an attempt to stock up at Sainsbury's for a fortnight.

Hannah walked slowly down the road, knowing that if she were caught they'd put her on the next flight home. She disappeared into the tube station, showed her travelcard to the ticket collector, went down in the lift and walked to the far end of the brightly-lit platform as the train rumbled into the station.

At Leicester Square she changed to the Piccadilly line,

and when the train pulled in to South Kensington, Hannah was among the first to reach the escalator. She didn't run up the steps, which would have been her natural inclination, because running attracted attention. She stood quietly on the escalator, studying the advertisements on the wall so that no one could see her face. The new fuel-injected Rover 200, Johnnie Walker whisky, a warning against AIDS, and Andrew Lloyd Webber's *Sunset Boulevard* at the Adelphi glared back at her. Once she'd emerged into the sunlight, Hannah quickly checked left and right before she crossed Harrington Road and walked towards the Norfolk Hotel, an inconspicuous medium-sized hostelry that she had carefully selected. She had checked it out the day before, and could walk straight to the ladies' rest room without having to ask for directions.

Hannah pushed the door open, and after quickly checking to confirm she was alone, chose the end cubicle, locked the door, and flicked open the catch of the battered suitcase. She began the slow process of changing identity.

Two sets of footsteps entered and left while she was undressing. During that time, Hannah sat hunched up on the lavatory seat, continuing only when she was confident she was alone.

The exercise took her nearly twenty minutes. When she emerged, she checked herself in the mirror and made a few minor adjustments.

And then she prayed, but not to their God.

Hannah left the ladies' room and made her way slowly up the stairs and back into the lobby of the hotel. She handed over her little case to the hall porter, telling him she'd collect it again in a couple of hours. She pushed a pound coin across the counter, and in return she received a little red ticket. She followed a tour party through the revolving doors and seconds later was back on the pavement.

She knew exactly where she was going and how long it would take to reach the front door, as she'd carried out a dry-run the previous day. She only hoped her Mossad instructor was right about the internal layout of the building. After all, no other agent had ever been inside before.

Hannah walked slowly along the pavement towards the Brompton Road.

She knew she couldn't afford to hesitate once she reached the front door. With twenty yards to go, she nearly decided to walk straight past the building. But once she reached the steps she found herself climbing them and then boldly knocking on the door. A few moments later, the door was opened by a bull of a man who towered a full six inches over her. Hannah marched in, and to her relief the guard stepped to one side, looked up and down the road and then slammed the door closed.

She walked down the corridor towards the dimly lit staircase without ever looking back. Once she reached the end of the fading carpet, she slowly climbed the wooden staircase. They'd assured her that it was the second door on the left on the first floor, and when she reached the landing she saw a door to the left of her, with peeling brown paint and a brass handle that looked as if it hadn't been polished for months. She turned the handle slowly and pushed the door open. As she entered, she was greeted by a babble of noise that suddenly ceased. The occupants of the room all turned to stare at her.

How could they know that Hannah had never been there before, when all they could see were her eyes?

Then one of them began talking again, and Hannah quietly took a seat in the circle. She listened carefully, and found that even when three or four of them were speaking at once she could understand almost every word. But the tougher test came when she decided to join in the conversation herself. She volunteered that her name was Sheka and that her husband had just arrived in London, but had only been allowed to bring one wife. They nodded their understanding and expressed their disbelief at British Immigration's inability to accept polygamy.

For the next hour, she listened to and discussed with them their problems. How dirty the English were, how decadent, all dying of AIDS. They couldn't wait to go home and eat proper food, drink proper water. And would it ever stop raining? Without warning, one of the black-clad women rose and bade her friends farewell. When a second got up to join her, Hannah realised this was her chance to leave. She followed the two women silently down the stairs, remaining a few paces behind. The massive man who guarded the entrance opened the door to let the three of them out. Two of them climbed into the back of a large black Mercedes and were whisked away, while Hannah turned west and began to retrace her steps to the Norfolk Hotel.

T. Hamilton McKenzie spent most of the night trying to work out what the man with the quiet voice could possibly want. He had checked his bank statements. He only had about $230,000 in cash and securities, and the house was probably worth another quarter of a million once the mortgage had been paid off – and this certainly wasn't a sellers' market, so that might take months to realise. All together, he could just about scrape up half a million. He doubted if the bank would advance him another cent beyond that.

Why had they selected him? There were countless

fathers at Columbus School who were worth ten or twenty times what he was – Joe Ruggiero, who never stopped reminding everybody that he owned the biggest liquor chain in Columbus, must have been a millionaire several times over. For a moment, McKenzie wondered if he was dealing with a gang that had simply picked the wrong man, amateurs even. But he dismissed that idea when he considered the way they'd carried out the kidnap and the follow-up. No, he had to accept that he was dealing with professionals who knew exactly what they wanted.

He slipped out of bed at a few minutes past six and, staring out of the window, discovered there was no sign of the morning sun. He tried to be as quiet as he could, although he knew that his motionless wife must surely be awake – she probably hadn't slept a wink all night. He took a warm shower, shaved, and for reasons he couldn't explain to himself, put on a brand new shirt, the suit he only wore when he went to church, and a flowered Liberty tie Sally had given him two Christmases before and which he had never had the courage to wear.

He then went down to the kitchen and made coffee for his wife for the first time in fifteen years. He took the tray back to the bedroom where he found Joni sitting upright in her pink nightgown rubbing her tired eyes.

McKenzie sat on the end of the bed and they drank black coffee together in silence. During the previous eleven hours they had exhausted everything there was to say.

He cleared the tray away and returned downstairs, taking as long as he could to wash and tidy up in the kitchen. The next sound he heard was the thud of the paper landing on the porch outside the front door.

He dropped the dishcloth, rushed out to get his copy of the *Dispatch* and quickly checked the front page, wondering if the press could have somehow got hold of the story. Clinton dominated the headlines, with trouble in Iraq flaring up again. The President was promising to send in more troops to guard the Kuwaiti border if it proved necessary.

'They should have finished off the job in the first place,' McKenzie muttered as he closed the front door. 'Saddam is not a man who works by the book.'

He tried to take in the details of the story but couldn't concentrate on the words. He gathered from the editorial that the *Dispatch* thought Clinton was facing his first real crisis. The President doesn't begin to know what a crisis is, thought T. Hamilton McKenzie. After all, his daughter had slept safely in the White House the previous night.

He almost cheered when the clock in the hall eventually struck eight. Joni appeared at the bottom of the stairs, fully dressed. She checked his collar and brushed some dandruff off his shoulder, as if he were about to leave for a normal day's work at the university. She didn't comment on his choice of tie.

'Come straight home,' she added, as she always did.

'Of course I will,' he said, kissing his wife on the cheek and leaving without another word.

As soon as the garage door swung up, he saw the flickering headlights and swore out loud. He must have forgotten to turn them off the previous night when he had been so cross with his daughter. This time he directed his anger at himself, and swore again.

He climbed in behind the wheel, put the key in the ignition and prayed. He switched the lights off and, after a short pause, turned the key. First quickly, then slowly, he tried to coax the engine into action, but it barely clicked as he pumped the accelerator pedal up and down.

'Not today!' he screamed, banging the steering wheel

with the palms of his hands. He tried a couple more times and then jumped out and ran back to the house. He didn't take his thumb off the bell until Joni opened the door with a questioning look on her face.

'My battery's flat. I need your car, quickly, quickly!'

'It's being serviced. You've been telling me for weeks to have it attended to.' T. Hamilton McKenzie didn't wait to offer an opinion. He turned his back on his wife, ran down the drive into the road and began searching the tree-lined avenue for the familiar yellow colour with a sign reading 444 4444 attached to the roof. But he realised there was a hundred to one chance of finding a cab driving around looking for a fare that early in the morning. All he could see was a bus heading towards him. He knew the stop was a hundred yards away, so he began running in the same direction as the bus. Although he was still a good twenty or thirty yards short of the stop when it passed him, the bus pulled in and waited.

McKenzie climbed up the steps, panting. 'Thank you,' he said. 'Does this bus go to Olentangy River Road?'

'Gets real close, man.'

'Then let's get going,' said T. Hamilton McKenzie. He checked his watch. It was 8.17 a.m. With a bit of luck he might still make the meeting on time. He began to look for a seat.

'That'll be a dollar,' said the driver, staring at his retreating back.

T. Hamilton McKenzie rummaged in his Sunday suit.

'Oh, my God,' he said. 'I've left . . .'

'Don't try that one, man,' said the driver. 'No cash, no dash.'

McKenzie turned to face him once again. 'You don't understand, I have an important appointment. A matter of life and death.'

'So is keeping my job, man. I gotta stick by the book. If

you can't pay, you've gotta debus 'cause that's what the regulations say.'

'But –' spluttered McKenzie.

'I'll give you a dollar for that watch,' said a young man seated in the second row who'd been enjoying the confrontation.

T. Hamilton McKenzie looked at the gold Rolex that had been presented to him for twenty-five years' service to the Ohio State University Hospital. He whipped it off his wrist and handed it over to the young man.

'It *must* be a matter of life and death,' said the young man as he exchanged the prize for a dollar. He slipped the watch onto his wrist. T. Hamilton McKenzie handed the dollar on to the driver.

'You didn't strike a good bargain there, man,' he said, shaking his head. 'You could have had a week in a stretch limo for a Rolex.'

'Come on, let's get going!' shouted McKenzie.

'It's not me who's been holding us up, man,' said the driver as he moved slowly away from the kerb.

T. Hamilton McKenzie sat in the front seat wishing it were he who was driving. He looked at his watch. It wasn't there. He turned round and asked the youth, 'What's the time?' The young man looked proudly at his new acquisition, which he hadn't taken his eyes off for one moment.

'Twenty-six minutes after eight and twenty seconds.'

McKenzie stared out of the window, willing the bus to go faster. It stopped seven times to drop and pick up passengers before they finally reached the corner of Independence, by which time the driver feared the watchless man was about to have a heart attack. As T. Hamilton McKenzie jumped off the steps of the bus, he heard the clock on the town hall strike 8.45 a.m.

'Oh God, let them still be there,' he said as he ran

towards the Olentangy Inn, hoping no one would recognise him. He stopped running only when he had reached the path that led up to reception. He tried to compose himself, aware that he was badly out of breath and sweating from head to toe.

He pushed through the swing door of the coffee shop and peered around the room, having no idea who or what he was looking for. He imagined that everyone was staring back at him.

The coffee shop had about sixty café tables in twos and fours, and he would have guessed it was about half full. Two of the corner tables were already taken, so McKenzie headed to the one that gave him the best view of the door.

He sat and waited, praying that they hadn't given up on him.

It was when Hannah arrived back at the crossing on the corner of Thurloe Place that she first had the feeling someone was following her. By the time she had reached the pavement on the South Kensington side, she was convinced of it.

A tall man, young, evidently not very experienced at shadowing, bobbed rather obviously in and out of doorways. Perhaps he thought she wasn't the type who would ever be suspicious. Hannah had about a quarter of a mile in which to plan her next move. By the time the Norfolk came in sight, she knew exactly what needed to be done. If she could get into the building well ahead of him, she estimated she only needed about thirty, perhaps forty-five, seconds at most, unless the porters were both fully occupied. She paused at the front window of a chemist's shop and stared at the array of beauty products that filled the shelves. She turned to look towards the lipsticks in the corner and saw his reflection in the brightly polished window. He was standing by a newspaper stand at the entrance to South Kensington tube station. He picked up a copy of the *Daily Mail* – amateur, she thought – which gave her the chance to cross the road before he could collect his change. She had reached the front door of the hotel by the time he had passed the chemist. Hannah didn't run up the steps, as it would have acknowledged his existence, but mistakenly pushed the revolving door so sharply that she sent an unsuspecting old lady tumbling onto the pavement much sooner than she'd intended.

The two porters were chatting as she shot across the lobby. The red ticket and another pound were already in her hand before she reached the porters' desk. Hannah slammed the coin down on the counter, which immediately attracted the older man's attention. When he spotted the pound, he quickly took the ticket, retrieved Hannah's little case and returned it to her just as her pursuer was coming through the revolving doors. She headed in the direction of the staircase at the end of the corridor, clutching the little case close to her stomach so the man following her would be unaware that she was carrying anything. When she reached the second step of the staircase she did run, as there was no one else in sight. Once down the staircase she bolted across the corridor and into the comparative safety of the ladies' room.

This time she was not alone. A middle-aged woman was leaning over a washbasin to check her lipstick. She didn't give Hannah so much as a glance when she disappeared into one of the cubicles. Hannah sat on the top of the lavatory, her knees tucked under her chin as she waited for the woman to finish her handiwork. It was two or three minutes before she finally left. Once Hannah heard the door close, she lowered her feet onto the cold marble floor, opened the battered suitcase to check everything was there and, satisfied that it was, changed back into her T-shirt, baggy sweater and jeans as quickly as she could.

She'd just managed to get her sneakers on when the door opened again, and she watched the lower part of two stockinged legs cross the floor and enter the cubicle next to hers. Hannah shot out, and buttoned up her jeans, before checking herself quickly in the mirror. She ruffled her hair a little and then began checking round the room. There was a large receptacle in the corner for depositing dirty towels. Hannah removed the plastic lid, took out all the towels that were there and forced her little case to the bottom, then quickly covered it with the towels and put the lid back in place. She tried to forget she had carried the bag from Leningrad to Tel Aviv to London – halfway across the world. She cursed in her native tongue before checking her hair in the mirror again. Then she strolled out of the ladies' room, attempting to appear calm, even casual.

The first thing Hannah saw when she stepped into the corridor was the young man sitting at the far end reading the *Daily Mail*. With luck, he wouldn't even give her a second thought. She had reached the bottom of the stairs when he glanced up. Rather good-looking, she thought, staring back at him for a second too long. She turned and began to climb the staircase. She was away; she'd made it.

'Excuse me, miss,' said a voice from behind her. Don't panic, don't run, act normally. She turned and smiled. He smiled back, almost flirting with her, and then blushed.

'Did you by any chance see an Arab lady when you were in the rest room?'

'Yes, I did,' replied Hannah. 'But why do you ask?' she demanded. Always put the enemy on the defensive whenever possible was the standard rule.

'Oh, it's not important. Sorry to have bothered you,' he said, and disappeared back around the corner.

Hannah climbed the stairs, returned to the lobby and headed straight for the revolving doors.

Pity, she thought once she was back on the pavement. He looked rather sexy. She wondered how long he would sit there, who he was working for, and to whom he would eventually be reporting.

Hannah began to retrace her steps home, regretting that she couldn't drop into Dino's for a quick spaghetti bolognese and then take in Frank Marshall's latest film, which was showing at the Cannon. There were still times when she yearned to be just a young woman in London. And then she thought of her mother, her brother, her sister, and once again told herself all of that would have to wait.

She sat alone for the first part of the tube journey, and was beginning to believe that if they sent her to Baghdad – as long as no one wanted to go to bed with her – she could surely now pass herself off as an Iraqi.

When the train pulled in to Green Park two youths hopped on. Hannah ignored them. But as the doors clamped shut she became aware that there was no one else in the carriage.

After a few moments, one of them sauntered over towards her and grinned vacantly. He was dressed in a black bomber jacket with the collar covered in studs, and his jeans were so tight they made him look like a ballet dancer. His spiky black hair stood up so straight that it looked as if he had just received convulsive shock therapy. Hannah thought he was probably in his early twenties. She glanced down at his feet to see that he was wearing heavy-duty army boots. Although he was a little overweight, she suspected from his movements that he was quite fit. His friend stood a few paces away, leaning against the railing by the door.

'So what do you say to my mate's suggestion of a quick strip?' he asked, removing a flick-knife from his pocket.

'Get lost,' Hannah replied evenly.

'Oh, a member of the upper classes, eh?' he said, offering the same vacant grin. 'Fancy a gang bang, do we?'

'Fancy a thick lip, do you?' she countered.

'Don't get clever with me, lady,' he said as the train pulled in to Piccadilly Circus.

His friend stood in the doorway so that anyone who might have considered entering the end carriage thought better of it.

Never seek attention, never cause a scene: the accepted rule if you work for any branch of the secret service, especially when you're stationed abroad. Only break the rules in extreme circumstances.

'My friend Marv fancies you. Did you know that, Sloane?'

Hannah smiled at him as she began planning the route she would have to take out of the carriage once the train pulled in to the next station.

'Quite like you myself,' he said. 'But I prefer black birds. It's their big bums, you know. They turn me on.'

'Then you'll like your friend,' said Hannah, regretting her words the moment she had said them. Never provoke.

She heard the click as a long thin blade shot out and flashed in the brightly lit carriage.

'Now there are two ways we can go about this, Sloane – quietly or noisily. It's your choice. But if you don't feel like co-operating, I might have to make a few etchings in that pretty face of yours.' The youth by the door began laughing. Hannah rose and faced her tormentor. She paused before slowly undoing the top button of her jeans.

'She's all yours, Marv,' said the young man as he turned to face his friend. He never saw the foot fly through the air as Hannah swivelled 180 degrees. The knife went flying out of his hand and shot across the floor to the far end of the carriage. A flat arm came down across his neck and he slumped to the ground in a heap, looking like a sack of potatoes. She stepped over his body and headed towards Marv.

'No, no, miss. Not me. Owen's always been the trouble-maker. I wouldn't have done nothin', not me, nothin'.'

'Take off your jeans, Marvin.'

'What?'

She straightened the fingers of her right hand.

'Anything you say, miss.' Marvin quickly undid his zip and pulled off his jeans to reveal a grubby pair of navy Y-fronts and a tattoo on his thigh that read 'Mum'.

'I do hope your mother doesn't have to see you like that too often, Marvin,' Hannah said as she picked up his jeans. 'Now the pants.'

'What?'

'You heard me, Marvin.'

Marvin slowly pulled off his Y-fronts.

'How disappointing,' said Hannah as the train pulled in to Leicester Square.

As the doors squelched closed behind her Hannah thought she heard, 'You filthy bitch, I'll . . .'

As she walked down the passage to the Northern line, Hannah couldn't find a litter bin in which to dispose of Marvin's grubby clothing. They had all been removed some time before after a sudden outbreak of IRA bombs in the London Underground. She had to carry the jeans and pants all the way to Chalk Farm, where she finally deposited them in a skip on the corner of Adelaide Road, then strolled quietly back home.

As she opened the front door, a cheery voice called

from the kitchen, 'Lunch is on the table, my dear.' Mrs Rubin walked through to join Hannah and declared, 'I've had the most fascinating morning. You wouldn't believe what happened to me at Sainsbury's.'

'What will it be, honey?' asked a waitress who wore a red skirt and a black apron and held a pad in her hand.

'Just black coffee, please,' said T. Hamilton McKenzie.

'Coming right up,' she said cheerfully.

He was about to check the time when he was reminded once again that his watch was on the wrist of a young man who was now probably miles away. McKenzie looked up at the clock above the counter. Eight fifty-six. He began to check everyone as they came through the door.

A tall, well-dressed man was the first to walk in, and as he scanned the room McKenzie became quite hopeful and willed him to look in his direction. But the man walked towards the counter and took a seat on a stool, with his back to the restaurant. The waitress returned and poured the nervous doctor a steaming black coffee.

Next to enter the room was a young woman, carrying a shopping bag with a long rope handle. She was followed a moment later by another smartly-dressed man who also searched the room with his eyes. Once again, T. Hamilton McKenzie's hopes were raised, only to be dashed when a smile of recognition flickered across the man's face. He too headed for the counter and took the stool next to the man who had come in a few moments earlier.

The girl with the shopping bag slipped into the place opposite him. 'That seat's taken,' said T. Hamilton McKenzie, his voice rising with every word.

'I know, Dr McKenzie,' said the girl. 'It's been taken by me.'

T. Hamilton McKenzie began to perspire.

'Coffee, honey?' asked the waitress who appeared by their side.

'Yes, black,' was all she said, not glancing up.

McKenzie looked at the young woman more carefully. She must have been around thirty – still at an age when she didn't require his professional services. From her accent, she was undoubtedly a native of New York, though with her dark hair, dark eyes and olive skin her family must surely have emigrated from southern Europe. She was slight, almost frail, and her neatly-patterned Laura Ashley dress of autumn browns, which could have been purchased in any one of a thousand stores across the country, made certain she would be forgettable in any crowd. She didn't touch the coffee that was placed in front of her.

McKenzie decided to go on the attack. 'I want to know how Sally is.'

'She's fine, just fine,' said the woman calmly. She reached down and with a gloved hand removed a single sheet of paper from her bag. She passed it over to him. He unfolded the anonymous-looking sheet:

Dear Daddy

They are treating me well but please agree to whatever they want.

Love Sal.

It was her writing, no question of that, but she would never have signed herself 'Sal'. The coded message only made him more anxious.

The woman leaned across and snatched the letter back.

'You bastards. You won't get away with it,' he said, staring across at her.

'Calm down, Dr McKenzie. No amount of threats or rhetoric is going to influence us. It's not the first time we've carried out this sort of operation. So, if you hope to see your daughter again . . .'

'What do you expect me to do?'

The waitress returned to the table with a fresh pot of coffee, but when she saw that neither party had taken a sip she said, 'Coffee's getting cold, folks,' and moved on.

'I've only got about $200,000 to my name. You must have made some mistake.'

'It's not your money we're after, Dr McKenzie.'

'Then what *do* you want? I'll do anything to get my daughter back safely.'

'The company I represent specialises in gathering skills, and one of our clients is in need of your particular expertise.'

'But you could have called and made an appointment like anyone else,' he said in disbelief.

'Not for what we have in mind, I suspect. And, in any case, we have a time problem, and we felt Sally might help us get to the front of the queue.'

'I don't understand.'

'That's why I'm here,' said the woman. Twenty minutes later, when both cups of coffee were stone cold, T. Hamilton McKenzie understood exactly what was expected of him. He was silent for some time before he said, 'I'm not sure if I can do it. To begin with, it's professionally unethical. And do you realise just how hard –'

The woman leaned down and removed something else from her bag. She tossed a small gold earring over to his side of the table. 'Perhaps this will make it a little easier for you.' T. Hamilton McKenzie picked up his daughter's earring. 'Tomorrow you get the other earring,' the woman continued. 'On Friday the first ear. On Saturday the other ear. If you keep on worrying about your ethics, Dr McKenzie, there won't be much of your daughter left by this time next week.'

'You wouldn't . . .'

'Ask John Paul Getty III if we wouldn't.'

T. Hamilton McKenzie rose from the table and leaned across.

'We can speed the whole process up if that's the way you want it,' she added, displaying not the slightest sign of fear.

McKenzie slumped back into his seat and tried to compose himself.

'Good,' she said. 'That's better. At least we now seem to understand each other.'

'So what happens next?' he asked.

'We'll be back in touch with you sometime later today. So make sure you're in. Because I feel confident that by then you'll have come to terms with your professional ethics.'

McKenzie was about to protest when the woman stood up, took a five-dollar bill out of her bag and placed it on the table.

'Can't have Columbus's leading surgeon washing up the dishes, can we?' She turned to leave and had reached the door before it struck McKenzie that they even knew he had left the house without his wallet.

T. Hamilton McKenzie began to consider her proposition, not certain if he had been left with any alternative.

But he was certain of one thing. If he carried out their demands, then President Clinton was going to end up with an even bigger problem.

6

A QUIET MAN sat on a stool at the end of the bar emptying the final drops in his glass. The glass had been almost empty of Guinness for some time, but the Irishman always hoped that the movement would arouse some sympathy in the barman, and he might just be kind enough to pour a drop more into the empty glass. But not this particular barman.

'Bastard,' he said under his breath. It was always the young ones who had no heart.

The barman didn't know the customer's real name. For that matter, few people did except the FBI and the San Francisco Police Department.

The file at the SFPD gave William Sean O'Reilly's age as fifty-two. A casual onlooker might have judged him to be nearer sixty-five, not just because of his well-worn clothes, but from the pronounced lines on his forehead, the wrinkled bags under his eyes and the extra inches around his waist. O'Reilly blamed it on three alimonies, four jail sentences and going too many rounds in his youth as an amateur boxer. He never blamed it on the Guinness.

The problem had begun at school when O'Reilly discovered by sheer chance that he could copy his classmates' signatures when they signed chits to withdraw pocket money from the school bank. By the time he had completed his first year at Trinity College, Dublin, he could forge the signatures of the provost and the bursar so well that even they believed that they had awarded him a bursary.

While at St Patrick's Institution for Offenders, Bill was introduced to the banknote by Liam the Counterfeiter. When they opened the gates to let him out, the young apprentice had nothing left to learn from the master. Bill discovered that his mother was unwilling to allow him to return to the bosom of the family, so he forged the signature of the American Consul in Dublin and departed for the brave new world.

By the age of thirty, he had etched his first dollar plate. The work was so good that, during the trial that followed its discovery, the FBI acknowledged that the counterfeit was a masterpiece which would never have been detected without the help of an informer. O'Reilly was sentenced to six years and the crime desk of the *San Francisco Chronicle* dubbed him 'Dollar Bill'.

When Dollar Bill was released from jail, he moved on to tens, twenties and later fifties, and his sentences increased in direct proportion. In between sentences he managed three wives and three divorces. Something else his mother wouldn't have approved of.

His third wife did her best to keep him on the straight and narrow, and Bill responded by producing documents only when he couldn't get any other work – the odd passport, the occasional driver's licence or social security claim – nothing really criminal, he assured the judge. The judge didn't agree and sent him back down for another five years.

When Dollar Bill was released this time, nobody would touch him, so he had to resort to doing tattoos at fairgrounds and, in desperation, pavement paintings which, when it didn't rain, just about kept him in Guinness.

Bill lifted the empty glass and stared once again at the barman, who returned a look of stony indifference. He failed to notice the smartly-dressed young man who took a seat on the other side of him.

'What can I get you to drink, Mr O'Reilly?' said a voice he didn't recognise. Bill looked round suspiciously. 'I'm retired,' he declared, fearing that it was another of those young plain-clothes detectives from the San Francisco Police Department who hadn't made his quota of arrests for the month.

'Then you won't mind having a drink with an old con, will you?' said the younger man, revealing a slight Bronx accent.

Bill hesitated, but the thirst won.

'A pint of draught Guinness,' he said hopefully.

The young man raised his hand and this time the barman responded immediately.

'So what do you want?' asked Bill, once he'd taken a swig and was sure the barman was out of earshot.

'Your skill.'

'But I'm retired. I already told you.'

'And I heard you the first time. But what I require isn't criminal.'

'So what are you hoping I'll knock up for you? A copy of the *Mona Lisa*, or is it to be the Magna Carta?'

'Nearer home than that,' said the young man.

'Buy me another,' said Bill, staring at the empty glass that stood on the counter in front of him, 'and I'll listen to your proposition. But I warn you, I'm still retired.'

After the barman had filled Bill's glass a second time, the young man introduced himself as Angelo Santini, and began to explain to Dollar Bill exactly what he had in mind. Angelo was grateful that at four in the afternoon there was no one else around to overhear them.

'But there are already thousands of those in circulation,' said Dollar Bill when Angelo had finished. 'You could buy a good reproduction from any decent tourist shop.'

'Maybe, but not a perfect copy,' insisted the young man.

Dollar Bill put down his drink and thought about the statement.

'Who wants one?'

'It's for a client who's a collector of rare manuscripts,' Angelo said. 'And he'll pay a good price.'

Not a bad lie, as lies go, thought Bill. He took another sip of Guinness. 'But it would take me weeks,' he said, almost under his breath. 'In any case, I'd have to move to Washington.'

'We've already found a suitable place for you in Georgetown, and I'm sure we can lay our hands on all the materials you'd need.'

Dollar Bill considered this claim for a moment, before taking another gulp and declaring, 'Forget it – it sounds too much like hard work. As I explained, it would take me weeks and, worse, I'd have to stop drinking,' he added, placing his empty glass back on the counter. 'You must understand, I'm a perfectionist.'

'That's exactly why I've travelled from one side of the country to the other to find you,' said Angelo quietly. Dollar Bill hesitated and looked at the young man more carefully.

'I'd want $25,000 down and $25,000 on completion, with all expenses paid,' said the Irishman.

The young man couldn't believe his luck. Cavalli had authorised him to spend up to $100,000 if he could guarantee the finished article. But then he remembered that his boss never trusted anyone who didn't bargain.

'$10,000 when we reach Washington and another $20,000 on completion.'

Dollar Bill toyed with his empty glass.

'$30,000 on completion if you can't tell the difference between mine and the original.'

'But we'll need to tell the difference,' said Angelo. 'You'll get your $30,000 if no one else can.'

Scott heard the phone ringing when he was at the foot of the stairs. His mind was still going over the morning lecture he had just given, but he leaped up the stairs three at a time, pushed open the door of his apartment and grabbed the phone, knocking his mother to the floor.

'Scott Bradley,' he said as he picked up the photograph and replaced it on the sideboard.

'I need you in Washington tomorrow. My office, nine o'clock sharp.'

Scott was always impressed by the way Dexter Hutchins never introduced himself, and assumed that the work he did for the CIA was more important than his commitment to Yale.

It took Scott most of the afternoon to rearrange his teaching schedule with two understanding colleagues. He couldn't use the excuse of not feeling well, as everyone on campus knew he hadn't missed a day's work through illness in nine years. So he fell back on 'woman trouble', which always elicited sympathy from the older professors, but didn't lead them to ask too many questions.

Dexter Hutchins never gave any details over the phone as to why Scott was needed, but as all the morning papers had carried pictures of Yitzhak Rabin arriving in Washington for his first meeting with President Clinton, he made the obvious assumption.

Scott removed the file that was lodged between Tax and Torts and extracted everything he had about the new

Israeli Prime Minister. His policy towards America didn't seem to differ greatly from that of his predecessor. He was better educated than Shamir, more conciliatory and gentler in his approach, but Scott suspected that if it came to a knife fight in a downtown bar, Rabin was the one who would come out unmarked.

He leaned back and started thinking about a blonde named Susan Anderson who had been present at the last briefing he had been asked to attend with the new Secretary of State. If she was at the meeting, the trip to Washington might prove worthwhile.

The following morning a black limousine with smoked windows pulled up outside Ohio State University Hospital. The chauffeur parked in the space reserved for T. Hamilton McKenzie, as he had been instructed to do.

His only other orders were to pick up a patient at ten o'clock and drive him to the University of Cincinnati and Homes Hospital.

At 10.10, two white-coated orderlies wheeled a tall, well-built man in a chair out through the swing doors and, seeing the car parked in the Dean's space, guided him towards it. The driver jumped out and quickly opened the back door. Poor man, he thought, his head all covered in bandages and only a small crack left for his lips and nostrils. He wondered if it had been burns.

The stockily-built man clambered from the wheelchair into the back, sank into the luxurious upholstery and stretched out his legs. The driver told him, 'I'm going to put on your seatbelt,' and received a curt nod in response.

He returned to his seat in the front and lowered his window to say goodbye to the two orderlies and an older, rather distinguished-looking man who stood behind them. The driver had never seen such a drained face.

The limousine moved off at a sedate pace. The chauffeur had been warned not, under any circumstances, to break the speed limit.

T. Hamilton McKenzie was overcome with relief as he watched the car disappear down the hospital drive. He hoped the nightmare was at last coming to an end. The operation had taken him seven hours, and the previous night had been the first time he had slept soundly for the past week. The last order he had received was to go home and wait for Sally's release.

When the demand had been put to him by the woman who left five dollars on the table at the Olentangy Inn, he had considered it impossible. Not, as he had suggested, on ethical grounds, but because he had thought he could never achieve a true likeness. He had wanted to explain to her about autografting, the external epithelium and the deeper corium, and how unlikely it was that . . . But when he saw the unnamed man in his private office, he immediately realised why they had chosen him. He was almost the right height, perhaps a shade short – an inch, no more – and he might have been five to ten pounds too light. But shoe lifts and a few Big Macs would sort out both of those problems.

The skull and features were remarkable and bore a stunning resemblance to the original. In fact in the end it had only proved necessary to perform rhinoplasty and a partial thickness graft. The results were good, very good. The surgeon assumed that the man's red hair was irrelevant because they could shave his head and use a wig. With a new set of teeth and good make-up, only his immediate family would be able to tell the difference.

McKenzie had had several different teams working with him during the seven hours in the operating theatre. He'd told them he needed fresh help whenever he began to tire. No one ever questioned T. Hamilton McKenzie inside the hospital, and only he had seen the final result. He had kept his side of the bargain.

She parked the Ford Taurus – America's most popular car – a hundred yards from the house, but not before she'd swung it round to face the direction in which she would be leaving.

She changed her shoes in the car. The only time she had nearly been caught was when some mud had stuck to the soles of her shoes and the FBI had traced it to within yards of a spot she had visited a few days before.

She swung her bag over her shoulder and stepped out onto the road. She began to walk slowly towards the house.

They had chosen the location well. The farmhouse was several miles from the nearest building – and that was an empty barn – at the end of a track that even desperate lovers would have thought twice about.

There was no sign of anyone being in the house, but she knew they were there, waiting, watching her every move. She opened the door without knocking and immediately saw one of them in the hall.

'Upstairs,' he said, pointing. She did not reply as she walked past him and began to climb the stairs.

She went straight into the bedroom and found the young girl sitting on the end of the bed reading. Sally turned and smiled at the slim woman in the green Laura Ashley dress, hoping that she had brought another book with her.

The woman placed a hand in her bag and smiled shyly, before pulling out a paperback and passing it over to the young girl.

'Thank you,' said Sally, who took the book, checked the cover and then quickly turned it over to study the plot summary.

While Sally became engrossed by the promised story, the woman unclipped the long plaited rope that was attached to the two sides of her shopping bag.

Sally opened the book at the first chapter, having already decided she would have to read every page very slowly. After all, she couldn't be sure when the next offering might come.

The movement was so fast that she didn't even feel the rope go round her neck. Sally's head jerked back and with one flick her vertebra was broken. Her chin slumped onto her chest.

Blood began to trickle out of her mouth, down her chin and onto the cover of *A Time to Love and a Time to . . .*

The driver of the limousine was surprised to be flagged down by a traffic cop just as he was about to take the exit ramp onto the freeway. He felt sure he hadn't broken the speed limit. Then he spotted the ambulance in his rear-view mirror, and wondered if they simply wanted to pass him. He looked to the front again to see the motorcycle cop was firmly waving him onto the hard shoulder.

He immediately obeyed the order and brought the car to a standstill, puzzled as to what was going on. The ambulance drew in and stopped behind him. The cop dismounted from his motorcycle, walked up to the driver's door and tapped on the window. The chauffeur touched a button in the armrest and the window slid silently down.

'Is there a problem, officer?'

'Yes, sir, we have an emergency on our hands,' the

policeman said without raising his visor. 'Your patient has to return to the Ohio State University Hospital immediately. There have been unforeseen complications. You're to transfer him to the ambulance and I will escort them back into the city.'

The wide-eyed driver agreed with a series of consenting nods. 'Should I go back to the hospital as well?' he asked.

'No, sir, you're to continue to Cincinnati and report to your office.'

The driver turned his head to see two paramedics dressed in white overalls standing by the side of the car. The policeman nodded and one of them opened the back door while the other released the seatbelt so that he could help the patient out.

The driver glanced in the rear-view mirror and watched the paramedics guide the well-built man towards the ambulance. The siren on the motorcycle brought his attention back to the policeman who was now directing the ambulance up the exit ramp so that it could cross the bridge over the highway and begin its journey back into the city.

The whole changeover had taken less than five minutes, leaving the driver in the limousine feeling somewhat dazed. He then did what he felt he should have done the moment he saw the policeman, and telephoned his headquarters in Cincinnati.

'We were just about to call you,' said the girl on the switchboard. 'They don't need the car any longer, so you may as well come straight back.'

'Suits me,' said the driver. 'I just hope the client pays the bill.'

'They paid cash in advance last Thursday,' she replied. The driver clicked the phone back on its cradle and began his journey to Cincinnati. But something was nagging in the back of his mind. Why had the policeman stood so close to the door that he couldn't get out, and why hadn't he raised his visor? He dismissed such thoughts. As long as the company had been paid, it wasn't his problem.

He drove up onto the freeway, and didn't see the ambulance ignore the signpost to the city centre and join the stream of traffic going in the opposite direction. The man behind the wheel was also contacting his headquarters.

'It went as planned, boss,' was all he replied to the first question.

'Good,' said Cavalli. 'And the chauffeur?'

'On his way back to Cincinnati, none the wiser.'

'Good,' Cavalli repeated. 'And the patient?'

'Fine, as far as I can tell,' said the driver, glancing in the rear-view mirror.

'And the police escort?'

'Mario took a detour down a side road so he could get changed into his Federal Express uniform. He should catch up with us within the hour.'

'How long before the next switch?'

The driver checked the milometer. 'Must be about another ninety miles, just after we cross the state line.'

'And then?'

'Four more changes between there and the Big Apple. Fresh drivers and a different car each time. The patient should be with you around midnight tomorrow, though he may have to stop off at a rest room or two along the way.'

'No rest rooms,' said Cavalli. 'Just take him off the highway and hide him behind a tree.'

7

DOLLAR BILL'S NEW HOME turned out to be the basement of a house in Georgetown, formerly an artist's studio. The room where he worked was well lit without glare and, at his request, the temperature was kept at sixty-six degrees with a constant humidity.

Bill attempted several 'dry runs' as he called them, but he couldn't get started on the final document until he had all the materials he needed. 'Nothing but perfection will do,' he kept reminding Angelo. He would not have his name associated with anything that might later be denounced as a forgery. After all, he had his reputation to consider.

For days they searched in vain for the right pen nibs. Dollar Bill rejected them all until he was shown a picture of some in a small museum in Virginia. He nodded his approval and they were in his hands the following afternoon.

The curator of the museum told a reporter from the *Richmond Times Dispatch* that she was puzzled by the theft. The pens were not of any historic importance or particularly valuable. There were far more irreplaceable objects in the next display case.

'Depends who needs them,' said Dollar Bill when he was shown the press cutting.

The ink was a little easier once Bill had found the right

shade of black. When it was on the paper he knew exactly how to control the viscosity by temperature and evaporation to give the impression of old age. Several pots were tested until he had more than enough to carry out the job.

While others were searching for the materials he needed, Dollar Bill read several books from the Library of Congress and spent a few minutes every day in the National Archives until he discovered the one mistake he could afford to make.

But the toughest requirement proved to be the parchment itself, because Dollar Bill wouldn't consider anything that was less than two hundred years old. He tried to explain to Angelo about carbon dating.

Samples were flown in from Paris, Amsterdam, Vienna, Montreal and Athens, but the forger rejected them all. It was only when a package arrived from Bremen with a selection dated 1781 that Dollar Bill gave a smile which only Guinness normally brought to his lips.

He touched, caressed and fondled the parchment as a young man might a new lover but, unlike a lover, he pressed, rolled and flattened the object of his attentions until he was confident it was ready to receive the baptism of ink. He then prepared ten sheets of exactly the same size, knowing that only one would eventually be used.

Bill studied the ten parchments for several hours. Two were dismissed within a moment, and four more by the end of the day. Using one of the four remaining sheets, the craftsman worked on a rough copy that Angelo, when he first saw it, considered perfect.

'Perfect to the amateur eye, possibly,' Bill said, 'but a professional would spot the seventeen mistakes I've made within moments. Destroy it.'

During the next week three copies of the text were

executed in the basement of Dollar Bill's new home in Georgetown. No one was allowed to enter the room while he was working, and the door remained locked whenever he took a break. He worked in two-hour shifts and then rested for two hours. Light meals were brought to him twice a day and he drank nothing but water, even in the evening. At night, exhausted, he would often sleep for eight hours without stirring.

Once he had completed the three copies of the forty-six-line text, Dollar Bill declared himself satisfied with two of them. The third was destroyed.

Angelo reported back to Cavalli, who seemed pleased with Dollar Bill's progress, although neither of them had been allowed to see the two final copies.

'Now comes the hard part,' Bill told Angelo. 'Fifty-six signatures, every one requiring a different nib, a different pressure, a different shade of ink, and every one a work of art in itself.'

Angelo accepted this analysis, but was less happy to learn that Dollar Bill insisted on a day off before he began to work on the names because he needed to get paralytically drunk.

Professor Bradley flew into Washington on Tuesday evening and booked himself into the Ritz Carlton – the one luxury the CIA allowed the schizophrenic agent/professor. After a light dinner in the Jockey Club, accompanied only by a book, Scott retired to his room on the fifth floor. He flicked channels from one bad movie to another before falling asleep thinking about Susan Anderson.

He woke at six-thirty the next morning, rose, and read the *Washington Post* from cover to cover, concentrating on the articles dealing with Rabin's visit. He got dressed watching a CNN report on the Israeli Prime Minister's speech at a White House dinner that had taken place the previous evening. Rabin assured the new President he wanted the same warm relationship with America that his predecessor had enjoyed.

After a light breakfast, Scott strolled out of the hotel to find a company car waiting for him.

'Good morning, sir,' were the only words his driver spoke on the entire journey. It was a pleasant trip out of the city that Wednesday morning, but Scott smiled wryly as he watched commuters blocking all three lanes going in the opposite direction.

When he arrived at Dexter Hutchins' office ten minutes before his appointment, Tess, the Deputy Director's secretary, waved him straight through.

Dexter greeted Scott with a firm handshake and a cursory attempt at an apology.

'Sorry to pull you in at such short notice,' he said, removing the butt of a cigar from his mouth, 'but the Secretary of State wants you to be present for his working meeting with the Israeli Prime Minister. They're having one of the usual official lunches, rack of lamb and irrelevant small talk, and they expect to start the working session around three.'

'But why would Christopher want me there?' asked Scott.

'Our man in Tel Aviv says Rabin is going to come up with something that isn't officially on the agenda. That's all he could find out. No details. You know as much about the Middle East as anyone in the department, so Christopher wants you around. I've had Tess put the latest data together so that you'll be right up to date by the time we get to this afternoon's meeting.' Dexter Hutchins picked up a pile of files from the corner of his desk and handed them to Scott. The inevitable 'Top

Secret' was stamped on each of them, despite the fact that a lot of the information they contained could be found strewn across the Foreign Desk of the *Washington Post*.

'The first file is on the man himself and Labour Party policy; the others are on the PLO, Lebanon, Iran, Iraq, Syria, Saudi Arabia and Jordan, all in reference to our current defence policy. If Rabin's hoping to get more money out of us, he can think again, especially after Clinton's speech last week on domestic policy. There's a copy in the bottom file.'

'Marked "Top Secret", no doubt,' said Scott.

Dexter Hutchins raised his eyebrows as Scott bundled up the files and left without another word. Tess unlocked a door that led to a small empty office next to her own. 'I'll make sure you're not disturbed, Professor,' she promised.

Scott turned the pages of the first file, and began to study a report on the secret talks that had been taking place in Norway between the Israelis and the PLO. When he came to the file on the Iraq–Iran conflict there was a whole section he'd written himself only two weeks before, recommending a surprise bombing mission on the Mukhbarat headquarters in Baghdad if the UN inspection team continued to be frustrated in their efforts to check Iraqi defence installations.

At twelve o'clock, Tess brought in a plate of sandwiches and a glass of milk as he began to read the reports on no-fly zones beyond the 36th and 32nd parallels in Iraq. When he had finished reading the President's speech, Scott spent another hour trying to puzzle out what change of course or surprise the new Prime Minister of Israel might have in mind. He was still deep in thought when Dexter Hutchins stuck his head round the door and said, 'Five minutes.'

In the car on the way to the State Department, Dexter asked Scott if he had any theories about what the Israeli leader might be going to surprise them with.

'Several, but I need to observe the man in action before I try to second guess. After all, I've only seen him once before, and on that occasion he still thought Bush might win the election.'

When they arrived at the C Street entrance it took almost as long for the two men from the CIA to reach the seventh floor as it always did for Scott to penetrate the inner sanctum of Langley.

At 2.53 they were ushered into an empty conference room. Scott selected a chair against the wall, just behind where Warren Christopher would be seated but slightly to his left so he would have a clear view of Prime Minister Rabin across the table. Dexter sat on Scott's right.

At one minute to three, five senior staffers entered the room, and Scott was pleased to see that Susan Anderson was among them. Her fine fair hair was done up in a coil, making her look rather austere, and she wore a tailored blue suit that accentuated her slim figure. The spotted white blouse with the little bow at the neck would have frightened off most men; it appealed to Scott.

'Good afternoon, Professor Bradley,' she said when Scott stood up. But she took a seat on the other side of Dexter Hutchins, and informed him that the Secretary of State would be joining them in a few moments.

'So how are the Orioles doing?' Scott asked, leaning forward and looking straight across at Susan, trying not to stare at her slim shapely legs. Susan blushed. From some file, Scott had recalled that she was a baseball fan, and when she wasn't accompanying the Secretary of State abroad, she never missed a game. Scott knew only too well that they had lost their last three matches.

'Doing about as well as Georgetown did in the NCAAs,' came back her immediate reply.

Scott could think of no suitable reply. Georgetown had failed to make the national tournament for the first time in years.

'Fifteen all,' said Dexter, who was obviously enjoying sitting on the high stool between them.

The door suddenly swung open and Warren Christopher entered the room accompanied by the Prime Minister of Israel, and followed by officials from both countries. They split down each side of the long table, taking their places according to seniority.

When the Secretary of State reached his seat at the centre of the table, in front of the American flag, he spotted Scott for the first time, and nodded an acknowledgement of his presence.

Once everyone was settled, the Secretary of State opened the meeting with a predictably banal speech of welcome, most of which could have been used for anyone from Yeltsin to Mitterrand. The Prime Minister of Israel responded in kind.

For the next hour they discussed a report on the meeting in Norway between representatives of the Israeli government and the PLO.

Rabin expressed his conviction that an agreement was progressing satisfactorily, but it remained vital that any further exchanges should continue in the utmost secrecy, as he feared that if his political opponents in Jerusalem got to hear of it, they could still scupper the whole plan before he was ready to make a public announcement.

Christopher nodded his agreement, and said it would be appreciated by the State Department if any such announcement could be made in Washington. Rabin smiled, but made no concession. The game of poker had begun. If he was to deliver the Americans such a public relations coup, he would expect something major in return. Only one more hand remained to be dealt before the home team discovered what that 'something' was.

It was during 'any other business' that Rabin raised the subject no one had anticipated. The Prime Minister circled around the problem for a few minutes, but Scott could see exactly where he was heading. Christopher was obviously being given the opportunity, if he wanted it, to kill any discussion stone dead before Rabin raised it officially.

Scott scribbled a note on a piece of paper and passed it over to Susan. She read his words, nodded, leaned across and placed the note on the blotting pad in front of the Secretary of State. He unfolded the single sheet, glanced at the contents but showed no sign of surprise. Scott assumed that Christopher had also worked out the size of the bombshell that was about to be dropped.

The Prime Minister had switched the discussion to the role of Israel in relation to Iraq, and reminded the Secretary of State three times that they had gone along with the Allied policy on Operation Desert Storm, when it was Tel Aviv and Haifa that were being hit by Scuds, not New York or Little Rock. It amused Scott that at the last meeting Rabin had said 'New York or Kennebunkport'.

He went on to say he had every reason to believe that Saddam was, once again, developing a nuclear weapon, and Tel Aviv and Haifa still had to be the first candidates for any warhead.

'Try not to forget, Mr Secretary, that we've already had to take out their nuclear reactors once in the past decade,' the Prime Minister said. 'And if necessary, we'll do so again.'

Christopher nodded, but made no comment.

'And were the Iraqis to succeed in developing a nuclear weapon,' continued Rabin, 'no amount of compensation or sympathy would help us this time. And I'm not willing to risk the consequences of that happening to the Israeli people while I'm Prime Minister.'

Christopher still offered no opinion.

'For over two years since the Gulf War ended, we have waited for the downfall of Saddam Hussein, either at the hands of his own people or, at least, by some outside influence encouraged by you. As each month goes by, the Israeli people are increasingly wondering if Operation Desert Storm was ever a victory in the first place.'

Christopher still didn't interrupt the Israeli Prime Minister's flow.

'The Israeli Government feels it has waited long enough for others to finish the job. We have therefore prepared a plan to assassinate Saddam Hussein.' He paused to allow the implications of his statement to sink in. 'We have at last found a way of breaching Saddam's security, and possibly of being invited into his bunker. Even so, this will still be a more difficult operation than those which led to the capture of Eichmann and the rescue of the hostages at Entebbe.'

The Secretary of State looked up. 'And are you willing to share this knowledge with us?' he asked quietly.

Scott knew what the reply would be even before the Prime Minister spoke, and so, he suspected, did Christopher.

'No, sir, I am not,' replied Rabin, looking down at the page in front of him. 'The only purpose of my statement is to ensure we do not clash with your colleagues from the CIA, as we have information which suggests that they are currently considering such a plan themselves.'

Dexter Hutchins thumped his knee with a clenched

fist. Scott hastily wrote a two-word note and passed it across to Susan. She removed her glasses, read the message and looked back at him. Scott nodded firmly, so she once again leaned forward and placed the note in front of the Secretary of State. He glanced at Scott's words, and this time he reacted immediately.

'We have no such plan,' said Christopher. 'I can assure you, Prime Minister, that your information is not correct.' Rabin looked surprised. 'And may I add that we naturally hope you will not consider any such action yourselves without keeping President Clinton fully informed.'

It was the first time the President's name had been brought into play, and Scott admired the way the Secretary of State had applied pressure without any suggestion of a threat.

'I hear your request,' replied the Prime Minister, 'but I must tell you, sir, that if Saddam is allowed to continue developing his nuclear arsenal, I cannot expect my people to sit by and watch.'

Christopher had reached the compromise he needed, and perhaps even gained a little time. For the next twenty minutes the Secretary of State tried to steer the conversation onto more friendly territory, but everyone in that room knew that once their guests had departed only one subject would come under discussion.

When the meeting was concluded the Secretary instructed his own staff to wait in the conference room while he accompanied the Prime Minister to his limousine. He returned a few minutes later with only one question for Scott.

'How can you be so sure Rabin was bluffing when he suggested we were also preparing a plan to eliminate Saddam? I watched his eyes and he gave away nothing,' said Christopher.

'I agree, sir,' replied Scott. 'But it was the one sentence he delivered in two hours that he read word for word. I don't even think he had written it himself. Some adviser had prepared the statement. And, more important, Rabin didn't believe it.'

'Do you believe the Israelis have a plan to assassinate Saddam Hussein?'

'Yes, I do,' said Scott. 'And what's more, despite what Rabin says about restraining his people, I suspect it was his idea in the first place. I think he knows every detail, including the likely date and place.'

'Do you have any theories on how they might go about it?'

'No, sir, I don't,' replied Scott.

Christopher turned to Susan. 'I want to meet with Ed Djerijian and his senior Middle Eastern people in my office in one hour, and I must see the President before he departs for Houston.'

Christopher turned to leave, but before he reached the door, he glanced back. 'Thank you, Scott. I'm glad you were able to get away from Yale. It looks as if we're going to be seeing a lot more of you over the next few weeks.' The Secretary of State disappeared out of the room.

'May I add my thanks, too,' said Susan as she gathered up her papers and scurried after her master.

'My pleasure,' said Scott, before adding, 'Care to join me for dinner tonight? Jockey Club, eight o'clock?'

Susan stopped in her tracks. 'You must do your research more thoroughly, Professor Bradley. I've been living with the same man for the past six years and . . .'

'. . . and I heard it wasn't going that well lately,' interjected Scott. 'In any case, he's away at a conference in Seattle, isn't he?'

She scribbled a note and passed it over to Dexter Hutchins. Dexter read the two words and laughed before passing it on to Scott: 'He's bluffing.'

When the two of them had been left alone, Dexter Hutchins also had one question that he needed answering.

'How could you be so sure that we aren't planning to take Saddam out?'

'I'm not,' admitted Scott. 'But I am certain that the Israelis don't have any information to suggest we are.'

Dexter smiled and said, 'Thanks for coming down from Connecticut, Scott. I'll be in touch. I've got a hunch the plane to Washington is going to feel like a shuttle for you over the next few months.' Scott nodded, relieved that the term was just about to end and no one would expect to see him around for several weeks.

Scott took a cab back to the Ritz Carlton, returned to his room and began to pack his overnight case. During the past year he'd considered a hundred ways that the Israelis might plan to assassinate Saddam Hussein, but all of them had flaws because of the massive protection that always surrounded the Iraqi President wherever he went. Scott felt certain also that Prime Minister Rabin would never sanction such an operation unless there was a good chance that his operatives would get home alive. Israel didn't need that sort of humiliation on top of all its other problems.

Scott flicked on the evening news. The President was heading to Houston to carry out a fund-raiser for Senator Bob Krueger, who was defending Lloyd Bentsen's seat in the special May elections. His plane had been late taking off from Andrews. There was no explanation as to why he was behind schedule – the new President was quickly gaining a reputation for working by Clinton Standard Time. All the White House correspondent was willing to say was that he had been locked in talks with the Secretary of State. Scott switched off the news and checked his watch. It was a little after seven, and his flight wasn't scheduled until 9.40. Just enough time to grab a bite before he left for the airport. He had only been offered sandwiches and a glass of milk all day, and considered that the CIA at least owed him a decent meal.

Scott went downstairs to the Jockey Club and was taken to a seat in the corner. A noisy congressman was telling a blonde half his age that the President had been locked in a meeting with Warren Christopher because 'they were discussing my amendment to the defence budget'. The blonde looked suitably impressed, even if the maître d' didn't.

Scott ordered the smoked salmon, a sirloin steak and a half bottle of Mouton Cadet before once again going over everything the Israeli Prime Minister had said at the meeting. But he concluded that the shrewd politician had given no clues as to how or when – or even whether – the Israelis would carry out their threat.

On the recommendation of the maître d', he agreed to try the house special, a chocolate soufflé. He convinced himself that he wasn't going to be fed like this again for some time and, in any case, he could work it off in the gym the next day. When he had finished the last mouthful, Scott checked his watch: three minutes past eight – just enough time for a coffee before grabbing a taxi to the airport.

Scott decided against a second cup, raised his hand and scribbled in the air to indicate that he'd like the check. When the maître d' returned, he had his MasterCard ready.

'Your guest has just arrived,' said the maître d', without indicating the slightest surprise.

'My guest . . .?' began Scott.

'Hello, Scott. I'm sorry I'm a little late, but the

President just went on and on asking questions.'

Scott stood up and slipped his MasterCard back into his pocket before kissing Susan on the cheek.

'You did say eight o'clock, didn't you?' she asked.

'Yes, I did,' said Scott, as if he had simply been waiting for her.

The maître d' reappeared with two large menus and handed them to her customers.

'I can recommend the smoked salmon and the steak,' she said without even a flicker of a smile.

'No, that sounds a bit too much for me,' said Susan. 'But don't let me stop you, Scott.'

'No, President Clinton's not the only one dieting,' said Scott. 'The consommé and the house salad will suit me just fine.' Scott looked at Susan as she studied the menu, her glasses propped on the end of her nose. She had changed from her well-cut dark blue suit into a calf-length pink dress that emphasised her slim figure even more. Her blonde hair now fell loosely on to her shoulders and for the first time in his memory she was wearing lipstick. She looked up and smiled.

'I'll have the crab cakes,' she told the maître d'.

'What did the President have to say?' asked Scott, as if they were still in a State Department briefing.

'Not a lot,' she said, lowering her voice. 'Except that if Saddam were to be assassinated he feels that he would become the Iraqis' number-one target.'

'A human enough response,' suggested Scott.

'Let's not talk politics,' said Susan. 'Let's talk about more interesting things. Why do you feel Ciseri is underrated and Bellini overrated?' she enquired. Scott realised Susan must have also read his internal file from cover to cover.

'So that's why you came. You're an art freak.'

For the next hour they discussed Bellini, Ciseri,

Caravaggio, Florence and Venice, which kept them fully occupied until the maître d' reappeared by their side.

She recommended the chocolate soufflé, and seemed disappointed that they both rejected the suggestion.

Over coffee, Scott told his guest about his life at Yale, and Susan admitted that she sometimes regretted she had not taken up an offer to teach at Stanford.

'One of the five universities you've honoured with your scholarship.'

'But never Yale, Professor Bradley,' she said before folding her napkin. Scott smiled. 'Thank you for a lovely evening,' she added as the maître d' returned with the check.

Scott signed it quickly, hoping she couldn't see, and that the CIA accounts department wouldn't query why it was a bill for three people.

When Susan went to the ladies' room Scott checked his watch. Ten twenty-five. The last plane had taken off nearly an hour before. He walked down to the front desk and asked if they could book him in for another night. The receptionist pressed a few keys on the computer, studied the result and said, 'Yes, that will be fine, Professor Bradley. Continental breakfast at seven and the *Washington Post* as usual?'

'Thank you,' he said as Susan reappeared by his side.

She linked her arm in his as they walked towards the taxis parked in the cobblestone driveway. The doorman opened the back door of the first taxi as Scott once again kissed Susan on the cheek.

'See you soon, I hope.'

'That will depend on the Secretary of State,' said Susan with a grin as she stepped into the back of the taxi. The doorman closed the door behind her and Scott waved as the car disappeared down Massachusetts Avenue.

Scott took a deep breath of Washington air and felt that after two meals a walk round the block wouldn't do him any harm. His mind switched constantly between Saddam and Susan, neither of whom he felt he had the full measure of.

He strolled back into the Ritz Carlton about twenty minutes later, but before going up to his room he returned to the restaurant and handed the maître d' a twenty-dollar bill.

'Thank you, sir,' she said. 'I hope you enjoyed both meals.'

'If you ever need a day job,' Scott said, 'I know an outfit in Virginia that could make good use of your particular talents.' The maître d' bowed. Scott left the restaurant, took the lift to the fifth floor and strolled down the corridor to room 505.

When he removed his key from the lock and pushed the door open he was surprised to find he'd left a light on. He took his jacket off and walked down the short passageway into the bedroom. He stopped and stared at the sight that met him. Susan was sitting up in bed in a rather sheer negligé, reading his notes on the afternoon's meeting, her glasses propped on the end of her nose. She looked up and gave Scott a disarming smile.

'The Secretary of State told me that I was to find out as much as I possibly could about you before our next meeting.'

'When's your next meeting?'

'Tomorrow morning, nine sharp.'

8

BUTTON GWINNETT WAS PROVING to be a problem. The writing was spidery and small, and the *G* sloped forward. It was several hours before Dollar Bill was willing to transfer the signature onto the two remaining parchments. In the days that followed, he used fifty-six different shades of ink and subtle changes of pressure on the dozen nibs he tried out before he felt happy with Lewis Morris, Abraham Clark, Richard Stockton and Caesar Rodney. But he felt his masterpiece was undoubtedly John Hancock, in size, accuracy, shade and pressure.

The Irishman completed two copies of the Declaration of Independence forty-eight days after he had accepted a drink from Angelo Santini at a downtown bar in San Francisco.

'One is a perfect copy,' he told Angelo, 'while the other has a tiny flaw.'

Angelo stood looking at the two documents in amazement, unable to think of the words that would adequately express his admiration.

'When William J. Stone was asked to make a copy back in 1820, it took him nearly three years,' said Dollar Bill. 'And, more important, he had the blessing of Congress.'

'Are you going to tell me the one difference between the final copy you've chosen and the original?'

'No, but I will tell you it was William J. Stone who pointed me in the right direction.'

'So what's next?' asked Angelo.

'Patience,' said the craftsman, 'because our little soufflé needs time to rise.'

Angelo watched as Dollar Bill transferred the two parchments carefully onto a table in the centre of the room where he had rigged up a water-cooled Xenon lamp. 'This gives out a light similar to daylight, but of much greater intensity,' he explained. He flicked the switch on and the room lit up like a television studio. 'If I've got my calculations right,' said Bill, 'that should achieve in thirty hours what nature took over two hundred years to do for the original.' He smiled. 'Certainly enough time to get drunk.'

'Not yet,' said Angelo, hesitating. 'Mr Cavalli has one more request.'

'And what might that be?' asked Dollar Bill in his warm Irish brogue.

He listened to Mr Cavalli's latest whim with interest. 'I feel I ought to be paid double in the circumstances,' was the forger's only response.

'Mr Cavalli has agreed to pay you another ten thousand,' said Angelo.

Dollar Bill looked down at the two copies, shrugged his shoulders and nodded.

Thirty-six hours later, the chairman and the chief executive of Skills boarded a shuttle for Washington.

They had two assessments to make before flying back to New York. If both came out positively, they could then arrange a meeting of the executive team they hoped would carry out the contract.

If, however, they came away unconvinced, Cavalli

would return to Wall Street and make two phone calls. One to Mr Al Obaydi, explaining why it would be impossible to fulfil his request, and the second to their contact in the Lebanon to tell him that they could not deal with a man who had demanded that ten per cent of the money be lodged in a Swiss bank account in his name. Cavalli would even supply the number of the account they had opened in Al Obaydi's name in Geneva, and thus the blame for failure would be shifted from the Cavallis to the Deputy Ambassador from Iraq.

When the two men stepped out of the main terminal, a car was waiting to ferry them into Washington. Crossing the 14th Street bridge they proceeded east on Constitution Avenue where they were dropped outside the National Gallery, a building that neither of them had ever visited before.

Once inside the East Wing, they took a seat on a little bench against the wall just below the vast Calder mobile and waited.

It was the clapping that first attracted their attention. When they looked up to see what was causing the commotion, they watched as flocks of tourists quickly stood to one side, trying to make a clearing.

When they saw him for the first time, the Cavallis automatically stood. A group of bodyguards, two of whom Antonio recognised, was leading the man through a human passage while he shook hands with as many people as possible.

The chairman and the chief executive took a few paces forward to get a better view of what was taking place. It was remarkable: the broad smile, the gait and walk, even the same turn of the head. When he stopped in front of them and bent down to speak to a little boy for a moment they might, if they hadn't known the truth, have believed it themselves.

When the man reached the front of the building, the bodyguards led him towards the third limousine in a line of six. In moments he had been whisked away, the sound of sirens fading into the distance.

'That two-minute exercise cost us one hundred thousand dollars,' said Tony as they made their way back towards the entrance. As he pushed through the revolving door a little boy rushed past him shouting at the top of his voice, 'I've just seen the President! I've just seen the President!'

'Worth every penny,' said Tony's father. 'Now all we need to know is whether Dollar Bill also lives up to his reputation.'

Hannah received an urgent call asking her to attend a meeting at the embassy when there was still another four months of her course to complete. She assumed the worst.

In the exams which were conducted every other Friday, Hannah had consistently scored higher marks than the other five trainee agents who were still in London. She was damned if she was going to be told at this late stage that she wasn't up to it.

The unscheduled appointment with the Councillor for Cultural Affairs, a euphemistic title for Colonel Kratz, Mossad's top man in London, was for six that evening.

At her morning tutorial, Hannah failed to concentrate on the works of the Prophet Mohammed, and during the afternoon she had an even tougher time with The British Occupation and Mandate in Iraq, 1917–32. She was glad to escape at five o'clock without being set any extra work.

The Israeli Embassy had, for the past two months, been forbidden territory for all the trainee agents unless specifically invited. If you were summoned you knew it was simply to collect your return ticket home: we no longer have any use for you. 'Goodbye,' and, if you were lucky, 'Thank you.' Two of the trainees had already taken that route during the past month.

Hannah had only seen the embassy once, when she was driven quickly past it on her first day back in the capital. She wasn't even sure of its exact location. After consulting an A–Z map of London, she discovered it was in Palace Green, Kensington, slightly back from the road.

Hannah stepped out of the High Street Kensington underground station a few minutes before six. She strolled up the wide pavement into Palace Green and on as far as the Philippine Embassy before turning back to reach the Israeli Mission just before the appointed hour. She smiled at the policeman as she climbed the steps up to the front door.

Hannah announced her name to the receptionist, and explained she had an appointment with the Councillor for Cultural Affairs. 'First floor. Once you reach the top of the stairs, it's the green door straight in front of you.'

Hannah climbed the wide staircase slowly, trying to gather her thoughts. She felt a rush of apprehension as she knocked on the door. It was immediately opened with a flourish.

'A pleasure to meet you, Hannah,' said a young man she had never seen before. 'My name is Kratz. Sorry to call you in at such short notice, but we have a problem. Please take a seat,' he added, pointing to a comfortable chair on the other side of a large desk. Not a man given to small talk, was Hannah's first conclusion.

Hannah sat bolt upright in the chair and stared at the man opposite her, who looked far too young to be the Councillor for Cultural Affairs. But then she recalled the real reason for the Colonel's posting to London. Kratz had a warm, open face, and if he hadn't been going prematurely bald at the front, he might even have been described as handsome.

His massive hands rested on the desk in front of him as he looked across at Hannah. His eyes never left her and she began to feel unnerved by such concentration.

Hannah clenched her fists. If she was to be sent home she would at least state her case, which she had already prepared and rehearsed.

The Councillor hesitated as if he were deciding how to express what needed to be said. Hannah wished he would get on with it. It was worse than waiting for the result of an exam you knew you had failed.

'How are you settling in with the Rubins?' Kratz enquired.

'Very well, thank you,' said Hannah, without offering any details. She was determined not to hold him up from the real purpose of their meeting.

'And how's the course working out?'

Hannah nodded and shrugged her shoulders.

'And are you looking forward to going back to Israel?' asked Kratz.

'Only if I've got a worthwhile job to go back to,' Hannah replied, annoyed that she had lowered her guard. She wished Kratz would look away for just a moment.

'Well, it's possible you may not be going back to Israel,' said Kratz.

Hannah shifted her position in the chair.

'At least, not immediately,' added Kratz. 'Perhaps I ought to explain. Although you have four more months of your course to complete' – he opened a file that lay on the desk in front of him – 'your tutor has informed us that you are likely to perform better in the final exams than any of the other five remaining agents, as I'm sure you know.'

It was the first time she had ever been described as an agent.

'We have already decided you'll be part of the final team,' Kratz said, as if anticipating her question. 'But, as so often happens in our business, an opportunity has arisen which we feel you are the best-qualified person to exploit at short notice.'

Hannah leaned forward in her chair. 'But I thought I was being trained to go to Baghdad.'

'You are, and in good time you will go to Baghdad, but right now we want to drop you into a different enemy territory. No better way of finding out how you'll handle yourself under pressure.'

'Where do you have in mind?' asked Hannah, unable to disguise her delight.

'Paris.'

'Paris?' repeated Hannah in disbelief.

'Yes. We have picked up information that the head of the Iraqi Interest Section has asked his government to supply him with a second secretary. The girl has been selected and will leave Baghdad for Paris in ten days' time. If you are willing to take her place, she will never reach Charles de Gaulle airport.'

'But they'd know I was the wrong person within minutes.'

'Unlikely,' said Kratz, taking out a thicker file from a drawer of his desk and turning a few pages. 'The girl in question was educated at Putney High School and then went on to Durham University to study English, both on Iraqi government grants. She wanted to remain in England but was forced to return to Baghdad when student visas were rescinded just over two years ago.'

'But her family . . .'

'Father was killed in the war with Iran and the mother has gone to live with her sister, just outside Karbala.'

'Brothers and sisters?'

'A brother in the Republican Guard, no sisters. It's all in the file. You'll be given a few days to study the background before you have to make up your mind. Tel Aviv is convinced we've a good chance of dropping you in her place. Your detailed knowledge of Paris is an obvious bonus. We would only leave you there for three to six months at the most.'

'And then?'

'Back to Israel in final preparation for Baghdad. By the way, if you decide to take on this assignment, our primary purpose is not to use you as a spy. We already have an agent in Paris. We simply want you to assimilate everything around you and get used to living with Arabs and thinking like them. You must not keep any records, or even make notes. Commit everything to memory. You will be debriefed when we take you out. Never forget that your final assignment is far more important to the state of Israel than this could ever be.' He smiled for the first time. 'Perhaps you'd like a few days to think it over.'

'No, thank you,' said Hannah. This time it was Kratz who looked anxious. 'I'm happy to take on the job, but I have a problem.'

'What's that?' asked Kratz.

'I can't type, and certainly not in Arabic.'

The young man laughed. 'Then we'll have to lay on a crash course for you. You'd better leave the Rubins' immediately and get yourself moved into the embassy by tomorrow night. They won't ask you for an explanation, and don't offer any. Meanwhile, study this.' He passed over a manila folder with the name 'Karima Saib' written across the top in bold letters. 'Within ten days you must know its contents by heart. The knowledge you retain may save your life.'

Kratz rose from his side of the desk and walked round to accompany Hannah to the door. 'Just one more thing,' he said as he opened the door for her. 'I believe this is yours.'

The Councillor for Cultural Affairs handed Hannah a small, battered suitcase.

In a car on the way to Georgetown, Cavalli explained to his father that within a hundred yards of the gallery the sirens would have been turned off and the limousines would peel away one after another as they reached the next six intersections, losing themselves in the normal morning traffic.

'And the actor?'

'With his wig removed and wearing dark glasses, no one would give Lloyd Adams a second look. He'll be taking the Metroliner back to New York this afternoon.'

'Clever.'

'Once their licence plates have been switched, the six limos will return to the city in a couple of days with their original New York plates.'

'You've done a highly professional job,' said his father.

'Yes, but that was only the dress rehearsal of a single scene. What we're planning in four weeks' time is to put on a three-act opera with the whole of Washington as our invited audience.'

'Try not to forget that we're being paid one hundred million for our troubles,' the old man reminded him.

'If we deliver, it will be good value for money,' said Cavalli as the car drove past the Four Seasons Hotel. The chauffeur turned left down a side street and came to a halt outside a quaint old wooden house. Angelo was waiting by a little iron gate at the top of a small flight of stone steps. The chairman and chief executive got out of the car and followed Angelo down the steps at a brisk pace, without speaking.

The door at the bottom was already open. Once they were inside, Angelo introduced them to Bill O'Reilly. Bill led them down the corridor to his room. When he reached the locked door he turned the key as if they were about to enter Aladdin's cave. He opened the door and paused for just a moment before switching on the lights, then led his little party to the centre of the room, where the two manuscripts awaited their inspection. He explained to his visitors that only one was a perfect copy of the original.

Bill passed both men a magnifying glass, then took a pace backwards to await their judgement. Tony and his father were not quite sure where to start, and began studying both documents for several minutes without uttering a word. Tony took his time as he went over the opening paragraph, 'When in the course of human events . . .', while his father became fascinated by the signatures of Francis Lightfoot Lee and Carter Braxton, whose colleagues from Virginia had left them so little room at the foot of the parchment to affix their names.

After some time, Tony's father stood up to his full height, turned towards the little Irishman and handed back the magnifying glass, and said, 'Maestro, all I can say is that William J. Stone would have been proud to know you.'

Dollar Bill bowed, acknowledging the ultimate forger's compliment.

'But which one is the perfect copy and which one has the mistake?' asked Cavalli.

'Ah,' said the forger. 'It was also William J. Stone who

pointed me in the right direction for solving that little conundrum.'

The Cavallis waited patiently for Dollar Bill to continue his explanation. 'You see, when Timothy Matlock engrossed the original in 1776, he made three mistakes. Two he was able to correct by simple insertions.' Dollar Bill pointed to the word 'represtative', where the letters *e* and *n* were missing, and then to the word 'only', which had been omitted a few lines further down. Both of the corrections had been inserted with a /\.

'But,' continued Dollar Bill, 'Mr Matlock also made one spelling mistake which he did not correct. On one of the copies, you will find, I *have*.'

9

HANNAH LANDED AT Beirut airport the night before she was due to fly to Paris. No one from Mossad accompanied the new agent, to avoid the risk of compromising her. Any Israeli found in the Lebanon is automatically arrested on sight.

Hannah had taken over an hour to be cleared by customs, but she finally emerged carrying a British passport, hand luggage and a few Lebanese pounds. Twenty minutes later she booked herself into the airport Hilton. She explained to the receptionist that she would only be staying one night and paid her bill in advance with the Lebanese pounds. She went straight to her room on the ninth floor and did not venture out again that evening.

She received just one phone call, at 7.20. To Kratz's question she simply replied 'Yes,' and the line went dead.

She climbed into bed at 10.40, but couldn't sleep for more than an hour at a time. She occasionally flicked on the television to watch spaghetti Westerns dubbed into Arabic. In between she managed to catch moments of restless sleep. She rose at ten to seven the following morning, ate a slab of chocolate she found in the tiny fridge, cleaned her teeth and took a cold shower.

She dressed in clothes taken from her hand luggage of a type which the file had indicated Karima favoured, and sat on the corner of the bed staring at herself in the mirror. She didn't like what she saw. Kratz had insisted that she crop her hair so that she looked like the one blurred photograph of Miss Saib they had in their possession. They also expected her to wear steel-rimmed spectacles, even if the glass in them didn't magnify. She had worn the spectacles for the past week but still hadn't got used to them, and often simply forgot to put them on or, worse, mislaid them.

At 8.19 a.m. she received a second phone call to let her know the plane had taken off from Amman with the 'cargo' on board.

When Hannah heard the morning cleaners chatting in the corridor a few moments later, she opened the door and quickly switched the sign on the knob outside to 'Do Not Disturb'. She waited impatiently in her room for a call saying either 'Your baggage has been mislaid,' which meant she was to return to London because they had failed to kidnap the girl, or 'Your baggage has been retrieved,' the code to show they had succeeded. If it was the second message she was to leave the room immediately, take the hotel minibus to the airport and go to the bookshop on the ground floor, where she was to browse until she was contacted.

A courier would then arrive at Hannah's side and leave a small package containing Saib's passport with the photograph changed, the airline ticket in Saib's name and any baggage tickets and personal items that had been found on her.

Hannah was then to board the flight to Paris as quickly as possible with only the one piece of hand luggage she had brought with her from London. Once she had landed at Charles de Gaulle she was to pick up Karima Saib's luggage from the carousel and get herself to the VIP carpark. She would be met by the Iraqi Ambassador's chauffeur, who would take her to the

Jordanian Embassy, where the Iraqi Interest Section was currently located, the Iraqi Embassy in Paris being officially closed. From that moment, Hannah would be on her own, and at all times she was to obey the instructions given by the embassy staff, particularly remembering that in direct contrast to Jewish women, Arab women were subservient to men. She must never contact the Israeli Embassy or attempt to find out who the Mossad agent in Paris was. If it ever became necessary, he would contact her.

'What do I do about clothes if Saib's don't fit?' she had asked Kratz. 'We know I'm taller than she is.'

'You must carry enough in your overnight bag to last for the first few days,' he had told her, 'and then purchase what you will need for six months in Paris.' Two thousand French francs had been supplied for this purpose.

'It must be some time since you've been shopping in Paris,' she had told him. 'That's just about enough for a pair of jeans and a couple of T-shirts.' Kratz had reluctantly handed over another five thousand francs.

At 9.27 the phone rang.

When Tony Cavalli and his father entered the boardroom, they took the remaining chairs at each end of the table, as the chairman and chief executive of any distinguished company might. Cavalli always used the oak-panelled room in the basement of his father's house on 75th Street for such meetings, but no one present believed they were there to conduct a normal board meeting. They knew there would be no agenda and no minutes.

In front of each of the six places where the board members were seated was a notepad, pencil and a glass of water, as there would have been at a thousand such meetings across America that morning. But at this particular gathering, in front of every place were also two long envelopes, one thin and one bulky, neither giving any clue as to its contents.

Tony's eyes swept the faces of the men seated round the table. All of them had two things in common: they had reached the top of their professions, and they were willing to break the law. Two of them had served jail sentences, albeit some years before, while three of the others would have done so had they not been able to afford the finest lawyers available. The sixth was himself a lawyer.

'Gentlemen,' Cavalli began, 'I've invited you to join me this evening to discuss a business proposition that might be described as a little unusual.' He paused before continuing, 'We have been requested by an interested party to steal the Declaration of Independence from the National Archives.'

Tony paused for a moment as uproar broke out immediately and the guests tried to outdo each other with one-liners.

'Just roll it up and take it away.'

'I suppose we could bribe *every* member of the staff.'

'Set the White House on fire. That would at least cause a diversion.'

'Write in and tell them that you won it on a game show.'

Tony was content to wait for his colleagues to run out of wisecracks before he spoke again.

'Exactly my reaction when we were first approached,' he admitted. 'But after several weeks of research and preparation, I hope you will at least grant me an opportunity to present my case.'

They quickly came to order and began concentrating on Tony's every word, though 'scepticism' would have best described the expression on their faces.

'During the past weeks, my father and I have been working on a draft plan to steal the Declaration of Independence. We are now ready to share that knowledge with you, because I must admit that we have reached a point where we cannot advance further on this project without the professional abilities of everyone seated around this table. Let me assure you, gentlemen, that your selection has not been a random exercise.

'But first I would like you all to see the Declaration of Independence for yourself.' Tony pressed a button underneath the table and the doors behind him swung open. The butler entered the room carrying two thin sheets of glass, a parchment held between them. He placed the glass frame on the centre of the table. The six sceptics leaned forward to study the masterpiece. It was several moments before anyone offered an opinion.

'Bill O'Reilly's work, would be my guess,' said Frank Piemonte, the lawyer, as he leaned over to admire the fine detail of the signatures below the text. 'He once offered to pay me in forged bills, and I would have accepted if I'd got him off.'

Tony nodded, and after they had all spent a little more time studying the parchment, he said, 'So, allow me to reword my earlier statement. We are not so much planning to steal the Declaration of Independence as to replace the original with this copy.' A smile settled on the lips of two of the previously sceptical guests.

'You will now be aware,' said Tony, 'of the amount of preparation that has gone into this exercise so far, and, indeed, the expense my father and I have been put to. But the reason we have continued is because we feel the rewards if we are successful far outweigh the risk of being caught. If you will open the thin envelopes in front of you, I believe the contents will make my point more clearly. Inside each envelope you will find a piece of paper on which is written the sum of money you will receive if you decide to become a member of the executive team.'

While the six men tore open the thinner of their two envelopes, Tony continued, 'If you feel, on discovering the amount involved, that the reward does *not* warrant the risk, now is the time to leave. I trust that those of us who remain may have confidence in your discretion because, as you will be only too aware, our lives will be in your hands.'

'And theirs in ours,' said the chairman, speaking for the first time.

A ripple of nervous laughter broke out around the table as each of the six men eyed the unsigned cheque in front of him.

'That figure,' said Tony, 'is the payment you will receive should we fail. If we succeed, the amount will be tripled.'

'So will the jail sentence if we get caught,' said Bruno Morelli, speaking for the first time.

'Summing up, gentlemen,' said Cavalli, ignoring the comment, 'if you decide to join the executive team, you will receive ten per cent of that payment in advance when you leave tonight, and the remaining sum within seven days of the contract being completed. This would be paid into any bank of your choice in any country of your choosing.

'Before you make your decision, there's one further thing I'd like you all to see.' Once again Tony pressed a button under the table, and this time the doors opened at the far end of the room. The sight that greeted them caused two of the guests to immediately stand, one to gasp and the remaining three to simply stare in disbelief.

'Gentlemen, I am happy that you were able to join me

today. I wanted to assure you all of my commitment to this project, and I hope you'll feel able to be part of the executive team. I'll have to leave you now, gentlemen,' said the man standing next to the chairman in the Ozark accent that had become so familiar to the American people during the past few months, 'so that you can study Mr Cavalli's proposition in greater detail. You can be confident that I'll do everything I can to help make the change this country needs. But for now, I have one or two pressing engagements. I feel sure you'll understand.' The actor smiled, and shook hands warmly with everyone around the table before strolling out of the boardroom.

Spontaneous applause broke out after the door had closed behind him. Tony allowed himself a smile of satisfaction.

'Gentlemen, my father and I will now leave you for a few minutes to consider your decision.'

The chairman and chief executive rose without another word and left the room.

'What do you think?' asked Tony as he poured his father a whisky and water from the cabinet in his study.

'A lot of water,' he replied. 'I have a feeling we may be in for a long night.'

'But did they buy it?'

'Can't be certain,' replied the old man. 'I was watching their faces while you were giving the presentation, and sure as hell, they didn't doubt the work you've put in. They were all impressed by the parchment and Lloyd Adams' performance, but other than Bruno and Frank they didn't give much away.'

'Let's start with Frank,' said Tony.

'First in then out, as Frank always is, but he likes money far too much to walk away from an offer as good as this.'

'You're that confident?' said Tony.

'It's not just the money,' replied his father. 'Frank's not going to have to be there on the day, is he? So he'll get his share whatever happens. I've never yet met a lawyer who would make a good field commander. They're too used to being paid whether they win or lose.'

'If you're right, Al Calabrese may turn out to be a problem. He's got the most to lose.'

'As our trade union leader, he'll certainly have to be out there on centre stage most of the day, but I suspect he won't be able to resist the challenge.'

'And what about Bruno? If –' began the chief executive, but he was cut short as the doors swung open and Al Calabrese walked into the room. 'We were just talking about you, Al.'

'Not too politely, I hope.'

'Well, that depends on . . .' said Tony.

'On whether I'm in?'

'Or out,' said the chairman.

'I'm in up to my neck is the answer,' said Al, smiling. 'So you'd better have a foolproof plan to present to us.' He turned to face Tony. 'Because I don't want to spend the rest of my life on top of America's most wanted list.'

'And the others?' asked the chairman, as Bruno Morelli brushed past them without even saying goodnight.

10

HANNAH NERVOUSLY GRABBED the ringing phone. 'This is Reception, madam. We were just wondering if you'll be checking out before midday, or do you require the room for an extra night?'

'No, thank you,' said Hannah. 'I'll have left by twelve, one way or the other.'

Two minutes later, the phone rang again. It was Colonel Kratz. 'Who were you speaking to a moment ago?'

'Reception were asking me when I would be checking out.'

'I see,' said Kratz. 'Your baggage has been retrieved,' was all he added.

Hannah replaced the phone and stood up. She felt a shot of adrenalin go through her body as she prepared for her first real test. She picked up her overnight bag and left the room, switching the sign on the door to 'Clean Me Please'.

Once she had reached the foyer, she had to wait only a few minutes before the hotel minibus returned from the airport on its circular journey. She sat alone in the back for the short trip to the departure area, then headed straight for the bookshop as instructed. She began to browse among the hardbacks, struck by how many American and British authors were obviously read by the Lebanese.

'Do you know where I can get some money changed, miss?' Hannah turned to find a priest smiling at her, who had spoken in Arabic with a slight mid-Atlantic accent. Hannah apologised and replied in Arabic that she didn't know where the currency exchange was, but perhaps the girl at the counter could help him.

As she turned back, Hannah became aware of someone else standing by her side. He removed a copy of *A Suitable Boy* from the shelf and replaced it with a small package. 'Good luck,' he whispered, and was gone even before she had seen his face. Hannah removed the package from the shelf and strolled slowly out of the bookshop. She began to search for the check-in counter for Paris. It turned out to be the one with the longest queue.

When she reached the front, Hannah requested a non-smoking seat.

The girl behind the counter checked her ticket and then began tapping away on her computer terminal. She looked puzzled. 'Were you unhappy with the seat previously allocated to you, Miss Saib?'

'No, it's just fine,' said Hannah, cursing herself for having made such a simple mistake. 'Sorry to have bothered you.'

'The flight will be boarding at Gate 17 in about fifteen minutes,' the girl added with a smile.

A man pretending to read the Vikram Seth novel he had just purchased watched as the plane took off. Satisfied he had carried out his instructions, he went to the nearest phone booth and rang first Paris and then Colonel Kratz to confirm that 'The bird has flown.'

The man in the priest's collar also watched Miss Saib board her plane, and he too made a phone call. Not to Paris or London, but to Dexter Hutchins in Langley, Virginia.

* * *

Cavalli and his father walked back into the room and once again resumed their places at each end of the table. One seat was empty.

'Too bad about Bruno,' said the chairman, licking his lips. 'We'll just have to find someone else to make the sword.'

Cavalli opened one of the six files in front of him. It was marked 'Transport'. He passed a copy to Al Calabrese.

'Let's start with the Presidential motorcade, Al. I'm going to need at least four limos, six motorcycle cops, two or three staff cars, two vans with surveillance cameras and a counter-assault team in a black Chevy Suburban – all of them able to pass the most eagle eye. I'll also want an additional van that would normally carry the White House media pool – the death-watch. Don't forget, the motorcade will be under far more scrutiny than last week, when we only had to turn on the sirens at the last moment, and then for just a few seconds. There's bound to be someone in the crowd who either works in government or is a White House junkie. It's often children who spot the most elementary mistakes and then tell their parents.'

Al Calabrese opened his file to find dozens of photographs of the President's motorcade leaving the White House on its way to the Hill. The photographs were accompanied by as many pages of notes.

'How long will it take you to have everything in place?' asked Cavalli.

'Three weeks, maybe four. I've got a couple of big ones in stock that would pass muster, and a bulletproof limo that the government often hires when minor heads of state are visiting the capital. I think the last crest we had to paint on the door was Uruguay, and the poor guy never even got to see the President – he ended up just getting twenty-five minutes with Warren Christopher.'

'But now for the hard part, Al. I need six outriders, riding police motorcycles, and all wearing the correct uniform.'

Al paused. 'That could take longer.'

'We haven't got any longer, Al. A month's going to be the outside for all of us.'

'It's not that easy, Tony. I can't exactly put an ad in the *Washington Post* asking for police –'

'Yes you can, Al. In a moment you'll all see why. Most of you round this table must be wondering why we've been honoured by the presence of Johnny Scasiatore, a man nominated for an Oscar for his direction of *The Honest Lawyer*.' What Cavalli didn't add was that since the police had found Johnny in bed with a twelve-year-old girl, the studios hadn't been in touch quite as frequently as in the past.

'I was beginning to wonder myself,' admitted Johnny.

The chief executive smiled. 'The truth is, you're the reason we'll be able to pull this whole plan off. Because you're going to direct the entire operation.'

'You're going to steal the Declaration of Independence and make a movie of it at the same time?' asked Johnny in disbelief. Cavalli waited for the laughter that broke out around the table to die down.

'Not exactly. But everyone in Washington on that day is going to believe that you are making a movie, not of us stealing the Declaration of Independence, but of the President visiting Congress. The fact that he drops into the National Archives on the way to the Capitol is something they won't ever need to know.'

'I'm lost already,' said Frank Piemonte, the team's lawyer. 'Can you take it a little slower?'

'Sure, Frank, because this is where you come in. I need a city permit to close down the route between the White

House and Congress for one hour on any day I choose in the last week in May. Deal direct with the city's motion picture and television office.'

'What reason do I give?' asked Piemonte.

'That Johnny Scasiatore, the distinguished director, wants to film the President of the United States on his way to the Senate to address a joint session of Congress.' Piemonte looked doubtful. 'Clint Eastwood managed it last year, so there's no reason why you shouldn't.'

'Then you'd better put $250,000 into the Fraternal Order of Police, Lodge No. 1,' suggested Piemonte. 'And the Mayor will probably expect the same amount for her re-election fund.'

'You can bribe any city official you know,' continued Tony, 'and I also want every member of the City Police Force on our books squared for the day – all they have to believe is that we're making a movie about the new President.'

'Do you have any idea what mounting an operation like this is likely to cost?' asked Johnny Scasiatore.

'Looking at the budget of your last film, and the return we made on our investment, I'd say yes,' replied Tony. 'And by the way, Al,' he added, turning his attention back to the old Teamster Union boss, 'sixty cops are due for retirement from the DCPD in April. You can employ as many of them as you need. Tell them it's a crowd scene and pay them double.' Al Calabrese added a note to his file.

'Now, the key to the operation's success,' continued Tony, 'is the half-block from the intersection of 7th Street and Pennsylvania Avenue to the delivery entrance of the National Archives.' He unfolded a large map of Washington and placed it in the centre of the table, then ran his finger along Constitution Avenue. 'Once they leave you, Johnny, it's for real.'

'But how do we get in and out of the Archives?'

'That's not your problem, Johnny. Your contribution ends when the six motorcycles and the Presidential motorcade turn right onto 7th Street. From then on, it's up to Gino.'

Until that moment, Gino Sartori, an ex-Marine who ran the best protection racket on the West Side, had not spoken. His lawyer had told him many times: 'Don't speak unless I tell you to.' His lawyer wasn't present, so he hadn't opened his mouth.

'Gino, you're going to supply me with the heavy brigade. I need eight Secret Service agents to act as the counter-assault team, preferably government-trained and well-educated. I only plan to be in the building for about twenty minutes, but we're going to have to be thinking on our feet for every second of that time. Debbie will continue to act as a secretary and Angelo will be dressed in naval uniform and carrying a small black case. I'll be there as the President's assistant, along with Dollar Bill as the President's physician.'

His father looked up, frowning. 'You're going to be inside the National Archives building when the document is switched?'

'Yes,' replied Tony firmly. 'I'll be the only person who knows every part of the plan, and I'm sure not watching this one from the sidewalk.'

'A question,' said Gino. 'If, and I only say if, I am able to supply the twenty or so people you need, tell me this: when we reach the National Archives, are they just going to open the doors, invite us in, and then hand over the Declaration of Independence?'

'Something like that,' replied Cavalli. 'My father taught me that the successful conclusion of any enterprise is always in the preparation. I still have one more surprise for you.' Once again he had their undivided attention. 'We have our own Special Assistant to the President in the White House. His name is Rex Butterworth, and he's on temporary assignment from the Department of Commerce for six months. He returns to his old job when the Clinton nominee has completed his contract in Little Rock and joins the President's staff. That's another reason why we have to go in May.'

'Convenient,' said Frank.

'Not particularly,' said Cavalli. 'It turns out that the President has forty-six Special Assistants at any one time, and when Clinton made his interest in commerce clear, Butterworth volunteered for the job. He's fixed a few overseas contracts for us in the past, but this will be the biggest thing he's done for us yet. For obvious reasons, it will also have to be his last assignment.'

'Can he be trusted?' asked Frank.

'He's been on the payroll for fifteen years, and his third wife is proving rather expensive.'

'Show me one who isn't,' said Al.

'Butterworth's looking for a big payday to get himself out of trouble, and this is it. And that brings me on to you, Mr Vicente, and your particular expertise as one of the biggest tour operators in Manhattan.'

'That's the legit side of my business,' replied the elderly man who sat on the right of the chairman, as befitted his oldest friend.

'Not for what I have in mind,' promised Tony. 'Once we have the Declaration in our possession, we'll need it kept out of sight for a few days and then smuggled abroad.'

'As long as no one realises it's been removed and I'm told well in advance where you want it delivered, that should be simple.'

'You'll get a week,' said Cavalli.

'I'd prefer two,' said Vicente, raising an eyebrow.

'No, Nick, you get a week,' the chief executive repeated.

'Can you give me a clue what distance it will have to travel?' Vicente asked, turning the pages of the file Tony had passed across to him.

'Several thousand miles. And as far as you're concerned it's COD, because if you fail to deliver, none of us gets paid.'

'That figures. But I'll still need to know how it has to be transported. For starters, will I have to keep the Declaration between two sheets of glass the whole time?'

'I don't know myself yet,' replied Cavalli, 'but I'm hoping you'll be able to roll it up and deposit it in a cylindrical tube of some kind. I'm having one specially made.'

'Does that explain why I've got several sheets of blank paper in my file?' asked Nick.

'Yes,' said Tony. 'Except those sheets aren't paper but parchment, each one of them 29¾ inches by 24¼ inches, the exact size of the Declaration of Independence.'

'So now all I've got to hope is that every customs agent and coastguard patrol won't be looking for it.'

'I want you to assume the whole world will be looking for it,' replied Cavalli. 'You aren't being paid this sort of money for doing a job I could handle with one call to Federal Express.'

'I thought you might say something like that,' said Nick. 'Still, I had the same problem when you wanted the Vermeer of Russborough stolen, and Irish Customs still haven't worked out how I got the painting out of the country.'

Cavalli smiled. 'So now we all know what's expected of us. And I think in future we should meet at least twice a week to start with, every Sunday at three o'clock and every Thursday at six, to make sure none of us falls behind schedule. One person out of synch and nobody else will be able to move.' Tony looked up and was greeted by nods of agreement.

It always fascinated Cavalli that organised crime needed to be as efficiently run as any public company if it hoped to show a dividend. 'So we'll meet again next Thursday at six?'

All five men nodded and made notes in their diaries.

'Gentlemen, you may now open the second of your two envelopes.' Once again, the five men ripped open their envelopes, and each pulled out a thick wad of thousand-dollar bills.

The lawyer began to count each note.

'Your down-payment,' Tony explained. 'Expenses will be met at the end of every week, receipts whenever possible. And, Johnny,' said Tony, turning to the director, 'this is not *Heaven's Gate* we're financing.' Scasiatore managed a smile.

'Thank you, gentlemen,' said Tony, rising. 'I look forward to seeing you all next Thursday at six o'clock.'

The five men rose and made their way to the door, each stopping to shake hands with Tony's father before he left. Tony accompanied them to their cars. When the last one had been driven away, he returned to find his father had moved to the study and was toying with a whisky while staring at the perfect copy of the Declaration that Dollar Bill had intended to destroy.

11

'CALDER MARSHALL, PLEASE.'

'The Archivist can't be interrupted right now. He's in a meeting. May I ask who's calling?'

'It's Rex Butterworth, Special Assistant to the President. Perhaps the Archivist would be kind enough to call me back when he's free. He'll find me at the White House.'

Rex Butterworth put the phone down without waiting to hear what usually happened once it was known the call had come from the White House: 'Oh, I feel sure I can interrupt him, Mr Butterworth, can you hold on for a moment?'

But that wasn't what Butterworth wanted. No, the Special Assistant needed Calder Marshall to phone back himself, because once he had gone through the White House switchboard, Marshall would be hooked. Butterworth also realised that, as one of forty-six Special Assistants to the President, and in his case only on temporary assignment, the switchboard might not even recognise his name. A quick visit to the little room that housed the White House telephone operators had dealt with that problem.

He drummed his fingers on the desk and gazed down with satisfaction at the file in front of him. One of the

President's two schedulers had been able to supply him with the information he needed. The file revealed that the Archivist had invited each of the last three Presidents – Bush, Reagan and Carter – to visit the National Archives, but due to 'pressing commitments' none of them had been able to find the time.

Butterworth was well aware that the President received, on average, 1,700 requests every week to attend some function or other. The latest letter from Mr Marshall, dated January 22nd 1993, had evoked the reply that although it was not possible for the President to accept his kind invitation at the present time, Mr Clinton hoped to have the opportunity to do so at some date in the future – the standard reply that about 1,699 requests in the weekly postbag were likely to receive.

But on this occasion, Mr Marshall's wish was about to be granted. Butterworth continued to drum his fingers on the desk as he wondered how long it would take Marshall to return his call. Less than two minutes would have been his guess. He allowed his mind to wander back over the events of the past week.

When Cavalli had first put the idea to him, he had laughed more loudly than any of the six men who had gathered round the table at 75th Street. But after studying the parchment for over an hour and still not being able to identify the mistake, and then later meeting with Lloyd Adams, he began to believe, like the other sceptics, that switching the Declaration might just be possible.

Over the years, Butterworth had served the Cavalli family well. Meetings had been arranged with politicians at a moment's notice, words were dropped in the ears of trade officials from someone thought to be well placed in Washington, and the odd piece of inside information had been passed on, ensuring that Butterworth's income was commensurate with his own high opinion of his true worth.

As he lay awake that night thinking about the proposition, he also came to the conclusion that Cavalli couldn't take the next step without him, and more important, his role in the deception would probably be obvious within minutes of the theft being discovered, in which case he could end up spending the rest of his life in Leavenworth. Against that possibility he had to weigh the fact that he was fifty-seven years old, had only three years to go before retirement, and a third wife who was suing him for a divorce he couldn't afford. Butterworth no longer dreamed of promotion. He was now simply trying to come to terms with the fact that he was probably going to have to spend the rest of his life alone, eking out some sort of existence on a meagre government pension.

Cavalli was also aware of these facts, and the offer of a million dollars – a hundred thousand the day he signed up, a further nine hundred thousand on the day the exchange took place – and a first-class ticket to any country on earth, almost convinced Butterworth that he should agree to Cavalli's proposition.

But it was Maria who tilted the balance in Cavalli's favour.

At a trade conference in Brazil the previous year, Butterworth had met a local girl who answered most of his questions during the day and the rest of them at night. He'd phoned her the morning after Cavalli's first approach. Maria seemed pleased to hear from him, a pleasure which became more vocal when she learned that he'd be leaving the service and, having come into 'a reasonable inheritance', was thinking of settling down somewhere abroad.

The President's Special Assistant joined the team the following day.

He had spent most of the hundred thousand dollars by the end of the week, clearing his debts and getting up to date with his first two wives' alimony. With only a few thousand left, there was now nothing to do but commit himself wholeheartedly to the plan. He didn't give a moment's thought to changing his mind, because he knew he could never hope to repay the money. He hadn't forgotten that the man he had replaced on Cavalli's payroll *had* once neglected to repay a far smaller sum after making certain promises. Once had been enough: Cavalli's father had had him buried under the World Trade Center when he'd failed to secure the promised contract for the building. A similar departure did not appeal to Butterworth.

The phone rang on Butterworth's desk, as he had predicted, in under two minutes, but he allowed it to continue ringing for some time before he picked it up. His temporary secretary announced that there was a Mr Marshall on the line and asked if he wanted to take the call.

'Yes, thank you, Miss Daniels.'

'Mr Butterworth?' enquired a voice.

'Speaking.'

'This is Calder Marshall over at the National Archives. I understand you phoned while I was in a meeting. Sorry I wasn't available.'

'No problem, Mr Marshall. It's just that I wondered if it would be possible for you to drop by to the White House. There's a private matter I'd like to discuss with you.'

'Of course, Mr Butterworth. What time would be convenient?'

'I'm up to my eyes the rest of this week,' Butterworth

said, looking down at the blank pages in his diary, 'but the President's away at the beginning of next week, so perhaps we could schedule something for then?'

There was a pause which Butterworth assumed meant Marshall was checking his diary. 'Would Tuesday, 10 a.m. suit you?' the Archivist eventually asked.

'Let me check my other diary,' said Butterworth, staring into space. 'Yes, that looks fine. I have another appointment at 10.30, but I'm confident we'll have covered everything I need to go over with you by then. Perhaps you would be kind enough to come to the Pennsylvania Avenue entrance of the Old Executive Office building. There'll be someone there to meet you and after you've cleared security they'll bring you up to my office.'

'The Pennsylvania Avenue entrance,' said Marshall. 'Of course.'

'Thank you, Mr Marshall. I look forward to seeing you next Tuesday at ten o'clock,' said Butterworth before replacing the receiver.

The President's Special Assistant smiled as he dialled Cavalli's private number.

Scott promised Dexter Hutchins he would be around when Dexter's son came to Yale for his admission interview.

'He's allowing me to tag along,' said Dexter, 'which will give me a chance to bring you up to date on our little problem with the Israelis. And I may even have found something to tempt you.'

'Dexter, if you're hoping that I'll get your son into Yale in exchange for a field job, I think I ought to let you know I have absolutely no influence with the Admissions Office.' Dexter's laugh crackled down the phone. 'But I'll still be happy to show you both over the place and give the boy any help I can.'

Dexter Jr could not have turned out to be more like his father: five foot ten, heavily built, a perpetual five o'clock shadow and the same habit of calling everything that moved 'sir'. When, after an hour strolling round the grounds, he left his father for his interview with the head of the Admissions Office, the Professor of Constitutional Law took the Deputy Director of the CIA back to his rooms.

Even before the door was closed, Dexter had lit up a cigar. After a few puffs he said, 'Have you been able to make any sense of the coded message sent by our operative in Beirut?'

'Only that everyone who joins the intelligence community has some strange personal reason for wanting to do so. In my case, it's because of my father and a Boy Scout determination to balance the books morally. In the case of Hannah Kopec, Saddam Hussein wipes out her family, so she immediately offers her talents to Mossad. With that powerful a motive, I wouldn't want to cross her path.'

'But that's exactly what I'm hoping you will do,' said Dexter. 'You're always saying you want to be tested in the field. Well, this could be your opportunity.'

'Am I hearing you properly?'

'Yale's spring term is about to end, right?'

'Yes. But that doesn't mean I don't have a lot of work to do.'

'Oh, I see. A happy amateur, twelve times a year when it suits you, but the moment you might have to get your hands dirty . . .'

'I didn't say that.'

'Well then, hear me out. First, we know Hannah Kopec was one of eight girls selected from a hundred to go to London for six months to study Arabic. This followed a year's intensive physical course at Herzliyah, where they covered the usual self-defence, fieldcraft and surveillance work. The reports on her were excellent. Second, a chat with her host's wife at Sainsbury's in Camden Town, wherever the hell that is, and we discover that she left suddenly, despite the fact that she was almost certainly meant to return to Israel as part of the team that was working on the assassination of Saddam. That's when we lose sight of her. Then we get one of those breaks that only come from good detective work. One of our agents who works at Heathrow spots her in duty free, when she's buying some cheap perfume.

'After she boards a plane for the Lebanon he phones our man in Beirut, who shadows her from the moment she arrives. Not that easy, I might add. We lost her for several hours. Then, out of nowhere, up she pops again, but this time as Karima Saib, who Baghdad are under the impression is on her way to Paris as second secretary to the Ambassador. Meanwhile, the real Miss Saib is abducted at Beirut airport and is now being held at a safe house somewhere across the border on the outskirts of Tel Aviv.'

'Where's all this leading, Dexter?'

'Patience, Professor,' he said, relighting the stub of his cigar, which hadn't been glowing for several minutes. 'Not all of us are born with your academic acuity.'

'Get on with it,' said Scott with a smile, 'because my academic acuity hasn't been stretched yet.'

'Now I come to a bit you're going to enjoy. Hannah Kopec has not been placed in the Iraqi Interest Section of the Jordanian Embassy in Paris to spy.'

'Then why bother to put her there in the first place? In any case, how can you be certain?' asked Scott.

'Because the Mossad agent in Paris – how shall I put

it? – does a little work for us on the side, and he hasn't even been informed of her existence.'

Scott scowled. 'So why *has* the girl been placed in the embassy?'

'We don't know, but we sure as hell would like to find out. We think Rabin can't give the go-ahead to strike Saddam while Kopec is still in France, so the least we need to know is when she's expected back in Israel. And that's where you come in.'

'But we must have a man in Paris already.'

'Several, actually, but every one of them is known by Mossad at a hundred paces, and, I suspect, even by the Iraqis at ten. So, if Hannah Kopec is in Paris without the Mossad sleeper knowing, I'd like you to be in Paris without our people knowing. That is, if you feel you can spare the time away from Susan Anderson.'

'She broke away from me the day her boyfriend returned from his conference. I don't know what it is I do to women. She called me last week to tell me they're getting married next month.'

'All the more reason for you to go to Paris.'

'On a wild goose chase.'

'This goose may just be about to lay us a golden egg, and in any case, I don't want to read about another brilliant Israeli coup on the front page of the *New York Times* and then have to explain to the President why the CIA knew nothing about it.'

'But where would I even start?'

'In your own time, you try to make contact with her. Tell her you're the Mossad agent in Paris.'

'But she would never believe –'

'Why not? She doesn't know who the agent is, only that there is one. Scott, I need to know –'

The door swung open and Dexter Jr came in.

'How did it go?' asked his father. The young man

walked across the room and slumped into an armchair, but did not utter a word.

'That bad, eh son?'

'Mr Marshall, how nice to meet you,' said Butterworth, thrusting out his hand to greet the Archivist of the United States.

'It's nice to meet you, too, Mr Butterworth,' Calder Marshall replied nervously.

'Good of you to find the time to come over,' said Butterworth. 'Do have a seat.'

Butterworth had booked the Roosevelt Room in the West Wing for their meeting. It had taken a lot of persuading of a particularly officious secretary who knew Mr Butterworth's station in life only too well. She reluctantly agreed to release the room for thirty minutes, and then only because he was seeing the Archivist of the United States. She also agreed to his second request, as the President would be out of town that day. The Special Assistant had placed himself at the top of a table that usually seated twenty-four, and beckoned Mr Marshall to be seated on his right, facing Tade Stykal's portrait of *Theodore Roosevelt on Horseback*.

The Archivist must have been a shade over six foot, and as thin as most women half his age would have liked to be. He was almost bald except for a semicircle of grey tufts around the base of his skull. He wore an ill-fitting suit that looked as if it normally experienced outings only on a Sunday morning. From his file, Butterworth knew the Archivist was younger than himself, but he vainly felt that if they had been seen together, no one would have believed it.

He must have been born middle-aged, thought Butterworth, but the Special Assistant had no such disparaging thoughts about the quality of the man's mind. After a *magna cum laude* at Duke University, Marshall had written a book on the history of the Bill of Rights that was now considered to be the standard text for every undergraduate studying American history. It had made him a small fortune – not that one could have guessed it by the way he dressed, thought Butterworth.

On the table in front of him was a file stamped 'Confidential', and above that the name 'Calder Marshall' in bold letters. Despite the fact that the Archivist was wearing horn-rimmed glasses with thick lenses, Butterworth felt he could hardly have missed it.

Butterworth paused before he began a speech he'd prepared every bit as assiduously as the President had his inauguration address. Marshall sat, fingers intertwined, nervously waiting for Butterworth to proceed.

'You have, over the past sixteen years,' began the Special Assistant, 'made several requests for the President to visit the National Archives.' Butterworth was pleased to observe that Marshall was looking hopeful. 'And, indeed, this particular President wishes to accept your invitation.' Mr Marshall's smile broadened. 'To that end, in our weekly meeting, President Clinton asked me to convey a private message to you, which he hoped you would understand must be in the strictest confidence.'

'In the strictest confidence. Of course.'

'The President felt sure he could rely on your discretion, Mr Marshall. So, I feel I can let you know that we're trying to clear some time during the last week of this month for him to visit the Archives, but nothing, as yet, has been scheduled.'

'Nothing, as yet, has been scheduled. Of course.'

'President Clinton has also requested that it be a

strictly private visit, which would not be open to the public or the press.'

'Not be open to the press. Of course.'

'After the explosion at the World Trade Center, one can't be too careful.'

'Can't be too careful. Of course.'

'And I would be obliged if you did not discuss any aspect of the visit with your staff, however senior, until we are able to confirm a definite date. These things have a habit of getting out and then, for security reasons, the visit might have to be cancelled.'

'Have to be cancelled. Of course. But if it's to be a private visit,' said the Archivist, 'is there anything the President particularly wants to see, or will it just be the standard tour of the building?'

'I'm glad you asked that question,' said Mr Butterworth, opening the file in front of him. 'The President has made one particular request, apart from which he will be in your hands.'

'In my hands. Of course.'

'He wants to see the Declaration of Independence.'

'The Declaration of Independence. That's easy enough.'

'That is not the request,' said Butterworth.

'Not the request?'

'No. The President wishes to see the Declaration, but not as he saw it when he was a freshman at Georgetown, under a thick pane of glass. He wishes the frame to be removed so he can study the parchment itself. He hopes you will grant this request, if only for a few moments.'

This time the Archivist did not immediately say 'Of course.' Instead he said, 'Most unusual,' and added, 'Hopes I would grant him this request, if only for a few moments.' There was a long pause before he said, 'I'm sure that will be possible, of course.'

'Thank you,' said Mr Butterworth, trying not to sound too relieved. 'I know the President will be most appreciative. And, if I could impress on you again, not a word until we've been able to confirm the date.'

Butterworth rose and glanced at the long-case clock at the far end of the room. The meeting had taken twenty-two minutes. He would still be able to escape from the conference room before he was thrown out by the officious woman from Scheduling.

The Special Assistant to the President guided his guest towards the door.

'The President wondered if you would like to see the Oval Office while you're here?'

'The Oval Office. Of course, of course.'

12

HAMID AL OBAYDI was left alone in the centre of the room. After two of the four guards had stripped him naked, the other two had expertly checked every stitch of his clothing for anything that might endanger the life of their President.

On a nod from the man who appeared to be the chief guard, a side door opened and a doctor entered the room, followed by an orderly who carried a chair in one hand and a rubber glove in the other. The chair was placed behind Al Obaydi, and he was invited to sit. He did so. The doctor first checked his nails and ears before instructing him to open his mouth wide while he tapped every tooth with a spatula. He then placed a clamp in his jaw so that it opened even wider, which allowed him to look into every crevice. Satisfied, he removed the clamp. He then asked Al Obaydi to stand up, turn round, place his legs straight and wide while bending over until his hands touched the seat of the chair. Al Obaydi heard the rubber glove being placed on the doctor's hand and felt a sudden burst of pain as two fingers were thrust up his rectum. He cried out and the guards facing him began to laugh. The fingers were extracted just as abruptly, repeating the jab of pain a second time.

'Thank you, Deputy Ambassador,' said the doctor, as if he had just checked Al Obaydi's temperature for a mild dose of 'flu. 'You can get dressed now.' Al Obaydi knelt down and picked up his pants as the doctor and the orderly left the room.

As he dressed, Al Obaydi couldn't help wondering if each member of the Security Council went through the same humiliation every time Saddam called a meeting of the Revolutionary Command Council.

The order to return to Baghdad to give Sayedi an update on the latest position, as the Ambassador to the UN had described the summons, filled Al Obaydi with considerable apprehension, despite the fact that following his most recent meeting with Cavalli he felt he had the answers to any questions the President might put to him.

Once Al Obaydi had reached Baghdad after a seemingly endless journey through Jordan – direct flights having been suspended as part of the UN sanctions – he hadn't been allowed to rest or even given the chance to change his clothes. He'd been driven direct to Ba'ath headquarters in a black Mercedes.

When Al Obaydi had finished dressing, he checked himself in a small mirror on the wall. His apparel was, on this occasion, modest compared with the outfits he'd left in his apartment in New York: Saks Fifth Avenue suits, Valentino sweaters, Church's shoes and a solid gold Cartier watch. All this had been rejected in favour of the one set of cheap Arab clothing he retained in the bottom drawer of his wardrobe in Manhattan.

When Al Obaydi turned away from the mirror, one of the guards beckoned him to follow as the door at the end of the room opened for the first time. The contrast to the bare, almost barrack-room surroundings of the examination room took him by surprise. A thickly carpeted, ornately painted corridor was well lit by chandeliers that hung every few paces.

The Deputy Ambassador followed the guard down the corridor, becoming more aware with each step of the massive gold-painted door that loomed up ahead of him. But when he was only a few paces away, the guard opened a side door and ushered him into an ante-room that echoed the opulence of the corridor.

Al Obaydi was left alone in the room, but no sooner had he taken a seat on the large sofa than the door opened again. Al Obaydi jumped to his feet only to see a girl enter carrying a tray, in the centre of which was a small cup of Turkish coffee.

She placed the coffee on a table beside the sofa, bowed and left as silently as she had come. Al Obaydi toyed with the cup, aware that he had fallen into the Western habit of preferring cappuccino. He drank the muddy black liquid simply out of a nervous desire to be doing something.

An hour passed slowly: he became increasingly nervous, with nothing in the room to read and only a massive portrait of Saddam Hussein to stare at. Al Obaydi spent the time going over every detail of what Cavalli had told him, wishing he could refer to the file in his small attaché case, which the guards had whisked away long before he'd reached the examination room.

During the second hour, his confidence began to drain away. During the third, he started to wonder if he would ever get out of the building alive.

Then suddenly the door swung open and Al Obaydi recognised the red-and-yellow flash on the uniform of one of Saddam's Presidential Guards: the Hemaya.

'The President will see you now,' was all the young officer said, and Al Obaydi rose and followed him quickly down the corridor towards the gold-painted door.

The officer knocked, opened the massive door and stood on one side to allow the Deputy Ambassador to join a full meeting of the Revolutionary Command Council.

Al Obaydi stood and waited, like a prisoner in the dock hoping to be told by the judge that he might at least be allowed to sit. He remained standing, well aware that no one ever shook hands with the President unless invited to do so. He stared round at the twelve-man council, noticing that only two, the Prime Minister, Tariq Aziz, and the State Prosecutor, Nakir Farrar, were wearing suits. The other ten members were dressed in full military uniform but did not wear sidearms. The only hand gun, other than those worn by General Hamil, the Commander of the Presidential Guard, and the two armed soldiers directly behind Saddam, was on the table in front of the President, placed where other heads of state would have had a memo pad.

Al Obaydi became painfully aware that the President's eyes had never left him from the moment he had entered the room. Saddam waved his Cohiba cigar at the Deputy Ambassador to indicate that he should take the vacant seat at the opposite end of the table.

The Foreign Minister looked towards the President, who nodded. He then turned his attention to the man who sat nervously in the far chair.

'This, Mr President, as you know, is Hamid Al Obaydi, our Deputy Ambassador at the United Nations, whom you honoured with the responsibility of carrying out your orders to steal the Declaration of Independence from the American infidels. On your instructions, he has returned to Baghdad to inform you, in person, of what progress he has made. I have not had an opportunity to speak to him, Mr President, so you will forgive me if I appear, like yourself, to be a seeker after information.'

Saddam waved his cigar again to let the Foreign Minister know that he should get on with it.

'Perhaps I could start, Deputy Ambassador' – Al Obaydi was surprised by such a formal address, as their two families had known each other for generations, but he accepted that to show friendship of any kind in front of Saddam was tantamount to an admission of conspiracy – 'by asking you to bring us all up to date on the President's imaginative scheme.'

'Thank you, Foreign Minister,' replied Al Obaydi, as if he had never met the man before. He turned back to face Saddam, whose black eyes remained fixed on him.

'May I begin, Mr President, by saying what an honour it has been to be entrusted with this task, especially remembering the idea had emanated from Your Excellency personally.' Every member of the Council was now concentrating his attention on the Deputy Ambassador, but Al Obaydi noticed that from time to time each of them would glance in Saddam's direction to see how he was reacting.

'I am happy to be able to report that the team led by Mr Antonio Cavalli . . .'

Saddam raised a hand and looked towards the State Prosecutor, who opened a thick file in front of him.

Nakir Farrar, the State Prosecutor, was feared second only to Saddam in the Iraqi regime. Everyone knew of his reputation. A first-class honours degree in jurisprudence at Oxford, President of the Union, and a bencher at Lincoln's Inn. That was where Al Obaydi had first come across him. Not that Farrar had ever acknowledged his existence. He had been tipped to be the first QC Iraq had ever produced. But then came the invasion of the Nineteenth Province and the British expelled the high-flyer, despite several appeals from people in high places. Farrar returned to a city he had deserted at the age of eleven, and immediately offered his remarkable talent for Saddam Hussein's personal use. Within a year

Saddam had appointed him State Prosecutor. A title, it was rumoured, he had selected himself.

'Cavalli is a New York criminal, Mr President, who, because he has a law degree and heads a private legal practice, creates a legitimate front for such an operation.' Saddam nodded and turned his attention back to Al Obaydi.

'Mr Cavalli has completed the preparation stage and his team is now ready to carry out the President's orders.'

'Do we have a date yet?' asked Farrar.

'Yes, State Prosecutor. May 25th. Clinton has a full day's schedule at the White House, with his speechwriters in the morning, and his wife's health-policy task unit in the afternoon, and he' – the Iraqi Ambassador to the UN had warned Al Obaydi never to refer to Clinton as 'the President' – 'will therefore not be involved in any public engagements that day, which would have made our task impossible.'

'And tell me, Deputy Ambassador,' said the State Prosecutor, 'did Mr Cavalli's lawyer succeed in getting a permit to close down the road between the White House and the National Archives during the time when Clinton will be involved in these internal meetings?'

'No, State Prosecutor, he did not,' came back Al Obaydi's reply. 'The Mayor's Office did, however, grant a permit for filming to take place on Pennsylvania Avenue from 13th Street east. But the road can only be closed for forty-five minutes. It seems this Mayor was not as easy to convince as her predecessor.'

A few members of the Council looked puzzled. 'Not as easy to convince?' asked the Foreign Minister.

'Perhaps "persuade" would be a better word.'

'And what form did this persuasion take?' asked General Hamil, who sat on the right of the President and knew only one form of persuasion.

'A $250,000 contribution to her re-election fund.'

Saddam began to laugh, so the others round the table followed suit.

'And the Archivist, is he still convinced it's Clinton who will be visiting him?' asked the State Prosecutor.

'Yes, he is,' said Al Obaydi. 'Just before I flew out Cavalli had taken eight of his own men over the building posing as a Secret Service preliminary reconnaissance team, carrying out a site survey. The Archivist could not have been more co-operative, and Cavalli was given enough time to check out everything. That exercise should make the switching of the Declaration on May 25th far easier for him.'

'But if, and I only say if, they succeed in getting the original out, have they made arrangements for passing the document over to you?' asked the State Prosecutor.

'Yes,' replied Al Obaydi confidently. 'I understand that the President wants the document to be delivered to Barazan Al-Tikriti, our venerated Ambassador to the United Nations in Geneva. When he has received the parchment, and not before, I will authorise the final payment.'

The President nodded his approval. After all, the venerated Ambassador in Geneva was his half-brother. The State Prosecutor continued his questioning.

'But how can we be sure that what is handed to us will be the original, and not just a first-class copy?' he demanded. 'What's to prevent them from making a show of walking in and out of the National Archives, but not actually switching the documents?'

A smile appeared on Al Obaydi's lips for the first time. 'I took the precaution, State Prosecutor, of demanding such proof,' he replied. 'When the fake replaces the original, it will continue to be displayed for the general public to view. You can be assured that I shall be among the general public.'

'But you have not answered my question,' said the State Prosecutor sharply. 'How will you know ours is the original?'

'Because on the original document penned by Timothy Matlock, there is a simple spelling mistake, which has been corrected on the copy executed by Bill O'Reilly.'

The State Prosecutor reluctantly sat back in his chair when his master raised a hand.

'Another criminal, Excellency,' explained the Foreign Minister. 'This time a forger, who has been responsible for making the copy of the document.'

'So,' said the State Prosecutor, leaning forward once again, 'if the incorrect spelling is still on the document displayed in the National Archives on May 25th, you will know we have a fake and will not pay out another cent. Is that right?'

'Yes, State Prosecutor,' said Al Obaydi.

'Which word on the original has been incorrectly spelt?' demanded the State Prosecutor.

When the Deputy Ambassador told him, all Nakir Farrar said was, 'How appropriate,' and then closed the file in front of him.

'However, it will still be necessary for me to have the final payment to hand,' continued Al Obaydi, 'should I be satisfied that they have carried out their part of the bargain, and that we are in possession of the original parchment.'

The Foreign Minister looked towards Saddam who, again, nodded.

'It will be in place by May 25th,' said the Foreign Minister. 'I would like the opportunity to go over some of the details with you before your return to New York.

As long as that meets with the President's approval?'

Saddam waved a hand to indicate that such a request was not important to him. His eyes remained fixed on Al Obaydi. The Deputy Ambassador wasn't sure if he was meant to leave or await further questioning. He favoured caution, and remained seated and silent. It was some time before anyone spoke.

'You must be curious, Hamid, about why I place such importance on this scrap of useless paper.' As the Deputy Ambassador had never met the President before, he was surprised to be called by his first name.

'It is not for me to question Your Excellency's reasoning,' replied Al Obaydi.

'Nevertheless,' continued Saddam, 'you would be less than human not to wonder why I am willing to spend one hundred million dollars and at the same time risk international embarrassment should you fail.'

Al Obaydi noted the word 'you' with some discomfort.

'I would be fascinated to know, Sayedi, if you felt able to confide in such an unworthy soul.'

Twelve members of the Council looked towards the President to gauge his reaction to the Deputy Ambassador's comment. Al Obaydi felt immediately that he had gone too far. He sat, terrified, during what felt like the longest silence in his life.

'Then I shall let you share my secret, Hamid,' said Saddam, his black eyes boring into the Deputy Ambassador. 'When I captured the Nineteenth Province for my beloved people, I found myself at war not with the traitors we had invaded, but the combined strength of the Western world – and that despite an agreement previously reached with the American Ambassador. "Why?" I had to ask, when everyone knew that Kuwait was run by a few corrupt families who had little interest in the welfare of their own people. I'll tell you why. In one word, oil. Had it been coffee beans that the Nineteenth Province was exporting, you would never have seen as much as an American rowing boat armed with a catapult enter the Gulf.'

The Foreign Minister smiled and nodded.

'And who were the leaders who ganged up against me? Thatcher, Gorbachev and Bush. That was less than three years ago. And what has happened to them since? Thatcher was removed by a coup carried out by her own supporters; Gorbachev was deposed by a man he himself had sacked only a year before and whose own position now looks unstable; Bush suffered a humiliating defeat at the hands of the American people. While I remain the Supreme Leader and President of my country.'

There followed a burst of applause which died instantly when Saddam began speaking again.

'That, of course, would be ample reward for most people. But not me, Hamid. Because Bush's place has been taken by this man Clinton, who has learned nothing from his predecessor's mistakes, and who now also wishes to challenge my supremacy. But this time it is my intention to humiliate him along with the American infidels long before they are given the opportunity to do so. And I shall go about this in such a way that will make it impossible for Clinton to recover any credibility in his lifetime. I intend to make Clinton and the American people the laughing stock of the world.'

The heads continued nodding.

'You have already witnessed my ability to turn the greed of their own people into a willingness to steal the most cherished document in their nation's history. And you, Hamid, are the chosen vessel to ensure that my genius will be acknowledged.' Al Obaydi lowered his head.

'Once I am in possession of the Declaration I shall

wait patiently until the fourth of July, when the whole of America will be spending a peaceful Sunday celebrating Independence Day.' No one in the room uttered a word while the President paused.

'I shall also celebrate Independence Day, not in Washington or New York, but in Tahrir Square, surrounded by my beloved people. When I, Saddam Hussein, President of Iraq, will in front of the entire world's media burn to a cinder the American Declaration of Independence.'

Hannah lay awake in her barrack-room bed, feeling not unlike the child she had been some thirteen years before when she had spent her first night at boarding school.

She had collected Karima Saib's cases from the carousel at Charles de Gaulle airport, dreading what she might find inside them.

A driver had picked her up as promised, but as he had been unwilling to make any attempt at conversation she had no idea what to expect when they pulled up outside the Jordanian Embassy. Hannah was surprised by its size.

The beautiful old house which was set back from the boulevard Maurice Barrès was formerly the home of the late Aga Khan. The Iraqi annexe had been allocated two complete floors, tangible proof that the Jordanians did not wish to get on the wrong side of Saddam.

On entering the annexe to the embassy, the first person she met was Abdul Kanuk, the Chief Administrator. He certainly didn't look like a diplomat, and when he opened his mouth she realised he wasn't. Kanuk informed her that the Ambassador and his senior secretary Muna Ahmed were tied up in meetings and that she was to unpack and then wait in her room until called for.

The cramped accommodation was just about large enough for a bed and two suitcases, and might, she thought, have been a store room before the Iraqi delegation moved in. When she eventually forced open Karima Saib's suitcase she quickly discovered that the only things that fitted from her wardrobe were her shoes. Hannah didn't know whether to be relieved, because of Saib's taste, or anxious about how little of her own she had to wear.

Muna Ahmed, the senior secretary, joined her in the kitchen for supper later that evening. It seemed that secretaries in the embassy were treated on the same level as servants. Hannah managed to convince Muna that it was better than she had expected, especially since they were only able to use the annexe to the Jordanian Embassy. Muna explained that as far as the Corps Diplomatique of France was concerned, the Iraqi Ambassador was to be treated only as a Head of Interest Section, although they were to address him at all times as 'Your Excellency' or 'Ambassador'.

During the first few days in her new job, Hannah sat in the room next to the Ambassador's on the other side of Muna's desk. She spent most of her time twiddling her fingers. Hannah quickly discovered that no one took much interest in her as long as she completed any work the Ambassador had left for her on his dictating machine. In fact that soon became Hannah's biggest problem, as she had to slow down in order to make Muna look more efficient. The only thing Hannah ever forgot was to keep wearing her see-through glasses.

In the evenings, over supper in the kitchen, Hannah learned from Muna everything that was expected of an Iraqi woman abroad, including how to avoid the advances of Abdul Kanuk, the Chief Administrator. By the second week, her learning curve had already slowed down, and increasingly Hannah found the Ambassador was relying on her skills. She tried not to show too much initiative.

Once they had finished their work, Hannah and Muna were expected to remain indoors, and were not allowed to leave the building at night unless accompanied by the Chief Administrator, a prospect that didn't tempt either of them. As Muna had no interest in music, the theatre or even going to cafés, she was happy to pass the time in her room reading the speeches of Saddam Hussein.

As the days slowly passed Hannah began to hope that the Mossad agent in Paris would contact her so that she could be pulled out and sent back to Israel to prepare for her mission – not that she had any clue who the Mossad agent was. She wondered if they had one in the embassy. Alone in her room, she often speculated. The driver? Too slow. The gardener? Too dumb. The cook? Certainly possible – the food was bad enough to believe it was her second job. Abdul Kanuk, the Chief Administrator? Hardly, since, as he pointed out at least three times a day, he was a cousin of Barazan Al-Tikriti, Saddam Hussein's half-brother and the UN Ambassador in Geneva. Kanuk was also the biggest gossip in the embassy, and supplied Hannah with more information about Saddam Hussein and his entourage in one night than the Ambassador managed in a week. In truth, the Ambassador rarely spoke of Sayedi in her presence, and when he did he was always guarded and respectful.

It was during the second week that Hannah was introduced to the Ambassador's wife. Hannah quickly discovered that she was fiercely independent, partly because she was half Turkish, and didn't consider that it was necessarily her duty always to stay inside the embassy compound. She did things that were thought extreme by Iraqi standards, like accompanying her husband to cocktail parties, and she had even been known to pour herself a drink without waiting to be asked. She also went – which was more important for Hannah – twice a week to swim at the nearby public baths in the boulevard Lannes. The Ambassador agreed, after a little persuasion, that it would be acceptable for the new secretary to accompany his wife.

Scott arrived in Paris on a Sunday. He had been given a key to a small flat on the avenue de Messine, and they had opened an account for him at the Société Générale on boulevard Haussmann in the name of Simon Rosenthal.

He was to telephone or fax Langley only after he had located the Mossad agent. No other operative had been informed of his existence, and he had been told not to make contact with any field agent he had worked with in the past who was now stationed in Europe.

Scott spent the first two days discovering the nine places from which he could observe the front door of the Jordanian Embassy without being seen by anyone in the building.

By the end of a week he had begun to realise for the first time what agents really meant by the expression 'hours of solitude'. He even started to miss some of his students.

He developed a routine. Every morning before breakfast he would run for five miles in the Parc Monceau, before he began the morning shift. Every evening he would spend two hours in a gym on rue de Berne before cooking supper, which he ate alone in his flat.

Scott began to despair of the Mossad agent ever leaving the embassy compound, and to wonder if Miss Kopec was even in there. The Ambassador's wife seemed to be the only woman to come and go as she pleased.

And then without warning, on the Tuesday of his second week, someone else left the building accompanying the Ambassador's wife. Was it Hannah Kopec? He only caught a fleeting glimpse as the car sped away.

He followed the chauffeur-driven Mercedes, always remaining at an angle that would make it difficult for the Ambassador's driver to spot him in his rear-view mirror. The two women were dropped outside the swimming pool on the boulevard Lannes. He watched them get out of the car. In the photographs he had been shown at Langley, Hannah Kopec had had long black hair. The hair was now cropped, but it was unquestionably her.

Scott drove a hundred yards further down the road, turned right and parked the car. He walked back, entered the building and purchased a spectator's ticket at a cost of two francs. He strolled up to the balcony which overlooked the pool. By the time he had selected an obscure seat in the gallery the Mossad agent was already swimming up and down. It only took moments for Scott to realise how fit she was, even if the Iraqi version of a swimsuit wasn't all that alluring. Her pace slowed when the Ambassador's wife appeared at the edge of the pool, after which she ventured only an occasional dog-paddle from one side to the other.

Some forty minutes later, when the Ambassador's wife left the pool, Kopec immediately quickened her pace, covering each length in under a minute. When she had swum ten lengths she pulled herself out of the water and disappeared towards the changing room.

Scott returned to his car, and when the two women reappeared he allowed the Mercedes to overtake him before following them back to the embassy.

Later that night he faxed Dexter Hutchins at Langley

to let him know he had seen her, and would now try to make contact.

The following morning, he bought a pair of swimming trunks.

It was on the Thursday that Hannah first noticed him. He was doing the crawl at a steady rate, completing each length in about forty seconds, and looked as if he might once have been a useful athlete. She tried to keep up with his pace but could only manage five lengths before he stretched away. She watched him pull himself out of the water after another dozen lengths and head off in the direction of the men's changing room.

On Monday morning the following week, the Ambassador's wife informed Hannah that she wouldn't be able to go for their usual swim the next day as she would be accompanying the Ambassador on his visit to Saddam Hussein's half-brother in Geneva. Hannah had already been told about the trip by the Chief Administrator, who seemed to know even the finest details.

'I can't think why you haven't been invited to join the Ambassador as well,' said the cook that evening. The Chief Administrator was silenced for about two minutes until Muna left the kitchen to go to her room. Then he revealed a piece of information that disturbed Hannah.

The following day Hannah was given permission to go swimming by herself. She was glad to have an excuse to get out of the building, especially as Kanuk was in charge of the delegation in the Ambassador's absence. He had taken the Mercedes for himself, so she made her own way to the boulevard Lannes by Métro. She was disappointed to find that the man who swam so well was nowhere to be seen when she started off on her thirty lengths. Once she had completed her exercise she clung onto the side, tired and slightly out of breath. Suddenly, she was aware that he was swimming towards her in the outside lane. When he touched the end he turned smoothly and said distinctly, 'Don't move, Hannah, I'll be back.'

Hannah assumed he must be someone who remembered her from her days as a model, and her immediate reaction was to make a run for it. But she continued to tread water as she waited for him to return, thinking he might perhaps be the Mossad agent Kratz had referred to.

She watched him swimming towards her, and became more apprehensive with each stroke. When he touched the edge he came to a sudden halt and asked, 'Are you alone?'

'Yes,' she replied.

'I thought I couldn't see the Ambassador's wife. She usually displaces a great deal of water without much forward motion. By the way, I'm Simon Rosenthal. Colonel Kratz instructed me to make contact. I have a message for you.'

Hannah felt stupid shaking hands with the man while they were both clinging onto the edge of the pool.

'Do you know the avenue Bugeaud?'

'Yes,' she replied.

'Good. See you at the Bar de la Porte Dauphine in fifteen minutes.'

He pulled himself out of the pool in one movement and disappeared in the direction of the men's changing room before she had a chance to reply.

A little over fifteen minutes later Hannah walked into the Bar de la Porte Dauphine. She searched around the room and almost missed him perched behind one of the high-backed wooden chairs directly below a large, colourful mural.

He rose to greet her and then ordered another coffee.

He warned her that they must spend only a few minutes together, because she ought to return to the embassy without delay. As she sipped the first real coffee she had tasted in weeks, Hannah took a closer look at him, and began to recall what it was like just to enjoy a drink with someone interesting. His next sentence snapped her back into the real world.

'Kratz plans to pull you out of Paris in the near future.'

'Any particular reason?' she asked.

'The date of the Baghdad operation has been settled.'

'Thank God,' said Hannah.

'Why do you say that?' asked Scott, risking his first question.

'The Ambassador expects to be called back to Baghdad to take up a new post. He intends to ask me to go with him,' replied Hannah. 'Or that's what the Chief Administrator is telling everyone, except Muna.'

'I'll warn Kratz.'

'By the way, Simon, I've picked up two or three scraps of information that Kratz might find useful.'

He nodded and listened as Hannah began to give him details of the internal organisation of the embassy, and of the comings and goings of diplomats and businessmen who publicly spoke out against Saddam while at the same time trying to close deals with him. After a few minutes he stopped her and said, 'You'd better leave now. They might begin to miss you. I'll try and arrange another meeting whenever it's possible,' he found himself adding.

She smiled, rose from the table and left, without looking back.

Later that evening, Scott sent a coded message to Dexter Hutchins in Virginia to let him know that he had made contact with Hannah Kopec.

A fax came back an hour later with only one instruction.

13

ON MAY 25TH 1993, the sun rose over the Capitol a few minutes after five. Its rays crept along the White House lawn and minutes later seeped unnoticed into the Oval Office. A few hundred yards away, Cavalli was slapping his hands behind his back.

Cavalli had spent the previous day in Washington, checking the finer details for what felt like the hundredth time. He had to assume that something must go wrong and, whatever it turned out to be, it would automatically become his responsibility.

Johnny Scasiatore walked over and handed Cavalli a steaming mug of coffee.

'I had no idea it could be this cold in Washington,' Cavalli said to Johnny, who was wearing a sheepskin jacket.

'It's cold at this time of the morning almost everywhere in the world,' replied Johnny. 'Ask any film director.'

'And do you really need six hours to get ready for three minutes of filming?' Cavalli asked incredulously.

'Two hours' preparation for a minute's work is the standard rule. And don't forget, we'll have to run through this particular scene twice, in somewhat unusual circumstances.'

Cavalli stood on the corner of 13th Street and

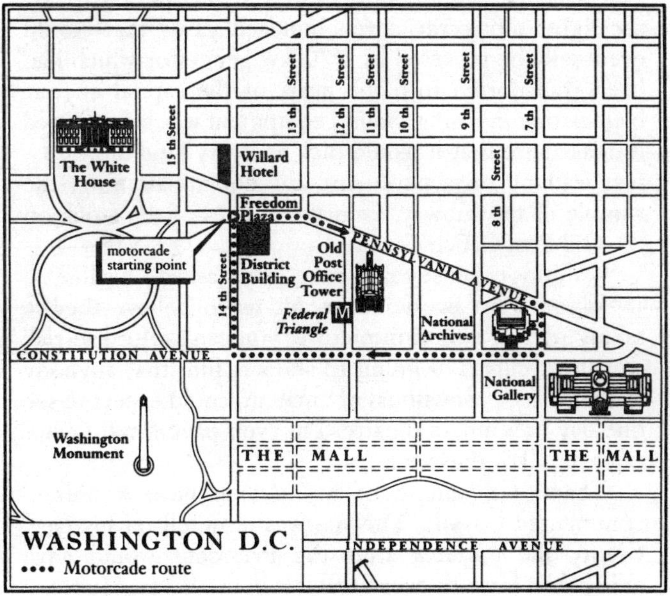
15 th Street
13 th Street
12 th Street
11 th Street
10 th Street
9 th Street
7 th Street
8 th Street
14 th Street
The White House
Willard Hotel
Freedom Plaza
motorcade starting point
District Building
Old Post Office Tower
Federal Triangle
M
PENNSYLVANIA AVENUE
National Archives
CONSTITUTION AVENUE
National Gallery
Washington Monument
THE MALL
THE MALL
INDEPENDENCE AVENUE
WASHINGTON D.C.
•••• Motorcade route

Pennsylvania Avenue and eyed the fifty or so people who came under Johnny's direction. Some were preparing a track along the pavement that would allow a camera to follow the six cars as they travelled slowly down Pennsylvania Avenue. Others were fixing up massive IK arc lights along the seven hundred yards that would eventually be powered by a 200kw generator which had been transported into the heart of the capital at four o'clock that morning. Sound equipment was being tested to make sure that it would pick up every kind of noise – feet walking on a pavement, car doors slamming, the rumble of the subway, even the chimes of the clock on the Old Post Office Tower.

'Is all this expense really necessary?' asked Cavalli.

'If you want everyone except us to believe they're taking part in a motion picture, you can't afford to risk any short-cuts. I'm going to shoot a film that anybody watching us, professional or amateur, could expect to see one day in a movie theatre. I'm even paying full equity rates for all of the extras.'

'Thank God none of my people have a union,' commented Cavalli. The sun was now full on his face, twenty-one minutes after the President would have enjoyed its warmth over breakfast in the White House.

Cavalli looked down at the checklist on his clipboard. Al Calabrese already had all his twelve vehicles in place on the kerbside, and the drivers were standing around in a huddle drinking coffee, sheltered from the wind by one of the walls of Freedom Plaza. The six limousines glistened in the morning sun as passers-by, cleaners and janitors leaving offices and early-morning commuters coming up from the Federal Triangle Metro slowed to admire the spectacle. A painter was just touching up the Presidential Seal on the third car while a girl was unfurling a flag on the right-hand fender.

Cavalli turned to see a police truck, tailboard down, parked in front of the District Building. Barriers were being lifted off and carried onto the pavement to make sure innocent passers-by did not stray onto the set during those crucial three minutes when the filming would be taking place.

Lloyd Adams had spent the previous day going over his lines one last time and dipping into yet another book on the history of the Declaration of Independence. That night he had sat in bed replaying again and again a video of Bill Clinton on his Georgia Avenue walk, noting the tilt of the head, the Razorback accent, the way he subconsciously bit his lower lip. The Monday before, Adams had purchased a suit that was identical to the one the President had worn to welcome the British Prime Minister in February – straight off the rack from Dillard's Department Store. He chose a red, white and blue tie, a rip-off of the one Clinton wore on the cover of the March issue of *Vanity Fair*. A Timex Ironman had been the final addition to his wardrobe. During the past week a second wig had been made, this time a little greyer, which Adams felt more comfortable with. The director and Cavalli had taken him through a dress rehearsal the previous evening: word perfect – though Johnny had commented that his collapse at the end of the scene was a bad case of overacting. Cavalli felt the Archivist would be far too overwhelmed to notice.

Cavalli asked Al Calabrese to go over the breakdown of his staff yet again. Al tried not to sound exasperated, as he had gone over it in great detail during their last three board meetings: 'Twelve drivers, six outriders,' he rattled off. 'Four of them are ex-cops or military police and all of them have worked with me before. But as none of them are going into the National Archives, they've simply been told they're involved in a movie. Only those working directly under Gino Sartori know what we're really up to.'

'But are they fully briefed on what's expected of them once they reach the Archives?'

'You'd better believe it,' replied Al. 'We went over it at least half a dozen times yesterday, first on a map in my office, and then we came down here in the afternoon and walked the route. They drive down Pennsylvania Avenue at ten miles an hour while they're being filmed and continue east until they reach 7th Street. Then they take a sharp right, when they'll be out of sight of everyone involved in the filming, not to mention the police. Then they turn right again at the delivery entrance of the National Archives, where they'll come to a halt in front of the loading dock. Angelo, Dollar Bill, Debbie, you and the counter-assault team leave their vehicles and accompany the actor into the building, where they'll be met by Calder Marshall.

'Once your party has entered the building the cars will go back up the ramp and take a right on 7th Street, another right on Constitution Avenue and then right on 14th Street before returning to the location where the filming began. By then, Johnny will be ready for a second take. On the signal from you that the Declaration of Independence has been exchanged for a fake, the second take will begin immediately, except this time we'll be picking up the thirteen operatives we dropped outside the National Archives.'

'And, if all goes to plan, the Declaration of Independence as well,' said Cavalli. 'Then what happens?' he asked, wanting to be sure that nothing had changed since their final board meeting in New York.

'The limos leave Washington by six separate routes,' continued Al. 'Three of them return to the capital during the afternoon, but not until they've changed their licence plates; two others go on to New York, and one drives to a destination known only to you; that will be the vehicle carrying the Declaration.'

'If it all runs as smoothly as that, Al, you'll have earned your money. But it won't, and that's when we'll really find out how good you are.' He nodded as Al left to grab a mug of coffee and rejoin his men.

Cavalli checked his watch: 7.22. When he looked up he saw Johnny heading towards him, red in the face. Thank God I don't have to work in Hollywood, thought Cavalli.

'I'm having trouble with a cop who says I can't put my lighting equipment on the sidewalk until 9.30 a.m. That means I won't be able to begin filming until after ten, and if I've only got forty-five minutes to start with –'

'Calm down, Johnny,' said Cavalli, and checked his list of personnel. He looked up and began to search the crowd of workers that was flowing off Freedom Plaza onto the pavement. He spotted the man he needed. 'You see the tall guy with grey hair practising his charm on Debbie?' he said, pointing.

'Yeah,' said Johnny.

'That's Tom Newbolt, ex-Deputy Chief of the DCPD, now a security consultant. We've hired him for the day. So go and tell him what your problem is, and then we'll find out if he's worth the five thousand dollars his company is charging me.'

Cavalli smiled as Johnny stormed off in Newbolt's direction.

Angelo stood over the slumbering body. He leaned across, grabbed Dollar Bill's shoulders, and began to shake him furiously.

The little Irishman was belching out a snore that

sounded more like an old tractor than a human being. Angelo leaned closer, only to find Dollar Bill smelt as if he had spent a night in the local brewery.

Angelo realised that he should never have left Bill the previous evening, even for a moment. If he didn't get the bastard to the Archives on time, Cavalli would kill them both. He even knew who'd carry out the job, and the method she would use. He went on shaking, but Dollar Bill's eyes remained determinedly closed.

At eight o'clock a klaxon sounded and the film crew took a break for breakfast.

'Thirty minutes. Union regulations,' explained Johnny when Cavalli looked exasperated. The crew surrounded a parked trailer – another expensive import – on the pavement, where they were served eggs, ham and hash browns. Cavalli had to admit that the crowds gathered behind the police barriers and the passers-by lingering on the pavement never seemed to doubt for a moment that this was a film crew getting ready for a shoot.

Cavalli decided to use the thirty-minute break to check for himself that, once the cars had turned right on 7th Street, they could not be seen by anyone involved in the filming back on Pennsylvania Avenue.

He strode briskly away from the commotion, and when he reached the corner of 7th Street he turned right. It was as if he'd entered a different world. He joined a group of people who were quite unaware of what was taking place less than half a mile away. It was just like Washington on a normal Tuesday morning. He was pleased to spot Andy Borzello sitting on the bench in the bus shelter near the loading dock entrance to the National Archives, reading the *Washington Post*.

By the time Cavalli had returned, the film crew were beginning to move back and start their final checks; no one wanted to be the person responsible for a retake.

The crowds at the barriers were growing thicker by the minute, and the police spent a considerable amount of their time explaining that a film was going to be shot, but not for at least another couple of hours. Several people looked disappointed at this information and moved on, only to allow others to take up the places they had vacated.

Cavalli's cellular phone began ringing. He pressed the talk button and was greeted by the sound of his father's Brooklyn vowels. The chairman was cautious over the phone, and simply asked if there were any problems.

'Several,' admitted Tony. 'But none so far that we hadn't anticipated or can't overcome.'

'Don't forget, cancel the entire operation if you're not satisfied with the response to your nine o'clock phone call. Either way, he mustn't be allowed to return to the White House.' The line went dead. Cavalli knew that his father was right on both counts.

Cavalli checked his watch again: 8.43. He strolled over to Johnny.

'I'm going across to the Willard. I don't expect to be too long, so just keep things rolling. By the way, I see you got all your equipment on the sidewalk.'

'Sure thing,' said Johnny. 'Once Newbolt talked to that cop, he even helped us carry the damn stuff.'

Cavalli smiled and began walking towards the National Theater on the way to the Willard Hotel. Gino Sartori was coming in the opposite direction.

'Gino,' Cavalli said, stopping to face the ex-Marine. 'Are all your men ready?'

'Every one of the bastards.'

'And can you guarantee their silence?'

'Like the grave. That is, if they don't want to end up digging their own.'

'So where are they now?'

'Coming from eight different directions. All of them are due to report to me by nine-thirty. Smart dark suits, sober ties, and holsters that aren't too obvious.'

'Let me know the moment they're all signed in.'

'Will do,' said Gino.

Cavalli continued his journey to the Willard Hotel, and after checking his watch again began to lengthen his stride.

He strolled into the lobby, and found Rex Butterworth marching nervously up and down the centre of the hall as if his sole aim in life was to wear out the blue-and-gold carpet. He looked relieved when he saw Cavalli, and joined him as he strode towards the elevator.

'I told you to sit in the corner and wait, not parade up and down in front of every freelance journalist looking for a story.'

Butterworth mumbled an apology as they stepped into the elevator and Cavalli pressed button eleven. Neither of them spoke again until they were safely inside 1137, the room in which Cavalli had spent the previous night.

Cavalli looked more carefully at Rex Butterworth now they were alone. He was sweating as if he had just finished a five-mile jog, not travelled up eleven floors in an elevator.

'Calm down,' said Cavalli. 'You've played your part well so far. Only one more phone call and you're through. You'll be on your flight to Rio before the first outrider even reaches the National Archives. Now, are you clear about what you have to say to Marshall?'

Butterworth took out some handwritten notes, mouthed a few words and said, 'Yes, I'm clear and I'm ready.' He was shaking like a jelly.

Cavalli dialled the private number of the Archivist's office half a mile away, and when he heard the first ring, passed the receiver over to Butterworth. They both listened to the continuing ringing. Eventually Cavalli put his hand out to take back the receiver. They would have to try again in a few minutes' time. Suddenly there was a click and a voice said, 'Calder Marshall speaking.'

Cavalli went into the bathroom and picked up the extension. 'Good morning, Mr Marshall. It's Rex Butterworth at the White House, just checking everything's all set up and ready your end.'

'It certainly is, Mr Butterworth. Every member of my staff has been instructed to be at their desks by nine o'clock sharp. In fact, I've seen most of them already, but only my deputy and the Senior Conservator know the real reason I've asked them all not to be late this morning.'

'Well done,' said Butterworth. 'The President is running on time and we anticipate he will be with you around ten, but I'm afraid he still has to be back at the White House by eleven.'

'By eleven, of course,' said the Archivist. 'I only hope we can get him round the whole building in fifty minutes, because I expect there are many of my staff who would like to meet him.'

'We'll just have to hope that fifty minutes is enough time to fit them all in,' said Butterworth. 'Can I assume that there are still no problems with the President's personal request?'

'None that I'm aware of,' said Marshall. 'The Conservator is quite happy to remove the glass so that the President can study the parchment in its original form. We'll keep the Declaration in the vault until the President has left the building. I hope to have the document back on view to the general public a few minutes after he departs.'

'It sounds to me as if you have everything under control, Mr Marshall,' said Butterworth, the sweat pouring off his forehead. 'I'm just off to see the President, so I'm afraid I'll be out of contact for the rest of the morning, but let's talk again this afternoon and you can tell me how it all went.'

Cavalli placed the phone on the side of the bath and bolted back into the bedroom, coming to a halt in front of the President's Special Assistant. Butterworth looked terrified. Cavalli shook his head frantically from side to side.

'Actually, now that I look at my schedule, Mr Marshall, I see you won't be able to reach me again today because I promised my wife I'd leave the office a little earlier than usual to prepare for our annual vacation which begins tomorrow.'

'Oh. Where are you going?' asked Marshall, innocently.

'Off to see my mother in Charleston. But I feel confident that the President's visit to the Archives will be a great success. Why don't we get together as soon as I'm back?'

'I would enjoy that,' said Marshall. 'And I do hope you have a pleasant break in South Carolina; the azaleas should still be blooming.'

'Yes, I suppose they will,' said Butterworth as he watched Cavalli pulling a finger across his throat. 'My other line is ringing,' he added, and without another word put the phone down.

'You said too much, you fool. We don't ever want him trying to contact you again.'

Butterworth looked apprehensive.

'How long will it be before the White House wonders where you are?' asked Cavalli.

'At least a week,' replied Butterworth. 'I really am due for my annual leave, and even my boss thinks I'm going to Charleston.'

'Well, that's something you did right,' said Cavalli, as he handed Butterworth a one-way ticket to Rio de Janeiro and a letter of confirmation that the sum of nine hundred thousand dollars had been deposited in the Banco do Brazil.

'I have to get back to the set,' said Cavalli. 'You stay put for ten minutes and then take a taxi to Dulles airport. And when you get to Brazil, don't spend all the money on a girl. And Rex, don't even think about coming back. If you do, it won't just be the Feds who are waiting for you at the airport.'

Angelo had somehow managed to get Dollar Bill dressed, but he still stank of Guinness, and he certainly didn't look like the President's personal physician – or anybody else's physician for that matter.

'Sorry, lad. Sorry, lad,' Dollar Bill kept repeating. 'I hope this won't get you into any trouble.'

'It will if you don't sober up in time to play your part and see that the parchment is transferred into the special cylinder. Because if Cavalli ever finds out I wasn't with you last night, you're dead, and more important, so am I.'

'Settle down, lad, and just make me a Bloody Mary. Two parts tomato juice and one part vodka. I'll be as right as rain in no time, you'll see.' Angelo looked doubtful as the little man's head fell back on the pillow.

As Cavalli closed the door of room 1137, a woman pushing a large laundry basket passed him in the corridor.

He took the lift to the ground floor and walked

straight out of the hotel. The first thing he saw as he left the Willard and crossed the plaza that divided the hotel from Pennsylvania Avenue was that the morning traffic was backed up for half a mile down 15th Street.

Al and Johnny came running towards him from different directions. 'What's going on?' were Cavalli's first words.

'Normal morning traffic coming in from Virginia, the police assure us, except we're blocking a lane and a half with our twelve vehicles and six outriders.'

'Damn, my mistake,' said Cavalli. 'I should have anticipated it. So what do you suggest, Al?'

'I send my boys over to Atlantic Garage on 13th and F until the police get the traffic on the move again, and then bring them back nearer the starting time.'

'It's a hell of a risk,' said Johnny. 'That permit only allows me to film for forty-five minutes, and they aren't going to stretch it by a second.'

'But if my cars stay put you might never get started at all,' said Al.

'OK, Al, you get moving, but make sure you're back on the grid by 9.50.' Cavalli checked his watch. 'That's twenty-seven minutes.' Al began running towards the parked cars.

Cavalli turned his attention to the director. 'What time are you bringing the actor out?'

'Nine-fifty-five, or the moment the last car is back in place. He's being made up in that trailer over there,' said Johnny.

Cavalli watched as the sixth limousine pulled away, and was relieved to see the traffic start to flow again.

'And Gino's Secret Service agents, what will happen to them now that the cars have gone?'

'Most of them are hanging around with the extras, but they aren't looking too convincing.'

Cavalli's cellular phone began to ring. 'I have to get back or you won't have a film, real or otherwise,' said Johnny. Cavalli nodded and said 'Yes,' into the mouthpiece as the director rushed away. Something caught Cavalli's eye as he tried to concentrate on the voice on the other end of the line.

'The helicopter is all set to take off at ten o'clock sharp, boss; but it loses its slot at seven minutes past. The traffic cops won't let it go up after that, however much you gave to the Fraternal Order of Police.'

'We're still running to schedule, despite some problems,' said Cavalli, 'so take her up at ten and just hover over the route. Marshall and his staff must be able to see and hear you when we arrive at the Archives. That's all I care about.'

'OK, boss. Understood.'

Cavalli checked his watch again. It was 9.36 and the traffic was now flowing smoothly. He walked over to the officer co-ordinating the shoot for the city's motion picture and television office.

'Don't worry,' said the Lieutenant even before Cavalli had opened his mouth. 'The traffic will be stopped and the detour signs in place by 9.59. We'll have you moving on time, I promise.'

'Thank you, officer,' said Cavalli, and quickly dialled Al Calabrese.

'I think you'd better start getting your boys back . . .'

'Number one has already left with two outriders. Number two's just about to go; after that, they leave at twenty-second intervals.'

'You should have been an army general,' said Cavalli.

'You can blame the government for that. I just didn't get the right education.'

Suddenly, Pennsylvania Avenue was ablaze with lights. Cavalli, like everyone else, shielded his eyes and then, just as suddenly, the lights were switched off, making the morning sun appear like a dim lightbulb.

'Good sparks,' Cavalli heard the director shout. 'I could only spot one that didn't function. The seventh on the right.'

Cavalli stood on the pavement and looked towards the corner of 13th Street, where he could see the first of Al's limousines with two outriders edging its way back through the traffic. The sight of the shining black limo made him feel nervous for the first time.

A tall, well-built, bald man wearing dark glasses, a dark blue suit, white shirt and a red, white and blue striped tie was walking towards him. He stopped by Cavalli's side as the first of the two outriders and the leading police car drew in to the kerb.

'How are you feeling?' asked Cavalli.

'Like all first nights,' said Lloyd Adams. 'I'll be just fine once the curtain goes up.'

'Well, you sure knew your lines word perfect last night.'

'My lines aren't the problem,' said Adams. 'It's Marshall's I'm worried about.'

'What do you mean?' asked Cavalli.

'He's not been able to attend any of our rehearsals, has he?' replied the actor. 'So he doesn't know his cues.'

The second car drew into line, accompanied by two more outriders, as Al Calabrese came running across the pavement and Lloyd Adams strode off in the direction of the trailer.

'Can you still do it in eleven minutes?' asked Cavalli, looking at his watch.

'As long as Chief Thomas's finest don't foul things up like they do every other morning,' said Al. He headed on towards the cars and immediately began to organise the unfurling of the Presidential flag on the front of the third car before checking on any specks of dirt that might have appeared on the bodywork after one trip round the block.

The staff van drew up in line. Scasiatore immediately swung round on his high stool and, through a megaphone, told the actor, the secretary, the Lieutenant and the physician to be ready to climb into the third and fourth cars.

When the director asked for the Lieutenant and the physician, Cavalli suddenly realised that he hadn't seen Dollar Bill or Angelo all morning. Perhaps they'd been waiting in the trailer.

The fourth limousine drew up as Cavalli's eyes swept the horizon, searching for Angelo.

The klaxon sounded again for several seconds, this time to warn the film crew that they had ten minutes left before shooting. The noise almost prevented Cavalli from hearing his phone ringing.

'It's Andy reporting in, boss. I'm still outside the National Archives. Just to let you know it's no busier than when you checked up an hour ago.'

'At least someone's awake,' said Cavalli.

'There can't be more than twenty or thirty people around at the moment.'

'Glad to hear it. But don't call me again unless something goes wrong.' Cavalli flicked off the phone and tried to remember what it was that had been worrying him before it rang. Eleven vehicles and six outriders were now in place. One vehicle was still missing. But something else was nagging at the back of Cavalli's mind. He became distracted when an officer standing in the middle of Pennsylvania Avenue began shouting at the top of his voice that he was ready to stop the traffic whenever the director gave the word. Johnny stood up on his chair and pointed frantically to the twelfth car, which remained obstinately stuck in traffic a couple of hundred yards away.

'If you divert the traffic now,' shouted Johnny, 'that one's never going to end up in the motorcade.'

The officer remained in the middle of the road and waved the traffic through as fast as he could in the hope of getting the limousine there quicker, but it didn't make a lot of difference.

'Extras on the street!' shouted Johnny, and several people who Cavalli had supposed were members of the public strolled onto the pavement and began walking up and down professionally.

Johnny stood up on his chair again and this time turned to face the crowd huddled behind the barriers. An aide handed him a megaphone so that he could address them.

'Ladies and gentlemen,' he began. 'This is a short cut for a movie about the President going to the Hill to address a joint session of Congress. I'd be grateful if you could wave, clap and cheer as if it were the real President. Thank you.' Spontaneous applause broke out, which made Cavalli laugh for the first time that morning. He hadn't noticed that the former Deputy Police Chief had crept up behind him during the director's address. He whispered in his ear, 'This is going to cost you a whole lot of money if you don't pull it off first time.'

Cavalli turned to face the ex-policeman and tried not to show how anxious he felt.

'The hold-up, I mean. If you don't get the shoot done this morning, the authorities aren't going to let you go through this charade again for one hell of a time.'

'I don't need to be reminded of that,' snapped Cavalli. He turned his attention back to Johnny, who had climbed down from his chair and was walking over to take his seat on the tracking dolly, ready to move as soon as the twelfth vehicle was in place. Once again, the aide passed Johnny the megaphone. 'This is a final check. Check your positions, please. This is a final check. Everyone ready in car one?' There was a sharp honk in reply. 'Car two?' Another honk. 'Car three?' Another sharp honk from the driver of Lloyd Adams' car. Cavalli stared in through the window as the bald actor removed the top of his wig box. 'Car four?' Not a sound came from car four.

'Is everyone in car four who should be in car four?' barked the director.

It was then that Cavalli remembered what had been nagging at him: he still hadn't seen Angelo or Dollar Bill all morning. He should have checked earlier. He hurried towards the director as a naval Lieutenant jumped out of a car which he'd left stranded in the middle of the road. He was six foot tall, with short-cropped hair, wearing a white uniform with a sword swinging by his side and medals for service in Panama and the Gulf on his chest. In his right hand he carried a black box. A policeman began chasing after him while Dollar Bill, carrying a small leather bag, followed a few yards behind at a slower pace. When Cavalli saw what had happened he changed direction and walked calmly out into the middle of the road, and the naval officer came to a halt by his side.

'What the hell do you think you're playing at?' barked Cavalli.

'We got held up in the traffic,' said Angelo lamely.

'If this whole operation fails because of you . . .'

Angelo turned the colour of his uniform as he thought about what had happened to Bruno Morelli.

'And the sword?' snapped Cavalli.

'A perfect fit.'

'And our physician. Is *he* fit?'

'He'll be able to do his job, I promise you,' Angelo said, looking over his shoulder.

'Which car are you both in?'

'Number four. Directly behind the President.'

'Then get in, and right now.'

'Sorry, sorry,' Dollar Bill said, as he arrived panting. 'My fault, not Angelo's. Sorry, sorry,' he repeated as the back door of car four was held open for him by the Lieutenant, who was gripping his sword. Once Dollar Bill was safely in, Angelo joined the would-be physician and slammed the door behind him.

The policeman who'd been chasing Angelo took his notebook out as Cavalli turned round looking for Tom Newbolt. Tom was already running across the road.

'Leave him to me,' was all he said.

The second van with surveillance cameras on board screeched to a halt to complete the line. The front window purred down. 'Sorry, boss,' said the driver. 'Some jerk just dumped his car right in front of me.' The clock on the Old Post Office Tower struck ten. At that moment, on a signal from the co-ordinating officer, several policemen walked out into the road. Some held up the traffic coming down Pennsylvania Avenue while others placed diversion signs to direct the cars away from where the filming was taking place.

Cavalli turned his attention to the other end of Pennsylvania Avenue, a mere seven hundred yards away. It was still bumper to bumper with slow-moving traffic.

'Come on, come on!' he shouted out loud as he checked his watch and waited impatiently for the all clear.

'Any moment now,' shouted back the officer, who was standing in the middle of the road.

Cavalli looked up to see the blue-and-white police helicopter hovering noisily overhead.

Neither he nor the officer spoke again until a couple of minutes later when they heard a sharp whistle blow three times from the far end of Pennsylvania Avenue. Cavalli checked his watch. They'd lost six precious minutes.

'I'll kill Angelo,' he said. 'If –'

'All clear!' shouted the co-ordinating officer. He turned to face Cavalli, who gave the director a thumbs-up sign.

'You've still got thirty-nine minutes,' bellowed the officer. 'That should easily be enough time to complete the shoot twice.' But Cavalli didn't hear the last few words as he ran to the second car, pulled open the door and jumped into the seat next to the driver.

And then a nagging thought hit him. Looking out of the side window, Cavalli began to scan the crowd once again.

'Lights!' screamed the director, and Pennsylvania Avenue lit up like Christmas Eve at Macy's.

'OK, everybody, we're going to shoot in sixty seconds.'

The limousines and motorcycles switched on their engines and began revving up. The extras strolled up and down while the police continued to divert commuters away from the scene. The director leaned back over his chair to check the lights and see if the seventh in line was working.

'Thirty seconds.' Johnny looked at the driver of the first car and said through the megaphone, 'Don't forget to take it easy. My tracking dolly can only manage ten miles an hour going backwards. And walkers,' – the director checked up and down the pavement – 'please look as if you're walking, not auditioning for *Hamlet*.'

The director turned his attention to the crowd. 'Now, don't let me down behind the barriers. Clap, cheer and wave, and please remember we're going to do the whole exercise again in about twenty minutes, so stick around if you possibly can.

'Fifteen seconds,' said the director as he swung back to face the first car in line. 'Good luck, everybody.'

Tony stared at Scasiatore, willing him to get on with it. They were now eight minutes late – which with this particular President, he had to admit, added an air of authenticity.

'Ten seconds. Rolling. Nine, eight, seven, six, five, four, three, two, one – action!'

The woman pushing the laundry basket down the corridor ignored the 'Do Not Disturb' sign on Room 1137 and walked straight in.

A rather overweight man, sweating profusely, was seated on the edge of the bed. He was jabbing out some numbers on the phone when he looked round and saw her.

'Get out, you dumb bitch,' he said, and turned back to concentrate on redialling the numbers.

In three silent paces she was behind him. He turned a second time just as she leaned over, took the phone cord in both hands and pulled it round his neck. He raised an arm to protest as she flicked her wrists in one sharp movement. He slumped forward and fell off the bed onto the carpet, just as the voice on the phone said, 'Thank you for using AT & T.'

She realised that she shouldn't have used the phone cord. Most unprofessional – but nobody called her a dumb bitch.

She replaced the phone on the hook and bent down, deftly hoisting the Special Assistant to the President onto her shoulder. She dropped him into the laundry basket. No one would have believed such a frail woman could have lifted such a heavy weight. In truth the only use she had ever made of a degree in physics was to apply the principles of fulcrums, pivots and levers to her chosen profession.

She opened the door and checked the passageway. At this hour it was unlikely there'd be many people around. She wheeled the basket down the corridor until she reached the housekeepers' elevator, faced the wall and waited patiently. When the lift arrived she pressed the button that would take her to the garage.

When the lift came to a halt on the lower ground floor she wheeled the basket out and over to the back of a Honda Accord, the second-most popular car in America.

Shielded by a pillar, she quickly transferred the Special Assistant from the basket into the boot of the car. She then wheeled the basket back to the lift, took off her baggy black uniform, dropped it into the laundry basket, removed her carrier bag with the long cord handle and despatched the laundry basket to the twenty-fifth floor.

She straightened up her Laura Ashley dress before climbing into the car and placing her carrier bag under the front seat. She drove out of the car park onto F Street, and had only travelled a short distance before she was stopped by a traffic cop.

She wound the window down.

'Follow the diversion sign,' he said, without even looking at her.

She glanced at the clock on her dashboard. It was 10.07.

14

AS THE LEAD POLICE CAR moved slowly away from the kerb, the director's tracking dolly began running backwards at the same pace along its rails. The crowds behind the barriers started to cheer and wave. If they had been making a real film the director would have called 'Cut' after twenty seconds because that fool of a co-ordinating officer was still standing in the middle of the road, hands on hips, oblivious to the fact that he wasn't the star of the movie.

Cavalli didn't notice the officer as he concentrated on the road ahead of him. He phoned through to Andy, who he knew would still be seated on the bench on 7th Street reading the *Washington Post*.

'Not much action this end, boss. A little activity at the bottom of the ramp, but no one on the street is showing any real interest. Is everything all right your end? You're running late.'

'Yes, I know, but we should be with you in about sixty seconds,' said Cavalli, as the director reached the end of his private railroad track and put one thumb in the air to indicate that the cars could now accelerate to twenty-five miles per hour. Johnny Scasiatore jumped off the dolly and walked slowly back down Pennsylvania Avenue so he could prepare himself for the second take.

Cavalli flicked the phone off and took a deep intake of

breath as the motorcade passed 9th Street; he stared at the FDR Monument that was set back on a grass plot in front of the main entrance of the Archives. The first car turned right on 7th Street; a mere half-block remained before they would reach the driveway into the loading dock. The lead motorcycles speeded up and when they were opposite Andy standing on the pavement, they swung right and drove down the ramp.

The rest of the motorcade formed a line directly opposite the delivery entrance, while the third limousine drove down the ramp to the loading dock.

The counter-assault team were the first onto the street, and eight of them quickly formed a circle facing outwards around the third car.

After the eight men had stared in every direction for a few seconds, Cavalli jumped out of the second car, ran across to join them and opened the back door of the third car so that Lloyd Adams could get out.

Calder Marshall was waiting on the loading dock, and walked forward to greet the President.

'Nice to meet you, Mr Marshall,' said the actor, thrusting out his hand. 'I've been looking forward to this occasion for some time.'

'As, indeed, have we, Mr President. May I on behalf of my staff welcome you to the National Archives of the United States. Will you please follow me.'

Lloyd Adams and his entourage dutifully followed Marshall straight into the spartan freight elevator. As one of the Secret Service agents kept his finger on the 'open' button, Cavalli gave the order for the motorcade to return to its starting point. Six motorcycles and the twelve vehicles moved off and began the journey back to rejoin the director and prepare for the second shoot.

The whole exercise of getting the actor into the building and the motorcade started on its return journey had taken less than two minutes, but Cavalli was dismayed to see that a small crowd had already gathered on the far side of the road by the Federal Trade Commission, obviously sensing something important was taking place. He only hoped Andy could deal with the problem.

Cavalli quickly slipped into the elevator, wedging himself behind Adams. Marshall had begun a short history of how the Declaration of Independence had ended up in the National Archives.

'Most people know that John Adams and Thomas Jefferson drafted the Declaration that was approved by Congress on July 4th 1776. Few, however, know that the second and third Presidents died on the same day, July 4th 1826 – fifty years to the day after the official signing.' The elevator doors opened on the ground floor and Marshall stepped out into a marble corridor and led them in the direction of his office.

'The Declaration had a long and turbulent journey, Mr President, before it ended up safely in this building.'

When they reached the fifth door on the left, Marshall guided the President and his staff into his office, where coffee awaited them. Two of the Secret Service agents stepped inside while the other six remained in the corridor.

Lloyd Adams sipped his coffee as Marshall ignored his in favour of continuing the history lesson. 'After the signing ceremony, on August 2nd 1776, the Declaration was filed in Philadelphia, but because of the danger of the document being captured by the British, the engrossed parchment was taken to Baltimore in a covered wagon.'

'Fascinating,' said Adams in a soft drawl. 'But had it been captured by the British infantry, copies would still have been in existence, no doubt?'

'Oh certainly, Mr President. Indeed, we have a good

example of one in this building executed by William J. Stone. However, the original remained in Baltimore until 1777, when it was returned to the relative safety of Philadelphia.'

'In another wagon?' asked the President.

'Indeed,' said Marshall, not realising his guest was joking. 'We even know the name of the man who drove it, a Mr Samuel Smith. Then, in 1800, by direction of President Adams, the Declaration was moved to Washington, where it first found a home in the Treasury Department, but between 1800 and 1814 it was moved all over the city, eventually ending up in the old War Office building on 17th Street.'

'And, of course, we were still at war with Britain at that time,' said the actor.

Cavalli admired the way Adams had not only learned his lines, but done his research so thoroughly.

'That is correct, Mr President,' said the Archivist. 'And when the British fleet appeared in Chesapeake Bay, the Secretary of State, James Monroe, ordered that the document be moved once again. Because, as I am sure you know, Mr President, it is the Secretary of State who is responsible for the safety of the parchment, not the President.'

Lloyd Adams did know, but wasn't sure if the President would have, so he decided to play safe. 'Is that right, Mr Marshall? Then perhaps it should be Warren Christopher who is here today to view the Declaration, and not me.'

'The Secretary of State was kind enough to visit us soon after he took office,' Marshall replied.

'But he didn't want the document moved again,' said the actor. Marshall, Cavalli, the Lieutenant and the physician dutifully laughed before the Archivist continued.

'Monroe, having spotted the British advancing on Washington, despatched the Declaration on a journey up the Potomac to Leesburg, Virginia.'

'August 24th,' said Adams, 'when they razed the White House to the ground.'

'Precisely,' said Marshall. 'You are well informed, sir.'

'To be fair,' said the actor, 'I've been well briefed by my Special Assistant, Rex Butterworth.'

Marshall showed his recognition of the name, but Cavalli wondered if the actor was being just a little too clever.

'That night,' continued Marshall, 'while the White House was ablaze, thanks to Monroe's foresight the Declaration was stored safely in Leesburg.'

'So when did they bring the parchment back to Washington?' asked Adams, who could have told the Archivist the exact date.

'Not for several weeks, sir. On September 17th 1814, to be precise. With the exception of a trip to Philadelphia for the centennial celebrations and its time in Fort Knox during World War II, the Declaration has remained in the capital ever since.'

'But not in this building,' said Adams.

'No, Mr President, you are right again. It has had several other homes before ending up here, the worst being the Patent Office, where it hung opposite a window and was for years exposed to sunlight, causing the parchment irreparable damage.'

Bill O'Reilly stood in the corner, thinking how many hours of work he had had to do and how many copies he had had to destroy during the preparation stage because of that particular piece of stupidity. He cursed all those who had ever worked in the Patent Office.

'How long did it hang there?' asked Adams.

'For thirty-five years,' said Marshall, with a sigh that

showed he was every bit as annoyed as Dollar Bill that his predecessors had been so irresponsible. 'In 1877 the Declaration was moved to the State Department library. Not only was smoking common at the time, but there was also an open fireplace in the room. And, I might add, the building was damaged by fire only months after the parchment had been moved.'

'That was a close one,' said Adams.

'After the war was over,' continued Marshall, 'the Declaration was taken from Fort Knox and brought back to Washington in a Pullman carriage before it was housed in the Library of Congress.'

'I hope it wasn't exposed to the light once again,' said Adams as Cavalli's phone rang.

Cavalli slipped into the corner and listened to the director tell him, 'We're back on the starting line, ready to go whenever you are.'

'I'll call when I need you,' was all Cavalli said. He switched his phone off and returned to listen to the Archivist's disquisition.

'. . . in a Thermapane case equipped with a filter to screen out damaging ultra-violet light.'

'Fascinating. But when did the document finally reach this building?' asked Adams.

'On December 13th 1952. It was transported from the Library of Congress to the National Archives in a tank under the armed escort of the US Marine Corps.'

'First a covered wagon, and finally a tank,' said the actor, who noticed that Cavalli kept glancing at his watch. 'Perhaps the time has come for me to see the Declaration in its full glory.'

'Of course, Mr President,' said the Archivist.

Marshall led the way back into the corridor, followed by the actor and his entourage.

'The Declaration can normally be seen by the public

in the rotunda on the ground floor, but we shall view it in the vault where it is stored at night.' When they reached the end of the corridor the Archivist led the President down a flight of stairs while Cavalli kept checking over the route that would allow them the swiftest exit if any trouble arose. He was delighted to find that the Archivist had followed his instructions and kept the corridors clear of any staff.

At the bottom of the steps, they came to a halt outside a vast steel door at which an elderly man in a long white coat stood waiting. His eyes lit up when he saw the actor.

'This is Mr Mendelssohn,' said Marshall. 'Mr Mendelssohn is the Senior Conservator and, I confess, the real expert on anything to do with the parchment. He will be your guide for the next few minutes before we visit the rest of the building.'

The actor stepped forward, and once again thrust out his hand. 'Good to meet you, Mr Mendelssohn.'

The elderly man bowed, shook the actor's hand, and pushed the steel door open.

'Please follow me, Mr President,' he said in a mid-European accent. Once inside the tiny vault, Cavalli watched his men spread out in a small circle, their eyes checking everything except the President. Bill O'Reilly, Angelo and Debbie also took their places as they had rehearsed the previous evening.

Cavalli quickly glanced at Dollar Bill, who looked as if it was he who might be in need of a physician.

Mendelssohn guided the actor towards a massive block of concrete that took up a large area of the far wall.

He patted the slab of concrete and explained that the protective shell had been built at a time when the nation's greatest fear had been a nuclear attack.

'The Declaration is covered in five tons of interlocking leaves of metal, embedded in the fifty-five-ton concrete and steel vault you see before you. I can assure you, Mr President,' Mendelssohn added, 'if Washington was razed to the ground, the Declaration of Independence would still be in one piece.'

'Impressive,' said Adams, 'most impressive.'

Cavalli checked his watch; it was 10.24, and they'd already been inside the building for seventeen minutes. Although the limousines were waiting, he had no choice but to allow the Conservator to carry on at his own pace. After all, their hosts were aware of the limitations on the President's time if they were still hoping to show him round the rest of the building.

'The entire system, Mr President,' continued the Conservator enthusiastically, 'is worked electronically. At the press of a button, the Declaration, which is always exhibited and stored in an upright position, travels up from this level through interlocking doors which open before the document finally comes to rest in a case of solid bronze, protected by ballistically tested glass and plastic laminate. Ultra-violet filters in the laminate give the inner layer a slightly greenish hue.' The actor looked lost, but Mr Mendelssohn continued, quite unconcerned. 'We are presently standing some twenty-two feet below the exhibit hall, and as the mechanics can be worked manually, I am able to stop the machinery at any time. With your permission, Mr Marshall.'

The Archivist nodded, and the Conservator touched a button that neither the actor nor Cavalli had spotted until that moment. The five-ton leaves began to slide apart above their heads, and a sudden whirling and clanking sounded as the massive brass frame that housed the parchment began its daily journey towards the ceiling. When the frame had reached desk height, Mr Mendelssohn pressed a second button, and the whirling sound instantly ceased. He then raised an open palm in the direction of the casing.

Lloyd Adams took a pace forward and stared across at the nation's most important historic document.

'Now, remembering your personal wish, Mr President, we in turn have a small request of you.'

The actor seemed uncertain what his lines were meant to be, and glanced towards Cavalli in the wings.

'And what might that request be?' prompted Cavalli, apprehensive of any change of plan at this late stage.

'Simply,' said Mr Mendelssohn, 'that while the Archivist and I are removing the outer casing of the Declaration, your men will be kind enough to turn and face the wall.'

Cavalli hesitated, aware that the Secret Service would never allow a situation to arise where they could not see the President at all times.

'Let me make it easier for you, Mr Mendelssohn,' said Adams. 'I'll be the first to comply with your request.' The actor turned away from the document, and the rest of the team followed suit.

In the brief space of time that the team were unable to see what was going on behind them, Cavalli heard twelve distinct clicks and the exaggerated sighs of two men not used to moving heavy weights.

'Thank you, Mr President,' said Calder Marshall. 'I hope that didn't put you to too much inconvenience.'

The thirteen intruders turned round to face the massive frame. The bronze casing had been lifted over to leave the impression of an open book.

Lloyd Adams, with Cavalli and Dollar Bill a pace behind, stepped forward to admire the original while Marshall and the Conservator continued to stare at the old parchment. Suddenly, without warning, the actor reeled back, clutching his throat, and collapsed to the ground. Four of the Secret Service agents immediately surrounded Adams while the other four bundled the Archivist and the Conservator out of the vault and into the corridor before they could utter a word. Tony had to admit Johnny was right – it had been a bad case of over-acting.

Once the door was closed, Cavalli turned to see Dollar Bill already staring at the parchment, his eyes alight with excitement, the Lieutenant by his side.

'Time for us to get to work, Angelo,' said the Irishman. He stretched his fingers out straight. The Lieutenant removed a pair of thin rubber gloves from the doctor's bag and pulled them over his hands. Dollar Bill wiggled his fingers like a concert pianist about to begin a recital. Once the gloves were in place, Angelo bent down again and lifted a long, thin knife out of the bag, placing the handle firmly in Dollar Bill's right hand.

While these preparations were being carried out, Dollar Bill's eyes had never once left the document. Those who remained in the room were so silent that it felt like a tomb as the forger leaned over towards the parchment and placed the blade of the knife gently under the top right-hand corner. It peeled slowly back, and he transferred the knife to the left-hand corner, and that too came cleanly away. Dollar Bill passed the knife back to Angelo before he began rolling the parchment up slowly and as tightly as he could without harming it.

At the same time, Angelo flicked back the handle of his dress sword and held the long shaft out in front of him. Cavalli took a pace forward and slowly pulled out Dollar Bill's counterfeit copy from the specially constructed chamber where the sword's blade would normally have lodged.

Cavalli and Dollar Bill exchanged their prizes and reversed the process. While Cavalli slid the original

Declaration inch by inch down the scabbard of the dress sword, Dollar Bill began to unroll his fake carefully onto the backplate of the laminated glass, the moist chemical mixture helping the document to remain in place. The counterfeiter sniffed loudly. The strong smell suggested thymol to his sensitive nose. Dollar Bill gave his copy one more long look, checked the spelling correction and then took a pace backward, reluctantly leaving his masterpiece to the tender care of the National Archives and its concrete prison.

Once he had completed his task Dollar Bill walked quickly over to the side of Lloyd Adams. Debbie had already undone his collar, loosened his tie and applied a little pale foundation to his face. The forger bent down on one knee, took off the rubber gloves and dropped them into a physician's bag full of make-up as Cavalli dialled a number on his cellphone.

It was answered even before he heard a ring, but Cavalli could only just make out a faint voice.

'Take two,' said Cavalli firmly, and rang off before pointing at the door. One of the Secret Service agents swung the steel grid wide open and Cavalli watched carefully as Mr Mendelssohn came charging through the gap and headed straight to the brass encasement, while Marshall, who was pale and quivering, went immediately to the side of the President.

Cavalli was relieved to see a smile come across the lips of the Conservator as he leaned over the fake Declaration. With the help of Angelo, he pulled the brass casing across and gave the manuscript a loving stare before fixing the lid back into place, then quickly tightened the twelve locks around the outside of the casing. He pressed one of the buttons and the whirling and clanking noise began again as the massive brass frame slowly disappeared back into the ground.

Cavalli turned his attention to the actor and watched as two of the Secret Service agents helped him to his feet, while Dollar Bill fastened his physician's bag.

'What chemical is it that protects the parchment?' asked Dollar Bill.

'Thymol,' replied the Archivist.

'Of course, I should have guessed. With the President's allergy problem, I might have expected this reaction. Don't panic. As long as we get him out in the fresh air as quickly as possible, he'll be back to normal in no time.'

'Thank God for that,' said Marshall, who hadn't stopped shaking.

'Amen,' said the little Irishman as the actor was helped towards the door.

Marshall quickly rushed to the front and led them back up the stairs, with the Secret Service agents following as close behind as possible.

Cavalli left Lloyd Adams stumbling behind him while he caught up with the Archivist. 'No one, I repeat, no one, must hear about this incident,' he said, running by Marshall's side. 'Nothing could be more damaging to the President when he has only been in office for such a short time, especially remembering what Mr Bush went through after his trip to Japan.'

'After his trip to Japan. Of course, of course.'

'If any of your staff should ask why the President didn't complete his tour of the building, stick to the line that he was called back to the White House on urgent business.'

'Called back on urgent business. Of course,' said Marshall, who was now whiter than the actor.

Cavalli was relieved to find his earlier orders about no staff being allowed in the lower corridor while the President was in the building still remained in force.

Once they had reached the freight elevator, and all the group were inside, they descended to the level of the loading dock. Cavalli sprinted out ahead of them and up the ramp onto 7th Street.

He was annoyed to find that there was still a small crowd on the far pavement, and no sign of the motorcade. He looked anxiously to his right, where Andy was now standing on the bench, pointing towards Pennsylvania Avenue. Cavalli turned to look in the same direction and saw the first motorcycle escort turning right into 7th Street.

He ran back down the ramp to find Lloyd Adams next to a Federal Express pick-up box, being propped up by two Secret Service agents.

'Let's make it snappy,' said Cavalli. 'There's a small crowd out there and they're beginning to wonder what's going on.' He turned to face the Archivist, who was standing next to the Conservator on the loading dock.

'Please remember, the President was called back to the White House on urgent business.' They both nodded vigorously. Four of the Secret Service agents rushed forward just as the third car, engine running, pulled up to the loading dock at the bottom of the ramp.

Cavalli opened the door of the third limousine and frantically waved the actor in. The lead riders on the motorcycles held up the traffic as the final car came to a halt at the mouth of the delivery entrance. As Lloyd Adams was assisted into the limousine, the small crowd on the other side of the road began pointing and clapping.

One of the Secret Service agents nodded back in the direction of the building. Angelo jumped into the second car, still clinging onto the sword, while Dollar Bill and the secretary piled into the fourth. By the time Cavalli had joined Angelo in the back of the second car and given the signal to move, the motorcycle escort was already in the middle of 7th Street holding up the traffic to allow the motorcade to proceed towards Constitution Avenue.

As the sirens blared and the limousines began their journey down 7th Street, Cavalli looked back and was relieved to see there was no longer any sign of Marshall or Mendelssohn.

He quickly switched his attention to the east side of 7th Street, where Andy was explaining to the crowd that it had not been the President but simply a rehearsal for a movie, nothing more. Most of the onlookers showed their obvious disappointment and quickly began to disperse.

Then he thought he saw him again.

As Cavalli's car sped down Constitution Avenue, the lead police car was already turning right into 14th Street, accompanied by two of the outriders. The sirens had been turned off, and the rest of the motorcade peeled off one by one as they reached their allotted intersections.

The first car swung right on 9th Street and right again back onto Pennsylvania Avenue before heading away in the direction of the Capitol. The third continued on down Constitution Avenue, keeping to the centre lane, while the fourth turned left onto 12th Street and the sixth right at 13th.

The fifth turned left on 23rd Street, crossing Memorial Bridge and following the signs to Old Town, while the second car turned left at 14th Street and headed towards the Jefferson Memorial and onto the George Washington Parkway.

Cavalli, who was seated in the back of the second car, dialled the director. When Johnny answered the phone, the only words he heard were, 'It's a wrap.'

15

SCOTT PRAYED THAT the Ambassador's wife would be unable to get away on Thursday, or might still be in Geneva. He remembered Dexter Hutchins saying, 'Patience is not a virtue when you work for the CIA, it's nine-tenths of the job.'

When he stopped at the end of the pool Hannah told him that the Ambassador's wife hadn't returned from Switzerland. They didn't bother to swim another length, but agreed to meet later at the amusement park in the bois de Vincennes.

The moment he saw her walking across the road he wanted to touch her. There were no instructions in any of the CIA handbooks on how to deal with such a situation, and no agent had ever raised the problem with him during the past nine years.

Hannah briefed him on everything that was happening at the embassy, including 'something big' taking place in Geneva that she didn't yet know the details of. Scott told her in reply to her question that he had reported back to Kratz, and that it wouldn't be long before she was taken out. She seemed pleased.

Once they began to talk of other things, Scott's training warned him that he ought to insist she return to the embassy. But this time he left Hannah to make the decision as to when she should leave. She seemed to relax for the first time, and even laughed at Scott's stories about the macho Parisians he met up with in the gym every evening.

As they strolled around the amusement park, Scott discovered it was Hannah who won the teddy bears at the shooting gallery and didn't feel sick on the big dipper.

'Why are you buying cotton candy?' he asked.

'Because then no one will think we're agents,' she replied. 'They'll assume we're lovers.'

When they parted two hours later he kissed her on the cheek. Two professionals behaving like amateurs. He apologised. She laughed and disappeared.

Shortly after ten o'clock, Hamid Al Obaydi joined a small crowd that had formed on the pavement opposite a side entrance of the National Archives. He had to wait some twenty minutes before the door opened again and Cavalli came running up the ramp just as the motorcade reappeared on the corner of 7th Street. Cavalli gave a signal and they all came rushing out to the waiting cars. Al Obaydi couldn't believe his eyes. The deception completely fooled the small crowd, who began waving and cheering.

As the first car disappeared around the corner, a man who had been there all the time explained that it was not the President but simply the rehearsal for a film.

Al Obaydi smiled at this double deception while the disappointed crowd drifted away. He crossed 7th Street and joined a long line of tourists, schoolchildren and the simply curious who had formed a queue to see the Declaration of Independence.

The thirty-nine steps of the National Archives took as many minutes to ascend, and by the time the Deputy Ambassador entered the rotunda the river of people had thinned to a tributary which flowed on across the marble hall to a single line up a further nine steps, ending in a trickle under the gaze of Thomas Jefferson and John Hancock. Before him stood the massive brass frame that housed the Declaration of Independence.

Al Obaydi noted that when a person reached the parchment, they were only able to spend a few moments gazing at the historic document. As his foot touched the first of the steps his heart started beating faster, but for a different reason from everyone else waiting in the queue. He removed from his inside pocket a pair of spectacles whose glass could magnify the smallest writing by a degree of four.

The Deputy Ambassador walked across to the centre of the top step and stared at the Declaration of Independence. His immediate reaction was one of horror. The document was so perfect it must surely be the original. Cavalli had fooled him. Worse, he had succeeded in stealing ten million dollars by a clever deception. Al Obaydi checked that the guards on each side of the encasement were showing no particular interest in him before putting on the spectacles.

He leaned over so that his nose was only an inch from the glass as he searched for the one word that had to be spelt correctly if they expected to be paid another cent.

His eyes widened in disbelief when he came to the sentence: 'Nor have We been wanting in attentions to our British brethren.'

The Ambassador's wife returned from Geneva with her husband the following Friday. Hannah and Scott had managed to steal a few hours together that morning.

It had been less than three weeks since he had first seen her in the public baths in the boulevard Lannes.

Little more than a fortnight since that first hastily arranged meeting at the café on the avenue Bugeaud. That was when the lies had begun; small ones to start with, that grew larger until they had spun themselves into an intricate web of deceit. Now Scott longed to tell her the truth, but as each day passed it became more and more impossible.

Langley had been delighted with the coded messages, and Dexter had congratulated him on doing such a first-class job. 'As good a junior field officer as I can remember,' Dexter admitted. But Scott had discovered no code to let the Deputy Director know he was falling in love.

He had read Hannah's file from cover to cover, but it gave no clue as to her real character. The way she laughed – a smile that could make you smile however sad or angry you were. A mind that was always fascinating and fascinated by what was happening around her. But most of all a warmth and gentleness that made their time apart seem like an eternity.

And whenever he was with her, he was suddenly no more mature than his students. Their clandestine meetings had rarely been for more than an hour, perhaps two, but it made each occasion all the more intense.

She continued to tell him everything about herself with a frankness and honesty that belied his deceit, while he told her nothing but a string of lies about being a Mossad agent whose front, while he was stationed in Paris, was writing a book, a travel book, which would never be published. That was the trouble with lies – each one created the next in a never-ending spiral. And that was the trouble with trust; she believed his every word.

When he returned home that evening, he made a decision he knew Langley would not approve of.

* * *

As the car edged its way into the outside lane of the George Washington Memorial Parkway bound for the airport the driver checked the rear-view mirror and confirmed no one was following them. Cavalli breathed a deep sigh of relief, though he had two alternative plans worked out if they were caught with the Declaration. He'd realised early on that it would be necessary to get as far away from the scene of the crime as quickly as possible. It had always been a crucial part of the plan that he would hand over the document to Nick Vicente within two hours of its leaving the National Archives.

'So let's get on with it,' said Cavalli, turning his attention to Angelo, who was seated opposite him. Angelo unbuckled the sword that hung from the belt around his waist. The two men then faced each other like Japanese sumo wrestlers, each waiting for the other to make the first move. Angelo placed the sword firmly between his legs, the handle pointing towards his boss. Cavalli leaned over and snapped the top back. Then, with the nail of his right thumb and forefinger, he extracted the thin black plastic cylinder from its casing. Angelo pressed the handle back in place and hitched the sword onto his belt.

Cavalli held the twenty-six-inch-long slim plastic cylinder in his hands.

'It must be tempting to have a look,' said Angelo.

'There are more important things to do at the moment,' said Cavalli, placing the cylinder on the seat next to him. He picked up the carphone, pressed a single digit followed by 'Send', and waited for a response.

'Yes?' said a recognisable voice.

'I'm on my way, and I'll have something to export when I arrive.' There was a long silence, and Cavalli wondered if he had lost the connection.

'You've done well,' came back the eventual reply. 'But are you running to schedule?'

Cavalli looked out of the window. The exit sign for Route 395 South flashed past. 'I'd say we're about a couple of minutes from the airport. As long as we make our allocated time slot, I still hope to be with you around one o'clock.'

'Good, then I'll have Nick join us so that the contract can be picked up and sent on to our client. We'll expect you around one.'

Cavalli replaced the phone and was amused to find Angelo was dressed only in a vest and underpants. He smiled and was about to comment when the phone rang. Cavalli picked it up.

'Yes,' he said.

'It's Andy. I thought you'd like to know it's back on display to the general public and the queues are as long as ever. By the way, an Arab stood around in the crowd the whole time you were in the building, and then joined the line to see the Declaration.'

'Well done, Andy. Get yourself back to New York. You can fill me in on the details tomorrow.'

Cavalli put the phone down and considered Andy's new piece of information as Angelo was completing a Windsor knot on a tie no lieutenant would have been seen dead in. He still didn't have his trousers on.

The smoked glass between the driver and the passengers slid down.

'We're just coming up to the terminal, sir. No one has followed us at any point.'

'Good,' said Cavalli as Angelo hurriedly pulled on his trousers. 'Once you've changed your licence plates, drive back to New York.'

The driver nodded as the limousine came to a halt outside Signature Flight Support.

Cavalli grabbed the plastic tube, jumped out of the car, ran through the terminal and out onto the tarmac. His eyes searched for the white Learjet. When he spotted it, a door opened and the steps were lowered to the ground. Cavalli ran towards them as Angelo followed, trying to pull on his jacket in the high wind.

The Captain was waiting for them on the top step. 'You've just made it in time for us to keep our slot,' he told them. Cavalli smiled, and once they had both clicked on their seatbelts, the Captain pressed a button to allow the steps to swing back into place.

The plane lifted off seventeen minutes later, banking over the Kennedy Center, but not before the steward had served them each a glass of champagne. Cavalli rejected the offer of a second glass as he concentrated on what still needed to be done before he could consider his role in the operation was finished. His thoughts turned once again to Al Obaydi, and he began to wonder if he'd underestimated him.

When the Learjet landed at La Guardia fifty-seven minutes later, Cavalli's driver was waiting by his car, ready to whisk them into the city.

As the driver continually switched lanes and changed direction on the highway that would eventually take them west over the Triborough Bridge, Cavalli checked his watch. They were now lost in a sea of traffic heading into Manhattan, only eighty-seven minutes after leaving Calder Marshall outside the delivery entrance of the National Archives. Roughly the time it would take a Wall Street banker to have lunch, Cavalli thought.

Cavalli was dropped outside his father's 75th Street brownstone just before one, leaving Angelo to go on to the Wall Street office and monitor the checking-in calls as each member of the team filed his report.

The butler held open the front door of No. 23 as Tony stepped out of the car.

'Can I take that for you, sir?' he asked, eyeing the plastic tube.

'No, thank you, Martin,' said Tony. 'I'll hold onto it for the moment. Where's my father?'

'He's in the boardroom with Mr Vicente, who arrived a few minutes ago.'

Tony jogged down the staircase that led to the basement and continued across the corridor. He strode into the boardroom to find his father sitting at the head of the table, deep in conversation with Nick Vicente. The chairman stood up to greet his son, and Tony passed him the plastic tube.

'Hail, conquering hero,' were his father's first words. 'If you'd pulled off the same trick for George III, he would have made you a knight. "Arise, Sir Antonio." But as it is, you'll have to be satisfied with a hundred million dollars' compensation. Is it permissible for an old man to see the original before Nick whisks it away?'

Cavalli laughed and removed the cap from the top of the cylinder before slowly extracting the parchment and placing it gently on the boardroom table. He then unrolled two hundred years of history. The three men stared down at the Declaration of Independence and quickly checked the spelling of 'Brittish'.

'Magnificent,' was all Tony's father said as he began licking his lips.

'Interesting how the names on the bottom were left with so little space for their signatures,' observed Nick Vicente after he had studied the document for several minutes.

'If they'd all signed their names the same size as John Hancock, we would have needed a Declaration of twice the length,' added the chairman as the phone on the boardroom table started to ring.

The chairman flicked a button on his intercom. 'Yes, Martin?'

'There's a Mr Al Obaydi on the private line, says he would like to have a word with Mr Tony.'

'Thank you, Martin,' said the chairman, as Tony leaned over to pick up the call. 'Why don't you take it in my office, then I can listen in on the extension.'

Tony nodded and left the room to go next door, where he picked up the receiver on his father's desk. 'Antonio Cavalli,' he said.

'Hamid Al Obaydi here. Your father suggested I call back around this time.'

'We are in possession of the document you require,' was all Cavalli said.

'I congratulate you, Mr Cavalli.'

'Are you ready to complete the payment as agreed?'

'All in good time, but not until you have delivered the document to the place of our choosing, Mr Cavalli, as I'm sure you will recall was also part of the bargain.'

'And where might that be?' asked Cavalli.

'I shall come to your office at twelve o'clock tomorrow, when you will receive your instructions.' He paused. 'Among other things.' The line went dead.

Cavalli put the phone down and tried to think what Al Obaydi could possibly mean by 'Among other things.' He walked slowly back to the boardroom to find his father and Nick poring over the Declaration. Tony noticed that the parchment had been turned round.

'What do you think he meant by "Among other things"?' Tony asked.

'I've no idea,' replied his father as he gave the parchment one last look and then began slowly to roll it up.

'No doubt I'll find out tomorrow,' said Tony as the

chairman handed the document to his son, who carefully slipped it back into its plastic container.

'So where's its final destination to be?' asked Nick.

'I'll be given the details at twelve o'clock tomorrow,' said Tony, a little surprised that his father hadn't reported his phone conversation with Al Obaydi to his oldest friend.

16

HE LAY WATCHING HER, his head propped up in the palm of his hand, as the first sunlight of the morning crept into the room. She stirred but didn't wake as Scott began to run a solitary finger down her spine. He couldn't wait for her to open her eyes and revive his memories of the previous night.

When Scott had, in those early days, watched Hannah walking from the Jordanian Embassy, dressed in those drab clothes so obviously selected with Karima Saib's tastes in mind, he thought she still looked stunning. Some packages, when you remove the brightly-coloured wrapping, fail to live up to expectation. When Hannah had first taken off the dowdy little two-piece suit she had been wearing that day, he had stood there in disbelief that anyone could be so beautiful.

He pulled back the single sheet that covered her and admired the sight that had taken his breath away the night before. Her short-cropped hair; he wondered how the long flowing strands would look when they fell on her shoulders as she wanted them to. The nape of her neck, the smooth olive skin of her back, and the long, shapely legs.

His hands were like a child's that had opened a stocking full of presents and wanted to touch everything at once. He ran his fingers down her shoulders to the arch of her back, hoping she would turn over. He moved a little closer, leaned across and began to circle her firm breasts with a single finger. The circles became smaller and smaller until he reached her soft nipple. He heard her sigh, and this time she did turn and fall into his arms, her fingers clinging to his shoulders as he pulled her closer.

'It's not fair, you're taking advantage of me,' she said drowsily as his hand moved up the inside of her thigh.

'I'm sorry,' he said, removing his hand and kissing her cheek.

'Don't be sorry. For heaven's sake, Simon, I want you to take advantage of me,' she said, pulling his body closer to her. He continued to stroke her skin, all the time discovering new treasures.

When he entered her, she sighed a different sigh, the sigh of morning love, calmer and more gentle than the demands of the night, but every bit as enjoyable.

For Scott it had been a new experience. Although he had made love many more times than he cared to remember, it had never been with the same excitement.

When they finished making love, she rested her head on his shoulder and he brushed a hair from her cheek, praying the next hour would go slowly. He hated the thought of her returning to the embassy that morning as he knew she eventually must. He didn't want to share her with anybody.

The room was now bathed in the morning sun, which only made him wonder when he would next be allowed to spend a whole night with her.

The Head of Interest Section had been called straight back to Geneva on urgent business, and had taken only one secretary with him, leaving Hannah in Paris on her own for the weekend. She only wished she could tell

Simon what it was all about, so he could pass the information on to Kratz.

She had double-locked her room and left the embassy compound by the fire escape. Hannah told him that she had felt like a schoolgirl creeping out of her dormitory to join a midnight feast.

'Better than any feast I can remember,' were his last words before they fell asleep in each other's arms.

The day had begun when they had gone shopping together in the boulevard Saint-Michel and bought clothes she couldn't wear and a tie he would never have considered before he met her. They'd had lunch at a corner café and taken two hours to eat a salad and drink a bottle of wine. They had strolled down the Champs-Élysées, hand in hand as lovers should, before joining the queue to see the Clodion exhibition at the Louvre. A chance to teach her something he thought he knew about, only to find it was he who did the learning. He bought her a floppy tourist hat in the little shop at the base of the Eiffel Tower and was reminded that she always looked stunning whatever she wore.

They had dinner at Maxim's but only ate one course, as they both knew by then that all they really wanted to do was return to his little flat on the Left Bank.

He remembered how he had stood there mesmerised as Hannah removed each garment until she became so embarrassed that she began to take off his clothes. It was almost as if he didn't want to make love to her, because he hoped the anticipation might go on forever.

Of all the women, including the occasional promiscuous student, with whom he had had one-night stands, casual affairs, even sometimes what he had imagined was love, he had never known anything like this. And afterwards, he discovered something else he had never experienced before: the sheer joy of just lying in her arms was every bit as exhilarating as making love.

His finger ran down the nape of her neck. 'What time do you have to be back?' he asked, almost in a whisper.

'One minute before the Ambassador.'

'And when's he expected?'

'His flight's due in from Geneva at 11.20. So I'd better be at my desk before twelve.'

'Then we still have time to make love once more,' he said as he placed a finger on her lips.

She bit the finger gently.

'Ow,' he said mockingly.

'Only once?' she replied.

Debbie brought the Deputy Ambassador through to Cavalli's office at twenty past twelve. Neither man commented on the fact that Al Obaydi was late. Tony indicated the chair on the other side of his desk, and waited for his visitor to be seated. For the first time, he felt strangely uneasy about the Arab.

'As I mentioned yesterday,' Cavalli began, 'we are now in possession of the document you require. We are therefore ready to exchange it for the sum agreed.'

'Ah, yes, ninety million dollars,' said the Iraqi, placing the tips of his fingers together just below his chin while he considered his next statement. 'Cash on delivery, if I remember correctly.'

'You do,' said Cavalli. 'So now all we need to know is where and when.'

'We require the document to be delivered to Geneva by twelve o'clock next Tuesday. The recipient will be a Monsieur Pierre Dummond of the bankers Dummond et cie.'

'But that only gives me six days to find a safe route out of the country and . . .'

'Your God created the world in that time, if I remember correctly,' said Al Obaydi.

'The Declaration will be in Geneva by Tuesday midday,' said Cavalli.

'Good,' said Al Obaydi. 'And if Monsieur Dummond is satisfied that the document is authentic, he has been given instructions to release the sum of ninety million dollars by wire transfer to any bank of your choice in the world. If, on the other hand, you fail to deliver, or the document proves to be a fake, we will have lost ten million dollars, with nothing to show for it but a three-minute film made by a world-famous director. In that eventuality, a package similar to this one will be posted to the Director of the FBI and the Commissioner of the IRS.'

Al Obaydi removed a thick envelope from his inside pocket and tossed it across the table. Cavalli's expression did not change as the Deputy Ambassador rose, bowed and walked out of the room without another word.

Cavalli felt sure he was about to discover what 'Among other things' meant.

He ripped open the bulky yellow envelope and allowed the contents to spill out onto his desk. Photographs, dozens of them, and documents with banknote serial numbers attached to them. He glanced at the photographs of himself in deep conversation with Al Calabrese on the pavement in front of the National Café, another of himself with Gino Sartori in the centre of Freedom Plaza, and yet another with the director sitting on the dolly as they talked to the former Chief of the DC Police Department. Al Obaydi had even taken a photograph of Rex Butterworth entering the Willard Hotel and of the actor, bald-headed, sitting in the third car, and later getting into the limo outside the Archives' loading dock.

Cavalli began drumming his fingers on the table. It was then that he remembered the nagging doubt at the back of his mind. It was Al Obaydi he had seen in the crowd the previous day. He had underestimated the Iraqi. Perhaps the time had come to call their man in the Lebanon and inform him of the Swiss bank account he had opened in the Deputy Ambassador's name.

No. That would have to wait until the ninety million had been paid in full.

'What do I do, Simon, if he offers me the job?'

Scott hesitated. He had no idea what Mossad would expect her to do. He knew exactly what *he* wanted her to do. It was no use putting the question to Dexter Hutchins in Virginia, because they wouldn't have hesitated to tell him to continue using Hannah for their own purposes.

Hannah turned towards what Scott laughingly described as the kitchen. 'Perhaps you could ask Colonel Kratz what I should do,' she suggested when he didn't reply. 'Explain to him that the Ambassador wants me to take Muna's place, but that another problem has arisen.'

'What's that?' asked Scott anxiously.

'The Ambassador's term of office comes to an end early next month. He may well be asked to stay in Paris, but the Chief Administrator is telling everyone that he's going to be called back to Baghdad and promoted to Deputy Foreign Minister.'

Scott still didn't offer an opinion.

'What's the matter, Simon? Are you incapable of making a decision at this time in the morning?' Scott still said nothing. 'You're just as pathetic on your feet as you are in bed,' she teased.

Scott decided the time had come to tell her everything. He wasn't going to wait another minute. He walked out of the kitchen, took her in his arms and stroked her hair. 'Hannah, I need to –' he had begun, when the phone rang. He broke away to answer it.

He listened for a few moments before saying to Dexter Hutchins, 'Yes, sure. I'll call you back as soon as I've had time to think about it.' What was the man doing up in the middle of the night, wondered Scott as he replaced the receiver.

'Another lover, lover?' Hannah asked with a smile.

'My publishers wanting to know when my manuscript will be finished. It's already overdue.'

'And what will your answer be?'

'I'm currently distracted.'

'Only currently?' she said, pressing her finger on his nose.

'Well, perhaps permanently,' he admitted.

She kissed him gently on the cheek and whispered, 'I must get back to the embassy, Simon. Don't come down with me, it's too risky.'

He held her in his arms and wanted to protest but settled for 'When will I see you again?'

'Whenever the Ambassador's wife feels in need of a swim,' Hannah said. She broke away. 'But I'll keep on reminding her how good it is for her figure, and that perhaps she ought to be taking even more exercise.' She laughed and left without another word.

Scott stood by the window, waiting for her to re-appear. He hated the fact that he couldn't just phone, write or make contact with her whenever he felt like it. He longed to send her flowers, letters, cards and notes to let her know how much he loved her.

Hannah ran out onto the pavement, a smile on her face. She looked up and blew Scott a kiss before she vanished around the corner.

Another man, who was cold and tired from hours of waiting, also watched her, not from a window in a warm room but from a doorway on the opposite side of the road.

The moment Scott disappeared from sight, the man stepped out of the shadows and followed the Ambassador's second secretary back to the embassy compound.

17

'I DON'T BELIEVE YOU,' she said.

'I fear that the truth of the matter is you don't want to believe me,' said Kratz, who had flown in from London that morning.

'But he can't be working for any enemy of Israel.'

'If that's the case, perhaps you can explain why he passed himself off as a Mossad agent?'

For the last two hours Hannah had tried to think of a logical reason why Simon would have deceived her, but had to admit that she had been unable to come up with a convincing answer.

'Have you told us everything you passed on to him?' Kratz demanded.

'Yes,' she said, suddenly feeling ashamed. 'But have you checked with all the friendly agencies?'

'Of course we have,' said Kratz. 'No one in Paris has ever heard of the man. Not the French, not the British, and certainly not the CIA. Their Head of Station told me personally that they have never had anyone on their books called Simon Rosenthal.'

'So what will happen to me now?' asked Hannah.

'Do you wish to continue working for your country?'

'You know I do,' she said, glaring back at him.

'And are you still hoping to be included in the team for Baghdad?'

'Yes, of course I am. Why would I have put myself through all this in the first place if I didn't want to be part of the final operation?'

'Then you will also want to abide by the oath you swore in the presence of your colleagues in Herzliyah.'

'Nothing would make me break that oath. You know that. Just tell me what you expect me to do.'

'I expect you to kill Rosenthal.'

Scott was delighted when Hannah confirmed on Thursday afternoon that she would be able to slip away for dinner on Friday evening, and might even find it possible to stay overnight. It seemed that the Ambassador had been called away to Geneva again. Something big was happening, but she still didn't know exactly what.

Scott had already decided that three things were going to take place when they next met. First, he would cook the meal himself, despite Hannah's comments about his inadequate kitchen. Second, he was going to tell her the truth about himself, whatever interruptions occurred. And third . . .

Scott felt more relaxed than he had in weeks once he had decided to 'come clean', as his mother had described it whenever he'd tried to get away with something. He knew that he would be recalled to the States once he had informed Dexter of what had happened, and that a few weeks later he would be quietly discharged. But that was no longer of any significance, because third, and most important of all, he was going to ask Hannah to come back to America with him, as his wife.

Scott spent the afternoon shopping in the market for freshly baked bread, the finest wild mushrooms, succulent lamb chops and tiny ripe oranges. He returned home to prepare a feast he hoped she would never forget. He had also prepared a speech he believed she would, in time, find it possible to forgive.

During the evening, Scott found himself looking up at the kitchen clock every few moments. He felt robbed if she was ever more than a few minutes late. She had failed to turn up for their previous meeting, though he accepted that she had no way of letting him know when something unexpected came up. He was relieved to see her walk through the door soon after the clock had struck eight.

Scott smiled when Hannah removed her coat, and he saw she was wearing the dress he had chosen for her when they'd gone shopping together for the first time. A long blue dress that hung loosely off the shoulders, and made her appear both elegant and sexy.

He immediately took her in his arms, and was surprised by her response. She seemed distant, almost cold. Or was he being over-sensitive? Hannah broke away and stared at the table laid for two with its red-and-white check tablecloth and two sets of unmatching cutlery.

Scott poured her a glass of the white wine he had selected to go with the first course before he disappeared into the kitchen to put the final touches to his culinary efforts, aware that he and Hannah always had so little time together.

'What are you cooking?' she asked, in a dull, flat voice.

'Wait and see,' he replied. 'But I can tell you the starter is something I learned when –' He stopped himself. 'Many years ago,' he added rather lamely.

He didn't see her grimace at his failure to finish the original sentence.

Scott returned to join her a few moments later, carrying two plates of piping-hot wild mushrooms, with a small slice of garlic bread. 'But not too much garlic,' he promised her, 'for obvious reasons.' No witty or sharp response came flying back, and he wondered if she was unable to stay overnight. He might have questioned her more closely had he not been concentrating on the dinner as well as wanting to get his speech over with.

'I wish we could get out of Paris and see Versailles, like normal people,' said Scott as he dug his fork into a mushroom.

'That would be nice,' she said.

'And even better . . .' She looked up and stared at him.

'A weekend at the Colmendor. I promised myself long ago when I first read the life of Matisse at . . .' He hesitated once again, and she lowered her head. 'And that's only France,' he said, trying to recover. 'We could take a lifetime over Italy. They have a hundred Colmendors.'

He looked hopefully towards her but her eyes remained staring at the half-empty plate.

What had he done? Or was *she* fearful of telling *him* something? He dreaded the thought of learning that she was going to Baghdad when all he wanted to do was take her to Venice, Florence and Rome. If it was Baghdad that was making her anxious, he would do everything in his power to change her mind.

Scott cleared away the plates to return a few moments later with the succulent lamb Provençal. 'Madam's favourite, if I remember correctly.' But he was rewarded only with a weak smile.

'What is it, Hannah?' he asked as he took the seat opposite her. He leaned across to touch her hand, but she removed it quickly from the table.

'I'm just a little tired,' she replied unconvincingly. 'It's been a long week.'

Scott tried to discuss her work, the theatre, the Clodion exhibition at the Louvre and even Clinton's attempts to bring the three living Beatles together, but with each new effort he received the same bland response. They continued to eat in silence until his plate was empty.

'And now, we shall end on my *pièce de résistance*.' He expected to be playfully chastised about his efforts as a chef; instead he received only the flicker of a smile and a distant, sad look from those dark, beautiful eyes. He disappeared into the kitchen and returned immediately, carrying a bowl of freshly sliced oranges with a touch of Cointreau. He placed the delicate morsels in front of her, hoping they would change her mood. But while Scott continued with his monologue Hannah remained an unreceptive audience.

He removed the bowls, his empty, hers hardly touched, and returned moments later with coffee, hers made exactly as she liked it: black, with a touch of cream floating across the top, and no sugar. His black, steaming, with too much sugar.

Just as he sat down opposite her, determined this was the moment to tell her the truth, she asked for some sugar. Scott jumped up, somewhat surprised, returned to the kitchen, tipped some sugar into a bowl, grabbed a teaspoon and came back to see her snapping closed her tiny evening bag.

After he had sat down and placed the sugar on the table he smiled at her. He had never seen such sadness in those eyes before. He poured them both a brandy, whirled his round the balloon, took a sip of his coffee and then faced her. She had not touched her coffee or brandy, and the sugar she had asked for remained in the centre of the table, its little mound undented.

'Hannah,' Scott began softly, 'I have something important to tell you, and I wish I had told you a long time ago.' He looked up, to find her on the verge of tears.

He would have asked her why, but feared that if he allowed her to change the subject he might never tell her the truth.

'My name is not Simon Rosenthal,' he said quietly. Hannah looked surprised, but not in the way he had expected – more anxious than curious. He took another sip of coffee and then continued. 'I have lied to you from the day we met, and the more deeply I fell in love with you, the more I lied.'

She didn't speak, for which he was grateful, because on this occasion, like his lectures, he needed to proceed without interruption. His throat began to feel a little dry, so he sipped his coffee again.

'My name is Scott Bradley. I am an American, but not from Chicago as I told you when we first met. I'm from Denver.' A puzzled look came into Hannah's eyes, but she still didn't interrupt him. Scott ploughed on.

'I am not Mossad's agent in Paris writing a travel book. Far from it, though I confess the truth is much stranger than the fiction.' He held her hand and this time she didn't try to remove it. 'Please, let me explain, and then perhaps you'll find it in your heart to forgive me.' His throat suddenly felt drier. He finished his coffee and quickly poured himself another cup, taking an extra teaspoonful of sugar. She still hadn't touched hers. 'I was born in Denver, where I went to school. My father was a local lawyer who ended up in jail for fraud. I was so ashamed that when my mother died, I took a post at Beirut University because I could no longer face anyone I knew.' Hannah looked up and her eyes began to show sympathy. It gave Scott the confidence to go on.

'I do not work for Mossad in any capacity, nor have I ever done so.' Her lips formed a straight line. 'My real job is nowhere near as romantic as that. After Beirut I returned to America to become a university professor.'

She looked mystified, and then her expression suddenly changed to one of anxiety.

'Oh, yes,' he said, his words beginning to sound slightly slurred, 'this time I'm telling the truth. I teach Constitutional Law at Yale. Let's face it, no one would make up a story like that,' he added, trying to laugh.

He drank more coffee. It tasted less bitter than the first cup.

'But I am also what they call in the trade a part-time spy, and as it's turned out, not a very good one. Despite many years of training and lecturing other people on how it should be done.' He paused. 'But that was only in the classroom.'

She looked more anxious.

'You need have no fears,' he said, trying to reassure her. 'I work for the good side, though I suppose even that depends on where you're looking from. I'm currently a temporary Field Officer with the CIA.'

'The CIA?' she stammered in disbelief. 'But they told me . . .'

'What did they tell you?' he asked quickly.

'Nothing,' she said, and lowered her head again.

Had she already known about his background, or perhaps guessed his original story didn't add up? He didn't care. All he wanted to do was tell the woman he loved everything about himself. No more lies. No more deceit. No more secrets. 'Well, as I'm confessing, I mustn't exaggerate,' he continued. 'I go to Virginia twelve times a year to discuss with agents the problems they've faced while working in the field. I was full of bright ideas to assist them in the peace and comfort of Langley, but I'll treat them with more respect now I've experienced some of the problems they come up against, especially having made such a mess of things myself.'

'It can't be true,' she said suddenly. 'Tell me you're making it up, Simon.'

'I'm afraid not, Hannah. This time it's all true,' he said. 'You must believe me. I only ended up in Paris after years of demanding to be tested in the field, because, with all my theoretical knowledge, I assumed I'd be a whizz if they just gave me the chance to prove myself. Scott Bradley, Professor of Constitutional Law. Infallible in the eyes of his adoring students at Yale and the senior CIA operatives at Langley. There'll be no standing ovation after this performance, of that we can both be sure.'

Hannah stood and stared down at him. 'Tell me it's not true, Simon,' she said. 'It mustn't be true. Why did you choose me? Why me?'

He stood and took her in his arms. 'I didn't choose you, I fell in love with you. They chose me. My people . . . my people needed to find out why Mossad had put you . . . put you in the Jordanian Embassy attached to the Iraqi Interest Section.' He was finding it difficult to remain coherent, and couldn't understand why he felt so sleepy.

'But why you?' she asked, clinging on to him for the first time that evening. 'Why not a regular CIA agent?'

'Because . . . because they wanted to put someone in . . . someone who wouldn't be recognised by any of the professionals.'

'Oh, my God, who am I meant to believe?' she said, breaking away. She stared helplessly at him.

'You can believe me, because I'll prove . . . prove all I've said is true.' Scott began to move away from the table. He felt unsteady as he walked slowly over to the sideboard, bent down to pull open the bottom drawer, and after some rummaging around removed a small leather case with the initials S.B. printed in gold on the top right-hand corner. He smiled a triumphant smile and turned back. He attempted to steady himself by resting one hand on the sideboard. He looked towards the blurred figure of the woman he loved, but could no longer see the desperate look on her face. He tried to remember how much he had already told her and how much she still needed to know.

'Oh, my darling, what have I done?' she said, her eyes now pleading.

'Nothing, it's all been my fault,' said Scott. 'But we'll have the rest of our lives to laugh about it. That, by the way, was a proposal. Feeble, I agree, but I couldn't love you any more than I do. You must surely realise that,' he added as he tried to take a pace towards her. She stood staring at him helplessly as he lurched forward before attempting to take a second step. Then he tried again, but this time he stumbled and collapsed across the table, finally landing with a thud on the floor at her feet.

'I can't blame you if you don't feel the same way as . . .' were his final words, as the leather case burst open, disgorging its contents all around a body that was suddenly still.

Hannah fell on her knees and took his head in her hands. She began to sob uncontrollably. 'I love you, of course I love you, Simon. But why didn't you trust me enough to tell me the truth?'

Her eyes rested on a small photo lodged between his fingers. She snatched it from his grasp. Written on the back were the words 'Katherine Bradley – Summer '66'. It must have been his mother. She grabbed the passport that lay by the side of his head and quickly turned the pages, trying to read through her tears. Male. Date of birth: 11.7.56. Profession: University Professor. She turned another page and a photo from *Paris Match* fell out. She stared at herself modelling an Ungaro suit from the spring collection of 1990.

'No, no. Don't let it be true,' Hannah said as she lifted him back into her arms. 'Let it be just more lies.'

And then her eyes settled on the envelope simply addressed 'Hannah'. She lowered his body gently to the ground, picked up the envelope and ripped it open.

My dearest Hannah,

I have tried to think of a hundred ways to begin this letter. There's one simple way. I love you. And, as important, I have never loved before, and now I know I can never love anyone like this again.

'No!' she screamed, 'No!' almost unable to read his words through her tears.

You are not only my lover but my closest friend. I'll never want or need anyone else ever again. I rejoice at the thought of spending the rest of my life with you, and wonder how I deserve to be so lucky.

'Please, God, no,' she wept as her head fell on his chest. 'I love you, too, Simon. I love you so much.'

I want three daughters and two sons and I must warn you that I won't settle for less. We'll discuss grandchildren later. I fear I'll be irascible and tiresome in old age, but I'll never stop loving you. Don't let's wait

'No, no, no . . .' Hannah cried as she bent down to kiss him. She suddenly leaped up and rushed over to the phone. She dialled 17 and screamed, 'Please God, let one pill not be enough. Answer, answer, answer!' she shrieked at the phone as the door of Scott's apartment flew open. Hannah turned to see Kratz and another man whom she didn't recognise come bursting in.

She dropped the phone on the floor and ran towards them, throwing herself at Kratz and knocking him to the ground.

'You bastard, you bastard!' she screamed. 'You made me kill the only person I ever really loved! I hope you rot in hell!' she said as her fists pumped down into his face.

The unknown man moved quickly across and threw Hannah to one side, before the two of them picked up Scott's limp body and carried him out of the room.

Hannah lay in the corner, weeping.

An hour passed, maybe two, before she crawled slowly back to the table, opened her bag and removed the second pill.

18

'WHITE HOUSE.'

'Mr Butterworth, please.'

There was a long silence. 'I don't show anyone by that name, sir. Just a moment and I'll put you through to Personnel.'

The Archivist waited patiently, made aware as each second passed that the new telephone system ordered by the Clinton administration was clearly overdue.

'Personnel office,' said a female voice. 'How can I help you?'

'I'm trying to locate Mr Rex Butterworth, Special Assistant to the President.'

'Who's calling?'

'Marshall, Calder Marshall, Archivist.'

'Of – ?'

'Of the United States of America.'

There was another long silence.

'The name Butterworth rings no bells with me, sir, but I'm sure you realise there are more than forty Special and Deputy Assistants to the President.'

'No, I didn't realise,' admitted Marshall. There followed another long silence.

'According to our records,' said the female voice, 'he seems to have returned to the Department of Commerce. He was a Schedule A – just here on temporary assignment.'

'Would you have a number where I might reach him?'

'No, I don't. But if you call the department locator at the Commerce Department, I'm sure they will find him for you.'

'Thank you for your help.'

'Glad to have been of assistance, sir.'

Hannah could never recall how long she had lain huddled up in the corner of Simon's room. She couldn't think of him as Scott, she would always think of him as Simon. An hour, possibly two. Time no longer had any relevance for her. She could remember crawling back to the centre of the room, avoiding overturned chairs and tables that would have looked more appropriate in a nightclub that had just experienced a drunken brawl.

She removed the pill from her bag and flushed it down the lavatory, the automatic action of any well-drilled agent. She then began to search among the debris for any photographs she could find and, of course, the letter addressed simply to 'Hannah'. She stuffed these few mementoes into her bag and tried, with the help of a fallen chair, to get back on her feet.

Later that night she lay in her bed at the embassy, staring up at the blank white ceiling, unable to recall her journey back, the route she had taken or even if she had climbed the fire escape or entered by the front door. She wondered how many nights it would be before she managed to sleep for more than a few minutes at a time. How much time would have to pass before he wasn't her every other thought?

She knew Mossad would want to take her out, hide her, protect her – as they saw it – until the French police had completed their investigation. Governments would have their diplomatic arms twisted up their diplomatic backs. The Americans would expect a lot in return for killing one of their agents, but eventually a bargain would be struck. Hannah Kopec, Simon Rosenthal and Professor Scott Bradley would become closed files. For all three of them were numbers: interchangeable, dispensable and, of course, replaceable.

She wondered what they would do with his body, the body of the man she loved. An honourable but anonymous grave, she suspected. They would argue that it must be in the interest of the greater good. Wherever they buried him, she knew they would never allow her to find his grave.

She wouldn't have dropped the pill in the coffee in the first place if Kratz hadn't talked again and again of the thirty-nine Scuds that had landed on the people of Israel, and in particular of the one which had killed her mother, her brother and her sister.

She might even have drawn back at the last moment if they hadn't threatened to carry out the job themselves, should she refuse. They promised her that if that was the case, it would be a far more unpleasant death.

Just as Hannah was about to take the first pill out of her bag, she had asked Simon for some sugar, one last lifeline. Why hadn't he grabbed at it? Why didn't he question her, tease her about her weight, do anything that would have made her have second thoughts? But then why, why had he waited so long to tell her the truth?

If he had only realised that she had things to tell him, too. The Ambassador had been called back to Iraq – a promotion, he explained. He was, as Kanuk had been telling everyone, to become Deputy Foreign Minister, which meant that in the absence of Muhammad Saeed Al-Zahiaf, he would be working directly with Saddam Hussein.

His place at the embassy was to be taken by a Hamid

Al Obaydi, the number two at the United Nations, who had recently rendered some great service for Iraq, of which she would eventually learn. The Ambassador had offered her the choice of remaining in Paris to serve under Al Obaydi, or returning to Iraq and continuing to work with him. Only days before, Mossad would have considered such an offer an irresistible opportunity.

Hannah so wanted to tell Simon that she no longer cared about Saddam, that he had made it possible for her to overcome her hatred of the Scuds, even made the death of her family a wound that might in time be healed. She knew that she was no longer capable of killing anyone, as long as she had someone to live for.

But now that Simon was dead, her desire for revenge was even stronger than before.

'Department of Commerce.'

'Rex Butterworth, please.'

'What agency?'

'I'm not sure I understand,' said the Archivist.

'What agency is Mr Butterworth with?' asked the operator, pronouncing each word slowly, as if she were addressing a four-year-old.

'I have no idea,' admitted the Archivist.

'We don't show anyone by that name.'

'But the White House told me –'

'I don't care what the White House told you. If you don't know which agency –'

'May I have the Personnel Office?'

'Just a minute.' It turned out to be far longer than a minute.

'Office of Personnel.'

'This is Calder Marshall, Archivist of the United States. May I speak to the director?'

'I'm sorry, but he's not available. Would you like to speak to his executive assistant, Alex Wagner?'

'Yes. That would be just fine,' said Marshall.

'She's not in today. Could you call again tomorrow?'

'Yes,' said Marshall with a sigh.

'Glad to have been of assistance, sir.'

When Kratz's car screeched to a halt outside the Centre Cardio-vasculaire on bois Gilbert there were three doctors, two orderlies and a nurse waiting for them on the hospital steps. The embassy must have pulled out every stop.

The two orderlies ran forward and lifted the body gently but firmly out of the back seat of the car, carrying Scott quickly up the steps before placing him on a waiting trolley.

Even as the trolley was being wheeled down the corridor the three doctors and the nurse surrounded the body and began their examination. The nurse quickly removed Scott's shirt and trousers while the first doctor opened his mouth to check his breathing. The second, a consultant, lowered his ear onto Scott's chest and tried to listen for a heartbeat, while the third checked his blood pressure; none of them looked hopeful.

The consultant turned to the Mossad leader and said firmly, 'Don't waste any time with lies. How did it happen?'

'We poisoned him, but he turned out not to be –'

'I'm not interested,' he said. 'What poison did you administer?'

'Ergot alkaloid,' said Kratz.

The consultant switched his attention to one of his assistants. 'Ring the Hospital Widal and get me details of its action and the correct antidote, fast,' he said as the orderlies crashed through the rubber doors and into a private operating theatre.

The first doctor had managed to keep Scott's mouth open during the short journey and create an airway. He had already pressed down the tongue to leave a clear passageway to the larynx. Once the trolley had come to a stop in the theatre he inserted a clear angled plastic tube of about five inches in length to ensure the tongue could not be swallowed.

The nurse then placed a mask over Scott's nose and mouth that was connected to an oxygen supply on the wall. Attached to the side of the mask was a rubber bag, which she began pumping regularly every three or four seconds with her left hand as she held his head steady with her right. Scott's lungs were immediately filled with oxygen.

The consultant placed an ear over Scott's heart again. He could still hear nothing. He raised his head and nodded to an orderly who began rubbing paste on different parts of Scott's chest. Another nurse followed him, placing small electronic discs on the paste marks. The wires from the discs were connected to a heart monitor machine that stood on a table by the side of the trolley.

The fine line that ran across the machine and registered the strength of the heartbeat produced a weak signal.

The consultant smiled below his mask, as the nurse continued to pump oxygen into the patient's mouth and nose.

Suddenly, without warning, the heart machine gave out a piercing sound. Everyone in the operating theatre turned to face the monitor, which was now showing a thin, flat line running from one side of the screen to the other.

'Cardiac arrest!' shouted the consultant. He jumped

forward and placed the heel of his hand over Scott's sternum, and with both arms firmly locked he began to rock backwards and forwards as he tried to push a volume of blood from the heart to resuscitate his patient. Like a proficient weightlifter, he was able to pump away with his arms at a rate of forty to fifty times a minute.

A houseman wheeled forward the defibrillator. The consultant placed two large electric clamps onto the front and side of Scott's chest.

'Two hundred joules,' said the consultant. 'Stand clear.' They all took a pace back as a shock was transferred from the electric discharge machine and ran through Scott's body.

They stared at the monitor as the consultant jumped forward again and continued to pump Scott's chest with the palms of his hands, but the thin green line did not respond. 'Two hundred joules, stand clear,' he repeated firmly, and they all stood back again to watch the effect of the electric shock. But the line remained obstinately flat. The consultant quickly returned to pumping Scott's chest with his hands.

'Three hundred and sixty joules, stand clear,' said the consultant in desperation, but the nurse who raised the number on the dial knew the patient was already dead.

The consultant pressed a button, and they all watched the highest shock allowed pass through Scott's body, assuming that must be the end. They turned their attention to the monitor.

'We've lost him,' was on the consultant's lips, when to their astonishment they saw the line begin to show a faint flicker. He leaped forward and began pumping away with the palms of his hands as the flicker continued to show irregular fibrillation. 'Three hundred and sixty joules, stand clear,' he said once again. The button was pressed and their attention returned to the monitor. Fibrillation returned to a normal rhythm. The youngest doctor cheered.

The consultant quickly located a vein in Scott's left arm and jabbed a needle directly into it, leaving a cannula sticking out to which a saline drip was quickly attached.

Another doctor rushed into the theatre and, facing his superior, said, 'The antidote is GTN.'

A nurse went straight over to the poisons cabinet and extracted a phial of glyceryl trinitrate, which she passed to the consultant, who had a syringe ready. He extracted the blue liquid from the phial, shot a little into the air to be sure it was flowing freely, then pumped the antidote into a side valve of the intravenous drip. He turned to watch the monitor. The flicker maintained a constant rhythm.

The consultant turned to the senior nurse and said, 'Do you believe in miracles?'

'No,' she replied. 'I'm a Jew. Miracles are only for Christians.'

Hannah began to form a plan, a plan that would brook no interference from Kratz. She had made the decision to accept the job as senior secretary to the Ambassador, and to accompany him back to Iraq.

As the hours passed, her plan began to take shape. She was aware there would be problems. Not from the Iraqi side, but from her own people. Hannah knew that she would have to circumvent Mossad's attempts to take her out, which meant that she could never leave the embassy, even for one moment, until the time came for the Ambassador to return to Iraq. She would use all the techniques they had taught her over the past two years to defeat them.

When she was in Iraq, Hannah would make herself

indispensable to the Ambassador, bide her time and, once she had achieved her objective, happily die a martyr's death.

She had been left with only one purpose in life now that Simon was dead. To assassinate Saddam Hussein.

'Department of Commerce.'

'Alex Wagner, please,' said the Archivist.

'Who?'

'Alex Wagner. Office of Personnel.'

'Just a minute.' Another stretched minute.

'Personnel.'

'This is Calder Marshall, Archivist of the United States. I called yesterday for Ms Wagner and you told me to try again today.'

'I wasn't here yesterday, sir.'

'Well, it must have been one of your colleagues. Is Ms Wagner available?'

'Just a minute.'

This time the Archivist waited several minutes.

'Alex Wagner,' said a brisk female voice.

'Ms Wagner, my name is Calder Marshall. I'm the Archivist of the United States, and it's extremely important that I contact Mr Rex Butterworth, who was recently detailed to the White House by the Commerce Department.'

'Are you a former employer of Mr Butterworth's?' asked the brisk voice.

'No, I am not,' replied Marshall.

'Are you a relative?'

'No.'

'Then I'm afraid I cannot help you, Mr Marshall.'

'Why's that?' asked the Archivist.

'Because the Privacy Act prohibits us from giving

out any personal information about government employees.'

'Can you tell me the name of the Commerce Director, or is that covered by the Privacy Act too?' the Archivist asked.

'Dick Fielding,' said the voice abruptly.

'Thank you for your assistance,' said the Archivist.

The phone went dead.

When Scott woke, his first memory was of Hannah. And then he slept.

When he woke a second time, all he could make out were blurred figures who appeared to be bending over him. And then he slept.

When he woke again, the blurs began to take some shape. Most of them seemed to be dressed in white. And then he slept.

When he woke the next time it was dark and he was alone. He felt so weak, so limp, as he tried to remember what had happened. And then he slept.

When he woke, for the first time he could hear their voices, soothing, gentle, but he could not make out the words, however hard he tried. And then he slept.

When he woke again, they had propped him up in bed. They were trying to feed him a warm, tasteless liquid through a plastic straw. And then he slept.

When he woke, a man in a long white coat, with a stethoscope and a warm smile, was asking in a pronounced accent, 'Can you hear me?' He tried to nod, but fell asleep.

When he woke, another doctor – this time he could see him clearly – was listening attentively as Scott attempted his first words. 'Hannah. Hannah,' was all he said. And then he slept.

He woke again, and an attractive woman with short dark hair and a caring smile was leaning over him. He returned her smile and asked the time. It must have sounded strange to her, but he wanted to know.

'It's a few minutes after three in the morning,' the nurse told him.

'How long have I been here?' he managed.

'Just over a week, but you were so close to death. I think in English you have the expression "touch and go". If your friends had been a moment –' And then he slept.

When he woke, the doctor told Scott that when he'd first arrived they thought it was too late, and twice he'd been pronounced technically dead. 'Antidotes and electrostimulation of the heart, combined with a rare determination to live and one nurse's theory that you might be a Gentile, defied the technical pronouncement,' he declared with a smile.

Scott asked if someone called Hannah had been to see him. The doctor checked the board at the end of his bed. There had been only two visitors that he was aware of, both of them men. They came every day. And then Scott slept.

When he woke, the two men the doctor had mentioned were standing one on each side of his bed. Scott smiled at Dexter Hutchins, who was trying not to cry. Grown men don't cry, he wanted to say, especially when they work for the CIA. He turned to the other man. He had never seen a face so full of shame, so ridden with guilt, or eyes so red from not sleeping. Scott tried to ask what had caused him such unhappiness. And then he slept.

When he woke, both men were still there, now resting on uncomfortable chairs, half asleep.

'Dexter,' he whispered, and they both woke immediately. 'Where's Hannah?'

The other man, who Scott noticed was recovering from a black eye and a broken nose, took some time answering his question. And then Scott slept, never wanting to wake again.

19

'DEPARTMENT OF COMMERCE.'

'The Director, please.'

'Who's calling?'

'Marshall, Calder Marshall.'

'Is he expecting your call?'

'No, he is not.'

'Mr Fielding only takes calls from people who have previously booked to speak to him.'

'What about his secretary?' asked Marshall.

'She never takes calls.'

'So how do I get a booking with Mr Fielding?'

'You have to speak to Miss Zelumski in reservations.'

'Can I be put through to Miss Zelumski, or do I have to make a reservation to speak to her as well?'

'There is no need to be sarcastic, sir. I'm only doing my job.'

'I'm sorry. Perhaps you'd put me through to Miss Zelumski.'

Marshall waited patiently.

'Miss Zelumski speaking.'

'I'd like to reserve a call to speak to Mr Fielding.'

'Is it domestic, most-favoured status or foreign?' asked a bored-sounding voice.

'It's personal.'

'Does he know you?'

'No, he doesn't.'

'Then I can't help. I only deal with domestic, most-favoured status or foreign.'

The Archivist hung up before Miss Zelumski was given the chance to say 'Glad to have been of assistance, sir.'

Marshall tapped his fingers on the desk. The time had come to play by new rules.

Cavalli had checked into the Hôtel de la Paix in Geneva the previous evening. He had booked a modest suite overlooking the lake. Neither expensive nor conspicuous. After he had undressed, he climbed into bed and tuned in to CNN. He watched for a few moments, but found that the news of Bill Clinton having his hair cut on board Air Force One while it was parked on a runway at Los Angeles airport was getting more coverage than the Americans shooting down a plane in the no-fly zone over Iraq. It seemed the new President was determined to prove to Saddam that he was every bit as tough as Bush.

When Cavalli woke in the morning, he jumped out of bed, strolled across to the window, opened the curtains and admired the fountain in the centre of the lake whose water spouted like a gushing well high into the air. He turned to see that an envelope had been pushed under the door. He tore it open to discover a note confirming his appointment to 'take tea' with his banker, Monsieur Franchard, at eleven o'clock that morning. Cavalli was about to drop the card into the waste-paper basket when he noticed some words scribbled on the bottom:

I do hope you find the brand appropriate.
Have a good party. N.V.

After a light breakfast in his room, Cavalli packed his suitcase and hanging bag before going downstairs. The doorman answered his questions in perfect English, and confirmed the directions to Franchard et cie. In Switzerland hall porters know the location of banks, just as their London counterparts can direct you to theatres and football grounds.

As Cavalli left the hotel and started the short walk to the bank, he couldn't help feeling something wasn't quite right. And then he realised that the streets were clean, the people he passed were well-dressed, sober and silent. A contrast in every way to New York.

Once he reached the front door of the bank, Cavalli pressed the discreet bell under the equally discreet brass plate announcing 'Franchard et cie'.

A doorman responded to the call. Cavalli walked into a marble-pillared hall of perfect proportions.

'Perhaps you would like to go straight to the tenth floor, Mr Cavalli? I believe Monsieur Franchard is expecting you.'

Cavalli had only entered the building twice before in his life. How did they manage it? And the porter turned out to be as good as his word, because when Cavalli stepped out of the lift, the chairman of the bank was waiting there to greet him.

'Good morning, Mr Cavalli,' he said. 'Shall we go to my office?'

The chairman's office was a modest, tastefully decorated room, Swiss bankers not wishing to frighten away their customers with a show of conspicuous wealth.

Cavalli was surprised to see a large brown parcel placed in the centre of the boardroom table, giving no clue as to its contents.

'This arrived for you this morning,' the banker

explained. 'I thought it might have something to do with our proposed meeting.'

Cavalli smiled, leaned over and pulled the parcel towards him. He quickly ripped off the brown-paper covering to find a packing case with the words 'TEA: BOSTON' stamped across it.

With the help of a heavy silver letter-opener which he picked up from a side table, Cavalli prised the wooden lid slowly open. He didn't notice the slight grimace that came over the chairman's face.

Cavalli stared inside. The top of the box was filled with styrofoam packing material, which he cupped out with his hands and scattered all over the boardroom table.

The chairman quickly placed a waste-paper basket by his side, which Cavalli ignored as he continued to dig into the box until he finally came to some objects wrapped in tissue-paper.

He removed a piece of the tissue-paper to reveal a teacup in the Confederate colours of the First Congress.

It took Cavalli several minutes to unwrap an entire tea set, which he laid out on the table in front of the puzzled banker. Once it was unpacked, Cavalli also appeared a little mystified. He dug into the box again, and retrieved an envelope. He tore it open and began reading the contents out loud.

> This is a copy of the famous tea set made in 1777 by Pearson and Son to commemorate the Boston Tea Party. Each set is accompanied by an authentic copy of the Declaration of Independence. Your set is number 20917, and has been recorded in our books under the name of J. Hancock.

The letter had been signed and verified by the present chairman, H. William Pearson VI.

Cavalli burst out laughing as he dug deeper into the wooden box, removing yet more packing material until he came across a thin plastic cylinder. He had to admire the way Nick Vicente had fooled the US Customs into allowing him to export the original. The banker's expression remained one of bafflement. Cavalli placed the cylinder in the centre of the table, before going over in considerable detail how he wanted the meeting at twelve to be conducted.

The banker nodded from time to time, and made the occasional note on the pad in front of him.

'I would also like the plastic tube placed in a strongbox for the time being. The key to the box should be handed over to Mr Al Obaydi when, and only when, you have received the full payment by wire transfer. The money should then be deposited in my No. 3 account in your Zurich branch.'

'And are you able to tell me the exact sum you anticipate receiving from Mr Al Obaydi?' asked the banker.

'Ninety million dollars,' said Cavalli.

The banker didn't raise an eyebrow.

The Archivist looked up the name of the Commerce Secretary in his government directory, then picked up his phone and pressed one button. 482 2000 was now programmed into his speed dial.

'Department of Commerce.'

'Dick Fielding, please.'

'Just a moment.'

'Office of the Director.'

'This is Secretary Brown.'

The Archivist had to wait only a few seconds before the call was put through.

'Good morning, Mr Secretary,' said an alert voice.

'Good morning, Mr Fielding. This is Calder Marshall, Archivist of the United States of America.'

'I thought . . .'

'You thought . . .?'

'I guess I must have picked up the wrong phone. How may I help you, Mr Marshall?'

'I'm trying to trace a former employee of yours. Rex Butterworth.'

'I can't help you on that one.'

'Why? Are you bound by the Privacy Act as well?'

Fielding laughed. 'I only wish I was.'

'I don't understand,' said the Archivist.

'Last week we sent Butterworth a merit bonus, and it was returned, "No forwarding address".'

'But he has a wife.'

'She got the same response to her last letter.'

'And his mother in South Carolina?'

'She's been dead for years.'

'Thank you,' said Calder Marshall, and put the phone down. He knew exactly who he had to call next.

Dummond et cie is one of Geneva's more modern banking establishments, having been founded as late as 1781. Since then the bank has spent over two hundred years handling other people's money, without religious or racial prejudice. Dummond et cie had always been willing to deal with Arab sheik or Jewish businessman, Nazi Gauleiter or British aristocrat, in fact anyone who required their services. It was a policy that had reaped dividends in every trading currency throughout the world.

The bank occupied twelve floors of a building just off the place de la Fusterie. The meeting that had been arranged that Tuesday at noon was scheduled to take place in the boardroom on the eleventh floor, the floor below the chairman's office.

The chairman of the bank, Pierre Dummond, had held his present position for the past nineteen years, but even he had rarely experienced a more unlikely coupling than that between an educated Arab from Iraq and the son of a former Mafia lawyer from New York.

The boardroom table could seat sixteen, but on this occasion it was only occupied by four. Pierre Dummond sat in the centre of one of the long sides under a portrait of his uncle, the former chairman, François Dummond. The present chairman wore a dark suit of elegant cut and style that would not have looked out of place had it been worn by any of the chairmen of the forty-eight banks located within a square mile of the building. His shirt was of a shade of blue that was not influenced by Milan fashions, and his tie was so discreet that, moments after leaving the room, only a remarkably observant client would have been able to recall its colour or pattern.

On Monsieur Dummond's right sat his client, Mr Al Obaydi, whose dress, although slightly more fashionable, was nonetheless equally conservative.

Opposite Monsieur Dummond sat the chairman of Franchard et cie, who, any observer would have noticed, must have shared the same tailor as Monsieur Dummond. On Franchard's left sat Antonio Cavalli, wearing a double-breasted Armani suit, who looked as if he had dropped in on the wrong meeting.

The little carriage clock that sat on the Louis-Philippe mantelpiece behind Monsieur Dummond completed twelve strokes. The chairman cleared his throat and began the proceedings.

'Gentlemen, the purpose of this meeting, which was called at our instigation but with your agreement, is to exchange a rare document for an agreed sum of money.' Monsieur Dummond pushed his half-moon spectacles further up his nose. 'Naturally, I must begin, Mr Cavalli, by asking if you are in possession of that document?'

'No, he is not, sir,' interjected Monsieur Franchard, as prearranged with Cavalli, 'because he has entrusted the document's safekeeping to our bank. But I can confirm that, as soon as the sum has been transferred, I have been given power of attorney to release the document immediately.'

'But that is not what we agreed,' interrupted Dummond, who leaned forward, feigning shock, before adding, 'My client's government has no intention of paying another cent without full scrutiny of the document. You agreed to deliver it here by midday, and in any case we still have to be convinced of its authenticity.'

'That is understood by my client,' said Monsieur Franchard. 'Indeed, you are most welcome to attend my office at any time convenient to you in order to carry out such an inspection. Following that inspection, the moment you have transferred the agreed amount the document will be released.'

'This is all very well,' countered Monsieur Dummond, pushing his half-moon spectacles back up his nose, 'but your client has failed to keep to his original agreement, which in my view allows my client's government' – he emphasised the word 'government' – 'to reconsider its position.'

'My client felt it prudent, in the circumstances, to protect his interest by depositing the document in his own bank for safekeeping,' came back the immediate reply from Monsieur Franchard.

Anyone watching the two bankers sparring with each other might have been surprised to learn that they played chess together every Saturday night, which Monsieur

Franchard invariably won, and tennis after lunch on Sunday, which he regularly lost.

'I cannot accept this new arrangement,' said Al Obaydi, speaking for the first time. 'My government has charged me to pay only a further forty million dollars if the original agreement is breached in any way.'

'But this is ridiculous!' said Cavalli, his voice rising with every word. 'We are quibbling over a matter of a few hours at the most and a building less than half a mile away. And as you well know, the figure agreed on was ninety million.'

'But you have since broken our agreement,' said Al Obaydi, 'so the original terms can no longer be considered valid by my government.'

'No ninety million, no document!' said Cavalli, banging his fist on the table.

'Let us be realistic, Mr Cavalli,' said Al Obaydi. 'The document is no longer of any use to you, and I have a feeling you would have settled for fifty million in the first place.'

'That is not the –'

Monsieur Franchard touched Cavalli's arm. 'I would like a few minutes alone with my client, and, if I may, the use of a telephone.'

'Of course,' said Monsieur Dummond, rising from his place. 'We will leave you. Please press the button under the table the moment you wish us to return.'

Monsieur Dummond and his client left the room without another word.

'He's bluffing,' said Cavalli. 'He'll pay. I know it.'

'I don't think so,' said Franchard.

'What makes you say that?'

'The use of the words "my government".'

'What does that tell us that we didn't already know?'

'The expression was repeated four times,' said

Franchard, 'which suggests to me that the financial decision has been taken out of the hands of Mr Al Obaydi, and only forty million has been deposited by his government with Dummond et cie.'

Cavalli began pacing round the room, but stopped by the phone which rested on a small side table.

'I presume that's bugged,' said Cavalli, pointing at the phone.

'No, Mr Cavalli, it is not.'

'How can you be so sure?' asked his client.

'Monsieur Dummond and I are currently involved in several transactions, and he would never allow our relationship to suffer for the sake of one deal. And in any case, he sits on the opposite side of the table from you today but, like every Swiss banker, that won't stop him from thinking of you as a potential customer.'

Cavalli checked his watch. It was 6.20 a.m. in New York. His father would have been up for at least an hour. He jabbed out the fourteen numbers and waited.

His father answered the phone, sounding wide awake, and after preliminary exchanges listened carefully to his son's account of what had taken place in the bank's boardroom. Cavalli also repeated Monsieur Franchard's view of the situation. The chairman of Skills didn't take long considering what advice he should give his son, advice which took Cavalli by surprise.

He replaced the phone and informed Monsieur Franchard of his father's opinion.

Monsieur Franchard nodded as if to show he agreed with the older man's judgement.

'Then let's get on with it,' said Cavalli reluctantly. Monsieur Franchard pressed the button under the boardroom table.

Monsieur Dummond and his client entered the room a few moments later and returned to the seats they had previously occupied. The old banker pushed his half-moon spectacles up his nose once again and stared over the top of them as he waited for Monsieur Franchard to speak.

'If the transaction is completed within one hour, we will settle for forty million dollars. If not, the deal is off and the document will be returned to the United States.'

Dummond removed his spectacles and turned to glance at his client. He was pleased that Franchard had picked up the significance of 'my government', a phrase he had recommended Mr Al Obaydi should use as often as possible.

'White House?'

'Yes, sir.'

'May I speak to the President's scheduler, please?'

'Can I ask who's calling?'

'Marshall, Calder Marshall, Archivist of the United States. And before you ask, yes, I do know her, and yes, she is expecting my call.'

The line went dead. Marshall wondered if he had been cut off.

'Patty Watson speaking.'

'Patty, this is Calder Marshall. I'm the –'

'Archivist of the United States.'

'I don't believe it.'

'Oh, yes, I'm a great fan of yours, Mr Marshall. I've even read your book on the history of the Constitution, the Bill of Rights and the Declaration. How can I help you? – Are you still there, Mr Marshall?'

'Yes, Patty, I am. I only wanted to check on the President's schedule on the morning of May 25th this year.'

'Certainly, sir. I'll just be a moment.'

The Archivist did not have long to wait.

'Ah yes, May 25th. The President spent the morning in the Oval Office with his speech writers, David Kusnet and Carolyn Curiel. He was preparing the text for his address on the GATT at the Chicago Council on Foreign Relations. He took a break to have lunch with Senator Mitchell, the Majority Leader. At three, the President –'

'Did President Clinton remain in the White House the whole morning?'

'Yes, sir. He didn't leave the White House all day. He spent the afternoon with Mrs Clinton in discussions with her health-policy task unit.'

'Could he have slipped out of the building without even you knowing, Patty?'

The scheduling secretary laughed. 'That's not possible, sir. If he had done that, the Secret Service would have informed me immediately.'

'Thank you, Patty.'

'Glad to have been of assistance, sir.'

Once the meeting at Dummond et cie had broken up, Cavalli returned to his hotel room to wait for Franchard to call and confirm that the sum of forty million dollars had been deposited in his No. 3 account in Zurich.

As long as the transaction was closed within the hour, he would still have easily enough time to catch the 4.45 out of Geneva for Heathrow and make the early-evening connection to New York.

Cavalli began to get a little anxious after thirty minutes passed and there had been no call, and even more so after forty. After fifty, he found himself pacing around the room, staring out at the fountain, and checking his watch every few moments.

When the phone eventually rang, he grabbed it.

'Mr Cavalli?' enquired a voice.

'Speaking.'

'Franchard here. The document has been verified and taken away. It might interest you to know that Mr Al Obaydi studied one word on the parchment for some time before he agreed to transfer the money. The agreed sum has been credited to your No. 3 account in Zurich as you specified.'

'Thank you, Monsieur Franchard,' said Cavalli without further comment.

'My pleasure, as always, Mr Cavalli. And is there anything else we can do for you while you're here?'

'Yes,' replied Cavalli. 'I need to transfer a quarter of a million dollars to a bank in the Cayman Islands.'

'The same name and account as the last three transactions?' asked the banker.

'Yes,' replied Cavalli. 'And the Zurich account, presently registered in the name of Mr Al Obaydi: I want to withdraw one hundred thousand dollars from it and . . .'

Monsieur Franchard listened carefully to his client's further instructions.

'State Department.'

'Can I speak to the Secretary of State?'

'Just a moment.'

'Office of the Secretary.'

'This is Calder Marshall. I'm the Archivist of the United States. It's vitally important that I speak with Secretary Christopher.'

'I'll put you through to his executive assistant, sir.'

'Thank you,' said Marshall, and waited for a very short time.

'This is Jack Leigh. I'm executive assistant to the Secretary. How may I help you, sir?'

'To start with, Mr Leigh, how many executive assistants does the Secretary of State have?'

'Five, sir, but there is only one senior to me.'

'Then I need to speak to the Secretary of State urgently.'

'Right now he's out of the office. Perhaps the Deputy Secretary can help?'

'No, Mr Leigh, he cannot help.'

'Well, I'll certainly let Secretary Christopher know you called, sir.'

'Thank you, Mr Leigh. And perhaps you'd be kind enough to pass a message on to him?'

'Of course, sir.'

'Would you let him know that my resignation will be on his desk tomorrow morning by nine a.m. This call is simply to apologise for the harm it will undoubtedly do to the President, particularly given the short period of time he has been in office.'

'You haven't spoken to anyone from the media about this, have you, sir?' asked the executive assistant, sounding anxious for the first time.

'No, I have not, Mr Leigh, and I shall not do so until noon tomorrow, which should give the Secretary ample time in which to prepare answers to any questions that he and the President will undoubtedly be asked by the press when they learn my reason for resigning.'

'I'll have the Secretary get back to you as quickly as I can, sir.'

'Thank you, Mr Leigh.'

'Glad to have been of assistance, sir.'

* * *

She flew into the Cayman Islands that morning and took a taxi to Barclays Bank in Georgetown. She checked her account to find it had been credited with three payments of two hundred and fifty thousand dollars. One on March 9th, another on April 27th, and a further one on May 30th.

There was one still to come. But, to be fair, Cavalli might not learn of the death of T. Hamilton McKenzie until he had returned from Geneva.

'And we have another package for you, Miss Webster,' said the smiling West Indian behind the counter.

Far too familiar, she thought. Once again the time had come for her to move her account to another bank in another country, in another name. She dropped the package into her carrier bag, threw it over her shoulder and left without a word.

She didn't attempt to open the thick brown envelope until she had called for coffee at the end of an unhurried meal at a hotel she would never book into. She then carefully slit open the top of the bulky package with her bread knife, allowing the contents to spill out onto the table.

The usual photos, from every angle, plus addresses past and present, and the daily habits and haunts of the intended victim. Cavalli never left any room for mistakes.

She studied the photos of a little fat man sitting on a bar stool. He looked harmless enough. The contract was always the same. To be carried out within fourteen days. Payment two hundred and fifty thousand dollars to account specified.

It wasn't Columbus or Washington this time, but San Francisco. She hadn't been to the West Coast in years, and she tried to remember if they had a Laura Ashley store.

* * *

'National Archives.'

'Mr Marshall, please.'

'Who's calling?'

'Christopher. Warren Christopher.'

'And you're with which agency?'

'I have a feeling he'll know.'

'I'll put you through, sir.' The Secretary waited patiently.

'Calder Marshall speaking.'

'Calder, it's Warren Christopher.'

'Good morning, Mr Secretary.'

'Good morning, Calder. I've just received your letter of resignation.'

'Yes, sir. I thought it was the only course of action I could take in the circumstances.'

'Very commendable, I feel sure, but have you let anyone else into your confidence?'

'No, sir. I intended to brief my staff at eleven and hold a press conference at twelve, as stated in my letter. I hope that doesn't inconvenience you, sir.'

'Well, I wondered if before you did that, you might find the time to have a meeting with the President and myself?'

Marshall hesitated only because the request had taken him by surprise.

'Of course, sir. What time would suit you?'

'Shall we say ten o'clock?'

'Yes, sir. Where would you like me to come?'

'The North Entrance of the White House.'

'The North Entrance, of course.'

'Jack Leigh, my executive assistant, will meet you in the West Wing reception area and accompany you to the Oval Office.'

'The Oval Office.'

'And Calder . . .'

'Yes, Mr Secretary?'

'Please do not mention your resignation to anyone until you've seen the President.'

'Until I've seen the President. Of course.'

'Thank you, Calder.'

'Glad to have been of assistance, sir.'

20

'I'D LIKE TO BEGIN by thanking you all for attending this meeting at such short notice,' said the Secretary of State. 'And, in particular, Scott Bradley, who has only recently recovered from . . .' Christopher hesitated for a moment, '. . . a near-tragic accident. I know we are all delighted by the speed of his recovery. I should also like to welcome Colonel Kratz, who is representing the Israeli Government, and Dexter Hutchins, the Deputy Director of the CIA.

'Only two of my staff are with me today: Jack Leigh, my executive assistant, and Susan Anderson, one of my senior Middle East advisers. The reason for numbers being limited on this occasion will become all too obvious to you. The issue we are about to discuss is so sensitive that the fewer people who are aware of it, the better. To suggest in this instance that silence is golden would be to underestimate the value of gold.

'Perhaps, at this juncture, I could ask the Deputy Director of the CIA to bring us up to date on the latest situation. Dexter.'

Dexter Hutchins unlocked his briefcase and removed a file marked 'For the Director's Eyes Only'. He placed the file on the table in front of him and turned its cover.

'Two days ago, Mr Marshall, the Archivist of the United States, reported to the Secretary of State that the Declaration of Independence had been stolen from the National Archives; or, to be more accurate, had been switched for a quite brilliant copy that had not only passed the scrutiny of Mr Marshall, but also that of the Senior Conservator, Mr Mendelssohn.

'It was only when Mr Marshall attempted to re-contact a Mr Rex Butterworth, who had been temporarily assigned to the White House as a Special Assistant to the President, that he became worried.'

'If I could just interject, Mr Hutchins,' said Jack Leigh, 'and point out that though Mr Butterworth was a former employee of the Commerce Department, should the press ever get hold of this you can be certain they would only refer to him as a "Special Assistant to the President".' Warren Christopher nodded his agreement.

'When Calder Marshall discovered that Butterworth hadn't returned after his vacation,' continued Dexter Hutchins, 'and that he had also left without giving a forwarding address, he naturally became suspicious. Under the circumstances, he considered it prudent to ask Mr Mendelssohn to check and see if the Declaration had in any way been tampered with. After putting the parchment through several preliminary tests – a separate memorandum has been sent to all of you on this – he came to the conclusion that they were still in possession of the original document.

'But Mr Marshall, a cautious man, remained sceptical, and contacted the President's scheduler, Miss Patty Watson – details also enclosed. Following that conversation, he asked the Conservator to carry out a more rigorous scrutiny.

'Mr Mendelssohn spent several hours alone that evening going over the parchment word by word with a magnifying glass. It was when he came to the sentence, "Nor have We been wanting in attentions to our British brethren", that the Conservator realised that the word "British" had been spelt correctly, and not with two *ts* as in the original Declaration executed by Timothy Matlock. When this piece of news was imparted to Mr Marshall, he immediately offered his resignation to the Secretary of State, a copy of which you all have.'

'If I could come in here, Dexter,' said Secretary Christopher. 'Just for the record, the President and I saw Mr Marshall in the Oval Office yesterday. He could not have been more co-operative. He assured us that he and his colleague, Mr Mendelssohn, will say and do nothing in the immediate future. He did add, however, his feeling of disgust at continuing to display a counterfeit copy of the Declaration to the general public. He made us both, that is to say the President and myself, agree that should we fail to recover the original document before its disappearance becomes common knowledge, we would confirm that his resignation had been dated May 25th 1993 and accepted by myself as custodian of the Declaration. He wished it to be confirmed in writing that he had in no way connived to deceive his staff or the nation he served. "I am not in the habit of being deceitful," were his final words before leaving the Oval Office.

'If it is possible,' continued Christopher, 'for a public servant to make the President and the Secretary of State feel morally inferior, Mr Marshall achieved it with considerable dignity. However, that does not change the fact that if we don't get the original parchment back before its theft becomes public knowledge, the media are going to roast the President and myself slowly over a spit. One thing's also for sure: the Republicans, led by Dole, will happily wash their collective hands in public. Carry on, Dexter.'

'Under the Secretary of State's instructions, we immediately formed a small task force at Langley to profile every aspect of the problem we are facing. But we quickly discovered that we were working under some severe restrictions. To begin with, because of the sensitivity of the subject and the people involved, we could not do what we automatically would have done in normal circumstances, namely consult the FBI and liaise with the DC Police Department. That, we felt, would have guaranteed us the front page of the *Washington Post*, and probably the following morning. We mustn't forget that the FBI is still smarting over the Waco siege, and they'd like nothing better than for the CIA to replace them on the front pages.

'The next problem we faced was having to tiptoe round people we'd usually bring in for questioning, for fear that they too might discover our real purpose. However, we have been able to come up with several leads without talking to any members of the public. Following a routine check of permit records at the DCPD, we discovered that a movie was being made in Washington on the same day as the document was stolen. The director of that movie was Johnny Scasiatore, who is currently on bail facing an indecency charge. Three others involved in the enterprise turn out to have criminal records. And some of those people fit the descriptions Mr Marshall and Mr Mendelssohn have given us of the group who arrived at the National Archives posing as the Presidential party. They include a certain Bill O'Reilly, a well-known forger who has spent several years in more than one of our state penitentiaries, and an actor who played the President so convincingly that both Mr Marshall and Mr Mendelssohn accepted it was him without question.'

'Surely we can discover who that was,' said Christopher.

'We already have. His name is Lloyd Adams. But we daren't bring him in.'

'How did you find him?' asked Leigh. 'After all, there are quite a few actors who can manage a passable resemblance to Clinton.'

'Agreed,' said the Deputy Director, 'but only one who's been operated on by America's leading plastic surgeon within the past few months. We have reason to believe that the ringleaders killed the surgeon and his daughter, which is why his wife reported everything she knew to the local Chief of Police.

'However, the whole operation would never have got off the ground without the inside help of Mr Rex Butterworth, who was last seen on the morning of May 25th and has since disappeared off the face of the earth. He booked a flight to Brazil, but he never showed. We have agents across the globe searching for him.'

'None of this is of any importance if we are no nearer to finding out where the original Declaration is at this moment, and who took it,' said Christopher.

'That's the bad news,' replied Dexter. 'Our agents spend hours on routine investigations that many American citizens consider a waste of taxpayers' money. But just now and then, it pays off.'

'We're all listening,' said Christopher.

'The CIA keeps under surveillance several foreign diplomats who work at the United Nations. Naturally, they would be outraged if any of them could prove what we were up to, and if we ever think they're onto us we back off immediately. In the case of Iraqis at the UN, we have people shadowing them round the clock. Our problem is that we can't operate within the UN complex itself, because if we were caught inside that building it would cause an international outcry. So, occasionally, their representatives are bound to slip our net.

'But we believe it was not a coincidence that Iraq's Deputy Ambassador to the United Nations, a Mr Hamid

Al Obaydi, was in Washington on the day the Declaration was switched, and took several photographs of the bogus filming that was taking place. The agent who was tracking Al Obaydi at the time also reported that, at 10.37, after the Declaration had gone back on display in the National Archives, Al Obaydi joined the public queue, waiting over an hour to view the parchment. But here's the clincher. He studied the document once, and then he looked at it a second time, with glasses.'

'Perhaps he's near-sighted,' said Susan.

'Our agent reports that he's never before or since seen him wearing glasses of any kind,' replied Dexter Hutchins. 'Now for the *really* bad news,' he continued.

'That wasn't it?' said Christopher.

'No, sir. Al Obaydi flew on to Geneva a week later and was spotted by our local station officer leaving a bank.' Dexter referred to his notes. 'Franchard et cie. He was carrying a plastic cylinder, and I quote, "a little over two feet in length and about two inches in diameter".'

'Who's going to tell the President?' said Christopher, putting his hands over his eyes.

'He took this cylinder by car straight to the Palais des Nations, and it hasn't been seen since.'

'And Barazan Al-Tikriti, Saddam's half-brother, is the Iraqi Ambassador to the United Nations in Geneva,' said Susan.

'Don't remind me,' said Christopher. 'But what I want to know is, why the hell didn't your man jump Al Obaydi when it was obvious what he was carrying? I would have found a way of keeping the Swiss in line.'

'We would have done so if we'd known what he was carrying, but at that stage we weren't even aware the Declaration had been stolen, and our surveillance was just routine.'

'So what you're telling us, Mr Hutchins, is that the Declaration could well be in Baghdad by now,' said Leigh. 'Because if it was sent through the diplomatic pouch, the Swiss wouldn't have let us get anywhere near it.'

No one spoke for several moments.

'Let's work on the worst-case scenario,' said the Secretary of State finally. 'The Declaration is already in Saddam's possession. So what's his next move likely to be? Scott, you're our man of logic. Can you second-guess what he might get up to?'

'No, sir, Saddam's not a man you can second-guess. Especially after his failed attempt to assassinate George Bush on his visit to Kuwait in April. Although the whole world accused him of being behind the plot, how did he react? Not with the usual bellicose shouting and screaming about the lies of the American imperialists, but with a reasoned, coherent statement from his Ambassador at the UN denying any personal involvement. Why? The press tells us it's because Saddam is hoping Clinton will be more reasonable in the long term than Bush. I don't believe it. I suspect Saddam realises that Clinton's position doesn't differ greatly from that of his predecessor. I don't think that's his reasoning at all. No, I suspect he believes that with the Declaration in his possession, he has a weapon so powerful that he can humiliate the United States, and in particular the new President, as and when he pleases.'

'When and how, Scott? If we knew that . . .'

'I have two theories on that, sir,' replied Scott.

'Let's hear them both.'

'Neither is going to make you feel any happier, Mr Secretary.'

'Nevertheless . . .'

'First he sets up a press conference, inviting the

world's media to attend. He selects some public place in Baghdad where he is safely surrounded by his own people, and then he tears up, burns, destroys, does whatever he likes to the Declaration. I have a feeling it would make prime-time television.'

'But we'd bomb Baghdad to the ground if he tried that,' said Dexter Hutchins.

'I doubt it,' said Scott. 'How would our allies, the British, the French, not to mention the other friendly Arab nations, react to our bombing innocent civilians because Saddam had stolen the Declaration of Independence from right under our eyes?'

'You're right, Scott,' said Warren Christopher. 'The President would be vilified as a barbarian if he retaliated by bombing innocent Iraqis after what a lot of the world would consider nothing more than a public relations coup, though I must tell you, in the strictest confidence, that we *do* have plans to bomb Baghdad if Saddam continues to undermine the UN inspection teams' attempts to examine Iraqi nuclear installations.'

'Has a date been decided on?' asked Scott.

Christopher hesitated. 'Sunday June 27th,' he said.

'The timing might well turn out to be unfortunate for us,' said Scott.

'Why? When do you think Saddam is likely to move?' asked Christopher.

'That's not so easy to answer, sir,' replied Scott, 'because you have to think the way he thinks. What makes that almost impossible is that he's capable of changing his mind from hour to hour. But if he thinks the problem through logically, my guess is he'll be considering two alternatives. Either on some symbolic date, maybe an anniversary associated with the Gulf War, or . . .'

'Or . . .?' said Christopher.

'Or he intends to hold on to it as a bargaining chip to allow him to retake the oilfields in Kuwait. After all, he's always claimed he had an agreement with us on that in the first place.'

'Either scenario is too horrific to contemplate,' said the Secretary of State. Turning to the Deputy Director, he asked, 'Have you begun to form any plan for getting the document back?'

'Not at the moment, sir,' replied Dexter Hutchins, 'as I suspect the parchment will be every bit as well protected as Saddam himself, and frankly we only learned of its likely destination last night.'

'Colonel Kratz,' said Christopher, turning his attention to the Mossad man, who had not uttered a word. 'Your Prime Minister informed us a few weeks ago that he was considering a plan to take out Saddam at some time in the near future.'

'Yes, sir, but he recognises your present dilemma, and all our activities have been shelved until the problem over the Declaration has been resolved, one way or the other.'

'I have already informed Mr Rabin how much I appreciate his support, especially as he can't even tell his own cabinet the true reason for his change of heart.'

'But we have our own problem, sir,' said the Israeli.

'Make my day, Colonel.'

The burst of laughter that followed helped to ease the tension for a moment – but only for a moment.

'We have been training an agent who was going to be part of the team for the final operation to eliminate Saddam, a Hannah Kopec.'

'The girl who . . .' said Christopher, half-glancing towards Scott.

'Yes, sir. She was totally blameless. But that is not the problem. After she returned to the Iraqi Embassy that evening, we were unable to get anywhere near Miss Kopec to let her know what had happened, because during the next few days she never once left the building, night or day. She and the Iraqi Ambassador have since returned to Baghdad under heavy guard. However, Agent Kopec remains under the misapprehension that she has killed Scott Bradley, and we suspect her only interest now is to eliminate Saddam.'

'She'll never get anywhere near him,' said Leigh.

'I wish I believed that,' said Scott quietly.

'She is a bold, imaginative and resourceful young woman,' said Kratz. 'And, worse, she has the assassin's greatest weapon.'

'Namely?' said Christopher.

'She no longer cares about her own survival.'

'Can this get any worse?' asked Christopher.

'Yes, sir. She knows nothing about the disappearance of the Declaration, and we have no way of contacting her to let her know.'

The Secretary of State paused for a moment, as if he was coming to a decision. 'Colonel Kratz, I want to put something to you which is likely to stretch your personal loyalty.'

'Yes, Mr Secretary,' said Kratz.

'This plan to assassinate Saddam. How long have you been working on it?'

'Nine months to a year,' replied Kratz.

'And it obviously entailed you getting a person or persons into Saddam's palace or bunker?'

Kratz hesitated.

'Yes or no will suffice,' said Christopher.

'Yes, sir.'

'My question is extremely simple, Colonel. May we therefore take advantage of the year's preparation you've already carried out and – dare I suggest – steal your plan?'

'I would have to take advice from my government before I could consider . . .'

Christopher took an envelope from his pocket. 'I will be happy to let you see Mr Rabin's letter to me on this subject, but first allow me to read it to you.'

The Secretary opened the envelope and extracted the letter. He placed his glasses on the end of his nose and unfolded the single sheet.

From the Prime Minister

Dear Mr Secretary,
You are correct in thinking that the Prime Minister of the State of Israel is Chief Minister and Minister of Defence while at the same time having overall responsibility for Mossad.

However, I confess that when it comes to any ideas we may be considering for future relations with Saddam, I have only been kept in touch with the outline proposals. I have not yet been fully briefed on the finer details.

If you believe on balance that such information as we possess may make the difference between success or failure with your present difficulties, I will instruct Colonel Kratz to brief you fully and without reservation.

Yours
Yitzhak Rabin

Christopher turned the letter around and pushed it across the table.

'Colonel Kratz, let me assure you on behalf of the United States Government that I believe such information as you have in your possession may make the difference between success and failure.'

PART TWO

'Nor have We been wanting
in attentions to
our Brittish brethren.'

21

THE DECLARATION OF INDEPENDENCE was nailed to the wall behind him.

Saddam continued puffing at his cigar as he lounged back in his chair. All of them seated around the table waited for him to speak. He glanced to his right.

'My brother, we are proud of you. You have served our country and the Ba'ath Party with distinction, and when the moment comes for my people to be informed of your heroic deeds, your name will be written in the history of our nation as one of its great heroes.'

Al Obaydi sat at the other end of the table, listening to the words of his leader. His fists, hidden under the table, were clenched to stop himself shaking. Several times on the journey back to Baghdad he had been aware that he was being shadowed. They had searched his luggage at almost every stop, but they had found nothing, because there was nothing to find. Saddam's half-brother had seen to that. Once the Declaration had reached the safety of their mission in Geneva he hadn't even been allowed to pass it over to the Ambassador in person. Its guaranteed route in the diplomatic pouch made it impossible to intercept even with the combined efforts of the Americans and the Israelis.

Saddam's half-brother now sat on the President's right-hand side, basking in his leader's eulogy.

Saddam swung himself slowly back round and stared down at the other end of the table.

'And I also acknowledge,' he continued, 'the role played by Hamid Al Obaydi, whom I have appointed to be our Ambassador in Paris. His name must not, however, be associated with this enterprise, lest it harm his chances of representing us on foreign soil.'

And thus it had been decreed. Saddam's half-brother was to be acknowledged as the architect of this triumph, while Al Obaydi was to be a footnote on a page, quickly turned. Had Al Obaydi failed, Saddam's half-brother would have been ignorant of even the original idea, and Al Obaydi's bones would even now be rotting in an unmarked grave. Since Saddam had spoken no one round that table, except for the State Prosecutor, had given Al Obaydi a second look. All other eyes, and smiles, rested on Saddam's half-brother.

It was at that moment, in the midst of the meeting of the Revolutionary Command Council, that Al Obaydi came to his decision.

Dollar Bill sat slouched on a stool, leaning on the bar in unhappy hour, happily sipping his favourite liquid. He was the establishment's only customer, unless you counted the slip of a woman in a Laura Ashley dress who sat silently in the corner. The barman assumed she was drunk, as she hadn't moved a muscle for the past hour.

Dollar Bill wasn't at first aware of the man who stumbled through the swing doors, and wouldn't have given him a second look had he not sat himself on the stool next to his. The intruder ordered a gin and tonic. Dollar Bill had a natural aversion to any man who drank gin and tonic, especially if they occupied the seat next to his when the rest of the bar was empty. He considered moving but decided on balance that he didn't need the exercise.

'So how are you, old timer?' the voice next to him asked. Dollar Bill didn't care to think of himself as an 'old timer', and refused to grace the intruder with a reply.

'What's the matter, not got a tongue in your head?' the man asked, slurring his words. The barman turned to face them when he heard the raised voice, and then returned to drying the glasses left over from the lunchtime rush.

'I have, sir, and it's a civil one,' replied Dollar Bill, still not so much as glancing at his interrogator.

'Irish. I should have known it all along. A nation of stupid, ignorant drunks.'

'Let me remind you, sir,' said Dollar Bill, 'that Ireland is the land of Yeats, Shaw, Wilde, O'Casey and Joyce.' He raised his glass in their memory.

'I've never heard of any of them. Drinking partners of yours, I suppose?' This time the young barman put his cloth down and began to pay closer attention.

'I never had that honour,' replied Dollar Bill, 'but, my friend, the fact that you have not heard of them, let alone read their works, is your loss, not mine.'

'Are you accusing me of being ignorant?' said the intruder, placing a rough hand on Dollar Bill's shoulder.

Dollar Bill turned to face him, but even at that close range he couldn't focus clearly through the haze of alcohol he had consumed during the past two weeks. He did, however, observe that, although he appeared to be part of the same alcoholic haze, the intruder was somewhat larger than himself. Such a consideration had never worried Dollar Bill in the past.

'No, sir, it was not necessary to accuse you of ignorance. For you have been condemned by your own utterances.'

'I won't take that from anyone, you Irish drunk,' said

the intruder. Keeping his hand on Dollar Bill's shoulder, he swung at him and landed a blow on the side of his jaw. Dollar Bill staggered back off his high stool, falling to the floor in a heap.

The intruder waited some time for Bill to rise to his feet before he aimed a second blow to the stomach. Once again, Dollar Bill ended up on the floor.

The young man behind the bar had already begun dialling the number his boss had instructed he should call if ever such a situation arose. He only hoped they would come quickly as he watched the Irishman somehow get back on his feet. This time it was his turn to aim a punch at the intruder's nose, a punch which ended up flying through the air over his assailant's right shoulder. A further blow landed on the side of Dollar Bill's throat. Down he went a third time, which in his days as an amateur boxer would have been considered a technical knock-out; but as there seemed to be no referee present to officiate, he rose once again.

The young barman was relieved to hear a siren in the distance, and was praying they weren't on their way to another call when suddenly four policemen came bursting through the swing doors.

The first one caught Dollar Bill just before he hit the ground for a fourth time, while two of the others grabbed the intruder, thrust his arms behind his back and forced a pair of handcuffs on him. Both men were bundled out of the bar and thrown into the back of a waiting police van. The siren continued its piercing sound as the two drunks were driven away.

The barman was grateful for the speed with which the San Francisco Police Department had come to his aid. It was only later that night that he remembered he hadn't given them an address.

* * *

As Hannah sat alone at the back of the plane bound for Amman, she began to consider the task she had set herself.

Once the Ambassador's party had left Paris, she had returned to the traditional role of an Arab woman. She was dressed from head to toe in a black abayah, and apart from her eyes, her face was covered by a small mask. She spoke only when asked a question directly, and never posed a question herself. She felt her Jewish mother would not have survived such a regime for more than a few hours.

Hannah's one break had come when the Ambassador's wife had enquired where she intended to stay once they had returned to Baghdad. Hannah explained that she had made no immediate plans as her mother and sister were living in Karbala, and she could not stay with them if she hoped to hold on to her job with the Ambassador.

Hannah had hardly finished the second sentence before the Ambassador's wife insisted that she come and live with them. 'Our house is far too large,' she explained, 'even with a dozen servants.'

When the plane touched down at Queen Alia airport, Hannah looked out of the tiny window to watch a large black limousine that would have looked more in place in New York than Amman driving towards them. It drew up by the side of the aircraft and a driver in a smart blue suit and dark glasses jumped out.

Hannah joined the Ambassador and his wife in the back of the car and they sped away from the airport in the direction of the border with Iraq.

When the car reached the customs barrier, they were waved straight through with bows and salutes, as if the border didn't exist. They travelled a further mile and passed a second customs post on the Iraqi side, where they were treated in much the same manner as the first, before joining the six-lane highway to Baghdad.

On the long journey to the capital, the speedometer rarely fell below seventy miles per hour. Hannah soon became bored with the beating sun and the sight of miles and miles of flat sand that stretched to the horizon and beyond, with only the occasional cluster of palm trees to break the monotony. Her thoughts returned to Simon and what might have been . . .

Hannah dozed off as the air-conditioned limousine sped quietly along the highway. Her mind drifted from Simon to her mother, to Saddam, and then back to Simon.

She woke with a start to find they were entering the outskirts of Baghdad.

It had been many years since Dollar Bill had seen the inside of a jail, but not so long that he had forgotten how much he detested having to associate with drug peddlers, pimps and muggers.

Still, the last time he had been foolish enough to get himself involved in a bar-room brawl, he had started it. But even then he only ended up with a fifty-dollar fine. Dollar Bill felt confident that the jails were far too overcrowded for any judge to consider the thirty-day mandatory sentence for such cases.

In fact he had tried to slip one of the policemen in the van fifty dollars. They normally happily accepted the money, opened the back door of the van and kicked you out. He couldn't imagine what the San Francisco police were coming to. Surely with all the muggers and drug addicts around they had more important things to deal with than mid-afternoon middle-aged bar-room drunks.

As Dollar Bill began to sober up, the stench got to him, and he hoped that he'd be among the first to be put up in front of the night court. But as the hours passed, and he became more sober and the stench became greater, he began to wonder if they might end up keeping him overnight.

'William O'Reilly,' shouted the police Sergeant as he looked down the list of names on his clipboard.

'That's me,' said Bill, raising his hand.

'Follow me, O'Reilly,' the policeman barked as the cell door clanked open and the Irishman was gripped firmly by the elbow.

He was marched along a corridor that led into the back of a courtroom. He watched the little line of derelicts and petty criminals who were waiting for their moment in front of the judge. He didn't notice a woman a few paces away from him, tightly gripping the rope handle of a holdall.

'Guilty. Fifty dollars.'

'Can't pay.'

'Three days in jail. Next.'

After three or four cases were dispensed with in this cursory manner within as many minutes, Dollar Bill watched the man who had shown no respect for the canon of Irish literature take his place in front of the judge.

'Drunk and disorderly, disturbing the peace. How do you plead?'

'Guilty, Your Honour.'

'Any previous known record?'

'None,' said the Sergeant.

'Fifty dollars,' said the judge.

It interested Dollar Bill that his adversary had no previous convictions, and was also able to pay his fine immediately.

When it came to Dollar Bill's own turn to plead, he couldn't help thinking, as he looked up at the judge, that he appeared to be awfully young for the job. Perhaps he really was now an 'old timer'.

'William O'Reilly, Your Honour,' said the Sergeant, looking down at the charge sheet. 'Drunk and disorderly, disturbing the peace.'

'How do you plead?'

'Guilty, Your Honour,' said Dollar Bill, fingering a small wad of bills in his pocket as he tried to remember the location of the nearest bar that served Guinness.

'Thirty days,' said the judge, without raising his head. 'Next.'

Two people in the courtroom were stunned by the judge's decision. One of them reluctantly loosened her grip on the rope handle of her holdall, while the other stammered out, 'Bail, Your Honour?'

'Denied.'

22

THE TWO MEN REMAINED SILENT until David Kratz had come to the end of his outline plan.

Dexter was the first to speak. 'I must admit, Colonel, I'm impressed. It just might work.'

Scott nodded his agreement, and then turned to the Mossad man who only a few weeks before had given Hannah the order that he should be killed. Some of the guilt had been lifted since they had been working so closely with each other, but the lines on the forehead and the prematurely grey hair of the Israeli leader remained a perpetual reminder of what he had been through. During their time together Scott had come to admire the sheer professional skill of the man who had been put in charge of the operation.

'I still need some queries answered,' said Scott, 'and a few other things explained.'

The Israeli Councillor for Cultural Affairs to the Court of St James nodded.

'Are you certain that they plan to put the safe in the Ba'ath Party headquarters?'

'Certain, no. Confident, yes,' said Kratz. 'A Dutch company completed some building work in the basement of the headquarters nearly three years ago, and among their final drawings was a brick construction, the dimensions of which would house the safe perfectly.'

'And is this safe still in Kalmar?'

'It was three weeks ago,' replied Kratz, 'when one of my agents carried out a routine check.'

'And does it belong to the Iraqi Government?' asked Dexter Hutchins.

'Yes, it has been fully paid for, and is now legally the property of the Iraqis.'

'Legally that may be the position, but since the Gulf War the UN has imposed a new category of sanctions,' Scott reminded him.

'How can a safe be considered a piece of military equipment?' asked Dexter.

'Exactly the Iraqis' argument,' replied Kratz. 'But, unfortunately for them, when they placed the original order with the Swedes, among the explicit specifications was the requirement that the safe "must be able to withstand a nuclear attack". The word "nuclear" was all that was needed to start the bells ringing at the UN.'

'So how do you plan to get round that problem?' asked Scott.

'Whenever the Iraqi Government submits a new list of items that they consider do not break UN Security Council Resolution 661, the safe is always included. If the Americans, the British and the French didn't raise any objection, it could slip through.'

'And the Israeli Government?'

'We would protest vociferously in front of the Iraqi delegation, but not behind closed doors to our friends.'

'So let us imagine for one moment that we're in possession of a giant safe that can withstand a nuclear attack. What good does that do us?' asked Scott.

'Someone has to be responsible for getting that safe from Sweden to Baghdad. Someone has to install it when they get there, and someone has to explain to Saddam's people how to operate it,' said Kratz.

'And you have someone who is six feet tall, a karate expert, and speaks fluent Arabic?'

'We did have, but she was only five feet ten.' The two men stared at each other. Scott remained silent.

'And how were you proposing to assassinate Saddam?' asked Dexter quickly. 'Lock him up in the safe and hope he would suffocate?'

Kratz realised the comment had been made to take Scott's mind off Hannah, so he responded in kind. 'No, we discovered that was the CIA's plan, and dismissed it. We had something more subtle in mind.'

'Namely?' asked Scott.

'A tiny nuclear device was to be planted inside the safe.'

'And the safe would be in the passage next to where the Revolutionary Command Council meet. Not bad,' said Dexter.

'And the device was to be set off by a five-foot-ten, Arabic-speaking Jewish girl?' asked Scott.

Kratz nodded.

'Thirty days? What did I do to deserve thirty days, that's what I want to know.' But no one was listening as Dollar Bill was hustled out of the courtroom, along the corridor and then out through a door at the rear of the building, before being pushed into the back seat of an unmarked car. Three men with military-style haircuts, Ray-Bans, and small earplugs connected to wires running down the backs of their collars, accompanied him.

'Why wasn't I given bail? And what about my appeal? I have the right to a lawyer, damn it. And by the way, where are you taking me?' However many questions he asked, Dollar Bill received no answers.

Although he was unable to see anything out of the

smoked-glass side windows, Dollar Bill could tell by looking over the driver's shoulder when they reached the Golden Gate Bridge. As they proceeded along Route 101, the speedometer touched fifty-five for the first time, but the driver never once exceeded the speed limit.

When twenty minutes later the car swung off the highway at the Belvedere exit, Dollar Bill had no idea where he was. The driver continued up a small, winding road, until the car slowed down as a massive set of wrought-iron gates loomed up in front of them.

The driver flashed his lights twice and the gates swung open to allow the car to continue its journey down a long, straight gravel drive. It was another three or four minutes before they came to a halt in front of a large country house which reminded Dollar Bill of his youth in County Kerry, when his mother had been a scullery maid up at the manor house.

One of Dollar Bill's escorts leaped out of the car and opened the door for him. Another ran ahead of them up the steps and pressed a bell, as the car sped away across the gravel.

The massive oak door opened to reveal a butler in a long black coat and a white bow tie.

'Good evening, Mr O'Reilly,' he declared in a pronounced English accent even before Dollar Bill had reached the top step. 'My name is Charles. Your room is already prepared. Perhaps you'd be kind enough to accompany me, sir.' Dollar Bill followed him into the house and up the wide staircase without uttering a word. He would have tried some of his questions on Charles, but as he was English, Dollar Bill knew he couldn't expect an honest reply. The butler guided him into a small, well-furnished bedroom on the first floor.

'I do hope you will find that the clothes are the correct fitting, sir,' said Charles, 'and that everything else is to your liking. Dinner will be served in half an hour.'

Dollar Bill bowed and spent the next few minutes looking round the suite. He checked the bathroom. French soap, safety razors and fluffy white towels; even a toothbrush and his favourite toothpaste. He returned to the bedroom and tested the double bed. He couldn't remember when he had last slept on anything so comfortable. He then checked the wardrobe and found three pairs of trousers and three jackets, not unlike the ones he had purchased a few days after returning from Washington. How did they know?

He looked in the drawers: six shirts, six pairs of pants and six pairs of socks. They had thought of everything, even if he didn't care that much for their choice of ties.

Dollar Bill decided to join in the game. He took a bath, shaved and changed into the clothes provided. They were, as Charles had promised, the correct fitting.

He heard a gong sound downstairs, which he took as a clear signal that he had been summoned. He opened the door, stepped into the corridor and proceeded down the wide staircase to find the butler standing in the hall.

'Mr Hutchins is expecting you. You'll find him in the drawing room, sir.'

'Yes, of course I will,' said Dollar Bill, and followed Charles into a large room where a tall, burly man was standing by the fireplace, the stub of a cigar in the corner of his mouth.

'Good evening, Mr O'Reilly,' he said. 'My name is Dexter Hutchins. We've never met before, but I've long been an admirer of your work.'

'That's kind of you, Mr Hutchins, but I don't have the same advantage of knowing what you do to pass the unrelenting hour.'

'I do apologise. I am the Deputy Director of the CIA.'

'After all these years, I get to have dinner in a large

country house with the Deputy Director of the CIA simply because I was involved in a bar-room brawl. I'm tempted to ask, what do you lay on for mass murderers?'

'I must confess, Mr O'Reilly, that it was one of my men who threw the first punch. But before we go any further, what would you like to drink?'

'I don't think Charles will have my favourite brew,' said Dollar Bill, turning to face the butler.

'I fear the Guinness is canned and not on tap, sir. If I had been given a little more notice . . .' Dollar Bill bowed again and the butler disappeared.

'Don't you think I'm entitled to know what this is all about, Mr Hutchins? After all . . .'

'You are indeed, Mr O'Reilly. The truth is, the government is in need of your services, not to mention your expertise.'

'I didn't realise that Clintonomics had resorted to forgery to help balance the budget deficit,' said Dollar Bill as the butler returned with a large glass of Guinness.

'Not quite as drastic as that, but every bit as demanding,' said Hutchins. 'But perhaps we should have a little dinner before I go into any details. I fear it's been a long day for you.' Dollar Bill nodded and followed the Deputy Director through to a small dining room, where the table had been set for two. The butler held a chair back for Dollar Bill, and when he was comfortably seated asked, 'How do you like your steak done, sir?'

'Is it sirloin or entrecôte?' asked Dollar Bill.

'Sirloin.'

'If the meat is good enough, tell the chef to put a candle under it – but only for a few moments.'

'Excellent, sir. Yours, Mr Hutchins, will I presume be well done?'

Dexter Hutchins nodded, feeling the first round had definitely gone to Dollar Bill.

'I'm enjoying this charade enormously,' said Dollar Bill, taking a gulp of Guinness. 'But I'd like to know what the prize is, should I be fortunate enough to win.'

'You might equally well be interested to know what the forfeit will be if you are unfortunate enough to lose.'

'I should have realised this had to be too good to last.'

'First, allow me to fill you in with a little background,' said Dexter Hutchins as a lightly grilled steak was placed in front of his guest. 'On May 25th this year, a well-organised group of criminals descended on Washington and carried out one of the most ingenious crimes in the history of this country.'

'Excellent steak,' said Dollar Bill. 'You must give my compliments to the chef.'

'I certainly will, sir,' said Charles, who was hovering behind his chair.

'This crime consisted of stealing from the National Archives, in broad daylight, the Declaration of Independence, and replacing it with a brilliant copy.'

Dollar Bill looked suitably impressed, but felt it would be unwise to comment at this stage.

'We have the names of several people involved in that crime, but we cannot make any arrests for fear of making those who are now in possession of the Declaration aware that we might be after them.'

'And what's this got to do with me?' asked Dollar Bill, as he devoured another succulent piece of meat.

'We thought you might be interested to know who had financed the entire operation, and is now in possession of the Declaration of Independence.'

Until that moment, Dollar Bill had learned nothing new, but he had long wanted to know where the document had ended up. He had never believed Angelo's tale of 'in private hands, an eccentric collector'. He put his knife and fork down and stared across the table at the

Deputy Director of the CIA, who had at last captured his attention.

'We have reason to believe that the Declaration of Independence is currently in Baghdad, in the personal possession of Saddam Hussein.'

Dollar Bill's mouth opened wide, although he remained silent for some considerable time. 'Is there no longer honour among thieves?' he finally said.

'There still could be,' said Hutchins, 'because our only hope of returning the parchment to its rightful home rests in the hands of a small group who are willing to risk their lives by switching the document, in much the same way as the criminals did originally.'

'If I had known . . .' Dollar Bill paused. 'How can I help?' he asked quietly.

'At this moment, we are in urgent need of a perfect copy of the original. And we believe you are the only person who is capable of producing one.'

Dollar Bill knew exactly where there was a perfect copy, hanging on a wall in New York, but couldn't admit as much without bringing on himself even greater wrath than Mr Hutchins was capable of.

'You made mention of a prize,' said Dollar Bill.

'And a forfeit,' said Dexter Hutchins. 'The prize is that you remain here at our West Coast safe house, in what I think you will agree are pleasant surroundings. While you are with us, you will produce a counterfeit of the Declaration that would pass an expert's eye. If you achieve that, you will go free, with no charges preferred against you.'

'And the forfeit?'

'After coffee has been served you will be released and allowed to leave whenever you wish.'

'Released,' repeated Dollar Bill in disbelief, 'and allowed to leave whenever I wish?'

'Yes,' said the Deputy Director.

'Then why shouldn't I just enjoy the rest of this excellent meal, return to my humble establishment in Fairmont, and forget we ever met?'

The Deputy Director removed an envelope from an inside pocket. He extracted four photographs and pushed them across the table. Dollar Bill studied them. The first was of a girl aged about seventeen lying on a slab in a morgue. The second was of a middle-aged man huddled foetus-like in the boot of a car. The third was of a heavily-built man dumped by the side of a road. And the fourth was of an older, distinguished-looking man. A broken neck was all the four of them had in common. Dollar Bill pushed the photos back across the table.

'Four corpses. So what?'

'Sally McKenzie, Rex Butterworth, Bruno Morelli, and Dr T. Hamilton McKenzie. And we have every reason to believe someone out there is planning the same happy ending for you.'

Dollar Bill speared the last pea left on his plate and downed the final drop of Guinness. He paused for a moment as if searching for inspiration.

'I'll need paper from Bremen, pens from a museum in Richmond, Virginia, and nine shades of black ink that can be made up for me by a firm in Cannon Street, London EC4.'

'Anything else?' asked Dexter Hutchins once he had finished writing down Dollar Bill's shopping list on the back of the envelope.

'I wonder if Charles would be kind enough to bring me another large Guinness. I have a feeling it may be my last for some considerable time.'

23

BERTIL PEDERSSON, the chief engineer of Svenhalte AC, was at the factory gate in Kalmar to greet Mr Riffat and Mr Bernstrom when the two men arrived that morning. He had received a fax from the United Nations the previous day confirming their flight times to Stockholm, and had checked with the arrivals desk at the airport to be informed that their plane had touched down only a few minutes late.

As they stepped out of their car, Mr Pedersson came forward, shook hands with both men and introduced himself.

'We are pleased to meet you at last, Mr Pedersson,' said the shorter of the two men, 'and grateful to you for making the time to see us at such short notice.'

'Well, to be frank with you, Mr Riffat, it came as quite a surprise to us when the United Nations lifted the restrictions on Madame Bertha.'

' "Madame Bertha"?'

'Yes, that is how we at the factory refer to the safe. I promise you, gentlemen, that despite your neglect, she has been a good girl. Many people have come to admire her, but nobody touches,' Mr Pedersson laughed. 'But I feel sure that after such a long journey you will want to see her for yourself, Mr Riffat.'

The short, dark-haired man nodded, and they both

accompanied Pedersson as he led them across the yard.

'You responded most quickly to the UN's sudden change of heart, Mr Riffat.'

'Yes, our leader had given orders that the safe should be delivered to Baghdad the moment the embargo was lifted.'

Pedersson laughed again. 'I fear that may not be so easy,' he said once they reached the other side of the yard. 'Madame Bertha was not built for speed, as you are about to discover.'

The three men continued to walk towards a large, apparently derelict building, and Pedersson strode through an opening where there must once have been a door. It was so dark inside that the two foreigners were unable to see more than a few feet in front of them. Pedersson switched on a single light, which was followed by what sounded like the sigh of an unrequited lover.

'Mr Riffat, Mr Bernstrom, allow me to introduce you to Madame Bertha.' The two men stared at the massive structure that stood majestically in the middle of the old warehouse floor.

'Before I make a formal introduction,' Pedersson continued, 'first let me tell you Madame Bertha's vital statistics. She is nine feet tall, seven feet wide and eight feet deep. She is also thicker skinned than any politician, about six inches of solid steel to be precise, and she weighs over five tons. She was built by a specialist designer, three craftsmen and eight engineers. Her gestation from conception to delivery was eighteen months. But then,' he whispered, 'to be fair, she is almost the size of an elephant. I lower my voice only because she can hear every word I say, and I have no wish to offend her.'

Mr Pedersson did not see the puzzled looks that came over the faces of his two visitors. 'But, gentlemen, you have only seen her exterior, and I can promise you that what she has to offer is more than skin deep.

'First, I must tell you that Madame Bertha will not allow anyone to enter her without a personal introduction. She is, gentlemen, not a promiscuous lady, despite what you may have been told about the Swedes. She requires to know three things about you before she will consider revealing her innermost parts.'

Although the two guests remained puzzled as to what he meant, they did not interrupt Mr Pedersson's steady flow.

'And so, gentlemen, to begin with you must study Bertha's chest. You will observe three red lights above three small dials. By knowing the six-number code on all three dials, you will be able to turn one of the lights from red to green. Allow me to demonstrate. First number to the right, second to the left, third to the right, fourth to the left, fifth to the right, sixth to the left. The first number for the first dial is 2, the second is 8, the third zero, the fourth 4, the fifth 3 and the sixth 7. 2-8-0-4-3-7.'

'The date of Sayedi's birthday,' said the tall, fair-haired visitor.

'Yes, I worked that one out, Mr Bernstrom,' said Pedersson. 'The second,' he said, turning his attention to the middle dial, 'is 1-6-0-7-7-9.' He turned the final number to the left.

'The day Sayedi became President.'

'We also managed that one, Mr Riffat. But I confess the third sequence fooled me completely. No doubt you will know what our client has planned for that particular day.' Mr Pedersson began twirling the third dial: 0-4-0-7-9-3.

Pedersson looked hopefully towards Mr Bernstrom, who shrugged his shoulders. 'I've no idea,' he lied.

'You will now note, gentlemen, that after entering the correct figures on all three dials, only one of Madame Bertha's lights has turned green, while two still remain obstinately red. But now that you have discovered her three codes, she will consider a more personal relationship. You will observe that below the three dials there is painted a small white square about the size of your hand. Watch carefully.' Pedersson took a pace forward and placed his right hand firmly on the white square. He left it there for several seconds, until the second light turned green.

'Even when she knows your palm print, she still won't open her heart. Not until I have spoken to her. If you look even more closely, gentlemen, you will see that the white square conceals a thin wire mesh, which houses a voice activator.' Both men stepped forward to look.

'At the present time, Bertha is programmed to react only to my vocal cords. It doesn't matter what I say, because as soon as she recognises the voice, the third light will turn green. But she will not even consider listening to me unless the first two lights are already green.'

Pedersson stepped forward and placed his lips opposite the wire mesh. 'Two gentlemen have come from America to see you, and desire to know what you look like inside.'

Even before he had finished the sentence, the third red light had flicked to green, and a noisy unclamping sound could be heard.

'Now, gentlemen, we come to the part of the demonstration of which my company is particularly proud. The door, which weighs over a ton, is nevertheless capable of being opened by a small child. Our company has developed a system of phosphor-bronze bearings that are a decade ahead of their time. Please, Mr Riffat, why don't you try for yourself?'

The shorter man stepped forward, gripped the handle of the safe firmly, and pulled. All three lights immediately turned red, and a noisy clamping sound began again.

Pedersson chuckled. 'You see, Mr Riffat, unless Madame Bertha knows you personally, she clams up and sends you back to the red-light district.' He laughed at a joke his guests suspected he had told many times before. 'The hand that opens the safe,' he continued, 'must be the same one that passed the palm-print test. A good safety device, I think you'll agree.' Both men nodded in admiration as Pedersson quickly fiddled with the three dials, placed his hand on the square and then spoke to Madame Bertha. One by one the three lights dutifully turned from red to green.

'She is now prepared to let me, and me alone, open her up. So watch carefully. Although, as I said, the door weighs a ton, it can be opened with the gentlest persuasion, thus.'

Pedersson pulled back the ton of massive steel with no more exertion than he would have used to open the front door of his home. He jumped inside the safe and began walking around, first with his arms outstretched to show that he could not touch the sides while standing in the centre, and then with his hands above his head, showing he was unable to reach the roof. 'Do please enter, gentlemen,' he cried from inside.

The two men stepped up gingerly to join him.

'In this case, three is not a crowd,' said Pedersson, laughing again. 'And you will be happy to discover that it is impossible for me to get myself locked in.' He gripped the handle on the inside of the safe and pulled the great door shut.

Two of the occupants did not find this part of the experiment quite so appealing.

'You see, gentlemen,' continued Pedersson, who could not hide the satisfaction in his voice, 'Bertha cannot lock herself again unless it is my hand on the outside handle.' With one small push, the door swung open and Pedersson stepped out, closely followed by his two customers.

'I once had to spend an evening inside her before the system was perfected – a sort of one-night stand, you might call it,' said Pedersson. He laughed even louder as he pushed the door back in place. The three lights immediately flashed to red and the clamps noisily closed in place.

He turned to face them. 'So, gentlemen, you have been introduced to Madame Bertha. Now, if you would be kind enough to accompany me back to my office, I will present you with a delivery note and, more important, Bertha's bible.'

As they returned across the yard, Pedersson explained to his two visitors that the book of instructions had been treated by the company as top secret. They had produced one in Swedish, which the company retained in its own safe, and another in Arabic, which Pedersson said he would be happy to hand over to them.

'The bible itself is 108 pages in length, but simple enough to understand if you are an engineer with a first-class honours degree.' He laughed again. 'We Swedish are a thorough race.'

Neither of the men felt able to disagree with him.

'Will you require anyone to accompany Madame Bertha on her journey?' Pedersson asked, his eyes expressing hope.

'No, thank you,' came back the immediate reply. 'I think we can handle the problem of transport.'

'Then I have only one more question for you,' Pedersson said, as he entered his office. 'When do you plan to take her away?'

'We hoped to collect the safe this afternoon. We understood from the fax you sent to the United Nations that your company has a crane that can lift the safe, and a trolley on which it can be moved from place to place.'

'You are right in thinking we have a suitable crane, and a trolley that has been specially designed to carry Madame Bertha on short journeys. I am also confident I can have everything ready for you by this afternoon. But that doesn't cover the problem of transport.'

'We already have our own vehicle standing by in Stockholm.'

'Excellent, then it is settled,' said Mr Pedersson. 'All I need to do in your absence is to programme out my hand and voice so that she can accept whoever you select to take my place.' Pedersson looked forlorn for a second time. 'I look forward to seeing you again this afternoon, gentlemen.'

'I'll be coming back on my own,' said Riffat. 'Mr Bernstrom will be returning to America.'

Pedersson nodded and watched the two men climb into their car before he walked slowly back to his office. The phone on his desk was ringing.

He picked it up, said, 'Bertil Pedersson speaking,' and listened to the caller's request. He placed the receiver on his desk and ran to the window, but the car was already out of sight. He returned to the phone. 'I am so sorry, Mr Al Obaydi,' said Pedersson, 'the two gentlemen who came to see the safe have just this moment left, but Mr Riffat will be returning this afternoon to take her away. Shall I let him know you called?'

Al Obaydi put the phone down in Baghdad, and began to consider the implications of what had started out as a routine call.

As Deputy Ambassador to the UN, it was his responsibility to keep the sanctions list up to date. He had hoped to pass on the file within a week to his as-yet-unappointed successor.

In the past two days, despite phones that didn't connect and civil servants who were never at their desks – and even when they were, were too terrified to answer the most basic questions – he was almost in a position to complete the first draft of his report.

The problem areas had been: agricultural machinery, half of which the UN Sanctions Committee took for granted was military equipment under another name; hospital supplies, including pharmaceuticals, on which the UN accepted most of their requests; and food, which they were allowed to purchase – although most of the produce that came across the border seemed to disappear on the black market long before it reached the Baghdad housewife.

A fourth list was headed 'miscellaneous items', and included among these was a massive safe which, when Al Obaydi checked its measurements, turned out to be almost the size of the room he was presently working in. The safe, an internal report confirmed, had been ordered before the planned liberation of the Nineteenth Province, and was now sitting in a warehouse in Kalmar, waiting to be collected. Al Obaydi's boss at the UN had confessed privately that he was surprised that the Sanctions Committee had lifted the embargo on the safe, but this did not deter him from assuring the Foreign Minister that they had only done so as a result of his painstaking negotiating skills.

Al Obaydi sat at his laden desk for some time, considering what his next move should be. He wrote a short list of headings on the notepad in front of him:

1 M.o.I.
2 State Security
3 Deputy Foreign Minister
4 Kalmar

Al Obaydi glanced at the first heading, M.o.I. He had remained in contact with a fellow student from London University days who had risen to Permanent Secretary status at the Ministry of Industry. Al Obaydi felt his old friend would be able to supply the information he required without suspecting his real motive.

He dialled the Permanent Secretary's private number, and was delighted to find that someone was at his desk.

'Nadhim, it's Hamid Al Obaydi.'

'Hamid, I heard you were back from New York. The rumour is that you've got what remains of our embassy in Paris. But one can never be sure about rumours in this city.'

'For once, they're accurate,' Al Obaydi told his friend.

'Congratulations. So, what can I do for you, Your Excellency?'

Al Obaydi was amused that Nadhim was the first person to address him by his new title, even if he was being sarcastic.

'UN sanctions.'

'And you claim you're my friend?'

'No, it's just a routine check. I've got to tie up any loose ends for my successor. Everything's in order as far as I can tell, except I'm unable to find out much about a gigantic safe that was made for us in Sweden. I know we've paid for it, but I can't discover what is happening about its delivery.'

'Not this department, Hamid. The responsibility was taken out of our hands about a year ago after the file was marked "High Command", which usually means for the President's personal use.'

'But someone must be responsible for a movement order from Kalmar to Baghdad,' said Al Obaydi.

'All I know is that I was instructed to pass the file on to our UN office in Geneva, as we don't have an embassy in Oslo. I'm surprised you didn't know that, Hamid. More your department than mine, I would have thought.'

'Then I'll have to get in touch with Geneva and find out what they're doing about it,' said Al Obaydi, not adding that New York and Geneva rarely informed each other of anything they were up to. 'Thanks for your help, Nadhim.'

'Any time. Good luck in Paris, Hamid. I'm told the women are fabulous, and despite what you hear, they like Arabs.'

Al Obaydi put the phone down and stared at the list on his pad. He took even longer deciding if he should make the second call.

The correct course of action with the information he now possessed would be to contact Geneva, alert the Ambassador of his suspicions and let Saddam's half-brother once again take the praise for something he himself had done the work on. He checked his watch. It was midday in Switzerland. He asked his secretary to get Barazan Al-Tikriti on the phone, knowing she would log every call. He waited for several minutes before a voice came on the line.

'Can I speak to the Ambassador?' he asked politely.

'He's in a meeting, sir,' came back the inevitable reply. 'Shall I disturb him?'

'No, no, don't bother. But would you let him know that Hamid Al Obaydi called from Baghdad, and ask him if he would be kind enough to return my call.'

'Yes, sir,' said the voice, and Al Obaydi replaced the phone. He had carried out the correct procedure.

He opened the sanctions file on his desk and scribbled on the bottom of his report: 'The Ministry of Industry have sent the file concerning this item direct to Geneva. I phoned our Ambassador there, but was unable to make contact with him. Therefore, I cannot make any progress from this end until he returns my call. Hamid Al Obaydi.'

Al Obaydi considered his next move extremely carefully. If he decided to do anything, his actions must once again appear on the surface to be routine, and well within his accepted brief. Any slight deviation from the norm in a city that fed on rumour and paranoia, and it would be him who would end up dangling from a rope, not Saddam's half-brother.

Al Obaydi looked down at the second heading on his notepad. He buzzed his secretary and asked her to get General Saba'awi Al-Hassan, Head of State Security, on the line. The post was one that had been held by three different people in the last seven months. The General was available immediately, there being more Generals than Ambassadors in the Iraqi regime.

'Ambassador, good morning. I've been meaning to call you. We ought to have a talk before you take up your new appointment in Paris.'

'My thoughts exactly,' said Al Obaydi. 'I have no idea who we still have representing us in Europe. It's been a long time since I served in that part of the world.'

'We're a bit thin on the ground, to be honest. Most of our best people have been expelled, including the so-called students whom we've always been able to rely on in the past. Still, not a subject to be discussed over the phone. When would you like me to come and see you?'

'Are you free between four and five this afternoon?'

There was a pause before the General said, 'I could be with you around four, but would have to be back in my office by five. Do you think that will give us enough time?'

'I feel sure you'll be able to brief me fully in that period, General.' Al Obaydi put the phone down on another routine call.

He stared at the third name on the list, one he feared might prove a little harder to bluff.

He spent the next few minutes rehearsing his questions before dialling an internal number. A Miss Saib answered the phone.

'Is there a particular subject you wish to raise with the Deputy Foreign Minister?' she asked.

'No,' replied Al Obaydi, 'I'm phoning at his specific request. I'm due for a little leave at the end of the week, and the Deputy Foreign Minister made it clear he wished to brief me before I take up my new post in Paris.'

'I'll come back to you with a time as soon as I've had a chance to discuss your request with the Minister,' Miss Saib promised.

Al Obaydi replaced the phone. Nothing to raise any suspicions there. He looked back at his pad and added a question mark, two arrows and another word to his list.

Kalmar ← ? → Geneva

Some time in the next forty-eight hours, he was going to have to decide which direction he should take.

The first question Kratz put to Scott on the journey from Kalmar to Stockholm was the significance of the numbers 0-4-0-7-9-3. Scott snapped out of a daydream where he was rescuing Hannah on a white charger, and returned to the real world, which looked a lot less promising.

'The fourth of July,' he responded. 'What better day could Saddam select to humiliate the American people, not to mention a new President.'

'So now at least we know when our deadline is,' said Kratz.

'Yes, but we've only been left with eleven days,' replied Scott. 'One way or the other.'

'Still, we've got Madame Bertha,' said Kratz, trying to lighten the mood.

'True,' said Scott. 'And where do you intend to take her on her first date?'

'All the way,' said Kratz. 'That is to say, Jordan, which is where I'm expecting you to join up with us again. In fact, my full team is already in Stockholm waiting to pick her up before they begin the journey to Baghdad. All the paperwork has been sorted out for us by Langley, so there should be no hold-ups on the way. Our first problem will be crossing the Jordanian border, but as we have all the requisite documents demanded by the UN, a few extra dollars supplied to the right customs official should ensure that his stamping hand lands firmly on the correct page of all our passports.'

'How much time have you allocated for the journey to Jordan?' Scott asked, remembering his own tight schedule.

'Six or seven days, eight at the outside. I've got a six-man team, all with considerable field experience. None of them will have to drive for more than four hours at a time without then getting sixteen hours' rest. That way there will be no need to stop at any point, other than to fill up with petrol.' They passed a sign indicating ten kilometres to Stockholm.

'So I've got a week,' said Scott.

'Yes, and we must hope that that's enough time for Bill O'Reilly to complete a perfect new copy of the Declaration,' said Kratz.

'It ought to be a lot easier for him a second time,' said Scott. 'Especially as every one of his requests was dealt with within hours of his asking. They even flew over nine shades of black ink from London on Concorde the next morning.'

'I wish we could put Madame Bertha on Concorde.'

Scott laughed. 'Tell me more about your back-up team.'

'The best I've ever had,' said Kratz. 'All of them have had front-line experience in several official and unofficial wars. Five Israelis and one Kurd.'

Scott raised an eyebrow.

'Few people realise,' continued Kratz, 'that Mossad has an Arab section, not large in numbers, but once we've trained them, only the Gurkhas make better killers. The test will be if you can spot which one he is.'

'How many are coming over the border with us?'

'Only two. We can't afford to make it look like an army. One engineer and a driver. At least, that's how they'll be described on the manifest, but they only have one job description as far as I'm concerned, and that's to get you into Baghdad and back out with the Declaration in the shortest possible time.'

Scott looked straight ahead of him. 'And Hannah?' he said simply.

'That would be a bonus if we got lucky, but it's not part of my brief. I consider the chances of your even seeing her are remote,' he said as they passed a 'Welcome to Stockholm' sign.

Scott began thumping Bertha's bible up and down on his knees. 'Careful with that,' said Kratz. 'It still needs to be translated, otherwise you won't know how to go about a proper introduction to the lady. After all, it will only be your palm and your voice she'll be opening her heart to.'

Scott glanced down at the 108-page book and wondered how long it would take him to master its secrets, even after it had been translated into English.

Kratz suddenly swung right without warning and drove down a deserted street that ran parallel to a disused railway line. All Scott could see ahead of him was a tunnel that looked as if it led nowhere.

When he was a hundred yards from the entrance, Kratz checked in his rear-view mirror to see if anyone was following them. Satisfied they were alone, he flashed his headlights three times. A second later, from what appeared to be the other end of a black hole, he received the same response. He slowed down and drove into the tunnel without his lights on. All Scott could now see was a torch indicating where they should pull up.

Kratz followed the light and came to a halt in front of what appeared to be an old army truck. It was stationed just inside the far end of the tunnel.

He jumped out of the car and Scott quickly followed, trying to accustom himself to the half-light. Then he saw three men standing on each side of the vehicle. The man nearest them came to attention and saluted. 'Good morning, Colonel,' he said.

'Put your men at ease, Feldman, and come and meet Professor Bradley,' said Kratz. Scott almost laughed at the use of his academic title among these men, but there were no smiles on the faces of the six soldiers who came forward to meet him.

After Scott had shaken hands with each of them he took a walk round the truck. 'Do you really believe this old heap is capable of carrying Madame Bertha to Baghdad?' he asked Kratz in disbelief.

'Sergeant Cohen.'

'Sir,' said a voice in the dark.

'You're the trained mechanic. Why don't you brief Professor Bradley?'

'Yes, sir.' Another figure appeared out of the gloom. Scott couldn't see his features clearly, as he was covered in grease, but from his accent he would have guessed he had spent most of his life in London. 'The Heavy Expanded Mobile Tactical Truck, or HEMTT, was built in Wisconsin. She has five gears, four forward, one reverse. She can be used on all terrains in most weather conditions in virtually any country. She weighs twenty tons and can carry up to ten tons, but with that weight on board you cannot risk driving over thirty miles per hour. Any higher than that and she would be impossible to stop, even though if pushed she can top 120 miles per hour.'

'Thank you, Cohen. A useful piece of kit, I think you'll agree,' said Kratz, looking back at Scott. 'We've wanted one of these for years, and then suddenly you arrive on the scene and Uncle Sam offers us the prototype model overnight. But then, at a cost of nearly a million dollars of taxpayers' money, you'd expect the Americans to be choosy about who they loan one out to.'

'Would you care to join us for lunch, Professor?' asked the man who had been introduced as Feldman.

'Don't tell me the HEMTT cooks as well,' said Scott.

'No, sir, we have to rely on the Kurd for that. Aziz's speciality is hamburger and French fries. If you've never had the experience before, it can be quite tasty.'

The eight of them sat cross-legged on the ground, using the reverse side of a backgammon board as a table. Scott couldn't remember enjoying a burnt hamburger more. He was also glad of the chance to chat to the men he would be working with on the operation. Kratz began to talk through the different contingency plans they would have to consider once they had reached the Jordan–Iraq border. It didn't take more than a few minutes for Scott to realise how professional these men were, or to see their desire to be part of the final team. He grew confident that the operation was in good hands, and that Kratz's team had not been chosen at random.

After a third hamburger he was sorry when the Mossad Colonel reminded him he had a flight to catch. He rose and thanked the cook for a memorable meal.

'See you in Jordan, sir,' said Sergeant Cohen.

'See you in Jordan,' said Scott.

As Scott was being driven to the airport, he asked Kratz, 'How are you going to select the final two?'

'They'll decide for themselves. Nothing to do with me, I'm only their commanding officer.'

'What do you mean?'

'They're going to play round-robin backgammon on the way to Jordan. The two winners get a day trip to Baghdad, all expenses paid.'

'And the losers?'

'Get a postcard saying "Wish you were here".'

24

HANNAH GATHERED UP all the files that the Deputy Foreign Minister would require for his meeting with the Revolutionary Command Council.

By working hours that no one else knew existed, and completing tasks the Minister had never thought would get done, Hannah had quickly made herself indispensable. Whenever the Minister needed something, it was there on his desk: she could anticipate his every need, and never sought praise for doing so. But, despite all this, she rarely left the office during the day or the house at night, and certainly seemed to be no nearer to coming into contact with Saddam. The Ambassador's wife tried valiantly to help on the social side, and on one occasion she even invited a young soldier round to dinner. He was good looking, Hannah thought, and seemed to be pleasant enough, although he hardly opened his mouth all evening and left suddenly without a word. Perhaps she was unable to hide the fact that she no longer had any interest in men.

Hannah had sat in on several meetings with individual Ministers, even members of the Command Council, including Saddam's half-brother, the Iraqi Ambassador to the UN in Geneva, but she felt no nearer to Saddam himself than she had been when she lived in a cul-de-sac in Chalk Farm. She was becoming despondent, and began to fear that her frustration might become obvious for all to see. As an antidote she channelled her energies into generating reports on interdepartmental spending, and set up a filing system that would have been the envy of the mandarins in Whitehall. But one of the many things Mossad had taught her during her arduous days of training was always to be patient, and ready, because in time an opening would appear.

It was early on a Thursday morning, when most of the Minister's staff had begun their weekends, that the first opening presented itself. Hannah was typing up her notes from a meeting the Deputy Minister had had the previous day with the newly-appointed Head of Interest Section in Paris, a Mr Al Obaydi, when the call came through. Muhammad Saeed Al-Zahiaf, the Foreign Minister, wished to speak to his deputy.

A few moments later, the Deputy Minister came rushing out of his office, barking at Hannah to follow him. Hannah grabbed a notepad and chased after the Minister down the long passageway.

Although the Foreign Minister's office was only at the other end of the corridor, Hannah had never been inside it before. When she followed her Minister into the room, she was surprised to find how modern and dull it was, with only the panoramic view over the Tigris as compensation.

The Foreign Minister did not bother to rise, but hastily motioned his subordinate into a chair on the opposite side of the desk, explaining that the President had requested a full report on the subject they had discussed at the Revolutionary Council the previous evening. He went on to explain that his own secretary had gone home for the weekend, so Miss Saib should take down a record of their meeting.

Hannah could not believe the discussion that followed. Had she not been aware that she was listening to two Ministers who were loyal members of the Revolutionary Command Council, she would have dismissed their conversation as an outrageous piece of propaganda. The President's half-brother had apparently succeeded in stealing the Declaration of Independence from the National Archives in Washington, and the document was now nailed to a wall of the room in which the Council met.

The discussion concentrated on how the news of this triumph should be released to an astonished world, and the date that had been selected to guarantee the greatest media coverage. Details were also discussed as to which square in the capital the President should deliver his speech from before he publicly burned the document, and whether Peter Arnett or Bernard Shaw of CNN should be granted special access to film the President standing next to the parchment the night before the burning ceremony took place.

After two hours the meeting broke up and Hannah returned with the Deputy Minister to his office. Without so much as a glance in her direction, he ordered her to make a fair copy of the decisions that had been taken that morning.

It took Hannah the rest of the morning to produce a first draft, which the Minister read through immediately. After making a few changes and emendations, he told her to produce a final copy to be delivered to the Foreign Minister with a recommendation that it should, if it met with his approval, be sent on to the President.

As she walked home through the streets of Baghdad that evening, Hannah felt helpless. She wondered what she could possibly do to warn the Americans. Surely they were planning some counter-measures in order to try to recapture the Declaration, or would at least be preparing some form of retaliation once they knew the day that had been selected for the public burning.

Did they even know where it was at that moment? Had Kratz been informed? Had Mossad been called in to advise the Americans on the operation they had themselves been planning for the past year? Were they now trying to get in touch with her? What would Simon have expected her to do?

She stopped at a cigarette kiosk and purchased three postcards of Saddam Hussein addressing the Revolutionary Command Council.

Later, in the safety of her bedroom, she wrote the same message to Ethel Rubin, David Kratz and the Professor of Arabic Studies at London University. She hoped one of them would work out the significance of the date in the top right-hand corner and the little biro'd square full of stars she had drawn on the wall by the side of Saddam's head.

'What time is the flight for Stockholm expected to depart?' he asked.

'It shouldn't be long now,' said the girl behind the SAS desk at Charles de Gaulle. 'I'm afraid it's only just landed on its inward journey, so it's difficult for me to be more precise.'

Another opportunity to turn back, thought Al Obaydi. But following his meeting with the Head of State Security and, the next morning, with the Deputy Foreign Minister, he felt confident that they had both considered what he had told them no more than routine. Al Obaydi had dropped into the conversation the fact that he was due for some leave before taking up his new appointment in Paris.

After Al Obaydi had collected his luggage from the carousel, he deposited all the large cases in storage, retaining only one bulky briefcase. He then took a seat in the corner of the departure lounge and thought about his actions during the past few days.

The Head of State Security hadn't had a lot to offer. The truth – not that he was going to admit it – was that he had enough problems at home without worrying about what was going on abroad. He had supplied Al Obaydi with an out-of-date instruction book on what precautions any Iraqi citizen should take when in Europe, including not to shop at Marks and Spencers or to mix socially with foreigners, and an out-of-date collection of photographs of known Mossad and CIA agents active on the Continent. After looking through the photographs, Al Obaydi wouldn't have been surprised to find that most of them had long retired, and that some had even died peacefully in their beds.

The following day, the Deputy Foreign Minister had been courteous without being friendly. He had given him some useful tips about how to conduct himself in Paris, including which embassies would be happy to deal with him despite their official position, and which would not. When it came to the Jordanian Embassy itself and the Iraqi annexe, he gave Al Obaydi a quick briefing on the resident staff. He had left Miss Ahmed there to guarantee some sort of continuity. He described her as willing and conscientious, the cook as awful but friendly, and the driver as stupid but brave. His only guarded warning was to be wary of Abdul Kanuk, the Chief Administrator, a wonderful title which did not describe his true position, his only qualification being that he was a distant cousin of the President. The Deputy Foreign Minister was careful not to voice a personal opinion, but his eyes told Al Obaydi everything he needed to know. As he left, the

Minister's secretary, Miss Saib, had presented him with another file. This one turned out to be full of useful information about how to get by in Paris without many friends. Places where he would be made welcome and others he should avoid.

Perhaps Miss Saib should have listed Sweden as somewhere to avoid.

Al Obaydi felt little apprehension about the trip, as he had no intention of remaining in Sweden for more than a few hours. He had already contacted the chief engineer of Svenhalte AC, who assured him he had made no mention of his earlier call to Mr Riffat when he returned that afternoon. He was also able to confirm that Madame Bertha, as he kept calling the safe, was definitely on her way to Baghdad.

'Would passengers travelling to Stockholm . . .' Al Obaydi made his way through the departure lounge to the exit gate and, after his boarding card had been checked, was shown to a window seat in economy. This section of the journey would not be presented as a claim against expenses.

On the flight across northern Europe, Al Obaydi's mind drifted from his work in Baghdad back to the weekend, which he had spent with his mother and sister. It was they who had helped him make the final decision. His mother had no interest in leaving their comfortable little home on the outskirts of Baghdad, and even less in moving to Paris. So now Al Obaydi accepted that he could never hope to escape: his only future rested in trying to secure a position of power within the Foreign Ministry. He was in no doubt that he could now perform a service for the President that would make him indispensable in Saddam's eyes; it might even present him with the chance of becoming the next Foreign Minister. After all, the Deputy was due for retirement in a couple of years, and sudden promotion never surprised anyone in Baghdad.

When the plane landed at Stockholm, Al Obaydi disembarked, using the diplomatic channel to escape quickly.

The journey to Kalmar by taxi took just over three hours, and the newly-appointed Ambassador spent most of the time gazing aimlessly out of the grubby window, pondering the unfamiliar sight of green hills and grey skies. When the taxi finally came to a halt outside the works entrance of Svenhalte AC, Al Obaydi was greeted by the sight of a man in a long brown coat who looked as if he had been standing there for some time.

Al Obaydi noticed that the man had a worried expression on his face. But it turned to a smile the moment the Ambassador stepped out of the car.

'How agreeable to meet you, Mr Al Obaydi,' said the chief engineer in English, the tongue he felt they would both feel most comfortable in. 'My name is Pedersson. Won't you please come to my office?'

After Pedersson had ordered coffee – how nice to taste cappuccino again, Al Obaydi thought – his first question proved just how anxious he was.

'I hope we did not do wrong?'

'No, no,' said Al Obaydi, who had himself been put at ease by the chief engineer's gushing words and obvious anxiety. 'I assure you this is only a routine check.'

'Mr Riffat was in possession of all the correct documents, both from the UN and from your government.'

Al Obaydi was becoming painfully aware that he was dealing with a group of highly-trained professionals.

'You say they left here on Wednesday afternoon?' Al Obaydi asked, trying to sound casual.

'Yes, that is correct.'

'How long do you imagine it will take them to reach Baghdad?'

'At least a week, perhaps ten days in that old truck, if they make it at all.'

Al Obaydi looked puzzled. 'An old truck?'

'Yes, they came to pick up Madame Bertha in an old army truck. Though, I must confess, the engine had a good sound to it. I took some pictures for my album. Would you like to see them?'

'Pictures of the truck?' said Al Obaydi.

'Yes, from my window, with Mr Riffat standing by the safe. They didn't notice.'

Pedersson opened the drawer of his desk and took out several pictures. He pushed them across his desk with the same pride that another man might have displayed when showing a stranger snapshots of his family.

Al Obaydi studied the photographs carefully. Several of them showed Madame Bertha being lowered onto the truck.

'There is a problem?' asked Pedersson.

'No, no,' said Al Obaydi, and added, 'Would it be possible to have copies of these photographs?'

'Oh yes, please keep them, I have many,' said the chief engineer, pointing to the open drawer.

Al Obaydi picked up his briefcase, opened it and placed the pictures in a flap at the front before removing some photographs of his own.

'While I'm here, perhaps you could help me with one more small matter.'

'Anything,' said Pedersson.

'I have some photographs of former employees of the state, and it would be helpful if you were able to remember if any of them were among those who came to collect Madame Bertha.'

Once again, Pedersson looked unsure, but he took the photographs and studied each one at length. He repeated, 'No, no, no,' several times, until he came to one which he took longer over. Al Obaydi leaned forward.

'Yes,' said Pedersson eventually. 'Although it must have been taken some years ago. This is Mr Riffat. He has not put on any weight, but he has aged and his hair has turned grey. A very thorough man,' Pedersson added.

'Yes,' said Al Obaydi, 'Mr Riffat is a very thorough man,' he repeated as he glanced at the details in Arabic printed on the back of the photograph. 'It will be a great relief for my government to know that Mr Riffat is in charge of this particular operation.'

Pedersson smiled for the first time as Al Obaydi downed the last drop of his coffee. 'You have been most helpful,' the Ambassador said. He rose before adding, 'I feel sure my government will be in need of your services again in the future, but I would be obliged if you made no mention of this meeting to anyone.'

'Just as you wish,' said Pedersson as they walked back down to the yard. The smile remained on his face as he watched the taxi drive out of the factory gate, carrying off his distinguished customer.

But Pedersson's thoughts did not match his expression. 'All is not well,' he muttered to himself. 'I do not believe that gentleman feels Madame Bertha is in safe hands, and I am certain he is no friend of Mr Riffat.'

It surprised Scott to find that he liked Dollar Bill the moment he met him. It didn't surprise him that once he had seen an example of his work, he also respected him.

Scott landed in San Francisco seventeen hours after he had taken off from Stockholm. The CIA had a car waiting for him at the airport. He was driven quickly up into Marin County and deposited outside the safe house within the hour.

After snatching some sleep, Scott rose for lunch, hoping to meet Dollar Bill straight away, but to his disappointment the forger was nowhere to be seen.

'Mr O'Reilly takes breakfast at seven and doesn't appear again before dinner, sir,' explained the butler.

'And what does he do for sustenance in between?' asked Scott.

'At twelve, I take him a bar of chocolate and half a pint of water, and at six, half a pint of Guinness.'

After lunch, Scott read an update on what had been going on at the State Department during his absence, and then spent the rest of the afternoon in the basement gym. He staggered out of the session around five, nursing several aches and pains from excessive exercise and one or two bruises administered by the judo instructor.

'Not bad for thirty-six,' he was told condescendingly by the instructor, who looked as if he might have been only a shade younger himself.

Scott sat in a warm bath trying to ease the pain as he turned the pages of Madame Bertha's bible. The document had already been translated by six Arabic scholars from six universities within fifty miles of where he was soaking. They had been given two non-consecutive chapters each. Dexter Hutchins had not been idle since his return.

When Scott came down for dinner, still feeling a little stiff, he found Dollar Bill standing with his back to the fire in the drawing room, sipping a glass of water.

'What would you like to drink, Professor?' asked the butler.

'A very weak shandy,' Scott replied before introducing himself to Dollar Bill.

'Are you here, Professor, out of choice, or were you simply arrested for drunk driving?' was Dollar Bill's first question. He had obviously decided to give Scott just as hard a time as the judo instructor.

'Choice, I fear,' replied Scott with a smile.

'From such a reply,' said Dollar Bill, 'I can only deduce you teach a dead subject or one that is no use to living mortals.'

'I teach Constitutional Law,' Scott replied, 'but I specialise in Logic.'

'Then you manage to achieve both at once,' said Dollar Bill as Dexter Hutchins entered the room.

'I'd like a gin and tonic, Charles,' said Dexter as he shook Scott's hand warmly. 'I'm sorry I didn't catch up with you earlier, but those guys in Foggy Bottom haven't been off the phone all afternoon.'

'There are many reasons to be wary of your fellow creatures,' Dollar Bill observed, 'and by asking for a gin and tonic, Mr Hutchins has just demonstrated two of them.'

Charles returned a moment later carrying a shandy and a gin and tonic on a silver tray, which he offered to Scott and the Deputy Director.

'In my university days, logic didn't exist,' said Dollar Bill after Dexter Hutchins had suggested they go through to dinner. 'Trinity College, Dublin would have no truck with the subject. I can't think of a single occasion in Irish history when any of my countrymen have ever relied on logic.'

'So what did you study?' asked Scott.

'A lot of Fleming, a little of Joyce, with a few rare moments devoted to Plato and Aristotle, but I fear not enough to engage the attention of any member of the board of examiners.'

'And how is the Declaration coming on?' asked Dexter, as if he hadn't been following the conversation.

'A stickler for the work ethic is our Mr Hutchins,

Professor,' said Dollar Bill as a bowl of soup was placed in front of him. 'Mind you, he *is* a man who would rely on logic to see him through. However, as there is no such thing in life as a free meal, I will attempt to answer my jailer's question. Today, I completed the text as originally written by Timothy Matlock, Assistant to the Secretary of Congress. It took him seventeen hours you know. I fear it has taken me rather longer.'

'And how long do you think it will take you to finish the names?' pressed Dexter.

'You are worse than Pope Julius II, forever demanding of Michelangelo how long it would take him to finish the ceiling of the Sistine Chapel,' said Dollar Bill as the butler removed the soup bowls.

'The names,' demanded Dexter. 'The names.'

'Oh, impatient and unsubtle man.'

'Shaw,' said Scott.

'I grow to like you more by the minute,' said Dollar Bill.

'The names,' repeated Dexter as Charles placed an Irish stew on the table. Dollar Bill immediately helped himself.

'Now I see why you are the *Deputy* Director,' said Dollar Bill. 'Do you not realise, man, that there are fifty-six names on the original document, each one of them a work of art in itself? Let me demonstrate to you, if I may. Paper, please, Charles. I require paper.'

The butler took a pad that lay next to the telephone and placed it by O'Reilly's side. Dollar Bill removed a pen from his inside pocket and began to scribble.

He showed his two dinner companions what he had written: 'Mr O'Reilly may have the unrestricted use of the company helicopter whenever he wishes.'

'What does that prove?' asked Dexter.

'Patience, Mr Hutchins, patience,' said Dollar Bill, as

he retrieved the piece of paper and signed it first with the signature of Dexter Hutchins, and then, changing his pen, wrote 'Scott Bradley'.

Once again he allowed them to study his efforts.

'But how . . .?' said Scott.

'In your case, Professor, it was easy. All I needed was the visitors' book.'

'But *I* didn't sign the visitors' book,' said Dexter.

'I confess it would be a strange thing for you to do when you are the Deputy Director,' said Dollar Bill, 'but, in your case nothing would surprise me. However, Mr Hutchins, you do have the infuriating habit of signing and dating the inside cover of any book you have purchased recently. I suspect in the case of first editions it will be the nearest you get to posterity.' He paused. 'But enough of this idle banter. You can both see for yourself the task I face.' Without warning, Dollar Bill folded his napkin, rose from the table leaving his half-finished stew, and walked out of the room. His companions jumped up and quickly followed him across to the west wing without another word being spoken. After they had climbed a small flight of stone steps they entered Dollar Bill's make-shift study.

On an architect's drafting board below a bright light rested the parchment. Both men walked across the room, stood over the board and studied the completed script. It had been inscribed above a large empty space covered in tiny pencil crosses that awaited the fifty-six signatures.

Scott stared in admiration at the work.

'But why didn't you . . .'

'Take up a proper occupation?' asked Dollar Bill, anticipating the question. 'And have ended up as a schoolmaster in Wexford, or perhaps have climbed to the dizzy heights of being a councillor in Dublin? No, sir, I would prefer the odd stint in jail rather than be considered by my fellow men as mediocre.'

'How many days before you have to leave us, young man?' Dexter Hutchins asked Scott.

'Kratz phoned this afternoon,' Scott replied, turning to face the Deputy Director. 'He says they caught the Trelleborg–Sassnitz ferry last night. They're now heading south, hoping to cross the Bosphorus by Monday morning.'

'Which means they should be at the border with Iraq by next Wednesday.'

'The perfect time of year to be sailing the Bosphorus,' said Dollar Bill. 'Especially if you hope to meet a rather remarkable girl when you reach the other side,' he added, looking up at Scott. 'So, I'd better have the Declaration finished by Monday, hadn't I, Professor?'

'At the latest,' said Hutchins as Scott stared down at the little Irishman.

25

WHEN AL OBAYDI ARRIVED back in Paris he collected his bags from the twenty-four-hour storage depot, then joined the queue for a taxi.

He gave the driver an address, without saying it was the Iraqi annexe to the Jordanian Embassy – one of the tips in Miss Saib's 'do's and don'ts' in Paris. He hadn't warned the staff at the embassy that he would be arriving that day. He wasn't officially due to take up his appointment for another fortnight, and he would have gone straight on to Jordan that evening if there had been a connecting flight. Once he had realised who Mr Riffat was, he knew he would have to get back to Baghdad as quickly as possible. By reporting direct to the Foreign Minister, he would have gone through the correct channels. This would protect his position, while at the same time guaranteeing that the President knew exactly who was responsible for alerting him to a possible attempt on his life, and which Ambassador, however closely related, had left several stones unturned.

The taxi dropped Al Obaydi outside the annexe to the embassy in Neuilly. He pulled his cases out of the back without any help from the driver, who remained seated obstinately behind the wheel of his car.

The embassy front door opened just an inch, and was then flung wide, and a man of about forty came running down the steps towards him, followed by two girls and a younger man.

'Excellency, Excellency,' the first man exclaimed. 'I am sorry, you must forgive me, we had no idea you were coming.' The younger man grabbed the two large cases and the girls took the remaining three between them.

Al Obaydi was not surprised to learn that the first man down the steps was Abdul Kanuk.

'We were told you would be arriving in two weeks' time, Excellency. We thought you were still in Baghdad. I hope you will not feel we have been discourteous.'

Al Obaydi made no attempt to interrupt the non-stop flow of sycophancy that came pouring out, feeling the man must eventually run out of steam. In any case, Kanuk was not a man to get on the wrong side of on his first day.

'Would Your Excellency like a quick tour of our quarters while the maid unpacks your bags?'

As there were questions Al Obaydi felt only this man could answer, he took advantage of the offer. Not only did he get the guided tour from the Chief Administrator, but he was also subjected to a stream of uninterrupted gossip. He stopped listening after only a few minutes; he had far more important things on his mind. He soon longed to be shown to his own room and left alone to be given a chance to think. The first flight to Jordan was not until the next morning, and he needed to prepare in his mind how he would present his findings to the Foreign Minister.

It was while he was being shown round what would shortly be his office looking out over a Paris that was turning from the half-light of dusk to the artificial light of night, that the Administrator said something Al Obaydi didn't quite catch. He felt he should have been paying closer attention.

'I'm sorry to say that your secretary is on holiday, Excellency. Like the rest of us, Miss Ahmed wasn't expecting you for another fortnight. I know she had planned to be back in Paris a week ahead of you, so that she would have everything ready by the time you arrived.'

'It's not a problem,' said Al Obaydi.

'Of course, you'll know Miss Saib, the Deputy Foreign Minister's secretary?'

'I came across Miss Saib when I was in Baghdad,' replied Al Obaydi.

The Chief Administrator nodded, and seemed to hesitate for a moment.

'I think I'll have a rest before dinner,' the Ambassador said, taking advantage of the temporary halt in an otherwise unending flow.

'I'll have something sent up to your room, Excellency. Would eight suit you?'

'Thank you,' said Al Obaydi, in an attempt to put an end to the conversation.

'Shall I place your passport and tickets in the safe, as I always did for the previous Ambassador?'

'A good idea,' said Al Obaydi, delighted to have at last found a way of getting rid of the Chief Administrator.

Scott put the phone down and turned to face Dexter Hutchins, who was leaning back in the large leather chair at his desk, his hands clasped behind his head and a questioning look on his face.

'So where are they?' asked Dexter.

'Kratz wouldn't give me the exact location, for obvious reasons, but at his current rate of progress he feels confident they'll reach the Jordanian border within the next three days.'

'Then let's pray that the Iraqi Ministry of Industry is as inefficient as our experts keep telling us it is. If so, the advantage should be with us for at least a few more days. After all, we did move the moment sanctions were lifted, and until you showed up in Kalmar, Pedersson hadn't heard a peep out of anyone for the past two years.'

'I agree. But I worry that Pedersson might be the one weak link in Kratz's chain.'

'If you're going to take these sorts of risks, no plan can ever be absolutely watertight,' said Dexter.

Scott nodded.

'And if Kratz is less than three days from the border, you'll have to catch a flight for Amman on Monday night, assuming Mr O'Reilly has finished his signatures by then.'

'I don't think that's a problem any longer,' said Scott.

'Why? He still had a lot of names to copy when I last looked at the parchment.'

'It can't be that many,' said Scott, 'because Mr Mendelssohn flew in from Washington this morning in order to pass his judgement, and that seems to be the only opinion Bill is interested in.'

'Then let's go and see for ourselves,' said Dexter as he swung himself up out of his chair.

As they left the office and made their way down the corridor, Dexter asked, 'And how's Bertha's bible coming along? I turned a few pages of the introduction this morning and couldn't begin to get a grasp of why the bulbs turn from red to green.'

'Only one man knows Madame Bertha more intimately than I do, and at this moment he's pining away in Scandinavia,' said Scott as they climbed the stone steps to Dollar Bill's private room.

'I also hear that Charles has designed a special pair of trousers for you,' Dexter said.

'And they're a perfect fit,' replied Scott with a smile.

As they reached the top of the steps, Dexter was about to barge in when Scott put an arm on his shoulder.

'Perhaps we should knock? He might be . . .'

'Next you'll be wanting me to call him "sir".'

Scott grinned as Dexter knocked quietly, and when there was no reply, eased the door open. He crept in to see Mendelssohn stooping over the parchment, magnifying glass in hand.

'Benjamin Franklin, John Morton and George Clymer,' muttered the Conservator.

'I had a lot of trouble with Clymer,' said Dollar Bill, who was looking out of the window over the bay. 'It was the damn man's squiggles, which I had to complete in one flow. You'll find a couple of hundred of them in the waste-paper basket.'

'May we approach the bench?' asked Dexter. Dollar Bill turned and waved them in.

'Good afternoon, Mr Mendelssohn. I'm Dexter Hutchins, Deputy Director of the CIA.'

'Could you possibly be anything else?' asked Dollar Bill.

Dexter ignored the comment and asked Mendelssohn, 'What's your judgement, sir?'

Dollar Bill continued to stare out of the window.

'It's every bit as good as the copy we currently have on display at the National Archives.'

'You are most generous, sir,' said Dollar Bill, who turned round to face them.

'But I don't understand why you have spelt the word "British" correctly, and not with two *t*s as it was on the original,' said Mendelssohn, returning his attention to the document.

'There are two reasons for that,' said Dollar Bill as six suspicious eyes stared back at him. 'First, if the exchange is carried out successfully, Saddam will not be able to claim he still has his hands on the original.'

'Clever,' said Scott.

'And second?' asked Dexter, who remained suspicious of the little Irishman's motives.

'It will stop the Professor from bringing back this copy and trying to pass it off as the original.'

Scott laughed. 'You always think like a criminal,' he said.

'And you'd better be thinking like one yourself over the next few days, if you're going to get the better of Saddam Hussein,' said Dollar Bill as Charles entered the room, carrying a pint of Guinness on a silver tray.

Dollar Bill thanked Charles, removed his reward from the tray and walked to the far side of the room before taking the first sip.

'May I ask . . .?' began Scott.

'I once spilt the blessed nectar all over a hundred-dollar etching that I had spent some three months preparing.'

'So what did you do then?' asked Scott.

'I fear that I settled for second best, which caused me to end up in the slammer for another five years.' Even Dexter joined in the laughter. 'However, on this occasion I raise my glass to Matthew Thornton, the final signatory on the document. I wish him good health wherever he is, despite the damn man's *ts*.'

'So, am I able to take the masterpiece away now?' asked Scott.

'Not yet, young man,' said Dollar Bill. 'I fear you must suffer another evening of my company,' he added before placing his drink on the window ledge and returning to the document. 'You see, the one problem I have been fighting is time. In Mr Mendelssohn's judgement, the parchment has an 1830s feel about it. Am I right, sir?'

The Conservator nodded, and raised his arms as if

apologising for daring to mention such a slight blemish.

'So what can be done about that?' asked Dexter Hutchins.

Dollar Bill flicked on a switch and the Xenon lamps above his desk shone down on the parchment and filled the room with light, making it appear like a film set.

'By nine o'clock tomorrow morning the parchment will be nearer 1776. Even if, because you have failed to give me enough time, I miss perfection by a few years, I remain confident that there'll be no one in Iraq who'll be able to tell the difference, unless they are in possession of a Carbon 14 dating machine, and know how to use it.'

'Then we can only hope that the original hasn't already been destroyed,' said Dexter Hutchins.

'Not a chance,' said Scott.

'How can you be so confident?' asked Dexter.

'The day Saddam destroys that parchment, he will want the whole world to witness it. Of that I'm sure.'

'Then, I'm thinking a toast might be in order,' said the Irishman. 'That is, with my gracious host's permission.'

'A toast, Bill?' said the Deputy Director, sounding surprised. 'Who do you have in mind?' he asked suspiciously.

'To Hannah,' said the little Irishman, 'wherever she may be.'

'How did you know?' asked Scott. 'I've never mentioned her name.'

'No need to, when you write it on everything from the backs of envelopes to steaming windows. She must be a very special lady, Professor.' He raised his glass and repeated the words, 'To Hannah.'

The Chief Administrator sat and waited patiently until the maid had removed the Ambassador's dinner tray. He then closed his door at the other end of the corridor.

He waited for another two hours, until he felt certain all the embassy staff had gone to bed. Confident he would be the only one left awake, he crept back down to his office and looked up a telephone number in Geneva. He dialled the code slowly and deliberately. It rang for a long time before it was eventually answered.

'I need to speak to the Ambassador,' he whispered.

'His Excellency retired to bed some time ago,' said a voice. 'You'll have to call back in the morning.'

'Wake him. Tell him it's Abdul Kanuk in Paris.'

'If you insist.'

'I do insist.'

The Chief Administrator waited for some time before a sleepy voice eventually came on the line.

'This had better be good, Abdul.'

'Al Obaydi has arrived in Paris unannounced, and two weeks before he was expected.'

'You woke me in the middle of the night to tell me this?'

'But he didn't come direct from Baghdad, Excellency. He made a slight detour.'

'How can you be so sure?' said the voice, sounding a little more awake.

'Because I am in possession of his passport.'

'But he's on holiday, you fool.'

'I know. But why spend the day in a city not known for attracting tourists?'

'You're talking in riddles. If you've got something to tell me, tell me.'

'Earlier today, Ambassador Al Obaydi paid a visit to Stockholm, according to the stamp on his passport, but he returned to Paris the same evening. Not my idea of a holiday.'

'Stockholm . . . Stockholm . . . Stockholm . . .' repeated

the voice on the other end of the line, as if trying to register its significance. A pause, and then, 'The safe. Of course. He must have gone on to Kalmar to check on Sayedi's safe. What has he found out that he thought worth hiding from me, and does Baghdad know what he's up to?'

'I have no idea, Excellency,' said the Administrator. 'But I do know he's flying back to Baghdad tomorrow.'

'But if he's on holiday, why would he return to Baghdad so quickly?'

'Perhaps being the Head of Interest Section in Paris is not reward enough for him, Excellency. Could he have his eyes on some greater prize?'

There was a long pause before the voice in Geneva said, 'You did well, Abdul. You were right to wake me. I shall have to phone Kalmar first thing in the morning. First thing,' he repeated.

'You did promise, Excellency, should I once again manage to bring to your attention . . .'

Tony Cavalli waited until Martin had poured them both a drink.

'Arrested in a bar-room brawl,' said his father after he had listened to his son's report.

'Yes,' said Cavalli, placing a file on the table by his side, 'and what's more, he was sentenced to thirty days.'

'Thirty days?' said his father in disbelief. The old man paused before he added, 'What instructions have you given Laura?'

'I've put her on hold until July 15th, when Dollar Bill will be released,' Tony replied.

'So where have they locked him up this time? The county jail?'

'No. According to the records at the district court in

Fairmont, they've thrown him back into the state pen.'

'For being involved in a bar-room brawl,' said the older man. 'It doesn't make sense.' He stared up at the Declaration of Independence on the wall behind his desk and didn't speak again for some moments.

'Who have we got on the inside?'

Cavalli opened the file on the table by his side and extracted a single sheet of paper. 'One senior officer and six inmates,' he said, passing his research across, pleased to have anticipated his father's question.

The old man studied the list of names for some time before he began licking his lips. 'Eduardo Bellatti must be our best bet,' he said, looking up at his son. 'If I remember correctly, he was sentenced to ninety-nine years for blowing away a judge who once got in our way.'

'Correct, and what's more, he's always been happy to kill anyone for a packet of cigarettes,' said Tony. 'So, if he takes care of Dollar Bill before July 15th, it would also save us a quarter of a million dollars.'

'Something isn't quite right,' said his father as he toyed with a whisky, which he hadn't touched. 'Perhaps it's time to dig a little deeper,' he added, almost as if he was talking to himself. He checked down the list of names once again.

Al Obaydi woke early the following morning, restless to be on his way to Baghdad so that he could brief the Foreign Minister on everything he'd learned. Once he was back on Iraqi soil he would prepare a full, written report. He went over the outline again and again in his mind.

He would first explain to the Foreign Minister that, while he was carrying out a routine sanctions check, he had learned that the safe that had been ordered by the President was already on its way to Baghdad. On discovering this, he had become suspicious that an enemy of the state might be involved in an assassination attempt on the life of the President. Not being certain who could be trusted, he had used his initiative, and even his own time and money, to discover who was behind the plot. Within moments of his reporting the details to the Foreign Minister, Saddam was sure to find out whose responsibility the safe was and, more important, who had failed to take care of the President's well-being.

A tap on the door interrupted his thoughts. 'Come in,' he called, and a maid entered carrying a breakfast tray of two pieces of burnt toast and a cup of thick Turkish coffee. Once she had closed the door behind her, Al Obaydi rose, had a cold shower – not by choice – and dressed quickly. He then poured the coffee down the washbasin and ignored the toast.

The Ambassador left his room and walked down one flight of stairs to his office, where he found the Chief Administrator standing behind his desk. Had he been sitting in his chair a moment before?

'Good morning, Excellency,' he said. 'I hope you had a comfortable night.'

Al Obaydi was about to lose his temper, but Kanuk's next question took him by surprise.

'Have you been briefed on the bombings in Baghdad, Excellency?'

'What bombings?' asked Al Obaydi, not pleased to be wrong-footed.

'It seems that at two o'clock this morning the Americans launched several Tomahawk Missiles at Mukhbarat headquarters in the centre of the city.'

'And what was the result?' Al Obaydi asked anxiously.

'A few civilians were killed,' replied the Chief Administrator matter-of-factly, 'but you'll be glad to know that our beloved leader was not in the city at the time.'

'That is indeed good news,' said Al Obaydi. 'But it makes it even more imperative that I return to Baghdad immediately.'

'I have already confirmed your flight reservations, Excellency.'

'Thank you,' said Al Obaydi, staring out of the window at the Seine.

Kanuk bowed low. 'I will see that you are met at the airport when you return, Excellency, and that this time everything is fully prepared for your arrival. Meanwhile, I'll go and fetch your passport. If you'll excuse me.'

Al Obaydi sat down behind his desk. He wondered how long he would be merely Head of Interest Section in Paris once Saddam learned who had saved his life.

Tony dialled the number on his private line.

The phone was picked up by the Deputy Warden, who confirmed in answer to Cavalli's first question that he *was* alone. He listened to Cavalli's second question carefully before he replied.

'If Dollar Bill's anywhere to be found in this jailhouse, then he's better hidden than Leona Helmsley's tax returns.'

'But the county court files show him as being registered with you on the night of June 16th.'

'He may have been registered with us, but he sure never showed up,' said the voice on the other end of the line. 'And it doesn't take eight days to get from San Francisco County Court to here, unless they've gone back to chaining cons up and making them walk the whole way. Perhaps that wouldn't be such a bad idea,' he added with a nervous laugh.

Cavalli didn't laugh. 'Just be sure you keep your mouth shut and your ears open, and let me know the moment you hear anything,' was all he said before putting the phone back down.

Cavalli remained at his desk for an hour after his secretary had left, working out what needed to be done next.

26

THE SECOND EMERGENCY meeting between the Foreign Minister and his deputy took place on the Tuesday morning, again at short notice. This time it was an unexpected direct call from the President that had both Ministers rushing off to the palace.

All Hannah had been able to piece together from the several phone calls that had gone back and forth that morning was that at some point Saddam's half-brother had called from Geneva, and from that moment the Deputy Foreign Minister appeared to forget the report he was preparing on the American bombing of Mukhbarat headquarters. He fled from the room in a panic, leaving secret papers strewn all over his desk.

Hannah remained at her desk in the hope that she might pick up some more information as the day progressed. While both Ministers were at the palace, she continued to check through old files, aware that she now had enough material to fill several cabinets at Mossad headquarters, but no one to pass her findings on to.

The two Ministers returned from the palace in the late afternoon, and the Deputy Foreign Minister seemed relieved to find Miss Saib was still at her desk.

'I need to make a written report on what was agreed at the meeting this morning with the President,' he said, 'and I cannot overstress the importance of confidentiality in this matter. It would not be an exaggeration to suggest that if anything I am about to tell you became public knowledge, we could both end up in jail, or worse.'

'I hope, Minister,' said Hannah as she put her glasses back on, 'that I have never given you cause for concern in the past.'

The Minister stared across at her, and then began dictating at a rapid pace.

'The President invited the Foreign Minister and myself to a confidential meeting at the palace this morning – date this memo today. Barazan Al-Tikriti, our trusted Ambassador in Geneva, contacted the President during the night to warn him that, after weeks of diligent surveillance, he has uncovered a plot by a group of Zionists to steal a safe from Sweden and use it as a means of illegally entering Iraq. The safe was due for delivery to Baghdad following the lifting of an embargo under UN Security Council Resolution 661. The President has ordered that General Hamil be given the responsibility for dealing with the terrorists' – Hannah thought she saw the Deputy Foreign Minister shudder – 'while the Foreign Ministry has been asked to look into the role played in this particular conspiracy by one of its own staff, Hamid Al Obaydi.

'Our Ambassador in Geneva has discovered that Al Obaydi visited the engineering firm of Svenhalte AC in Kalmar, Sweden, on Monday June 28th, without being directed to do so by any of his superiors. During that visit he was informed of the theft of the safe and the fact that it was being transported to Baghdad. Following his trip to Kalmar, Al Obaydi stayed overnight at our Interest Section in Paris, when he would have had every opportunity to inform Geneva or Baghdad of the Zionist plot, but he made no attempt to do so.

'Al Obaydi left Paris the following morning and, although we know he boarded a flight to Jordan, he has not yet shown up at the border. The President has ordered that if Al Obaydi crosses any of our national frontiers, he should be arrested and taken directly to General Hamil at the headquarters of the Revolutionary Command Council.'

Hannah's pencil flew across the pages of her shorthand notebook as she tried to keep up with the Minister.

'The safe,' continued the Deputy Foreign Minister, 'is currently being transported aboard an old army truck, and is expected to arrive at the border with Jordan some time during the next forty-eight hours.

'All customs officers have received a directive to the effect that the safe is the personal property of the President, and therefore when it reaches the border it must be given priority to continue its journey on to Baghdad.

'Our Ambassador in Geneva, having had a long conversation with a Mr –' the Minister checked his notes '– Pedersson, is convinced that the group accompanying the safe are agents of the CIA, Mossad, or possibly even the British SAS. Like the President, the Ambassador feels the infiltrators' sole interest is in recovering the Declaration of Independence. The President has given orders that the document should not be moved from its place on the wall of the Council Chamber, as this could alert any internal agent to warn the terrorist group not to enter the country.

'Twenty of the President's special guards are already on their way to the border with Jordan,' continued the Minister. 'They will be responsible for monitoring the progress of the safe, and will report directly to General Hamil.

'Once the agents of the West have been apprehended

and thrown in jail, the world's press will be informed that their purpose was to assassinate the President. The President will immediately appear in public and on television, and will make a speech denouncing the American and Zionist warmongers. Sayedi believes that neither the Americans nor the Israelis will ever admit to the real purpose of their raid, but that they will be unable to deny the President's claim. Sayedi feels this whole episode can be turned into a public relations triumph, because if the assassination attempt is announced on the same day that the President publicly burns the Declaration of Independence, it will make it even harder for the Americans to retaliate.

'Starting tomorrow, the President requires a situation update every morning at nine and every evening at six. Both the Foreign Minister and myself are to report to him direct. If Al Obaydi is picked up, the President is to be informed immediately, whatever the time, night or day.'

Hannah's pencil hadn't stopped scribbling across her note pad for nearly twenty minutes. When the Deputy Minister finally came to an end, she tried to take in the full significance of the information she now possessed.

'I need one copy of this report drafted as quickly as possible, no further copies to be made, nothing put on tape, and all your shorthand notes must be shredded once the memo has been handed to me.' Hannah nodded as the Deputy Foreign Minister picked up the phone and dialled the internal number of his superior.

Hannah returned to her room and began typing up the dictation slowly, at the same time trying to commit the salient points to memory. Forty-five minutes later she placed a single copy of the report on the Minister's desk.

He read the script carefully, adding the occasional note in his own hand. When he was satisfied that the memo fully covered the meeting that had taken place that morning, he set off down the corridor to rejoin the Foreign Minister.

Hannah returned to her desk, aware that the team bringing the safe from Sweden were moving inexorably towards Saddam's trap. And if they had received her postcard . . .

When Al Obaydi landed in Jordan, he could not help feeling a sense of triumph.

Once he had passed through customs at Queen Alia airport and was out on the road, he selected the most modern taxi he could find. The old seventies Chevy had no air conditioning and showed 187,000 miles on the clock. He asked the driver to take him to the Iraqi border as quickly as possible.

The car never left the slow lane on its six-hour journey to the border, and because of the state of the roads Al Obaydi was unable to sleep for more than a few minutes at a time. When the driver eventually reached the highway, he still couldn't go much faster because of the oil that had been spilt from lorries carrying loads they had illegally picked up in Basra, to sell at four times the price in Amman. Loads that Al Obaydi had assured the United Nations Assembly time and again were a figment of the Western world's imagination. He also became aware of trucks travelling in the opposite direction that were full of food that he knew would be sold to black-marketeers, long before any of it reached Baghdad.

Al Obaydi checked his watch. If the driver kept going at this speed he wouldn't reach the border before the customs post closed at midnight.

* * *

When Scott landed at Queen Alia airport later that day and stepped on to the tarmac, the first thing that hit him was a temperature of ninety-five degrees. Even dressed in an open-neck shirt, jeans and sneakers, he felt roasted before he had reached the airport terminal. Once he'd entered the building, he was relieved to find it was air conditioned, and his one bag came up on the carousel just as quickly as it would have done in the States. He checked his watch and changed it to Central Eastern time.

The immigration officer hadn't seen many Swedish passports before, but as his father had been an engineer, he wished Mr Bernstrom a successful trip.

As Scott strolled through the green channel, he was stopped by a customs official who was chewing something. He instructed the foreigner to open his bulky canvas bag. After rummaging around inside, the only thing the officer showed any interest in was a long, thin cardboard tube that had been wedged along the bottom of the bag. Scott removed the cap on the end of the tube, pulled out the contents and unrolled a large poster, which was greeted by the official with such puzzled amazement that he even stopped chewing for a moment. He waved Scott through.

Once Scott had reached the main concourse, he walked out onto the road in search of a taxi. He studied the motley selection of cars that were parked by the side of the pavement. They made New York Yellow Cabs look like luxury limousines.

He instructed the driver parked at the front of the queue to take him to the Roman theatre in the centre of the city. The eleven-mile journey into Amman took forty minutes, and when Scott was dropped outside the third-century theatre he handed the driver two ten-dinar notes – enough, the experts at Langley had told him, to cover the cost of the trip. The driver pocketed the notes but did not smile.

Scott checked his watch. He was still well in time for the planned reunion. He walked straight past the ancient monument that was, according to his guidebook, well worth a visit. As instructed by Kratz, he then proceeded west for three blocks, occasionally having to step off the pavement into the road to avoid the bustling crowds. When he reached a Shell petrol station he turned right, leaving the noisy shoppers behind. He then took the second turning on the left, and after that another to the right. The roads became less crowded with locals and more full of potholes with each stride he took. Another left, followed by another right, and he found himself entering the promised cul-de-sac. At the end of the road, when he could go no further, he came to a halt outside a scrapyard. He smiled at the sight that greeted him.

By the time Al Obaydi reached the border, it was already pitch dark. All three lanes leading to the customs post were bumper to bumper with waiting lorries, covered with tarpaulins for the night. The taxi driver came to a halt at the barrier and explained to his passenger that he would have to hire an Iraqi cab once he was on the other side. Al Obaydi thanked the driver and gave him a handsome tip before going to the front of the queue outside the customs shed. A tired official gave him a languid look and told him the border was closed for the night. Al Obaydi presented his diplomatic passport and the official quickly stamped his visa and ushered him through, aware that there would be no little red notes accompanying such a document. Al Obaydi felt exhilarated as he strolled the mile between the two customs posts. He walked to the front of another queue, produced his passport once again, and received another smile from the customs officer.

'There is a car waiting for you, Ambassador,' was all the official said, pointing to a large limousine that was parked near the highway. A smiling chauffeur stood waiting. He touched the peak of his cap and opened the back door.

Al Obaydi smiled. The Chief Administrator must have warned them that he would be coming over the border late that night. He thanked the customs official, walked over to the highway and slipped into the back of the limousine. Someone else was already there, who also appeared to be waiting for him. Al Obaydi began to smile again, when suddenly an arm shot across his throat and threw him to the floor. His hands were pinned behind his back, and a pair of handcuffs clicked into place.

'How dare you?' shouted Al Obaydi. 'I am an Ambassador!' he screamed as he was hurled back up onto the seat. 'Don't you realise who I am?'

'Yes, I do,' came back the reply. 'And you're under arrest for treason.'

Scott had to admit that the HEMTT carrying Madame Bertha looked quite at home among the colourful collection of old American cars and lorries piled high on three sides of the scrapyard. He ran across to the truck and jumped up into the cab on the passenger side. He shook hands with Kratz, who seemed relieved to see him. When Scott saw who was seated behind the wheel, he said, 'Good to see you again, Sergeant Cohen. Am I to assume you play a mean game of backgammon?'

'Two doubles inside the board clinched it for me in the final game, Professor, though God knows how the Kurd even reached the semi-final,' Cohen said as he switched on the engine. 'And because he's a mate of mine, the others are all claiming I fixed the dice.'

'So where's Aziz now?' asked Scott.

'On the back with Madame Bertha,' said the Sergeant. 'Best place for him. Mind you, he knows the back streets of Baghdad like I know the pubs in Brixton, so he may turn out to be useful.'

'And the rest of the team?' asked Scott.

'Feldman and the others slipped over the border during the night,' said Kratz. 'They're probably in Baghdad waiting for us by now.'

'Then they'd better keep well out of sight,' said Scott, 'because after the bombing last Sunday, I suspect death might prove the least of their problems.'

Kratz offered no opinion as Sergeant Cohen eased the massive vehicle slowly out of the yard and onto the street; this time the roads became wider with each turning he took.

'Are we keeping to the plan that was agreed in Stockholm?' asked Scott.

'With two refinements,' said Kratz. 'I spent yesterday morning phoning Baghdad. After seven attempts, I got through to someone at the Ministry of Industry who knew about the safe, but it's the age-old problem with the Arabs: if they don't see the damn thing in front of their eyes, they don't believe it exists.'

'So our first stop will have to be the Ministry?' said Scott.

'Looks like it,' replied Kratz. 'But at least we know we've got something they want. Which reminds me, have you brought the one thing they don't want?'

Scott unzipped his bag and pulled out the cardboard tube.

'Doesn't look a lot to be risking your life for,' said Kratz as Scott slipped it back into his bag.

'And the second refinement?' asked Scott.

Kratz removed a postcard from his inside pocket and passed it over to Scott. A picture of Saddam Hussein addressing the Revolutionary Command Council stared back at him. A little biro'd square full of stars had been drawn in by the side of his head. Scott turned the card over and studied her unmistakable handwriting: 'Wish you were here.'

Scott didn't speak for several moments.

'Notice the date, did you?'

Scott looked at the top right-hand corner: 4.7.93.

'So, now we know where it is, and she's also confirmed exactly when Saddam intends to let the rest of the world into his secret.'

'Who's Ethel Rubin?' asked Scott. 'And how did you get your hands on the card?'

'The lady Hannah was billeted with in London. Her husband is Mossad's legal representative in England. He took the card straight to the embassy the moment it arrived and they sent it overnight in the diplomatic pouch. It reached our embassy in Amman this morning.'

Once they had reached the outskirts of the town, Scott began to study the barren terrain as the lorry continued its progress along the oil-covered, potholed roads.

'Sorry to be going so slowly, Professor,' said Cohen, 'but if I throw my brakes on with the road in this condition, Madame Bertha might travel another hundred yards before the wheels even have a chance to lock.'

Kratz went over every contingency he could think of as Cohen drove silently towards the border. The Mossad leader ended up by describing the layout of the Ba'ath headquarters once again.

'And the alarm system?' asked Scott when he had come to an end.

'All you have to remember is that the red buttons by

the light switches activate the alarm, but at the same time close all the exits.'

Scott nodded, but it was some time before he asked his next question. 'And Hannah?'

'Nothing's changed. My first task is to get you in and then back out with the original document. She still remains an unlikely bonus, although she obviously knows what's going on.'

Neither of them spoke again until Sergeant Cohen pulled off the highway into a large gravel layby packed with lorries. He parked the vehicle at an angle so that only the most inquisitive could observe what they were up to, then jumped out of the cab, pulled himself over the tailboard and grinned at the Kurd who was lounging against the safe. Between them they removed the tarpaulin that covered the massive structure as Scott and Kratz climbed up to join them in the back of the truck.

'What do you think, Professor?' asked Aziz.

'She hasn't lost any weight, that's for sure,' said Scott, as he tried to remember the nightly homework he had done in preparation for this single exam.

He stretched his fingers and smiled. All three bulbs above the white square were red. He first turned all three dials to a code that only he and a man in Sweden were aware of. He then placed his right hand on the white square, and left it there for several seconds. He leaned forward, put his lips up against the square and spoke softly. 'My name is Andreas Bernstrom. When you hear this voice, and only this voice, you will unlock the door.' Scott waited as the other three looked on in bemused silence. He then swivelled the dials. All three bulbs remained red.

'Now we discover if I understood the instructions,' said Scott. He bit his lip and advanced again. Once more he twiddled the dials, but this time to the numbers selected by Saddam, ending with 0-4-0-7-9-3. The first light went from red to green. Aziz smiled. Scott placed the palm of his hand in the white square and left it there for several seconds. The second light switched to green.

Scott heard Kratz sigh audibly as he stepped forward again. He put his lips to the white square so they just touched the thin wire mesh. 'My name is Andreas Bernstrom. It's now time for the safe to –' The third light turned green even before he had completed the sentence. Cohen offered up a suppressed cheer.

Scott grasped the handle and pulled. The ton of steel eased open.

'Not bad,' said Cohen. 'What do you do for an encore?'

'Use you as a guinea-pig,' said Scott. 'Why don't you try and close the safe, Sergeant?'

Cohen took a step forward and with both hands shoved the door closed. The three bulbs immediately began flashing red.

'Easy, once you get the hang of it,' he said.

Scott smiled and pulled the door back open with his little finger. Cohen stared open-mouthed as the lights returned to green.

'The lights might flash red,' said Scott, 'but Bertha can only handle one man at a time. No one else can open or close the safe now except me.'

'And I was hoping it was because he was a Jew,' said Aziz.

Scott smiled as he pushed the door of the safe closed, swivelled the dials and waited until all three bulbs turned red.

'Let's go,' said Kratz, who Scott felt sounded a little irritated – or was it just the first sign of tension? Aziz threw the tarpaulin back over Madame Bertha while his colleagues jumped over the side and returned to the cab.

No one spoke as they continued their journey to the border until Cohen let out a string of expletives when he spotted the queue of lorries ahead of them. 'We're going to be here all night,' he said.

'And most of tomorrow morning, I expect,' said Kratz. 'So we'd better get used to it.' They came to a halt behind the last lorry in the queue.

'Why don't I just drive on up front and try to bluff my way through?' said Cohen. 'A few extra dollars ought to . . .'

'No,' said Kratz. 'We don't want to attract undue attention at any time between now and when we cross back over that border.'

During the next hour, while the truck moved forward only a couple of hundred yards, Kratz went over his plans yet again, covering any situation he thought might arise once they reached Baghdad.

Another hour passed, and Scott was thankful for the evening breeze that helped him doze off, although he realised that he would soon have to wind the window up if he wished to avoid freezing. He began to drift into a light sleep, his mind switching between Hannah and the Declaration, and which, given the choice, he would rather bring home. He realised that Kratz was in no doubt why he had volunteered to join the team when the chances of survival were so slim.

'What's this joker up to then?' said Cohen in a stage whisper. Scott snapped awake and quickly focused on a uniformed official talking to the driver of the lorry in front of them.

'It's a customs official,' said Kratz. 'He's only checking to see that drivers have the right papers to cross the border.'

'Most of this lot will only have two little bits of red paper about five inches by three,' said Cohen.

'Here he comes,' said Kratz. 'Try and look as bored as he does.'

The officer strolled up to the cab and didn't even give Cohen a first look as he thrust a hand through the open window.

Cohen passed over the papers that the experts at Langley had provided. The official studied them and then walked slowly round the lorry. When he returned to the driver's side, he barked an order at Cohen that none of them understood.

Cohen looked towards Kratz, but a voice from behind rescued them.

'He says we're to go to the front of the queue.'

'Why?' asked Kratz suspiciously. Aziz repeated the question to the official.

'We're being given priority because of the letter signed by Saddam.'

'And who do we thank for that?' asked Kratz, still not fully convinced.

'Bill O'Reilly,' said Scott, 'who was only too sorry he couldn't join us on the trip. But he's been given to understand that it's quite impossible to get draught Guinness anywhere in Iraq.'

Kratz nodded, and Sergeant Cohen obeyed the official's instructions, allowing himself to be directed into the lane of oncoming traffic as he began an unsteady two-mile journey to the front of the queue. Vehicles legally progressing towards Amman on the other side of the road found they had to swerve onto the loose rubble of the hard shoulder if they didn't want a head-on collision with Madame Bertha.

As Cohen completed the last few yards to the border post, an angry official came running out of the customs shed waving a fist. Once again it was Aziz who came to their rescue, by recommending that Kratz show him the letter.

After one look at the signature, the fist was quickly exchanged for a salute.

'Passport,' was the only other word he uttered.

Kratz passed over three Swedish and one Iraqi passport with two red notes attached to the first page of each document. 'Never pay above the expected tariff,' he had warned his team. 'It only makes them suspicious.'

The four passports were taken to a little cubicle, studied, stamped and returned by the official, who even offered them the suggestion of a smile. The barrier on the Jordanian side was raised, and the lorry began its mile-long journey towards the Iraqi checkpoint.

27

HAMID AL OBAYDI was dragged into the Council Chamber by two of the Presidential Guards and then dumped in a chair several yards away from the long table.

He raised his head and looked around at the twelve men who made up the Revolutionary Command Council. None of their eyes came into contact with his, with the exception of the State Prosecutor.

What had he done that these people had decided to arrest him at the border, handcuff him, throw him in jail, leave him to sleep on the stone floor and not even offer him the chance to use a lavatory?

Still dressed in the suit he had crossed the border in, he was now sitting in his own excrement.

Saddam raised a hand, and the State Prosecutor smiled.

But Al Obaydi did not fear Nakir Farrar. Not only was he innocent of any trumped-up charge, but he also had information they needed. The State Prosecutor rose slowly from his place.

'Your name is Hamid Al Obaydi?'

'Yes,' replied Al Obaydi, looking directly at the State Prosecutor.

'You are charged with treason and the theft of state property. How do you plead?'

'I am innocent, and Allah will be my witness.'

'If Allah is to be your witness, I'm sure he won't

mind me asking you some simple questions.'

'I will be most happy to answer anything.'

'When you returned from New York earlier this month, you carried on with your work in the Foreign Ministry. Is that correct?'

'It is.'

'And was one of your responsibilities checking the government's latest position with reference to UN sanctions?'

'Yes. That was part of my job as Deputy Ambassador to the UN.'

'Quite so. And when you carried out these checks, you came across certain items on which embargoes had been lifted. Am I right?'

'Yes, you are,' said Al Obaydi confidently.

'Was one of those items a safe?'

'It was,' said Al Obaydi.

'When you realised this, what did you do about it?'

'I telephoned the Swedish company who had built the safe to ascertain what the latest position was, so that I could enter the facts in my report.'

'And what did you discover?'

Al Obaydi hesitated, not sure how much the Prosecutor knew.

'What did you discover?' insisted Farrar.

'That the safe had been collected that day by a Mr Riffat.'

'Did you know this Mr Riffat?'

'No, I did not.'

'So what did you do next?'

'I rang the Ministry of Industry, as I was under the impression that they were responsible for the safe.'

'And what did they tell you?'

'That the responsibility had been taken out of their hands.'

'Did they also tell you into whose hands the responsibility had been entrusted?' asked the Prosecutor.

'I don't remember exactly.'

'Well, let me try and refresh your memory – or shall I call the Permanent Secretary to whom you spoke on the phone that morning?'

'I think he may have said that it was no longer in their hands,' said Al Obaydi.

'Did he tell you whose hands it was in?' repeated the Prosecutor.

'I think he said something about the file being sent to Geneva.'

'It may interest you to know that the official has submitted written evidence to confirm just that.'

Al Obaydi lowered his head.

'So, once you knew that the file had been passed on to Geneva, what did you do next?'

'I phoned Geneva and was told the Ambassador was not available. I left a message to say that I had called,' said Al Obaydi confidently, 'and asked if he would call back.'

'Did you really expect him to call back?'

'I assumed he would.'

'You assumed he would. So what did you write in your report, in the sanctions file?'

'The file?' asked Al Obaydi.

'Yes. You were making a report for your successor. What information did you pass on to him?'

'I don't remember,' said Al Obaydi.

'Then allow me to remind you once again,' said the Prosecutor, lifting a slim brown file from the table. ' "The Ministry of Industry have sent the file concerning this item direct to Geneva. I phoned our Ambassador there, but was unable to make contact with him. Therefore, I cannot make any progress from this end until he returns my call. Hamid Al Obaydi." Did you write that?'

'I can't remember.'

'You can't remember what the Permanent Secretary said to you; you can't remember what you wrote in your own report when property of the state might have been stolen, or worse . . . But I shall come to that later. Perhaps you would like to check your own handwriting?' said the Prosecutor as he walked from the table and thrust the relevant sheet in front of Al Obaydi's face. 'Is that your writing?'

'Yes, it is. But I can explain.'

'And is that your signature at the bottom of the page?'

Al Obaydi leaned forward, studied the signature and nodded.

'Yes or no?' barked the Prosecutor.

'Yes,' said Al Obaydi quietly.

'Did you, that same afternoon, visit General Al-Hassan, the Head of State Security?'

'No. He visited me.'

'Ah, I have made a mistake. It was he who visited you.'

'Yes,' said Al Obaydi.

'Did you alert him to the fact that an enemy agent might be heading towards Iraq, having found a way of crossing the border with the intention of perhaps assassinating our leader?'

'I couldn't have known that.'

'But you must have suspected something unusual was going on?'

'I wasn't certain at that time.'

'Did you let General Al-Hassan know of your uncertainty?'

'No. I did not.'

'Was it because you didn't trust him?'

'I didn't know him. It was the first time we had met.

The previous . . .' Al Obaydi regretted the words the moment he had said them.

'You were about to say?' said the Prosecutor.

'Nothing.'

'I see. So, let us move on to the following day, when you paid a visit – because I feel confident that he didn't visit you – to the Deputy Foreign Minister.' This induced some smiles around the table, but Al Obaydi did not see them.

'Yes, a routine call to discuss my appointment to Paris. He was, after all, the former Ambassador.'

'Quite. But is he not also your immediate superior?'

'Yes, he is,' said Al Obaydi.

'So, did you tell *him* of your suspicions?'

'I wasn't sure there was anything to tell him.'

'Did you tell him of your suspicions?' asked the Prosecutor, raising his voice.

'No, I did not.'

'Was he not to be trusted either? Or didn't you know him well enough?'

'I wasn't sure. I wanted more proof.'

'I see. You wanted more proof. So what did you do next?'

'I travelled to Paris,' said Al Obaydi.

'On the next day?' asked the State Prosecutor.

'No,' said Al Obaydi, hesitating.

'On the day after, perhaps? Or the day after that?'

'Perhaps.'

'Meanwhile, the safe was on its way to Baghdad. Is that right?'

'Yes, but –'

'And you *still* hadn't informed anyone? Is that also correct?'

Al Obaydi didn't reply.

'Is that also correct?' shouted Farrar.

'Yes, but there was still enough time –'

'Enough time for what?' asked the State Prosecutor.

Al Obaydi's head sank again.

'For you to reach the safety of our embassy in Paris?'

'No,' said Al Obaydi. 'I travelled on to –'

'Yes?' said Farrar. 'You travelled on to where?'

Al Obaydi realised he had fallen into the trap.

'To Sweden, perhaps?'

'Yes,' said Al Obaydi. 'But only because –'

'You wanted to check the safe was well on its way? Or was it, as you told the Foreign Minister, that you were simply going on holiday?'

'No, but . . .'

' "Yes but, no but." Were you on holiday in Sweden? Or were you representing the state?'

'I was representing the state.'

'Then why did you travel economy, and not charge the state for the expense that was incurred?'

Al Obaydi made no reply.

The Prosecutor leaned forward. 'Was it because you didn't want anyone to know you were in Sweden, when your superiors thought you were in Paris?'

'Yes, but in time . . .'

'After it was too late, perhaps. Is that what you're trying to tell us?'

'No. I did not say that.'

'Then why did you not pick up a phone and ring our Ambassador in Geneva? He could have saved you all the expense and the trouble. Was it because you didn't trust him either? Or perhaps he didn't trust you?'

'Neither!' shouted Al Obaydi, leaping to his feet, but the guards grabbed him by the shoulders and threw him back onto the chair.

'Now that you've got that little outburst out of the way,' said the Prosecutor calmly, 'perhaps we can continue. You travelled to Sweden, to Kalmar to be exact, to keep an appointment with a Mr Pedersson, whom you did seem willing to phone.' The Prosecutor checked his notes again. 'And what was the purpose of this visit, now that you have confirmed it was not a holiday?'

'To try and find out who it was who had stolen the safe.'

'Or was it to make sure the safe was on the route you had already planned for it?'

'Certainly not,' said Al Obaydi, his voice rising. 'After all, it was I who discovered that Riffat was the Mossad agent Kratz.'

'You *knew* that Riffat was a Mossad agent?' queried the Prosecutor in mock disbelief.

'Yes, I found out when I was in Kalmar,' said Al Obaydi.

'But you told Mr Pedersson that Mr Riffat was a thorough man, a man who could be trusted,' said the State Prosecutor, checking his notes. 'Am I right? So now at last we've found someone you can trust.'

'It was quite simply that I didn't want Pedersson to know what I'd discovered.'

'I don't think you wanted *anyone* to know what you had discovered, as I shall go on to show. What did you do next?'

'I flew back to Paris.'

'And did you spend the night at the embassy?'

'Yes, I did, but I was only stopping overnight on my way to Jordan.'

'I'll come to your trip to Jordan in a moment, if I may. But what I should like to know now is why, when you were back at our embassy in Paris, you didn't immediately call our Ambassador in Geneva to inform him of what you had discovered? Not only was the Ambassador in residence, but he took a call from another member of the embassy staff after you had gone to bed.'

Al Obaydi suddenly realised how Farrar knew everything. He tried to collect his thoughts.

'My only interest was getting back to Baghdad to let the Foreign Minister know the danger our leader might be facing.'

'Like the imminent dropping of American bombs on Mukhbarat headquarters?' suggested the State Prosecutor.

'I could not have known what the Americans were planning,' shouted Al Obaydi.

'I see,' said Farrar. 'It was no more than a happy coincidence that you were safely tucked up in bed in Paris while Tomahawk missiles were showering down on Baghdad.'

'But I returned to Baghdad immediately I learned of the bombing,' insisted Al Obaydi.

'Perhaps you wouldn't have been in quite such a hurry to return if the Americans had succeeded in assassinating our leader.'

'But my report would have proved . . .'

'And where is that report?'

'I intended to write it on the journey from Jordan to Baghdad.'

'How convenient. And did you advise your trustworthy friend Mr Riffat to ring the Minister of Industry to find out if he was expected?'

'No, I did not,' said Al Obaydi. 'If any of this were true,' he added, 'why would I have worked so hard to see that our great leader secured the Declaration?'

'I'm glad you mentioned the Declaration,' said the State Prosecutor softly, 'because I'm also puzzled by the role you played in that particular exercise. But first, let me ask you, did you trust our Ambassador in Geneva to see that the Declaration was delivered to Baghdad?'

'Yes, I did.'

'And did it reach Baghdad safely?' asked the Prosecutor, glancing at the battered parchment, still nailed to the wall behind Saddam.

'Yes, it did.'

'Then why not entrust the knowledge you had acquired about the safe to the same man, remembering that it was his responsibility?'

'This was different.'

'It certainly was, and I shall show the Council just how different. How was the Declaration paid for?'

'I don't understand,' said Al Obaydi.

'Then let me make it easier for you. How was each payment dealt with?'

'Ten million dollars was to be paid once the contract had been agreed, and a further forty million when the Declaration was handed over.'

'And how much of that money – the state's money – did you keep for yourself?'

'Not one cent.'

'Well, let us see if that is totally accurate, shall we? Where did the meetings take place for the exchange of these vast sums of money?'

'The first payment was made to a bank in New Jersey, and the second to Dummond et cie, one of our banks in Switzerland.'

'And the first payment of ten million dollars, if I understand you correctly, you insisted should be in cash?'

'That is not correct,' said Al Obaydi. 'The other side insisted that it should be in cash.'

'How convenient. But then, once again, we only have your word for that, because our Ambassador in New York has stated it was you who insisted the first payment had to be in cash. Perhaps he misunderstood you as well. But let us move on to the second payment, and do correct me if I have misunderstood you.' He paused. 'That was paid direct into Franchard et cie?'

'That is correct,' said Al Obaydi.

'And did you receive, I think the word is a "kickback", after either of these payments?'

'Certainly not.'

'Well, what *is* certain is that, as the first payment was made in cash, it would be hard for anyone to prove otherwise. But as for the second payment . . .' The Prosecutor paused to let the significance of his words sink in.

'I don't know what you're talking about,' snapped Al Obaydi.

'Then you must be having another lapse of memory, because during your absence, when you were rushing back from Paris to warn the President of the imminent danger to his life, you received a communication from Franchard et cie which, because the letter was addressed to our Ambassador in Paris, ended up on the desk of the Deputy Foreign Minister.'

'I've had no communication with Franchard et cie.'

'I'm not suggesting you did,' said the Prosecutor, as he strode forward to within a foot of Al Obaydi. 'I'm suggesting *they* communicated with *you*. Because they sent you your latest bank statement in the name of Hamid Al Obaydi, dated June 25th 1993, showing that your account was credited with one million dollars on February 18th 1993.'

'It's not possible,' said Al Obaydi defiantly.

'It's not possible?' said the Prosecutor, thrusting a copy of the statement in front of Al Obaydi.

'This is easy to explain. The Cavalli family is trying to get revenge because we didn't pay the full amount of one hundred million as originally promised.'

'Revenge, you claim. The money isn't real? It doesn't

exist? This is just a piece of paper? A figment of our imagination?'

'Yes,' said Al Obaydi. 'That is the truth.'

'So perhaps you can explain why one hundred thousand dollars was withdrawn from this account on the day after you had visited Franchard et cie?'

'That's not possible.'

'Another impossibility? Another figment of the imagination? Then you have not seen this withdrawal order for one hundred thousand dollars, sent to you by the bank a few days later? The signature on which bears a remarkable resemblance to the one on the sanctions report which you accepted earlier was authentic.'

The Prosecutor held both documents in front of Al Obaydi so they touched the tip of his nose. He looked at the two signatures and realised what Cavalli must have done. The Prosecutor proceeded to sign his death warrant, even before Al Obaydi had been given the chance to explain.

'And now you are no doubt going to ask the Council to believe that it was Cavalli who also had your signature forged?'

A little laughter trickled round the table, and Al Obaydi suspected that the Prosecutor knew that he had only spoken the truth.

'I have had enough of this,' said the one person in the room who would have dared to interrupt the State Prosecutor.

Al Obaydi looked up in a last attempt to catch the attention of the President, but with the exception of the State Prosecutor the Council were looking towards the top of the table and nodding their agreement.

'There are more pressing matters for the Council to consider.' He waved a hand as if he were swatting an irritating fly.

Two soldiers stepped forward and removed Al Obaydi from his sight.

'That was a whole lot easier than I expected,' said Cohen, once they had passed through the Iraqi checkpoint.

'A little too easy, perhaps,' said Kratz.

'It's good to know that we've got one optimist and one pessimist on this trip,' said Scott.

Once Cohen was on the highway he remained cautious of pushing the vehicle beyond fifty miles per hour. The lorries that passed in the opposite direction on their way to Jordan rarely had more than two of their four headlights working, which sometimes made them appear like motorcycles in the distance, so overtaking became hazardous. But his eyes needed to be at their most alert for those lorries in front of him: for them, one red tail-light was a luxury.

Kratz had always thought the three-hundred-mile journey from the border to Baghdad would be too long to consider covering in one stretch, so he had decided they should have a rest about forty miles outside the Iraqi capital. Scott asked Cohen what time he thought they might reach their rest point.

'Assuming I don't drive straight into a parked lorry that's been abandoned in the middle of the road or disappear down a pothole, I'd imagine we'll get there around four, five at the latest.'

'I don't like the sight of all these army vehicles on the road. What do you think they're up to?' asked Kratz, who hadn't slept a wink since they crossed the border.

'A battalion on the move, I'd say, sir. Doesn't look that unusual to me, and I don't think we'd need to worry about them unless they were going in the same direction as us.'

'Perhaps you're right,' said Kratz.

'You wouldn't give them a second thought if you'd crossed the border legally,' said Scott.

'Possibly. But Sergeant,' Kratz said, turning his attention back to Cohen, 'let me know the moment you spot anything you consider unusual.'

'You mean, like a woman worth a second glance?'

Kratz made no comment. He turned to ask Scott a question, only to find he had dozed off again. He envied Scott's ability to sleep anywhere at any time, especially under such pressure.

Sergeant Cohen drove on through the night, not always in a straight line, as he circumvented the occasional burned-out tank or large crater left over from the war. On and on they travelled, through small towns and seemingly uninhabited sleeping villages, until a few minutes past four, when Cohen swung off the highway and up a track that could have only considered one-way traffic. He drove for another twenty minutes, finally coming to a halt when the road ended at an overhanging ledge.

'Even a vulture wouldn't find us here,' said Cohen as he turned off the engine. 'Permission to have a smoke and a bit of shut-eye, Colonel?'

Kratz nodded and watched Cohen jump out of the cab and offer Aziz a cigarette before disappearing behind a palm tree. He checked the surrounding countryside carefully, and decided Cohen was right. When he returned to the truck, he found Aziz and the Sergeant were already asleep, while Scott was sitting on the ledge watching the sun come up over Baghdad.

'What a peaceful sight,' he said as Kratz sat down beside him, almost as though he had been talking to someone else. 'Only God could make a sunrise as beautiful as that.'

'Something isn't right,' muttered Kratz under his breath.

28

SADDAM NODDED TO THE PROSECUTOR. 'Now we have dealt with the traitor, let us move on to the terrorists. What is the latest position, General?'

General Hamil, known as the Barber of Baghdad, opened the file in front of him – he kept a file on everybody, including those sitting around the table. Hamil had been educated at Sandhurst and returned to Iraq to receive the King's Commission, only to find there was no King to serve. So he switched his loyalty to the new President, Abdul Karim Qasim. Then a young Captain changed sides in the 1963 coup and the Ba'ath Party took power. Once again Hamil switched his loyalty, and was rewarded with an appointment to the personal staff of the new Vice-President, Saddam Hussein. Since that day he had risen rapidly through the ranks. He was now Saddam's favourite General, and Commander of the Presidential Guard. He had the distinction of being the only man, with the exception of the President's bodyguards, allowed to wear a side-arm in Saddam's presence. He was Saddam's executioner. His favourite hobby was to shave his victims' heads before they were hanged, with a blunt cut-throat razor that he never bothered to sharpen. Some of them disappointed him by dying before he could get the rope around their necks.

Hamil studied his file for a few moments before offering an opinion. 'The terrorists,' he began, 'crossed the border at 21.26 last night. Four passports were presented to the immigration officer for stamping. Three were of Swedish origin, and one was from Iraq.'

'I'll skin that one personally,' said Saddam.

'The four men are travelling in a truck that appears to be quite old, but as we are unable to risk taking too close a look, I cannot be sure if we are dealing with a Trojan horse or not. The safe that you ordered, Mr President, is undoubtedly on the back of the truck.

'The truck has driven non-stop through the night at a steady pace of around forty miles per hour in the direction of Baghdad, but at 4.09 this morning it turned off into the desert, and we ceased to monitor its movements, as that particular path leads nowhere. We believe they have simply come off the road to rest before travelling on to the capital later this morning.'

'How many miles are they from Baghdad at this moment?' asked the Minister of the Interior.

'Forty, perhaps fifty – an hour to an hour and a half at the most.'

'So, if we now have them trapped in the desert, General, why don't we just send troops in and cut them off?'

'While they are still bringing the safe to Baghdad?' interrupted Saddam. 'No. That way lies our only danger.'

'I'm not sure I understand, Sayedi,' said the Minister of the Interior, turning to face his leader.

'Then I will explain, *Minister*,' Saddam said, exaggerating the final word cruelly. 'If we arrest them in the desert, who will believe us when we tell the world they are terrorists? The Western press will even claim that we planted their passports on them. No, I want them arrested right here in the Council Chamber, when it will be impossible for Mossad to deny their involvement and, more important, we will have exposed their plot and made fools of them in the eyes of the Zionist people.'

'Now I understand your profound wisdom, Sayedi.'

Saddam waved a hand and turned his attention to the Minister of Industry.

'Have my orders been carried out?'

'To the letter, Excellency. When the terrorists arrive at the Ministry, they will be made to wait, and will be treated curtly, until they produce the documentation that claims to come from your office.'

'They presented such a letter at the border,' interrupted General Hamil, still looking down at his file.

'The moment such a letter is presented to my office,' continued the Minister for Industry, 'a crane will be supplied so that the safe can be transferred into this building. I fear that we will have to remove the doors on the front of the building, but only –'

'I am not interested in the doors,' said Saddam. 'When do you anticipate that the safe will arrive outside the building?'

'Around midday,' said General Hamil. 'I shall personally take over the entire operation once the safe is inside the building, Mr President.'

'Good. And make sure the terrorists see the Declaration before they are arrested.'

'What if they were to try to destroy the document, Excellency?' asked the Interior Minister, attempting to recover some lost ground.

'Never,' said Saddam. 'They have come to Baghdad to steal the document, not to destroy their pathetic piece of history.' Two or three people round the table nodded their agreement. 'None of you except General Hamil and his immediate staff will come anywhere near this building for the next twenty-four hours. The fewer people who know what's really happening, the better. Don't even brief the officer of the day. I want the security to appear lax. That way they will fall right into our trap.'

General Hamil nodded.

'Prosecutor,' said Saddam, turning his attention to the other end of the table, 'what will the international community say when they learn I have arrested the Zionist pigs?'

'They are terrorists, Excellency, and for terrorists, there can be only one sentence. Especially after the Americans launched their missiles on innocent civilians only days ago.'

Saddam nodded. 'Any other questions?'

'Just one, Your Excellency,' said the Deputy Foreign Minister. 'What do you want to do about the girl?'

'Ah, yes,' said Saddam, smiling for the first time. 'Now that she has served her purpose, I must think of a suitable way to end her life. Where is she at the moment?'

As the truck began its slow journey back along the tiny desert path, with Aziz taking his turn behind the wheel and Cohen in the back with Madame Bertha, Scott felt the atmosphere inside the cab had changed. When they pulled off the highway to rest, he still believed they were in no real danger. But the grim silence of morning made him suddenly aware of the task they had set themselves.

They had Kratz to thank for the original idea, and mixed with his particular cocktail of imagination, discipline, courage, and the assumption that no one knew what they were up to, Scott felt they had a better than even chance of getting away with it, especially now they knew exactly where the Declaration was situated.

When they reached the main road, Aziz jokingly asked, 'Right or left?'

Scott said 'Left,' but Aziz turned dutifully right.

As they travelled along the highway towards Baghdad the sun shone from a cloudless sky that would have delighted any tourist board, although the burned-out tanks and the craters in the road might not have been considered obvious attractions. No one spoke as the miles sped by: there was no need for them to go over the plans another time. That would be like an Olympian training on the morning of a race – either too late, or no longer of any value.

For the last ten miles, they joined an expressway that was equal to anything they might have found in Germany. As they crossed a newly reconstructed bridge over the Euphrates, Scott began to wonder how close he was to Hannah, and whether he could get himself into the Foreign Ministry without alerting Kratz, let alone the Iraqis.

When they reached the outskirts of Baghdad, with its glistening skyscrapers and modern buildings, they could have been entering any major city in the world – until they saw the people. There were lines of cars at petrol pumps in a land where the main asset was oil, but their length was dwarfed only by the queues for food. All four of them could see that sanctions were biting, however much Saddam denied it.

They drove nearer to the city centre, along the road that passed under the Al-Naser, the massive archway of two crossed swords gripped by casts of Saddam's hand. There was no need to direct Aziz to the Ministry of Industry. He wished he still lived in Baghdad, but he hadn't entered the city since his father had been executed for his part in the failed coup of 1987. Looking out of the window at his countrymen, he could still smell their fear in his nostrils.

As they passed the bombed-out remains of the Mukhbarat headquarters, Scott noticed an unmanned ambulance parked outside the Iraqi intelligence centre. It was strategically placed for the CNN television cameras rather than for any practical purpose, he suspected.

When Aziz saw the Ministry of Industry building looming up ahead of him, he pointed it out to Scott, who remembered the façade from the mass of photographs supplied by Kratz. But Scott's eyes had moved up to the gun turrets on top of the Foreign Ministry, a mere stone's throw away.

Aziz brought the lorry to a halt a hundred yards beyond the entrance to the Ministry. Scott said, 'I'll be as quick as I can,' as he jumped out of the cab and headed back towards the building.

As he climbed the steps to the Ministry, he did not see a man in a window of the building opposite who was speaking on the telephone to General Hamil.

'The truck has stopped about a hundred metres beyond the Ministry. A tall, fair-haired man who was in the front of the vehicle is now entering the building, but the other three, including Kratz, have remained with the safe.'

Scott pushed through the swing doors and strolled past two guards who looked as if they didn't move more than a few feet every day. He walked over to the information desk and joined the shortest of three queues. The one-handed clock above the desk indicated that it was approximately 9.30.

It took another fifteen minutes before Scott reached the counter. He explained to the girl that his name was Bernstrom and that he needed to see Mr Kajami.

'Do you have an appointment?' she asked.

'No,' said Scott. 'We called from Jordan to warn him that a safe the government had ordered was on its way to Baghdad. He asked us to inform him the moment it arrived.'

'I will see if he's in,' said the receptionist. Scott waited, staring up at a massive portrait of Saddam Hussein in uniform holding a Kalashnikov. It dominated the otherwise blank grey walls of the reception area.

The girl listened carefully to whoever it was on the other end of the line before saying, 'Someone will be down to see you in a few minutes.' She turned her attention to the next person in the queue.

Scott hung around for another thirty minutes before a tall, thin man wearing a smart Western suit stepped out of the lift and walked over to him.

'Mr Bernstrom?'

'Yes?' said Scott, as he swung round to face the man.

'Good morning,' he said confidently in English. 'I am Mr Ibrahim, Mr Kajami's personal assistant. How can I help you?'

'I have brought a safe from Sweden,' said Scott. 'It was ordered by the Ministry some years ago, but, due to the UN sanctions, could not be delivered any earlier. We were told that when we reached Baghdad we should report to Mr Kajami.'

'Do you have any papers to verify your claim?'

Scott removed a file from his bag and showed Mr Ibrahim its contents.

The man read through each document slowly until he came to the letter signed by the President. He read no further. Looking up, he asked, 'May I see this safe, Mr Bernstrom?'

'Certainly,' said Scott. 'Please follow me.' He led the official out onto the street and took him over to the truck.

Cohen stared down at them. When Kratz gave the order, he whipped the tarpaulin off the safe so that the civil servant could inspect Madame Bertha for himself.

Scott was fascinated by the fact that those passing in

the street didn't give the safe a second look. If anything, they quickened their pace. Fear manifested itself among these people by their lack of curiosity.

'Please come with me, Mr Bernstrom,' said Ibrahim. Scott accompanied him back to the reception area, where he returned upstairs without another word.

Scott was left waiting for another thirty minutes before Ibraham came back.

'You are to take the safe to Victory Square, where you will see a barrier with a tank in front of a large white building. They are expecting you.'

Scott was about to ask where Victory Square was when Ibrahim turned and walked away. He went back to the truck, and joined Kratz and Aziz in the front before passing on the news. Aziz didn't need to be told the way.

'No special treatment there, I'm glad to see,' said Kratz.

Scott nodded his agreement as Aziz eased the truck back into the road. The traffic was much heavier now. Lorries and cars were honking their horns, managing to move only a few inches at a time.

'It must be an accident,' said Scott, until they turned the corner and saw the three bodies hanging from a makeshift gallows: a man wearing an expensive designer suit, a woman perhaps a little younger, and another much older woman. It was hard to be certain, with their heads shaven.

Mr Kajami sat at his desk, dialled the number that had been passed to him, and waited.

'Deputy Foreign Minister's Office, Miss Saib speaking.'

'This is the Minister of Industry calling. Could you put me through to the Deputy Foreign Minister.'

'I'm afraid he's out of the office at the moment, Mr Kajami. Shall I ask him to return your call, or would you like to leave a message?'

'I will leave a message, but perhaps he could also call me when he gets back.'

'Certainly, Minister.'

'Could you let him know that the safe has arrived from Sweden and can therefore be crossed off the sanctions list.' There was a long pause. 'Are you still there, Miss Saib?'

'Yes. I was just writing down what you said, sir.'

'If he needs to see the relevant forms we still have them at the Ministry, but if it's the safe he wants to check on, it's already on its way to the Ba'ath headquarters.'

'I understand, sir. I'll see he gets the message just as soon as he comes in.'

'Thank you, Miss Saib.'

Kajami replaced the phone on the hook, glanced across his desk at the Deputy Foreign Minister and smiled.

29

AZIZ BROUGHT THE TRUCK to a halt in front of a tank. A few soldiers were moving around, but there didn't appear to be a great deal of activity.

'I was expecting a bigger show of force than this,' said Kratz. 'It's the Ba'ath Party headquarters, after all.'

'Saddam's probably at the palace, or even out of Baghdad,' suggested Aziz as two soldiers advanced towards the truck. The first one shouted 'Out!' and they obeyed slowly. Once all four of them were on the ground, the soldier ordered them to stand a few yards away from the truck while a couple of other soldiers jumped up on the back and removed the tarpaulin.

'This one's a Major,' whispered Aziz as a portly man covered in battle ribbons and carrying a mobile phone advanced towards them. He stopped and looked up at the safe suspiciously before turning to Kratz and introducing himself as Major Saeed.

'Open,' was all he added.

Kratz pointed to Scott, who climbed up onto the back of the lorry while several more soldiers surrounded it to watch him perform the opening ceremony. Once Scott had pulled the great door open, the Major joined him on the back of the truck, but not until one of the soldiers had given him a hand-up. He stood a pace back and ordered two of his men to go inside. They appeared apprehensive at first, but once they had entered the safe they began touching the sides and even jumping up to try to reach the roof. A few moments later, Saeed joined them, and banged the walls with his swagger stick. He then stepped back out, jumped heavily off the truck and turned towards Scott.

'Now we wait for a crane,' he said, sounding a little more friendly. He dialled a number on the phone.

Cohen climbed into the cab and sat behind the wheel, the keys still in the ignition, while Aziz remained on the back with the safe. Scott and Kratz leaned against a wall, trying to appear bored, while having a conversation on the alternatives they now faced.

'We must find some way of getting into the building ahead of the safe,' said Kratz. Scott nodded his agreement.

The clock in Victory Square had struck 12.30 before Aziz spotted the tall, thin structure progressing slowly round the massive statue of Saddam. The four of them watched as soldiers ran out into the street to hold up the flow of traffic and allow the vast crane to continue its progress uninterrupted.

Scott explained to the Major that the truck now needed to be moved to a position opposite the front door. He agreed without a phone call. When the truck was parked exactly where Scott wanted it, Major Saeed finally conceded that the doors would have to come off their hinges if they were ever going to get the safe and its trolley inside the building.

This time he did make a phone call, and to Scott's question, 'How long?' he simply shrugged his shoulders and replied, 'Must wait.'

Scott was determined to use the 'must wait' period, and explained to Major Saeed that he needed to walk the route that the safe would travel once they had entered the building.

The Major hesitated, made a further phone call, held on for some time before he received an answer, and then, pointing to Scott, said, 'You, only.'

Scott left Kratz to organise the crane as it prepared to lift the safe off the lorry, and followed the Major into the building.

The first thing that Scott noticed as he walked down the carpeted corridor was its width and solid feel. Every few paces there were soldiers lounging against the wall who sprang to attention the moment they saw Major Saeed.

At the end of the corridor was an elevator. The Major produced a key and turned it in a lock on the wall. The doors of the elevator opened slowly. It struck Scott that the size of the safe must have been determined by the width of the lift. He doubted if there would be much more than an inch to spare all round once they had succeeded in getting Madame Bertha on board.

The Major pressed a button marked '– 6', which, Scott noted, was as far down as they could go. The lift dropped slowly. When the doors opened Scott followed Major Saeed into a long corridor. This time he had the feeling that the passageway had been built to survive an earthquake. They came to a halt outside a pair of heavy, reinforced doors, guarded by two soldiers carrying rifles.

Saeed asked a question, and both guards shook their heads. 'The Chamber is empty, so we can go straight through,' he explained, then proceeded to unlock the door. Scott followed him into the Council Chamber.

His eyes searched quickly round the room. The first thing he saw on the far wall was another massive portrait of Saddam, this time in a dark double-breasted suit. Then he spotted one of the red alarm buttons next to a light switch that Kratz had warned him about. The

Major hurried on through the Chamber, giving the impression of a man who hadn't the right to be there, while Scott went as slowly as he felt he could get away with. And then he saw it, just for a moment, and his heart sank: the Declaration of Independence was nailed to the wall, a corner torn and some of the signatures looking distinctly blurred.

The Major unlocked the far door and Scott reluctantly followed him through into the adjoining corridor. They continued for only a few more paces before coming to a halt in front of a massive recess of inlaid brick that Scott didn't need to measure to realise had been purpose-built in anticipation of the arrival of the safe.

Scott took some time measuring the space, as he tried to think of how he could get a longer look at the Declaration. After a few minutes, Major Saeed tapped him on the shoulder with his swagger stick and indicated that it was time for them to return to the courtyard. Scott reluctantly followed him back down the short corridor and into the Council Chamber, which the Major scurried through while Scott lingered to measure the doors. He was pleased to discover that they would have to be taken off their hinges. He stood a pace back as if considering the problem. The Major returned and slapped the side of his leg with his swagger stick, muttering something under his breath that Scott suspected wasn't altogether flattering.

Scott stole a glance to the right, and confirmed his worst fears: even if he were able to exchange the two documents, it would take an even greater genius than Dollar Bill to repair the damage that Saddam had already inflicted.

'Come. Come. We must go,' said the Major.

'And so must these doors,' said Scott, and turning, added, 'and those two as well,' pointing to the pair at the other end of the Chamber. But Major Saeed was already striding off down the long corridor towards the open lift.

Hannah put the phone down and tried to stop herself trembling. They had warned her many times at Herzliyah that however tough you think you are, and however well trained you've been, you will still tremble.

She checked her watch. Her lunch break was due in twenty minutes, and although she rarely left the building during the day except on official business, she knew she could no longer sit in that office and just wait for events to happen all around her.

The Deputy Foreign Minister had left for the palace at eight that morning, and had told her not to expect him back until five at the earliest. A muscle in her cheek twitched as she began to type out the Minister of Industry's message.

For fifteen minutes, she sat at her desk and planned how the hour could be best spent. As soon as she was clear in her mind what needed to be done, she picked up her phone and asked a girl on the switchboard to cover her calls during the lunch break.

Hannah put on her glasses, left the room and walked quickly down the corridor, remaining close to the wall with her head bowed, so that those passing didn't give her a second look.

She took the stairs rather than the lift, slipped across the hall past reception, through the swing doors and out onto the steps of the Foreign Ministry.

'Saib's just left the building,' said a voice from the other side of the road into a mobile phone. 'She's going in the direction of Victory Square.'

Hannah continued walking towards the square. The crowds were so large and noisy that she feared another public hanging must have taken place. When she reached the end of the road and turned the corner, she averted her eyes as she made a path between those who were standing, staring, some even laughing at the spectacle.

'Quite a high-up official,' someone joked. Another more serious voice said that he had heard he was a diplomat recently back from America who had been caught with his fingers in the till. A third, an elderly woman, wept when someone suggested that the other two were the man's innocent mother and sister.

Once Hannah could see the barrier she slowed her pace. She stopped and stared across the road at the Ba'ath Party headquarters. She was pleased to be hidden in such a large crowd, even if it did occasionally obscure her view.

'She's facing the Ba'ath Party headquarters. Everyone else is looking in the opposite direction.'

Hannah's eyes settled on the truck that was surrounded by soldiers, and then she saw the massive safe that was perched on the back of the vehicle and the two young men who were attaching large coils of steel to its base. One was Middle Eastern in appearance, the other vaguely European. And then she saw Kratz – or was it Kratz? Whoever it was disappeared behind the far side of the truck. She waited for the man to reappear. When he did, a few moments later, she was left in no doubt that it was the Mossad leader.

She realised that she could not wait around in such a public place for much longer, and decided to return to her office and consider what needed to be done next. She gave Kratz one last look as a group of cleaners came out of the building, walked across the tarmac and passed by the barrier without any of the soldiers paying them the slightest attention.

Hannah began to walk away from Victory Square, just

as Major Saeed and Scott emerged from the building into the courtyard.

'She's on the move again, but she doesn't seem to be returning to the Ministry.' The man on the mobile phone listened for a moment and then replied, 'I don't know, but I'll follow her and report back.'

When Scott stepped back into the courtyard he was pleased to see that Kratz had already got the crane into position to lift the safe off the truck. Aziz and Cohen were fastening long steel coils around the body of Madame Bertha while the specially constructed trolley, of which Mr Pedersson was so proud, had been placed on the ground between the front door and the side of the truck.

Scott looked up at the crane that was taller than the building itself and back down at the operator, sitting in his wide cab near the base. Once Cohen and Aziz had jumped off the truck Kratz gave the operator the thumbs-up.

Scott pointed at the safe and beckoned to Kratz, who walked over, looking puzzled. He thought the operation was going rather well.

'What's the problem?' he asked. Scott continued pointing at the safe, and with exaggerated movements indicated how he thought it would have to be moved, while whispering to Kratz: 'I've seen the Declaration.' He moved to the other side of the safe. Kratz followed, now also pretending to take a close interest in the safe.

'Great news,' said Kratz. 'So where is it?'

'The news is not so great,' said Scott.

'What do you mean?' asked Kratz anxiously.

'It's in the Council Chamber, exactly where Hannah said it would be. But it's nailed to the wall,' replied Scott.

'Nailed to the wall?' said Kratz under his breath.

'Yes, and it looks as if it's beyond repair,' said Scott, as he heard the crunch of a gear shifting into place. He watched as the steel cords tightened, followed by a raucous revving of the engine. But Madame Bertha refused to budge an inch. The revving noise became even louder a second time, but she still remained unmoved by their solicitations.

The operator pushed the long gear lever forward another notch, and tried a third time. Finally Bertha rose an inch off the back of the lorry, swaying gently from side to side. Some of the soldiers started to cheer, but they stopped immediately when the Major turned to stare in their direction.

Kratz nodded and Cohen ran across the tarmac and lowered the tailboard, before getting into the cab and jumping behind the wheel of the truck. He switched on the engine, pushed the gear lever into first and moved the vehicle slowly forward until the safe was left dangling in mid-air. Aziz and Kratz then pushed the trolley a few yards across the tarmac so that it was directly below the dangling safe, Kratz gave the thumbs-up a second time, and the crane operator slowly began lowering the five tons of steel, inch by inch, until it came to rest on the trolley, causing the large rubber wheels to compress abruptly.

The safe now rested in front of the double doors, waiting for the carpenter to arrive before it could progress on its inward journey. The Major shrugged his shoulders even before Kratz had mouthed the question.

As Cohen backed the lorry into a parking space designated by the Major, an Iraqi, dressed in a dishdash and a red-and-white keffiyeh and carrying a tool bag appeared at the barrier.

Once the guards had thoroughly checked the tool bag,

tipping all its contents out onto the ground, they allowed him through. The carpenter gathered up his tools, took one look at the safe, another at the double doors, and understood immediately why his boss had described the problem as urgent. Scott stood back and watched the craftsman as he began to unscrew the hinges on one of the doors.

'So where's Dollar Bill's counterfeit at the moment?' asked Kratz.

'Still in my bag,' said Scott. 'I'm going to have to do some work on it, or they'll spot the difference the moment I've exchanged it for the original.'

'Agreed,' said Kratz. 'You'd better get on with it while the carpenter's working on the door. I'll try and keep the Major occupied.'

Kratz sauntered over to the carpenter and started chatting to him while Scott disappeared into the front of the truck carrying his bag. Once the Major saw what Kratz was doing he ran across to join them.

Scott stared through the cab window as he extracted Dollar Bill's copy from the cylinder and tried to recall where the main damage was on the original. First he made a tear in the top right-hand corner, then he spat on the names of John Adams and Robert Treat Paine. After he had studied his handiwork he decided he hadn't gone far enough and, placing the copy on the floor, he rubbed the soles of his shoes gently over the surface. He glanced up to see the Major ordering Kratz to let the carpenter get on with his job. Kratz shrugged his shoulders as Scott rolled up the copy of the Declaration and returned it to the cylinder, before sliding it down the specially-sewn long thin pocket on the inside of his trouser leg. A perfect fit.

A few moments later the carpenter got off his knees and smiled to show he had completed his task. At the

Major's command four soldiers stepped forward and removed the doors. They carried them a few paces away and leaned them up against an outside wall.

The Major ordered several more soldiers to push the trolley as Scott guided Madame Bertha through the doorway. Kratz and Aziz tried to follow, but the Major waved an arm firmly to indicate that only Scott could enter the building. It was Scott's turn to shrug his shoulders.

Inch by inch, they eased the trolley down the long corridor. The lift doors had been left open, but it still took forty hands to lever the five tons of metal safely inside. Scott knew from his research that this part of the building had been built to survive a nuclear attack, but he wondered if the lift would ever recover from having to carry the five-ton safe down six floors. He was only thankful that Madame Bertha was going down, not up.

The lift doors slowly closed and the Major quickly led Scott through a side door and down the back stairs, followed by a dozen soldiers. When they reached the basement, the doors of the lift were already open and Madame Bertha stood there, majestically waiting. The Major pointed to the floor with his swagger stick: ten of the soldiers fell to their knees and began pulling the trolley inch by inch until they finally managed to coax it into the corridor. The lift was then sent up to – 5, and six of the soldiers ran back up the stairs, jumped into the empty lift and returned to the basement so they could push the safe from the other side.

The carpenter had already removed the first set of doors they would encounter when the safe entered the Council Chamber, but was still working on the second set when the trolley reached the entrance. The delay gave Scott an opportunity to supervise the moving of the large table up against the side wall and the placing of the chairs on the table so that the safe would have a clear passage into the far corridor.

As he went back and forth Scott had several opportunities to stare at the Declaration, even study the spelling of the word 'Brittish'. He quickly realised that the parchment was in an even worse condition than he had thought.

Once the doors were finally removed, the soldiers began pushing the safe across the Chamber and out into the short corridor on the last few yards of its journey. When they had reached the end of the corridor opposite the specially prepared recess, Scott supervised the last few inches of its move until they could push the five tons of steel no further. Madame Bertha had finally come to her resting place against the far wall.

Scott smiled, and Major Saeed made another phone call.

The old woman explained to Hannah that the next shift was to be at three o'clock that afternoon, and they would be expected to have the Council Chamber ready for the meeting that was to take place at six the following day. They hadn't been able to do a proper job on the first shift that morning because of that safe.

Hannah had followed the cleaners, watching as they peeled off one by one and went their separate ways. She selected an old woman carrying the heaviest bags, and offered to help her across the road. They quickly got into conversation, and Hannah continued to carry the bags all the way to her front door, explaining that she only lived a few streets away.

'Come inside, my dear,' the old lady said.

'Thank you,' replied Hannah, feeling more like the wolf than Little Red Riding Hood.

Slipping a small whisky into the old woman's coffee had proved harmless enough, and it certainly loosened her tongue. Two Valium dropped in the cleaner's second coffee ensured that it would be several hours before she woke. Mossad had taught Hannah five different ways of breaking into a car, a hotel room, a briefcase, even a small safe, so a drugged old woman's handbag was no great challenge. She removed the special pass and slipped out of the house.

'She's now heading back in the direction of the Ministry,' said the voice into the mobile phone. 'We've checked the old woman. She passed out and probably won't come round until this time tomorrow. The only thing that's been taken is her security pass.'

When Hannah arrived back at her desk there was no sign that the Deputy Foreign Minister had returned, so she checked with the switchboard. There had only been three calls: two said they would call back tomorrow, and the third didn't leave a message.

Hannah replaced the handset and typed out a note explaining that she had gone home as she wasn't certain whether the Deputy Foreign Minister would be returning that day. As long as he didn't check his messages until after five o'clock, there would be no reason for him to become suspicious.

In the privacy of her little room, Hannah exchanged her office clothes for the traditional black abaya with a pushi covering her face. She checked herself in the mirror before once again leaving the building, silently and anonymously.

'I'm almost sure it's her coming out of the Ministry,' said the voice into the mobile phone, 'but she's changed into traditional dress and is no longer wearing glasses. She's heading towards Victory Square again. I'll keep you briefed.'

Hannah was back in Victory Square a few minutes before the first cleaner was expected to arrive for work. Although the crowd was now smaller, she was still able to remain inconspicuous. She looked across the road towards the courtyard. The safe was no longer to be seen, and the crane too had disappeared. The truck was now backed up against the wall. Hannah strained to see if Kratz was one of the figures sitting in the front of the truck, but she couldn't penetrate the haze of smoke.

Hannah turned her attention to a building she had never entered but felt she knew so well. A full-scale plan of each floor was attached to a board in the operations room of Mossad's headquarters in Herzliyah, and you couldn't take the second paper of any exam on Iraq without being able to draw every floor of the building in detail. Information was added all the time, from the strangest sources: escaped refugees, former diplomats, ex-Cabinet Ministers who were Kurds or Shi'ites, even the former British Prime Minister Edward Heath.

The first cleaner arrived a few minutes before three, presented her pass and then hurried across the tarmac before disappearing into a side door of the building. The second appeared a few moments later, and followed the same procedure. When Hannah spotted the third making her way along the far side of the pavement, she slipped across the road and filed in behind her as she walked towards the barrier.

'She's crossed the road, reached the barrier, and the guard is now checking her pass,' said the voice into the mobile phone. 'As instructed, they've let her through. She's now walking across the tarmac and following another woman through the side door. She's in, the door's closed. We've got her.'

* * *

'Now you open the safe,' said Major Saeed.

Scott swivelled the dials to their coded numbers, and the first bulb turned green. The Major was impressed. Scott then placed the palm of his hand on the white square, and a few seconds later the middle bulb turned green. The Major was mesmerised. Scott leaned forward and spoke into the voice box, and the third light turned green. The Major was speechless.

Scott pulled the handle and the door swung open. He jumped inside and immediately extracted the cardboard tube from the inside of his trouser leg.

The Major spotted it at once, and flew into a rage. Scott quickly flicked off the cap, took out the poster of Saddam Hussein and unpeeled it, letting the backing paper fall to the ground before he strolled to the far side of the safe and fixed the portrait of Saddam to the wall. A smile returned to the Major's face as Scott bent down, rolled up the backing paper and slid it into the tube.

'Now I teach you,' said Scott.

'No, no, not me,' said Major Saeed. He held his phone up in the air and said, 'We must go back upstairs.'

Scott felt like swearing as he stepped out of the safe, dropping the tube and allowing it to roll across the floor to the darkest corner. The plan he had so carefully prepared with Kratz would no longer be possible. He reluctantly left the open safe and joined the Major as he marched quickly towards the Council Chamber, this time not allowing Scott any opportunity to hold him up.

Hannah joined the other cleaners inside the building, and told them that her mother had been taken ill and that she had been sent to cover for her. She tried to assure them that it was not the first time she had done so, and was surprised when they asked no questions. She assumed that they were fearful of being involved with a stranger.

Hannah picked up a box of cleaning equipment and made her way down the back stairs. The plan displayed on the walls at Herzliyah was proving impressively accurate, even if nobody had managed the exact number of steps to the basement.

When she reached the door that led into the bottom corridor she could hear voices coming from the direction of the Council Chamber. Whoever it was must be heading for the lift. Hannah backed up against the wall so she could just see them through the thick pane of wire-mesh glass in the centre of the door.

The two men passed. Hannah didn't recognise the Major, but when she saw who was with him, her legs gave way and she almost collapsed onto the ground.

Once they were back in the courtyard, the Major dialled a number. Scott strolled over to Kratz, who was standing behind the truck.

'Did you manage to switch the Declaration?' were Kratz's first words.

'No, I didn't have time. It's still on the wall of the Chamber.'

'Damn. And the copy?'

'I left it in the tube on the floor of the safe. I couldn't risk bringing it out.'

'So how are you going to get back into the building?' asked Kratz, looking towards the Major. 'You were meant to use the time –'

'I know. But it turns out he's not the one who'll be in charge of the safe. He's getting in touch with whoever it is I'll have to instruct.'

'Not what we needed. I suspect that with the Major

our first plan would have been a lot easier,' said Kratz. 'I'd better brief the others so we can work on an alternative if things go wrong again.'

Scott nodded his agreement, and he and the Mossad leader strolled over to the truck where Aziz and Cohen were sitting in the cab smoking. As the Colonel climbed into the front, two cigarettes were quickly stubbed out. Kratz explained why they were still waiting, and warned them that this could be the Professor's last chance to get back into the Council Chamber. 'So when he comes out next time,' he explained, 'we must be ready to go. With a little luck, we might still make the border by midnight.'

How could he possibly be alive? Hannah thought. Hadn't she killed him? She had seen his dead body carried out of the room. She tried to organise her thoughts, which ranged from absolute joy to utter fear. She recalled her senior instructor telling her, 'When you're in the front line, never be surprised by anything.' She felt she now had the right to contradict him, if she was ever given the chance.

Hannah pushed open the door and crept into the corridor, which was deserted except for a pair of soldiers chatting by the entrance to the Chamber. She realised she couldn't hope to get past them without being questioned.

With a pace to go, she was told to stop, and came to a halt between them. After they had checked the cleaning box thoroughly, the one with two stripes on his arm said, 'You know it's our duty to search you as well?' Hannah made no comment while he bent down, lifted her long black robe and placed his hands on her ankles. The second one let out a raucous laugh as he put his fingers round the front of her neck, and began moving his hands down over her shoulders and across her breasts, while his colleague moved his hands up her legs and onto her thighs. As the first soldier reached the top of her legs, his colleague pinched her nipples. Hannah pushed them both away and stepped into the Chamber. They made no attempt to follow, although their laughter increased in volume.

The table had been returned to the centre of the room and the chairs casually rearranged around it. She began by straightening the table before placing the chairs at an equal distance from each other. She was still trying to take in the fact that Simon was alive. But why would the CIA send him to Baghdad? Unless . . . she stared up at the massive portrait of Saddam Hussein as she straightened his chair at the head of the table. Then her eyes came to rest on the document that was nailed next to his picture.

The American Declaration of Independence was fixed to the wall in exactly the place the Deputy Foreign Minister had claimed it was.

30

TWO CARS SWEPT UP TO the barrier and were ushered quickly through without the suggestion of a check. Scott watched carefully as a large group of soldiers surrounded the vehicles.

When a tall, heavily-built man stepped out of the second car, Aziz said under his breath, 'General Hamil, the Barber of Baghdad. He carries a cut-throat razor on his keyring.'

Kratz nodded. 'I know his complete life history,' he said. 'Even the name of the young Lieutenant he's currently living with.'

Major Saeed was now standing to attention, saluting the General, and Scott didn't need to be told that this man was of a different rank and calibre to the one he had been dealing with until then. He studied the face of the man dressed in an immaculate tailored uniform with several more rows of battle ribbons than the Major, wearing black leather gloves and carrying a swagger stick. It was a cruel face. The troops who stood around him were unable to disguise their fear.

The Major pointed to Scott and said, 'You, come.'

'I've got a feeling he means you,' said Kratz.

Scott nodded and strolled across to join them.

'Mr Bernstrom,' the General said, removing the glove from his right hand, 'I am General Hamil.' Scott shook his hand. 'I am sorry to have kept you waiting. But don't let me hold you up any longer. Please show me your safe, which Major Saeed seems so impressed by.'

Without another word the General turned and began walking towards the building, leaving Scott with little choice but to follow. For the first time in his life, Scott was terrified.

Hannah picked up a duster and some polish and began to rub in small circles on the table while taking a more careful look at the Declaration of Independence. The parchment was in such terrible condition that she doubted if it could be repaired even if Simon were able to get it back to Washington.

She peered round the door into the short corridor, and spotted the safe she had seen on the truck earlier that day. It was open, but was guarded by two more thugs, chatting as much as the other two who were stationed at the door of the Council Chamber.

Hannah made her way slowly down the corridor, dusting and polishing the ledge of the wooden skirting until she was opposite the safe and had a clear view inside. She took a pace forward and peered in as if she had never seen anything like it in her life before. One of the soldiers kicked her and she fell into the safe. The inevitable raucous laughter followed. She was about to turn round and retaliate when she saw the long cardboard cylinder in one corner, almost hidden in the shadow. She leaned across and rolled it quickly towards her until it was safely under her long skirt. She wondered if she could use it to get a message to Simon. Hannah left her duster and polish on the floor of the safe, stepped out backwards and bolted down the corridor, as if to escape the guards.

Once she was back in the Chamber she removed

another rag from the cleaning box and began polishing the table until she was in a position where no one could see her from either passageway. She then lowered herself slowly onto her knees until she was below the table, and let the cardboard tube fall to the floor in front of her. She quickly flicked off the cap, to find the cylinder wasn't empty. She pulled out the parchment, unrolled it and studied it in disbelief: a magnificent copy of the Declaration of Independence, obviously made by a craftsman, even if someone had tried to deface it. She realised immediately that Simon must have been hoping to find some way of switching the copy for the original.

Kratz watched Scott follow General Hamil into the building, then walked slowly across to the truck and climbed into the cab. He stared through the front window. No one was taking any particular interest in what they were up to.

'This is too easy,' he said. 'Far too easy.' Cohen and Aziz looked straight ahead, but didn't offer an opinion. 'If Hamil is involved, they must suspect something. The time has come for us to find out who knows what.'

'What do you have in mind, sir?' asked Cohen.

'I have a feeling that our switchboard Major isn't fully aware of what's going on. Either they haven't briefed him, or they think he's not up to the job.'

'Or both,' suggested Aziz.

Kratz nodded. 'Or both. So let's find out. Aziz, I want you and Cohen to take a stroll down to the barrier. Tell the guards that you're going for something to eat, and that you'll be back in a few minutes. If they refuse to let you through, we've got a real problem, because that will mean they know what we're up to. In which case, come back to the cab and I'll start working on what we have to do next.'

'And if they let us through?' asked Cohen.

'Get out of sight,' said Kratz, 'but keep in visual contact with the truck. That shouldn't be too hard, with these gawking crowds. If Professor Bradley comes out with his cardboard tube and I rest my arm on the window ledge as I'm doing now, get back here fast, because we won't want to be hanging about. And by the way, Cohen: if I'm not around for any reason, and the Professor should suggest a detour to the Foreign Ministry, overrule him.' Cohen nodded, without a clue what the Colonel was talking about. 'But if you spot that we're in trouble, keep well out of the way for one hour, and then pray that the whopper works.'

'Understood, sir,' said Cohen.

'Take the keys with you,' said Kratz. 'Now get going.'

Kratz stepped back down onto the tarmac, strolled over to where Major Saeed was listening to one of his interminable phone calls, and placed himself a few feet to his left as if wanting to attract his attention. At the same time he looked over his shoulder to watch Aziz and Cohen walking towards the barrier.

Kratz continued to try and attract the Major's attention as Aziz came to a halt at the barrier and started joking with one of the guards.

A few moments later Kratz saw both of his men step under the barrier. Within seconds they were lost in the crowd.

Major Saeed came off the phone. 'What is the problem this time?' he asked. Kratz took out a cigarette and asked the Major for a light.

'Don't smoke,' he said, and waved him away.

Kratz walked slowly back to the cab and took his place behind the steering wheel, his eyes never leaving the open doorway of the Ba'ath Party headquarters.

* * *

Hannah stared at the Declaration hanging on the wall. It was only a few paces away from her. She waited until she heard another roar of laughter from the soldiers before walking over to the document and quickly trying to remove the nails. Three came out with the minimum of effort, but the one at the top right-hand corner refused to budge, and the Declaration continued to dangle from it. After a few more seconds, she felt she was left with no choice but to ease the document over the head of the nail. Once the parchment was in her hand she went back to the table, placed the original on the floor and returned quickly to attach the copy to the wall.

She hardly glanced at her handiwork before she turned back to the table, knelt on the ground, and rapidly rolled up the original, replacing it in the cylinder. Once again she tucked it under her skirt. It had been the longest two minutes of her life. She remained on her knees, trying to think. She knew she couldn't risk trying to get the tube out of the building, as the guards might decide to 'search' her again. There was no alternative. She walked quickly back down the short corridor and was in the safe even before the two soldiers had stopped talking. She let the cylinder fall to the floor, then pushed it back into the darkest corner, exactly where she had first seen it. Then she picked up the duster and polish she had left behind, stepped back out of the safe and showed them to the soldiers, and ran back down the corridor towards the Chamber.

Hannah knew she must get out of the building as quickly as possible, and somehow pass a message to Simon.

And then she heard the voices.

The lift doors slid apart at the basement floor. The General stepped out into the corridor and headed towards the Council Chamber.

'And just how large is this safe?' he asked Scott.

'Nine feet in height, seven feet in width and eight feet in depth,' responded Scott immediately. 'You could hold a private meeting in there if you wished to, General.'

'Is that so?' said Hamil. 'But I am informed the safe can only be operated by one person. Is that true?'

'That is correct, General. We followed the exact specifications your government requested.'

'I am also told that the safe can withstand a nuclear attack. Is that the case?'

'Yes,' replied Scott. 'The safe has a six-inch skin and would be unaffected by any explosion other than a direct hit. In any other circumstances, everything in the safe would be preserved, even if the building it was standing in was completely demolished.'

'Impressive,' said the General as the guards sprang to attention and he touched the rim of his beret with his swagger stick. He marched into the Chamber and Scott followed, annoyed to find there was a woman polishing the table. He certainly didn't need her hanging around when he came back out. The General didn't even look at Hannah as he strode through the Chamber.

Scott glanced across at the parchment before he followed the General out of the room.

'Ah,' Hannah heard the General say when he was still several yards from the end of the corridor. 'Pure statistics don't do your safe justice, Mr Bernstrom.' The two soldiers remained rigidly at attention as the General studied the safe for some time, before stepping inside. When he saw the cardboard tube on the floor he bent down and picked it up.

'Just to protect the picture,' explained Scott as he stepped in to join him. He pointed to the portrait of Saddam Hussein.

'You are a thorough man, Mr Bernstrom,' said Hamil.

'You would have made an excellent colonel in one of my regiments.' He laughed and passed the cardboard tube over to Scott.

Hannah listened intently to every word, and concluded that she must get out of the building as quickly as possible and alert Kratz to what she had done.

'Would you like me to show you how to programme the safe?' she heard Scott ask as she reached the entrance of the Chamber.

'No, no, not me,' said General Hamil. 'The President will be the only one who will be allowed to operate the safe.' Those were the last words Hannah heard as she walked out of the Chamber, past the guards, and continued purposefully down the long corridor.

When she reached the doors that led to the staircase she turned back to see the General striding into the Chamber and, some way behind him, Scott following. He was holding the tube.

Hannah wanted to scream with delight.

Scott realised he would never be given a chance to carry out the switch once Saddam was in the building. When he reached the Chamber he allowed the General to get a few paces ahead of him. His eyes swept the room, and he was relieved to find the cleaner was no longer anywhere to be seen. The guards sprang to attention as the General strode out of the Council Chamber into the far corridor.

Scott stared at the alarm button on the wall ahead of him. 'Don't look round,' he begged under his breath as he kept his eyes on the retreating back of the General. With a yard to go before he reached the door, Scott lunged forward and jabbed his thumb on the red button. The doors immediately slammed closed and clamped with a deafening noise.

Hannah was just about to push open the door that led to the back stairs when the alarm gave out a piercing sound and all the exits were immediately bolted. She turned to discover she was alone in the corridor with General Hamil and four of his republican guards.

The General smiled at her. 'Miss Kopec, I believe. I'm delighted to make your acquaintance. I fear it will be a couple of minutes before Professor Bradley is able to join us.'

The guards surrounded Hannah as the General looked up at a television screen above the door. He watched as Scott, inside the Chamber, pressed a button on the side of his watch. Scott then ran over to the wall, quickly extracted the copy of the document from the tube, and checked it against the original. He felt he had done a fair job back in the cab of the truck, but he spat on Lewis Morris and John Witherspoon for good measure, then spent a few seconds rubbing the parchment on the stone floor before comparing it once again to the one on the wall. He looked at his watch: forty-five seconds. He began to pull the nails out of the wall, but was unable to get the top right-hand one to budge, so he eased the Declaration over its head. Sixty seconds.

Hannah stared up at the television screen in horror, watching Simon undo all her work, while the General made a phone call.

Once Scott had removed the document from the wall he placed it on the table. He then fastened the copy that he had taken out of the cardboard cylinder back on the wall, easing the parchment over the nail in the top right-hand corner, which still stubbornly refused to budge. Ninety seconds. He picked up Dollar Bill's copy from the table, rolled it up and dropped it into the cylinder. One hundred and ten seconds. He walked over to the door that led to the lifts and stood inhaling deeply for a moment before the alarm stopped and the doors swung open.

Scott knew that it would take them a few minutes

before the source of the alarm could be checked, so when he saw the General, he shrugged his shoulders and smiled.

Kratz sat on the front seat of the truck, keeping a wary eye on Major Saeed. There was a ringing sound: Saeed pressed a button and placed his phone to his ear. Suddenly, without warning, he turned, whipped out his pistol and looked anxiously towards the cab. He barked out an order, and within seconds every soldier in sight surrounded the truck, their rifles pointing directly at Kratz.

The Major rushed up. 'Where are the other two?' he demanded. Kratz shrugged his shoulders. Saeed turned on his heels and ran into the building, shouting another order as he went.

Kratz placed his right hand over his left wrist and slowly began to unpeel the plaster, a second skin, secreted beneath his watch. He delicately removed the tiny green pill stuck to the plaster and transferred it to the palm of his hand. Sixty or seventy eyes were staring at him. He began coughing, and slowly put his hand up to his mouth, lowered his head and swallowed the pill.

Saeed came rushing back out of the building and began barking new orders. Within seconds, a car pulled up beside the truck.

'Out!' the Major screamed at Kratz, who stepped down onto the tarmac and allowed a dozen fixed bayonets to guide him towards the back door of the car. He was pushed onto the seat, and two men in dark suits took a place on each side of him. One quickly turned him and tied his hands behind his back, while the other blindfolded him.

Cohen and Aziz watched from the other side of the square as the car sped away from them.

31

THE GENERAL RETURNED Scott's smile.

'I won't introduce you to Miss Saib,' he said, 'as I believe you've already met.'

Scott looked blank as he stared at the woman dressed in a black abaya and a pushi that covered her face. She was surrounded by four soldiers, their bayonets drawn.

'We have a lot to thank Miss Saib for, because of course it was she who led us to you in the first place, not to mention her postcard to Mrs Rubin that helped you find the Declaration so quickly. We did try to make it as easy as possible for you.'

'I don't know Miss Saib,' said Scott.

'Oh, come, Professor – or should I call you Agent Bradley? I admire your gallantry, but while you may claim not to know Miss Saib, you certainly know Hannah Kopec,' the General said as he ripped off Hannah's pushi.

Scott stared at Hannah, but still said nothing.

'Ah, I see you do remember her. But then, it would be hard to forget someone who tried to kill you, wouldn't it?'

Hannah's eyes pleaded with Scott.

'How touching, my dear, he's forgiven you. But I fear I don't share his forgiving nature.' The General turned to see Major Saeed running towards him. He listened carefully to what the Major whispered to him, then began banging his swagger stick rapidly against his long leather boots.

'You're a fool!' he shouted at the top of his voice, and suddenly struck the Major across the face with his swagger stick.

He turned back to face Scott. 'It seems,' he said, 'that the reunion I had planned for you and your friends will have to wait a little longer, because although we have Colonel Kratz safely locked up, the Jew and the Kurdish traitor have escaped. But it can only be a matter of time before we catch them.'

'How long have you known?' asked Hannah quietly.

'You made the mistake so many of our enemies make, Miss Kopec, of underestimating our great President,' replied the General. 'He dominates the affairs of the Middle East to a far greater extent than Gorbachev did the Russians, Thatcher the British, or Bush the American people. I ask myself, how many citizens in the West any longer believe the Allies won the Gulf War? But then, you were also stupid enough to underrate his cousin, Abdul Kanuk, our newly appointed Ambassador to Paris. Perhaps he wasn't quite that stupid when he followed you all the way to your lover's flat and stood in a doorway the rest of the night before following you back to the embassy. It was he who informed our Ambassador in Geneva what "Miss Saib" was up to.

'Of course, we needed to be sure, not least because our Deputy Foreign Minister found it so hard to accept such a tale about one of his most loyal members of staff. Such a naïve man. So, when you came to Baghdad, the Ambassador's wife invited Miss Saib's brother to dinner. But, sadly, he didn't recognise you. Your cover, as the more vulgar American papers would describe it, was blown. Those same papers keep asking pathetically, "Why doesn't Mossad assassinate President Saddam?" If only they knew how many times Mossad has tried and failed. What Colonel Kratz didn't tell you at your training school in Herzliyah, Miss Kopec, was that you are the seventeenth Mossad agent who has attempted to infiltrate our ranks during the past five years, and all of them have experienced the same tragic end as your Colonel is about to. And the real beauty of the whole exercise is that we don't have to admit we killed any of you in the first place. You see, the Jewish people are unwilling to accept, after Entebbe and Eichmann, that such a thing could possibly happen. I feel sure you will appreciate the logic of that, Professor.'

'I'll make a bargain with you,' said Scott.

'I'm touched, Professor, by your Western ethics, but I fear you have nothing to bargain with.'

'We'll trade Miss Saib if you release Hannah.'

The General burst out laughing. 'Professor, you have a keen sense of the ridiculous, but I won't insult you by suggesting that you don't understand the Arab mind. Do allow me to explain. You will be killed, and no one will comment because, as I have already explained, the West is too proud to admit that you even exist. Whereas we in the East will throw our hands in the air and ask why Mossad has kidnapped a gentle, blameless secretary on her way to Paris, and is now holding her in Tel Aviv against her will. We even know the house where she is captive. We have already arranged for sentimental pictures of her to be released to every paper in the Western world, and a distraught mother and son have been coached for weeks by one of your own public relations companies to face the Western press. We'll even have Amnesty International protesting outside Israeli embassies across the world on her behalf.'

Scott stared at the General.

'Poor Miss Saib will be released within days. Both of

you, on the other hand, will die an unannounced, unheralded and unmourned death. To think that all you sacrificed your lives for was a scrap of paper. And while we are on that subject, Professor, I will relieve you of the Declaration.'

The four soldiers stepped forward and thrust their bayonets at Scott's throat as the General snatched the cardboard tube from his grasp.

'You did well to switch the documents in two minutes, Professor,' said the General, glancing up at the television screen above him. 'But you can be assured that it remains our intention to burn the original very publicly on the fourth of July, and I feel confident that we will destroy President Clinton's flimsy reputation along with it.' The General laughed. 'You know, Professor, I have for many years enjoyed killing people, but I shall gain a particular pleasure from your deaths, because of the appropriate way you will be departing this world.'

The soldiers surrounded Hannah and Scott and forced them back into the Chamber and on towards the short corridor. The General followed them down the passage. They all came to a halt in front of the open safe.

'Allow me,' said General Hamil, 'to inform you of one statistic you failed to mention, Professor, when you briefed me on this amazing feat of engineering. Perhaps you simply didn't know, although I am bound to admit that you have done your homework thoroughly. But did you realise that one person locked in a safe of this size, with a capacity of 504 cubic feet, can only hope to survive for six hours? I do not yet know the exact length of time two people can hope to survive while sharing the same amount of oxygen. But I will very shortly.' He removed a stopwatch from his pocket, waved his swagger stick, and the soldiers hurled first Hannah and then Scott into the safe. The smile remained on the General's face as two of the soldiers pushed the massive door closed. The lights all began flashing red.

The General clicked his stopwatch.

When the car came to a halt, Kratz reckoned that the distance they had travelled was under a mile. He heard the door open and felt a shove on his arm to indicate he should get out of the car. He was pushed up three stone steps before entering a building and walking into a long corridor. His footsteps echoed on the wooden floor. Then he was guided into a room on his left, where he was pushed down onto a chair, tied and gagged. His shoes and socks were removed. When he heard the door close, he sensed he was alone.

It was a long time – he couldn't be sure just how long – before the door opened again. The first voice he heard was General Hamil's. 'Remove the gag,' was all he said.

Kratz could hear him pacing round the chair, but at first the General said nothing. Kratz began to concentrate. He knew the pill was good for two hours, no more, and he suspected that it was already forty or fifty minutes since they had driven him away from Ba'ath headquarters.

'Colonel Kratz, I have waited some time for the privilege of making your acquaintance. I have long admired your work. You are a perfectionist.'

'Cut the crap,' said Kratz, 'because I don't admire you or your work.'

He waited for the first slap of gloves across his face or for a fist to come crashing into his jaw, but the General simply continued to circle the chair.

'You mustn't be too disappointed,' said the General. 'I feel sure, after all you've heard about us, that you must have expected at least some electric shocks by now, perhaps the Chinese water torture, even the rack, but I fear – unlike Mossad, Colonel – that when dealing with people of your seniority we long ago dispensed with such primitive methods. We have found them to be outmoded, a thing of the past. Worse, they just don't get results. You Zionists are tough and well trained. Few of you talk, very few. So we've had to resort to more scientific methods to gain the information we need.'

If it was still within the hour, thought Kratz, he had judged it well.

'A simple injection of PPX will ensure that we learn everything we want to know,' continued the General, 'and once we have the information we require, we'll simply kill you. So much more efficient than in the past, and with all the environmental complaints one gets nowadays, so much more tidy. Though, I must confess, I miss the old methods. So you'll appreciate why I couldn't resist locking Miss Kopec and Professor Bradley in their safe, especially as they hadn't seen each other for so long.'

Kratz's hand was pressed back and held against the arm of the chair. He felt fingers searching for a vein, and when the needle went in, he flinched. He began counting: one, two, three, four, five, six . . .

He was about to find out if one of Europe's leading chemists had, as she claimed, found the antidote for the Iraqis' latest truth drug. Mossad had tracked down the supplier in Austria. Strange how many people think there are no Jews left in Austria.

. . . thirty-seven, thirty-eight, thirty-nine . . .

The drug was still in its testing stage, and needed to be proved under non-laboratory conditions. If a person could remain fully in control of his senses while appearing to be under hypnosis, then they would know their antidote was a success.

. . . one minute, one minute one, one minute two, one minute three . . .

The test would come when they stuck the second needle in, and that might be anywhere. Then the trick was to show no reaction whatsoever, or the General would immediately realise that the original injection had failed to have the required effect. The training programme for this particular 'realistic experience' was not universally popular among agents, and although Kratz had experienced 'the prick', as it was affectionately known, once a month for the past nine months, you only had a single chance in 'non-laboratory conditions' to discover if you could pass the test.

. . . one minute thirty-seven, one minute thirty-eight, one minute thirty-nine . . .

The injection was meant to take effect after two minutes, and every agent had been taught to expect the second needle at some time between two and three minutes, thus the counting.

. . . one minute fifty-six, one minute fifty-seven . . .

Relax, it must come at any moment. Relax.

Suddenly the needle was jabbed in and out of the big toe on his left foot. Kratz stopped gritting his teeth; even his breathing remained regular. He had won the Israeli Pincushion Award, First Class. Mossad made jokes about everything.

32

'. . . AND ALL THAT TIME I really thought you were dead.'

'We had no way of letting you know,' said Scott.

'Still, it's no longer of any importance, Simon,' said Hannah. 'Sorry. "Scott" will take a bit of getting used to. I may not be able to manage it in the time we've got left.'

'We may have more time left than you think,' said Scott.

'How can you say that?'

'One of the contingency plans that Kratz and I worked on was that if any of us were caught and tortured while someone else was still free, we'd hold out for one hour before telling them the whopper.'

Hannah knew exactly what Mossad meant by the whopper, even if on this occasion she didn't know the details.

'Although I have to admit this is one scenario we never considered,' said Scott. 'In fact, the exact opposite. We thought that if we were able to convince them we had another purpose for bringing the safe to Baghdad, they'd immediately evacuate the building and clear the surrounding area.'

'And what would that have achieved?'

'We hoped that with the building empty, even if we'd been captured, the other agents who came over the border a day ahead of us might have a clear hour to get into the Council Chamber and remove the Declaration.'

'But wouldn't the Iraqis have taken the document away with them?'

'Not necessarily. Our plan was that we would tell them exactly what would happen to their beloved leader if the safe was closed by anyone other than me. We felt that would cause panic, and they'd probably leave everything behind.'

'So Kratz drew the short straw.'

'Yes,' said Scott quietly. 'Not that his original plan is relevant any longer, after I was stupid enough to hand over the Declaration to Hamil. So now we'll have to use the time to get out, not in.'

'But you didn't hand it over,' said Hannah. 'The Declaration is still on the wall of the Chamber.'

'I'm afraid not,' said Scott. 'Hamil was right. I switched the copies after I set the alarm off. So I ended up giving Hamil back the original.'

'No, you didn't,' said Hannah. 'It's because you believed you switched the original that you fooled Hamil as well as yourself.'

'What are you talking about?' said Scott.

'I'm the one responsible,' said Hannah. 'I found the cardboard tube in the safe and switched the two documents, thinking I could get out of the building and then pass on a message to let Kratz know what I'd done. The trouble was, you and General Hamil arrived just as I was about to leave. So, when you locked yourself in the Chamber, you put the original back on the wall, and then you handed over the copy to Hamil.'

Scott took her in his arms again. 'You're a genius,' he said.

'No I'm not,' said Hannah. 'So you'd better let me in on the secret of what you've planned for this particular scenario. To start with, how do we get out of a locked safe?'

'That's the beauty of it,' said Scott. 'It isn't locked. It's programmed so that it can only be opened and closed by me.'

'Who dreamed that one up?'

'A Swede who would happily take our place, but he's stuck in Kalmar. The first thing I have to do is discover which wall is the door.'

'That's easy,' said Hannah. 'It has to be exactly opposite me because I'm sitting below the picture of Saddam, remember?'

Scott and Hannah began the short crawl on their hands and knees to the other side of the safe. 'Now we go to the right-hand corner,' he said, 'so that when we push, the leverage will be easier.'

Hannah nodded, and then remembered they couldn't see each other. 'Yes,' she said.

Scott checked the luminous dial of his watch. 'But not quite yet,' he added. 'We'll have to give Kratz a little more time.'

'Enough time to tell me what the whopper is?' asked Hannah.

'Good,' said the General, when Kratz didn't react to the needle being jabbed into his big toe. 'Now we can find out all we need to know. But to begin with, some simple questions. Your Mossad rank?'

'Colonel,' said Kratz. The secret was to tell them only facts you felt confident they already knew.

'Your initiation number?'

'78216,' he said. If in doubt, assume they know, otherwise you could be caught out.

'And your official position?'

'Councillor for Cultural Affairs to the Court of St James in London.' You are allowed three testing lies and one whopper, but no more.

'What are the names of your three colleagues who accompanied you on this mission?'

'Professor Scott Bradley, an expert on ancient manuscripts,' – the first testing lie – 'Ben Cohen, and Aziz Zeebari.' The truth.

'And the girl, Hannah Kopec, what is her rank in Mossad?'

'She is still a trainee.'

'How long has she been with Mossad?'

'Just over two years.'

'And her role?'

'To be placed in Baghdad to discover where the Declaration of Independence was located.' The second lie.

'You are doing well, Colonel,' said the General, looking at the long, thin cardboard tube he held in his right hand.

'And was this your overall responsibility as her commanding officer?'

'No. I was simply to accompany the safe from Kalmar.' The third lie.

'But surely that was nothing more than an excuse to locate the Declaration of Independence?'

Kratz hesitated. Experts had been able to show that even under the influence of a truth drug a highly trained agent would still hesitate when asked a secret he had never revealed in the past.

'What was the true purpose of your bringing the safe to Baghdad, Colonel?'

Kratz still remained silent.

'Colonel Kratz,' said the General, his voice rising with every word, 'what was the real reason you brought the safe to Baghdad?'

Kratz counted to three before he spoke.

'To blow up the Ba'ath Party headquarters with a tiny nuclear device secreted in the safe, in the hope of killing the President along with all the members of the Revolutionary Command Council.' The whopper.

How Kratz wished he could see the General's face. It was Hamil who was hesitating now.

'How was the bomb to be activated?'

Again Kratz did not reply.

'I will ask you once again, Colonel. How was the bomb to be activated?'

Still Kratz said nothing.

'When will it go off?' shouted the General.

'Two hours after the safe has been closed by anyone other than the Professor.'

The General checked his watch, rushed to the only phone in the room and shouted to be put through to the President immediately. He waited until he heard Saddam's voice. He didn't notice that Kratz had fainted and fallen from his chair to the floor.

Scott eased himself into the corner before once again checking the little sulphur dots on his watch. It was 5.19. He and Hannah had been in the safe for an hour and seventeen minutes.

'I'm going to push now. If you hear anything, shove as hard as you can. If there's anyone still out there our only hope will be to take them by surprise.'

Scott began to exert the minimum amount of pressure on the corner of the door with the tips of his fingers, and it eased open an inch. He stopped and listened, but could hear nothing. He took a look through the tiny crack, and could see no one. He pushed another inch. Still no sound. Both of them now had a clear view of the corridor.

Scott looked at Hannah and nodded, and together they shoved as hard as they could. The ton of steel shot open. They both leaped into the corridor, but there was no one to be seen. There was an eerie silence.

Scott and Hannah walked slowly down the short corridor, keeping to the sides until they reached the Chamber. Still no sound. Scott put a foot into the Chamber and glanced to his left. The Declaration of Independence was still hanging on the wall next to the portrait of Saddam.

Hannah moved silently to the far end of the Chamber and looked into the long corridor. She then turned back to Scott and nodded. Scott checked the spelling of 'Brittish' before saying a silent hallelujah. He pulled out three of the nails, then eased the Declaration over the remaining nail in the top right-hand corner, trying to forget that he had spat on a national treasure and rubbed it in the dust. He gave Saddam one last look before rolling up the parchment and joining Hannah in the corridor.

Hannah slid along the wall, then pointed to the lift. She pulled a finger across her throat to show Scott she wanted to avoid using it in favour of the back stairs. He nodded his agreement and followed her out of the side door.

They moved quickly but silently up the six flights of stairs until they reached the ground floor. Hannah beckoned Scott into the side room where the cleaners had collected their boxes. She had reached the window on the far side of the room and was on her knees even before Scott had closed the door. He joined her and they stared out on a deserted Victory Square. There was no one to be seen in any direction.

'God bless Kratz,' said Scott.

Hannah nodded and beckoned him to follow her again. She led him back into the corridor and guided him quickly to the side door. Scott opened the door tentatively and slipped out ahead of her. A moment later she joined him on the tarmac.

He pointed to a group of palm trees halfway across the courtyard, and she nodded once again. They covered the twenty yards to its relative safety in under three seconds. Scott turned to look back at the building and saw the truck standing up against the wall. He assumed that, in the panic, it was just something else that had been left behind.

He tapped Hannah on the shoulder and indicated that he wanted to return to the building. They covered the ground at the same pace as before, ducking back inside the door. Scott led Hannah to the main corridor, where they found the front door was swinging on its hinges. He looked through the gap and pointed to the truck, mimed to which side he would go and touched her shoulder. Again they sprinted across the tarmac as if reacting to a starting pistol.

Scott jumped behind the wheel as Hannah leaped in the other side.

'Where the hell –' was Scott's first reaction when he discovered the ignition key wasn't in place. They began frantically to search the glove compartment, under the seats, on the dashboard. 'The bastards must have taken the key with them.'

'Simon, look out!' screamed Hannah. Scott turned to see a figure leaping up onto the footplate.

Hannah moved quickly into position to attack the intruder, but Scott blocked her.

'Good afternoon, miss,' said the stranger. 'Sorry we haven't been properly introduced,' he added before turning to Scott. 'Move over, Professor,' he said as he put the key back in the ignition. 'If you recall, it was agreed that I'd do the driving.'

'What in heaven's name are you doing here, Sergeant?' asked Scott.

'Now that's what I call a real American welcome,' replied Cohen. 'But, to answer your question, I was just obeying orders. I was told if you came out of that door carrying a cardboard tube, I was to get myself back here and move the hell out of it, but not under any circumstances to allow you to make a detour to the Foreign Ministry. By the way, where's the tube?'

'Look out!' shouted Hannah again, as she turned and saw an Arab charging towards them from the other side.

'That one won't do you any harm,' said Cohen, 'he's bloody useless. Doesn't even know the difference between a Diet Coke and a Pepsi.' Aziz leaped onto the running board and said to Scott, 'I think we've got about another twenty minutes, Professor, before they work out that there's no bomb in the safe.'

'Then let's get out of here,' said Scott.

'But where to?' asked Hannah.

'Aziz and I have already done a recce, sir. As soon as the sirens sounded we knew that Kratz must have sold them the whopper, because they couldn't move fast enough to get themselves below. Soldiers and police first seems to be the rule out here. Aziz and I have had the run of the city centre for the last hour. In fact the only person we bumped into was one of our own agents, Dave Feldman. He'd already sussed out the best route to give us a chance of avoiding any military.'

'Not bad, Cohen,' said Scott.

Cohen turned suddenly and stared at the Professor.

'I didn't do it for you, sir, I did it for Colonel Kratz. He got me out of jail once, and he's the only officer that's ever treated me like a human being. So whatever it is that you're holding in your hands, Professor, it had bloody well better be worth his life.'

'Thousands have given their lives for it over the years,' said Scott quietly. 'It's the American Declaration of Independence.'

'Good God,' said Cohen. 'How did the bastards get their hands on that?' He paused briefly. 'Am I meant to believe you?'

Scott nodded and unrolled the parchment. Cohen and Aziz stared in disbelief for several seconds.

'Right then, we'd better get you home, Professor, hadn't we?' said Cohen. 'Aziz will take over while we're in his neck of the woods.' He jumped out of the cab and the Kurd came running round to take his place behind the wheel. Once Cohen had clambered over the tailboard, he banged the roof of the truck and Aziz switched the engine on.

They accelerated round the courtyard, drove straight through the barrier and out onto Victory Square. The only other vehicles to be seen had long since been abandoned, and there was no sign of anyone on the streets.

'The area has been cleared for three miles in every direction, so it will be a little time before we come across anything,' Aziz said as he turned left into Kindi Street. He quickly moved the lorry up to sixty miles per hour, a speed only Saddam had ever experienced before on that particular road.

'I'm going to take the old Baquba Road out of the city, travelling through the areas where we're least likely to see any sign of the military,' explained Aziz as he passed the fountain made famous by Ali Baba. 'I'm still hoping to reach the highway out of Baghdad within the magic two hours.'

Aziz took a sudden right, switching gears but hardly losing any speed as he continued through what gave every impression of being a ghost town. Scott looked up at the sun as they crossed a bridge over the Tigris; in an hour or so it would have disappeared behind the highest buildings, and their chances of remaining undetected would greatly improve.

Aziz swung past Karmel Junblat University and into Jamila Street. There were still no people on the roads or pavements, and Scott felt that if anyone did see them now they would assume they were part of an army unit on patrol.

It was Hannah who spotted the first person: an old man, bent double, sitting on the edge of the pavement as if nothing in particular had taken place. They drove past him at sixty miles per hour, but he didn't even look up.

Aziz swung into the next road and found himself facing a group of young looters carrying off televisions and electronic equipment. They scattered when they saw the truck. Around the next corner there were more looters, but still no sign of police or soldiers.

When Aziz spotted the first dark-green uniforms he swerved quickly right, down a side street that on any other Wednesday would have been packed with shoppers and where a vehicle would have been lucky to average more than five miles per hour. But today Aziz managed to keep the speedometer above fifty. He turned right again, and they saw some of the first of the locals who had ventured back onto the streets. Once they had reached the end of the road, Aziz was able to join the main thoroughfare out of Baghdad. The traffic was still light.

Aziz eased the truck across into the outside lane, checking his rear-view mirror every few seconds and complying with the speed limit of fifty miles per hour. 'Never get stopped for the wrong reasons,' Kratz had warned him a thousand times.

When Aziz switched his sidelights on, Scott's hopes began to rise. Although the two hours had to be up, he doubted that anybody would be out searching for them yet, and it was well understood that with every mile out of Baghdad the citizens became less and less loyal to Saddam.

Once Aziz had left the Baghdad boundary sign behind him he pushed the speedometer up to sixty. 'Give me twenty minutes, Allah,' he said. 'Give me twenty minutes and I'll get them to Castle Post.'

'Castle Post?' said Scott. 'We're not on a Red Indian scouting mission.'

Aziz laughed. 'No, Professor, it's the site of a First World War British Army post, where we can hide for the night. If I can get there before –' All three of them spotted the first army lorry coming towards them. Aziz swung off to the left, skidded into a side road, and was immediately forced to drop his speed.

'So now where are we heading?' asked Scott.

'Khan Beni Saad,' said Aziz, 'the village where I was born. It will only be possible for us to stay for one night, but no one will think of looking for us there. Tomorrow, Professor, you will have to decide which of the six borders we're going to cross.'

General Hamil had been pacing around his office for the past hour. The two hours had long passed, and he was starting to wonder if Kratz might have got the better of him. But he couldn't work out how.

He was even beginning to regret that he had killed the man. If Kratz had still been alive, at least he could have fallen back on the tried and trusted method of torture. Now he would never know how he would have responded to his particular shaving technique.

Hamil had already ordered a reluctant lieutenant and his platoon back to the basement of the Ba'ath headquarters. The lieutenant had returned swiftly to report that the safe door was wide open and the truck had disappeared, as had the document that had been hanging on the wall. The General smiled. He remained confident that he was in possession of the original Declaration, but he extracted the parchment from the cylinder and laid it on his desk to double-check. When he came to the word 'British', he turned first white, and then, by several degrees, deeper and deeper shades of red.

He immediately gave an order to cancel all military leave, and then commanded five divisions of the elite guard to mount a search for the terrorists. But he had no way of knowing how much start they had on him, how far they might have already travelled, and in which direction.

However, he did know that they couldn't remain on the main roads in that truck for long, without being spotted. Once it was dark, they would probably retreat into the desert to rest overnight. But they would have to come out the following morning, when they must surely try to cross one of the six borders. The General had already given an order that if even one of the terrorists managed to cross any border, guards from every customs post would be arrested and jailed, whether they were on duty or not. The two soldiers who were supposed to have closed the safe door had already been shot for not carrying out his orders, and the Major detailed to supervise the moving of the safe had been immediately arrested. At least Major Saeed's decision to take his own life had saved Hamil the trouble of a court martial: within an hour the Major had been found hanging in his cell. Obviously leaving a coil of rope in the middle of the floor below a hook in the ceiling had proved to be a compelling enough hint. And as for the two young medical students who'd been responsible for the injections, and who had witnessed his conversation with Kratz, they were already on their way to the southern borders, to serve with a less than elite regiment. They were such nice-looking boys, the General thought; he gave them a week at the most.

Hamil picked up the phone and dialled a private number that would connect him to the palace. He needed to be certain that he was the first person to explain to the President what had taken place that afternoon.

33

SCOTT HAD ALWAYS CONSIDERED his own countrymen to be an hospitable race, but he had never experienced such a welcome as Aziz's family gave to the three strangers.

Khan Beni Saad, the village in which Aziz was born, had, he told them, just over 250 inhabitants at the last count, and barely survived on the income it derived from selling its small crop of oranges, tangerines and dates to the housewives of Kirkuk and Arbil.

The chief of the tribe, who turned out to be one of Aziz's uncles, immediately opened his little stone home to them so that they could make use of the one bath in the village. The women of the house – there seemed to be a lot of them – kept boiling water until all of the visitors were pronounced clean.

When Scott finally emerged from the chief's home, he found a table had been set up under a clump of citrus trees in the Huwaider fields. It was laden with strange fish, meat, fruit and vegetables. He feared they must have gathered something from every home in the village.

Under a clear starlit night, they devoured the fresh food and drank mountain water that, if bottled, a Californian would happily have paid a fortune for.

But Scott's thoughts kept returning to the fact that tomorrow they would have to leave these idyllic

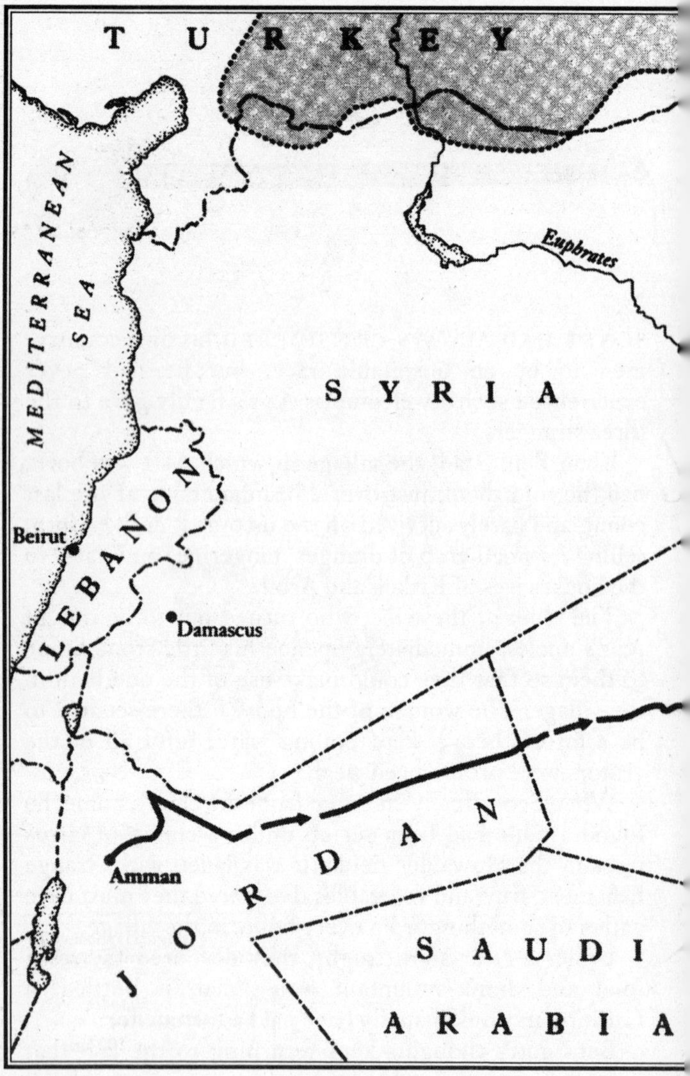

TURKEY
MEDITERRANEAN SEA
Euphrates
SYRIA
LEBANON
Beirut
Damascus
Amman
JORDAN
SAUDI ARABIA

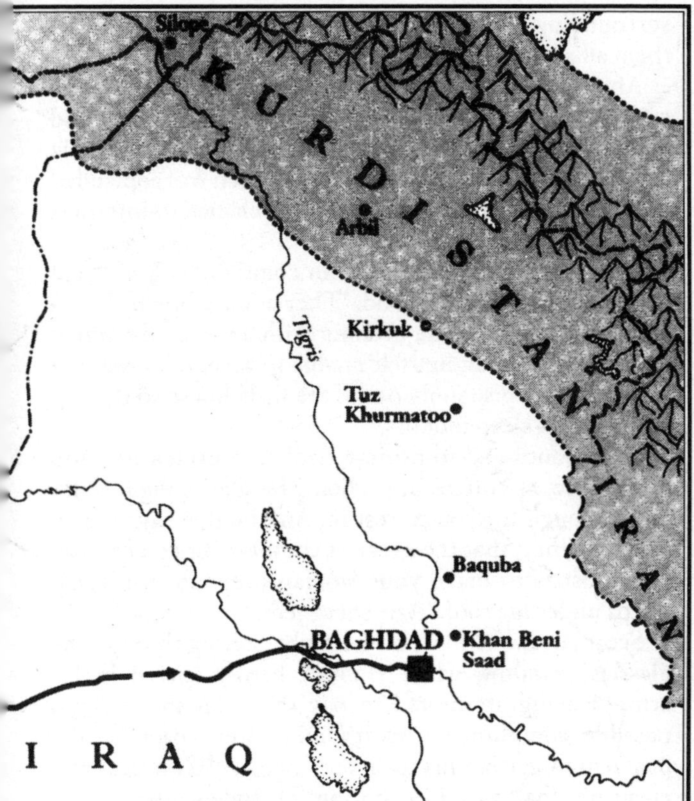

Silope
KURDISTAN
Arbil
Tigris
Kirkuk
Tuz Khurmatoo
IRAN
Baquba
BAGHDAD
Khan Beni Saad
IRAQ
Regions inhabited by the Kurdish nation
0
50 miles
0
100 kms

surroundings, and that he would somehow have to get them all across one of the six borders.

After coffee had been served in various different-sized cups and mugs, the chief rose from his place at the head of the table to make a speech of welcome, which Aziz translated. Scott made a short reply which was applauded even before Aziz had been given the chance to interpret what he had said.

'That's one thing they have in common with us,' said Hannah, taking Scott's hand. 'They admire brevity.'

The chief ended the evening with an offer for which Scott thanked him, but felt unable to accept. He wanted to order all of his family out of the little house so that his guests could sleep indoors.

Scott continued to protest until Aziz explained, 'You must agree, or you insult his home by suggesting it is not good enough for you to rest in. And by the way, it is an Arab tradition that the greatest compliment you can pay your host is to make your woman pregnant while she sleeps under his roof.' Aziz shrugged.

Scott lay awake most of the night, staring through the glassless window, while Hannah hardly stirred in his arms. Having attempted to pay the chief the greatest possible compliment, Scott's mind went back to the problem of getting his team over one of the borders and ensuring that the Declaration of Independence was returned safely to Washington.

When the first ray of light crept across the woven rug that covered their bed, Scott released Hannah and kissed her on the forehead. He slipped from under the sheets to find that the little tin bath was already full of warm water, and the women had begun boiling more urns over an open fire.

Once Scott was dressed, he spent an hour studying maps of the country, searching for possible routes across

Iraq's six borders. He quickly dismissed Syria and Iran as impossible, because the armies of both would be happy to slaughter them on sight. He also felt that to return over the Jordanian border would be far too great a risk. By the time Hannah had joined him he had also dismissed Saudi Arabia as too well guarded, and was now down to only five routes and two borders.

As his hosts began to prepare breakfast, Scott and Hannah wandered down into the village hand in hand, as any lovers might on a summer morning. The locals smiled, and some bowed. Although none could hold a conversation with them, they all spoke so eloquently with their eyes that they both understood.

Once they had reached the end of the village, they turned and strolled back up the path towards the chief's house. Cohen was frying eggs on an open fire, and Hannah stopped to watch how the women baked the thin, circular pieces of bread which, covered in honey, were a feast in themselves. The chief, once again sitting at the head of the table, beckoned Scott to the place beside him. Cohen had already taken a seat on a stool and was about to begin his breakfast when a goat walked up and tugged the eggs straight off the plate. Hannah laughed and cracked Cohen another egg before he had a chance to voice his opinion.

Scott spread some honey on a piece of warm bread, and a woman placed a mug of goat's milk in front of him.

'Worked out what we have to do next, have you, Professor?' asked Cohen as Hannah dropped a second fried egg on to his plate. In one sentence, he had brought them all back to reality.

A villager came up to the table, knelt by the side of the chief and whispered in his ear. The message was passed on to Aziz.

'Bad news,' Aziz told them. 'There are soldiers blocking all the roads that lead back to the main highway.'

'Then we'll have to go across the desert,' said Scott. He unfolded his map and spread it across the table. Alternative routes were highlighted by a dozen blue felt-tip lines. He pointed to a path leading to a road which would take them to the city of Khalis.

'That is not a path,' said Aziz. 'It was once a river, but it dried up many years ago. We could walk along it, but we would have to leave the truck behind.'

'It won't be enough to leave the truck,' said Scott. 'We'll have to destroy it. If it were ever found by Saddam's soldiers, they would raze the village to the ground and massacre your people.'

The chief looked perplexed as Aziz translated all Scott had said. The old man stroked the rough morning stubble on his chin and smiled as Scott and Hannah listened to his judgement, unable to understand a word.

'My uncle says you must have his car,' Aziz translated. 'It is old, but he hopes that it still runs well.'

'He is kind,' said Scott. 'But if we cannot drive a truck across the desert, how can we possibly go by car?'

'He understands your problem,' said Aziz. 'He says you must take the car to pieces bit by bit, and his people will carry it the twelve miles across the desert until you reach the road that leads to Khalis. Then you can put it together again.'

'We cannot accept such a gesture,' said Scott. 'He is too generous. We will walk and find some form of transport when we reach Huwaider.' He pointed to the first village along the road.

Aziz translated once again: his uncle looked sad and murmured a few words. 'He says it is not really his car, it was his brother's car. It now belongs to me.'

For the first time, Scott realised that Aziz's father had been the village chief, and how much his uncle was willing to risk to save them from being captured by Saddam's troops.

'But even if we could take the car to pieces and put it together again, what about army patrols once we reach that road?' he asked. 'By now thousands of Hamil's men are bound to be out there searching for us.'

'But not on those roads,' Aziz replied. 'The army will stick to the highway. They realise that's our only hope of getting across the border. No, our first problem will come when we reach the roadside check at Khalis.' He moved his finger a few inches across the map. 'There's bound to be at least a couple of soldiers on duty there.'

Scott studied the different routes again while Aziz listened to his uncle.

'And could we get as far as Tuz Khurmatoo without having to use the highway?' asked Scott, not looking up from the map.

'Yes, there's a longer route, through the hills, that the army would never consider, because they'd run the risk of being attacked by the Peshmerga guerrillas so near the border with Kurdistan. But once you've gone through Tuz Khurmatoo it's only a couple of miles to the main highway, though it's still another forty-five miles from there, with no other way of crossing the border.'

Scott held his head in his hands and didn't speak for some moments. 'So if we took that route we would be committed to crossing the border at Kirkuk,' he eventually said. 'Where both sides could prove to be unfriendly.'

The chief started tapping Kirkuk on the map with his finger while talking urgently to his nephew.

'My uncle says Kirkuk is our best chance. Most of the inhabitants are Kurdish and hate Saddam Hussein. Even the Iraqi soldiers have been known to defect and become Kurdish Peshmergas.'

'But how will they know which side we're on?' asked Scott.

'My uncle will get a message to the Peshmergas, so that when you reach the border they will do everything they can to help you to cross it. It's not an official border, but once you're in Kurdistan you'll be safe.'

'The Kurds sound our best bet,' said Hannah, who had been listening intently. 'Especially if they believe our original mission was to kill Saddam.'

'It might just work, sir,' said Cohen. 'That is, if the car's up to it.'

'You're the mechanic, Cohen, so only you can tell us if it's possible.'

Once Aziz had translated Scott's words the chief rose to his feet and led them to the back of his house. He came to a halt beside a large oblong object covered by a black sheet. He and Aziz lifted off the cover. Scott couldn't believe his eyes.

'A pink Caddy?' he said.

'A classic 1956 Sedan de Ville, to be exact, sir,' said Cohen, rubbing his hands with delight. He opened the long, heavy door and climbed behind the vast steering wheel. He pulled a lever under the dashboard and the bonnet flicked up. He got out, lifted the bonnet and studied the engine for some minutes.

'Not bad,' he said. 'If I can nick a few parts from the truck, I'll give you a racing car within a couple of hours.'

Scott checked his watch. 'I can only spare you an hour if we're hoping to cross the border tonight.'

Scott and Hannah returned to the house and once again pored over the map. The road Aziz had recommended was roughly twelve miles away, but across terrain that would be hard going even if they were carrying nothing.

'It could take hours,' Scott said.

'What's the alternative if we can't use the highway?' asked Hannah.

While she and Scott continued working on the route and Cohen on the car, Aziz rounded up thirty of the strongest men in the village. At a few minutes past the hour, Cohen reappeared in the house, his hands, arms, face and hair covered in oil.

'It's ready to be taken apart, Professor.'

'Well done. But we'll have to get rid of the truck first,' said Scott as he rose from the table.

'That won't be possible, sir,' said Cohen. 'Not now that I've removed one or two of the best parts of its engine. That Cadillac should be able to do over a hundred miles per hour,' he said, with some pride. 'In third gear.'

Scott laughed, and accompanied by Aziz went in search of the chief. Once again he explained the problem.

This time the chief's face showed no anxiety. Aziz translated his thoughts. ' "Do not fear, my friend," he says. "While you are marching across the desert we will strip the truck and bury each piece in a place Saddam's soldiers could never hope to discover in a thousand years." '

Scott looked apprehensive, but Aziz nodded his agreement. Without waiting for Scott's opinion the chief led his nephew to the back of the house, where they found Cohen supervising the stripping of the Cadillac and the distribution of its pieces among the chosen thirty.

Four men were to carry the engine on a makeshift stretcher, and another six would lift the chrome body onto their shoulders like pallbearers. Four more each carried a wheel with its white-rimmed tyre, while another four transported the chassis. Two held onto the red-and-white leather front seat, another two the back seat, and one the dashboard. Cohen continued to distribute the remaining pieces of the Cadillac until he came to the back of the line, where three children who looked no more than ten or eleven were given responsibility for two five-gallon cans of petrol and a tool bag. Only the roof was to be left behind.

Aziz's uncle led his people to the last house in the village so he could watch his guests begin their journey towards the horizon.

Scott shook hands with the chief, but could find no words adequate to thank him. 'Give me a call the next time you're passing through New Haven,' was what he would have said to a fellow American.

'I will return in better times,' he told the old man, and Aziz translated.

'My people wait for that day.'

Scott turned to watch Cohen, compass in hand, leading his improbable platoon on what appeared likely to be an endless journey. He took one of the five-gallon cans from the smallest of the children, and pointed back towards the village, but the little boy shook his head and quickly grabbed Scott's canvas bag.

Would history ever reveal this particular mode of transport for the Declaration of Independence, Scott wondered, as Cohen shouted 'Forward!'

General Hamil continued to pace round his office, as he waited for the phone to ring.

When Saddam had learned the news of Major Saeed's incompetence in allowing the terrorists to escape with the Declaration, he was only furious that he had not been able personally to end the man's life.

The only order he had given the General was that a message should be put out on state radio and television stations hourly, stating that there had been an attempt on his life which had failed, but that the Zionist terrorists were still at large. Full descriptions of the would-be assassins were given, and he asked his beloved countrymen to help him in his quest to hunt down the infidels.

Had the matter been less urgent, the General would have counselled against releasing such information, on the grounds that most of those who came across the terrorists might want to help them, or at best turn a blind eye. The only advice he did give his leader was to suggest that a large reward should be offered for their capture. Enlightened self-interest, he had found, could so often overcome almost any scruples.

The General came to a halt in front of a map pinned to the wall behind his desk, temporarily covering a portrait of Saddam. His eye passed down the many thin red lines that wriggled between Baghdad and Iraq's borders. There were a hundred villages on both sides of every one of the roads, and the General was painfully aware that most of them would be only too happy to harbour the fugitives.

And then he recollected one of the names Kratz had given him. Aziz Zeebari – a common enough name, yet it had been nagging at him the whole morning.

'Aziz Zeebari . . . Aziz Zeebari . . . Aziz Zeebari . . .' he repeated. And then he remembered. He had executed a man of that name who had been involved in an attempted coup about seven years before. Could it possibly have been the traitor's father?

The load-bearers halted every fifteen minutes to rest, change responsibilities and place the strain on yet-untested muscles. 'Pit stops', Cohen called them. They managed two miles in the first hour, and between them drank far more water than any car would have devoured.

When Scott checked his watch at midday, he estimated that they had only covered a little over two thirds of the distance to the road: it had been a long time since they had lost sight of the village but there was still no sign of life on the horizon. The sun beat down as they continued their journey, the pace slowing with each mile.

It was the eyes of a ten-year-old child that were the first to see movement. He ran to the front and pointed. Scott could see nothing as the little boy jogged ahead, and it was to be another forty minutes before they could all clearly see the dusty road. The sight made them quicken their pace.

Once they reached the side of the road, Aziz gave the order that the pieces of the car should be lowered gently to the ground, and a little girl, who Scott hadn't noticed before, handed out bread, goats' cheese and water while they rested.

Cohen was the first up and began walking around his platoon, checking on the various pieces. By the time he had returned to the chassis, they were all impatient to put the car together again.

Scott sat on the ground and watched as thirty untrained mechanics, under the direction of Sergeant Cohen, slowly bolted the old Cadillac together piece by piece. When the last wheel had been screwed on, Scott had to admit it *looked* like a car, but wondered if the old veteran would ever be able to start.

All the villagers surrounded the massive pink vehicle as Cohen sat in the driver's seat.

Aziz waited until the children had emptied their last drop of petrol into the tank. He then screwed on the big steel cap and shouted, 'Go for it!'

Cohen turned the key in the ignition.

The engine turned over slowly, but wouldn't catch. Cohen leaped out, lifted the bonnet and asked Aziz to take his place behind the wheel. He made a slight re-adjustment to the fan belt, checked the distributor and cleaned the spark plugs of the last few remaining grains of sand before screwing them in tightly. He stuck his head out from under the bonnet.

'Have a go, Kurd.'

Aziz turned the key and pressed the accelerator. The engine turned over a little more quickly but still didn't want to start. Sixty eyes stared beneath the bonnet, but offered no advice as Cohen spent several more minutes working on the distributor.

'Once again, and give it more throttle!' he shouted. Aziz switched on the ignition. The chug became a churn, and then suddenly a roar as Aziz pressed the accelerator – a noise only exceeded by the cheers of the villagers.

Cohen took Aziz's place in the front and lifted the gear lever on the steering column up into first. But the car refused to budge, as the wheels spun round and it bedded itself deeper and deeper into the sand. Cohen turned off the engine and jumped out. Sixty hands were flattened against the car as it was rocked backwards and forwards, and then, with one great shove, it was eased out of its deep trough. The villagers pushed it a further twenty yards and then waited for the Sergeant's next order.

Cohen pointed to the little girl who had distributed the food. She came shyly forward and he lifted her into the front of the car. With sign language, Cohen instructed her to kneel by the accelerator pedal and press down. Without getting into the car, Cohen leaned across, checked that the gears were in neutral, and switched on the engine. The little girl continued to push on the accelerator with both hands, and the engine revved into action. She immediately burst into tears, as the villagers cheered even louder. Cohen quickly lifted the little girl out onto the sand and then beckoned to Aziz.

'You're about half my weight, mate, so get in, put it into first gear and see if you can keep it going for about a hundred yards. If you can, we'll all jump in. If you can't, we'll have to push the bloody thing all the way to the border.'

Aziz stepped gingerly into the Cadillac. Sitting on the edge of the leather seat he gently lifted the lever into first gear and pressed down on the accelerator. The car inched forward and the villagers began to cheer again as Scott, Hannah and Cohen ran along beside it.

Hannah opened the passenger door, pushed the seat forward and jumped into the back as the car continued at its slow pace. Cohen leaped in after her and shouted, 'Second gear!'

Aziz pulled the lever down, across and up. The car lurched forward.

'That's third, you stupid Kurd!' shouted Cohen. He turned to see Scott running almost flat out. Cohen reached across to hold the door open as Scott threw his bag into the back. Scott leaped in and Cohen grabbed him round the shoulders. Scott's head landed in Aziz's lap, but although the Kurd swerved the car still kept going on the firmer sand. Aziz continued swinging the car from side to side to avoid the mounds of sand that had blown on to the road.

'I can see why there aren't likely to be any army patrols on this road,' was Cohen's only comment.

Scott turned back to see the villagers waving frantically. Returning their wave seemed inadequate after all they had done. He hadn't thanked them properly or even said goodbye.

The villagers didn't move until the car was out of sight.

* * *

General Hamil swung round, angry that anyone had dared to enter his office without knocking. His ADC came to a halt in front of his desk. He was shaking, only too aware of the mistake he had made. The General raised his swagger stick and was about to strike the young officer across the face when he bleated out, 'We've discovered the village that the traitor Aziz Zeebari comes from, General.'

Hamil lowered his arm slowly until the swagger stick came to rest on the officer's right shoulder. The tip pushed forward until it was about an inch away from the ball of his right eye.

'Where?'

'Khan Beni Saad,' said the young man in terror.

'Show me.'

The Lieutenant ran over to the map, studied it for a few moments and then placed a finger on a village about ten miles north-east of Baghdad.

General Hamil stared at the spot and smiled for the first time that day. He returned to his desk, picked up the phone and barked out an order.

Within an hour, hundreds of troops would be swarming all over the little village.

Even if Khan Beni Saad did only have a population of 250, the General felt confident someone would talk, however young.

Aziz was able to keep up a steady thirty miles per hour while Scott tried to work out where they were on the map. He couldn't pinpoint their exact location until they had been driving for nearly an hour, when they came across a crude handpainted signpost lying in the road that read 'Khalis 25km'.

'Keep going for now,' said Scott. 'But we'll have to

stop a couple of miles outside town so I can figure out how we get past the checkpoint.'

Scott's confidence in the old chief's judgement that there would be no army vehicles on that road was growing with every mile of flat desert road they covered. He continued to study the map carefully, now certain of the route that would have to be taken if they hoped to cross the border that day.

'So what *do* we do when we reach the checkpoint?' asked Cohen.

'Maybe it'll be easier than we think,' said Scott. 'Don't forget, they're looking for four people in a massive army truck.'

'But we *are* four people.'

'We won't be by the time we reach the checkpoint,' explained Scott, 'because by then you and I will be in the boot.'

Cohen scowled.

'Just be thankful it's a Caddy,' said Aziz, grinning as he tried to maintain the steady speed.

'Perhaps I should take over the wheel now,' said Cohen.

'Not here,' said Scott. 'While we're on these roads, Aziz stays put.'

It was Hannah who saw her first. 'What the hell does she think she's up to?' she said, pointing to a woman who had jumped out into the middle of the road and was waving her arms excitedly.

Scott gripped the side of the window ledge as Cohen leaned forward to get a clearer view.

'Don't stop,' said Scott. 'Swerve round her if you have to.' Suddenly Aziz began laughing.

'What's so funny, Kurd?' asked Cohen, keeping his eyes fixed on the woman, who remained determinedly in the middle of the road.

'It's only my cousin Jasmin.'

'Another cousin?' said Hannah.

'We are all cousins in my tribe,' Aziz explained as he brought the Cadillac to a halt in front of her. He leaped out of the car and threw his arms around the young woman, as the others joined them.

'Not bad,' said Cohen when he was finally introduced to cousin Jasmin, who hadn't stopped talking even when she shook hands with Scott and Hannah.

'So what's she jabbering on about, then?' demanded Cohen, before Aziz had been given the chance to translate his cousin's words.

'It seems the Professor was right. The soldiers have been warned to look out for an army truck being driven by four terrorists. But her uncle has already been in touch this morning to warn her we'd be in the Cadillac.'

'Then it must be a hell of a risk to try and get past them,' said Hannah.

'A risk,' agreed Aziz, 'but not a hell of a risk. Jasmin crosses this checkpoint twice a day, every day, to sell oranges, tangerines and dates from our village. So she's well known to them, and so is my uncle's car. My uncle says she must be in the Cadillac when we go through the checkpoint. That way they won't be suspicious.'

'But if they decide to search the boot?'

'Then they won't get their daily ration of cigarettes, or fruit for their families, will they? You see, they all take it for granted we must be smuggling something.'

Jasmin started chattering again and Aziz listened dutifully. 'She says you must all climb into the boot before someone passing spots us.'

'It's still a hell of a risk, Professor,' said Cohen.

'It's just as big a risk for Jasmin,' said Scott, 'and I don't see any other route.' He folded up the map, walked round to the back of the car, opened the boot and climbed in. Hannah and Cohen followed without another word.

'Not as comfortable as the safe,' remarked Hannah as she put her arms round Scott. Aziz wedged the bag between her and Cohen. Hannah laughed.

'One bang on the side of the door,' said Aziz, 'and I'll be stopping at the checkpoint.'

He slammed down the boot. Jasmin grabbed her bags from the side of the road and jumped in next to her cousin.

The three of them in the boot heard the engine splutter into action and begin its more stately progress over the last few miles towards Khalis.

Jasmin used the time to brief Aziz on her routine whenever she crossed the checkpoint.

34

THE CHIEF WAS HANGED FIRST. Then his brothers, one by one, in front of the rest of the village, but none of them uttered a word. Then they moved on to his cousins, until a twelve-year-old girl, who hoped to save her father's life, told them about the strangers who had stayed in the chief's house the previous night.

They promised the little girl that her father would be saved if she told them everything she knew. She pointed out into the desert to show them where they had buried the lorry. Twenty minutes of digging by the soldiers and they were able to confirm that she had been telling the truth.

They contacted General Hamil by field phone. He found it hard to believe that thirty of the Zeebari tribe had taken the chief's Cadillac to pieces and carried it bit by bit across the open desert.

'Oh, yes,' the little girl assured them. 'I know it's true because my brother carried one of the wheels all the way to the road on the other side of the desert,' she declared, pointing proudly towards the horizon.

General Hamil listened carefully to the information over the phone before ordering that the girl's father and brother should also be hanged.

He returned to the map on the wall and quickly pinpointed the only possible road they could have taken.

His eye moved along the path across a stretch of desert until it joined another winding road, and then he realised which town they would have to pass through.

He looked at the clock on his desk: 4.39. 'Get me the checkpoint at Khalis,' he instructed the young Lieutenant.

Aziz saw a stationary van in the distance being inspected by a soldier. Jasmin warned him it was the checkpoint and tipped out the contents of one of her bags onto the seat between them.

Aziz banged on the side of his door, relieved to see there were only two soldiers in sight, and that one of them was sleeping in a comfortable old chair on the other side of the road.

When the car came to a halt Scott could hear laughter coming from somewhere. Aziz passed a packet of Rothmans to the guard.

The soldier was just about to wave them through when the other guard stirred from his drowsy slumber like a cat who had been resting for hours on a radiator. He pushed himself up, moved slowly towards the car, and looked over it with admiration, as he had done many times before. He began to stroll around it. As he passed the boot he gave it a loving slap with the palm of his hand. It flicked open a few inches. Scott pulled it gently closed as Jasmin dropped a carton of two hundred Rothmans on the ground by her side of the car.

The border guard moved quickly for the first time that day. Jasmin gave him a smile as he retrieved the cigarettes, and whispered something in his ear. The soldier looked at Aziz and started laughing, as a large lorry stacked with crates of beer came to a halt behind them.

'Move on, move on,' shouted the first soldier, as the

sight of greater rewards caught his eye. Aziz quickly obeyed and lurched forward in second gear, nearly throwing Cohen and the holdall out of the back.

'What did you say to that soldier?' asked Aziz once they were out of earshot.

'I told him you were gay, but I would be returning on my own later.'

'Have you no family pride?' asked Aziz.

'Certainly,' said Jasmin. 'But he is also a cousin.'

On Jasmin's advice, Aziz took the longer southern route around the town. He was unable to avoid all the potholes, and from time to time he heard groans coming from the boot. Jasmin pointed to a junction ahead of them, and told Aziz that that was where he should stop. She gathered up her bags, leaving some fruit on the seat between them. Aziz came to a halt by a road that led back into the centre of the town. Jasmin jumped out, smiled and waved. Aziz waved back, and wondered when he would see his cousin again.

He drove on alone to the far side of the town, still unable to risk letting his colleagues out of the boot while the few locals around could observe what was going on.

Once Khalis was a couple of miles behind him, Aziz came to a halt at a crossroads which displayed two signposts. One read 'Tuz Khurmatoo 120km', and the other 'Tuz Khurmatoo 170km'. He checked in every direction before climbing out of the car, opening the boot and letting the three baggage passengers tumble out onto the road. While they stretched their limbs and took deep breaths of air, Aziz pointed to the signposts. Scott didn't need to look at the map to decide which road they would have to take.

'We must take the longer route,' he said, 'and hope that they still think we're in the truck.' Hannah slammed down the boot with feeling before they all four jumped back into the car.

Aziz averaged forty miles an hour on the winding road, his three passengers ducking out of sight whenever another vehicle appeared on the horizon.

The four of them devoured the fresh fruit Jasmin had left on the front seat.

When they passed a signpost indicating twenty kilometres to Tuz Khurmatoo Scott said to Aziz, 'I want you to stop a little way outside the village and go in alone before we decide if it's safe for us to drive straight through. Don't forget it's only another three miles beyond Tuz Khurmatoo to the highway, so the place could be swarming with soldiers.'

'And to the Kurdish border?' asked Hannah.

'About forty-five miles,' said Scott as he continued to study the map. Aziz drove for another twenty minutes before he came over the brow of a hill and could see the outline of a village nestling in the valley. A few moments later he pulled the car off the road and parked it under a row of citrus trees that sheltered them from the sun and the prying eyes of those in passing vehicles. Aziz listened carefully to Scott's instructions, got out of the car and jogged off in the direction of Tuz Khurmatoo.

General Hamil was too furious to speak when the young Lieutenant informed him that the Cadillac had passed through the Khalis checkpoint less than an hour before, and neither of the soldiers on duty had bothered to check the boot.

After a minimum of torture, one of them had confessed that the terrorists must have been helped by a young girl who regularly passed through the checkpoint.

'She will never pass through it again,' had been the General's sole observation.

The only other piece of information they were able to get out of the soldiers was that whoever had been driving the car was the girl's cousin, and a homosexual. Hamil wondered how they could possibly know that.

Once again, the General returned to the map on the wall behind his desk. He had already given orders for an army of helicopters, lorries, tanks and motorcycles to cover every inch of the road between Khalis and the border, but still no one had reported seeing a Cadillac on the highway. He was mystified, knowing they couldn't possibly have turned back or they would have run straight into his troops.

His eyes searched every route between the checkpoint and the border yet again. 'Ah,' he said finally, 'they must have taken the road through the hills.' The General ran his finger along a thin winding red line until it joined the main highway.

'So that's where you are,' he said, before bellowing out some new orders.

It was almost an hour before Cohen announced, 'One Kurd heading towards us, sir.'

As Aziz came running up the slope the grin remained on his face. He had been into Tuz Khurmatoo and he was able to reassure them that the village was going about its business as usual. But the government radio was blasting out a warning to be on the lookout for four terrorists who had attempted to assassinate the Great Leader, so all the main roads were now crawling with soldiers. 'They've got good descriptions of all four of us, but the radio bulletin an hour ago was still saying we were in the truck.'

'Right, Aziz,' said Scott, 'drive us through the village. Hannah, sit in the front with Aziz. The Sergeant and I will lie down in the back. Once we're on the other side of Tuz we'll keep out of sight and only continue on to the border after it's dark.'

Aziz took his place behind the wheel, and the Cadillac began its slow journey into Tuz.

The main road through the village must have been about three hundred yards long and just about wide enough to take two cars. Hannah looked at the little timber shops and the men who were growing old sitting on steps and leaning against walls. A dirty old Cadillac travelling slowly through the village, she thought, would probably be the highlight of their day, until she saw the vehicle at the other end of the road.

'There's a jeep coming towards us,' she said calmly. 'Four men, one of them sitting behind what looks like an anti-aircraft gun mounted on the back.'

'Just keep driving slowly, Aziz,' said Scott. 'And Hannah, keep talking us through it.'

'They're about a hundred yards away from us now and beginning to take an interest.' Cohen pointed to the tool bag and grabbed a wrench. Scott selected a spanner as they both turned over slowly and rested on their knees.

'The jeep has swung across in front of us,' said Hannah. 'We're going to be forced to stop in about five seconds.'

'Does it still look as if there are four of them?' asked Scott.

'Yes,' said Hannah. 'I can't see any more.'

The Cadillac came to a halt.

'The jeep has stopped only a few yards in front of us. One of the soldiers is getting out and another is following. Two are staying in the jeep. One is behind the mounted gun and the other is still at the wheel. We'll take the first two,' said Hannah. 'You'll have to deal with the two in the jeep.'

'Understood,' said Scott.

The first soldier reached the driver's side as the second passed the bumper on Hannah's right. Both Aziz and Hannah had their outside hands on the armrests, their doors already an inch open.

The instant Aziz saw the first soldier glance into the back and go for his gun, he swung his door open so fast that the crack of the soldier's knees sounded like a bullet as he collapsed to the ground. Aziz was out of the car and on top of him long before he had time to recover. The second soldier ran towards Hannah as Scott leaped out of the car. Hannah delivered one blow to his carotid artery and another to the base of his spine as he tried to pull out his gun. A bullet would not have killed him any quicker. The third soldier started firing from the back of the jeep. Cohen dived out into the road, and the fourth soldier jumped from behind the wheel and ran towards him, firing his pistol. Cohen hurled the wrench at him, causing him to step to one side and straight into the firing line of the mounted gun. The bullets stopped immediately, but Cohen was already at his throat. The soldier sank as if he had been hit by a ton of bricks, and his gun flew across the road. Cohen gave him one blow to the jugular vein and another to the back of the neck: he went into spasms and began wriggling on the ground. Cohen quickly turned his attention to the man seated behind the gun, who was lining him up in his sights. At ten yards' distance, Cohen had no hope of reaching him, so he dived for the side of the car as bullets sprayed into the open door, two of them ripping into his left leg. Scott was now running towards the jeep from the other side. As the soldier swung the gun round to face him, Scott propelled himself through the air and onto the top of the jeep.

Bullets flew everywhere as they tumbled clumsily off the back, Scott still clinging onto his spanner. They were both quickly on their feet, and Scott brought the spanner down across the gunner's neck – the soldier raised an arm to fend off the blow, but Scott's left knee jack-knifed into his crotch. The gunner sank to the ground as the second blow from the spanner found its mark and broke the soldier's neck cleanly. He lay splayed out on the road, looking like a breast-stroke swimmer halfway through a stroke. Scott stood over him, mesmerised, until Aziz dived at his legs and knocked him to the ground. Scott couldn't stop shaking.

'It's always hardest the first time,' was the Kurd's only comment.

The four of them were now facing outwards, covering every angle as they waited for the locals to react. Cohen climbed unsteadily up into the jeep, blood pouring from his leg, and took his place behind the mounted gun. 'Don't fire unless I say so,' shouted Scott as he checked up and down the road. There wasn't a person to be seen in either direction.

'On your left!' said Hannah, and Scott turned to see an old man dressed in a long white dishdash with a black-and-white spotted keffiyeh on his head, a thick belt hung loosely around his waist. He was walking slowly towards them, his hands held high in the air.

Scott's eyes never left the old man, who came to a halt a few yards away from the Cadillac.

'I have been sent by the village elders because I am the only one who speaks English,' he said. The man was trembling and the words came stumbling out. 'We believe you are the terrorists who came to kill Saddam.'

Scott said nothing.

'Please go. Leave our village and go quickly. Take the jeep and we will bury the soldiers. Then no one will ever know you were here. If you do not, Saddam will murder us all. Every one of us.'

'Tell your people we wish them no harm,' said Scott.

'I believe you,' said the old man, 'but please, go.'

Scott ran forward and stripped the tallest soldier of his uniform while Cohen kept his gun trained on the old man. Aziz stripped the other three while Hannah grabbed Scott's bag from the Cadillac before jumping into the back of the jeep.

Aziz threw the uniforms into the jeep and then leaped into the driving seat. The engine was still running. He put the vehicle into reverse and swung round in a semicircle as Scott took his place in the front. Aziz began to drive slowly out of Tuz Khurmatoo. Cohen turned the gun round in the direction of the village, at the same time thumping his left leg with his clenched fist.

Scott continued to look behind him as a few of the villagers moved tentatively out into the road and started to drag the soldiers unceremoniously away. Another climbed into the Cadillac and began to reverse it down a side road. A few moments later they had all disappeared from sight. Scott turned to face the road ahead of him.

'It's about another three miles to the highway,' said Aziz. 'What do you want me to do?'

'We've only got one chance of getting across that border,' said Scott, 'so for now pull over into that clump of trees. We can't risk going out onto the highway until it's pitch dark.' He checked the time. It was 7.35.

Hannah felt blood dripping onto her face. She looked up, and saw the deep wounds in Cohen's leg. She immediately tore off the corner of her yashmak and tried to stem the flow of blood.

'You all right, Cohen?' asked Scott anxiously.

'No worse than when I was bitten by a woman in Tangier,' he replied.

Aziz began laughing.

'How can you laugh?' said Hannah, continuing to clean the wound.

'Because he was the reason she bit me,' said Cohen.

After Hannah had completed the bandaging, the four of them changed into the Iraqi uniforms. For an hour they kept their eyes on the road, looking for any sign of more soldiers. A few villagers on donkeys, and more on foot, passed them in both directions, but the only vehicle they saw was an old tractor that chugged by on its way back to the village at the end of a day's service.

As the minutes slipped by, it became obvious that the villagers had kept to their promise and made no contact with any army patrols.

When Scott could no longer see the road in front of them, he went over his plan for the last time. All of them accepted that their options were limited.

The nearest border was forty-five miles away, but Scott now accepted the danger they could bring to any village simply by passing through it. He didn't feel his plan was foolproof, far from it, but they couldn't wait in the hills much longer. It would only be a short time before Iraqi soldiers were swarming all over the area.

Scott checked the uniforms. As long as they kept on the move, it would be hard for anyone to identify them in the dark as anything other than part of an army patrol. But once they reached the highway, he knew they couldn't afford to stay still for more than a few seconds. Everything depended on how close they could get to the border post without being spotted.

When Scott gave the order, Aziz swung the jeep onto the winding road to begin the three-mile journey to the highway. He covered the distance in five minutes, and during that time they didn't come across another vehicle. But once they hit the highway, they found the road was covered with lorries, jeeps, even tanks, travelling in both directions.

None of them saw the two motorcycles, the tank and three lorries that swung off the highway and headed at speed down the little road towards Tuz Khurmatoo.

Aziz went as fast as he could, while Cohen remained seated on the back behind the gun. Scott watched the road ahead of him, his beret pulled well down. Hannah sat below Cohen, motionless, a gun in her hand. The first road sign indicated that it was sixty kilometres to the border. For a moment Scott was distracted by an oil well that kept pumping away on the far side of the road. Nobody spoke as the distance to Kirkuk descended from fifty-five to forty-six, to thirty-two, but with each sign and each new oil well, the traffic became heavier and their speed began to drop rapidly. The only relief was that none of the passing patrols seemed to show any interest in the jeep.

Within minutes the little village was swarming with soldiers from Saddam's elite guard. Even in the dark, it took only ten bullets and as many minutes for them to find out where the Cadillac was, and another thirty bullets to discover the unfilled graves of the four dead soldiers.

General Hamil listened to the senior officer when he phoned in with the details. All he asked for was the radio frequency of the jeep that had been in Tuz Khurmatoo earlier that evening. The General slammed down the phone, checked his watch, and keyed in the frequency.

The single tone continued for some time.

* * *

'They must still be looking for a truck or a pink Cadillac,' Scott was saying when the radio phone began ringing. They all four froze.

'Answer it, Aziz,' said Scott. 'Listen carefully, and find out what you can.'

Aziz picked up the handset, listened to a short message, then said, 'Yes, sir,' in Arabic, and put the handset down.

'They've found the Cadillac, and are ordering all jeeps to report to their nearest army post,' he said.

'It can't be long before they realise it's not one of their men driving this jeep,' said Hannah. 'If they don't already know.'

'With luck we might still have twenty minutes,' said Scott. 'How far to the border?'

'Nine miles,' said Aziz.

The General knew it had to be Zeebari, or he would have responded with the elite guards' code number.

So now he knew what vehicle they were in, and which border they were heading for. He immediately picked up the phone and barked another order. Two officers accompanied him as he ran out of the room and into a large yard at the back of the building. The blades of his personal helicopter were already slowly rotating.

It was Aziz who first spotted the end of a long queue of oil tankers waiting to cross the unofficial border. Scott checked the inside track and asked Aziz if he could drive down such a narrow strip.

'Not possible, sir,' the young Kurd told him. 'We'd only end up in the ditch.'

'Then we've no alternative but to go straight down the middle.'

Aziz moved the jeep out into the centre of the road and tried desperately to maintain his speed. To begin with he was able to stay clear of the lorries and avoid the oncoming traffic. The first real trouble came four miles from the border, when an army truck heading towards them refused to move over.

'Shall I blast him off the road?' said Cohen.

'No,' said Scott. 'Aziz, keep going, but prepare to jump and take cover among the tankers, then we'll regroup.' Just as Scott was about to leap, the lorry swerved across the road and ended up in the ditch on the far side.

'Now they all know where we are,' said Scott. 'How many miles to the customs post, Aziz?'

'Three, three and a half at the most.'

'Then step on it,' said Scott, although he realised Aziz was already going as fast as he could. They had managed to cover the next mile in just over a minute when a helicopter swung above them, beaming down a search-light that lit up the entire road. The radio phone began ringing again.

'Ignore it,' shouted Scott as Aziz tried to keep the jeep on the centre of the road and maintain his speed. They passed the two-mile mark as the helicopter swung back, confident it had spotted its prey, and began to focus its beam directly on them.

'We've got a jeep coming up our backside,' said Cohen, as he swung round to face it.

'Get rid of it,' said Scott.

Cohen obliged, sending the first few shots through the windscreen and the next into the tyres, thankful for the light from above. The pursuing jeep swung across the road, crashing into an oncoming lorry. Another quickly took its place. Hannah reloaded the gun with a magazine of bullets that was lying on the floor while Cohen concentrated on the road behind them.

'One and a half miles to go,' shouted Aziz, nearly crashing into lorries on both sides of the road. The helicopter hovered above them and began to fire indiscriminately, hitting vehicles going in both directions.

'Don't forget that most of them haven't a clue who's chasing what,' said Scott.

'Thanks for sharing that piece of logic with me, Professor,' said Cohen. 'But I've got a feeling that helicopter knows exactly who he's chasing.' Cohen began to pepper the next jeep with bullets the moment it came into range. This time it simply slowed to a halt, causing the car behind to run straight into it and creating a concertina effect as one after another the pursuing jeeps crashed into the back of the vehicle in front of them. The road behind was suddenly clear, as if Aziz had been the last car through a green light.

'One mile to go,' shouted Aziz as Cohen swung round to concentrate on what was going on in front of him and Hannah reloaded the automatic gun with the last magazine of bullets. Scott could see the lights of a bridge looming up in front of him: the Kirkuk fortress on the side of the hill that Aziz had told them signalled the customs post was only about half a mile away. As the helicopter swung back and once again sprayed the road with bullets, Aziz felt the front tyre on his side suddenly blow as he drove onto the bridge.

Scott could now see the Kurdish checkpoint ahead of him as the helicopter swung even lower on its final attempt to stop them. A flurry of bullets hit the jeep's bonnet, ricocheted off the bridge and into the windscreen. As the helicopter swung away, Scott looked up and for a second stared into the eyes of General Hamil.

Scott looked back down and punched a hole in the shattered windscreen, only to discover he was faced with two rows of soldiers lined up in front of him, their rifles aiming straight at the jeep.

Behind the row of soldiers were two small exits for those wishing to enter Kurdistan and two entrances on the other side of the road for those driving out of Kirkuk.

The two exits to Kurdistan were blocked with stationary vehicles, while the two entrances had been left clear – although no one at that moment was showing any desire to enter Saddam's Iraq.

Aziz decided that he would have to swing across the road and risk driving the jeep at an acute angle through one of the small entrances, where he might be faced with an oncoming vehicle – in which case they would be trapped. He was still losing speed, and could feel that the rim of the front left-hand wheel was now touching the ground.

Once they were within range, Cohen opened fire on the line of soldiers in front of him. Some fired back, but he managed to hit several before the rest scattered.

With a hundred yards to go and still losing speed, Aziz suddenly swung the jeep across the road and tried to steer it towards the second entrance. The jeep hit the right-hand wall, careered into the short, dark tunnel and bounced onto the left-hand wall before lurching out into no-man's land, between the two customs posts.

Suddenly there were dozens of soldiers pursuing them from the Iraqi side. 'Keep going, keep going!' shouted Scott as they emerged from the little tunnel.

Aziz was still losing speed as he steered the jeep back to the left and pointed it in the direction of the border with Kurdistan, a mere four hundred yards away. He pressed his foot flat down on the accelerator but the speedometer wouldn't rise above two miles per hour. Another row of soldiers, this time from the Kurdish border, was facing them, their rifles pointing at the jeep. But none of them was firing.

Cohen swung around as a stray bullet hit the back of the jeep and another flew past his shoulder. Once again he fired a volley towards the Iraqi border, and those who could quickly retreated behind their checkpoint. The jeep trundled on for a few more yards before it finally whimpered to a halt halfway between the two unofficial barriers that the UN refused to recognise.

Scott looked towards the Kurdish border. A hundred Peshmergas were lined up, their rifles now firing – but not in the direction of the jeep. Scott turned back to see another line of soldiers tentatively advancing from the Iraqi side. He and Hannah began firing their pistols as Cohen let forth another burst which came to a sudden stop. The Iraqi soldiers had started to retreat again, but sensed immediately that their enemy had finally run out of ammunition.

Cohen leaped down off the jeep and quickly took out his pistol. 'Come on, Aziz!' he shouted as he rushed forward and crouched beside the driver's door. 'We'll have to cover them so the Professor can get his bloody Declaration across the border.'

Aziz didn't reply. His body was slumped lifelessly over the wheel, the horn sounding intermittently. The unanswered radio phone was still ringing.

'The bastards have killed my Kurd!' shouted Cohen. Hannah grabbed the canvas bag as Scott lifted Aziz out of the front of the jeep. Together, they began to drag him the last few hundred yards towards the border with Kurdistan.

Another line of Iraqi soldiers started to advance towards the jeep as Scott and Hannah carried the dead body of Aziz nearer and nearer to his Kurdish homeland.

They heard more shots whistle past them, and turned to see Cohen running towards the Iraqis screaming, 'You killed my Kurd, you bastards! You killed my Kurd!' One of the Iraqis fell, another fell, one retreated. Another fell, another retreated, as Cohen went on advancing towards them. Suddenly, he fell to his knees, but somehow he kept crawling forward, until a final volley rang out. The Sergeant collapsed in a pool of blood a few yards from the Iraqi border.

While Scott and Hannah carried the dead Kurd into the land of his people, Saddam's soldiers dragged the body of the Jew back into Iraq.

'Why were my orders disobeyed?' Saddam shouted.

For several moments no one around the table spoke. They knew the chances of all of them returning to their beds alive that night had to be marginal.

General Hamil turned the cover of a thick file, and looked down at the handwritten note in front of him.

'Major Saeed was to blame, Mr President,' stated the General. 'It was he who allowed the infidels to escape with the Declaration, and that is why his body is now hanging in Tohrir Square for your people to witness.'

The General listened intently to the President's next question.

'Yes, Sayedi,' he assured his master. 'Two of the terrorists were killed by guards from my own regiment. They were by far the most important members of the team. They were the two who managed to escape from Major Saeed's custody before I arrived. The other two were an American professor and the girl.'

The President asked another question.

'No, Mr President. Kratz was the commanding officer,

and I personally arrested the infamous Zionist leader before questioning him at length. It was during that interrogation that I discovered that the original plan had been to assassinate you, Sayedi, and I made certain that he, like those who came before him, failed.'

The General had no well-rehearsed answer to the President's next question, and he was relieved when the State Prosecutor intervened.

'Perhaps we can turn this whole episode to our advantage, Sayedi.'

'How can that be possible,' shouted the President, 'when two of them have escaped with the Declaration and left us with a useless copy that anyone who can spell "British" will immediately realise is a fake? No, it is I who will be made the laughing stock of the world, not Clinton.'

Everyone's eyes were now fixed on the Prosecutor.

'That may not necessarily be the case, Mr President. I suspect that when the Americans see the state of their cherished treasure, they will not be in a hurry to put it back on display at the National Archives.'

The President did not interrupt this time, so the Prosecutor continued.

'We also know, Mr President, that because of your genius, the parchment currently on display in Washington to an unsuspecting American public is, to quote you, "a useless copy that anyone who can spell 'British' will immediately realise is a fake".'

The President's expression was now one of concentration.

'Perhaps the time has come, Sayedi, to inform the world's press of your triumph.'

'My triumph?' said the President in disbelief.

'Why, yes, Sayedi. Your triumph, not to mention your magnanimity. After all, it was you who gave the order to hand over the battered Declaration to Professor Bradley after the gangster Cavalli had attempted to sell it to you.'

The President's expression turned to one of deep thought.

'They have a saying in the West,' added the Prosecutor, 'about killing two birds with one stone.'

Another long silence followed, during which no one offered an opinion until the President smiled.

PART THREE

'. . .we mutually pledge to each other our Lives, our Fortunes and our sacred Honor.'

35

THE OFFICIAL STATEMENT issued by the Iraqi government on July 2nd was that there was no truth in the report that there had been a shooting incident on the border posts at Kirkuk in which several Iraqi soldiers had been killed and more wounded.

The Kurdish leaders were unable to offer any opinion on the subject, as the only two satellite phones in Iraqi Kurdistan had been permanently engaged with requests for assistance from the State Department in Washington.

When Charles Streator, the American Ambassador in Istanbul, was telephoned and asked by the Reuters Bureau Chief in the Middle East why a US Air Force jet had landed at the American base in Silope on the Turkish border, and then returned to Washington with two unknown passengers as its cargo, His Excellency told his old friend that he had absolutely no idea what he was talking about. The Bureau Chief considered the Ambassador to be an honest man, although he accepted that it was part of the job to lie for his country.

The Ambassador had in fact been up all night following a call from the Secretary of State requesting that one of their helicopters should be despatched to the outskirts of Kirkuk to pick up five passengers, one American, one

Arab and three Israelis, who were then to be flown back to the base at Silope.

The Ambassador had called Washington later that morning to inform Warren Christopher that unfortunately only two people had managed to cross the border alive: an American named Scott Bradley and an Israeli woman, Hannah Kopec. He had no information on the other three.

The American Ambassador was totally thrown by the Secretary of State's final question. Did Professor Bradley have a cardboard tube in his possession? The Ambassador was only disappointed that the Reuters correspondent hadn't asked him the same thing, because then he would have been telling him the truth when he said, 'I've absolutely no idea what you're talking about.'

Scott and Hannah slept for most of the flight back to America. When they stepped off the plane at the military air base they found Dexter Hutchins at the bottom of the steps waiting to greet them. Neither of them was surprised when customs showed little interest in Scott's canvas bag. A CIA car whisked them off in the direction of Washington.

On the journey into the capital, Dexter warned them that they would be going direct to the White House for a top-level meeting, and briefed them on who else would be present.

They were met at the West Wing reception entrance by the President's Chief of Staff, who conducted them to the Oval Office. Scott couldn't help feeling that, as it was his first meeting with the President, he would have preferred to have shaved at some time during the last forty-eight hours, and not to have been dressed in the same clothes that he'd worn for the past three days.

Warren Christopher was there to greet them at the door of the Oval Office, and he introduced Scott to the President as if they were old friends. Bill Clinton welcomed Scott home, and thanked Hannah for the part she had played in securing the safe return of the Declaration.

Scott was delighted to meet Calder Marshall for the first time, Mr Mendelssohn for the second time, and to be reunited with Dollar Bill.

Dollar Bill bowed to Hannah. 'Now I understand why the Professor was willing to cross the earth to bring you back,' was all the little Irishman had to say.

The moment the handshakes were over, none of them could hide their impatience to see the Declaration. Scott unzipped his bag and carefully took out a bath towel, from which he extracted the document before handing it over to its rightful custodian, the Secretary of State. Christopher slowly unrolled the parchment. No one in the room was able to hide their dismay at the state the Declaration was in.

The Secretary passed the document over to the Archivist who, accompanied by the Conservator and Dollar Bill, walked across to the large window overlooking the South Lawn. The first word they checked was 'Brittish', and the Archivist smiled.

But it was only a few moments more before Calder Marshall announced their combined judgement. 'It's a fake,' was all he said.

'How can you be so certain?' asked the President.

'*Mea culpa*,' said Dollar Bill, looking a little sheepish.

'So does that mean that Saddam is still in possession of the original?' asked the Secretary of State in disbelief.

'No, sir, he has the copy Scott took to Baghdad,' said Dollar Bill. 'So clearly he was already in possession of a fake before Scott did the exchange.'

'Then who has the original?' the other four asked in unison.

'Alfonso Mario Cavalli would be my guess,' said Dollar Bill.

'And who's he?' asked the President, no wiser.

'The gentleman who paid me to make the copy that is currently in the National Archives,' said Dollar Bill, 'and to whom I released the only other copy, which I am now holding in my hands.'

'But if the word "Brittish" is spelt with two *t*s, how can you be so certain it's a fake?' asked Dexter Hutchins.

'Because, of the fifty-six signatures on the original Declaration, six have the Christian name George. Five of them signed *Geo*, which was the custom of the time. Only George Wythe of Virginia appended his full name. On the copy I presented to Cavalli I made the mistake of also writing *Geo* for Congressman Wythe, and had to add the letters *rge* later. Although the lettering is perfect, I used a slightly lighter shade of ink. A simple mistake, and discernible only to an expert eye.'

'And even then, only if they knew what they were looking for,' added Mendelssohn.

'I never bothered to tell Cavalli,' continued Dollar Bill, 'because once he had checked the word "Brittish" he seemed quite satisfied.'

'So, at some time Cavalli must have switched his copy with the original, and then passed it on to Al Obaydi?' said Dexter Hutchins.

'Well done, Deputy Director,' said Dollar Bill.

'And Al Obaydi in turn handed the copy on to the Iraqi Ambassador in Geneva, who had it delivered to Saddam in Iraq. And, as Al Obaydi had seen Dollar Bill's copy on display at the National Archives with "British" spelt correctly, he was convinced he was in possession of the original,' said Dexter Hutchins.

'You've finally caught up with the rest of us,' said Dollar Bill. 'Though to be fair, sir, I should have known what Cavalli was capable of doing when I said to you a month ago: "Is there no longer honour among thieves?" '

'So, where is the original now?' demanded the President.

'I suspect it's hanging on a wall in a brownstone house in Manhattan,' said Dollar Bill, 'where it must have been for the past ten weeks.'

The light on the telephone console to the right of the President began flashing. The President's Chief of Staff picked up an extension and listened. The normally unflappable man turned white. He pushed the hold button.

'It's Bernie Shaw at CNN for me, Mr President. He says Saddam is claiming that the bombing of Baghdad last weekend was nothing more than a smokescreen set up to give a group of American terrorists the chance to retrieve the Declaration of Independence, which a Mafia gang had tried to sell him and which he personally returned to a man called Bradley. Saddam's apparently most apologetic about the state the Declaration is in, but he has television pictures of Bradley spitting and stamping on it and nailing it to a wall. If you don't believe him, Saddam says you can check the copy of the Declaration that's on display at the National Archives, because anyone who can spell "British" will realise it's a fake. Shaw's asking if you have any comment to make, as Saddam intends to hold a press conference tomorrow morning to let the whole world know the truth.'

The President pursed his lips.

'My bet is that Saddam has given CNN an exclusive on this story, but probably only until tomorrow,' the Chief of Staff added.

'Whatever you do,' said Hutchins, 'try to keep it off the air for tonight.'

The Chief of Staff hesitated for a moment until he saw the President nodding his agreement. He pressed the button to re-engage the call. 'If you want to go on the air with a story like that, Bernie, it's your reputation on the line, not mine.'

The Chief of Staff listened carefully to Shaw's reply while everyone else in the room waited in silence.

'Be my guest,' were the last words the Chief of Staff offered before putting the phone down.

He turned to the President and told him: 'Shaw says he will have a crew outside the National Archives the moment the doors open at ten tomorrow morning, and, I quote: if the word "British" is spelt correctly, he'll crucify you.'

The President glanced up at the carriage clock that stood on the mantelpiece below the portrait of Abraham Lincoln. It was a few minutes after seven. He swivelled his chair round to face the Deputy Director of the CIA.

'Mr Hutchins,' he said, 'you've got fifteen hours to stop me being crucified. Should you fail, I can assure you there won't be a second coming for me in three years, let alone three days.'

36

THE LEAK STARTED in the early morning of Sunday July 4th, in the basement of number 21, the home of the Prestons, who were on vacation in Malibu.

When their Mexican housekeeper answered the door a few minutes after midnight, she assumed the worst. An illegal immigrant with no Green Card lives in daily fear of a visit from any government official.

The housekeeper was relieved to discover that these particular officials were only from the gas company. Without much prompting, she agreed to accompany them down to the basement of the brownstone and show them where the gas meters were located.

Once they had gained entry it only took a few moments to carry out the job. The loosening of two gas valves ensured a tiny leak which gave off a smell that would have alarmed any layman. The explosives expert assured his boss that there was no real cause for concern, as long as the New York Fire Department arrived within twenty minutes.

The senior official calmly asked the housekeeper to phone the fire department and warn them they had a gas leak in number 21 which, if not dealt with quickly, could cause an explosion. He told her the correct code to give.

The housekeeper dialled 911, and when she was finally put through to the fire department, stammered out the problem, adding that it was 21 East 75th, between Park and Madison.

'Get everyone out of the building,' instructed the Fire Chief, 'and we'll be right over.'

'Yes, sir,' said the housekeeper, not pausing for a moment before fleeing onto the street. The expert quickly repaired the damage he had caused, but the smell still lingered.

To their credit, seven minutes later a New York Fire Department hook and ladder, sirens blasting, sped into 75th Street. Once the Fire Chief had carried out an inspection of the basement of number 21 he agreed with the official – whom he had never met before – that safety checks would also have to be carried out on numbers 17, 19, 23 and 25, especially as the gas pipe ran parallel to the city's sewerage system.

The Deputy Director of the CIA then retired to the far side of the road to watch the Fire Chief go about his work. As the sirens had woken almost everyone in the neighbourhood, it wasn't proving too hard to coax the residents out onto the street.

Dexter Hutchins lit a cigar and waited. As soon as he had left the White House, he had begun rounding up a select team of agents who rendezvoused in a New York hotel two hours later for a briefing, or, to be more accurate, half a briefing. Because once the Deputy Director had explained to them that this was a Level 7 inquiry, the old-timers realised they would be told only half the story, and not the better half.

It had taken another two hours before they got their first break, when one of the agents discovered that the Prestons in number 21 were on vacation. Dexter Hutchins and his explosives expert had arrived on the doorstep of number 21 just after midnight. The Mexican immigrant without a Green Card turned out to be a bonus.

The Deputy Director relit his cigar, his eyes fixed on one particular doorway. He breathed a sigh of relief when Tony Cavalli and his father emerged in their dressing gowns, accompanied by a butler. He decided it would be sensible to wait for another couple of minutes before he asked the Fire Chief's permission to inspect number 23.

The whole operation could have been underway a lot earlier if only Calder Marshall hadn't balked at the idea of removing the fake Declaration from the vault of the National Archives and placing it at Dexter Hutchins' disposal. The Archivist made two stipulations before he finally agreed to the Deputy Director's request: should the CIA fail to replace the copy with the original before ten o'clock the following morning, Marshall's resignation statement, dated May 25th, would be released an hour before the President or the Secretary of State made any statement of their own.

'And your second condition, Mr Marshall?' the President had asked.

'That Mr Mendelssohn be allowed to act as custodian of the copy remaining with the Deputy Director at all times, so that he will be present should they locate the original.'

Dexter Hutchins realised he had little choice but to go along with Marshall's conditions. The Deputy Director stared across at the Conservator, who was standing between Scott and the explosives expert, on the pavement opposite number 23. Dexter Hutchins had to admit that Mendelssohn looked more convincing as an official from the gas company than anyone else in his team.

As soon as Hutchins saw two of his agents emerging from number 19 he stubbed out his cigar and strolled across the road in the direction of the Fire Chief. His three colleagues followed a few paces behind.

'All right for us to check on number 23 now?' he asked casually.

'Fine by me,' said the Fire Chief. 'But the owners are insisting the butler sticks with you.'

Hutchins nodded his agreement. The butler led the four of them into the lobby, down to the basement and directly to the cupboard that housed the gas supply. He assured them that there had not been the slightest smell of gas before he went to bed, some time after his master had retired.

The explosives expert carried out his job deftly, and in moments the basement stank of gas. Hutchins recommended to the butler that for his own safety he should return to the street. With a handkerchief covering his nose and mouth Martin reluctantly agreed, leaving them to try and locate the leak.

While the expert repaired the damage, Scott and Dexter began checking every room in the basement. Scott was the first to enter Cavalli's study and discover the parchment hanging on the wall, exactly where Dollar Bill had promised it would be. Within seconds the other two had joined him. Mendelssohn stared lovingly at the document. He checked the word 'Brittish' before lifting the glass frame gently off the wall and placing it on the boardroom table. Scott unzipped the large tool bag one of the agents had put together earlier in the evening, containing screwdrivers of all sizes, knives of all lengths, chisels of several widths and even a small drill, in fact everything that would be required by a professional picture framer.

The Conservator checked the back of the frame and requested a medium-sized screwdriver. Scott selected one and passed it across to him.

Mendelssohn slowly and methodically removed all eight of the screws that held the two large steel clamps to the back of the frame. Then he turned the glass over on its front. Dexter Hutchins couldn't help thinking that he might have shown a little more sense of urgency.

The Conservator, oblivious to the Deputy Director's impatience, rummaged around in the bag until he had selected an appropriate chisel. He wedged it between the two pieces of laminated glass at the top right-hand corner of the frame. At the same time, Scott extracted from the cylinder supplied by Mendelssohn the copy of the Declaration they had taken from the National Archives earlier that evening.

When the Conservator lifted the top piece of the laminated glass and rested it on the boardroom table, Scott could tell from the smile on his face that he believed he was staring down at the original.

'Come on,' said Dexter, 'or they'll start getting suspicious.'

Mendelssohn didn't seem to hear the Deputy Director's urgings. He once again checked the spelling of 'Brittish' and, satisfied, turned his attention to the five 'Geo's and one 'George' before glancing, first quickly and then slowly, over the rest of the parchment. The smile never left his face.

Without a word, the Conservator slowly rolled up the original, and Scott replaced it with the copy from the National Archives. Once Scott had the sheets of glass back in position he screwed the two steel clamps firmly in place.

Mendelssohn deposited the cylinder in the work bag while Scott hung the copy on the wall.

They both heard Dexter Hutchins' deep sigh of relief.

'Now for Christ's sake let's get out of here,' said the Deputy Director as six cops, guns drawn, burst into the room and surrounded them.

'Freeze!' said one of them. Mendelssohn fainted.

37

ALL FOUR WERE ARRESTED, handcuffed and had their rights read out to them. They were then driven in separate police cars to the Nineteenth Precinct.

When they were questioned, three refused to speak without an attorney present. The fourth pointed out to the Desk Sergeant that if the bag which had been taken from him was opened at any time other than in the presence of his attorney, a writ would be issued and a separate action taken out against the NYPD.

The Desk Sergeant looked at the smartly-dressed, distinguished-looking man and decided not to take any risks. He labelled the bag with a red tag and threw it in the night safe.

The same man insisted on his legal right to make one phone call. The request was granted, but not until another form had been completed and signed. Dexter Hutchins put a collect call through to the Director of the CIA at 2.27 a.m.

The Director confessed to his subordinate that he hadn't been able to sleep. He listened intently to Hutchins' report and praised him for not revealing his name or giving the police any details of the covert assignment. 'We don't need anyone to know who you are,' he added. 'We must be sure at all times not to embarrass the President.' He paused for a moment. 'Or, more important, the CIA.'

When the Deputy Director put the phone down, he and his three colleagues were hustled away to separate cells.

The Director of the CIA put on his dressing gown and went down to his study. After he had written up a short summary of the conversation he had had with his deputy, he checked a number on his desk computer. He slowly dialled the 212 area code.

The Commissioner of the New York City Police Department uttered some choice words when he answered the phone, until he was sufficiently alert to take in who it was sounding so wide awake on the other end of the line. He then switched on the bedside light and began to make some notes on a pad. His wife turned over, but not before she had added a few choice words of her own.

The Director of the CIA ended his part of the conversation with the comment, 'I owe you one.'

'Two,' said the Commissioner. 'One for trying to sort out your problem.'

'And the second?' asked the Director.

'For waking up my wife at three o'clock in the morning.'

The Commissioner remained seated on the edge of the bed while he looked up the home number of the Captain in charge of that particular precinct.

The Captain recognised his chief's voice immediately he picked up the phone, and simply said, 'Good morning, Commissioner,' as if it were a routine mid-morning call.

The chief briefed the Captain without making any mention of a call from the Director of the CIA or giving any clues about who the four men languishing in his night cells were – not that he was absolutely certain himself. The Captain scribbled down the salient facts on the back of his wife's copy of *Good Housekeeping*. He didn't bother to shower or shave, and dressed quickly in the clothes he had worn the previous day. He left his apartment in Queens at 3.21 and drove himself into Manhattan, leaving his car outside the front of the precinct a few minutes before four.

Those officers who were fully awake at that time in the morning were surprised to see their boss running up the steps and into the front hall, especially as he looked dishevelled, unshaven, and was carrying a copy of *Good Housekeeping* under his arm.

He strode into the office of the Duty Lieutenant, who quickly removed his feet from the desk.

The Lieutenant looked mystified when asked about the four men who'd been arrested earlier, as he'd only just finished interrogating a drug pusher.

The Desk Sergeant was called for and joined the Captain in the Duty Lieutenant's office. The veteran policeman, who thought he had seen most things during a long career in the force, admitted to booking the four men, but remained puzzled by the whole incident, because he couldn't think of anything to charge them with – despite the fact that one of the householders, a Mr Antonio Cavalli, had called within the last few minutes to ask if the four men were still being held in custody, as a complication had arisen. None of the residents had reported anything stolen, so theft did not apply. There could be no charge of breaking and entering, as on each occasion they had been invited into the buildings. There was certainly no assault involved, and trespass couldn't be considered, as they had left the premises the moment they were asked to do so. The only charge the Sergeant could come up with was impersonating gas company officials.

The Captain didn't show any interest in whether or

not the Desk Sergeant could find something to charge them with. All he wanted to know was: 'Has the bag been opened?'

'No, Captain,' said the Sergeant, trying to think where he had put it.

'Then release them on bail, pending further charges,' instructed the Captain. 'I'll deal with the paperwork.'

The paperwork took the Captain some considerable time, and the four men were not released until a few minutes after six.

When they ran down the precinct steps together, the little one with the pebble glasses was clinging firmly on to the unopened bag.

Antonio Cavalli woke with a start. Had he dreamed that he'd been dragged out of bed and onto the street in the middle of the night?

He flicked on the bedside light and picked up his watch. It was 3.47. He began to recall what had taken place a few hours earlier.

Once they were out on the street, Martin had accompanied the four men back into the house. Too many for a simple gas leak, Cavalli had thought. And what gas company official would smoke cigars and could afford a Saks Fifth Avenue suit? After they had been inside for fifteen minutes, Cavalli had become even more suspicious. He asked the Fire Chief if the men were personally known to him. The Chief admitted that, although they had been able to give him the correct code over the phone, he had never come across them before. He decided Mr Cavalli was right when he suggested that perhaps the time had come to make some checks with Consolidated Edison. Their switchboard informed him that they had no engineers out on call that night on 75th

Street. The Fire Chief immediately passed this information on to the police. A few minutes later six police officers had entered number 23 and arrested all four men.

After they had been driven away to the station, his father and Martin had helped Tony check every room in the house, but as far as they could see nothing was missing. They had gone back to bed around 1.45.

Cavalli was now fully awake, though he thought he could hear a noise coming from the ground floor. Was it the same noise that had woken him? Tony checked his watch again. His father and Martin often rose early, but rarely between the hours of three and four.

Cavalli swung out of bed and placed his feet on the ground. He still felt sure he could hear voices.

He slipped on a dressing gown and walked over to the bedroom door. He opened it slowly, went out onto the landing and peered over the balustrade. He could see a light shining from under the door of his father's study.

Cavalli moved swiftly down the one flight of stairs and silently across the carpeted hallway until he came to a halt outside the study. He tried to remember where the nearest gun was.

He listened carefully, but could hear no movement coming from inside. Then, suddenly, a gravelly voice began cursing loudly. Tony flung open the door to find his father, also in his dressing gown, standing in front of the Declaration of Independence and holding a magnifying glass in his right hand. He was studying the word 'British'.

'Are you feeling all right?' Tony asked his father.

'You should have killed Dollar Bill when I told you to,' was his father's only comment.

'But why?' asked Tony.

'Because they've stolen the Declaration of Independence.'

'But you're standing in front of it,' said Tony.

'No I'm not,' said his father. 'Don't you understand what they've done?'

'No, I don't,' admitted Tony.

'They've exchanged the original for that worthless copy you put in the National Archives.'

'But the copy on the wall was the other one made by Dollar Bill,' said Tony. 'I saw him present it to you.'

'No,' said his father. 'Mine was the original, not a copy.'

'I don't understand,' said Tony, now completely baffled. The old man turned and faced his son for the first time.

'Nick Vicente and I switched them when you brought the Declaration back from Washington.' Tony stared at his father in disbelief. 'You didn't think I'd allow part of our national heritage to fall into the hands of Saddam Hussein?'

'But why didn't you tell me?' asked Tony.

'And let you go to Geneva knowing you were in possession of a fake, while the deal still hadn't been closed? No, it was always part of my plan that you would believe the original had been sent to Franchard et cie, because if you believed it, Al Obaydi would believe it.'

Tony said nothing.

'And you certainly wouldn't have put up such a fight over the loss of fifty million if you'd known all along that the document you had in Geneva was a counterfeit.'

'So where the hell is the original now?' asked Tony.

'Somewhere in the offices of the Nineteenth Precinct, would be my bet,' replied his father. 'That is, assuming they haven't already got clean away. And that's what I intend to find out right now,' he added as he walked over to his desk and picked up the phone book.

The chairman dialled seven digits and asked to speak to the duty officer. He checked his watch as he waited to be put through. It was 4.22.

When the Desk Sergeant came on the line, Cavalli explained who he was, and asked two questions. He listened carefully to the replies, then put the phone back on the hook.

Tony raised an eyebrow.

'They're still locked up in the cells, and the bag's been placed in a safe. Have we got anybody on the Nineteenth Precinct payroll?' asked his father.

'Yes, a lieutenant who's done very little for us lately.'

'Then the time has come for him to pay his dues,' said his father as he began walking towards the door.

Tony passed him, taking the stairs three at a time on the way back to his bedroom. He was dressed within minutes, and walked back down the staircase, expecting to have to wait some time for his father to reappear, but he was already standing in the hallway.

His father unlocked the front door and Tony followed him out onto the pavement, passing him to look up the street in search of a Yellow Cab. But none chose to turn right down 75th Street at that time in the morning.

'We'll have to take the car,' shouted his father, who had already begun to cross the road in the direction of the all-night garage. 'We can't afford to waste another minute.' Tony dashed back into the house and removed the car keys from the drawer of the hall table. He caught up with his father long before he reached their parking space.

As Tony fastened his seatbelt, he turned and asked his father, 'If we do manage to get the Declaration back, what the hell do you intend to do then?'

'To start with, I'm going to kill Dollar Bill myself, so I

can be certain that he never makes another copy. And then –' Tony turned the key in the ignition.

The explosion that followed woke the entire neighbourhood for the second time that morning.

The four men came running down the precinct steps. The smallest of them was clinging on to a bag. A car whose engine had been turning over for the past hour swung across the road and came to a halt by their side. One of the men walked off into the half-light of the morning, still not certain why his expertise had been required in the first place.

Dexter Hutchins joined the driver in the front, while Scott and the Conservator climbed quickly into the back.

'LaGuardia,' said Dexter and then thanked the agent for sitting up half the night. Scott looked between the two front seats as the digital clock changed from 6:11 to 6:12.

The agent swung on to the outside lane.

'Don't break the speed limit,' ordered Dexter. 'We don't need any more delays at this stage.' The agent edged back into the centre lane.

'What time's the next shuttle?' asked Scott.

'Delta, seven-thirty,' replied the driver. Dexter picked up the phone and punched in ten numbers. When a voice at the other end said, 'Yes,' the Deputy Director replied, 'We're on our way, sir. We should have everything back in place by ten.'

Dexter replaced the phone and turned round to assure himself that the silent Conservator was still with them. He was clutching the bag that was now resting on his legs.

'Better take everything out of the bag other than the cylinder,' said Dexter. 'Otherwise we'll never get past security.'

Mendelssohn unzipped the bag and allowed Scott to remove the screwdrivers, knives, chisels and finally the drill, which he placed on the floor between them. He zipped the bag back up.

At 6.43 the driver pulled off the highway and followed the signs for LaGuardia. No one spoke until the car came to a halt at the kerb opposite the Marine Air terminal entrance.

As Dexter stepped out of the car, three men in tan Burberrys jumped out of a car that had drawn in immediately behind them, and preceded the Deputy Director into the terminal. Another man in a smart charcoal-grey suit, with a raincoat over his arm, held out an envelope as Dexter passed him. The Deputy Director took the package like a good relay runner, without breaking his stride, as he continued towards the departure lounge, where three more agents were waiting for him.

Once he had checked in, Dexter Hutchins would have liked to pace up and down as he waited to board the aircraft. Instead, he stood restlessly one yard away from the Declaration of Independence, surrounded by a circle of agents.

'The shuttle to Washington is now boarding at Gate Number 4,' announced a voice over the intercom. Nine men waited until everyone else had boarded the aircraft. When the agent standing by the gate nodded, Dexter led his team past the ticket collector, down the boarding ramp, and onto the aircraft. They took their seats, 1A–F and 2A–F. 2E was occupied only by the bag, 2D and 2F by two men who weighed five hundred pounds between them.

The pilot welcomed them aboard and warned them there might be a slight delay. Dexter checked his watch: 7.27. He began drumming his fingers on the armrest that divided him from Scott. The flight attendant offered every one of the nine men in the first two rows a copy of *USA Today*. Only Mendelssohn took up her offer.

At 7.39 the aircraft taxied out onto the runway to prepare for take-off. When it stopped, Dexter asked the flight attendant what was holding them up.

'The usual early-morning traffic,' she replied. 'The Captain has just told me that we're seventh in the queue, so we should be airborne in about ten to fifteen minutes.'

Dexter continued drumming his fingers on the armrest, while Scott couldn't take his eyes off the bag. Mendelssohn turned another page of his *USA Today*.

The plane swung round onto the take-off runway at 7.51, its jets revving before it moved slowly forward, then gathered speed. The wheels left the ground at 7.53.

Within moments the flight attendant returned, offering them all breakfast. She didn't get a positive response until she reached row seven. When later she gave the three crew members on the flight deck their usual morning coffee, she asked the Captain why rows three to six were unoccupied, especially as it was Independence Day.

The Captain couldn't think of a reason, and simply said, 'Keep your eye on the passengers in rows one and two.' He became even more curious about the nine men at the front of the aircraft when he was cleared for landing as soon as he announced to air traffic control that he was seventy miles away from Washington.

He began his descent at 8.33, and was at the gate on schedule for the first time in months. When he had turned the engine off, three men immediately blocked the gangway and remained there until the Deputy Director and his party were well inside the terminal. When Dexter Hutchins emerged into the Delta gate area, one agent played John the Baptist, while three others fell in behind, acting as disciples. The Director had obviously taken seriously that fine line between protection and drawing attention. Dexter spotted four more agents as he passed through the terminal, and suspected there were at least another twenty hidden at strategic points on his route to the car.

As Dexter passed under the digital clock, its red numbers clicked to 9:01. The doors slid open and he marched out onto the pavement. Three black limousines were waiting in line with drivers by their doors.

As soon as they saw the Deputy Director, the drivers of the first and third cars jumped behind their wheels and turned on their engines, while the driver of the second car held open the back door to allow Scott and Mendelssohn to climb in. The Deputy Director joined the agent in the front.

The lead car headed out in the direction of the George Washington Parkway, and within minutes the convoy was crossing the 14th Street bridge. As the Jefferson Memorial came into sight Dexter checked his watch yet again. It was 9.12. 'Easily enough time,' he remarked. Less than a minute later, they were caught in a traffic jam.

'Damn!' said Dexter. 'I forgot the streets would be cordoned off for the Independence Day parade.'

When they had moved only another half a mile in the next three minutes, Dexter told his driver they were left with no choice. 'Hit the sirens,' he said.

The driver flashed his lights, turned on his siren at full blast, and watched as the lead car veered into the inside lane and managed a steady forty miles per hour until they came off the freeway.

Dexter was now checking his watch every thirty seconds as the three cars tried to manoeuvre themselves from lane to lane, but some of Washington's citizens, unmoved by sirens and flashing lights, weren't willing to let them through.

The lead car swerved between two police barriers and turned into Constitution Avenue at 9.37. When Dexter saw the floats lining up for the parade, he gave the order to turn the sirens off. The last thing he needed was inquisitive eyes when they finally came to a halt outside the National Archives.

It was Scott who saw them first. He tapped Dexter on the shoulder and pointed ahead of him. A television crew was standing at the head of a long queue outside the front door of the National Archives.

'We'll never get past them,' said Dexter. Turning to Mendelssohn, he asked, 'Are there any alternative routes into the building?'

'There's a delivery entrance on 7th Street,' replied Mendelssohn.

'How appropriate,' said Dexter Hutchins.

'Drive past the front door and then drop me off on the corner,' said the Conservator. 'I'll cross Constitution and go in by the delivery entrance.'

'Drop you off on the corner?' said Dexter in disbelief.

'If I'm surrounded by agents, everyone will . . .' began Mendelssohn.

'Yes, yes, yes,' said the Deputy Director, trying to think. He picked up the phone and instructed the two other cars to peel off.

'We're going to have to risk it,' said Scott.

'I know,' said Dexter. 'But at least you can go with him. After all, you've never looked like an agent.' Scott wasn't sure whether he should take the remark as a compliment or not.

As they drove slowly past the National Archives, Dexter looked away from the impatient camera crew.

'How many of them?' he asked.

'About six,' said Scott. 'And I think that must be Shaw with his back to us.'

'Show me exactly where you want the car to stop,' said the Deputy Director, turning to face Mendelssohn.

'Another fifty yards,' came back the reply.

'You take the bag, Scott.'

'But . . .' began Mendelssohn. When he saw the expression on Dexter Hutchins' face, he didn't bother with a second word.

The car drew into the kerb and stopped. Scott grabbed the bag, jumped out, and held the door open for Mendelssohn. Eight agents were walking up and down the pavement trying to appear innocent. None of them was looking towards the steps of the National Archives. The two unlikely looking companions quickly crossed Constitution Avenue and began running up 7th Street.

When they reached the delivery entrance, Scott came face to face with an anxious Calder Marshall, who had been pacing back and forth at the bottom of the ramp.

'Thank God,' was all the Archivist said when he saw Scott and the Conservator running down the ramp. He led them silently into the open freight elevator. They travelled up two floors and then ran along the corridor until they reached the staircase that led down to the vault. Marshall turned to check that the two men were still with him before he began running down the steps, something no member of staff had ever seen him do before. Scott chased after the Archivist, followed by Mendelssohn. None of them stopped until they reached a set of massive steel doors.

Marshall nodded, and a slightly breathless Conservator leaned forward and pressed a code into a little box beside the door. The steel grid opened slowly to allow the three of them to enter the vault. Once they were inside, the Conservator pressed another button, and the door slid back into place.

They paused in front of the great concrete block that

had been built to house the Declaration of Independence, just as a priest might in front of an altar. Scott checked his watch. It was 9.51.

Mendelssohn pressed the red button and the familiar clanking and whirling sound began as the concrete blocks parted and the massive empty frame came slowly into sight. He touched the button again when the glass casing had reached chest height.

The Archivist and the Conservator walked forward while Scott unzipped the bag. The Archivist took two keys from his jacket pocket and passed one over to his colleague. They immediately set about unlocking the twelve bolts that were evenly spaced around the thick brass rim. Once they had completed the task they leaned over and heaved across the heavy frame until it came to rest like an open book.

Scott removed the container and passed it over to the Archivist. Marshall eased the cap off the top of the cylinder, allowing Mendelssohn to carefully extract its contents.

Scott watched as the Archivist and the Conservator slowly unpeeled the Declaration of Independence, inch by inch, onto the waiting glass, until the original parchment was finally restored to its rightful place. Scott leaned over and took one last look at the misspelt word before the two men heaved the brass cover back into place.

'My God, the British still have a lot to answer for,' was all the Archivist said.

Calder Marshall and the Conservator quickly tightened up the twelve bolts surrounding the frame and took a pace back from the Declaration.

They paused for only a second while Scott checked his watch again. 9.57. He looked up to find Marshall and Mendelssohn hugging each other and jumping up and down like children who had been given an unexpected gift.

Scott coughed. 'It's 9.58, gentlemen.' The two men immediately reverted to character.

The Archivist walked back over to the concrete block. He paused for a moment and then pressed the red button. The massive frame rose, continuing its slow journey upwards to the gallery to be viewed by the waiting public.

Calder Marshall turned to face Scott. A flicker of a smile showed his relief. He bowed like a Japanese warrior to indicate that he felt honour had been satisfied. The Conservator shook hands with Scott and then walked over to the door, punched a code into the little box and watched the grid slide open.

Marshall accompanied Scott out into the corridor, up the staircase and back down in the freight elevator to the delivery entrance.

'Thank you, Professor,' he said as they shook hands on the loading dock. Scott loped up the ramp and turned to look back once he had reached the pavement. There was no sign of the Archivist.

He jogged across 7th Street and joined Dexter in the waiting car.

'Any problems, Professor?' asked the Deputy Director.

'No. Not unless you count two decent men who look as if they've aged ten years in the past two months.'

The tenth chime struck on the Old Post Office Tower clock. The doors of the National Archives swung open and a television crew charged in.

The Deputy Director's car moved out into the centre of Constitution Avenue, where it got caught up between the floats for Tennessee and Texas. A police officer ran across and ordered the driver to pull over into 7th Street.

When the car came to a halt, Dexter wound down his window, smiled at the officer and said, 'I'm the Deputy Director of the CIA.'

'Sure. And I'm Uncle Sam,' the officer replied as he began writing out a ticket.

38

THE DEPUTY DIRECTOR of the CIA phoned the Director at home to tell him that it was business as usual at the National Archives. He didn't mention the traffic ticket.

The Conservator phoned his wife and tried to explain why he hadn't come home the previous night.

A woman holding a carrier bag with a rope handle contacted the Iraqi Ambassador to the UN on her mobile phone and let him know that she had killed two birds with one stone. She gave the Ambassador an account number for a bank in the Bahamas.

The Director of the CIA rang the Secretary of State and assured him that the document was in place. He avoided saying '*back* in place'.

Susan Anderson rang Scott to congratulate him on the part he had played in restoring the document to its rightful home. She also mentioned in passing the sad news that she had decided to break off her engagement.

The Iraqi Ambassador to the UN instructed Monsieur Franchard to transfer the sum of nine hundred thousand dollars to the Royal Bank of Canada in the Bahamas and at the same time to close the Al Obaydi account.

The Secretary of State rang the President at the White House to inform him that the press conference scheduled for eleven o'clock that morning had been cancelled.

A reporter on the *New York Daily News* crime beat filed his first-edition copy from a phone booth in an underground garage on 75th Street. The headline read 'Mafia Slaying in Manhattan'.

Lloyd Adams' phone never stopped ringing, as he was continually being offered parts in everything from endorsements to a feature film.

The Archivist did not return a call from one of the President's Special Assistants at the White House, inviting him to lunch.

A CNN producer called in to the news desk to let them know that it must all have been a hoax. Yes, he had verified the spelling of 'Brittish', and only Dan Quayle could have thought it had two *t*s.

Scott phoned Hannah and told her how he wanted to spend Independence Day.

THE END

In CONGRESS, July 4, 1776.

The unanimous Declaration
of the thirteen united
States of America

When, in the course of human events, it becomes necessary for one people to dissolve the political bands which have connected them with another, and to assume among the powers of the earth, the separate and equal station to which the Laws of Nature and of Nature's God entitle them, a decent respect to the opinions of mankind requires that they should declare the causes which impel them to the separation. — We hold these truths to be self-evident, that all men are created equal, that they are endowed by their Creator with certain unalienable Rights, that among these are Life, Liberty and the Pursuit of Happiness. — That to secure these rights, Governments are instituted among Men, deriving their just powers from the consent of the governed, — That whenever any Form of Government becomes destructive of these ends, it is the Right of the People to alter or to abolish it, and to institute new Government, laying the foundation on such principles and organizing its powers in such form, as to them shall seem most likely to effect their Safety and Happiness. Prudence, indeed, will dictate that Governments long established should not be changed for light and transient causes; and accordingly all experience hath shewn, that mankind are more disposed to suffer, while evils are sufferable, than to right themselves by abolishing the forms to which they are accustomed. But when a long train of abuses and usurpations, pursuing invariably the same Object evinces a design to reduce them under absolute Despotism, it is their right, it is their duty, to throw off such Government, and to provide new Guards for their future security. — Such has been the patient sufferance of these Colonies; and such is now the necessity which constrains them to alter their former Systems of Government. The history of the present King of Great Britain is a history of repeated injuries and usurpations, all having in direct object the establishment of an absolute Tyranny over these States. To prove this, let Facts be submitted to a candid world.— He has refused his Assent to Laws, the most wholesome and necessary for the public good. — He has forbidden his Governors to pass Laws of immediate and pressing importance, unless suspended in their operation till his Assent should be obtained; and when so suspended, he has utterly neglected to attend to them. —— —— He has refused to pass other Laws for the accommodation of large districts of people, unless those people would relinquish the right of Representation in the Legislature, a right inestimable to them and formidable to tyrants only. — He has called together legislative bodies at places unusual, uncomfortable, and distant from the depository of their Public Records, for the sole purpose of fatiguing them into compliance with his measures. — He has dissolved Repres/en\tative Houses repeatedly, for opposing with manly firmness his invasions on the rights of the people. — He has refused for a long time, after such dissolutions, to cause others to be elected; whereby the Legislative powers, incapable of Annihilation, have returned to the People at large for their exercise; the State remaining in the mean time exposed to all the dangers of invasion from without, and convulsions within. ——— He has endeavoured to prevent the Population of these States; for that purpose obstructing the Laws for Naturalization of

Foreigners; refusing to pass others to encourage their migrations hither, and raising the conditions of new Appropriations of Land. — He has obstructed the Administration of Justice, by refusing his Assent to Laws for establishing Judiciary Powers. — He has made Judges dependent on his Will alone, for the tenure of their offices, and the amount and payment of their salaries. ———— He has erected a multitude of New Offices, and sent hither swarms of Officers to harass our People, and eat out their substance. — He has combined us, in times of peace, Standing Armies without the Consent of our legislatures. — He has affected to unite the Military independent of and superior to the Civil power. — He has combined with others to subject us to a jurisdiction foreign to our constitution, and unacknowledged by our laws; giving his Assent to their Acts of pretended Legislation: — For quartering large bodies of armed troops among us: — For protecting them, by a mock Trial, from punishment for any Murders which they should commit on the Inhabitants of these States: — For cutting off our Trade with all parts of the world: — For imposing Taxes on us without our Consent: — For depriving us, in many cases, of the benefits of Trial by Jury: — For transporting us beyond Seas to be tried for pretended offences. — For abolishing the free System of English Laws in a neighbouring Province, establishing therein an Arbitrary government, and enlarging its Boundaries so as to render it at once an example and fit instrument for introducing the same absolute rule into these Colonies: — For taking away our Charters, abolishing our most valuable Laws, and altering fundamentally the Forms of our Governments: — For suspending our own Legislations, and declaring themselves invested with power to legislate for us in all cases whatsoever. — He has abdicated his Government here, by declaring us out of his Protection and waging War against us. — He has plundered our seas, ravaged our Coasts, burnt our towns, and destroyed the lives of our people. — He is at this time transporting large Armies of foreign Mercenaries to compleat the works of death, desolation and tyranny, already begun with circumstances of Cruelty and Perfidy scarcely paralleled in the most barbarous ages, and totally unworthy the Head of a civilized nation. — He has constrained our fellow Citizens taken Captive on the high Seas to bear Arms against their Country, to become the executioners of their friends and Brethren, or to fall themselves by their Hands. — He has excited domestic insurrections amongst us, and has endeavoured to bring on the inhabitants of our frontiers, the merciless Indian Savages, whose known rule of warfare, is an undistinguished destruction of all ages, sexes and conditions. In every stage of these Oppressions We have Petitioned for Redress in the most humble terms: Our repeated Petitions have been answered /only\ by repeated injury. A Prince, whose character is thus marked by every act which may define a Tyrant, is unfit to be the ruler of a free people. Nor have We been wanting in attentions to our Brittish brethren. We have warned them from time to time of attempts by their legislature to extend an unwarrantable jurisdiction over us. We have reminded them of the circumstances of our emigration and settlement here. We have appealed to their native justice and magnanimity, and we have conjured them by the ties of our common kindred to disavow these usurpations, which, would inevitably interrupt our connections and correspondence. They too have been deaf to the voice of justice and of consanguinity. We must, therefore, acquiesce in the necessity, which denounces our Separation, and hold them, as we hold the rest of mankind, Enemies in War, in Peace Friends. —

We, therefore, the Representatives of the **united States of America**, in General Congress, Assembled, appealing to the Supreme Judge of the world for the rectitude of our intentions, do, in the Name, and by Authority of the good People of these Colonies, solemnly publish and declare, that these United Colonies are, and of Right ought to be **Free and Independent States**; that they are Absolved from all Allegiance to the British Crown, and that all political connection between them and the State of Great Britain, is and ought to be totally dissolved; and that as Free and Independent States, they have full Power to levy War, conclude Peace, contract Alliances, establish Commerce, and to do all other Acts and Things which Independent States may of right do. — And for the support of this Declaration with a firm reliance on the protection of divine Providence, we mutually pledge to each other our Lives, our Fortunes and our sacred Honor.